We're suspended inside like bugs in flaming cotton candy. It's spectacular—a lurid, artificial sunrise.

I'm breathing like a racehorse at the end of its run. My faceplate fogs. I can barely see, but right away, I know for sure that there's trouble. The big ball has split early. There are only three Skyrines in my cherry glow. Others have spun off in fiery clumps, and who knows where they'll land?

The glow burns down closer and closer, brighter and brighter. With gut-check jerks we slow from four klicks per second to one klick per second to one klick per minute, until, just after the last of our puff burns out, just after our packs release and rocket away, smoking, sad, finished...

The three of us flex our knees and land with less-than-gentle thumps.

I pick myself up, surprised I'm still alive. Bad drops are usually fatal. Quick look around. Flat, immense.

Welcome to Mars. The Red.

No immediate threat.

Time to freely scream inside my helm and figure out what the hell went wrong.

Praise for
THE WAR DOGS TRILOGY

War Dogs

"Stuffed with adrenaline-pumping action and mystifying ambiguity, Bear's series launch is a tempest of rousing SF adventure with a dash of Peckinpah." —*Publishers Weekly*

"Packed with adventure and incident...conveyed with gritty realism." —*Kirkus*

Killing Titan

"Readers familiar with Haldeman's *The Forever War*, Heinlein's *Starship Troopers*, or Scalzi's Old Man's War series will feel right at home—this is actually a novel of big ideas and philosophical exploration." —*Booklist*

"*Killing Titan* keeps the thrills coming." —*Shelf Awareness*

Take Back the Sky

"A resoundingly satisfying conclusion, paying off all the bets Bear made in the earlier books, and then some." —*B&N Sci-Fi & Fantasy Blog*

"Bear's interstellar war epic comes to its action-packed conclusion." —*io9*

THE
WAR DOGS
TRILOGY

THE
WAR DOGS TRILOGY

GREG BEAR

www.orbitbooks.net

War Dogs copyright © 2014 by Greg Bear
Killing Titan copyright © 2015 by Greg Bear
Take Back the Sky copyright © 2016 by Greg Bear
Excerpt from *The Corporation Wars: Dissidence* copyright © 2016 by Ken MacLeod
Excerpt from *The Eternity Wars: Pariah* copyright © 2017 by Jamie Sawyer

Author photograph by Astrid Anderson Bear
Cover design by Lisa Marie Pompilio
Cover art by Shutterstock
Cover copyright © 2017 by Hachette Book Group, Inc.

Orbit
Hachette Book Group
1290 Avenue of the Americas
New York, NY 10104
orbitbooks.net

First Omnibus Edition: September 2017

Orbit is an imprint of Hachette Book Group.
The Orbit name and logo are trademarks of Little, Brown Book Group Limited.

The Hachette Speakers Bureau provides a wide range of authors for speaking events. To find out more, go to www.hachettespeakersbureau.com or call (866) 376-6591.

Library of Congress Control Number: 2017943900

ISBNs: 978-0-316-51333-3 (trade paperback), 978-0-316-51332-6 (ebook)

Printed in the United States of America

LSC-C

Printing 3, 2021

CONTENTS

WAR DOGS

This book is dedicated to my favorite Mustangers:
LCDR Dale F. Bear, USN, Retired
LCDR Richmond D. Garrett, USN, Retired

And by extension to all who served with them in
WW2, Korea, and Vietnam.

I also express my appreciation to those friends who helped
make this a better book, and I am honored to pass
along their own acknowledgments:

David Clark (Vietnam): "I'd like to list my military forebears,
men who served as an example for me. My father, Ken Clark,
WW2 Navy Signalman; Cecil 'Duke' Crowell, US Navy
hardhat diver, WW2; my grandfather Ernest Shultz, WWI
Navy aviation pioneer; and my great-great-uncle George
Booth, First Sergeant Company D, 155 PA Infantry, Army of
the Potomac,
American Civil War."

Donald E. McQuinn (Korea, Vietnam): "My gratitude to every
Marine of my past, and my thanks to our Marines of the present
and future in the full confidence that they'll never fail to
add luster to our Corps. Semper Fidelis."

Dan O'Brien (Iraq): "To the fallen Sailors and Marines of Kilo
3/12: Doc Noble, Cpl. McRae, Cpl. Zindars, and Lcpl. Lync,
and all the others who fell on the moonscapes of Iraq and
Afghanistan. No need to mention me, it seems trivial after
mentioning them."

I'm mentioning Dan anyway, because he helped, and he was
there.

Heartfelt thanks to all for so much.

GREG BEAR

DOWN TO EARTH

I'm trying to go home. As the poet said, if you don't know where you are, you don't know who you are. Home is where you go to get all that sorted out.

Hoofing it outside Skybase Lewis-McChord, I'm pretty sure this is Washington State, I'm pretty sure I'm walking along Pacific Highway, and this is the twenty-first century and not some fidging movie—

But then a whining roar grinds the air and a broad shadow sweeps the road, eclipsing cafés and pawnshops and loan joints—followed seconds later by an eye-stinging haze of rocket fuel. I swivel on aching feet and look up to see a double-egg-and-hawksbill burn down from the sky, leaving a rainbow trail over McChord field...

And I have to wonder.

I just flew in on one of those after eight months in the vac, four going out, three back. Seven blissful months in timeout, stuffed in a dark tube and soaked in Cosmoline.

All for three weeks in the shit. Rough, confusing weeks.

I feel dizzy. I look down, blink out the sting, and keep walking. Cosmoline still fidges with my senses.

Here on Earth, we don't say *fuck* anymore, the Gurus don't like it, so we say fidge instead. Part of the price of freedom. Out on the Red, we say fuck as much as we like. The angels edit our words so the Gurus won't have to hear.

SNKRAZ.

Joe has a funny story about *fuck*. I'll tell you later, but right now, I'm not too happy with Joe. We came back in separate ships, he did not show up at the mob center, and my Cougar is still parked outside Skyport Virginia. I could grab a shuttle into town, but Joe told me to lie low. Besides, I badly want time alone—time to stretch my legs, put down one foot after another. There's the joy of blue sky, if I can look up without keeling over, and open air without a helm—and minus the rocket smell—is a newness in the nose and a beauty in the lungs. In a couple of klicks, though, my insteps pinch and my calves knot. Earth tugs harsh after so long away. I want to heave. I straighten and look real serious, clamp my jaws, shake my head—barely manage to keep it down.

Suddenly, I don't feel the need to walk all the way to Seattle. I have my thumb and a decently goofy smile, but after half an hour and no joy, I'm making up my mind whether to try my luck at a minimall Starbucks when a little blue electric job creeps up behind me, quiet as a bad fart. Quiet is not good.

I spin and try to stop shivering as the window rolls down. The driver is in her fifties, reddish hair rooted gray. For a queasy moment, I think she might be MHAT sent from Madigan. Joe warned me, "For Christ's sake, after all that's happened, stay away from the doctors." MHAT is short for *Military Health Advisory Team*. But the driver is not from Madigan. She asks where I'm going. I say downtown Seattle. Climb in, she says. She's a colonel's secretary at Lewis, a pretty ordinary grandma, but she has these strange gray eyes that let me see all the way back to when her scorn shaped men's lives.

I ask if she can take me to Pike Place Market. She's good with that. I climb in. After a while, she tells me she had a son just like me. He became a hero on Titan, she says—but she can't really know that, because we aren't on Titan yet, are we?

I say to her, "Sorry for your loss." I don't say, *Glad it wasn't me.*

"How's the war out there?" she asks.

"Can't tell, ma'am. Just back and still groggy."

They don't let us know all we want to know, barely tell us all we *need* to know, because we might start speculating and lose focus.

She and I don't talk much after that. Fidging *Titan*. Sounds old and cold. What kind of suits would we wear? Would everything freeze solid? Mars is bad enough. We're almost used to the Red. Stay sharp on the dust and rocks. That's where our shit is at. Leave the rest to the generals and the Gurus.

All part of the deal. A really big deal.

Titan. Jesus.

Grandma in the too-quiet electric drives me north to Spring Street, then west to Pike and First, where she drops me off with a crinkle-eyed smile and a warm, sad finger-squeeze. The instant I turn and see the market, she pips from my thoughts. Nothing has changed since vac training at SBLM, when we tired of the local bars and drove north, looking for trouble but ending up right here. We liked the market. The big neon sign. The big round clock. Tourists and merchants and more tourists, and that ageless bronze pig out in front.

A little girl in a pink frock sits astride the pig, grinning and slapping its polished flank. What we fight for.

I'm in civvies but Cosmoline gives your skin a tinge that lasts for days, until you piss it out, so most everyone can tell I've been in timeout. Civilians are not supposed to ask probing questions, but they still smile like knowing sheep. *Hey, spaceman, welcome back! Tell me true, how's the vac?*

I get it.

A nice Laotian lady and her sons and daughter sell fruit and veggies and flowers. Their booth is a cascade of big and little peppers and hot and sweet peppers and yellow and green and red peppers, Walla Walla sweets and good strong brown and fresh green onions, red and gold and blue and russet potatoes, yams and sweet potatoes, pole beans green and yellow and purple and speckled, beets baby and adult, turnips open boxed in bulk and attached to sprays of crisp green leaf. Around the corner of the booth I see every kind of mushroom but the screwy kind. All that roughage dazzles. I'm accustomed to browns and pinks, dark blue, star-powdered black.

A salient of kale and cabbage stretches before me. I seriously consider kicking off and swimming up the counter, chewing through the thick leaves, inhaling the color, spouting purple and green. Instead, I buy a bunch of celery and move out of the tourist flow. Leaning against a corrugated metal door, I shift from foot to cramping foot, until finally I just hunker against the cool ribbed steel and rabbit down the celery leaves, dirt and all, down to the dense, crisp core. Love it. Good for timeout tummy.

Now that I've had my celery, I'm better. Time to move on. A mile to go before I sleep.

I doubt I'll sleep much.

Skyrines share flophouses, safe houses—refuges—around the major spaceports. My favorite is a really nice apartment in Virginia Beach. I could be heading there now, driving my Cougar across the Chesapeake Bay Bridge, top down, sucking in the warm sea breeze, but thanks to all that's happened—and thanks to Joe—I'm not. Not this time. Maybe never again.

I rise and edge through the crowds, but my knees are still shaky, I might not make it, so I flag a cab. The cabby is white and middle-aged, from Texas. Most of the fellows who used to cab here, Lebanese and Ethiopians and Sikhs, the younger ones at least, are gone to war now. They do well in timeout, better than white Texans. Brown people rule the vac, some say. There's a lot of brown and black and beige out there: east and west Indians, immigrant Kenyans and Nigerians and Somalis, Mexicans, Filipinos and Malaysians, Jamaicans and Puerto Ricans, all varieties of Asian—flung out in space frames, sticks clumped up in fasces—and then they all fly loose, shoot out puff, and drop to the Red. Maybe less dangerous than driving a hack, and certainly pays better.

I'm not the least bit brown. I don't even tan. I'm a white boy from Moscow, Idaho, a blue-collar IT wizard who got tired of working in cubicles, tired of working around shitheads like myself. I enlisted in the Skyrines (that's pronounced SKY-reen), went through all the tests and boot and desert training, survived first orbital, survived first drop on the Red—came home alive and relatively sane—and now I make good money. Flight pay and combat pay—they call it engagement bonus—and Cosmo-line comp.

Some say the whole deal of cellular suspension we call timeout shortens your life, along with solar flares and gamma rays. Others say no. The military docs say no but scandal painted a lot of them before my last deployment. Whole bunch at Madigan got augured for neglecting our spacemen. Their docs tend to regard spacemen, especially Skyrines, as slackers and complainers. Another reason to avoid MHAT. We make more than they do and still we complain. They hate us. Give them ground pounders any day.

"How many drops?" the Texan cabby asks.

"Too many," I say. I've been at it for six years.

He looks back at me in the mirror. The cab drives itself; he's in the seat for show. "Ever wonder why?" he asks. "Ever wonder what you're giving up to *them*? They ain't even human." Some think we shouldn't be out there at all; maybe he's one of them.

"Ever wonder?" he asks.

"All the time," I say.

He looks miffed and faces forward.

The cab takes me into Belltown and lets me out on a semi-circular drive, in the shadow of the high-rise called Sky Tower One. I pay in cash. The cabby rewards me with a sour look, even though I give him a decent tip. He, too, pips from my mind as soon as I get out. Bastard.

The tower's elevator has a glass wall to show off the view before you arrive. The curved hall on my floor is lined with alcoves, quiet and deserted this time of day. I key in the number code, the door clicks open, and the apartment greets me with a cheery pluck of ascending chords. Extreme retro, traditional Seattle, none of it Guru tech; it's from before I was born.

Lie low. Don't attract attention.

Christ. No way am I used to being a spook.

The place is just as I remember it—nice and cool, walls gray, carpet and furniture gray and cloudy-day blue, stainless steel fixtures with touches of wood and white enamel. The couch and chairs and tables are mid-century modern. Last year's Christmas tree is still up, the water down to scum and the branches naked, but Roomba has sucked up all the needles. Love Roomba. Also pre-Guru, it rolls out of its stair slot and checks me out, nuzzling my toes like a happy gray trilobite.

I finish my tour—checking every room twice, ingrained caution, nobody home—then pull an Eames chair up in front of the broad floor-to-ceiling window and flop back to stare out over the Sound. The big sky still makes me dizzy, so I try to focus lower down, on the green and white ferries coming and going, and then on the nearly continuous lines of tankers and big cargo ships. Good to know Hanjin and Maersk are still packing blue and orange and brown steel containers along with Hogmaw or Haugley or what the hell. Each container is about a seventh the size of your standard space frame. No doubt filled with clever goods made using Guru secrets, juicing our economy like a snuck of meth.

And for that, too—for *them*—we fight.

BACKGROUNDER, PART 1

ATS. All True Shit. So we're told.

The Gurus, whose real name, if it is their real name, is awful hard for humans to pronounce—made their presence known on Earth thirteen years ago, from the depths of the Yemeni desert, where their first scout ship landed. They wanted to establish a beachhead, make sure humans wouldn't find them and overrun them right away.

They made first contact with a group of camel herders who thought they were djinn, genies, and then, when they judged the time was right, reached out to the rest of humanity. As the story goes, they hacked into telecoms and satlinks, raised a fair pile of money by setting up anonymous trading accounts, then published online a series of pretty amazing puzzles that attracted the attention of the most curious and intelligent. They recruited a few, gave them a preliminary cover story—something about a worldwide brain trust hoping to set up offices in major capitals—and sent them around the planet to organize sanctuaries.

In another online operation, the Gurus and their new recruits led a second select group—military, clandestine services, political—on a merry geocache chase, in quest of something that might point to a huge breach of national security. There was a breach, of course.

It was the Gurus.

Working in this fashion, it became apparent to a few of our best and brightest that they were not dealing with an eccentric rich hermit with an odd sense humor. And there were genuine rewards, rich Easter eggs waiting to be cracked. Linking the most interesting puzzles led logically to some brilliant mathematical and scientific insights. One of these, quantum interlacing, showed the potential of increasing bandwidth in any Shannon-compliant network by a millionfold.

Only then did the Gurus reveal themselves—through another specially trained group of intermediaries. They came in peace. Of course. They planned on being even more helpful, in due time—piecing out their revelations in step sequence, not to upset proprietary apple carts all at once.

World leaders were gradually made aware of the game change, with astonishing tact and political savvy. Citizen awareness followed a few months later, after carefully coached preparation. It seemed the Gurus knew as much about our psychology and sociology as they did about the rules of the universe. They wanted to take things gradual.

And so over a period of six months, the Gurus came forward, moving out in ones and twos from their Yemeni Hadramaut beachhead to world capitals, economic centers, universities, think tanks—transforming themselves into both hostages and indispensable advisors.

The Gurus explained that they are here in tiny numbers because interstellar travel is fantastically difficult and expensive, even at their level of technology. So much had been guessed by our scientists. We still don't know how many Gurus came to Earth originally, but there are now, at best estimate—according to what our own governments will tell us—about thirty of them. They don't seem to mind being separated from each other or their own kind, but they keep their human contacts to a few dozen. Some call these select emissaries the Wait Staff.

It took the Gurus a while to drop the other shoe. You can see why, looking back. It was a very big shoe, completely slathered in dog shit.

Just as we were getting used to the new world order—just as we were proving ourselves worthy—the Gurus confessed they were not the only ones out there in the dark light-years. They explained that they had been hounded by mortal enemies from sun to sun, planet to planet, and were in fact now stretched thin—left weak, nearly defenseless.

Gurus were not just being magnanimous with their gifts of tech. They needed our help, and we needed to step up and help them, because these enemies were already inside the far, icy margins of our solar system, were, in fact, trying to establish their own beachhead, but not on Earth.

On Mars.

Some pundits started to call this enemy the Antagonists—Antags. The name stuck. We were told very little about them, except that they were totally bad.

And so our first bill came due. Skyrines were volunteered to help pay. As always.

———

THE SUN SETS watery yellow in a pall of Seattle gray. Night falls and ships' lights swim and dance in my tears. I'm still exuding slimy crap. Spacemen can't use drugs the first few days because our livers are overworked cleaning out residue. It comes out of our skin and sits on our breath like cheap gin and old sweat. Civilian ladies don't like the stink until we remind them about the money, then some put up with it.

It's quiet in the apartment. Empty. Spacemen are rarely alone coming or going or in the shit. If we're not in timeout, there's always that small voice in the ear, either a fellow Skyrine or your angel. But I don't really mind being alone. Not for a few hours. Not until Joe comes back and tells me how it all turned out. What the real secret was—about Muskies and the Drifter, the silicon plague, the tower of smart diamonds.

About Teal.

And the Voors, nasty, greedy SOBs who lost almost everything and maybe deserved to lose more. But they didn't deserve *us*.

I curl up in the Eames chair and pull up the blanket. I'm so tired, but I've got a lot on my mind. Pretty soon, I relive being in the shit.

It's vivid.

I HATE PHYSICS

Physics is what kills you, but biology is what wants you dead.

We're wide awake in the pressure tank at the center of our space frame, fresh from timeout, being pumped full of enthusiasm while the Cosmoline is sponged off by rotating cloths, like going through a car wash except in zero g.

This drop, we're told there are six space frames falling into insertion orbits. The first four frames hold two fasces, each fascis a revolving cylinder with three sticks like bullets. We call them rotisseries. Each stick carries a squad of Skyrines. That makes two hundred and forty of us, this drop. The fifth and sixth frames carry transport sleds with heavy weapons and vehicles and a couple of fountains. We won't see any of that until we're down on the Red.

Once we're sponged, we pull on skintights, do a final integrity check, strap on sidearms, receive palm-sized spent matter cassettes, then slip on puff packs and climb back into our sticks. Precise, fast, no time to think. Waiting in the stick is not good. The tubes are tight and dark. Our angels play soothing music, but that only makes it worse.

I start to twitch.

What's taking so long?

Then everything—and I mean *everything*—hisses and whines and squeals. I'm squashed against my tube on one side, then another, then top, then bottom, and altogether, we sing *hallelujah*, we're off!

The fasces spin outward from the frame, cylinders retro-firing to slow and get ready to discharge our sticks. I can't see anything but a diagram projected on the inside of my faceplate. Cheery. Colorful. All is well.

We've begun our drop.

The sticks shoot out of the rotisseries in precise sequence. Bite of atmosphere seems delayed. Feels wrong. Then it starts—the animal roar of entry. Just as the noise outside my stick becomes unbearable, thirty of us shoot from our tubes, out the end of the sticks, and desperately arrange ourselves, clinging to aero shields.

The shields buck in the upper atmosphere.

Over Mars.

The sky is filled with Red.

We ride ten to a shield for a few minutes in bouncy, herky-jerk free fall, at the end of which we all roll off. Comes a brief moment of white light and stove-grill heat. One side of my skintight flaps and then settles against my skin. Nice and toasty.

My drop pack spins out millions of threads like gossamer, almost invisibly thin. We call this puff. The threads expand to a lumpy ball fifty meters wide, which wobbles and snatches at Mars's thin, thin air—and then gloms on to other balls, other Skyrines enveloped in puff.

All around our jammed puffballs, curling thread tips burn away. We're suspended inside like bugs in flaming cotton candy. It's spectacular—a lurid, artificial sunrise. I'm breathing like a racehorse at the end of its run. My faceplate fogs. I can barely see, but right away, I know for sure that there's trouble. The big ball has split early. There are only three Skyrines in my cherry glow. Others have spun off in fiery clumps, and who knows where they'll land?

The glow burns down closer and closer, brighter and brighter. With gut-check jerks we slow from four klicks per second to one klick per second to one klick per minute, until, just after the last of our puff burns out, just after our packs release and rocket away, smoking, sad, finished...

The three of us flex our knees and land with less-than-gentle thumps.

I pick myself up, surprised I'm still alive. Bad drops are usually fatal. Quick look around. Flat, immense.

Welcome to Mars.

The Red.

No immediate threat.

Time to freely scream *fuck!* inside my helm and figure out what the hell went wrong.

———

I'M WITH TAK AND KAZAK. I think it was DJ and maybe Vee-Def and Michelin I saw thrashing away through the last of our puff sunrise. They may be no more than a klick or two off. The fasces apparently shot our sticks at the apex of insertion rather than low orbit. We've been separated from the rest of our platoon, and I have no idea how far away our company may be. They likely came down in a north-south fan, spread across more than a hundred klicks.

We could take days to reassemble.

There are no transport sleds nearby, and therefore no vehicles—no Skells or Tonkas or deuces.

Looks like we'll be hoofing it.

And no big weapons.

What's left of our packs falls, still smoking, a few hundred meters north. That's GPS north—no magnetic field on the Red. Good, I say to myself; sats are still up. We can receive our last-minute tactical and regroup in order. But then my angel loses the signal. The gyro is still good, however, and through my helm grid, I scope out the sun.

The Antags keep bringing down our orbital assets, nav and recon sats and other necessities. Newly arrived space frames keep spewing them out, along with Skyrines and transport sleds, but a lot of the time, when we arrive, we don't know right away where we are or what we're supposed to do. We're trained to just git along. Staying mobile makes you a tougher target. We call it drunkard's walk, but most of us drunkards are packed tight with prayer—that we're in range of the rest of our company, an intact sled, maybe a fountain, or at the very least we'll stumble over a stray tent box.

After four months transvac, the pre-drop cocktail of epi and histamines makes me feel terrific, barring a slight case of the wobbles. I pay no attention to how I feel, nor do Tak or Kazak. We're all sergeants. We've been here before. Our angels coordinate with fast, high-pitched screes, not likely to be heard more than a few tens of meters away. No joy. Nobody has the plan. No fresh recon. NCOs rule at last.

We know all there is to know, for now. But we don't even know where we've touched down.

We bump helms.

"What strength?" Tak asks.

"A squad, no more—in this sector," I say.

"Whatever fucking sector this is!" Kazak says.

"Northern lowlands," I guess. "Pressure's about right." I scuff brown dust along the flat, rocky hardpan and point north. "DJ and some others skipped over that way."

DJ is Engineering Sergeant Dan Johnson.

"Then let's find them," Tak says.

"Nothing here worth staying for," Kazak agrees. "Terrible

place for a fight—no high ground, almost no terrain. Can't dig fighting holes in this old shit. Where are we, fucking Hellas? Why drop us in the middle of nothing?"

No answer to that.

We walk, carrying less than five hours of breath and water, armed only with bolt-and-bullet pistols that resemble thick-barreled .45s. Tak Fujimori has an orange stripe on his helm. Tak is from Oakland. He went through vac training and jump school with me at SBLM and Hawthorne. He is compact and strong and very religious, though I'm not sure what religion. Maybe all of them.

Timur Nabiyev—Kazak—wears blue tape. He's from Kazakhstan, on exchange from Eurasian Defense. He trained with contingents of Chinese and Uyghurs in the cold desert of Tak-lamakan, specializing in dusty combat—then with Italians and French around Vesuvius and on the Canary Islands. Kazak is not religious except when he's on the Red, and then he's some sort of Baptist, or maybe Orthodox.

Out on the Red, we're all religious to one degree or another. Soviets once claimed they went into space and couldn't find God. They obviously never fell from high orbit in the middle of a burning bush.

The Red here is a wide, level orange desert shot through with purple and gray, and out there, to the northwest, one little scut of ridgeline, low and round. Otherwise, the horizon is unrelieved. Monstrously flat.

Skintights sport kinetic deflection layers around upper thighs and torso that can discourage rounds of 9mm or less, but no body armor can save us from Antag bolts and other shit, which closely matches what we deal. Not even our transports have more than rudimentary armor. Too damned heavy. Ours are made by Jeep, of course, mostly fold-out Skells with big wheels, but also Tonkas and Deuces and mobile weapons trucks called General Pullers—Chesties to those who love them. For important actions, even bigger weapons are delivered on wide-bed platforms called Trundles.

When a sled drops nearby. When we find them.

Sky still looks empty. Quiet.

No more drops for now.

We are forbidden from using radio, can't even uplink by laser until—if—our sats get replaced and can scope out the territory. Then up-to-data and maps will get lased from orbit, unless there's dust, in which case we may not get a burst for some time. Satellite microwave can penetrate all but the grainiest dust, but command prefers direct bursts of laser, and Antags could have sensors on every low ridge and rocky mound. If dust scatters our targeted beams, they're excellent at doing reverse Fourier, pinning our location to within a few meters and frying us like flies on a griddle. So we're hiking silent except for scree and touching helms.

If a fountain made it, it's going to be dormant and heavily camouflaged, waiting for our magic touch. Hard to find. But if we do find one, we'll replenish and maybe grab a nap before we're in the shit.

Or there is no shit.

Hard to know what will happen.

After all this time, we know almost nothing about the enemy except they're roughly our size, on average, with snouted helms, two long arms with hanging sleeves, three legs—or two legs and a tail—and they're not from around here. Only once have I seen their scant remains up close.

If we succeed, they're scrap and stain. If they succeed—

All physics.

I SCAN THE horizon over and over as we walk, nervous habit. The low line of atmosphere out there is brownish pink and clear except for a tan fuzzy patch near the distant ridge that doesn't seem to be going anywhere. Did I miss that the last time? I point it out to the others. Could be vehicular, could be a recent fountain drop; could be Antags.

We'll find DJ and the others, then head that direction. No sense rushing.

My angel, mounted above my left ear, follows my focus with little whirring sounds, then finishes laying out grids and comparing the negligible terrain to stored profiles. I look at Tak, then at Kazak. Their angels concur. We dropped over Marte Vallis in southern Elysium, within a few sols' hike of a small pedestal crater the angels label EM2543a, locally known as "Bridger," probably after some Muskie who died there.

The loess laps in low, snakelike waves across the hardpan. We cross over an X and then a Y and then a W of long, broad marks like roadways, some, we know—we've seen them from orbit and from the air—running for hundreds of klicks. These are not roads but wind-doodles, cryptic messages scrawled across the flats by millions of dust devils.

According to the angels, we are transiting a low plateau of ancient olivine. A second layer of flood basalt overlaps this one a few dozen klicks south. If we play tourist and venture that way, we will see that the edges of the upper plateau have sloughed, leaving irregular cliffs about ten meters high, with several meters of rubble at the base—quite fresh, less than fifty million years old.

My boot sensor is working for once and says the local dust is pH neutral. No signs of water outflow. Still, the basalt layers overlie deep, heavily fractured, and angled plates of ancient sandstone, probably the broken remains of a Noachian seabed. That means there could be underground water way below, shifting deep flows with no surface eruptions in our epoch. All same-same. Nary a sip for us. Mars is rarely generous.

Skintight injects more enthusiasm. Christ, I love it. I need it. We're experiencing our first sol! How exciting. A sol is one day on the Red, just a little longer than an Earth day. There won't be a pickup for at least seven or eight sols. Much longer if they can't find us, which seems likely. We're probably screwed.

But for the moment, none of us cares.

JOURNEYS END IN LOVERS MEETING

We walk north, saying little.

Skyrines rarely survive more than four drops. This is my fifth. So far, I'm as clear and frosty as a winter eve, but my skintight is already pulling back the encouragement.

I hate transitions.

As the cocktail slacks off, I start to think too much. Brain is not my friend. Leathery-winged shadows rustle in the back of my skull. I may or may not be psychic, but I can feel with knife-edge prickles that we're heading into opportunity—by which I mean trouble.

With his new eyes, Tak is the first to spot the body. He swings his arm and in turn I alert Kazak. We spread out and charge our sidearms.

In a few minutes, walking steady, no leaping, we surround the body. There's another about ten meters off, and another twenty beyond that. Three in all. The uniforms are Russian, probably with French equipment. Tak bends over the first and rolls it faceup. The skintight is still puffy. The helm plate is gruesome. Can't tell if it was male or female.

Tak pokes his finger at his own helm, then explodes his hands away. *Sploosh!* Germ needles. Poor bastard was feverish in seconds, crazy for the next four or five minutes, could have even shot his or her squad before falling over and fermenting. Tak finds where the little needle punctured the fabric and ta-da gestures at its feathery vanes. He doesn't try to pull it out. Fucking germ needles can poke up as well as prick down. They can be deployed from aerostats—large balloons—or dropped from orbit in exploding pods. Both systems spray silvery gray clouds over a couple of square kilometers. The needles, each about four centimeters long, shift their wide fletches and *find* you. Then they turn you into a balloon filled with bone chips and pus.

Real nightmare batwing shit.

Our angels scree the swollen suit, just in case the dead soldier's unit is still up for a chat. No luck. It's long since self-wiped. Since we haven't uplinked since the drop, and of course have not been briefed on recent engagements, we don't know anything about these guys or why they are here. They must have arrived many sols before us—maybe weeks. Why? There weren't supposed to be major operations before our arrival. Somebody's had second thoughts since we left Earth. Maybe these guys were shipped out on fast frames, taking only a month or two rather than four...They left before us, and now they're dead, and we don't know anything about why they are here.

It's getting tougher and tougher to stay focused.

At this point, we decide radio silence is stupid. Our only chance is to try to raise other Skyrines and hear if they've found something useful.

We split three different directions.

Only then do I see Engineering Sergeant Dan Johnson, DJ, waving his hands and descending a short slope made nasty by BB-sized pebbles. He manages to skitter down on his feet, then waves again and signs that he's found a tent box. We greet him with shoulder slaps and real joy. His angel screes ours, and now we're four instead of three.

"Anybody see sparkly?" DJ asks. "I saw sparkly coming down, above and outside."

We all agree that we saw no sparkly. Sparkly is bad—it's our term for space combat observed from a distance. Space frames and sticks being blown out of the sky.

"The puff was all fucked," Kazak says resentfully. "How could you tell?"

"Well, I saw *something*," DJ insists, but he doesn't push. We don't even want to think about it. He's found a tent box, he's leading us to it. The box is up on Bridger's pedestal. Craters on Mars often sit on rises caused by force of impact hardening the surrounding regolith, making them more resistant to erosion. Scientists call the rises pedestals, and this one is about two meters above the hardpan.

We're starting to really wear down by the time we reach the box and do a walk-around. The box is at least a month old, probably also Russian or French, and still has fresh purple striping— no interference since it was dropped, no booby traps, and no germ needles to render it useless. We make damned sure of that. Safety and sanctuary. We may be in the middle of nowhere important, off course and ultimately doomed, but at least we're good for the night, which is rolling over fast, and of course it's going to be cold and dry.

Still, we're about to sleep in a tent dropped for a dead squad. I'm not happy about that, but something similar happened on my last drop, and we all survived and took down something like sixty Antags—painted them on the sand from a couple of hundred meters. A good two weeks in the shit, and the nearest I've been to learning what an Antag looks like up close.

Bolts don't leave much to autopsy after the fighting is done: cuplike pieces of helm filled with grayish skull-bits—no teeth; shreds of light armor and suit, big, wide sleeves and leggings filled with crumbling bone and charred spines. Backbones, maybe. Our gunny ignored the tissue but scooped up some of the fabric and tech and packaged it for return. We heard no more about it. It's traditional in the Corps to keep grunts ignorant about who we fight, something about dehumanizing the enemy. Well, they ain't fucking human to begin with.

DJ and Tak break the tent box's seal. The stripes turn orange-pink and then brown—safe—and the tent inflates. It carries enough air to last the night, and because it's made for five, maybe a few hours into tomorrow. Strapped in a bag outside, we find a case of MREs with sacks of water and six vials of vodka. The MREs consist of hard sausage (Finnish, the label says—probably reindeer) and tubes containing something like borscht. A feast. We stuff the vodka in our hip packs, keeping our eyes on the black sky while the tent grows and the sun drops.

We talk without butting helms, but can barely hear each other through the thin, thin air. Not that there's much to say. The smudge on the horizon has not changed, other than turning a pretty shade of violet. It may only be a big dust devil. If so, the wind conditions out there have been stable for several hours.

I look higher, bending my neck to see the zenith. Much of the time the stars over the Red shine brighter and steadier than they ever do on Earth. Their beauty is lost on me. They judge. Worse, they send Antags. The stars are waiting for me to fuck up.

After we trigger and tune the sentinel, the tent is ready. We scoop dust in our gloves and fling it in slow plumes over the striped plexanyl to provide local color. Then we circle, pull short dusters from our thighs, and brush each other down, paying particular attention to wrinkles around our underarms and gear belts. Nobody wants to itch inside the tent all night, and nothing itches like fine Martian loess. We might not notice at first; six or eight hours after a drop, Cosmoline blocks itching and a lot of other sensations, so all seems smooth and cool and baby-powder sweet. During those hours I feel like a walking ghost or some other kind of disembodied asshole. But when sensation returns—and it always does—Mars dust can turn a miserable night on the Red into something truly special.

Assured that we are now relatively clean, one by one, we squeeze through the tent's canal into our little womb, like babies in reverse. When we're all in, and I've checked the seal and found it good, I crack my faceplate. Checker always takes first sniff. The tent air is okay, clean and cold. Like Russian steppes.

––––––

I'M BARELY AN hour into some crazy whimpering dream about mean kids when the tent wheeps intruder alert and we all jerk up, just as *something* slips through the entrance and plops down among us puppies. Beams flash. Kazak is loudly cursing in his eponymous patois. Then his beam illuminates a helm, a face— a human face—grinning like a bandit. Behind the faceplate, we recognize the broad nose, bushy unibrow, deep blue eyes, and somber, straight mouth.

"Shit, it's Vee-Def," Tak says. As we settle down, DJ passes Gunnery Sergeant Leonard Medvedev some water and an MRE.

Still all sergeants.

"Anybody get tactical?" Medvedev—Vee-Def—asks. As we dim our lights, the beams intersect a thin haze, and we realize there's dust in the tent. Vee-Def entered without brushing down. A severe breach.

"Fuckup," Kazak says.

"Nobody got tactical," Tak says.

"Anybody see a sled come down?" Vee-Def asks.

That's too stupid a question to answer. We're here in a Russian tent.

"How many tents?" he asks.

"How many do *you* see?" Tak asks.

More quiet.

"Sticks were all fucked," Vee-Def murmurs around a swig. His eyes are wide and scared. "I came down alone. Fucking puff was burning!"

"It's supposed to burn, man," DJ says.

"No, I mean there was sparkly and the sticks caught it. Looked like space frames, too. We may be all that's left!"

We're quiet for a few seconds.

"Bullshit," Tak says.

"I saw it, too," DJ reminds us, with a resentful glance.

Bad news takes a while to soak in when you're out on the Red, because just a little bad news means you're going to die, and this is a lot. Vee-Def feels the burn of bearing evil tidings. "I don't like Finnish sausage," he says, and offers around in pinched fingers a hard little tube of preserved reindeer.

No takers. We scratch ourselves with disdain.

Then Kazak starts giggling. "Is that your Tootsie Roll, man? Or you just glad to see us?"

It's dumb and not very funny. But for the moment we're warm, we're scratching, we're alive, and Vee-Def does what he does best, he sticks the sausage up his nose, or tries to, and then sneezes and snot comes out with the sausage and the sausage is good only for the family dog, which we were thoughtless enough to have left behind.

It's not good laughter. It's harsh and tired and angry. But it *is* laughter, and there may not be much to be had this trip. We don't say it, however. Not even Vee-Def is dumb enough to say more.

We're in the month-old tent of a dead platoon, our sticks got scattered, no transport sleds, our space frames may have caught sparkly, we have almost no tactical, comm seems to be down all over—even our angels are quiet.

We could be the Lost Patrol.

Morning will tell.

MARS WILL BE HEAVEN, SOMEDAY

I can't sleep for shit. I keep going over how fucked we are.

It's extreme on the Red. The air is just a millibar above a vacuum. It's always too damned cold. While there's quite a bit of water on Mars, overall most of it is tough to get at—locked up at the poles or cached beneath old seabeds or hidden in deep-flowing aquifers. That makes water a major strategic commodity. There's always a tiny residue of moisture in the air, enough to form high, icy clouds. There's more water in the air when the seasons melt the caps, which they do with monotonous regularity. Mars can be a cloudy world. I've even seen it snow, though the snow rarely makes it to the ground. That's called virga on Earth. Same on Mars.

On a large scale, weather on Mars is totally predictable. On a warrior's scale, not so much. There are always those scribbling dust devils, and big storms can block out the sun for months, covering the Red in dark brown murk so dense and fine you can't see your hand in front of your face. Imagine a near vacuum you can't see through. But the air does get warmer when the dust absorbs sunlight.

Making oxygen is the trick. Cracking water—hydrolysis—is comparatively easy; CO_2 and oxidized dust take more energy and time. That's why we need fountains. Fountains are big, often the size of a semi cab. We usually carry a couple with us on a drop, but they can also be delivered a few weeks before we arrive, on stealth chutes hundreds of meters wide, usually at night. They plop down on the Red and if the dust is deep enough—if they're not on impenetrable hardpan—they burrow in and almost immediately pop out solar collectors and extraction vanes and whirl the vanes to collect moisture from the air.

Fountains can stockpile enough volatiles over a few weeks to keep a company alive for two or three months. A big fountain can keep half a company in combat posture for six or eight months, refilling skintights with water and air.

Command can also decide to turn a fountain into a fuel depot, reserving its hydrogen and oxygen for propellant. We've all heard of fountains letting warriors suffocate on the Red for the greater strategic good—allowing someone else to get home again. Which do you need more? A return ticket, or enough to breathe? It's a nasty balance. Needless to say, Skyrines have a love-hate relationship with fountains.

To make matters more interesting, the longer a fountain has been on the surface, the more it becomes a prime target for Antag fire. Sometimes Antags let a fountain sit for weeks, working away, storing up volatiles, and when troops arrive and settle in, *then* they blow it up. Real sense of humor. Just as we start to party—scrap and stain on the Red.

If a fountain happens to locate a shallow aquifer or cached ice, it becomes a strategic reserve and may not announce its presence even to Skyrines, but instead shoots the news up to command and awaits instructions. Too valuable to waste on grunts.

OUTSIDE, THE DARK is complete and the air is clear. It's not as cold outside as on the southern highlands, but it's still plenty cold—about minus eighty Celsius. Inside the tent, curled up like puppies in a litter to conserve heat, we are truly womb brothers. Freudian, but not many Skyrines know dick about Freud, so traditionally, when we puppy up, we joke about bad porn instead. Unless we're too tired. There's a whole weird genre of porn down on the Big Blue Marble, about getting it on with Gurus or Antags. We aren't told what Gurus look like and don't know much about Antags, so they can be most anything we want. Why not prime green pussy? Some people down on the Blue Marble are just too strange to live. Interesting the Gurus don't seem to mind them.

In the dim light of a single beam, suppressed to a dull orange and hanging from the center of the tent, I study my mates. They seem to be asleep. I envy them that.

Tak is my friend, we go back a long ways, but I never feel entirely secure around him. He's quiet, movie-star handsome, lean and sharp, stronger and far more perceptive than me. Ever since Hawthorne, and in all our many battles, I've felt with a spooky prickle that someday he'll survive when I won't. Still, so far we've both survived, often because of what Tak does. He's damned good on the Red and a beast in a tussle.

Kazak is a very different sort. He's our barn door exchange student, a short, stocky guy with amazingly slanty eyes and even black fuzz on his crown that descends not so abruptly to a widow's peak. He came over from Kazakhstan a few years back and got promoted before the Skyrines found out he was a Tartar shithead and closed the barn door. Perfect teeth, long on the canines. A real *Canis lupus* with a feral smile. Not the brightest, but maybe the most steady and calm in a fight or a tough situation, he can be a quick judge of character, not always correctly, often with a Mongolian twist that's hard for the rest of us to figure. I can easily imagine him slapping raw meat under the saddle of his stocky pony and chewing on it in between Parthian shots with a compound bow. I have Polish and German blood in my family. Kazak denies fervently that his ancestors once raped and slaughtered mine. "Mongols so handsome, mother ladies just spread and bred," he says. Right. When things are loose, Kazak's sense of humor is murder. His practical jokes verge on felonies. PFCs have to stay on their toes around him.

Even for all that, most of us like him because he's *our* shithead and as shitheads go, he's kind of special. I've dropped with Kazak twice and sometimes he has this look that, when he has it, very reliably informs us that our Tartar shithead will take us *all* back home with him—a fierce wrinkle in one eye that makes me, too, want to bear his children.

Tonight, squinch-faced and snoring, he looks like a troubled baby. Still, he's snoring. I envy him that.

Being likable is a gift I do not reliably possess. I can turn it on sometimes, but I know when I'm doing it and feel guilty, people should just know I'm a good guy without the charm wave…But maybe I'm not such a good guy after all. Maybe default is truth. Nobody treats me as anything special, and I prefer it that way. Nobody but Joe and Tak and maybe Kazak. They're my best friends in this whole dust-fucked war.

An hour or more passes. I'm almost asleep, or maybe I'm dreaming I'm still awake, but I'm definitely awake when the alarm goes off again. Tak gets up on his knees by the membrane, ready to throttle whatever comes through. His face creases with handsome disappointment when a blue-stripe helm pokes in. Just another Skyrine, and this time it is Corporal Lindsay—Mitch—Michelin, his face blue with cold and hypoxia.

Tak raises his hands and flexes them. Finally, somebody we can boss around. Michelin is not the most compliant corporal, however. The entrance sucks shut as he pulls out his second boot, making our ears pop, and he falls on his back across DJ and Kazak. Then he claws his faceplate open and coughs until he's doubled. It's several minutes before he can say anything.

"No beacon!" he croaks. "Fuck. Almost died."

"You're welcome," Kazak says.

"Who's here?" Michelin asks, examining us with bloodshot eyes. He sees we're all superiors. It does not faze him. Tak hands the newcomer a tube of borscht and some reindeer sausage, then, more reluctantly, a bag of water. Now we're six, too many for the tent, if it's all we've got, but what can you do?

Michelin fixes his pink-eye gaze on Tak and grins. "Praise be, I'm in heaven. Master Sergeant Fujimori is here to service me. Who needs virgins?" His lips are still purple. He does not look good, but he's coming around. He holds up the Russian food tube. "What is this shit? Tastes like weak kimchee." And he erupts an enormous fart.

"Take that bloat outside," Tak requests, fastidious to a fault.

Michelin is too weak to apologize. After he's mumbled over our names and ranks, he falls into something like a nap, more like a brief coma, and then, twenty minutes later, flails for a moment before settling down, wide-eyed and shivering.

We're all awake now.

"Christ, our sticks must have shot their loads early," he says, rolls over, and asks if we have tactical.

"No," DJ says.

Then, with a shy smile, our lone corporal confesses he *might* have something. Turns out Michelin is the only one who got a solid burst before sparkly scrubbed the sky clean. Our angels share and we analyze his download, which includes broken uplink from previous drops.

"Still far from complete," Tak says.

"None of the fountains are putting out signal," DJ says. "Maybe they didn't make it down, maybe they got taken out—not one is talking."

We meditate on that.

"Tent can keep us going for eight more hours," DJ says. We give him the look. We do not need to hear what we already know. Tell us something new or something beautiful. DJ glances away, eyes losing focus, going dreamy. It's his safety.

Tak explores Michelin's burst beyond the negative on fountains. "Well, here's good news," he says. "Euro company before us"—the guys whose reindeer sausages and borscht lie heavy in our guts—"dropped a few tent boxes they didn't get a chance to use. No data on what went wrong…but there could still be six or seven inside ten klicks."

Our angels lock, and he shows us that the tents are widely spaced around the pedestal and the crater. We'll have to hike to avoid suffocation.

Few Skyrines keep it together when we can't breathe. No matter how tough our selection and training, we all tend to open our faceplates when oxy drops below threshold and claustrophobia takes over. True story. Skyrines typically want to die a few minutes early rather than slip into lung-searing delirium. Go figure.

"Rest up," Tak says.

After that, we're quiet for another half hour. I'm on the edge of a buzzing, insect-hive sort of sleep when the tent alarm goes off once more and Neemie squeezes in to join us—Staff Sergeant Nehemiah Benchley, from our second fire team, a strawberry blond surfer with a plump face and Asian wave tattoos that ripple like skin movies on his hands and neck. He's as ignorant as the rest of us. He reports the east is getting brighter, and he saw nobody else either during the drop or while walking. He cannot explain how he lasted this long. We don't inquire. Could be we're already dead. A hypnotically dumb idea that occurs far too often to warriors on the Red.

We drink up from what's left in the tent tubes, enjoy the luxury of a good piss in our recups, and for a few minutes, the tent smells of urine and ball-sweat. Not unpleasant, once you're used to it. Like a washroom in a Russian brothel. No disrespect. Dead Russians are saving us this night.

The tent announces in a stern, prerecorded voice—in Russian, Kazak translates—that there are far too many of us and we have depleted its resources.

The sky outside the tent is getting bright.

Time to move on.

GOD SAVES DRUNKARDS
AND BAKA DUDES

Morning is really cold.

We clap on our helms, seal up, query our angels, and one by one, through our faceplates, lift eyebrows or pook out lips, meaning all our angels are quiet. There are still no bit bursts, therefore no sats in the sky. Our angels have no good news, no news at all, and so they say nothing.

The tent is depleted. We birth out and just leave it there. No sense wasting strength trying to dig a hole and hide it, and it's useless to try to burn it under these conditions, because we'd have to supply the oxygen, and on top of all that, the tent's been out here for a month and if anybody cares they already know where it is. Likely nobody cares.

More Lost Patrol shit.

"We're at the butt end of a fight," Neemie opines into our gloom.

"Right," DJ says. "Tell us something ripping, Master Sergeant Venn."

"Ripping is as ripping does," I say. "We have no commander. We are on a hunt for gasps and sips and lunch. Not that I'm all that hungry." I look critically at Michelin and then at Vee-Def, who graces us with a dopey grin we can't really see behind his helm, but we know it's there.

We keep surveying the sky. From ground level all over Mars, you can spot space frames and other orbitals, especially before sunrise or after sunset, when the angles and contrast are best. This morning, nothing presents itself but a brilliant wall of stars. Air is very clear, and that means it's not going to get much warmer.

I look west because my left hand itches and it's on my western side. That little brown blurry patch is still there, up north a ways. Looks too far off to be of consequence, but it's the only steady attraction in our tight little theater. I touch helms with Tak. "Your ten," I say. He looks. His new eyes are better than ours. "What *is* that?"

"Dust devil," he says.

"It's been there since yesterday."

"What do *you* think it is?" DJ asks.

"A cute little twist in a Fiat...and she's got a keg," Kazak interposes.

"Could be wreckage," I say. "Could be a malfunctioning fountain. Could be anything."

"Ants," Vee-Def says, meaning Antags, Antagonists. Every word gets shorter as wars go on. Guys like Vee-Def do the shortening.

"*Could* be Antags," Kazak agrees. "But they would already be here if they cared about us, no? Why waste resources just to put us out of our misery—"

"Go see," Tak says, cutting off a bad ramble. He's a steady dude. When Tak makes a decision, others nod and agree. Neemie and Michelin move off first. The rest of us follow. I look back at the tent, our lifesaver, now useless junk. All across Mars there are thousands of tons of stuff that will get buried by dust and then dug up centuries from now and sold at auction. Our job is to make sure it's Sotheby's and not Ant-Bay. Ha-ha.

Talk of sparkly has gotten us downhearted. All we want is to find another tent. Not much hope for relief and certainly we can't hope for a pickup at this point.

We probably don't have enough reserves to reach the brown blur in the west. But maybe we're on a drop line, a regular pattern of deliveries in theater, across the plain. A mystical pilgrim's trail that will lead us to a few more days of life, and no asking God for more, that's already too much.

———

HIKING ON MARS in the morning chill is a treat I'd sell to any starry-eyed explorer for a hot shower.

Decades ago, a bunch of them came to Mars and set up parking lots full of white hamster mazes, then dug deep networks of rabbit tunnels. They claimed Mars and called it home. We call them all Muskies after a visionary entrepreneur, Elon Musk. From what little I've read, he founded an online bank, made cars and spaceships, promoted a vegan lifestyle, and fought for years with Blue Origin's Jeff Bezos, Virgin's Richard Branson, and a dozen other competitors around the world for launch facilities and orbital domination. Eventually, they pooled resources to fulfill the dream of putting people on Mars. But Musk had the name that stuck.

For almost twenty years, settlers kept crossing the vac and arriving on the Red, and then, abruptly, the migrations stopped—mostly because the best settlements maxed out and the others were starving or worse, like Jamestown in Virginia. But a few hundred stalwarts survived, and for a time Muskies were highly regarded, successful pioneers...Until people tired of spending money on the colonies, none of which ever made a return on investment.

So the investment stopped.

After the Gurus arrived and told us that Mars had maggots and we had to go out there and exterminate them before they grew into wasps, the Muskies became a liability. The brass decided we couldn't defend them, or save them if they got in trouble, once the Battle of Mars began in earnest. I've never seen a Muskie, even at a distance. There may be a couple of thousand left alive, but Earth hasn't done squat for them in years. As far as anyone knows, Antags don't bother with them, either.

The original settlers paid between $10 million and $100 million each for their *Mayflower* moment. Our strategy prof at SBLM likened them to the guy who lit out in the 1930s for the Pacific Islands to get away from the hurly-burly and ended up on Guadalcanal.

EVERY SKYRINE IS SOMEBODY'S BASTARD

We march. Radio silence isn't all that big a deal now, but we keep our talk to a minimum. The sky is still empty. Looks as if what's going to be here is already here.

Walking on lowland hardpan with only a softening of dust, or low ripples cut through by devil tracks, is easy enough, not like sand or deep dust, and we weigh about one-quarter what we would on Earth, so we could conceivably jump along like John Carter or a moon astronaut, but that's not recommended and not even all that much fun after the first few leaps, because you never know when your boot will come down on a stone big enough to turn your ankle. There are fucking rocks all over.

There's a lot of confusion still about how Mars came to be what it is today. Parts of Mars are pure nightmare, from a geologist's standpoint—so much evidence of big gushes and rivers and lakes and even oceans of past water, present water not so evident, but there all the same—so much difference between the southern highlands and the northern lowlands—plus the biggest visible impact basin in the solar system, Hellas Planitia, surrounded by peculiar terrain both older and younger than the impact… Smart people spend lifetimes trying to riddle it.

Mostly, I leave it to them. But I have my theories. I'm willing to believe all these little rocks fell out of some giant kid's pockets. He walked around in dirty sneakers for hundreds of thousands of years, picking up rocks and stuffing them in his dungarees. Whenever his balls chafed and tugged his pants leg, he dribbled a stony trail. Johnny Rocker. That explains all these ankle-turners.

We could legitimately pray for a thin cloud of fine silt to blow over, but the sky is not cooperating. Martian dust is a major heat-grabber. Temperatures rise, batteries last longer. Insolation—solar energy—drops quite a bit, but we aren't laying out solar panels and our skintights have little in the way of photovoltaic capacity.

DJ says he's in sight of the next Russian tent. He's quite an ace at finding tents. We knew roughly where it was, but he climbed the pedestal and located the tent box in an old gully. And then he reports it's got warning colors.

"Germ needles," he says.

The box is filled with shit that kills humans.

That leaves us with maybe two hours of breath.

———

By date of rank, I rule in this fragmented squad, but I don't give orders because nobody cares until we get our recon and tactical becomes important. Besides, if I go all commando voice—*Now, men! Listen up*—they're likely to ignore me and turn to Tak.

Which is fine by me.

I'd sure like to hear from Gamecock, our company commander—Lieutenant Colonel Harry Roost. I don't much like Roost—he can be a by-the-book hardass—but I respect him. He would be strong and direct out here, if not reassuring. We don't need a hand-holder. We need a lifesaver with a sense of purpose.

———

THINGS DO NOT get better. Before we reach the next tent box, Tak spots debris a few hundred meters off and we divert. As we get closer, all I see is a skipping series of strike marks, scorch and scatter—a few craters where chunks hit, while the rest went on and plowed long, shallow graves in the hardpan.

We gather around the edge of the strike zone and eyeball the extent. This was once an entire space frame, and it did not fall empty. It came down full of sticks and fasces. There are dead Skyrines everywhere. And a transport sled, split into pieces. Skell-Jeeps spill out of the shattered capsules like the bones of half-born babes. All useless. Even dangerous. Kazak warns us to stay clear of anything that looks like a reactor.

We gingerly poke around, looking for oxygen generators, tanks, packs of skintights, anything that could keep us going for a few more hours. Nobody talks. We don't examine the bodies. They came down hard and they're mostly just scattered rips of fabric, squashed helms…freeze-dried stain. They had probably just emerged from Cosmoline, woozy and sluggish, and were getting cleaned off, suiting up, attaching puff packs, prepping for the drop. The space frame must have just then been hit by ground-to-sky bolts or lasers, or sky-to-sky, no way of telling. When seen from a few dozen klicks, or from the ground: sparkly. Just as Michelin and Vee-Def said. Major sparkly to take down the company's frames and all our sats and, since we have yet to find a fountain, maybe all those as well.

The trunk of the frame might contain extra cargo. We give it a quick search. Nothing here, either. Pure Skyrine waste, nothing to see. Move along.

We have about half an hour. We'll be dead long before we reach the brown blur. Just keep marching toward the rough position of the next tent box. Kazak suggests we fan out, not to offer a compact target. We break into three groups.

"What's that tower of haze out there, really, do you think?" Tak asks. He's about ten meters away, skirting the pedestal's rim.

"Something stupid," DJ says, about thirty meters away. "Making itself obvious."

"Or something strong that doesn't give a fuck about being spotted," Vee-Def suggests.

That's possible, but I don't want to hear it. If it's strong and boastful, it doesn't belong to us. Antags are winning today.

"Maybe it's a secret sect of Muskies," Neemie says, moving closer.

"Shut up," I say. "And keep the spread."

We go wide again. Fifteen minutes of oxygen, give or take. Soon our angels will warn us we're down to last gasp and that will seal the deal. Maybe that's why we call them angels. They could be the last thing you hear.

Hey, Skyrine—it's a good day to die. They don't actually say that, but it might be cool if they did.

———

TIME TO DESCRIBE a skintight. It's a remarkable piece of equipment, even when it's failing, even when you know you're going to die. Your standard Mars-grade skintight is a flexible and seamless suit woven from a continuous monomolecular strand of carbon coilflex, set into a bilayer gel mostly comfy to the skin. Moisture is recycled or broken down into oxygen, depending on the need. In the field, the skintight absorbs skin waste and conveys it through tiny tubes to storage packs around the butt, which gives Skyrines a big-bootie profile. Every few days you remove the extract from the butt packs and throw it away—a useless lump of oil and dead skin and salt and other gunk.

The helm and the angel process video and tactical memory. Skintight fabric contains circuitry for battlefield diagnostic, which sends our health status to the angel for uplink, so that birds on high can tell our commanders how we're doing down on the Red.

Skintights do nearly everything except walk and fight and they do it quietly and without complaining. Some say they are like the still-suits in *Dune*, and they do bear a resemblance, but ours do a hell of a lot more than conserve and filter water.

Every Skyrine has a love-hate relationship with his skintight. Can't wait to get home and get it off, but then he misses the convenience of never having to worry about pee or crap or sweat, and feels, when naked, that one is minus a real friend, perhaps the best friend ever. Some old hands have to relearn bladder control when they're back in civvies. All the designers need do is make skintights sexually accommodating and Skyrines might never have to come home again.

Yeah.

That said, a skintight whose batteries are running down, whose oxygen is running out, whose water is turning sour, feels less like a friend and more like a jar full of pickle juice.

We are sinking deep in the jar.

THE WAY IT SPOZED TO BE

Immediately after drop, or on the way down, you're supposed to receive updated tactical and maps with known objectives and concentrations of Antag forces clearly laid out, appropriate to your squad's assigned chores.

Ideally, you'll drop within a short hike of a fountain or, barring that, a cluster of tent boxes, and somewhere in the vicinity your transport sled will also come down on stealth chutes, spiraling in within a couple of klicks of the company's drop zone, though they are pretty targets and often don't make it intact.

Skyrines are trained to make do with what they got. But when you got next to nothing…

Every Skyrine drops with at least one basic weapon, his sidearm. As I said, they look like fat .45s. Someone named them Yllas, don't know why. They don't shoot bees. They fire bullets and bolts. Bolts are deadly to anything they hit within five hundred meters. They home on whatever you're looking at with about ninety-nine percent accuracy. The pistols carry a small spent matter cassette and that has to be switched on to charge the plasma about thirty seconds before combat. A single spent matter cassette can charge and launch about sixty bolts. Gun captain—a rotating duty—collects all used cassettes. Spent matter waste is bad shit and we're supposed to be sensitive about ecological issues. In truth, however, there are a lot of cached bags of it out on the Red; no time in combat to search and recover if, for example, our gun captain gets zeroed. Vee-Def is supposed to be gun captain for this drop.

Kinetic rounds work in vac, of course—gunpowder supplies its own oxygen. But cold can reduce range, and target practice on Earth doesn't train you for Mars, where windage is usually very light, the thin air very cold, and the gravity drop much slower. Our other weapons, lasers and even weak-field disruptors, can be affected by heavy dust.

Skyrines have been trained to fight in nearly all conditions. Training is so you might not get killed before you gain experience. Newbies start on the Red with nothing but simulations and a month of Earth-based live fire—not nearly enough, in my opinion. You only really improve by doing.

———

AND HERE'S WHAT we think we know about the Antags, or at least, what we're told: They probably don't come from our solar system or anywhere near. That means they arrived on a big ship, tech unknown but capable of crossing interstellar distances. It's tough to visualize how huge interstellar space is. Vast, vast, long-long-long distance—repeat a trillion times until you feel really small and silly. Mostly empty light-years and deep cold.

But we haven't found that big ship, have no idea where it might be hiding, and can only vaguely guess how they get from there to Mars. Or anywhere else they take a fancy to. So far, just Mars, we're told.

But then the grandma said...

Titan! Jesus.

HEAVY HAND

Maybe I'm seeing things.

A couple of lights are floating up in the sky, competing with Phobos for my attention, bright enough to be space frames, but they could just as easily be Antag. Their *Grasshopper*-class boats are about that bright in orbit—clusters of pressurized tubes filled with transports and weapons and combatants.

Tak raises his hand. Michelin raises his and shouts there are sats still up—and then I see a thin blue line drop down quick, hit the dust, miss Vee-Def—then try again. This time the line touches him, then shifts over to Tak.

"Bit burst!" Tak shouts, loud enough to hear from five meters. We've been found.

I get my blue line next, and my angel is suddenly happy to show me where we are, where there might be supplies and weapons—the immediate logistical picture. Only three of us receive the laser lines, so our angels exchange for the next few seconds while we're chattering like schoolkids waiting for the bus.

"Something's coming," Tak says, having finished a quick

skim, tagging data he finds immediately important. To my surprise, it's not survival data—nothing to do with tents or sleds.

It's a warning.

"Big stuff coming down," Tak summarizes, concentrating so hard his eyes cross.

Michelin cranes his neck and looks up at the sky, squinting. He covers his helm with gray-gloved hands. Then he crouches. Instinct. We watch him, bemused.

"What is it?" Vee-Def asks. "Landing parties? Big Mojo?"

Big Mojo is rumored to have been seen once, four years ago: a kind of massive Antag orbital capable of shaving off huge, battalion-strength landers and dropping them to the Red. The lights we see aren't that bright. But they're also not what we're being warned about. Whatever's out there, whatever's on its way in, the mass is enormous, and there are nine to twelve of them, maybe more, separate objects tracked by our few remaining sats, which have finally and most kindly supplied us with what they know—just before we suffocate.

"Biggest may be a hundred million tons," DJ says, winnowing the numbers down to basics. "Others, smaller—five or six million."

"Jesus," Neemie says, his voice husky. His air is going fast. So is mine.

"Why tell us this shit now?" Michelin asks, lifting his head from his crouch.

"We're within five hundred klicks of point of impact," I say. "Approaching at more than forty klicks per second, which means they're moving in…I think fast…from outside Mars's orbit? Solar orbit? Extrasolar, from the Oort?"

Does that make sense? Wouldn't the Antags want to slow them down, whatever they are, or do they just plan on skimming atmo and making another go-around?

"What can we fucking do?" Michelin cries.

"How soon?" Neemie asks.

"Doesn't say."

Some lights now roll into view low in the west, very bright objects indeed, very big, one actually a crescent—and moving fast. Right for our collective noses, so it looks, so it feels.

Then, just as we are about to fall on our knees and wait for the big bright things to fly by or hit us square, Vee-Def finds practical info in the bit burst and shouts, "Three more Russian tents! A whole pallet! A hundred meters that way—" He points.

We run. No questions, no disagreement. We got maybe ten minutes of air.

I look over my shoulder and nearly take a header. But you can stumble quite a ways on Mars and still recover, if you're fast with your footwork. What I see, as I keep my footing and keep running, is that the objects in the sky are *tumbling*; the motion is obvious—bright, dark, crescent wobbling. Quick count: one scary big one, visually wider than Phobos but, I hope, I fear, much closer, and nine or ten smaller, but by now you can see all of them rolling around way up there like happy seals in an ocean swell.

Tak and Kazak find the pallet of three tent boxes and we cluster around as Vee-Def and DJ and Michelin slice the containment straps and separate the boxes, check the stripes—safe—then pop the seals. Two tents spring out, nearly hitting me and Michelin, and then roll and lie there, all innocent and beautiful. The third won't disengage from the box. Its air reserve is empty. It's not quite useless, however—Vee-Def harvests its water packs.

We got maybe four minutes to get one or both of the remaining tents to inflate before we climb inside, but even if we do that—

The first object hits the atmosphere. It draws a superfast ghostly white flame across the sky. The flame lingers and turns pale purple. The object strikes beyond the northwestern horizon.

It is *gone*. Not so bad. Then a brilliant flash seems to roll out of the west, quickly fades to a gloriously supernal mauve, while a pinkish dome shot through with coiling white clouds blooms at the center of the strike. The dome rises into perfect mushroom cap, supported by—nothing! No central pillar of smoke or cloud at first, but finally it seems to fill in, condense, and we see the mottled grayish stalk, tossing out curving streamers of purple and white.

We stand in awe. I'm gasping—Cheynes-Stokes breathing, not good.

The first tent has nearly inflated.

Then the ground shakes—*heaves* violently, tossing us like bowling pins. We end on our butts, clutching at the hardpan, while all around, dust leaps and pebbles and rocks do a crazy, jiggling dance.

A few dozen meters away, the hardpan *cracks open*, taking in the pallet and the bum tent—swallowing them whole. Almost gets DJ as well, but he scrambles toward us like a desert beetle. The crack stops a few arm-lengths from my faceplate. The sound is awful, a hard-packed, rhythmic pounding that shakes our skulls, our bones, makes the fabric of our skintights ripple, like standing too close to a Japanese drummer in full frenzy. My head pulses with each wave, and then—the waves seem to bounce off something and come back from the other side, from the east. What the fuck is that about?

We look west again.

A translucent wall of air passes over, buffets us, and suddenly we are surrounded by a muffled, pressing, scary quiet.

"Cone of silence!" Tak calls out, lying flat beside me.

"What?"

"We're in the cone! The shock wave's bounced against the upper air and arced over!" he says.

I have no idea what he means.

"More coming!" Michelin shouts. We all manage to look up. The sky, the horizon, is a soundless, eerie sort of awful, shot through with gray streaks spreading from that too-perfect mushroom cap, then obscuring it. That might have been the big one. If it wasn't, we won't survive, because it isn't over. A half dozen others *skip* this way and that across the sky and through the clouds like stones on a pond, finally plunging...

The shock is amazing. I'm tossed maybe five meters up and flip over and land on my back, hard enough to knock me silly. I try to breathe. Everything hurts. Broken ribs? If my skintight tears, I'm cold meat, but that may not matter, because the stars have fled—there's only a low gray ceiling, seemingly solid, impenetrable. But white specks fall *through* the ceiling.

I'm just a big ball of pain but then, old memories, I reacquire an agonized pair of childlike eyes and say, It's Christmas, look! Snow. Snow is falling all around. Flakes and chunks, some like grapple, some big as my fist. Falling all over, bouncing off me, off the hardpan. I don't bother to get up. Maybe I can't and I don't want to know that.

Pretty soon I'm buried in it.

Damn, we were almost in the tent.

Then come the rocks.

NOT YET A HERO, HUH?

I wake up and see Tak leaning over me, looking into my face.
Fingers do the ICU, UCME?

Yes. Yes.

It's heavy outside.

The air is like nothing I've ever felt on Mars, warm and dense.
My angel has been sounding a continuous wheep-wheep of
alarm. I get up on one elbow. There's a blanket of ice and snow
all around, punctuated by black rocks big as my fist, big as my
head—new rocks, flung from hundreds of klicks away. Some are
still smoking.

Impact heat.

Scattered between the snow and ice and the rocks are pools
of fizzing liquid water, bubbling like hot springs. Terrific. We've
made it to Yellowstone.

We're on Planet Perrier.

I try to say that over comm. I want to show Tak I'm still
clever, still able to make jokes, but I've bitten my tongue and my
mouth is full of blood and it splatters on my faceplate when I try
to talk.

Tak shakes his head. Holds up two fingers. I get up to help him find the others. DJ is buried in a drift. We shove aside rocks and ice. He's limp when we pull him out, but recovers enough to join our search. Kazak we find next. He's alert and looks as if he might have just had a refreshing nap. Leaps up out of the rubble, brushing snow and dust from his plate and shoulders.

Michelin is also still alive, but his helm took a rock or something and the plate is cracked, not yet through the seal. Still pressurized. All our skintights are okay, miracle of miracles. No rips.

We immediately try to relocate the other tents. Maybe the one has finished inflating. If it hasn't, or if both got swallowed by another crack or pierced by rocks, we're down to nothing, don't know how we lasted this long, must have been mere minutes yadayada all the shit that fills one's head as the body does, like a robot, like a trained dog, what it's supposed to do to keep your pretty soul wrapped in flesh.

We find the tent. It inflated, but then—ruptured, big holes where rocks went through. But the canisters still have air and we take turns charging our skintights. Just a few minutes' worth.

Where's Vee-Def? Neemie?

We find the second tent box. Shadows close in around my eyes like groping fingers. My lungs are awful balloons filled with fire.

Tak inflates the tent. The noise all around has returned. It's unrelenting. Mars is cosmically bitching: whistling, hissing, sighing—then, letting out with a shrill, high scream as something much too grand shoots overhead. More big stuff coming down? No way to know. The gray canopy of clouds still looks solid. The local pools still bubble and spit mud, local air still feels thick, but everything is cooling rapidly, and now the water is turning into steaming, crusty, carbonated ice—sinking into the dust or soaking into hardpan.

Fog suddenly condenses all around. It's like a big Walt Disney brush painting us over. We can't see much of anything. Wiping my faceplate, fingers streak away dust and water. The water vanishes from my fingertips and leaves just the dust. Never even had time to become mud.

I pick my way around and kick at the last of the snow, vanishing before it can liquefy. This stuff is not water! Like dry ice or something else. Weird.

Something in me remembers where Michelin was, and I turn just enough to walk back and find him. He's trying to get up. Tak bumps into me. We both check Michelin over. His eyes are wide, concerned. He swipes at the fog.

Tak holds up five fingers.

My cheeks hurt I'm grimacing so hard.

Kazak joins us. The fog begins to clear, swirling up and away in ghostly eddies. The sky shows patches of grainy black. Funny I haven't noticed the sound for a while, but it's down to a constant brumble-grumble with odd pops that make my ears hurt.

Then it gets real quiet. That's not much better, in my opinion. We all stand hands on shoulders, supporting each other, supporting Michelin, who's regaining his balance, some of his strength, touching his faceplate, no doubt wondering how he made it through.

Vee-Def and Neemie come stumbling out of the last unwinding mist. They spot us. Shamble our way. Tak holds up seven fingers. Praise Jesus. We gather around the one intact tent, brush ourselves off as best we can, and crawl one by one through the tent's tight canal. No immediate appointments. No place else to go. We are tired, lost, beat-up little puppies. Too many for the tent, regulation, but nobody cares. We've got air, water.

The ground is still vibrating as I manage to find some sleep. Then, maybe five minutes later, Michelin wakes us by flashing a beam around, and says, sitting up straight, hair on end, full of revelation, "That ice—some of it was dry ice, methane, ammonia—really *old* shit!"

"So?" Kazak asks, ticked off.

"The Antags dropped a fucking *comet*!" Michelin concludes, and stares around at us, one by one, jaw agape, impressed by his own intelligence.

We stare back. Fuck yeah. No disagreement.

"Heavy hand, man," Vee-Def says, shaking his head in admiration. "Taking charge."

NOT DEAD YET

Caught in a weird, ethereal glow as we wake, we untangle, sit up, and one by one, peer through the clear tent panels. Tak's face when he looks shines like hot bronze.

The sunrise is amazing. I've never seen such colors on Mars, like a Pacific island postcard, great streaky plumes of dust catching first light of morning, all red and orange and gold. Our resources are not encouraging. Plus, we're hungry. We don't complain, but now we think on it.

We suit up and emerge. The world outside doesn't seem to have changed substantially, after all the hurly-burly. The brown blur is back, just about where it was. The sky is a little lighter—more dust kicked up—but the snow is gone and the puddles have all fizzed away. It's once again a dry, desolate hardpan.

Dust settles quickly on Mars, once the wind stops.

We stand out in the cold like anyone would, wrapped in crossed arms, whapping our shoulders, waiting for salvation or at least something different. Skyrines do not stay impressed for long. About the only thing that would impress me now is a portal opening directly ahead and taking me straight to a Jack's

Popper Palace. Beer. Burgers and fries. I'm hungry enough that that would impress the hell out of me.

Kazak hears something. "Sounds like a mosquito."

"Skell coming," Vee-Def says. He has the best ears of our small bunch. Tak has the best eyes of anyone in the company; new eyes, brilliant blue. Even so, I spot the Skell-Jeep first, a little bug whining over the horizon. It flies a big chartreuse flag, the color most obvious out here—green and yellow severely lacking on Mars.

The Skell veers to avoid fresh pits and then it's upon us. Glory yet again—we have our division deputy commander! Lieutenant Colonel Hal Roost, Gamecock to his troops, is driving the Skell while a United Korean *sojang*, a major general, two small stars attached combat-style to a blaze strap on his chest, rides shotgun. The general cradles a Facilitator—a wide-mouthed rocket launcher. The general also has two Tchikoi flechette pistols strapped to his belt, wrapped in transparent Baggies with finger holes, dusty-desert fashion.

This pair is grim, abrupt, no congratulations, no small talk. Gamecock signals radio silence is still on. Our bad. We are, however, under the circumstances allowed to communicate by scree or laser, angels targeting each other, or by shouting in our helms, and that gives us a chance to clearly hear Gamecock announce that our forces are in temporary disarray.

"We took major sparkly on delivery. The drop was severely fidged. Some orbital jock must have spooked at the first G2O." Ground-to-orbit. That could explain our high stick release.

"Well, they're all dead now," Gamecock says. "Good to see you made it." Gamecock gestures over his shoulder. "We need to reevaluate our leisure activity. See that blur? That—is a game changer. Probably some sort of Antag factory. We don't know whether it came down with the dirty ice or was lying there waiting for supplies."

"Master Sergeant Venn saw it before the strike," Tak says.

Gamecock nods, good info. "Whatever, now it's got everything it needs to crank out adverse goodies."

And to think we were moving toward it. Like jacklighted deer, I guess.

We look at the Korean general, wondering if he'll contribute anything. His face, behind a dirty faceplate, is haggard. His skintight is exceptionally dirty. He's been out in the open for some time.

"Pardon," Gamecock says. "This is General Woo Jin Kwak. He dropped with an eastern platoon the week before we arrived. Lost most of his men. The survivors are south of here. Good news, they've found an old Chinese fountain and may have the codes to activate. So that's where we're going to regroup. Then, we're going to attempt to establish two-way with whatever sats are still working and conduct some recon. Learn what's going on. What's expected of us. For now, that Chinese fountain is our destination. And it is over *there*." He points south. "We'll know nothing more about the Antags until we have orders and command tells us go see," he says. "And to do that, we need to stay alive and accumulate resources."

"Leave now," Kwak says, and swings up his arm. Command structure among the signatories in our fight is not supertight, despite the fact we're supposed to be buddies and cooperate fully. Korean general and all, we don't move unless Lieutenant Colonel Roost tells us to.

"Climb up, travelers," Gamecock says.

The Skell-Jeep is big enough to carry us all, if three hang from the waist bars. Tak and Vee-Def and I hang. Gamecock drives us south. Judging by the bent frame and a skewed wheel that thumps us about, the Skell has taken a couple of tumbles and a roll or two since it popped out of its capsule. It's a real beach buggy ride.

Pretty soon, recent craters become more obvious. The comet chunks split before striking atmosphere. A lot of loose ice

WAR DOGS | 61

skipped around way up there, creating a total impact zone of maybe ten or twenty thousand square klicks. Just guessing. Pinpoint aim considering where comets usually dwell.

I'm asking myself—we're all amateur astronomers up here—how the Antags can maneuver fucking comets without our knowing, since trans-Martian space is scanned from Earth and the Moon every few hours. Maybe the Antags covered it in soot before moving it downsun. No matter. That level of theory is way above my pay grade, but I stuff it aside in a mental cubby to ponder later, perhaps before returning to timeout.

I like having things to ponder as the Cosmoline sinks in, the bigger and weirder the better. One of my favorite ponders is the Galouye question—is all this, the entire perceived universe, a gigantic computer simulation? There's a philosopher named Thaddeus Cronkle way down in London who claims he has proven that it is, and that we can run what some boffin or other called a Taylor algorithm to figure out which operating system is running the show. We're all Neos. Cool shit, that, real calming. Better than contemplating heaven, because all Skyrines go to heaven, not an exclusive club, and if it lets *us* in, I doubt it's much like what we've been told. Paradise, like Mars, is never what it's spozed to be.

The Skell takes us through even rougher scenery. There was fighting south of us before we dropped. Remnants of bivouacs lie all around, scattered as if by massive S2G—sky-to-ground—laser or bolts or torpedoes. We watch in respectful silence. There are bodies. Lots of bodies, and they may have taken orders from the Korean general.

He doesn't look left or right.

———

A BIVOUAC ON Earth means a temporary encampment where troops have not had time to pitch tents or set up any structure. On Mars, of course, there is rarely any sort of bivouac without tents or other cover. We steal words from the past and abuse them.

Gamecock does not enlighten as to our tactical. He's as lack-wit as the rest of us. And the general still doesn't do anything but sit there, his gloved hands grabbing the seat bars so tight they look like they might split. He's seen rough shit. The way he's not looking at the pits and debris, maybe he saw it here.

Tak, hanging on beside me, studies the field of recent battle with screw-lipped concentration, like he's constipated. Neemie is motion sick but holding it in. Only Vee-Def keeps a steely squint toward some far destination, wherever it may be. Heroic. Stoic. So unlike him.

The overloaded Skell climbs a slope and tops a barchan—a big sinuousity of blown sand about fifteen meters high—and rolls for a time along the crest, then turns with a sickening, tire-scurry lurch and descends, sideways, sliding, threatening to roll—but Gamecock corrects just before we hit the hardpan.

Without warning, just beyond the dust-deviled edge of sand, the lieutenant colonel takes us straight over rutted, ancient mud, nearly knocking me loose, and with another lurch, down into a deep furrow. He brakes the Skell to a trembling halt within five paces of a rough lean-to. The lean-to is made of capsule and tube parts and covers a big tent, a command tent.

Beyond the lean-to, the furrow splits, carving a Y in the flatness. Gamecock jumps from the Skell. We're quickly the center of attention as heavy rank emerges from the lean-to. This Y-shaped depression is our recon point. It is full of Asian and Russian brass—two Chinese generals and three Russian colonels. Boy are they happy to see us! Now there are sergeants and a corporal to boss around, along with Gamecock.

Kwak dismounts slowly, passes his weapons to a Russian colonel, and turns toward us. Face pale, resigned, he gathers strength to summon us into the command tent. Where is this honcho's staff? Each one of these officers should have security and staff and a whole lean-to or command tent apiece. Clearly, they have fallen on hard times.

I glance at Gamecock and then at Tak, whose constipation has relaxed into focused wonder, and share a silent fear that here, buckaroos, there are far too many cowboys and not nearly enough Indians.

Tak touches helms with me. "Why so many generals?" he asks.

"Somebody fucked up major ops," I guess.

THE STRAIGHT SKINNY—OR NOT

The lean-to is jury-rigged and works more as concealment than protection or support. The command tent beneath resembles an old hot air balloon, sagging and rippling under the curved and cracked aluminum and plastic. A one-person airlock replaces the birth canal entrance, but operates much the same way: you enter, wrap yourself in membrane, air is squeezed back into the tent, then you unzip an inner panel, unwind, and step inside. We make sure DJ and Vee-Def brush down thoroughly, not to disgrace us.

Tak and I silently assess the situation once we're in. This is not a place of safety or refuge. They've probably been using the tent mostly as a place to talk. First, the pressure is no better than it would be most of the way up Everest. Even so, the thin air smells of death—foul-sweet, clogging. None of the officers looks fit. Most have sustained crush or strike injuries. Wounds tend to get nasty in low pressure. Flesh needs oxygen at decent pressure to purify and heal, otherwise anaerobes move in. I long to seal up my skintight and leave. We all do.

Gamecock introduces us around the ragged circle. Despite wanting to gag, I'm in awe. Here we are, grunts from a fragmented squad, sharing the air—however foul—with commanding officers from three partner regions and five nations. These guys hang out with world leaders. Certainly a group worth rescuing, and that may improve our chances…

Major General Kwak proves adept at English and is in slightly better health than the others. He tells us, in a tight, pain-racked voice, that they have a little water, another day's worth of air, and—at the northern branch of the furrow—something that would be invaluable if it weren't broken: a Chinese fountain, covered with sand and dust, not by design, but by the local weather. It's at least two years old, from a previous drop.

"Can you fix?" he asks with a hopeful rise of one brow.

Gamecock and DJ confer in whispers. I can't hear what they're saying. I know that DJ had tech training on fountains but was never certified.

As a Russian named Efremov pushes out a sag in the tent, Kwak slowly steps over to a fold-out table supporting a small projector. "You must be asking, why are so many generals? Because commanders must study ground before committing troops to battle." He gives a wry shake of his head. "We arrived with many space frames, an orbital command station, many satellites. Seventy-five transport sleds, hundreds of vehicles. And now they are destroyed or scattered. We made emergency drop, and are now here."

These impressive combined ops did not include us. They must have arrived separately from our squadron, weeks before.

"We have not been able to establish comm with our other forces. We do not know where they may be, or how many survive. We were unfortunate…" Major General Kwak pauses, chest heaving as he works to suppress Cheynes-Stokes. With so many in the tent, long speeches are clearly not in order, but that's never stopped generals.

Kwak continues. "Our ships encountered Antagonist defenses in orbit with at least forty of their...snake-trains, upon their own insertion and entry." He looks less sure of his words and refers to a Russian colonel, who translates for us, "Snake-trains...The general refers to Antagonist resupply caravans. Carrying weapons, troops, great amounts of volatiles."

"Comets?" Gamecock asks.

"We think so, yes," Efremov says, and drops down on his knees. These few words and he's almost out for the count.

"Clearly, something large," Kwak resumes. Determined to finish this grim briefing, the general refocuses with shuddering effort. "There is only one of our satellites still in orbit, though that may be down now as well. No more frames will arrive for at least a week. Until we understand how our present forces are dispersed, and what strength remains, we are merely observers. Are we agreed on this intelligence, gentlemen?"

Everybody's agreed, if not happy.

A Colonel Orlov pushes up and struggles to do his bit. "Chinese fountain...inoperable. We lost engineers in the drop. But it may still be reworked—repaired."

"We have an engineer," Gamecock says. DJ looks apprehensive. "Do you have proper tools?"

"Possibly," Kwak says. "But not many spare parts."

The officers confer in Chinese and Russian. Then another officer enters the tent and looks around: an Indian with a swollen face, chapped and cracked lips and cheeks, his right arm badly broken and hanging in a crude cable sling. Lots of starboard breaks here. A command sled could have landed hard and injured everybody inside, all at once.

"We are in regard to repair and refit," Kwak tells him.

"Most excellent." The newcomer reaches out his left hand to

Roost, thinks better of that gesture—no good for Muslims, and who knows?—withdraws the hand, looks around with sunken eyes. "I am Brigadier Jawahar Lal Bhagati. Who here is capable of our salvation, and making do for all?"

The old fountain seems to be our last hope.

Gamecock puts a hand on DJ's shoulder. "Sir, this man is the best we have."

God help us.

"Most excellent!" says Bhagati. "We have scrounged tools, and may have the right codes to activate. Let us begin."

BRIEF HOPE

The next few hours, I'm designated quartermaster and scurry back and forth carrying tools and a few of the dwindling water packs. Still no food to speak of, but we can do without that for days longer.

DJ seems to be making progress with the fountain, but it's getting dark and very cold, minus one hundred Celsius, and we're not going to be able to stay outside much longer. Keeping warm drains batteries fast. During cold snaps or night, Skyrines are supposed to squeeze into a tent or at the very least huddle in a ditch and cover with dust. Last man pushes dust over the group and then burrows in as best he can. Back on Rainier, we trained extensively on how to huddle and cover. Like puppies, as I've said; puppies seem to know how to assume the most efficient piles.

Tak had corpsman training back at SBLM, and despite his own contusions and a couple of cracked ribs, he tends to the beat-up officers in the half-inflated tent with a steady, blue-eyed gaze that is equally good at calming horses.

Our squad, by the way, is code-named Trick and is made up, in full complement, of two fire teams. Tak and I are part of fire team one—weak-field disruptor, rapid-delivery bolt rifles, and multitrack launchers. If we arrive with all our weapons, of course. I don't know why we still use code names. We don't even know if Antags understand human languages. But we sure as hell don't know *their* languages. No one, as far as we've been informed, has ever intercepted comm between Antag units or their ships or equipment. Nothing to help us make a Rosetta. Maybe they just don't *talk*.

Which is one reason I don't like calling our enemy *Ants*. Ants communicate all sorts of ways. Ant colonies are a single organism, a single mind, mostly, with the individual insects we call "ants" acting both as muscle and neurons. Each ant serves as scout, worker, and a little bit of the colony brain. The colony as a whole gathers intel around its field of action and then solves problems like a distributed network. They communicate by touching feelers and sensing chemicals they leave behind, trails of clues that also serve as a kind of GPS. I'd hate to fight ants, especially big ones. Gamecock, like Vee-Def—like Joe—persists in calling our enemies Ants. Sometime I'll tell you about my nightmare of getting stung all over.

Christ, it's getting cold. I'm starting to feel comfortable, ready to settle in and go to sleep, so to keep awake, I walk back and forth in the ditch between the half-inflated command tent, where the generals and colonels are hanging out—with the exception of Gamecock—and back up to the northern branch of the Y to the broken Chinese fountain. My ankles are knotting, so my gait is more of a controlled stumble. Worse, there's a sickening smell in my helm. I hope it's not my own gangrene. At the very least, our skintights are well beyond pickle juice; the scrub filters are failing and the residue must be turning rancid, which is absorbing oxygen...Everything needs recharging, replacing. Including me.

Finally, I post myself by the fountain, too tired to move. Sleep is a soft and lovely thought. Lovely easeful death. Through a darkening tunnel, I watch DJ's feet. He's shoveled out an angle of dust at the base of the fountain and unscrewed a hatch, into which he's now shoved the upper half of his body. His feet twitch and every now and then he bends his knees. That's how I know he's still alive, still working.

Fountains are impressive pieces of equipment. They used to arrive by balloon bounce, but since they've gotten larger, more expensive, and more delicate, they're more often delivered by stealth chutes or even chemical fuel descent. This Chinese model is smaller than some and may have bounced down hard when it arrived. Maybe it wasn't packed right. At any rate, Colonel Orlov explains, on one of his own slow, painful passes up the trench, that some of its collection tanks have been crunched and its self-diagnostic unit has refused to activate, under the stubborn belief that it won't do any good. Fountains can get neurotic.

DJ's boots twitch, his knees flex, but other than that, he's a cipher.

The fountain suddenly decides to pop its top and push out a collection vane. Orlov and I give out a weak cheer. Kazak, Michelin, and Efremov join us, hopeful. But the vane doesn't unfold or spin, and it's no good if it doesn't spin.

DJ finally shoves out of the bay and shakes his helm. "All busted up inside," he calls out. We can barely hear him. Kazak and Michelin and I touch helms with him like footballers in a huddle. "The parts that work are unhappy, and if I reroute the bus, the parts that don't work will suck all the power. Drain it down to nothing. Don't know what more I can do. If anybody finds a parts kit, let me know, okay?"

We amble in slow lurches for the command tent, loopy from the smell in our suits. None of us wants to spend a night puppied with a bunch of senior officers, but we don't have any choice. Die outside or steal air and heat from the brass.

BLONDE ON A BUGGY

We're in serious trouble, no doubt about it. We barely make it through the night. I lie in our pile, moving only when Kazak kicks in his sleep. He kicks like a mule.

General Bhagati is doing poorly. Blood poisoning, best guess. His own once-friendly germs have decided he's a dead man. That happens a lot to warriors in battle. Germs seem to think we're all walking corpses.

First light, we seal our helms and leave the tent to stand under the pink dawn. The sunrise is abrupt and not at all spectacular—not that we care. Point comes when beauty is lost on a fellow. My head swims. Helm stinks like a refrigerator whose power has been out for a couple of days, skin itches all over, and I assume the others, like me, will soon consider just popping a faceplate and getting it over with. A miserable end for Trick Squad.

Where did it go wrong? I'll get into that later, I decide, when the freezing cold really sets in. You get warm, comfortable, and last thoughts come easier. At least the itching will go away. Maybe.

I sit on the edge of our ditch and catch occasional dim speech sounds from around the tent, but it doesn't mean much, mostly in Korean or Mandarin. I took some Mandarin in high school and junior college, but not much sticks with me. I wanted to take an internship in Shanghai but got turned down because of an ultraslight criminal record—boosting an uncle's truck when I was thirteen. Skyrines don't mind criminals. They beat that juvenile crap out of you, then raise you from petty crook to stone killer. Skyrines start out as Marines, but then we get shipped to the desert and mountain centers for a lot of additional training. There's also the entire Right Stuff gantlet, including a madhouse LSD psych evaluation that demands a Nuremberg trial. I remember that vividly, more than the routines of piss-poor torture, also known as VPP&T—Vacuum Physical Prep and Training. Hawthorne Depot, Rainier, Baker, Adams—Mauna Kea. Military medicine has been pushed to the ethical limits, and way beyond. Blood doping and juicing aren't allowed until you're a finalist, but then the docs really go to town. I added fifteen pounds of solid muscle, then was starved fifteen to make up for it. My body fat ratio...

Shit, I don't care. I'm sitting on the edge of the ditch, thinking vaguely about women—but not yet thinking about good old Mom. According to hallowed combat tradition, the last thing a mortally wounded grunt asks for is Mom, but in the vac and on the Red, nobody can hear that final whimper.

Michelin sits beside me. We bump helms and he says, very hoarse, "They're all down there yelling at DJ in Mandarin. I hate officers. He doesn't know Mandarin. I do, and they are talking shit. Blaming him for killing us all."

"How's he taking it?"

"DJ may know machines, but he is the densest piece of wood in the forest. He's mostly ignoring them."

My head is really spinning. My eyes take snapshots at the end of a long, dark pipe.

But I'm not yet blind.

"See that?" I ask, pointing north.

"What?"

"That." This could go on for a while, but Michelin manages to focus. He grabs my arm.

"*That*...is a vehicle!" he says.

"Not a Skell," I observe.

"Definitely not one of ours."

"Still, it's pretty big. Antag?"

"No idea. Not a Millie." Millies are millipede-like Antag transports, with dozens of segments mounted on big tires.

"We should let the others know," Michelin says.

We don't move. We're fascinated by the progress of the approaching vehicle. It's maybe ten meters long, a cylindrical carriage with big, curved, punch-blade tires. It's not one of ours, but it certainly isn't Antag.

We slowly remember that we've seen its like in old vids.

"It's a Muskie bus...isn't it?" Michelin says with boyish wonder.

A squad's spooky antennae can spread news quick and without words. The rest of our Skyrines, except for DJ and Gamecock, suddenly appear in the trench, climb to the edge, and squat next to us.

"What's so funny?" Kazak asks. Nobody's laughing, but he's hearing laughter, I guess.

"It's a Muskie colony transport," Michelin says. "A bus."

Gamecock joins us last. We let him shove into the center of our lineup. "Fidge this," he says. "DJ reports no possible joy with the fountain. I'm getting ready to hitch a ride with the Horseman." By which he means Death. But then he leans forward, squints, and sits up straight, squaring his shoulders. "Do you see *that*?" he asks.

"We all see it," I say.

"Then maybe it's real. Have you ID'd it?"

"It's a Muskie bus," Michelin says.

"Everyone sure it's not Ant faking a Muskie?" Gamecock asks. He sounds beyond tired. We're all near the end. My angel has been telling me every five minutes or so that the skintight filters have maxed out. I'm thinking about shutting it down, just to let myself fade in peace.

But there is that bus. If Gamecock sees it, too, and Michelin says it's a bus, it had better be a bus.

Meanwhile, as the shared hallucination is being scrupulously eyeballed by us ragged group of perch-crows, nobody seems willing to initiate and engage, not even Gamecock. Kazak and Tak do rock-paper-scissors. They come up evenly matched, rock against rock, three times. Spreading fingers is just too damned hard.

"Fate calls on us both," Kazak says. "Sir, Tak and I would like to go beg a cup of sugar."

Gamecock nods, but he's not agreeing, exactly; his carbon dioxide has shot way up and he's about to fall asleep, then die.

Tak punches his arm. "Sir!"

The lieutenant colonel pulls back. He looks around, behind, down into the ditch, across the broken fountain and the sagging command tent. "Am I in charge here?" he asks dreamily.

"Yes, sir," Michelin says. "You're all we got. The Russians are dead. The Indian is dying. Chinese and Koreans are huddled in the tent, and the tent is out of air."

While we're considering our lack of options, the cylinder out on the flats rolls forward again. Toward us, it seems. We've been surveilled and someone has decided to investigate. Bless them. Bless all Muskies. Survivors. Self-sufficient, quiet...mobile.

Gamecock finds a last grain of resolve and taps Kazak's helm. "Stand down, both of you. Let them come to us," he says. "DJ, go knock up the generals and tell them we have visitors and not to shoot."

DJ hustles, as much as he can move at all, down the slope into the ditch, where he pauses, gets his bearings, despite the fact there's really only one direction he can move—along the ditch—and then lurches forward again.

I turn my attention back to the flat. I don't trust superb coincidence. What in hell would a Muskie be doing out here? The nearest settlement is at least six hundred klicks northwest. Somewhere near the center of the comet impacts.

The bus is now about fifty meters off.

Gamecock raises one arm. Waves it slowly. The vehicle slows and stops again. My vision is almost gone. Through the fuzzy end of a dark gray barrel, I make out a few more details. There are patches all over the fuselage. The curved blades on all six tires are scratched and dented and look to be from different batches, varying in color from titanium gray-orange to rusty steel. Bus has been around for a while. A prospector? I've not heard of such out here, but even Muskies must have hard-core purists who can't stand to be around *anybody*. Pity if the bus is carrying just one gnarly old miner with a chaw-stained beard and the phys of King Tut.

DJ returns, it seems right away—but that could mean I've nodded off without knowing it. Tak is shaking me by my arm, and Kazak is trying to rouse Michelin, who's not responding.

"What's with the generals?" Gamecock asks DJ.

"Asleep or dead," he says. "That fountain was our last hope. Sorry, fellows."

"Not your fault," I manage to say. I can hear them okay, but I'm not sure they hear me. Sound is funny on Mars. Everything is funny, or soon will be. I'm hypoxic. I don't even notice that someone is approaching us on foot, not until a tall, slender figure in a lime-green skintight is almost upon us. Very tall. Maybe two meters.

Carrying slung tanks and a pressure hose.

The figure's helm lases ours. A female voice inquires, "Give refill? Or you walk a me back my buggy?"

We all try to walk, but it's a bust. We tumble over on the ridge and slide past her, if it *is* a her; I hope it's a her. Mother or female angel, *really* an angel. I'm good with either. Michelin directs her to Gamecock. She attaches her hose and pumps oxygen for a few seconds, and when his eyes flutter, she disconnects and makes rounds, giving us each a few minutes. My concentration returns, but my head hurts like hell. The tunnel is wider but I'm seeing double and can't stop blinking.

Then the female does her rotation again, charging our suits with at least an hour's worth of gasps. When she's finished with the second rotation, she steps up over the ridge and into the furrow. We all sit on the other side of the ridge and enjoy just breathing, waiting for our wits to reassemble. It's going to be a long wait.

Our savior comes back leading the Korean general. Tak follows. Our eyes meet. He shakes his head as he walks up the ridge.

"Sorry," the female says. She sounds young. "Coudna get t'em in time. We should get a my buggy and te hell out. Ot'ers sure come soon."

Her voice is high and a little hard on consonants and *s*'s. I had read about thinspeak...pronunciation adapted for high altitude or thinner air. Now I'm hearing it. Plus a true Muskie accent. She's the real thing. Through her faceplate I see a wisp of white-blond hair and large, blue-green eyes. She's very tall. Have I said that already?

"Are we the last?" Gamecock asks. "I mean, our company..."

"Havena seen else a-one. Sommat set off transponder an hour ago. I tracked a way off course and found you."

DJ must have activated the fountain's beacon. He may have inadvertently saved our lives. But likely he also announced our presence to anything that gives a damn within a hundred klicks.

We march to the buggy's airlock, helping each other along. DJ and Michelin tend to Major General Kwak.

"Second gen?" DJ asks the ranch wife as she returns to assist. We're all on radio comm now.

"Don't be rude," Tak says.

"Born a Mars," she confirms. "All guys? No fem?"

"No women," Gamecock says.

"Damn. Be good, now." She gives us each, one by one, a foot up into the lock. "Carry us all, buggy's got just juice enow make te eastern Drifter."

Great. Whatever that is.

Her eyes meet mine as she hands me up, right after the general. She's strong, despite being slender. "Welcome on't, *Master Sergeant Venn*." She sounds out my name precisely. It's on my chest strap.

I smile. "Thank you."

"Get te hell in," she says.

I am the last. She climbs up and seals the door. In the cramped lock, she hands out brushes unlike any we've seen—labeled "Dyson." Like magic, we're clean in a few minutes, with nary a speck kicked loose. She dumps the brushes down a little chute. "Gecko tech," she announces with that amazing smile as the lock finishes its cycle and she pushes open the inner hatch.

We tumble into the relatively spacious cabin, about two meters wide and four long. Forward, through the wedge-shaped windshield, I can see the ridge, the unmoving vane of the useless Chinese fountain…

The distant horizon.

The young woman—she can't be more than twenty-three, twenty-four Earth years, half that Martian—sits in the forward seat and takes the pilot's two-grip wheel. The bus responds with a whine, a deep groan, and a whir of electric motors, and we back away from the ridge, turn north, roll a short distance, then turn southeast.

We take seats on cushions or slings spaced along the bus's interior. Unmarked bins and plastic crates fill most of the cabin, leaving us with little space to call our own. We do not complain.

"Rough go soon," she says. "Strap in if you can, otherwise hang a tie-downs."

Vee-Def assumes a husky feminine voice. The husky part comes easy. "Buckle your seat belts, gentlemen, it's going to be a bumpy ride," he says. He's quoting someone, I don't know who, probably a movie star, but that's okay. Everything's okay.

Tak and Michelin and I try to treat the general's wounds, which have purple edges, not good; we don't know if he'll last more than a few hours. He slips in and out of consciousness, murmuring in Korean.

The young woman focuses on the drive. The bus does not appear to be equipped with other than the most rudimentary guidance. I can make out a kind of sighting telescope in the roof just behind the driver's seat, probably for taking star fixes. Grid lines on the lower half of the windshield. No side windows, no way for us in the back to look out at the passing spectacle that is Mars.

A bottle of tasteless water is passed around. Even the general takes a long drink.

I feel almost human.

"Remove t'ose skintights," our driver says.

"Yes, ma'am!" DJ says, grinning like a bandit.

"Scrub t'em out while t'ey charge a buggy taps," she continues. On Mars, among the Muskies, there are now several kinds of accents and dialects and even some newly birthing languages, we were briefly informed in basic. But we weren't instructed in any of them.

"Pull your pouches and toss t'em a recycle chute. I t'ink we have filters a fit, back a rear bulkhead, top right drawer. T'en, scrubbed and clean, climb in your suits again. We're going outside onced we get t'ere."

Those of us who can, follow her directions. We don't mind being bossed by a tall blond ranch wife. That's what our DI at Hawthorne called Muskie women, when he mentioned them at all. *"Don't think you're going to save all those ranch wives... They are off-limits. They do not fidging care. To you, they matter less than Suzy Rottencrotch."* That sort of shit. I am deliriously grateful. I feel the way a pound mutt must feel, rescued just before they seal the hatch on the death chamber.

We're all War Dogs, adopted by a very tall, strong ranch wife.

———

WE'VE STRIPPED TO Under Armour when the first big jolt hits. She wasn't kidding. We're off the plateau, off the hardpan, onto real washboard. And heading toward the eastern Drifter. Whatever that is.

"As Raisuli said, *It is good to know where one is going*," I quote. Skyrines headed for the Red dote on desert war movies, even flatties. Oddly, Vee-Def does not get the reference, which makes him sullen.

Tak and Kazak finish their chores first, scrubbing and repacking filters, despite the lurching and jolting, and suit up again, then move to the front. Michelin is next. I'm slower, luxuriating in the simplicity of being alive.

Glancing at the ranch wife, I feel the vague pressure of crotch interest. I'm reviving enough to ask what life is like for her, up here, and how I may be of assistance, that sort of hormonal shit. Feels good. But of course, Michelin has moved in first. Michelin imagines himself our Tango Foxtrot Romeo. Not even the obvious competition of Tak sidelines his self-assurance.

He's trying to strike up a conversation.

The ranch wife shakes her head, twice.

Michelin doesn't get that she's fully focused on the job at hand until she shoots out her long right arm and claps a spidery hand over his mouth. "Shut*T*up, please," she says. "You want a roll t'is t'ing?"

The long arm's reverse elbow swivel impresses us all. We goggle in admiration.

"No, ma'am," Michelin says. He grins like a sap back at us, then squats down behind the control cab—and promptly goes to sleep.

Major General Kwak is in severe pain. He doesn't complain, but we can't pull off his skintight, not around that splinted arm. I rummage in the rear bulkhead and find the medical kit in a drawer just below the filters, marked with a red cross, and with Tak's help administer some morphine. Nothing more modern in the way of painkillers, apparently, but this will do for now. The general regards us with tight eyes, nods his gratitude. Muzzes out. I start looking for a transfer bag or rolls of tape to repair his suit. Either we patch the skintight's arm, which is showing too much fray, or we bag him entire, or he's going to have to stay in the bus. Will the ranch wife mind us using her safety gear, depleting her reserves, air and water?

That leads me to ask myself, what is she doing out here all alone—and how do we possibly fit into those plans? She could just as easily dump us in a hole. We've never been of much use to Muskies. Maybe their neutrality has taken a more practical turn and they've gone over to the Antags. It's all about survival. I might do the same. How is it bad thoughts return so quick when you know you're not going to die, not right away?

More sharp lurches and nearly vertical ascents. The suspension squeaks and groans and the tire blades whang like steel drums, bending until they crimp, then snapping out on the uproll with an energy that makes the whole cabin shudder.

I can't sleep.

But then I wake up and the young woman has stopped the bus, climbed out of her seat, and is stepping gingerly back through our sprawled group. She sees my eyes are open, faces me, and says, "I have a make report and count for what I've used."

"Right," I say. "Can I help?"

"Doub*T* it." She gently nudges the general, who does not react. "Chinese?" she asks.

"Korean," I say. I'm on my feet, working out the tingles from being jammed up with the others. I bump my head on the cabin roof. How she manages to hand-over and stoop so gracefully is beyond me. She's beautiful. She's the most beautiful creature in the entire universe. Gosh.

She cocks me a hard side glance. "I'm a dust widow," she says. "Know what t'at means?"

I shake my head.

"I've gone t'rough t'ree husbands sin*T*s I war nine. Your atten*T*on mean as much to me as a sheet mite's. Understood, Sold*T*er?"

"Marine, ma'am. Skyrine."

Nine would be something like eighteen, in Earth years. And that no more than a few years ago, best guess.

"You know my name," I say. "What's yours?"

Another hard look. She grimly faces forward. "Teal Mackenzie Green," she says. "Nick for Tealullah."

"Nice name," I say.

Kazak is awake now, listening. Vee-Def and Tak confer in the farthest corner, under the bulkhead drawers. Our commander, Gamecock, is curled up like a pill bug. Kazak and I nudge him. He's cramped something fierce—that happens when skintights go sour. Lactic acid burn is a misery I wish on no one. He stretches as best he can, grimacing.

"Tell us about this Drifter," he says to Teal, the ranch wife, the dust widow, whose beauty is undiminished and maybe even enhanced now that she's scowled at me.

"Not till we get a shelter." She finishes the seal on her bright green suit, a bulky older model, likely custom-mod to fit. It has different-colored patches on limbs and torso. First owner was apparently shorter. "A wheel is jammed and we're about fifty meters a whar we need to be. Anybody fit a get out and push?"

We all volunteer. Gamecock picks the strongest, includes me and himself; we're jammed in the lock again and then outside, and none of us is sure the skintights will hold suck, after all they've been through.

PARADISE LAID UP

U.S. kids are taught that the first settlers on the Red were the superrich and a few of their friends. They made mistakes. A lot of them died. The survivors recruited others, paid for them to fly up—which got harder as news returned about how so many camps were consolidating, failing—disappearing. Mars is a hell of a long ways from Earth when there's trouble. Jamestown and Croatoan all over again.

But the tough got tougher. They learned and stuck it out and, gradually, the settlements began to expand. Began to really and truly succeed. The survivors became heroes.

Then arrived the third wave, including hard-core folks who found Earth too civilized, too restrictive—too stupid. Rugged individualists, political fanatics, IQ theorists seeking to isolate and improve the human gene pool. Diehard bigots and supremacists, happy to turn Mars into a spaghetti western. My high school history teacher, Mr. Wagner, fairly liberal, left his students with the impression that Mars was pretty much a lost cause. Still, it sounded exciting—romantic. Frontier towns with attitude. A boy could still dream.

Our strategy prof in basic at SBLM added a few more details: "Before the arrival of the Gurus, private sector colonies on Mars denied Earth's taxing authority, and even tried to declare their terrestrial and orbital assets exempt from government interference. After our war began, when the government took over all launch centers, the colonies protested, refused to pay their cable bills—stopped recognizing Earthly specie. Their access to interplanet broadband was cut. Blackout followed. Silence.

"We know where the settlements are, mostly, but we are not authorized to contact them, to intervene in their defense, or to commandeer their assets unless absolutely necessary—and only then with prior authorization from ISC."

Back then, International Space Command was in charge of our war effort, until Germany, Canada, and all of South America withdrew and the United States fragmented politically into war and pax states—those that accepted the story told to us by the Gurus, and those that did not. Forty U.S. states supported, those most likely to get richer from Guru tech and science. Ten did not, mostly in the South and Midwest. Cuba abstained and declared itself neutral, despite having achieved statehood just a few years before.

International Space Command regrouped and was renamed International Sky Defense, or just plain Sky Defense. Some of our equipment still carries the old logo. Most of the Northern Hemisphere countries joined in and contributed to the effort, India and China massively—big industrial needs, lots of Guru bennies. Two-thirds of our forces are now Asian. You learn quickly how tiny a slice Western civ cuts from Earth's pie.

The Sky War entered its thirteenth year and at the age of twenty-six I became a sergeant. Timeout does not add to seniority, only active duty on the Red. There are a lot of inequities in the Corps, but bitching gets you nowhere because, as always, brass is polished brighter than me and thee.

THE LAST OF my squad—so far as any of us know—has been rescued by a ranch wife who is taking us with her to a mysterious
site she calls the eastern Drifter. As I've said, I'm not completely
ignorant of Mars geology, but I have no idea what a Drifter might
be or what it might look like. Yet now, apparently, we are there.

The bus shudders to a halt on a rugged slope of dust-pocked
lava. Teal has pushed her vehicle as far as she can, two hundred
meters up this slope, beyond which rises an odd, knobby hill
about fifty meters high at its peak and, from what we can see,
about two hundred meters wide. Teal locks the wheel and joins
us in the rear.

Our skintights are now charged with sufficient air and water
to last us at least a few hours. The landscape we see as we exit the
bus's airlock is fascinating but tough to riddle. Thirty meters to
our left—north—is a mound of deep brown and black stone, not
lava, weathered almost smooth. To me the mound resembles a
half-sunken head. I make out a beetling overhang like a rumpled
brow. To the right of this head, south and west, lies an angled
ridge like a muscular black arm, its "hand" clenched into a fist,
protecting a kind of rocky harbor. A giant seems to have risen
out of the planet, head, neck, and one shoulder, then laid an arm
across the lava field, trying to shove itself up, but somehow got
stuck—freezing solid before it could climb out and walk away.

Sunken giant. Shit. For the first time in many hours, curiosity takes strong hold. We need to know what our ranch wife is
doing out in the middle of nowhere, on the edge of our tactical theater, not too far from our ODZ—Orbital Drop Zone. All
alone—except for us.

Teal completes her circuit, then butts helms with Gamecock
and makes her needs known. She'll go back to the wheel and
steer, but she wants us to roll the bus the last few dozen meters

into the curved embrace of the giant's arm. I hope there's something waiting there other than a metaphorical armpit.

I take position near the bus's right rear wheel, careful not to let the edges of the blades touch suit or gloves. No wonder our ride was rough. The wheels are worn almost razor-blade thin. Everything about the Muskies seems threadbare, last-ditch, desperate. And yet, the dust widow saved *us*.

Gamecock comes up beside me, along with Tak, and we decided how best to move the bus to where the lady wants it to go. Our effort is mighty, the progress slow, but we manage in about fifteen minutes to close the distance. Then Teal locks the brakes, steps out again through the airlock, holds up her hand, and marches off into the shadow of that massive, crooked arm with a wonderful, long-legged stride that combines hop and jog. A true princess of Mars.

The sun is just over the upper forearm and shines in our eyes, so we can't see her in the shadows. A minute or two later, she returns, shaping out of the darkness like a green ghost, and tells us to push some more.

We push.

Hard-packed sand and dust form a decent floor inside the arm. In the shadow of the wall, my eyes finally adjust and I see, set into the giant's upper chest (I can almost count the ribs), a solid metal gate about ten meters wide and nine meters high. Beside it is a smaller gate, more of a door. The big gate has been opened, I presume by Teal, exposing a black cavern. The gate's outer surface has rusted to a close match for natural Martian brown. Hardly visible at all, except up close. The stony wall surrounding the rusted gate is coated with a thick layer of lava, alternating rough and glassy, as if a melted flow slurped up the giant's arm. In the armpit and crook of the elbow lean two dramatic intrusions of massive, six-sided columnar basalt.

Vee-Def leans in to say, "Muskies are vegan, right?"

He probably saw a movie about cannibals on Mars.

"They certainly won't eat *your* stringy ass," Kazak assures him.

I am only half listening. The giant has faced wind, water, and lava for a long, long time—why not just wear away, sink down, give up? "It's still trying to swim," I tell myself.

Michelin emerges and lends a hand as we push the bus across the threshold, into a cramped, dark airlock barely wide enough to accommodate the wheels and skinny dudes sneaking around each side. He tells us the general is doing poorly, might not last more than a few hours unless we decant him into full medical. "He's got something he wants to say to Gamecock. His English is better than my Korean, but he's going in and out."

As our ranch wife comes through the narrow gap to the left, shining a bright single beam, I see glints and realize the roof is low, low indeed. How the bus fits at all puzzles me until I notice that it has hunkered down on its suspension and the bottom of the fuselage is now just a few centimeters above the lava floor. Teal's light reveals unnatural-looking grooves crisscrossing the walls and roof. I'm no expert, but the cavern, the lock, seems to have been dug, blasted, or melted out of a large mass of metal-bearing rock, leaving basalt columns as structural support.

Teal opens and climbs through a smaller hatch in the inner wall, and we stand around for a few minutes until the gate closes behind us. Then she returns and inspects the outer seal.

"Airtight," she says. "After I open te inner, we'll push and park beyond."

"Have you been here before?" Tak asks.

"No," she says. "But I know of it."

"Is this the eastern Drifter?" I ask.

She looks past me. "Get everyone out when we're t'rough."

"Our Korean general is going to need some help," I say.

"Stretcher in te boot." She taps the bus's stern, showing us the outlines of a flush equipment bay. In short order, with her help, I pull out a rolled and folded stretcher and prepare it. "From here is slope," she says. "Should make pushing easy."

With that, the tall young lady returns to the bus's midsection, lifts herself up, squeezes flat, and climbs in.

The inner lock door now pulls aside, back into the rock. Very neat engineering, I think. An echoing blat of the horn tells us to resume pushing. A few minutes later, we're inside a chamber about three meters below the floor of the outside entrance. DJ and I close the second gate behind the bus. This one has a thick polymer seal that grabs hold of the circular metal frame. Encouraging, but still no pressure.

The inner chamber is high, dark, possibly natural—a relatively smooth half ovoid about twenty meters across. What would leave a big egg-shaped hollow in the dense, metal-bearing stone? Hot gas? Steam? The floor is dust and sand, compacted from material that could have drifted in before the airlock was finished. In the gloom, we see nine other vehicles in a tight half circle pushed close to the northern wall. They look old and worn-out.

Teal clambers down from the bus, all arms and legs, with an unfamiliar, almost alien grace. She looks back at us, at me, gestures for us to follow—and is once more definitely human, definitely female.

Command would surely frown upon fraternization with Muskies, if they thought it likely or even possible. But the fact is, we've received no instruction about them one way or another.

We do know how to treat our sisters in the Corps. They're fellow Skyrines, no more, no less, *ever*, as long as we're in service. It's a hard code and both sides are held responsible. Tak and Kazak once served rough justice on a flagrant violator of the sister code, a corporal named Grover Sudbury. Sudbury had raped and beaten a female PFC in his crummy apartment outside the depot at Hawthorne. Tak excluded me because I had a list of sketchy fitness reports and might have been DD'd if caught.

But I saw the bastard after they had finished with him, crawling bloody and mewling across the deck of a second-floor walkway. They had finished by shoving him through a door that was closed at the time. Corporal Sudbury did not appear capable of standing, much less fit for duty. Months later, the Corps booted him in disgrace.

And then, Sudbury just vanished. Nobody ever heard from him again. Remember his name: Grover Sudbury. There have been a lot like him in the last couple of years, far more among civvies than Skyrines.

So I know when to stop thinking about sex. But I'm tired, pretty sure we're doomed, and the dust widow is exotic, not like women back on Earth—not like any female in the Corps. Great fun to watch.

We ferry the general out of the buggy on the stretcher. He's mostly out of it, awake but delirious. Vee-Def keeps him from plucking at his faceplate. I glance at my glove and wrist joins, usually the first to reveal increasing pressure. We're still in Mars normal.

Michelin stays close to the ranch wife. "Where exactly are we...?" He runs a glove along the dark stone walls.

"Te Drifter, I told you," she answers softly, reluctantly. Does she regret bringing us here? "Te eastern Drifter."

"But what *is* that?" Michelin asks, glancing around for assistance. We know as little as he does.

"Te garage will pressure, if t'ere pressure on t'other side. T'at's the inner lock. If a pressure, you strip, go naked—except for te general. Brush down now. Doan a want you bring in bat*T*le sand."

I'm not sure what she means, *battle sand*, with that brittle *T* of thinspeak—spent matter waste? What do the Muskies know about that? That's all she'll tell us until we open yet another smaller hatch, less rusty, quite thick, serious about keeping stuff in and out. An inner sanctum must lie beyond.

Gamecock has said little throughout our trek. Now he bumps helms with Tak and they seem to reach some agreement. I hope it doesn't mean we're about to commandeer this place or otherwise take charge.

As we open the thick hatch, enter the inner lock, and crowd in around the stretcher, I feel a deeper, almost creepy sense of awe. This formation is so very different from anything I know about Mars. The stone is remarkably dark and looks exceptionally dense and hard. Every few meters, ceiling and walls are shot through with glints of large metal crystals—wider than my hand. Nickel-iron, I guess. Beyond the polished crystals, there are more runs of grooves and other signs of excavation. Must have been a bitch to carve and finish. If the Muskies did all this, years ago, then they're a lot more accomplished than we were ever taught at SBLM.

Vee-Def comes close to me, grinning at whatever he is about to blurt. He bumps helms. "Vast!" he intones. "Fremen warriors! Vast!" At my recoil and grimace, he shouts, "Duncan Idaho, right?"

Neemie and Michelin ignore him. I doubt Vee-Def reads much, he's probably quoting one of the many movie versions. Never a drop of rain on Mars. Snow, yes, but never rain.

The fabric around my wrist finally dimples. The airlock is pressurizing. Our ears feel it next. Teal opens the opposite hatch. A tiny, dim light flicks on out there somewhere. It looks far away.

"Batteries on. Might still be good. If I don't pass out, join me?" She pops her faceplate. She doesn't pass out.

The dimple around my wrist gets deeper—we're surrounded by maybe two-thirds of a bar. Then she cracks open the hatch we just passed through and air rushes by, filling the garage.

"Go ahead," she says, once the wind subsides, and peels out of her own suit. In a few minutes, we're all naked. The relief is amazing. I do not want to ever put on a skintight again. Slumped and rumpled on the deck, our suits stink, but the air seems good, even fresh—not a bit stale.

Not that I'm paying much attention to the air. The ranch wife wears only squared-off panties. I cannot help myself. My God, she is amazing. I never knew a woman could be that tall, that slender, that spidery, and still be so beautiful. Even the general ogles her with a pained grin and asks us to remove his helm.

She doesn't seem to notice; possibly doesn't care. We're not part of her tribe. We're not Muskies.

Why bring us here? What use could we be?

And what the fuck *is* this place?

WHAT THE LOCALS RECOMMEND

We have ready access to the garage, and as little star lights flick on in the high ceiling we start to inventory supplies on the bus—Teal's buggy—and on the older vehicles, which it turns out are already pretty stripped down.

Then Teal wanders off, leaving us in the dim glow. She returns a few minutes later wearing dark green overalls—ill-fitting, made for a shorter individual, worn through at knees and elbows, but more decorous than near nudity. Draped over her forearm is a stack of similar clothing. She tosses it to the floor. As I pick one out of the pile and give it a shake, my fingers rub away green dust. I bend over and swipe the compacted floor with my palm, bringing away the same dust, along with a few grains of grit.

"Algae?" I ask nobody in particular. DJ and Vee-Def are scratching and trying to make their overalls fit.

Teal kneels beside the general and gives him more water. "Can you talk?" she asks him gently.

For the moment, his delirium has passed and his English

has returned. "Must tell them soon," he murmurs. "Looking for this. Looking for just this." The general settles back, closes his eyes. Teal scowls in concern. She glances my way, aware I've caught her lapse. Her face goes bland.

Tak and Kazak squat behind the general, taking it all in. Gamecock is probably waiting for the right moment to suggest to our hostess that careful, thorough recon might be a fine idea. He does not like the shadows. Nor do any of us.

The ranch wife seems to be deciding who our leader might be. She focuses on Tak—of course. I'm used to that. He and I have been on liberty together from Tacoma to Tenerife. Women always look his way first.

Tak, with a dignified nod, directs her to Gamecock.

"My name is Teal," she says to the colonel. "Nick for Tealullah Mackenzie Green."

Gamecock introduces himself as Lieutenant Colonel Harold Roost. After him, we all divulge our proper names and ranks—all but the general, who has drifted off again. Tak gives him another dose of morphine. Teal warns him, that's it, no more. Although I'm wondering if she prefers that the general would simply fade away…

"T'ere a much trouble here," Teal says as we rearrange, like kids around a campfire. She becomes the center of our attention, but we might be a pack of dogs, she might be talking to us just to relieve boredom, for all the emotion we seem to arouse. "We stay away a trouble, but now it comes a-doorstep, right a T'ird Town, my Green Camp."

"There's more than one town nearby?" Gamecock asks.

She doesn't answer this, but keeps talking, eyes over our heads, searching the darkness and stone. "I come here until te bad time passes."

"Bad time," the general says. Perversely, the morphine seems to perk him up. Maybe he drifts off to escape the pain.

"*S*T'ere a battle coming?" Teal asks Gamecock.

"We're stragglers from a bad drop," he says. "Waiting to regroup."

"So t'ere wor more..." She nods slowly. "Many?"

Gamecock lifts his lips, adds nothing.

"I figured," Teal says. "From te buggy, while heading sout'east...Kep rolling by broken ships, buggies, abodes—tents—bodies across te flat. Hundreds."

"Human?" Gamecock asks.

"Hard a know." She throws out her hands. "Couldna stop. I had a make speed a get here."

The general struggles to sit up. His eyes are bright, feverish. "Knew about this. Looking! Long time past," he says, "big strike. Big as a moon. Ice and stone metal core. Heat of impact tremendous, but shove ice deep, superheat steam, blow out... Biggest basin! Chunks not mix."

Teal watches him with a veiled glare, as if he is a snake trying to bite. She gently pushes him back down, then changes the subject. "Tell what you can, what a-happening a t'ere," she says to Gamecock.

"Major effort," Gamecock says. "Troops and supplies, survey parties."

"Robots?" she asks.

He shakes his head.

"Why na robots? Why people? Far Ot'ers supposed a be smart, from anot'er star, right?"

We've asked ourselves that same question. Same reason, I suppose, that robot football never caught on. Real bones, real snaps.

"Robots can't replace a Skyrine," Gamecock says.

Teal sniffs disdain. "Figure t'at out, save yourselves."

"Where's the fun?" Michelin says. "Life is being there."

"Deat' *S*'a never going home," Teal responds. *Death's never going home.* Right. She crouches again by the general, checks his neck pulse; her knees show through holes in the jumpsuit. Fascinating knees. "We stay ou*T* way. We'd like a know how long 'twill last."

The general's eyes flutter. "Hard battle coming."

Gamecock's face is stony, but I suspect he's still trying to figure out what he can say in front of this noncombatant, whether we need to commandeer her supplies, her vehicle... everything in these caverns.

It's Tak who speaks next, maybe out of turn, but what the hell. We owe our lives to her. "We dropped without tactical," he says. Gamecock swivels on his ankles to face him, brow wrinkled. "No complete update. We're pretty ignorant."

"*I* know," the general says, voice weak. "I tell more. But *she* must not listen," he says, staring at Teal.

Without a word, Teal rises and walks toward the darkness where she retrieved the jumpsuits. "Let me know when you're done," she calls.

We sit for a moment in silence, out of uniform, worn to nubs. The air in the hollow is cool, strangely sweet... Active environmental. All of it just adds to our enormous puzzle.

Gamecock looks down at the general's face, then up at the rest of us. "Get ready to listen," he says. Closer to the general's ear, he says, enunciating each word, "Sir, we're secure. You need to tell us what you know."

The general swings his head right and left, scanning us, the side of the bus—then looks straight up at the stone roof. "This is retreat, reservoir," he murmurs. "Place to hide." A wave of pain racks him.

"Maybe it is," Gamecock says.

"Much more," the general says, eyes searching for relief.

Gamecock gestures for Tak to give the general more morphine—
a half dose. Tak complies.

"What's the plan, sir?"

"Old plan, year old," the general says, eyes moist. "Land and
reinforce, lay forts and tunnels, claim low flats, establish networks of resources, fountains, depots. Big drops, rocket descent
pods. *Big* effort from Earth, funded by Russia, China. Lots of
my soldiers. Informed not much enemy orbital. All wrong. We
arrive, Russians first. All wrong. Lots of enemy orbital, recently
inserted, take us down, Antags have *big* ground presence, dominance. We fight. Lose big. We know so little!" He looks away,
ashamed. Nothing to be ashamed of.

"We were in transit when all that went down," Gamecock
says to the rest of us. "We were meant to be a backup or modest
supplemental to the big push."

"They could at least have told us," Kazak complains.

"Antag G2O mopped us from the sky. All but one of our
satellites were down." He pauses, then adds, "That's what must
have happened."

"No resources, no weapons, can't do much down here," the
general says. That seems to be it, then. We're all we've got, and
we're relying on the hospitality of a ranch wife and her peculiar
cave just to stay alive.

Michelin and Tak and I go back to the others. Gamecock
stays with the general, in case he has more to say.

"Muskies!" DJ says. "Bless 'em. Sure talk strange."

"Not that strange, after so many decades," I say, thinking on
Teal, idly considering what it might be like to go AWOL and
join the Muskies—not that we have another choice, right now.
Hardly any command. Hardly any AWOL involved.

"What the hell is this place?" Kazak asks.

"Surprised there's still air and water and power." Tak shakes
his head. "Don't know how long it's been empty."

"If it *is* empty," Vee-Def says, eyes searching. "Like the Mines of Moria. Orcs everywhere, man." He spreads his hands, makes crawly motions.

"Fuck that," DJ says.

Tak stretches his neck, then does a few yoga moves. I follow his lead. "She's not telling us much," he says, assuming downward dog.

"Why should she?" DJ asks. "What I'd like to know is, why is she out here all alone?" He puts on a squint-eyed frown that could be either suspicion or skepticism.

Gamecock and Michelin join us. "The general is out. We peeled back his skintight. Gangrene. He needs surgery."

"Good luck with that," Kazak says.

"He said something odd before he passed out. Mumbling in Korean and English, back and forth, about broken moons, uneven settling…" He shrugs. "I'm not sure this place is any kind of surprise to command."

"They've been looking for it?" I ask, again feeling that spooky prickle.

"We don't know what orders the first wave might have had. The general's not exactly making sense."

"Teal didn't look happy when he was talking," I say.

Gamecock glances between me and Tak, settles on me. "You've been studying her."

"Sorry," I say.

"Not at all. She's receptive."

"BS, sir," I say. "She glammed Tak."

"I'm a good judge," Gamecock says. "Go after her. Find out what this place has to offer, how long we can stay, how long we *should* stay. Whether we're alone. If this is a big ore concentration, then it's dead cert the Antags will have scoped it out."

"And we haven't?" Tak asks.

"No need asking our angels," Gamecock says. "They won't

carry strategic data we don't absolutely need, and that includes planet-wide gravimetry. Still, that kind of info has got to be pretty old…Why wouldn't the Antags know?" He shoves all this aside with a push of his palm. "Go," he tells me.

The others smile as I stand. I shove my hands into the overall pockets, feel something cold, then, surprised, pull out a metal disk about the size of a quarter. I hold it out, catch the light, see that it's featureless on one side like a slug, but made of what could be silver. Very white silver. And on the other side, there's a long, coiling string of tiny numbers and letters.

"Holy crap!" Neemie says, and grasps at the air. I pass him the slug. Neemie's father runs a rare coin shop in Detroit. He looks at it up close, turns it over, rubs it in his fingers, sniffs it. "It's platinum," he says. He passes it around and when everyone is done marveling, as much as any of us have the energy to marvel, Kazak hands it back to me.

"A sample of the local ore?" Gamecock asks.

No idea. I replace the purloined platinum in the pocket where I found it and move off after Teal.

———

THE DARKNESS BEYOND the antechamber to the buggy barn is broken only by occasional star lights, low-power jobs about the size of a grain of wheat. They look as if they might have been glowing for years.

I can see Teal's footprints in the damp green dust that lightly coats the tunnel floor and almost everything else. A few minutes and I arrive at a juncture connecting other tunnels, right, left, straight ahead, up…and down.

Way down. I pull back and lean against a wall, heart pounding against my ribs.

Almost fell into a shaft.

Maybe she wants us *all* dead. That would make sense, given the situation. Maybe she thinks, or was told, that there are troops out here looking into the family secrets. She could pick us up off the Red, fake concern, take us to the very place someone's looking for, but it's a mine where she can just dump us down a deep, deep hole…

I nearly died in a mine at Hawthorne. Joe pulled me back at the very last instant. Rocks rolled from under my boots into a pit, splashing into stagnant water dozens of meters down.

This hole is about four meters wide. With considerable care, I walk around it and try to pick up Teal's footprints on the other side, but the floor beyond is suddenly bare—no dust, no prints. However, I hear distant padding sounds…echoes of someone breathing. I hope it's Teal.

The walls are marked again by regular grooves, scoring the stony surface in a fashion that makes me think machines might have done the excavation, leaving grooves so that other machines could use them for stability or guidance. Maybe the machines are still down here. I imagine a mobile printer/depositor, serviced by a truck carrying buckets of slurry for different builds…going from place to place and building stuff for the miners.

Another thirty meters and I hear a voice off to one side, coming from a cubby. Teal emerges, rises to her full height, and looks down on me in the dim light.

"Are t'ey coming?" she asks.

"No," I say.

"Just you?"

"Just me." I take out the coin and hold it up in the palm of my hand. "Found this in a pocket. Any idea what it's for?"

She glances, sees the coiling string of numbers, gives a little shudder. "Caretaker," she says. "Must be his jumper."

"They left caretakers behind?"

"Maybe. Hang onna't." She moves on. I follow. She's slowed down a bit, as if she can't find what she's looking for.

"Do you mind my asking, again, maybe—have you been here before?"

"No," she says.

"How do you know where to go, what to do?"

She answers, "My fat'er told me."

"Was *he* ever here?"

"Na more questions."

"We're grateful, of course."

"W'afor t'ey send *you*?" she asks as we walk. She points behind us to the rest of my squad.

"They're concerned."

"T'ey t'ink I like you?"

No words for another ten or twelve paces. Then, Teal says, with a short intake of breath, "Your soldiers han't riven or forced. T'ey leave us be. I could guess it so. Flammarion lies on sa many t'ings."

There's a crater on Mars called Flammarion, also one on the Moon. They used to name craters after dead scientists. Flammarion was an astronomer some time ago, but what his or her namesake is doing here, or has done to Teal, or has told Teal about us, I can't even guess.

On we move another couple of dozen paces.

"T'was tip time I left Green Camp," Teal says. "Sa bad came a me. Ally Pecqua stole my widow's due, and Idol Gargarel…He chose me a make t'ird gen with te Voors."

"Third gen? Force you to have kids?" I don't know anything about Voors. Another settlement, I guess. Trading females. Doesn't sound appealing.

Teal looks sidewise, face cold in the faint blue light of the star bulbs—lost and cold and sad. I want to punch Ally what's-the-name and Idle Gargle in their throats for making her sad.

Teal continues, "I stole te buggy and just drove away. Stealing transport is killing crime in te basin. You're not te only ones in trouble on Mars.

"I'm not here a rescue you. You need a rescue *me*."

NOT YOUR FATHER'S FUTURE

Sitting in the Eames chair, looking out at the early morning gray, I tap fingers on my knees. Reach into my pocket. Fumble with the platinum coin. Then I get up to pee. Wander into the kitchen. Open the refrigerator. Nothing looks good. Most of it has spoiled. No fresh veggies. Should have picked some up in the market. Not thinking. Not planning ahead.

Walking ghost, out of my box.

I drink a glass of water from the tap. *Soon time a break and out*, Teal would say.

Walk some more and sync my terrestrial compass. Take advantage of my liberty, with or without company. But I don't want to. I don't know what to do with what I know. Could be dangerous to tell anybody. Joe told me to stay away from MHAT. Maybe I shouldn't even be *here*.

I can wallow in confusion and self-pity in the blue and steel apartment only so long before ape-shit darkness closes in and worse memories gibber and poke.

On top of the amazing, the good, and the awful that came after I acquired the coin, I have echoing in my head the jagged haunt of Teal's own story, of high frontier injustice and a young woman's flight, and how none of us could save her from the value of that primordial, metal-rich *Drifter*, nor from her betrayal of a hard ethic pushed way beyond the intent of the original Muskies.

Humans can be such shits.

A Skyrine shouldn't tangle in matters that have nothing to do with why we fight. Shouldn't invest in an outcome neither his own nor the war's. Stay in the box. But last night's fitful sleep, second night back—after a day spent in seclusion, squeezed into the leather chair, wrapped in soaking towels, seeping out through sweaty skin the last of the Cosmoline—staring out the window at the passing ships and ferries and pleasure boats, the pulse of Guru-motivated wealth and commerce, the whole, big, wide fidging world—

I heard echoes of Teal's voice, her accent, her choice of words. What Teal said before she betrayed her people's trust and led a wayward bunch of Skyrines to the Martian crown jewels:

You need a rescue me.

Despite everything, despite the Battle of Mars and our very real chances of losing the entire war, I can still hear her voice and believe, *insist*, that Teal is alive, can still be found, though I have no more power to return to Mars right now than one of those wheeling gulls.

Not unless I take another tour. Something I have vowed not to do. Something Joe would definitely discourage.

But there's one thing I did vow. I promised Teal that I will deliver the platinum token.

I just don't know to whom.

HOBOS AND DRIFTERS

The answer to where all the air comes from is a few hundred meters ahead, down a tunnel with many branches, most of them dark—no star lights. We don't go there.

Teal breaks into a lope. I have difficulty keeping up. She knows how to push and kick away from both floor and ceiling in the lesser gravity, not so Mars-bound as to have lost her terrestrial strength. I have no idea how Muskies raise their daughters; maybe there's universal Spartan discipline. The Green Camp big shots might insist their children train to become accomplished gymnasts. She sure moves like one.

Is her story, barely begun, a tale of patriarchal tragedy, rigorous discipline—or hypocrisy and cant, all *Scarlet Letter* and shit? I am truly both sympathetic and intrigued—but then I come up abruptly to where she stands on the edge of another shaft, actually a very large pit. I nearly bump into her. She blocks me with her outstretched arm, glaring at me yet again. Am I really that clumsy?

Beyond the rocky edge, a wide, echoing gloom fills with rising plumes of hot mist, fresh and moist and somehow electric.

Slurps and the wet claps of bursting bubbles echo through the steam. Nothing like it in my experience on Mars. For the first time, I feel that I am actually smelling a living planet, not just the dusty shell around a fossil egg.

Teal backs us away a couple of steps. "Onced t'ey called t'is Devil's Hole," she says. "I didna know t'was so close."

"Hot pools," I say. "Not sulfurous. Clean, sweet."

"T'ey *wor* sulfurous. Fat'er said you could not breat' here a-t'out a special mask. And still, t'ere's niter." She leans and points to a patina of white crystals flecking the black stone arch. "First team here suffocated. Bad air seeped inna t'eir suits. Second team took better suits and dosed te deep pools wit' oxyphores. Buggied in borax and potash from te farm flats, dropped oxidized dust and mine tailings inna pools. Oxyphores converted all into life, food—air."

Oxyphores—the green dust?

"T'ird team dug more garages, brought depositors and printers, made machines, explosives—carved and blasted deep. Too deep, as 'Turn out. Cut a stony barrier right inna hobo. Flow fast, alive. Deep flood. You know a hobo, what t'at is, Master Sergeant Venn?"

"Not in your sense, I suspect."

"Hesperian history. You learn geology in school?"

No need to tell all. "Fighting means knowing your ground."

"*Hobo* should be spelled with double aitch, *H2-obo*. Means anT'ient underground lake or river flowing, sloshing, around volcanic chimneys and hard, rocky roots, seek an old familiar bed a run free, flood or carve more, t'en, as always, up t'ere, freeze, dry up—blow away. But keep a flow deep down, down here. No matter how t'ey dam and block, hobo kept breaking t'rough, flood entire. No need for sa much water, we already had enough from te soft lands. Te miners struggled a pump and get back a work. T'ey failed.

"My fat'er was a tail end of fift' team. When t'ey pulled out, he set te sensors a let towns know when te hobo played down, sloshed ot'er way. T'ey planned a come back and resume mining. Ore a big lodes of iron, nickel, platinum, iridium, aluminum. Of course too much water, even for Martians. All could a let us build more towns. Many more. If we wor making more babies or bringing in more settlers. Neit'er which we do, now."

"Because of the fighting."

"Afore t'en. Te first troubles started afore I wor born."

"Troubles?"

"Come wit' me."

She takes me through a narrower tunnel. Here, the star lights seem brighter—the walls reflect their feeble glow. Beneath the green dust, my fingers feel the neutral warmth of pure metal in large patterns, irregular and beautiful crystalline shapes.

Then it hits me. During daylight, Mars dirt is warmer than the thin air for the first couple of centimeters, but gets colder the deeper you dig. Down here, something is keeping the Drifter's thick walls pleasant to the touch. The Drifter may be sitting above an old magma chamber, one of the last signs of Mars's youth.

This place is *fabulous*. I doubt it would be possible to over-rate its strategic importance. How could it have been kept secret from Earth? Or from the Antags, for that matter?

But if Gamecock heard the general right, maybe it isn't secret—not to Command. Someone could have spilled the beans and told Earth, and Earth could have finally decided to look up satellite gravimetry from decades past.

Confirm an anomaly.

Maybe command decided this is something worth finding and fighting for. Enough water and materials to support a couple of divisions, thousands of drops and ascents, for decades to come. No need for fountains.

Yet the Antags are still dropping comets.

And nobody told *us*.

My head reels trying to figure the ins and outs.

Teal comes to a ladder, metal rungs hammered into one side of a square, vertical shaft about three meters wide, rising into darkness. I can just make out a platform ten or fifteen meters above.

"Climb wit' me?" she asks. "I doan wan*T* go it alone."

"What's up there?"

"My father said a watchtower, dug inna rock near te top, face west."

"There's air?"

She gives me a tart look and takes to the rungs. There is indeed a platform about halfway up the shaft. I'm not at all good at orienting underground, not sure which way I'm pointed, but guess we're well up in the hill that rises over and beyond the sunken entrance—the "head" of the Drifter. The pure metal gives way to dark reddish stone streaked with black. The platform is rusty, coated in greenish powder, and creaks under our weight. Rust-colored water streaks and shimmers down the stone.

How long since the flood subsided? Days? Weeks? And who would be alerted that the Drifter was again open to mining and manufacture? How long until they all decide to return, in force, and find us?

Niter. Sulfur. Depositors and printers. They could easily make weapons, explosives.

Another ladder climb and we pass through a metal hatchway into a cubicle, bare rock on three sides, metal shutters on the fourth—and cold. Deep cold. Electric heaters have been mounted low in the stone walls, but not turned on. The chill sucks the heat from our bodies. We obviously won't be staying long.

"'Tis as I heard," Teal says, shivering, stooping—too tall for the cubicle. "T'is was built a guard over ot'er camps shoving in."

Where there are people, there will be competition. Conflict. It's what humans do best.

"Maybe we shoulda worn skintights," Teal mutters as she twists the plastic knurl. "Doan know if…"

With a ratcheting creak, the shutters pull up and aside. There's thick, dusty plex beyond, lightly fogged by decades of blowing sand—despite another set of shutters on the opposite side. Teal keeps turning the knurl and the outer shutters lift as well. The wide port provides a view of the sloping entrance to the northern garage and the rocky plain beyond. That damned brown blur still rises in the northwest. Odd. The comets should have wiped away any weather pattern.

I point it out to Teal. "That's been there since we arrived. Any idea what it might be?"

She shakes her head.

Because the plex sits under a meter of rock overhang, there's no view of the sky much above the horizon. And we can't look straight east or south.

Teal reaches up and unscrews a cover in the cubicle's roof. My fingers are numb. I can barely feel my face.

"T'ree-sixty," she says, swinging aside the cover and pulling down a shining steel periscope. She plucks at its metal bars, not to freeze her fingers. "As told."

"Who told?" I ask.

"Fat'er. Look quick," she says. "Canna stay long unless we find te control booth and gin te power."

I keep my eyes a couple of centimeters from the nearly solid rubber eyecups, but manage a circling, fish-eye view of the land around the promontory and the cubicle. Like a submarine under the sand!

Nothing…nothing…

Around once more, and then, to the southeast, I see a dusty

plume, much closer, and beneath that, approaching the Drifter: three vehicles, neither Antag nor Skyrine.

More buggies.

"Muskies coming," I say.

She gives me attitude about that name, but takes the view. She rotates the periscope several times, always pausing in the direction of the buggies' approach.

"From te Voor camp," she announces.

"Voor? Who are they?"

"Voors, Voortrekkers," she says. "You know not'ing of us!" She stows the scope, closes the shutters, and returns to the ladder, muttering, "Got a way gin main power."

Right. She descends from the lookout and I follow, fingers so numb I can barely hold on to the rungs. If we find a control room and power switches and equipment, maybe we'll also find the miners' stock of reserves: medical supplies, skintight repair kits, food. Enough to give us time to wait for reinforcements. Which have *got* to be on their way. This was supposed to be a big shove, right?

Maybe we've found what command was looking for all along.

PATRIOTS AND PIONEERS ALL

Teal is in the tunnel, running east. I reach the bottom of the shaft barely in time to see her disappear into darkness. Training tells me to get back to my squad—Voortrekker sounds suspiciously old-school—but I'm conflicted. I don't know what sort of trouble we could face, what exactly to tell Gamecock or Tak or the general, if he's still with us. Would the buggies carry miners returning to their digs—happy to see us, happy to have our help? Somehow, I don't think so. But can I trust Teal to tell the whole truth?

I doubt our angels will answer any of these local questions. They're rarely conversant on matters not immediately important to our operations, and settlers have never been an issue.

And why not?

How stupid is that?

The star lights here still glow, but dimmer, doubtless on fading battery power. I cross through many gaps filled with shadows. I'm feeling my way and my pace is slower than Teal's. The tunnel weaves for fifty or sixty meters through raw metal and then basalt and outcrops of what looks like pyrites—fool's gold, crystals of iron sulfide. Lots going on in the eastern Drifter.

The tunnel opens into what could be another buggy barn—but empty. The green dust here is thick and pools of moisture stain the floor's compacted sand. Teal stands on the far side, beside another lock hatch, feeling the seals with her long fingers, then pushes her face close to detect loss of air.

The temperature is cooler but not frigid.

"Western gate still tight," she says, glancing back at me. "And welded shut. My fat'er told me t'ere now only two gates, two ways in, sout'ern and nort'ern. When te Voors took te Drifter, t'ey wanted exclusive, made*T* defensible wit' small force."

"Do the Voors know we're here?"

"T'ey know *I'm* a-here," she says.

"How?"

She shakes her head and walks to our right, toward a glassed-in booth mounted high in the empty chamber, where a dispatcher or controller might sit, looking down upon the garage floor. She climbs the ladder and pushes on a door in the booth's side.

I stand below and look up. "Tell me what happens if they get in," I say.

"If t'ey find me, t'ey take me back. If t'ey find *you*, t'ey kill all."

"They can fucking try," I say.

"T'ey have guns," she announces, working to pry open the booth door. No go. It looks welded shut as well. She descends, eyes darting like a deer seeking a canebrake.

"We need to know the truth," I say. "Why did you come here? What if those buggies are just bringing back miners?"

"T'ey wouldna come back just now," she says.

"Why not? The hobo's down—"

"Because t'ey're *afraid*!" she cries. "You think t'is just a mine? You donna know a t'ing!"

"Afraid of what? Us?"

"Na!"

"What the fuck is going on?" I ask, voice a little too high. I try to stay in front of her and intercept one of her looks, but as she sets foot on the floor, and I push in, she grimaces, reaches out with a long, agile arm—and slaps me. I don't know a single Skyrine who reacts well to being slapped by anyone bigger than a child. My hand is up and about to return the favor when the look on her face collapses into anguish, and she lets out a piercing scream.

That stops us both cold. We face off in the middle of the chamber, breathing heavily. She twists about, hands out and clenched, stretched to the limit.

"We *have a* find it!" she cries. Her voice echoes—broken, lost, hollow. Then she falls to one knee, as if about to pray, and hangs her head. "It warna just the hobo drove out fift' team. My fat'er wouldna say all. Even so, he told me come here when if t'ere is na ot'er place a go. Drifter safer t'an Green Camp, if I wor put a te dust. But he said I must go alone."

This floors me. "Even so, you rescued us," I say, trying to reestablish common ground, common sympathies. "Maybe you thought, like you said, we might be able to help. You don't think anyone else can or will help...right?"

She shakes her head. "I doan know why I pick you. You're na our people. You're na even friends."

"We're *human*, goddammit!" I say. "We're fighting for everyone."

"Na for *us*," she says softly. "We doan want you here. Likely *t'ey* doan want you here."

"The Voors?"

Teal forces her calm, fixed face, stands, and wipes her cheeks with the back of her hand. Then, looking down and blinking, she reaches a decision. "Sorry. Na call for sa much at once*T*."

"Yeah," I say.

"If t'ere be power, we switch *T*'on afore Voors reach te sout'ern gate. T'en we lock and stop t'em outside."

Her lingo is getting too thick for me. One sound, inflected, passes for a page in a dictionary. "We haven't checked the eastern gate."

"Na time. T'ey're close."

"We're fighters," I say. "We should check and if necessary post watches at all the gates—"

"Voor buggies haul twen*T*'each. T'at wor sixty. You?—" She holds up one spread hand and three fingers. A stern look.

"Okay. But they're just settlers. What kind of weapons would they carry?"

Her withering glance away tells me I've asked exactly the wrong question. "T'ey find lost guns on te dust—maybe yours?"

"Nothing they're trained for. Nothing they have codes or charges for. They're not Skyrines."

Teal has this expression, avoiding looking at me, like she wants to tell all—but it's hard. Long years of indoctrination and resentment. No love for the Earth that cut them off and joined an interplanetary war. Then, her stiffness slides away. She's come this far. There's no turning back. She focuses, makes a face—she has to speak to me in a way I'll understand, and so she reaches back, speaks more slowly. "T'ey're *Voors*. Dutch, Germans, Africans, some Americans—whites only. Independent, old history. Smart, cruel—fat'er-rule. They came first a join Green Camp, t'en cause trouble, break wit' all, took a *trek—t'eir* trek—fifteen hundred kilometers. Claimed and routed a French camp—Algerians, Moroccans, some Europeans—cleaned t'em out, sent most a die on te dust. Rebuilt. Regimented. T'ey used French printers a make weapons, said a fight off solders from Eart' coming a destroy t'em. Na a body at Green Camp or

Robinson or Amazonia or McClain said naught a t'em. We'd all been cut from Eart' already, na more supplies, na more uplink— pushed on our own, we couldna afford te bigger fight." She takes a deep breath, shakes her head.

"Who found the Drifter first?"

"French camp. T'ey did sommat little mining, t'en pulled out. After, te Voors worked a hard five years until t'ey breached te lava dike and hobo surged. T'ey're the fourth and fift' teams. T'en...t'ey withdrew, but keep claim."

"What did they leave behind?"

"Buggies back at te north gate, clot'ing—some supplies. I doan know how else much."

"Your father was a Voor?"

"French. Voors let him live a-cor he war white. But t'ey sent his first wife out te dust. She wor African, a Muslim. Fat'er left Algerian camp just after Voors close te Drifter. Went te Green Camp..." She gets that distant look, too much history, too many nasty tales even before she was born. "Married my mot'er, and t'ere wor me."

The Drifter was closed due to the hobo for more than twenty years? Nine or ten Martian years? And we happen back just in time for the reopening! This isn't making even a skeletal sort of sense.

"The Voors, do they partner with Antags?" I ask.

She makes a face, I *would* think that—then shakes her head vigorously. "We call t'ose Far Ot'ers. We wor told Amazonia sent folks out te dust a meet t'em. Nobody's heard a t'ose since."

"If the Voors left good stuff here, what could we expect to find? Mining machinery? Food?"

"Fat'er say t'ere wor a printer-depositor, barrels of slurry, maybe safed food, surely spare parts, enow te gear up quick— all in upper chambers so na get swashed. T'ey keep all locked, wrapped, and sealed—stake and reclaim onced hobo sinks.

But…" She reaches into her pocket and takes out another platinum coin. Shows me a string of numbers and letters inscribed on both sides. Similar to the coin I found. Different numbers, however. "Codes te get in."

"That's how you got us in?"

She nods.

"And the power?"

"Hydro deep, far below. Where te hobo still flows." Saying all this, Teal looks sick with doubt and uncertainty. She has no idea what we're capable of.

"Where do we look for their cache?" I ask.

She walks off a few steps. "Fat'er show a chart, but t'wor old."

We work our way around the chamber, searching the deep shadows for exits, side tunnels—and find a dark hole hiding behind a basalt outcrop. No star lights, but wide enough to allow a buggy. The big tunnel cuts through metal and black rock. No grooves. Why?

"T'is was made near te end, I t'ink," Teal says. "Afore t'ey left."

If the Voors are indeed hard-core bigots, renegades, killers—patriots intent on making their own nation because they fit nowhere else…Are they also the most rational of pioneers? Would they attract and keep the best engineers, enough to plan and carry out a long-term drainage operation? Or did they just keep blasting pits and tunnels way down below until they tapped into the hobo? Ruining or drastically delaying their schemes of conquest, forcing them to abandon the Drifter…

Waiting, fuming—angrier and angrier.

"Your father was their chief mining engineer?"

"Geologist," Teal says.

"Did he go to Green Camp to offer them his expertise? After the Voors…"

"He told enow a keep t'em interested, so t'ey'd allow him

a stay. But he never told all. He kept saying te hobo would be down soon, because wit'na the Drifter and its promise, we have na value. Ally Pecqua and Idol Gargarel finally got tired, arrested him. T'en t'ey stole my widow's due, and he knew 'twas over for bot' us. When he wouldna tell more, t'ey sent him out te dust. I wor next. Sa I left."

"Was it always that bad?" I ask.

"Rationals love a correct and trouble. Cut off from Eart', t'ey only got harder and meaner."

Makes my neck hairs bristle. Still, though we owe Teal our lives, I have no way to verify her story, no way to know how a meeting with the Voors might turn out. Maybe they're just tough. Maybe they're fighters. Maybe we are better off with bigoted fighters than corrupt Muskies. I've certainly known enough bigoted good ol' boy Skyrines. Nasty boys in town, terrific in a fight.

SNKRAZ.

At the end of this wide tunnel lies a wider, square chamber, and within the chamber, a great big knobby shadow surrounded by even darker boxes and drums. The walls are equipped with shelves—some cut out of the rock. Right and left are smaller antechambers. Teal pokes in and out of them in sequence, silent.

Then she emerges from the last.

"Is that a printer?" I ask.

She nods. "Never seen one t'at old. 'Tis big."

"And the drums...slurry?"

"Plastic, metal, alumiclay, a t'ere—" She points. "Sinter chamber. Make almost any machine part. May gin up te buggy, te other buggies. If I can switch and ramp power."

"Where would we do that?" I'm acutely aware our time is running out. The Voor buggies were less than ten klicks away when last we looked.

"Track a star lights," she says. "T'ey'll get brighter. Te genera-
tor and t'ermal source should be near te emergency reserves."

"Your father said that?"

Another nod.

We walk together back up the slot, find a dark offshoot we
missed, venture along for a dozen meters.

"T'ere's a big battle out t'ere," Teal says. "You, te Far Ot'ers."

"Yes, ma'am." I walk a couple of steps behind her. She's liable
to fling her arms back as she feels around in the dark, and she's
strong. Don't need to lose teeth.

"You have any idea what Eart' did, cutting us off, cutting us loose? How many you have killed a loneliness and
Eart'-grief?"

"I'm not sure I understand."

"We're morna half crazed. Cost me my first husband. He had
Eart' family too."

"Oh?"

Her accent gets deeper. She's going home in memory. "He
worna used a narrow places. Came star-eyed, filled a freedom-
talk. Romanced my family and won me young, t'en spent most
a his time far-minding it, away in his t'oughts—back a Eart'.
Cut off, he lapsed, sorrowed, didna see us, didna see me. Vasted
up here." She pronounces this "vaysted," a portmanteau word,
a cruel bundle of her first husband's life. "Gone stir," she adds
softly. "After t'at, never saw me clear. Saw only his Eart' wife.
Tore t'ings, violent, til te camp passed judgment and sent him
out te dust. He just wanted a go home."

Not just the Voors are hard, apparently.

I'm not about to point out what we were told, about Muskies
not paying their cable bills. Not paying taxes. Or any of the rest
of it. Our lives may depend on this young woman's tolerance, if
not her favor.

Quiet minutes as we push along, until we see a single star

light hanging on its almost invisible wire—but brighter than the others. Another fifty meters, in darkness and complete silence except for our breath and padding boots, and here the star lights are brightest of all—five bunched together, as if marking a location. Should have brought Tak, I think, with his new eyes. But mine have caught a black hatchway she missed.

"Here," I say to Teal, who has gone on, perhaps distracted by her memories.

Doubling back, standing beside me, she pulls out her platinum, feels around the hatch—finds a small panel, slides it open, revealing a display and keypad. She lays the coin against the panel and punches in the string of numbers. The hatch clicks and together we pull it wide. Beyond brightly glow a lot more star lights, hundreds suspended from the ceiling, outlining the walls of another larger chamber, also square and about twenty meters on a side. The illumination is bright enough to dazzle for a few seconds, but we can clearly make out a medium-sized electrical panel, and beside this, the steel cap to a thermal source. Hot water from below ground? Nuclear? Likely not spent matter. That's never been shared off Earth. Just as well…

Teal seems to be following memorized instructions. In a few minutes, moving from station to station, she's got the station humming, buzzing, snapping inside its ranks of transformers, storage cells, fuel cells. The star lights brighten and the room lightens to clarity surrounded by stony gloom, except where a vein of that crystal-patterned nickel-iron reflects cloudy brilliance.

"Hydro still strong inna deep works," she says.

"Can we lock the southern gate?" I ask.

"Maybe," Teal says.

"Do you know how?" I ask.

"Control room," she says.

"This isn't it?"

"Substa*T*on for te nort'ern upper works. T'ere should be a substa*T*on for sout' and east, also big deeps and central digs—a main board for te whole installa*T*on."

In the new brightness, I see that Teal's face is still slick with tears. This was her father's domain. He worked here...For the Voors. Told her what he knew.

But all that he knew?

"You know where that is?"

Her large gray-green eyes flick, searching, looking beyond me. "Maybe," she says, and returns to the wide tunnel. At the junction, she points left. "T'is way."

She moves ahead. My squad's survival likely depends on what we find. I'm already remiss in not telling them what I know about the Voors. I judge we have about ten minutes to prepare for the new buggies' arrival. If this chancy operation succeeds, and nobody gets in our way, we might be able to rejoin the battle—the war. To live is to fight.

But I'm thinking on this woman, no doubt about it. Some points down the trail I'm going to find out all I can about the Muskies, about Teal's people at Green Camp, if she still thinks they're her people—whatever they call themselves. Little Green Men and Women. Maybe they're all just Martians now. Very romantic, that. More history. More culture and language.

More about what made her what she is.

The brighter lights reveal all we missed before: a sunken door, a fallen sign, a set of steps carved into the rock, leading up about fifteen meters through a smooth-cut corridor to another chamber. This one is lined and sealed by black, shrink-down plastic sheeting. Teal sets to removing the plastic, not an easy task, and I help. In a few minutes, we unveil a much wider shuttered viewport facing southeast—and beneath that, a dusty and decades-old control panel, sporting a holographic display panel—tiny projectors mounted on a strip above the panel—

The works. A southern watchtower to complement the northern—but also a command center.

I stand behind her as she takes a seat on a hard plastic chair. Most of the equipment here was likely made by the old, bulky printer-depositor; that is how Mars was furnished, replacing old-style manufacture and factories—but demanding slurries to feed the printers: solvents, polymers, powdered metals and ceramics...All the necessary materials that could be shot through a printer head onto a laser-hardened or heat-set or fusible object of manufacture. Including weapons.

All of which had to be shipped from Earth, or mined and purified on Mars.

Seven minutes. I'm trying to imagine the motions of the Voor buggies, the men inside—or men and women. How long will it take to get back to my squad? What can I deliver in the way of knowledge, strength, advantage, if I leave this command center before it's even up and running?

Teal looks at me, takes a deep breath, then flips open the cover to a number pad. Carefully, she lays the coin on the pad, then keys in the string.

We both jump as the panel powers up. Lights pick out projectors, which begin to whir and whine after so many decades of disuse. The panel sensors recognize our faces, find our eyes, the projectors align, and color patterns and even crude, unfocused images flicker before us. The first views are external and seem to fill the volume over the panel in exaggerated 3-D.

Teal waves her hand over a flat square in the center of the panel and brings one image forward, spreading it wide with her fingers. We now have a live view—I assume—of much of the southeastern slope of the Drifter, the rear shoulders and back of the swimming giant. She calls up other cameras, all external, and then, with a side glance, the first internals—thumbnails of dozens of chambers within the Drifter's bulk. At Teal's command, the thumbnails expand into brighter, more detailed images, rising between us and the dark walls. One shows a sloping surface made of crystals, surrounded by darkness but outlined by star lights. That view suddenly goes black: camera failure, security—or did Teal just delete it with a flick of her finger?

What she's summoned from this watchtower control panel is a tally of tunnels, shafts, digs, forming a map that turns slowly before us, expanding in jerks as more are added, as more old cameras return to life. The Drifter was a big operation, and it appears the flooding has not permanently damaged most of it.

Coins, codes, cameras everywhere…Multiple points of security. The miners had seriously worried about claim-jumpers, interlopers—maybe Skyrines or Antags, though it seems this place was left to the hobo before our war began.

Soon, the grand map finishes filling out. I recognize the upper works—the gates and tunnels we've passed through, along with where we are. There are many, many more tunnels and chambers, not yet explored, all in green. But there are also extensive and deeper excavations, some very deep, judging by the comparatively small profile of the upper works—and many of these are marked in blue and red.

Teal pokes her fingers through the blue and red traces. "My God," she breathes. "T'ere's na'one here, and 'tis still changing!" She shoots me another look, sees I have no idea what she's on about, then blanks the map and expands the southern garage and its "harbor," another encircling wall of lava.

The three Voor buggies are pulling up outside a wider, taller version of the northern gate through which Teal brought us earlier. She flicks through several vantages around the rocky harbor and sandy floor. "A t'ird of te eyes are down," she mutters. "Might come back onced t'ey warm. Can you see enow?"

The buggies have halted, having arranged themselves in a defensive triangle, tails together, noses pointed outward.

Nobody disembarks immediately. No way to know how many Voors we might face, what arms they carry, if any...

Then a hatch opens in the middle buggy and a stocky figure in patchwork skintight emerges, hesitates on the step, reluctantly descends.

"Voor?" I ask Teal.

"Looks like."

"Recognize him?"

The projectors whine and complain as she turns to frown at me. "I doan know any Voors."

"Is he a leader, a scout?"

She shakes her head.

Another figure climbs down, in similar skintight—taller than the first by a foot, broad across the shoulders, brawny. Not at all like Teal, but still homegrown, I guess, since there hasn't been a colonist transport for years...

And then a third, much smaller—skinny, even puny, and a fourth, about mid-sized. All look male to me. They stand out on the rock and sand before the southern gate, not moving after they've arranged themselves in a curve beside the middle buggy. I assume they're all Voors. There's a stiffness, a tension in their grouping— but nobody has emerged from the other buggies, not yet.

"Any comm?" I ask.

She shakes her head. "Not'ing like," she says. "Doan know about radio."

"They might not know we're here."

"T'ey know *summat* is here," she says.

"How?"

Silence.

"Would Green Camp sic Voors after you?" I ask.

"T'ey might."

"That bad?"

Another nod.

"To arrest you?"

"Common interest," Teal says with a lost downbeat. "Two years back, Green Camp and the Voors drew up a share claim, for when te hobo draws out. My fat'er helped make te deal, to stay important and keep us alive. Green Camp t'inks Voors might haply force t'at claim if others jump. T'ey might t'ink I'm jumping. If t'ey see *you*..."

Christ, I'm beginning to feel like I've stumbled into a Jack London novel. And fuck you if you think a Skyrine doesn't read old books.

The Voors haven't moved. By posture alone, they look apprehensive. Then they turn as the point buggy's lock hatch opens. Three more Voors descend, another varied group—also male.

From the last buggy, three more step down—making nine. Still nowhere near capacity for the buggies.

But then three figures in different skintights emerge from the lock of the middle buggy. All Skyrines, and all female, prominently displaying their sidearms.

Latecomers? Stragglers? Male and female needs transvac are sufficiently different that we often ride different sticks and join into combat-ready units in theater, on the Red.

Teal zooms in without my asking, and I manage to scan their blazes: U.S. Seventh Marines on one, ISD Second Interplanetary on the other two. I make out three flags: U.S., of course, and— among our favorite allies on the Red—Malaysian and Filipino.

From the other buggies, six more Skyrines descend, also female and heavily armed. Between them, I count four flechette guns, two armor-punching lasers, and a microwave disruptor, effective against Antag equipment in past engagements, but according to recent tech skinny, maybe no more. The last to step down from the point buggy is a Filipino gunnery sergeant, and she hefts a strong-field suppressor, about as big and impressive a weapon as any one of us can carry.

Teal sweeps over to a captain's parallel bars, and a stenciled name well known to me: Daniella Coyle. Captain Danny Coyle. I barely suppress a whoop. "Holy shit," I say. "Sisterhood is powerful!"

Teal is puzzled by my triumph. "T'ey're yours?" she asks.

"I am *theirs*," I say. "Outlaw ladies held up the Dodge stage. Time to make them welcome!"

BACKGROUNDER, PART 2

Now is not the time to get into all the branches and divisions
and shit, but while we're watching more internationals and
ladies arrive on our scene, light 'splainin' is in order.

International Sky Defense (ISD) is our overarching authority.
Its symbol is a flaming shield protecting a speckled blue marble,
Earth, kind of like SHAEF but spacey. At its highest level, ISD
Joint Command is staffed by politicians and retired military
commanders from all signatory nations. Joint Command, everyone assumes—but no one I've met actually knows—reports to
the Wait Staff, representatives of the Gurus.

Below Joint Command, each signatory nation assigns warriors
and resources and helps pay for ISD's orbital assets, transfer craft—
space frames, sleds, and such—and weapons, including R&D.

The United States "loans" Navy, Marine, Air Force, and
Army warriors to ISD. Other countries assign, we loan; same
difference. Skyrines sometimes combine not just with international units, but with other U.S. services, mostly Army or Air
Force—and since we're already under NAVSEC, the secretary
of the Navy, and he's mostly obedient to Joint Command, that

means we can run into warriors from just about any branch of service, and any signatory nation, recognize them more or less as partners, try hard to respect their command hierarchy, and work together efficiently, mostly without invoking esprit de corps, which can make Marines pugnacious.

Historically, that's how we see ourselves—Skyrines are nothing more nor less than Marines who ride rockets. Some say we're a touch more civilized than ground pounders, but frankly, I don't see or feel that, and once all the battles are won and the Antags have fled back across the sea of stars, we will happily revert to the well-trained, tightly disciplined, rudely judgmental bastards we have always been.

Even with all that, when we're off the field of battle and engaging in additional training or just plain R&R, we manage to get into some lovely threaps—that is, swedges, stoushes, dustups, squash-downs, knucklers, blennies, bruisers, fwappers, scratchers, jawbusts, jointers, joists, jaunts, jousts, teethers, chirps, flips, funsies, fisticuffs, ball-tug, dentals, gouges, or, in more common parlance, disagreements, tête-à-têtes, contretemps—fights.

Eskimos = twenty words for snow. Skyrines = twenty-plus phrases for getting scrappy, in that friendly sort of way where we rarely kill each other.

If you don't understand where fights will begin, and who is going to be on your side, and who is just *not*, you can get into trouble fast. Among the ISD signatories, U.S. Marines buddy up well with Filipinos, Koreans, Japanese, the few Guamanians we run into, Fijians (Pacific Islanders in general), New Zealanders (especially Maoris), and Australians. We get along okay with Brits and the French. The Italians have wine and MREs to die for and the most beautiful women I've ever seen in space, except for all the rest. We love the Indians and Pakistanis and Sri Lankans and Tibetans, and of course, there's Kazak and the 'stans, good people all.

Skyrines mostly get along with the Chinese, but we can have issues with Russians, though both are terrific at the beginning of a drunk and downright fierce on the Red.

Canada, Germany, Austria, Spain, most of Eastern Europe, all of South America, and Africa—but for Somalia, Ethiopia, and Yemen—are not signatory.

———

WHILE TRAINING AT Hawthorne, we used our one day of R&R to visit Lindy's 1881, a rough local bar in the small, square desert town. There, by severe happenstance, we met up with a stack of eleven Russian exchange officers. They had been invited to Hawthorne to lecture and critique U.S. training practices. What numbnuts depot clerk let them out all at once to do the town has never been revealed.

The encounter started off jovial. The Russians tried to explain, over beer and cold peppered vodka, how training at Socotra—off the tip of Yemen—and in Siberia was so much harsher and more realistic than anything we went through here at Hawthorne. Kazak disagreed and gave them the stink-eye. His people and theirs have history. It was obvious words would soon lead to deeds. After a few minutes of verbal give-and-take, Tak, Kazak, Michelin, myself, and four female Skyrines conferred how best to deploy a Fist Marine Division.

One of those sisters was then–First Lieutenant Coyle, chaperoning her brood and standing aloof from us grunts, but nodding to the music and enjoying the ambience—until she saw she could not get her chicks out fast enough to avoid the coming scuffle.

The sisters walked between their brothers and formed a loose line between them and the Russians. This encouraged the Russians to smirk and question our masculine courage. They gave each other encouraging looks and foresaw easy mayhem followed by another round of cold vodka.

The locals, a crusty, paunchy crew, well past their middle years, cleared chairs and tables and sat by with big grins.

Meanwhile, Michelin casually took post by the bar's rear exit.

The Russians led with three burly toughs. At a barely perceptible nod from Coyle, the sisters withered and allowed their line to dimple, then to break up. Brothers and sisters re-formed into flanks on both sides of the long bar, opening up space at the side of the establishment for our rear echelons to maneuver.

And so we did.

The Russians, no strangers to bar fights, observed these tactics through a vodka haze and finally recognized the seriousness of their plight. Smirks turned to frowns.

Kazak, with a wink at Tak and me, said something *very* offensive.

Game on.

Our Russian allies whipped out a steel grove of navy-issue Iglas—wickedly practical blades—and, from puffy pant legs, slowly pulled knotted climbing ropes and lengths of tow chain. Brows furrowed, knuckles white, balancing from foot to foot, they swayed one way, then another with choreographed precision, like flags in a wind, toward our flanks—admirable to see in men so full of Russian spirits.

And then—they chose their opponents and leaped.

Kazak gleefully ran Tartar interference through the melee, snatching at knotted ropes, taunting, dancing away with wiggling fingers from the slashing Iglas—sowing wholesale confusion. Tak and I worked around Kazak's quantum indeterminacy and doubled in at the conclusion of his feints, disarming four of the biggest Russians and dislocating their shoulders with precise sweeps-and-bows.

First Lieutenant Coyle and our sisters dealt summarily with the younger, less experienced, and thus meaner chain-wielders. After their wrists were snapped and they were disarmed, Coyle, with a lovely flourish, sent Russian officers reeling one by one down the length of the scarred wooden bar to the rear exit, where Michelin booted them through a banging, shivering screen door. Bruised and battered Russians piled up in the rear parking lot.

Just before our brave allies pushed off the oil-stained gravel to return for another round, earning our respect and doubtless forcing us to trade lives for Skyrine honor—U.S. Marine Brigadier General Romulus Potocki slammed through the front door, bellowed like a bull, and, before anyone could react, underhanded a stun grenade between the tables.

When the smoke cleared—everyone in the bar reeling and most of us bleeding from the ears—Potocki called us all to attention. Those who could still hear alerted to his presence, and the rest, observing them, followed suit. Even the Russians, slumping through the screen door and past Michelin, stood up straight, if they could.

All but one beardless stripling who had hidden behind an overturned table, and now rose with a howl to whip his chain around Tak's head.

At that, Coyle herself stomped the poor kid into a tight, dusty corner. And Potocki watched her do it.

A few minutes later, the MPs showed up.

Kazak and the ladies came through this deafer than posts but otherwise unscathed. I acquired a couple of Iglas and a slice across my bicep that took three days under Guru paste to heal. Med center restored everyone's ears.

Tak lost both eyes, but in short order—the next day—the Corps issued him a fresh pair, bright blue. Within hours he was better than ever. His raccoon-mask chain-whip welt took longer to fade—the rest of our time at Hawthorne. We became local heroes. Skyrines bowed theatrically in the mess. Attitude and spirit.

Most fun we had had in weeks. And we all had inappropriate dreams about First Lieutenant Coyle.

Five months later, on the Red, with nary a bitter word, some of us teamed up with those same Russians and seven hours after our drop engaged a dense Antag redoubt in the center of Chryse, near Shirley Patera. We reduced the enemy to smoke and chaff. Some of the Russians received decorations.

The kid who had chain-whipped Tak was not there. He had been demoted, by request of the Gurus in Moscow, and sent back to Novosibirsk to hump a desk.

I'm happy to see our sisters, delighted to see Coyle, and I hope she remembers me. We work well together.

HOPE IS THE THING THAT FLOATS

Teal and I descend from the watchtower, make our way as quickly as we can down the tunnels, and within ten minutes Teal has climbed into the southern garage booth and opened the outer gate. The three Voor buggies—plus the nine Voors and nine Skyrines—are soon inside an even bigger hollow, a hangar carved out of basalt, with rows of steel support beams shoring up the roof.

After the buggies park, three more Skyrines escort the drivers down from each. There are nowhere near sixty Voors, as Teal feared; there are only twelve. I'm curious why they would take three buggies.

The Voors, all pale males in their twenties or thirties, line up beside their vehicles. One is a skinny old dude, likely first gen. Their skintights are as cadged together as Teal's, but reddish brown, with black helms and leggings and white-tipped boots.

I finger in magnification and look more closely at the new blazes. The Skyrines are from First Battalion, which in the past has been assigned early recon and ground prep—sneaking around the Red in the dark before a battle, surveilling Antag positions, correcting and refining maps, choosing drop sites.

How these new arrivals have made their way into my lofty presence does not encourage confidence. Still, they have a strong-field suppressor. And they know how to handle the locals.

Before Teal and I descend, I give out a sharp, four-tone whistle, and Captain Coyle greets us at the bottom of the booth ladder, sharp-eyed, pistol drawn and charged. She's in her late thirties, whippet-wiry inside the skintight, red hair, plump cheeks, and black eyes visible through her helm. I am out of uniform, but I've strapped my blaze to my arm, and I pull up my sleeve to show the bump where I've been chipped and dattooed. Captain Coyle runs her glove over the dattoo, then consults her angel on name and rank and current disposition, while the other Skyrines listen in, all ears, some grinning—expecting their situation is about to improve. Maybe, maybe not.

Coyle is not yet reassured. With a side glance at Teal, standing a few meters back, she faces me. "Master Sergeant Michael Venn," she says, echoing the display in her helm. "Sixth Marines, out of Skyport Virginia last deployment. Have we met, Venn?"

"Affirmative, Captain."

"Can't recall just where. Can't read your chip, but the dattoo tells the tale. Are there more of us around here?"

I tell her about our broken squad, the Korean general, how we survived on Russian tents and could not save an assortment of top officers. The captain listens, stern-faced. "We came down about two days after you," she says, "maybe three hundred klicks south. Similar situation, looks like. Then we ran into these boys. Real charmers. SNKRAZ."

Sho 'Nuff KrayZ. Recent update from SNAFU, *Situation Normal, All Fucked Up,* which our alien sponsors do not like to hear.

Captain Coyle takes the suppressor from Gunnery Sergeant Maria Christina de Guzman—mid-twenties, oval-faced, small and supple and very fit looking, with strange, cold eyes—and tells her to prep the Voors. Here, in decent pressure and only a mild chill, Gunny de Guzman orders the Voors to strip to their Dutch undies. I don't know what "Dutch undies" means, but Sergeant Anita Magsaysay snickers and the others look pleased.

For their part, the Voors are tense and pasty-faced as they pull off their skintights.

I know that in Coyle's opinion, though she's being polite, I'm still under suspicion. No angel to lase, no read on my chip, dattoo purely surface, no bona fides other than a whistle that could have been compromised and a detached blaze that could belong to anybody; I could *be* anybody. I try to look relaxed and friendly.

Teal simply looks frightened. She obviously believes the Voors were sent to kill her. But under firm prodding, the Voors do as they are told, silent, resentful, eight of them young and skinny and scared, three in their thirties and not much fatter, one emaciated elder with burning eyes.

Sergeant Mazura b. Mustafa—of middle height, narrow face, big black eyes, and luxurious lips—binds the Voors' wrists with tough plastic straps. Several of the almost naked men study Teal as if trying to remember the sketchy portrait on a wanted poster. They could believe we're going to restore their liberty, allow them to continue their settler ways—do what they came here to do. After all, Earth policy is hands-off, live and let live, right?

Only now are we joined by Gamecock and Tak and DJ, who goggle at this turn of events. Gamecock approaches the captain, who opens her plate and shoots out a gloved hand. The ones in control, for now, begin to relax a little. DJ and Tak exchange friendly greetings with some of our sisters. They are polite but edgy, worn down from whatever they went through before they encountered the Voors—and from having to deal with these gentlemen on apparently less than cordial terms.

And those cold eyes. Something's different about some of our warriors in this gathering…

But I dismiss all doubts.

"Anyone speak Afrikaans?" Captain Coyle asks. She removes her helm and shakes out a short mop of sweaty black hair.

"I do, a little," Teal says. Four of our sisters, alerted to her presence, take this opportunity to gather around her, scoping her out, admiring her fashion sense, I suppose. Teal puts up with their curiosity, but after a few minutes, Coyle reins it in.

"Ah, Captain, first ranch wife we've seen!" Magsaysay complains.

"She's tall," says Lance Corporal Katy Suleiman.

"Taller than you, Shrimp," Mustafa says.

"Everyone's taller than Suleiman," Magsaysay observes.

"She's pretty, though," says Corporal Juana Maria Ceniza. She experimentally pinches the fabric on Teal's arm, eyes wary as a fox's.

"Cut that shit, Ash!" Coyle warns.

Ceniza lifts one brow, but pulls her hand away and backs off.

"Go on," the captain encourages.

"Radio talk mostly," Teal says, shivering at our ladies' interest. "*Taal*, t'ey call it."

"Their English is piss-poor," Coyle says.

"T'ey speak English well enow when t'ey want," Teal says. The Voors squint hard at her. One makes a rude gesture, which is knocked down by Corporal Firuzah Dawood, a short, stocky gal with a shaved scalp and a dancer's way of moving around the captives. Nothing escapes her, and she's not afraid to be brusque.

"You hitched a ride?" Gamecock asks Coyle.

"Not hardly, sir," Coyle says. "We saw them heading our way, took residence behind some rocks, and offered up a pigeon. No way of guessing their intentions. To our delight, they stopped."

"For little ol' me," Ceniza says. She grins, thrusts out a leg, mocks pulling up a skirt. Objectively, I assess that she might be the shapeliest of our sisters.

"As soon as they saw Ash—Corporal Ceniza—they screeched to a halt and came out mad as hornets, weapons drawn," Coyle says. "A bunch of gallant males surrounded her, and the boss man blessed her out—I think. Accused her of violating Muskie neutrality."

"Some sort of dispute with the condo association," Ceniza says. "Assholes were going to strip me on the Red." Her mates seem prepared to get angry all over again. They close in on the Voors, palming sidearms—but Captain Coyle raises a hand. The Voors bead sweat and glare.

"We popped out from hiding, desert fashion," Coyle continues. "They wisely decided not to go up against Sergeant de Guzman." Coyle returns to the gunny the strong-field suppressor, also known as a lawnmower. De Guzman, had she been so ordered, could have cut the Voor buggies into sausage slices with a few sweeps.

The eldest Voor, the one Coyle calls the boss man, raises his bound wrists. He's a small, skeletal guy with a high pale forehead, a fringe of wayward gray hair, a small, sharp nose, and a thin-lipped, white-stubbled face. "Talk, we talk, Colonel," he says to Gamecock, fellow male, trying to appear conciliatory if not actively friendly. His black eyes shine like aggies. "We need to *talk* what is happening."

"I'll listen in a moment," Gamecock says. "For now," and he looks hard at me, "I need to catch up on every little thing that's happened in the last hour." He turns to Captain Coyle. "And the last few days."

"Yes, sir," Coyle says. "The Voors appear to have something to add to that conversation."

"That we do, and damned essential!" the old Voor says.

Teal does not look happy, but there's little she can do. She's now effectively reduced to the same status as the Voors, until we find time to sit and share and get things straightened out.

Until we understand what the hell this Drifter station is, and what's going on around it, and what it implies both for the settlers and for our little war.

IN HEAVEN AS IT IS ON EARTH

In the early years of Mars colonies, idealism and pioneer spirit drew "investors" with promises of a new and better life under the hurtling moons of Mars, never closer than tens of millions of miles from Earth, often much farther. That appealed to an intriguing subset of humanity that held, even within that narrow purpose, many different opinions about life.

The first pioneers on Mars were packed into small, chemical fuel spaceships, up to twenty at a time, without benefit of Cosmoline sleep, to suffer in high-tech discomfort the months-long journey.

When they arrived—if they arrived, for as many as half died during those first voyages—they found supply and construction vessels at their landing sites, ready to be arranged into those famous white hamster mazes, while primitive versions of our fountains swept the air and soil of Mars for the ingredients essential to life.

High adventure.

Bravery and creativity and passion were essential to the success of those early settlements. Remarkably, nine out of ten of the new settlers survived the first few years, thanks to the genius and foresight of a small slate of terrestrial entrepreneurs, most of whom never made it to Mars.

They were too old. Age was the single greatest factor in casualty rates during transit. Men and women over forty were ten times more likely to sicken and die. Some said it was physical frailty; as I look back on those voyages through the lens of my own experience, I am more inclined to believe it was a fatal pining for Earth's basic luxuries—wide-open spaces, blue skies and clouds and rain, clumped dirt, clean, fresh air, the mineral tang of good water—that drove older travelers into decline.

So many pioneers had been convinced that a heaven of simulated reality would make up for all that was lacking on Mars. It did not. They should have studied the examples of pioneer families on the Great Plains, hunkering in the murky shadows of sod huts, the ladies—away from home and friends and society—driven to spooning laudanum while the men hunted or plowed hard, rocky fields, turning grim and leather-faced as weather and natives challenged, their children seemed to run wild as animals, and the last reserves of sanity dwindled.

Some dreamers believed that Mars could be terraformed—remade in Earth's image. Barring that long possibility, they imagined great domed frontier towns with outlaws and sheriffs and saloons, or their high-tech equivalents. One such dome was erected, inflatable, a thousand meters wide. It lasted six months before being destroyed by a double calamity of meteor strike and high wind. No others were built, but the concept will likely return if Mars ever finds peace.

But what I'm really working up to is an explanation for what the hell Voortrekkers and their ilk were doing on Mars.

People who build utopias need places to put their nowheres. The groups that followed the first waves of settlers to Mars were filled to overflowing with grumble. Not a few felt constrained by Earthly trends that discouraged bigotry and patriarchal dominance and denied power to those who espoused biblical or economic purities. People seeking to build personal empires hid behind these idealists, then rose up to take advantage of their lapses, their unmet necessities...by imposing order and discipline, which utopias typically lack and desperately need, especially when conditions get harsh and death looms.

Once these pragmatists were in power, all over the Earth hard-core malcontents took subscriptions for specialized settlements and shipped dozens or even hundreds of chosen ones—prepackaged and compatible seedling societies—to Mars.

And so we now face Voortrekkers, not the actual Forward Explorers of South African and Rhodesian history, but a group of dedicated reenactors that espoused many of those ancient hard-core attitudes.

No blacks, no wogs—hard ways for hard living.

Latter-day patriarchs running roughshod over history.

———

KAZAK AND MICHELIN have joined us in the southern garage. DJ is tending to the general.

Being outnumbered has done nothing to subdue the old Voor, who is already stepping up his rhetoric. His name is Paul de Groot. He's been on Mars for thirty-two years. "Listen up!" he shouts. We fall silent as his shrill voice rings across the hangar.

"Bit of a stinker, sir," Captain Coyle mutters to Gamecock.

"We are Trekboers! You've commanded my wagons, you'll know our names and where we stand!" De Groot makes a point of walking around his men, tapping their heads—a reach for some, as he is the shortest—and naming them. "This is Jan, this is Hendrik, this is Johannes, that is Shaun," and on down the list. The broad-shouldered brute I saw from the overlook is named Rafe. He has a quiet stealth that concerns me. Pent-up, strong, like a coiled snake. I wonder if he and the stinker are father and son. For all I know, they might *all* be his sons.

The Voors settle to parade rest. Teal looks even more miserable.

"Understood, sir," Gamecock says, breaking in just as Captain Coyle is about to lay down her share. The captain is not impressed by any of the Voors. "We're willing to come to an accommodation, providing it's mutually beneficial. We need information—"

"You're here a-learn what this pipe does!" de Groot cries out, though everyone else is quiet. He clamps his teeth with a click, levels his shoulders, and thrusts out his jaw. "Trekboers protect what's ours." His dialect is different from Teal's, but then, he's trying to speak English. To my ear, he's easier to understand.

Gamecock approaches him. "You were willing to murder us," he says. "That could explain our general lack of courtesy, don't you think?"

"No such!" de Groot says, but in a lower voice. "We have little to share and no kindness on principle."

"Leave that be," Gamecock says. "Captain Coyle tells me you have information that could go a long way to patching up our differences. If we can establish mutual trust...for now."

De Groot sniffs. "This is *our* pipe," he says. "Our station. We keep it under hold, patch and drain it, waiting, a-hope of return and mining. And living! But you can understand, we do not want its quality a-shouted any who listen. Strange ears, out on the dust!"

"We can agree on that," Gamecock says.

The old Voor turns to Teal. His face sharpens and his lips purse as if he is about to spit. "You are the *hoer*," he says. "Do you know this one?" he shouts to all of us, advancing until he sees the sisters and Gamecock have palmed their sidearms. Then he nods like a dip bird and backs off a step. "She betrayed her camp, and now she betrays all *us*. None should be here! *This* is our salvation, our hope. We follow *her*, a-stop her betrayal." He flings his arms at the heavy dark space. But then his bluster fades, he seems to deflate a little, and he nods at Rafe, the big fellow, who steps forward.

"We come from bad news," the broad-shouldered young Voor says softly. "Piet Retief Kraal and the Swellendam Pipe have been destroyed. The Far Comers have not bothered with us until now, but our *legerplaatze* are silent. And this woman's camp—silent a-well. It may be all were murdered by ice, rocks."

"The comet took out a *settlement*?" Gamecock asks.

"All we had, gone," Rafe confirms, sensing, hoping for a turn of sympathies. Shaun and Andres, both young and light-haired, lean against each other. Andres is shaking.

"We *think*," de Groot says, watching this emotion with gimlet eyes. "Same compass. No radio after. Shock nearly scrubbed our wagons. Our brothers wanted a-look, but I am hard man, *we* go on. If the *leger* is there, it is there. If it is gone…But the others, they disagree. They take a wagon and leave."

"The ranch wife saved you," Coyle says in a wondering undertone.

"*Hoer* has luck a-get out in just time," de Groot counters. His voice rises for effect, and he thrusts out his bound hands. "She *knew*. She's glove with the Far Comers!"

Our tall rescuer has frozen in place, face screwed up and drained of color. "T'at's a *lie*," she says very softly.

Rafe continues, "As *vader* says, what's done is out. We have a-decide new all soon, friend or foe, or we're over. We are finished, *dood*."

By which he means, I assume, we are dead.

"Now all listen," de Groot resumes, building up again, able to inflate and deflate apparently at will. He folds his twisty-tied hands in front of his crotch, lowers his head, gazes up at us under his brows. "This pipe is hope, but only if we fix and restore. And here the *hoer* could help, if she tells what she knows—and trims time so doing."

Gamecock has been listening without comment until now, but he quickly arranges us to block the Voors just as they move forward, despite their plastic shackles, to begin these labors.

"You are not in command here, sir," he reminds de Groot in a confidential voice.

"It's *our* pipe, damn!" the Voor named Shaun cries, and the others bristle, but de Groot shushes them, waves them down with his hands like a conductor with an orchestra. I swear that Rafe is just waiting for a chance to make a stupid move. Tak and I instinctively take a couple of steps left and right to flank him. He's big. They would all die, but maybe that's good enough for their pride under the circumstances—who can say? Humans are invariably wild animals. We learn that early in boot. I doubt it's any different on Mars.

"Do you know our history, this place?" de Groot asks. "Where we are, where we stand, where we suffered and suffer now?"

"We've left you alone," Gamecock says. "That's what you want, isn't it?"

"We stand in fear of soldiers taking all, and now—*she* brings you!" De Groot tries to jab a knobby finger at Teal, who narrows her eyes. The Voors are bound—she is not. I suppose that's a telling point.

"Where in hell are we, Venn?" Gamecock asks me, aside. "What is this place?"

"We could tell," de Groot says.

Gamecock looks between us, concentrates on me. "What have you learned?"

"Far from all I'd like to know, sir. This woman's father told her this mine, Drifter, pipe—whatever—was a place where she could retreat if things got bad at her camp. Apparently, they did."

"How?" Gamecock asks Teal.

"Long story," she says, swallowing hard, eyes still tracking the Voors.

Gamecock looks back at me. "Venn, what the hell is all this about?"

"The settlements, towns, laagers, whatever they call them— have had it rough, Colonel. They've managed to explore and build camps, but I think their population hasn't grown much."

"Hard times!" de Groot says. "Hardest for Voors!"

"You fight for what isna yours!" Teal cries, her brittle restraint snapping. "You raid and kill and *t'ieve!*" Gamecock is losing control of the discourse, but at least there's information emerging, of a kind. He looks at me to indicate he will interrupt if passions overflow, or if the talk is not useful.

I stand aside.

"We were told by her station, this *hoer* has left, she is angry, she is going a-our pipe," de Groot says.

Teal looks down. "Na such," she murmurs.

"Her *vader*, he was an engineer," Rafe says. "He left the Trek-boers long past. Went a-Green Camp."

"Lost the Trekboer way," de Groot adds firmly.

"You killed his wife!" Teal says, eyes up, accusing.

"At Green he lost his wife again!" de Groot says. "Man is good at losing wives."

"How many camps know about this place?" Gamecock breaks in.

"Just Voors and Green Camp," Teal says defiantly. "Te Voors killed most te Algerians."

"Not such," de Groot says. He's about to add something, but, looking around at all the brown faces, his Adam's apple bobs and he clamps his jaw.

"My fat'er told na else but me, and t'en Ally Pecqua took my intended and made him her own." An old story. Teal is intent on saying more, letting out her frustration. "Among te Rationals, wit'out a husband, I am a burden."

De Groot snorts. "Among Voors, women are *value*."

"White women," Teal says.

Our sisters study the Voors closely, eyes narrowed to slits. Rafe notices and nudges his father, who looks around, less smug but no less defiant.

"They were fools, but we partner," de Groot concludes with a deep sniff up his long nose.

Gamecock listens with a serious and sympathetic expression. To Teal, he says, "Your father told you how to get around this place, where to find food and resources."

Teal nods. Her eyes are dry, weeping done.

"You did not intend to bring others with you, including us."

"No. But t'ey woulda died out t'ere," she says, eyes like head-lamps in the shadow.

Gamecock turns first to Captain Coyle, whose expression is neutral with a touch of grim, then to de Groot, and observes his reaction. I watch Rafe, who cringes in anticipation. He knows de Groot just can't keep still and shut up.

"We *live*!" de Groot shouts. "We feed our people! We trek and settle and build, flee battles, *soldate*, but even so, lose families and land! And now, because of *your* war, the *laager* is *gone*!" He stares around as if his look could pierce us all. "We have waited years. When the water is down, the pipe is no longer flooded, we mine and build and make crops. Here there is much metal—but down below, vents, *vluchtige*—pockets of methane, ammonia—*stikstof*—nitrogen!"

"And sulfide," I explain under my breath to the colonel. "They seeded oxyphores in the pits."

Gamecock frowns. Biology is not his strength. Skipping over

that, I add the important point: "Enough water still flows to power the old generators. And they have a printer. Quite a few barrels of slurry—metal, ceramic, medical, and nutrient."

"How many?" Gamecock asks.

"Hard to know, sir. Lots. They finished most of the installation before the hobo—before the water rose and they left."

"Drifter. Pipe. Hobo," Gamecock says, trying to absorb the words.

"Why not just pump out the water and sell it?" Tak asks.

"Water iss *everywhere*," Rafe says. "We got water."

"That gives *suurstof*, oxygen, hydrogen," de Groot says. "But very little *stikstof*, not so much *metaal*, not like this, just ready to dig and melt. This pipe means *huise*, *kos*, food—life! But what is that now? *Nutteloos!* No use!"

His agony is honest. His eyes fill with tears. Everyone is still, quiet. The other Voors seem embarrassed. Rafe flexes his arms, tugging at his twisty-ties. Hard times indeed.

"I never wanted *t'at*," Teal says.

"You led them straight here!" Rafe says, not shouting, but with deep resentment.

"So did you," Captain Coyle reminds him.

"Not our choosing," Rafe says.

The tension is rising. Gamecock feels it. We all feel it. Teal can feel it most acutely. We're all that stands between her and de Groot's vengeance. These guys would love to resume their little gnome works without our interference.

"There's no point assigning blame," Gamecock says. "Save that for later. How many Voors left your buses, your wagons?"

"Trekboers. Many," Rafe says.

De Groot clamps his jaw. "They go where home was."

Too many to fit in one wagon. Coyle asks, "Can they walk that far?"

"They die," de Groot says. "When hope it is gone, we go on

trek, like our ancestors. Dutch go hard on them, they walk from Cape Town to the Big Karoo and the Little Karoo. Our way."

"*King Solomon's Mines*," I say.

"That is right," Rafe says sadly. "Ophir. Right here we are. We are no danger. Set us free!"

Gamecock lowers his eyebrows a notch. Coyle shakes her head.

Vee-Def and Kazak have gone back to the northern garage at Gamecock's murmured instructions and now rejoin us. They confer with Coyle and Gamecock, away from Voor ears, and after a minute, Gamecock motions for me and Tak to come aside with them. Tak repeats his report. "We've got a good line of sight to the northwest. Lots of activity—there's a big cloud out there. Venn saw it earlier, just after we dropped. Well, now it's bigger and closer. There are tunnels and hidey-holes all through this place. We really need a map or a native guide."

I tell them about the southern watchtower and the control panel. Gamecock sends DJ to check it out.

"I'm not sure any of the Voors have been here in years," Gamecock says.

"Teal might know more, but she's terrified," I say.

"They keep calling this a 'pipe,'" Kazak says, drawing closer. "What the hell does that mean?"

"Volcanic pipe, like where diamonds are mined," Tak says.

"I saw something on a display up in the watchtower," I say. "A cavern or room, bright, shiny, crystals all over."

"Diamonds—here?" Gamecock asks, incredulous.

"Don't know that, sir, or where it is, even if it's in this formation."

"The big fellow did grab on to calling this place Solomon's mine," Coyle says. She points to me. "Master Sergeant Venn seems to have a relationship with the ranch wife. She showed you around, didn't she?"

"She's just scared," I say.

"Assume nothing," Coyle says.

Gamecock is studying me. I don't like that.

"I don't think she trusts any of us," I say.

"She's got to be lonely," Gamecock says. "She came here with nobody, to get away—but then she picks us up. None of the settlements like us…" Something continues not to convince or impress him. I have to agree—there are major gaps in every one of these stories.

Tak and I regard each other with owlish resignation. The dust and activity out there is almost certainly Antag, and they're either heading our direction deliberately, out to get us in particular, or we're on the path to wherever they are going. Given the nature of this place, if the Antags have tracked all these buggies from orbit, homing in on the Drifter like dung beetles to a pile, they're going to be curious.

Likely the Drifter has distinct gravimetry and until now the Antags have ignored it, as we have, because there's been too much else to do. But if they're in complete charge, laying down a heavy, long-term hand, they may feel the freedom to send out targeted recon.

"I want to know as much as we can know about this place, as soon as possible," he says. "There could be a hell of a lot more at stake than just us and them. Keep letting Teal think we're on her side. We may *be* on her side, of course. Captain Coyle, you go with them—chaperone. Take the big one, Rafe, just to let the Voors feel they're not being left out."

"What about the old guy?" Coyle asks. "He's the boss. And he's real trigger." She means a natural killer, remorseless and cold. "He might know more than the others. And the others won't do anything without his say."

"Isolate him," Tak suggests. "Defuse him."

"Take him away, the rest will get anxious," Gamecock says.

"I'll bet he's told his son most of what he knows. Rafe's the one you want to get separate." He presses his hands together, then splits them apart. "I'm pretty sure we're all going to be together in the shit soon enough. If we can keep them in line...Get them to fight *with* us...Maybe we'll die another day. But right now, we need to do our best to uplink and get instructions," the colonel concludes with a sour look.

DJ returns. "I've scoped out the watchtower rooms," he says. "Beetling brows over the ports." He salutes a caveman ridge above his nose. "No line of sight to zenith. Maybe to the horizon, but that's the long way."

"Even if we had working lasers," Gamecock says.

"We have helm lasers," Tak says. "On a clear night, we *could* get a horizontal link—for a few seconds at least."

"How? You couldn't hold steady enough."

"The sats could spot dust twinkle and do Fourier, then downlink."

"Why would they?" Gamecock asks doubtfully. "Antags can spot twinkle as well."

"If any sats survive," I add.

"Well, what if some do?" Tak says. "Sir, we can't *not* take chances. We need to compare our own tactical in real time, the updates between Captain Coyle's launch and drop and ours— not just chew over old news. Our angels are terrible at computing command decisions, especially when the shit sets up. But you *know* they will. And then, we have to do what they say." We have been instructed to follow angelic orders, even barring updates. That threat chills us all—all except Coyle, who stays cool, indifferent.

I note this with a slight itch in the back of my head.

"We're the deciders," I say.

Gamecock considers. "Captain Coyle—you, me, Tak, let's draw in the dust. Michelin, you and whomever the captain assigns work the layout with Rafe. Venn, take Teal back to that watchtower and look around. Keep her away from the Voors. And get back in your skintights, all of you. DJ…go outside through the southern garage. Shoot some beams. See if we can raise a sat."

DJ looks unhappy.

"Twenty minutes," Gamecock tells him. "Then get the fidge back in here."

"Just say 'fuck,' sir," DJ grumbles. "Bloody Gurus can't fucking hear us."

"Assume nothing," Gamecock says. "Go."

BACKGROUNDER, PART 3

I sit in the apartment's high morning light, flipping the inscribed platinum disk between my fingers, basking in a multicolored and subdivided square of reflected spring sun—with coffee. The lone box of breakfast cereal has long since become a village of weevils, a movable feast—if I regard them as food rather than company.

Doesn't matter. I'm not hungry. The dubious delights of being alone have worn off. I'm waiting for Joe to show up and tell me the outcome, as far as it goes, of his part of our long story.

I feel weirdly biblical this morning. Smiting and being smitten.

Lo and behold, heavenly visitors came to Earth, and at first it was good, though many were sore amazed, and some were affrighted and did rise up and protest.

That's all I got. Never did get into that shit much.

But about two-thirds of us decided it was okay, why be a wallflower at the orgy? The second year after the Gurus outed themselves, the major industrial nations recorded near-zero unemployment. All who could work, worked—there was that much to do to exploit what little they had begun to reveal.

But everything is context. Before the real kicker, the mother of other dropped shoes—the announcement that the Antags were in our backyard—the Gurus led with an opening poke, a diagnostic of our will, of our submission.

Maybe.

Gurus seemed reasonable, mostly. They took a larger view. No surprise, given their celestial origins. They didn't mind their benefits expanding to all nations, even those that refused to acknowledge they were real. They also didn't mind satires or outright blasphemies against their persons or activities—seemed at times to encourage them. Lets off steam. So be it. They are not *really* God or gods, after all. Like us, mere mortals.

And yet, like the God of Abraham, shrouded in His secure sanctuary, the Gurus do not show themselves to the greater world. In the early years, speculation ran rampant, but those in the know managed to keep quiet about what they saw and experienced, in the presence of our visitors.

And to them—to the Wait Staff, just before the truly shitty boot dropped—was passed the first edict of Guru kind. Call it a firm request.

The Gurus made it clear, however magnanimous they might seem, that they found offensive any and all sexual profanity. Words that showed disrespect to the sacred biological functions of reproduction. Blaspheme against the Lord or Allah or Krishna or Buddha or Brahma if you will, but the F-word and its irreverent equivalents were a foul stench unto core Guru beliefs.

No physical punishment would ensue should that word continue to occupy its favored place in literature, entertainment, and common discourse—that was not Guru style—but they would be highly displeased, and if sufficiently highly displeased, they could reduce their revelations, perhaps even pack up and depart.

Some found that amusing. Upon threat of suppression, the floodgates opened. For a few months, the channels of human discourse overflowed with sexual profanity of an amazing level of creativity and vigor.

And then, as promised, the Gurus clammed up. For three months, nothing new passed to the outer world from the Wait Staff. So began the worldwide clampdown on the F-word. After all, geese with sensitive ears who laid golden eggs now rocked our economy. No reason to be ungrateful. For the first time in human history, humans managed to mostly clean up their language.

Way back in the twentieth century, creative types conjured substitutes for F-words by the dozens, like ersatz coffee or fake cigarettes—or bootleg gin—to avoid purely human censors. That talent was now revived. A young blogger in Beijing, whose reports, in admirable English, were popular worldwide, made up the word *fidge* as the new expletive of choice. He carefully explained—for sensitive eyes and ears—that nowise and nohow did *fidge* have a sexual connotation.

Fidge it became: fidge this, fidge that.

Gamecock was always extra cautious.

And that's not all. Don't know if there's any relation, but respecting reproduction...

Maybe you know about the lists, the unsolved disappearances all around the world. They seem to have begun about three years after the Gurus arrived. A select group of men and even a few women are vanishing. Some have been connected with or accused of sexual crimes. Violent stuff. Like Corporal Grover Sudbury. Remember him?

The disappearances continue to this day. Certainly not mystery number one, but interesting.

WAKEFUL THOUGHTS FOR SLEEPLESS GRUNTS

I think more this morning of the Red. How, wearing a skintight and standing on a flat, lifeless prairie of old lava and blown dust and sand, sometimes, even before a battle, I could feel free, liberated, useful; whereas here, in the apartment, the walls are closing in worse than any faceplate; the ample air seems denser and more confining than the sour smell of packed filters.

There's an untouched bowl of cereal on the table. It's still moving. The weevils are active. I don't know whether to throw them out or sit down and talk to them. I've got it bad. I'm shaking, and it's not just the pure caffeine of freshly ground black coffee, a luxury hardly ever available on Mars. I'm shaking because my extended cat whiskers tell me a moment is arriving that will both explain and traumatize. I do not want to know. I've switched off my phone, cut the intercom and buzzer; nobody in, nobody out who doesn't already have a key. No news. No updates. Just the closing in and restlessness and shivering. No more, please. I'm a man without a center. I have no idea where the hell I am. Waiting for Joe. Waiting for anybody who can tell me what the hell happened and how long I have to lie low.

Christ, I am well and truly fucked.

I look at the door, above the rise and beyond the small flight of stairs, framed by the upstairs loft, clearly illuminated by rising glory reflected from a glass-walled skyscraper a few hundred meters across the downtown neighborhood—blue-green windows redirecting the eastern sunrise.

Someone's coming. It won't be Joe. That much my whiskers tell me. Someone new. I get up on autopilot, shivering uncontrollably, and move toward the door.

As my toe lands on the first step, the doorbell rings its Big Ben chimes. Very retro. It takes me a long while to answer, but whoever or whatever is there is patient. I finally unlatch the door and swing it open, half expecting I will take aggressive action— at the very least, jump out and scream "Boo!"

But I don't.

A small, zaftig woman with black eyes, a stub nose, and a close-cropped patch of red hair looks at me without expression— relaxed, composed. She's wearing a light gray overcoat and a red and purple scarf. She smells like roses, old-lady perfume, but she can't be much older than me.

"Yeah?" I say.

"Joseph sent me," she says with a knowing grin. "He told me you'd be here," she adds, looking past me into the apartment. "He's sorry he couldn't make it. But he said you'll understand."

I'm staring, goggle-eyed.

The woman who smells like roses explains, into my silence, "He gave me the code to the downstairs entry. And the elevator."

Still staring.

"Can I come in?" she asks. Straightforward. Steady. She's dealt with fidged Skyrines before.

"Joe's okay?" I ask.

"I haven't heard from him in a few days."

"Where is he?"

"I don't know."

"Is he in trouble?"

"He is *always* in trouble."

"You're his girlfriend?"

"Do I look that stupid?" But again she smiles. It's a lovely, gentle smile. "He *invited* me to come talk with you. Have you got the coin?"

"I've got some coins," I say.

"One important coin. Silver?"

"You tell me," I say.

"Platinum," she says.

"Yeah."

"What's on the coin?"

"Numbers," I say.

"Good on you."

I seem to pass, for now. The woman says, "In case you're wondering, Teal's alive, last I heard, but that was a while ago."

"How do you know about Teal?"

She cocks her head, holds out one hand, may she come in? I stand aside, let her in, and close the door. My shaking has stopped. It's better not to be alone. What I know, what I think I know, I really do not want to keep to myself. This might be progress.

"I smell coffee," she says.

"I can't smell coffee. Fidging Cosmoline. Miss that."

"Do you smell my roses?" she asks.

"Yeah."

"Good. Pretty soon, you'll smell the coffee, too."

"Okay. Thanks."

"Not a problem."

I go to the kitchen and get down a mug, pour her what's left in the carafe. She doesn't follow, doesn't move far from the entry, just stands back there, craning her neck and looking around the apartment.

"You guys do okay."

"Thanks. It's not my place," I say, and deliver the cup.

"You might put on some clothes," she tells me, eyes fixed on my chin.

I look down. I'm naked.

"Right," I say. "Sorry."

"Did Joe tell you I'm a nurse?"

"Joe didn't say a thing about you," I say over my shoulder as I go to collect a robe.

"That's surprising. Vac and mini-g medicine, combat metabolism, oxydep—Injuries from anoxia and hypoxia."

"MHAT?" I ask from the bedroom.

"No. Not that there's anything wrong with MHAT. Good for warriors in trouble. But my billets were orbital."

"Active duty?"

"Indefinite furlough," she says. "I'm facing courts-martial."

"That's good," I say.

"Hmm."

"What's your name?"

"Puddin' tame," she says.

"Great. Just a friend of Joe's, or a friend of Teal's?"

"A friend to Mars," she says. "I hope."

I've put on a robe and cinch the tie as I return.

"Can I see the coin?" she asks.

I've been clenching it against my palm like Gollum—*my Precious*—as I once observed myself doing on Mars, in the Drifter, but, now, shyly enough, I drop the end of the tie, open my fingers, and hold it out.

She reaches.

I pluck it back and close my hand.

"Name, rank, serial number," I say.

"First Lieutenant Alice Harper, U.S. Marine Medical Services, awaiting dishonorable discharge."

"Disability?"

"Multiple cancers, all cured—but leading to profound Cosmoline sickness," she says. "Can't take the vac anymore." Then she adds, when I look dubious, "That's my real name and rank, *fuckhead.*"

Spoken like a true Skyrine.

Again, I hold out the coin. She picks it up between small, pretty fingers, nails cut close and clean and painted with clear polish, and turns it over, brings it to her eye, then hands it back.

"Looks good," she says.

"What does it mean? A second coin…"

"Tell me what happened," she says, and takes another step into the apartment. "May I sit?"

"Of course."

She sits on the couch.

And just as she does that, the awful reluctance returns. *I don't want to tell.* Telling is like making people die all over again. I stand in the living room, saying nothing, just looking out the window with a dumbass squint.

"I'm a good listener," she says. "Tell me what happened, and maybe I'll be able to tell you what the coin means."

I gather up my courage. I would like to know more. I already know some of it. Not a lot. Just enough. The Algerians and the Voors weren't the first to mine the Drifter. Not by three and a half billion years.

It's a big story getting bigger. Let's slip back into it slowly, like a scalding bath.

COMES THE HEAT

Teal and I return to the northern garage and put on our skin-tights. Scrubbed and recharged, my suit is almost comfortable. There's six hours of oxygen in the backpack, new filters—not pristine sweetness, but no longer pickle juice. Reassuring, if things get bad and we have to exit in a hurry.

"The Voors will kill you if t'ey can," Teal says under her breath. "T'ey hate brown people. And your fems are bossy, too."

"Brown people do better in the vac," I say.

"My fat'er t'ought so," she says. Teal's back is to me as we head toward the ladder leading to the cold high room, which I'm hoping is warming now that power is back on. She pauses at the bottom of the ladder. "Te Voors had all *t'is*," she says, shoulders tensed, back arched, everything in her posture asking me how stupid they must be. "Wealt' and food and metal and water power, as long as te hobo flowed. And 'tis still flowing, down t'ere, where 'tis safe and useful. But te Voors will never be happy. Na else wanted a work or trade wit' t'em, because of te wrong t'ey did te Algerians—and my fat'er."

I say nothing. My job is to look northwest. We climb the ladder in silence. The cold room is warming, just a little. The radiant heater mounted on one wall crackles as years of dust pop off.

Teal raises the shutter.

We both see at once. Where the steady brown blur had been, there's now a wide wall of dust, and it's no storm. Big movement all along the western horizon, an arc of at least thirty klicks, from one corner of the port to the other. Many things in motion.

What sort of things?

I close my helm's plate and dial down a pair of virtual binocs. The plate measures the angles of incident light from the front of the plate to the rear, does a transform algorithm, and voila— a lensless virtual magnification of the infrared projects into my eyes, along with my angel's analysis of what I might be seeing. More Guru tech.

Teal has pulled down the periscope, handling it gingerly. Not time enough to warm. Maybe it has its own magnification, but I doubt she's seeing all that I'm seeing. There's a phalanx of vehicles out there, deep in the dust cloud. The angel analyzes the most likely threat first, a large concentration of Antag vehicles. As well, aerostats are advancing slowly behind the dust, about fifty klicks from the Drifter: big suspended balloons, the smallest at least a hundred meters in diameter. But then the angel points up another, much smaller line of vehicles, moving at speed in front of the main mass, just before the leading edge of the dust. These outlines are more familiar, possibly not a threat—

The angel flashes purple, still collating—then chirps. Here's some good news. The advancing Antag front is driving a line of human transports. Not many, no more than twenty or thirty, but they're clipping along at a fair pace and will likely reach the arc that includes our position before the Antags.

"Not'ing but dust," Teal says, pushing back the scope. "What do you see?"

I've been quiet, except for clucking my tongue and tapping my gloved fingers, a habit when I see shit coming down. "Ants chasing rabbits," I say. "Cavalry, maybe." I don't say aloud, *but not enough, and followed right on their heels by a whole lot of Indians.* The biggest Antag push I've ever witnessed.

I try to raise Gamecock, but as before, RF is blocked by the density of metal and rock. I remember DJ is outside the southern gate trying to pick up a sat signal. He's on the wrong side of the Drifter and won't see what we see.

"Far Ot'ers? Do t'ey know we'or here?" Teal asks.

"No idea," I say, and lean in close to the plex, hoping my laser will carry that far. I murmur a message to the angel and it shoots a beam through the port, varying frequency to find a sweet spot. Not much chance it will get through, it tells me. Plex too thick. Too much dust between us and the advancing vehicles.

"No good?" Teal asks.

"Depends," I say. "We got to go. Shut the port. Don't want heat giving us away."

Teal closes the louvers. We descend and run back to the southern garage.

Gamecock and de Groot have agreed to a loose armistice, against the wishes of Captain Coyle, who does not enjoy being outranked. Gamecock has somehow convinced de Groot and the Voors to help us begin defensive prep. All the twisty-ties have been cut and discarded. Makes me nervous, but what the hell—it's our only option.

"I shot a helm burst east," I say.

"Might not have been a good idea, bringing them here," Coyle says.

"We need help," Gamecock says, frowning at her in puzzlement.

"Maybe." Coyle isn't happy about any of it. Again, her reaction seems wonky.

Kazak and Tak, with the help of Rafe and Andres, have sketched a crude map in the green dust of the key tunnels and external points of access, and when I pass along what I've seen, the Skyrines go into overdrive. Coyle orders three of her team lower into the Drifter to check out the supply situation, and asks Teal if she could act as a guide. Teal, with a glance at me, and to my nod, agrees. She trusts me. But fuck if I know what's going on.

They head out.

Rafe conferences with the Voors while de Groot talks over final things with Gamecock and Tak. If our forces received my burst and are speeding to join us, we'll open the northern gate and let them in—all the troops and as many of their vehicles and weapons as the garage can hold. Then we'll hunker down, hope the Antags pass us by—

But they won't. We sense that. They've laid down a heavy hand, they mean to stay, and that will take all the resources they can grab.

They still have eyes in the sky.

And they know we're here.

SHIT ALSO FLOATS, SOMETIMES

Before I exit, Teal returns with our three sisters. Her glum look leaves me with a strong impression that she suspects something is wrong, something that she does not feel at liberty to divulge. Does it involve our collaborating, even under necessity, with the Voors?

I wish I knew more about their history from an unprejudiced source, but on the other hand, Green Camp has been closer to the problem than anyone on Earth, and the tall dust widow is a serious, sober sort; she's suffered through her own kind of shit, her own kind of betrayal. Green Camp effectively forced her out on the Red. Then they alerted the Voors she was heading their way, all just to preserve a share of the Drifter, de Groot's pipe.

And now, she sees we're cozying up with her enemies.

Blows huge, all of it.

The generators are doing well, Coyle's team reports, and Teal agrees. Gamecock instructs Tak and me to post ourselves outside the northern gate, hiding behind the rock ridge, peeking over the top. We'll have a direct view of the approaching dust.

I check out the vehicle lock. It will only take three Skells or two Tonkas at a time, end to end. We won't be able to get all the vehicles inside, even those that will fit, before the Antags are upon us.

We pass through the personnel lock, which is big enough for maybe ten. Outside, it's coming up on mid-afternoon and very cold, but we aren't quite freezing; shivering knocks my teeth together, but that's okay, that's what we're used to. We can only hope the Antags and their sats don't spot our slim IR signatures and take potshots.

The wall of dust doesn't look any closer, but it does look higher. We can make out a few vehicles on the leading front with our naked eyes. Then the dust closes in. They must be fleeing in thick haze, and surely they know what's behind them. Makes me shiver.

Tak and I tap helms and talk to pass the time.

"How many days between space frames?" Tak asks. We both know the answer, but I say it anyway,

"Forty-three on average, depending on the season."

"How much equipment on the average sled?"

"Six hundred tons."

"How much of that is weaponry, how much transport and tents?"

We're not worried about fountains for the moment, because it's obvious we've found the mother lode of water and other resources.

"Forty percent transports, twenty weaponry," I say, rattling off the stats we're used to dealing with. Each delivery and drop can vary widely, and we won't know until we're updated; all this talk is snotsuck. But we're hoping our cavalry is traveling with platforms that can carry big hurt. Tons and tons of it, and lots of spent matter to mow down Antags.

"I could go for a steak," Tak says.

"Cue sad harmonica," I say, but grimace at the thought of sizzling meat.

"Play 'Danny Girl,' " he says. "The captain is hot."

"Captain Coyle is *not* hot. She's total big sister."

"Big Mama, you mean." Tak has *dignitas*, but he's no less male for all that. Irritating a watch partner is a true art form. Too little, and we might relax, become inattentive; too much, and we lose focus on the Red and start paying more attention to the argument.

"Guy can violate protocol on the Red anytime he wants," Tak says. "In his head."

"Hope angel doesn't note it."

"Duly observed. Angel, absolve me." Tak looks aside. "I heard Coyle went special ops."

"Something like that," I say. "And nothing about her after Hawthorne."

We think this over. Separate goals, separate orders. Special ops is like a hidden reef. Could protect, could sink.

Our angels are quiet. We never know what they record. So far, no Skyrine has ever had his loose talk or death video splattered over media; maybe we're too trusting. Or maybe we're too damned select and valuable to be messed with. Or—maybe we just can't afford to pay for the right video feed.

"How far?" Tak asks. We don't dare lase for range, a) because dust will absorb and scatter, and b) because the helm plates can guess almost as well with their incident angles and magnification transforms, like a camera finding focus. So Tak already knows.

But I say it anyway. "Five klicks for the lead group."

"Reinforcements. Transports and weapons."

Our angels now feed us rough approximations of what's stirring the closest dust. "Tonkas, four big ones," I say. "A bunch of Skells. A Chesty. And maybe a Trundle or two."

"Jeez. What's on the platforms? Stuff we trained with, or sci-fi crap we don't know how to use?"

Skyrines dream of that possibility. Major upgrades—MPHF, pronounced *mmph*, acronym for Mega Plus Hurt Factor—in our dreams these fabulous, decisive weapons are delivered by surprise, ready to link to our angels and upload instant training and serving suggestions. But training vids are the weakest link in Earth's military-industrial complex. Gurus leak us ideas for shit to use, but they don't tell us how best to use it.

Thinking there might be MPHF coming at us is too much to hope for. Hurts deep in my warrior soul. So we change the subject.

"That dust widow likes you, Venn," Tak says.

"She's in a tight angle." I tell him about her situation with the Voors.

"Shit," Tak says. "They want to paint her?"

"They would if they could."

"No wonder Coyle wanted them separated. I thought only enlightened nerds colonized Mars."

"Not hardly. Lots of folks wanted to get the hell off Earth. Rich and poor, nerds or just pissed-off."

"I do get the impression our guests don't much like brown people. Me, they don't know how to take."

"Nobody knows how to take you, Fujimori," I say. "Besides, why would any of them like Skyrines? Antags dropped shit on their settlement. It's our war, they claim, not theirs."

"Well, she likes *you*. What was it you found in those dungarees? What did Neemie say it was?"

"Platinum."

"Is there beaucoup platinum down there?"

"Maybe."

"Shit, let's do a *Dirty Dozen*!"

"You mean *Castle Keep*," I say. "Or maybe *Kelly's Heroes*."

Most Skyrines play Spex combat games or watch war movies when they're not crossing the vac or training or fighting. Some read. Tak does it all, but unlike Vee-Def, doesn't file away trivia.

Tak scoffs. "How far?"

"Three klicks and closing."

"See anything behind the Tonkas and the sleds?"

"Could be Millies. And high up, aerostats."

"Aerostats mean germ needles," Tak says.

"Wear a hat."

"Shit yes. Big steel sombrero." He holds his hands over his head, spreads them wide, pretends to hunker down more than we already are, squeezed into a narrow crevice in the rock.

Air support over Mars is difficult, because wings have to be so damned huge; anything like an airplane has to be big, clumsy, hard to maneuver—a perfect target. Antag aerostats are huge and even more clumsy, and in theory make good targets, but they seem to be cheap, easy to replace, and are surprisingly tough to shoot down. You pretty much have to slice away or burn out a few dozen meters of the aerostat's surface before it's fatally wounded and descends slowly to the dust, slumping like a big jellyfish on a terrestrial beach. We don't use them. I'm not sure why. We don't use germ needles, either. I'd say Antags know more about our biology than we do about theirs.

I rub the surface of the old basalt with my hand, feeling the age, trying to psych out some deeper truth.

Tak watches my hand. "Spirit of the Red? What you receiving?"

"Zip."

"Fucking superstition."

I'm not so sure. I keep seeing the coin, the platinum disk with its spiral of numbers, and it doesn't fit. It doesn't fit that some Voor miner would leave something so cool and valuable in his overalls—unless of course he died and nobody else knew. Still,

Teal seems to know. Possibly her father knew something and told her.

And maybe, just maybe, the previous owner of the dungarees was a caretaker, left behind...

And decided to go naked, without his dungarees?

Leaving his coin?

Maybe he's still down there, deep down, wallowing in green dust.

SNKRAZ.

"Three klicks," Tak says.

"Can't get a fix on how far behind the Antags are."

We're both thinking the same thing about the gates. Their outer doors will be like toilet tissue against Antag weapons.

"I say it's another five klicks. Gives us a minute or two to welcome reinforcements."

We enter the personnel lock and cycle through. We'll be back outside soon enough. The rocks look jagged enough to hide more than a few warriors. We're going to have to erect a slim sort of defense around both gates, set up a 360 atop the basalt hump-head, maybe find a kind of natural, high-point revetment for the lawnmower—the strong-field suppressor. It looks like a compact barbell with two handgrips and two nodes thrusting forward from the gray balls on each end. A triplex of spent matter cartridges hangs between the grips. Flip your guard and squeeze both grips and you spread tuned nasty over a wide arc.

We exit the inner lock hatch and stand before DJ, who is all alone and looks confused.

"Where is everybody?" he asks.

"Where's who?"

"*Everybody*. The Voor wagons are still over at the southern garage. The ranch wife's buggy..." He points. Teal's cylindrical vehicle is still parked beside the older hulks. "But all the people—gone."

"You passed through from there and didn't see anyone?"

"Just tunnels and dust."

"Where's the colonel and Captain Coyle?" Tak asks.

"Wherever they all went, I suppose," DJ says, exasperated and scared. "Nobody said a thing to me. How the hell should I know?"

I walk around the garage, examining the floor. There's a general trample of boot prints in the green dust, ours upon arrival, and then paths heading in several directions—nothing more.

"Goddamn Voors," DJ says.

"How the fuck could they overpower Skyrines when we have a lawnmower?" I ask. No answer. Tak is thoughtful.

Tak, DJ, and I are alone in the northern garage, with guests soon to arrive, and no plan how to greet them.

DRIFTERS AND HOBOS

Alice settles into our couch, draping her pleasingly plump arms along the back, feeling the leather with her well-manicured fingers.

"How did the Drifter get there?" I ask.

She looks at me. "Didn't Teal or Joe tell you?"

"I don't know what I don't know," I say.

"You're testing me."

"You test, I test. I'm asking meaningful questions. Doesn't that mean I'm on the mend, Doc?"

She lifts a corner of her lips, takes one last look at the platinum coin, and delicately deposits it on the glass table between us. I don't think she covets it. I think it scares her. "Nobody thought such a formation could exist," she says. "We've been telling ourselves an old, old story...trying to get it to make sense, not quite succeeding."

"Who's we?"

"Experts and doubters," she says.

"You do geology?"

"I used to analyze orbital surveys. For a year, I even guided tactical mapping. First time I went out on a space frame, crossing the vac, to get up close and personal with the Red, we were caught in a massive solar storm—about halfway. Lasted six days. Fourteen space frames, everyone got full dose. Cosmoline couldn't absorb near enough. We arrived and parked in orbit. Fortunately there was an Ant lull at the time, perhaps because they were too smart to go out when it's that hot. Our frames got shipped back before we could drop anybody. Twelve frames returned, but two are still out there, endlessly orbiting—dead. I rode a hawk down to SBLM, ended up spending six months in Madigan rehab. Ended my career. Officers don't rise in ranks if they're stuck on Earth."

"And for that, they court-martial you?"

"That came later," she says.

"At least you're alive," I say.

She looks out the window, moves one arm on the back of the couch, lifts her hand. "I returned to civilian life, paid to get bored and blow my head off inside a year. That's the gamble, right?"

All too familiar among those mustered out of service for whatever reason.

"So I expanded my study program. Took all the available courses on settler history—what few courses remain. Universities have been dropping them right and left as funding dries up. Gurus don't like them, I guess. I took more science, then geology, focusing on Mars in deep time. Lots of civilian science about Mars, even now. Peaceniks, pure space types, libertarians. I fell right in with them, after a time, once they got over suspicions I was a spy. But nobody saw *this* coming."

"You split sociology, history—and geology?"

"Pretty much. After that, I interviewed with settler advocacy groups in Sacramento and Paris. Got picked up by a splinter of Mars Plus in New Mexico."

"Sandia Space Studies," I say. "Isn't that Air Force?"

"Yeah."

"Teal got a message through to them? Or Joe?"

"One or the other, I don't know," Alice says. "But Joe told us you might have something interesting to say. Describe this Drifter to me again."

I do. I'm full of metaphors. I tell her it's like a huge mandrake root almost submerged in a sea of cold basalt, descending many miles into the Martian crust. A lot of metals. Very heavy, no doubt. "Why didn't it sink?" I ask.

"Everyone wants to know that. I assume they're checking all over the Red now for others like it." She watches me too intently.

"Probably," I say. I feign ignorance—easy for me at the best of times.

"But maybe not," Alice says, drawing herself up. "Did you ever think the Gurus don't want us to know about this Drifter? Or any Drifters?"

"Why?" I ask.

"Not wanting to find them could explain why we've never paid attention to our own gravimetry. Which I had a hell of a time digging up."

Okay. But we're dodging the main issue. "So what is it?" I ask.

"Best guess, and not a bad one, is that it's a chunk of big old moon," Alice says. "One of many, maybe the biggest, that hit Mars a few billion years ago. Nine hundred miles or so in diameter, about the size of Rhea around Saturn. Metal and rocky core. Thick layer of ice and other volatiles. Probably got deflected by another passing object in the outer system, then fell downsun, approached Mars, and broke up as it passed through the Roche limit—the distance before tidal forces break a body into smaller pieces. The biggest chunks swung around Mars half a revolution or so—then fell right about where Hellas is now. The impacts melted through the mantle and wobbled the whole planet, rang it like a bell—also melted half the crust. Pretty much created the division between the southern highlands and northern lowlands.

"The impact in Hellas instantly converted most of the volatiles to superheated steam and blew them off into space. Some of the rest bubbled out through the molten impact basin for the next few hundred thousand years. Like a soda bottle." She grows flushed describing all this. To her, it's sexy. "The Martian crust and mantle congealed, solidified. But the big chunks of moon weren't completely absorbed. A couple of plumes of upwelling magma kept thrusting up the chunks—the last, unabsorbed remains—and floated them in place, like feathers on a jet of air."

"Jesus," I say.

Alice takes a deep breath. "Those days are long gone," she says. "The plumes are a lot colder. Most are solid. The Drifter has been sinking for a couple of billion years—but its head still pokes through, and there are lots of deep vent tubes carved by superheated lava, pushing tunnels right through to the deep roots, down to the main bulk of all those spectacular metals. Sound about right?"

It does. Perfect, in fact.

"All right, do I pass?"

"You pass."

"So do tell," she says, attentive without being needy.

GO DOWN IN HISTORY,
DAMN YOU ALL

We've made our way to the southern garage and back, and now we stand beside Teal's buggy and the abandoned hulks. The tunnels between are deserted, as DJ described—as far as we could search. The weapons carried by Captain Coyle's squad are nowhere in sight, and so it seems likely that the tables have been turned and our Skyrines have been overpowered and taken away to be disposed of.

"The Voors must have had a weapons cache," Tak says, wandering around the walls. "They got the drop on the rest."

All we have are sidearms.

"No bodies, no blood," DJ observes.

No blood in the garage is a positive. Teal would likely be the first to get shot. After that, there are no positives. I'm not even sure we know how to open the gate and operate the locks fast enough to let in our reinforcements, if they arrive—if they *are* reinforcements and not prisoners driven ahead of the main column of Antags just to absorb our fire.

"We know the layout around here. I bet DJ can lead us through to the eastern gate," Tak says.

"Teal thought it was sealed," I say. "Like the western gate."

"Did you check?" Tak asks. "And what would it take to unseal it? The eastern garage makes the most sense."

"But the Voor wagons are still back at the southern gate!" DJ says.

"Maybe there was a wagon left outside," Tak says. "They could all fit into one now, right? Leave us behind, or kill us—get the hell out before the Ants arrive."

"I don't think they'd leave," I say. "It's too dangerous out there. If they get caught up in a battle, they're smoke and scrap, even if they have Coyle's weapons, which they can't use."

"Right," Tak says. "That could mean they have a dungeon down deep, hard to find—harder to get into. But how in hell did they overpower Coyle and Gamecock?"

I've considered all the possibilities, and one hypothesis remains unassailable, based on what little we know. I share it. There must have been one or more Voor wagons outside that Captain Coyle did not see and could not have commandeered. These latecomers could have arrived after the others, saw that something had gone wrong, and circled around to the eastern gate, then pushed stealthy raiders through the tunnels—where they got the drop on our comrades.

While those of us outside heard nothing.

I share this cheerful scenario. Tak considers with growing calm, not even frowning. The worse things seem, the calmer he looks.

"Shit, man," DJ says. "Why not leave somebody to take us out, too? We could *all* be stain by now."

"Because we don't matter," Tak says.

We quickly share the maps captured by our angels during explorations, with distances, elevations, quick video and photo notes on what was seen and where. Battlefield record keeping.

Nowhere near complete, but we come up with a good possibility for a passage to the eastern garage. And if the green dust in that tunnel is scuffed by lots of feet, we'll know we're on the right track.

Or we stay and let the reinforcements in. DJ says he might be able to operate the vehicle airlock from the control booth, but maybe not fast enough to get all the vehicles through...or any big weapons.

We're just churning.

I think I'm going to have to make the decision. I got my stripes before Tak. I get down on one knee. The others do the same, as if we're about to form a prayer triangle.

"Our buds out there don't even know we're here, unless they got my flash," I say. "We don't have time to get them all in, and besides, the doors won't hold long. Tak, you and DJ stay. I think I can operate Teal's bus. I'll go out and meet the approaching line, help them set up a defensive cordon around the northern gate, while DJ gets into the booth and you both try to cycle as many as you can. Maybe we can bring in enough to deal with the Voors."

Tak looks dubious but DJ looks energized. "Right!" he says. "They're looking for a place to turn and fight."

"What about the Antags?" Tak asks. "Won't they just cut through the small force, then blast the doors and swarm in?"

"Nothing better," I say. An old Skyrine nostrum. All that we deserve and nothing better. We glance at each other in the gloom. Tak and DJ tilt their heads, push out their lips, spit into the green dust.

Teal's buggy was not personally coded, as far as I could tell. Maybe she had an implant or a key fob, but I never saw her use it. The buggy was stolen anyway. We work our way to the buggy's hatch and push the big flat entrance button. The hatch opens. I climb into the lock. Then I look back at Tak and DJ. We nod. Last time into the breach.

As the big kahuna, our DI on Mauna Kea, told us on our graduation, *Last time no see anymore.*

Nothing better.

It's on.

ZULU TIME

I can barely see DJ in the upper booth through the buggy's front
windows. The bus's controls are not much different from a
Skell or a big Tonka—a two-handled wheel on a stick and foot
pedals. There's enough charge left in the batteries to get me out
the gate and maybe ten or twelve klicks beyond—no time to wait
for a full charge from the Drifter's generators.

Tak pulls the plug. DJ opens the inner doors. I rumble
through, learning as I go—and manage to just scrape the edge
of one door. Hope I haven't punched a hole, hope the door seals
tight on the way back...

Hiss surrounds the buggy, the suck of retrieved air. Pressure drops in the lock. My ears pop. When the hiss is down to
a light puff, DJ opens the outer doors and I shove the stick forward and to the left to go around the low end of the giant's arm.
The only communication I'm going to have is radio. Can't rely
on the helm laser this time—too much dust. So I start broadcasting across multiple shortwave digital bands. The dust looks
thick and the vehicles are likely tossing up big grains—enough to
interfere with microwave. But what the hell. If anybody human's

listening, I can rev up the bus motors and wind them down in a kind of dogtrot EM pulse.

Soon, in just a couple of minutes, that arc of fleeing Skyrines and the Antags chasing them will arrive at the Drifter's northern gate. If the Skyrines know we're here, if they got my laser burst, they'll be heading for the gate. If not, they'll sweep around this bump in the Red like waves around a rock.

The air in the buggy smells like sweat and electricity. The batteries are old; the wiring may be shorting out as well. And all those pads from our skintights are doubtless festering in the rear hopper.

Outside, the air is an amazingly beautiful shade of lavender, shot through with high stripes of pink. The dust raised by the oncoming tide sweeps over the buggy, over everything.

Then it gets dark, very dark—black in just a few seconds. Martian night falls almost instantly and the only residual light has to come through the dust tops down to where I am—which it doesn't. Everyone out there in the dark and the dust is traveling blind, chasing blind, fleeing blind. And I'm moving out, broadcasting like a sonofabitch, pumping the engines up and down...

Then, to my left, a Skell-Jeep rolls up and throws a beam, almost blinds me, and passes so close it grazes a tire. The buggy shivers and complains. No doubt they know I'm here, but do they think I'm a Muskie? Or the idiot Skyrine who lased them?

Another vehicle passes me—this time a Tonka. My radar is shooting quick blips. I can make out hazy return in the general scatter and I'm still rolling forward, chuckling like an idiot child, when something or someone dogtrots a shortwave carrier. No voice—just up-and-down frequency variation. Answering my motor pulses.

"Someone wishes to speak to us," my helm says. "They want to know where we come from."

I then go all out on the shortwave and tell them we're friendly, give a call sign I hope is still good, ask to speak with the ranking CO. A rough, raspy voice gets back to me in seconds. "Who the fuck are you, and what are you doing way out here in the boonies?"

My face lights up in a big grin. Even with all the distortion and drop-out, I know this guy. It's Joe—First Sergeant Joe Sanchez.

"No time," I say. "We've found a rock up ahead with a door in it, leading to a bunch of caves—a pretty good refuge, but you'll have to buy time to get us all inside. Can you form a line on me?"

I am the only game in town, the only hope they have. My radar shows a fair number of our vehicles—at least ten, if I count through the ghosts and guesses—now forming a dirty curve about two hundred meters from end to end, like a mitt flexing to intercept a ball.

"If you'll just hold still a minute," Joe says, "you beautiful bastard."

"Gladly, First Sergeant." I pull back the buggy's wheel and pump the brakes, about a kilometer from the northern gate. This is where we're going to have to hold until or if the Antags decide to halt and reconnoiter. Not likely. But a battle in the dusty dark is nobody's ideal.

"Time to plow a hole with whatever you've got," I say. "You have to make the Antags hesitate. Then we'll withdraw in proper order to the rock."

I send the coordinates.

"Do you know how many Ants are on our tail?" the familiar voice asks, weaker and more raspy. "We haven't taken time to look over our shoulder."

Night is upon us. Nobody can see shit. Maybe the Antags are having the same difficulty.

"Rough guess," I say, "a hundred times your force, airborne and ground."

"Pick targets for maximum disruption," the raspy voice orders.

Another voice responds: "Sir, we'll provoke immediate fire. I don't know how we've—"

Another voice, female, shrill: "Die screaming, sweatrag!"

"Just fucking light 'em up!"

Then the dust glows in bright, quick flickers, like lightning seen through a filthy window. That makes me want to cry. We're in a real fight. We're all going to die, finally, and it's the best feeling in the world—kill and be killed! I wish someone was in the buggy to share it with me. I wish Teal could see me now. Or my dad. My uncle Karl.

Anyone.

The murk starts to really glow, almost steady, like a weird sunrise. Our buds are lighting up with all they've got, and judging by the purple tinge, they're using at least one big bolt cutter.

God, it's *awful* pretty.

Thumps rise through the bus's tires, shaking the frame. I hear ascendant whines cut through the thin air—through the muffling dust—and rise beyond human hearing. A Chesty's twin disruptors are hitting targets, slicing and dicing and electrifrying. Other sounds, other weapons. The Antags are firing back, I think, but it doesn't sound coordinated. It sounds confused. Of course, what do I know. I'm a blind duck in a truck.

Happier and happier.

I start singing.

Someone on the shortwave joins in. We're an insane duet for about ten seconds.

The murk fades, then the dust pulses again with pink and purple and finally green. Another big transport rolls up and around—a Deuce and a half, four sets of whanging tires, twice as big as a Tonka. I cheer out loud. The first part of our line is withdrawing to the Drifter.

At the same time, someone raps on the outer hull of the buggy, hard. I rise out of the driver's seat and go back to see who it is. At this stage, I'm loopy enough not to mind if it's one of the far-traveled enemy. Any change, please, to break the goddamn suspense, the awful grind of not knowing shit. Someone's cycling through. I'm tapping my feet and pushing off against the ceiling not to fly around in the cabin.

The hatch opens. A Skyrine pushes inside—and it *is* Joe, finally! Old friend. Old training buddy. Veteran of four previous mutual actions on the Red. Only he's got a lieutenant colonel's silver oak leaf pinned to his chest—rather, half of one, and there's blood all over his skintight, mostly dry, but some still foaming from the vac. Apparently not his own.

"Master Sergeant Michael Venn, my lucky day," Lieutenant Colonel Joseph Sanchez says, opening his helm.

I snap back and salute him.

"Screw that, it's brevet." Joe doesn't bother to brush down before he moves up front. I don't care. The cabin is already full of dust. He glares through the windshield, observing the withdrawal, then flops down on the step behind the controls. "Comm flashed they'd intercepted a hinky beam from somebody with your name—is that right?"

"Yes, sir!"

"So did the goddamn Antags, I bet. Where did you find this heap?"

I explain quickly about Gamecock and the Sky Defense brass in their sad, sagging tent. "Teal, the previous driver—a ranch wife—picked us up and took us to a lucky rock with a big door in it. After she unlocked the door and let us in, we accepted a visit from Captain Daniella Coyle and eleven sisters, who themselves hitched a ride with twelve hostile settlers—Voors. But they're gone now. Coyle and all her team, the Voors, the rest of my team—Kazak and Vee-Def and Michelin—seem to have disappeared deeper into the rock. We don't know where any of them are."

Joe stares at me through bloodshot, pale blue eyes, then shakes his head. "Outstanding! A dozen Voors. As in Voortrekkers?"

"Sort of. There could be more, if there's an unsecured gate… if they got reinforcements and overpowered Captain Coyle. They may have all the weapons, including a lawnmower. Which they can't use."

"Outstanding to above!" He's feverish from exhaustion.

"Sir, have you got recent tactical?" A silver oak leaf stomps any invitation to intimacy, especially when there's blood.

"Recent as of forty-eight hours, but they got most of our sats, and our new ones are being swatted down faster than we can find them." He grips my shoulder with one hand, and we exchange tactical. I close my faceplate to make sure I got it all. Little angel alarms and flashing pink dots in the upper corner.

I got it—but the angel is not happy. Position-wise, we are screwed—we should not be anywhere near where we are. I open my faceplate. "Angel's frantic," I say.

"Fuck it. Take the wheel and get in line."

I get behind the wheel and roll us into the retreating caravan. Another volley of purple pulses lights up the dust; the platform will withdraw last.

"Have you uplinked any of this with orbital?" Joe asks.

"Maybe DJ sent up something, but unlikely."

He rubs the bridge of his nose. "Vinnie, tell me how long before it gets so bad we shit our pants." We monkey-grimace and laugh. The thing about skintights is it's no fun pissing or shitting your pants because it doesn't matter—that's what you do all the time. So to signal that we live in fear, to express that we've lost all hope and fuck the big stuff—we don't relax our rectums. We just laugh. But not too long.

Time for Joe's story.

"Big Hammer two days back, we dropped right around a comet strike zone, lots of sparkly, lost maybe two-thirds of our frames, but three sleds came down intact, carrying six Trundles, five General Pullers, fifteen Skells, and six Deuces, all fully charged—but only ninety-two Skyrines. Most of command hit hard. And so..." He taps the bloody half leaf. "We salvaged what we could."

Another pulse and we can see the outline of the Drifter ahead.

"How many can you cycle through at once, and how fast?" he asks.

"Ten troops through the personnel lock, plus maybe three Skells or two Tonkas through the big gate. A Chesty won't fit, and I doubt the Trundles will, either. There's another gate on the opposite side, about a mile around the head—the hill. Might be big enough to take more Tonkas and maybe the Chesty. If there's time, maybe we can unload the platform."

Joe doesn't take long to think it through. "Cycle all the troops first. We'll divert big stuff around the head."

My angel gives him precise southern gate coordinates and he passes them along. I broadcast plain and loud to the Drifter and hope DJ and Tak are on the alert and haven't been swept by Voors.

Then I look left, south, on the driver's side vid. Three banged-up Deuces and the Chesty are pulling out of line to go left around the head. I can just hear them rolling behind us. Rear vid shows four Skells and a Tonka passing our buggy to cross right over the lava and old mud, preceding us toward the Drift-er's arm. They're carrying troops and will go first.

"We're in sad shape, Vinnie," Joe says. "Save our sorry assets, and I'll hook you up with my seester."

"It would be my honor."

"She's ugly as sin."

"*Sin* rhymes with *Venn*, sir."

"Fuck you."

Outside, the dust is clearing, revealing night-dark sand and an amazing starry sky. We spin around and I scan the opposite line through my faceplate magnifier. The movement of Antags has stopped, but a few bolts are still being thrown out from the trundle to a largely quiet and unmoving line. They're just sitting and taking it, waiting, like a row of wolves curious as to why the rabbits have turned and bared their teeth.

Not scared. Just curious.

"It's a big drive," I say. "What are they hauling?"

"Major hurt, we assume. No time to stop and peek under their skirts."

The settling dust opens a space between us and the Antags. They have big black Millies, long and segmented like millipedes, little round wheels reaching out on a hundred legs. Haven't seen Millies that big before—at least fifty meters long and ten meters wide. Each looks like it can carry a couple of platoons, and there are *lots*. Plenty of parallel rollers as well, like big mas-sage wheels on a rope—some supporting hooks to anchor the aeros, which float a couple of hundred meters above the hardpan like fat, shadowy jellyfish. Weapon mounts squat on flatbeds very like our Trundles, ready to deploy tuned relaxers, neural exciters—cause us fits. We call them shit-rays. Could be used to ease capture. But mostly they're prelude to unbridled bouts of execution—converting paralyzed, befouled humans to stain on the Red.

"We ain't paid enough," Joe concludes, a sentiment so universal it doesn't even register.

I see one of our bigger bolts has carved a Millie right down the middle, lengthwise. At that distance, I can more imagine than actually see movement of the injured, the dying. Hope and imagination combine forces. *Die, die. Breathe out and boil whatever you have for lungs.*

"Why aren't they shooting?" I ask. It's unnatural, not returning heat.

"Patience," Joe says, shaking his head. He does not know, does not believe our luck, if luck it is and not a pregnant pause. The Antags have us right where they want us. Why not just blast away?

Are they afraid of damaging the Drifter?

"Two more Tonkas around the left," Joe says after the first pair have vanished beyond the left shoulder. They are followed by the General Puller—the Chesty. The big Trundle has stopped firing and is soon kicking up a plume behind the Chesty. If I were Joe, I'd station the Trundle and a couple of Deuces just around the northern slope of the Drifter.

And so he does.

But there's still no Antag response.

"I know just what they're going to do," Joe says. "They're going to wait until we're all inside, then they're going to nuke us from orbit and boil us like lobsters."

"Don't think that will work, Joe, sir," I say.

"Why the hell not?"

"Because it's big and deep."

And because they want the Drifter as much as we do?

"But nukes would seal us in, wouldn't they?"

"Maybe."

I ask myself what it would be like to live like moles forever, breathing green dust, struggling to raise crops in the faded glimmer of hydroelectric power from a hobo that's mostly drained away. What'll that give us, a couple of months before we start dining on raw Voor and I fight for Teal's honor, or the Antags dig us out—

Joe sees my pensive gaze. "Stop thinking, shithead," he says. "Sorry to engage your fucking intellect."

"Yes, sir."

"Is there food in there?"

"Some."

There've been no shots since our last platform-mounted bolt cutters. But now an aerostat is on the move above the northwestern horizon, like a small black cloud covering the stars. It will be over us in a few minutes.

Joe looks at me. The vehicles have no doubt piled up behind the lava ridge, at the northern gate. I very much doubt they can all cycle through before the aerostat rains needles.

"Tell them to abandon the last vehicles," I say to Joe. "Tell them to run to the lock and pack in like Vienna sausages. And do the same at the southern gate."

"Right," Joe says.

If the Antags can hear and understand, this will be fun. For them, this will be a rollicking slaughter of frantic little rats. Needles will do the trick—no need to waste energy or big ordnance. Then they can perch on the Drifter and wait out the survivors.

"Our turn, Vinnie," Joe says. We quickly round the clenched fist of the lava arm and come up on the Skells and Tonkas. Skyrines are leaping out and jogging toward the rusty gate. A quick glance behind shows the aero looming, no more than a few hundred meters until it can loose the first curtain of needles.

We seal helms and exit the buggy's rear lock together. The run is a blur—feet barely touching sand and dust and rock, skipping, stumbling, rolling and jouncing on the upswing, zigging by abandoned Skells and a Tonka, almost catching up with our fellows, around the rough point of the ridge, into the rocky harbor of the northern gate.

Get in line, except there is no line. Skyrines are bunched up waiting to cycle through. DJ must be crazy, I think, not opening the vehicle lock, the big gate—but then I see it yawn wide, the first crowd has cycled through, and another group packs in—all but twenty making it before there's absolutely no way to add more without crushing bone or getting caught in the hatch.

The lock closes.

Joe and I stay back. Eighteen others pace, cringing, in the embrace of the ridge.

"Find cover in the rocks!" I call over suit-to-suit.

Seven guys try to fit into one cubby large enough for two. Joe and I have found low ridges we can hide under, if we dig out some sand. I can see him across the harbor, not far from the gate.

Ten left out in the open.

The aero is at zenith. Three or four minutes at minimum until DJ can cycle and open a lock again.

We've done our best.

Puffs in the sand. Dozens of little plumes shoot up and fall back quick. The ten out in the open are running around like rats in a dog pit. I can barely hear their screaming. Then I can hardly see for all the needles, a gray haze of falling death. Our stragglers cover their heads with arms and groping hands, but it doesn't matter—one needle and you go crazy and then, at leisure, twitching on the dust, puff up until your skintight splits its seams.

I can't bear to watch.

Four gang up to yank two Skyrines from cover, but get kicked off, then give up and just stand slouched under the deluge, heads bowed, hands stiff by their sides. Needles make them flinch.

They look like hedgehogs.

Then they begin that slow, awful dance.

Four more flail out from cover, plucking needles that have swooped in and found them.

Big gate still sealed.

I close my eyes and pray.

LAST EXIT TO HELL

The apartment is cool, almost cold, and sunset outside the window is a faint gray-yellow over the Olympics beyond the sound. I've changed out of my robe into civvies, Hawaiian shirt, and jeans. Alice Harper stands by the big window, arms crossed. "Wherever man goes," she says, and clenches herself tighter, "history sucks."

Can't disagree. The bad shit builds as I resurrect these awful memories. I say, "Do you think Green Camp actually wanted to flush Teal out on the Red?" I want, I *need*, to change the subject.

"Absolutely," she says. "Rationals believe in tight intellectual order, total logic, everything determined, DNA is fate, blue-blooded pedigree is your only hope—Asians beat whites beat blacks and Hispanics. Like a bloody-minded religion, only don't tell them that. Everything statistical, mathematically sound… Atheists by law, strict dogmatists, reductionists…Techno-racists. Libertarianism pushed to the ultimate extreme." She lowers her arms.

I watch her, fascinated by her calm, her weird *enthusiasm*. I wish I could be like that, feel as she feels right now. *Anything* not to be *me*. I say, "Just doesn't make sense."

"Use your head. Someone like Teal who apparently insists on one man at a time…no sharesies…She's baggage. The top bitch would shove her out soon as spit."

That would be Ally Pecqua, I'm guessing. "Pretty harsh."

Alice Harper shrugs. "It only got worse when Earth cut the data and stopped sending supplies. Mars not making anybody money, couldn't pay their bills. Time to slice the umbilical. Might drive anyone over the edge."

"What in hell are we fighting for, then? If we don't give a shit about the Red, why not just leave it to the Antags?"

"Because Gurus…" She gives me a stern look. "Rhetorical question, right?"

My turn to shrug. "I'm still out there. In my head. I have to sort it out or I'll never come home."

"So tell me more. Tell me what happened with you and Teal," Alice says.

That's not easy. I'm having a hard time moving on, still locked on the image of my fellow Skyrines dancing under that curtain of darts, until the aero passes over, circling at the end of its dragline, and the rain stops.

It's coming back to me now in full force, that awfulness. I'm sweating heavy. I stink like a gymnasium full of wrestlers.

———

JOE BREAKS COVER and makes a run for the personnel lock gate. He starts pounding on it. Me and four guys join him, we're all pounding. I can't hear my fist hitting the hatch. I can't hear anything. I'm too busy looking down at my arms, my legs, too busy inspecting myself.

Then I stop. My heart stops.

There's a dart on my forearm.

Jesus.

Joe sees it, too. He doesn't pull it out, doesn't touch it, neither do I, because I'm not going crazy, it's only just pierced the skintight, might not have touched my skin, it was a ricochet, maybe, and hasn't yet pumped its poison.

Or it *has*, and adrenaline is just holding back the symptoms. Medics say that can happen.

My fingers reach down. Can't just leave it there.

Joe grabs my hand, then pushes his head in close to mine and looks through our faceplates straight into my eyes. "Don't," he says.

The smaller gate begins to grind open. We squeeze through the opening as it grows. The survivors are packed tight inside the lock by the time the aero is guided back over the shoulders of the Drifter. Everyone jostles, trying to get to the far side while the outer door closes. Joe makes a fence with his arms around me so nothing and nobody can jam the dart home.

My ears and throat feel pressure return.

The inner door opens and we spill out. Joe holds my clean arm, still gripping my hand, and we slowly spin like we're waltzing, because I'm trying to reach for the dart, and he's stopping me from doing that.

Pressure reaches Drifter max.

The other Skyrines see I'm darted. They stand clear of us, pushing at the inner door, which cracks open, slides slowly into the wall, and Skyrines exit, move through, but Joe still holds my hand, and I stop us spinning.

Hold out my darted arm.

"I'm not going to touch it," Joe says. "You know why."

"Up and down," I say, hardly able to draw breath. That's what the darts can do. Push up a *second* needle through the fletches and stick a would-be rescuer.

I'm on the couch with Alice.

I'm in the inner lock with Joe, my arm hurts, my muscles burn like fury.

I want to cry, *on the couch.*

I am crying, *in the lock, in my helm.* Sobbing like a baby.

We're through.

We're in the garage.

One of the Skyrines hands Joe a small needle-nose pliers. Good name. Part of someone's drop kit, maybe the gift of a relative before his transvac, use this, son, to pull out those sonofabitching things. Joe holds my arm steady, the tips of the pliers hover, he's shaking, I'm shaking, dear God don't push it down.

Jesus *don't even touch it.*

Then, he's got it. He lifts. He doesn't start shaking until the needle is out. He doesn't fling it aside. He doesn't drop it. Training kicks in after the near panic. Another Skyrine holds open a small silver bag. Joe deposits the dart into the bag and pats my shoulder. "We can't go back that way, not on foot," he says matter-of-factly.

The rocky harbor is littered with active darts.

———

ALICE LISTENS AND says nothing.

"I stink," I say.

"Please go on. Tell me what you can, what you feel like telling."

Christ, I *really* want Joe to walk through the apartment door. Jesus and God and Mary and Buddha and St. Emil Kapaun, I want that. If Joe doesn't come home, maybe I never will.

SKY BASIC

To go from an infant race of ground huggers to a force capable of fighting on other worlds, humans were handed a decent selection of Guru gifts, including of course spent matter technology, but also a thorough understanding of our own biology, chemistry, and psychology.

I suppose the Gurus knew us better than we knew ourselves. I've never met one—never met anyone who has—but I imagine them as wizened, wise, tall, and graceful, but tough sons of bitches to have survived their own long voyage across the awesome distances between the stars.

They knew our limits, political, biological, psychological. And so they helped us formulate Cosmoline, that greenish gel in which we are all packed and preserved like fruits in a can, not awake, not asleep, but not cold—not frozen—just quiet and contented while the space frames carry us to where we're going.

Some of us call it Warm Sleep. Old-timers will remember that Cosmoline was a patented petroleum-based product that helped keep rifles and guns and equipment from rusting. Not at all the same; a clever marketing wizard simply transferred the name and it stuck.

The chemistry behind our version of Cosmoline helped foster a thousand medical advances, of course. So it was one of those Guru swords that were already plowshares. In space, nobody had to rust or corrupt—not if they were wrapped in Cosmoline.

I've already described some of the side effects, but there are others, much worse. About one time in a hundred thousand, Cosmoline induces a complicated cascade of negative reactions. I've only seen it once. A space frame delivered a platoon of healthy Skyrines to orbit around the Red—along with one tube filled with corrupt Jell-O. Did the occupant die on impact? During the journey? Nobody explained, nobody asked questions. War is hell. We are all grateful not to remember the months we spend in the long rise to Mars.

Of far more concern to the usual breed of ecological worry-warts is spent matter tech. The Gurus knew how to suck all the life, if not quite all the energy, out of elements heavier than carbon and calcium. By reaching down to their inner electron shells and messing with a few quantum constants, atoms can be induced to give up a startling amount of nonnuclear energy. No neutrons, no deadly radiation, just remarkable amounts of pure power—but the resulting dead, *spent* mass is incredibly toxic. It's still matter, still behaves something like what it used to be, but that behavior is deceptive. Deadly. It's gone zombie. Spent matter waste has to be disposed of thoroughly and completely—in secure orbit. It should not be stockpiled on Earth or stored on Mars, and it should just not be shot willy-nilly into space.

Some have said that at the end of its energy draw, spent matter is toxic in terms of physics as well as chemistry. Dropped into the sun, into any star, spent matter might start a nasty chain reaction—literally slowing and then killing the sun's pulsing fusion heart. I don't know about that. But I do know that war is messy, and there are canisters of spent matter all over Mars, and probably in orbit as well, so the long-term consequences of Guru tech are still unknown. We should all hope the worrywarts are wrong and nothing will happen to the sun. But for the last couple of hundred years, some of those worrywarts have been spot-on.

Still, Gurus seemed delighted to help us recover from our own ignorance and greed...providing free visions of a boundless and bright future.

Until they told us about the Ants and recruited us to help fight their war. And their war became our war.

BACKING UP NOW

I thought I'd leap over to the good stuff, the easy stuff, all technical and shit, but that's not how it's going to be.

I just have to tough it out.

I cannot escape the burn from what happened in that embracing arm of sand-blasted lava, that little harbor of shelter outside the Drifter's western gate, filled with Joe's buddies. That may be the most horrible thing I've ever seen—Skyrines trying to pull each other out of cover to avoid the rippling curtains of plunging, swooping, *seeking* germ needles.

Fear is a drug you need to survive. Without fear, you die quicker; that's part of basic, that's what the old guys instill in us when we're fledglings waiting and eager to fly; fear is your friend, but only in controlled doses, never in such flooding waves that you panic. Panic kills you quicker than bullets. Panic turns you into doomed animals.

We panicked, all of us, in the embrace of that drowning giant's thick lava arm: those under cover, those out in the open, didn't matter. We would have killed each other rather than face the goddamned needles, and now that stokes my rage, the rage that eats me inside, that makes me less than a human being forever after, not just because I've seen my fellow Skyrines die horribly, but because I was forced to *want them to die* instead of me. I felt that little exultation that no needle was going to hit me, that I'd live to fuck again, maybe fuck their girlfriends, sympathy call, howdy, reporting to duty, sorry, ma'am, he's not coming back, but *I'm* here...

Fuck it! Fuck it all. I have so much rage at myself, at the Antags, at everything that made me grow up to be a Skyrine, a fighter across the stars, a heroic asshole coward who gave up being a sappy, naïve kid to fight in so many battles, only to finally panic on the Red, and then, like God is wagging His stony white finger at me, *shit*, that needle on my arm, just waiting to plunge in, you did not escape, you piss-scared little fuckwad, it's still *here*, and it's going to *get* you and eat you and you'll bloat up and burst, but only after you go crazy and somebody has to shoot you to keep you from hurting everyone.

Inside the dark, stone-walled garage...

Expletive expletive expletive. No words bad enough to convey that rage. No such language for what I am, what I feel. Just conjure up a deep, noisy silence, red with flashes of... why red? Not rage! Just deep, holy, animal disappointment, like what every gazelle must feel that falls to a lion, like any dinosaur that heard its sinews snapping and bones crunching under the razor teeth of a *T. rex*. First you panic, and then you die, one way or another.

I am no better than dead meat, broken, rotting, carrion, but I'm still here, still ambulatory. I just can't really tell the tale, not completely.

Not truthfully.

I died.

I did not die.

I keep trying to get back to the main current of our story, to the Drifter. But I'm going over history, technicalities, the kind of pop science deemed fit to stuff into a warrior's skull. Alice with her stiff, sad, not very sympathetic look confirms I'm just churning, I'm not getting my point across; she doesn't get it; she needs to change the subject.

"You were going to tell me about the caves," she says, looking out the big window. "I assume that means the crystals, the silicon plague. The Church," she adds.

She knows about the Church.

Okay. So that works. That knocks me loose. The beauty and strangeness and even those additional moments of horror, way down in the bowels of the Drifter. Sure. It's that easy, isn't it? Wonder trumps rage and panic.

Now my anger turns, quick as a bunny, into laughter. I laugh out loud, to her irritation, but it *is* funny. She wants the nougat center without the hard candy shell. Go straight to the point, skip all the spiky, nettle-wrapped stuff that makes us feel shitty and inadequate, that makes *me* feel and look and smell like a…

What? What am I now, other than a survivor, a lost Skyrine completely dead inside?

Something more.

Something *quite* different, thank you. Reliving the whole needle bit has reawakened snakes in my head. Snakes with broken glass for scales. But really, tell the truth, Vinnie old fellow—that isn't actually *it*, is it?

Strong tea. That's what DJ called it.

Green tea.

Ice moon tea.

Like Teal, only first gen, but nobody knows. There is redemption if I give in. But will it be *me* that survives?

My resolution sets up into concrete, but not the way either of us expected. "I'm done here," I tell her. "You aren't the one I need to talk to."

Alice turns her head, frowning. "I'm sorry," she says. "What can I do to—?"

"We're done. I won't explain."

"We need to know what you know," she says, angry roses on her cheeks.

"Get someone who's been there," I say. "Someone who doesn't think I'm crazy or about to be. I'll tell it to them, maybe."

"I don't think that," Alice says. "Honestly, I don't."

"Why did they send just you? Why not the whole committee?"

"There's a committee?" she asks.

"Yeah, there's a committee, all ready to overturn the system, set it right, just get them the information, listen to me confess to what I saw out there. Sure, they'll use us to overthrow the system— then shoot us in the back of the head and toss us aside. Like the Kronstadt sailors." Fidge me, how did *that* get in there?

"I don't understand," Alice says slowly. "You know that Joe wanted me to come here and talk to you."

"What's his moniker? His tag?"

"Sanka," Alice says. "Teal would say that was his nick."

I very slowly deflate. Letting out the snakes, maybe. Sucking down to what's actually going to happen, nothing I can do about it. I don't know what to think or feel.

"You know where he is," I say, but without conviction.

"I wish I did," Alice says. "There was just a delayed message. And there is no committee, not yet anyway…Just a beginning, a suspicion, that maybe there's something I can do, we can do."

"No committee?"

"None. We're too ignorant and stupid to be organized," she says, and I see she means it, and her tell is the cold disappointment that she's ineffective, that she's as ignorant as she says.

"Sorry," I say. But I still won't look at her. I wish she would go away and leave me to the Eames chair and the night and the endless lines of ferries and freighters. What we fight for.

"I wish Joe were here," Alice says softly. "Or another Sky-rine, like you say, someone who can understand what you've been through, because I *can't*. I won't say I can. I never will. *I don't want to feel what you're feeling, ever.* All right?"

That's honest. Still deflating. The snakes haven't left, but they've settled down a little.

The *other*, though…

My new memories, the oldest memories of all. Maybe I like it. Maybe this great, expanding volume of memories makes me more than what I am, provides a bigger refuge for my broken soul.

Alice's eyes are targeting *me*, holding me there in the chair, and suddenly, I like it, I like being targeted and pinned by this zaftig female in our clean steel and blue apartment, earned by all that money, all that comp. She's got some strength and she's not as arrogant as I thought.

Best of all, she doesn't want to understand.

Good. Fine.

But still silent. Frozen.

"I can leave you here and come back later," she says after a minute, "maybe when Joe gets here. Or I can just leave for good. Let you be."

I have no idea what expression suddenly comes to my face, but it makes her jump, startled. I lean forward, my voice a little high. "There's something very strange happening to us, to Earth, isn't there?" I ask. "With the Gurus and the Antags and going out to the Red."

"Hell, yes," she says, eyes flashing. "You're just starting to realize that?"

"Some things are coming together, maybe. I'm almost there now."

Another pause. We're watching each other, hawk and mouse, mouse and hawk.

"Then take me along, please, if you can, take me there with you," Alice says. "Maybe then we can start unwinding all the threads and figure out what we've got ourselves into. Maybe *then* there can be a committee, and you'll be on it."

I grit my teeth and shake my head. "No committees. We got a get out a here. I need a walk somewheres."

She narrows one eye at the accent. "Okay." She gets up, ready to go, but I'm still sitting.

"Yesterday, a grandma in a blue electric car gave me a ride and told me her son became a hero on Titan," I say. "Know anything about that?"

Alice shakes her head. But the merest shift in her frown says, maybe that wasn't good, maybe that shouldn't have happened.

"Why would she know that, why would anybody tell her?" I ask. Then my thoughts focus. "She said she was a colonel's secretary. At SBLM. Maybe that's how she knew. The brass told her. A security slip, too much sympathy, but they tell her."

Alice lifts her hand a few inches, noncommittal.

"Titan!" I say. "That's out around Saturn. That's out by the rings and shit, one and a half billion klicks across the vac. That's out where a *lot* of the moons are covered with ice, isn't it? Deep ice, with liquid oceans underneath—some of them?"

Alice takes a deep breath. "We both need a break," she says, standing. "I'll buy groceries, if you'll let me fix something to eat."

"There's not much here that isn't spoiled," I admit. The room feels lighter. The air is sweeter. Maybe I'm okay.

Maybe we're just putting off the rough shit for another couple of hours. But that's good, isn't it?

"Can I buy the groceries, Master Sergeant Venn?" she asks very softly.

"Yeah. I'll stay here."

She's firm. She insists. "I'd like you to accompany me to the market. I'd like you to go shopping with me, Vinnie."

I pretend to think that over. I'm acting like a child. To tell this story, to live as a whole man after this moment, I have to go back to being a child. Feels funny and right at the same time. All us Skyrines are children, before, during, and even *inside* the end. So the experienced ones tell us. The DIs and veterans.

"I went to the market soon as I got back," I say.

"What did you buy?"

"Celery."

"And obviously, nothing else. So…shall we go?"

I do like it at the market. There're other children, and the old bronze pig, and toys. Doughnuts. Pastries. Jerky. Fruit and candy. I need to stand up and walk around and maybe eat more celery.

Why celery? I think I know. Ritual. As a kid, I loved celery. My mother would hand me a stalk filled with bright orange Cheez Whiz, whenever she made a salad. She'd smile at me, perfect love, tree to apple, simple, no judgment. I was just a kid and she was my mom.

Welcome home.

I don't want to cry now or get lost in myself.

I get up. Alice takes gentle hold of my elbow.

"Let's go to the market," she says. "Let's walk there and then walk back. It's only a couple of miles. If you have the legs for it."

MOVING FORWARD AGAIN

I have the legs.

I enjoy the air, the streets, the hill down to the market, the climb back, though it makes my knees wobble. I enjoy walking beside Alice Harper, who takes it all without breaking a sweat or one little huff, Earth girl that she is; she looks zaftig, but it's muscle and no small determination all bundled up and concentrated.

I enjoy walking. I enjoy walking with her.

Nobody pays us much attention.

I'm starting to smell like a human being again.

At the old fish stall, where the guys and the ladies still flash naked biceps and fling salmon to each other, Alice buys whole cooked crab and clams and cod and snapper, and after, we walk down a hallway to a smaller indoor shop lined with dark wooden shelves, where she picks out herbs and spices and the clerk scoops them out of glass jars into little plastic bags; Alice is sure we don't have such back at the apartment—we don't—and she says she's going to make a good fish stew, *cioppino*, if that's

204 | GREG BEAR

okay, if I like fish stew. I probably do, I don't know. It's been so long since I've been served a home-cooked meal.

The walk back is easier. I carry the groceries.

This is nice.

But I still refuse to trust her. I just can't. It's far too dangerous, with what I have bottled up inside me.

———

I SIT ON a bar stool at the kitchen counter while Alice works. "This is a great kitchen," she says. "You guys should use it to do more than microwave pizza."

"We never spend a lot of time here," I say. "After a few days, after we stop stinking and get our land legs back, we go out."

"Hunting?" she asks with a wry face.

"Yeah," I say. "Or just looking. Cosmoline—takes the edge off for a while, you know. One of the downsides of transvac. Or the benefits, if you're a monk."

"Pushes you back from the responsibility of acting human?" she asks, with a quiet tone I can't read, and a side look as she chops the celery and tomatoes and begins to simmer a fish stock of scraps she bought at the market. I can smell again, it's mostly back. Being able to smell is half the job of coming home. I can smell Alice beneath the rose perfume. It's not like she smells sexy, not yet, but smelling her is a treat, a revelation.

"It's okay," I say. "We're not very good company for a few days. You'll vouch for that."

"I will," she says, terse but not judgmental. She puts a lid on the simmering pot, after adding more onions and celery. She snaps off a stalk and passes it across the counter to me. I hold it, look it over. Nothing like it on the Red. Nothing so crisp and fresh, nothing this crisp and alive, even after it's been pulled from the bunch and trimmed. Likely Teal has never bitten into a stalk of celery. Nothing like this for decades to come, probably.

If ever. How brave was that, for the Muskies to fly out to the Red, knowing what they'd leave behind, just to see something new, something few humans had ever seen?

"When company was coming," Alice says, apropos of nothing, "my mother used to lay out a tray of celery stuffed with Cheez Whiz."

That makes nice sparks burst in my head, lovely bits of glow, soft and gentle, like a thousand little night-lights following me around in the dark. "Really?"

"True salt of the Earth. Emphasis on the salt." Alice smiles and keeps adding to the pot. Onions, olive oil, garlic, saffron, so many fresh herbs I can't count, black pepper, white pepper... bewildering.

She turns down the heat, watching me with a light, open-lipped grin.

I lift the celery, fence the air.

"Yeah," she says, and taps the pot with a wooden spoon, also purchased at the market, and fences back. Celery crosses spoon. Spoon wins. I finish off my losing weapon.

"This will take a while," she says, putting down the spoon, "but I guarantee, it'll be the best you ever tasted." She reaches into the last canvas bag and lifts out a bottle of white wine, natural grapes, no GM stuff—not cheap. She pours a good splash into the pot.

Then, she asks, lifting the bottle, "Ready?"

My body does not cringe.

"We have juice glasses," I say.

"Poor boys."

It's getting dark outside. Another sol is passing—I mean, another day. So *unreal*. The apartment smells wonderful. I'm not sweating, I'm not shaking, my legs are almost back to normal, memories a little less jagged.

Not that the worst part is over. I was hoping *that* was the worst part, but I know it isn't. In jerks and starts, I try to continue. My voice is steady—for a while.

She pours a couple of juice glasses. We hoist, toast Earth, the Red, all of it: the dead, the living, the irrational and unfinished. Silent but comprehensive. The wine tastes good. Crisp, green, like rain over spring hills. Alice pours the fish stock through a spaghetti basket, puts aside the bones and shriveled fish heads— stuff that brings back bad memories. Could be like what fills the skintight of a Skyrine stuck with a germ needle...

Then she whisks the scraps aside and returns the stock to the pot, adds more vegetables, sluices in a little more wine.

"Never enough wine," she murmurs. "Fish and crabs come next, in a few minutes. Clams at the very last. They're still alive..."

She pulls back, regretting that bit of information, but it's not life and death per se, or going into the pot, that gets to me.

"Tender morsels," I say.

We return to couch and chair.

"How are the legs?" she asks. "Sore?"

"Steady."

Alice crosses her legs, holds up the last of her wine in the twilight, suspended in her fingers, city lights twinkling in the juice glass. I manage to say some things. Then more things. It doesn't hurt as much.

She gets up to add the fish and crab. In a few minutes, she adds the clams, and a few minutes later, serves it up. Oh my God. It is good. I eat four bowls. Airplanes pass in the night sky. A double-egg and hawksbill crosses the Sound, heading for SBLM. More Skyrines returning from the vac. I put down my bowl and stifle a tremendous belch. First time I've done that in modern memory.

"I'm ready," I say.

And she listens.

WHAT THE BIG BOYS WANT
YOU TO KNOW

There are thirty-two of us in the garage, including DJ, still up in the high booth, and Tak, who's standing clear of the new arrivals, the survivors, and standing clear of me; we might have more darts. Before they had to close up for good, before the shower of germ needles, they managed to bring in twenty-three of Joe's troops, three Skell-Jeeps, and two medium-sized Tonkas. Teal's buggy and a few of the smaller vehicles are still outside, some in the shelter of the giant's arm, but they all might as well be gone.

We don't know if any of the other vehicles and big weapons made it around to the southern gate.

Joe tells Tak to check us over and don't touch anyone.

One of the new Skyrines, the one with the needle pouch, fishes a handful of fresh pouches out of his leggings and gets ready to receive more. Tak does a thorough job of checking us over, telling us to spin, lift our arms and then our legs, show the soles of our boots. All our skintights are clean, no rips, no poke marks.

DJ descends from the booth.

"Got water? New filters?" Joe asks.

"I'll look," DJ says. He sounds sad, guilty to walk among the strung-out newbies, who are still shivering and wild-eyed. He climbs up into a Skell-Jeep and rummages through the bins, manages to retrieve a clutch of filter pads, then climbs onto a Tonka, accesses the heating system, drains clean water into a can, and passes it around.

One of the newbies—Corporal Vita Beringer, young, baby-faced, and almost completely zoned, is slowly, methodically trying to peel out of her skintight. Joe slaps her hand down, reseals a loose seam, tells her she's better off for now keeping it on. We don't know whether the Voors can selectively flush air in the Drifter—suffocate us. I know he's thinking that, but he doesn't say it out loud. He just knows when's the right time to be blunt, and when it's better to be quiet and soft. Gently persistent. Joe is good that way.

DJ tells me, in an aside, that he doubts the outer gate can withstand much of an assault. No news there. "They're pretty rusty," he says. "I wonder the Antags aren't already knocking."

"They're patient," I say. "No need to rush in."

Or is it some other reason? They can skip around the Drifter, leave it alone, leave us here, if they want. Island hopping. I suppose the Drifter is the closest thing to an island there is on the Red.

Joe approaches us, waves Tak over, tells us to gather behind a Tonka, away from the others. He and Tak served together three or four times, shared a few weeks of OCS prep at McGill. We huddle behind the Tonka like boys getting ready to play marbles and brief Joe on what little we know about the Drifter, transfer what little knowledge we have managed to collect.

"Thanks for the reception," he says. "Our drop was a shitty

blender. Sisters and brothers, different frames, broken platoons. All mixed up."

"De nada, sir," Tak says. "Par for this course."

Joe points down. "How deep is this thing?"

"More than a mile, maybe a lot more," I say. "Deep mining interrupted by a hobo—a wandering subsurface river. It's been flooded up to here for at least twenty years, Earth years—but now the water has subsided, opening up the workings. We haven't been down very far." I lift my hands. "It's mostly guesswork."

"How far has anyone gone?" Joe asks.

"DJ's been back and forth a couple of times to the southern gate," I say. "Teal took me through a few side tunnels. There are a couple of watchtowers, lookouts, up in the head—the mound. The western gate is welded shut. The eastern gate was supposed to be closed up and welded as well, but that could be where a second pack of Voors entered."

"We don't know that for sure," Tak says. "But it makes sense."

"Settler equipment and supplies?"

"A depositor mothballed in a side chamber. Looks to be in decent shape."

"Barrels of slurry?"

"Some. Maybe a lot."

"We have to check that out," Joe says. "We have to secure whatever resources we can find. So…DJ knows his way around."

"And can operate the southern gate," I say.

We'll end up repeating what Gamecock tried to do, but we have no choice. And maybe the newbies will do it better.

"First order of business—let's send a welcoming party to the southern garage. Then let's get the fuck away from here before Ants come knocking."

Tak calls over three of the survivors, a tall major named Jack Ackerly, an equally string-bean warrant officer named George

Brom, as well as a shorter corporal, a sister, Shelby Simca. As the trio stands at attention, Joe reaches to open his faceplate, as if to rub his eye or his nose, but Simca stops him with a cautionary hand.

"Dust, sir," she says. "We haven't had time to brush down."

"Right," Joe says. "Thanks. You two go with Corporal Johnson, DJ—accompany him to the southern gate and let in as many of our team and big vehicles as you can, post guard, then reconnoiter. Leave bread crumbs. One of you will return and report. We'll rendezvous halfway."

"Yes, sir," Simca says, and the trio runs off to gather up DJ. I'm sure he'll be delighted to have company.

Joe lays down more orders to the rest to form up, prep weapons, charge bolts, finish stripping the Skell-Jeeps and Tonkas of supplies—make ready to move out.

"Let's not join our friends right away," Joe says to the assembled troops. The specters of dead, bloated Skyrines on the other side of that lock are enough to motivate everybody. After what they've just been through, the newbies move fast.

Joe rejoins us behind the Tonka. "What the hell happened?" he asks. "Vinnie shot some of it at me on the Red, but we were distracted. Give it to me again, slower."

Tak takes a stab at summing up. "A month ago, Sky Defense must have dropped a battalion of Eurasians on the Red, to prep and defend fountains, cache weapons, get ready for later drops."

"You found them?" Joe asks.

"Some," Tak says. "All dead, at first. We found a few tents, one darted but two functional, enough to keep us alive. No working fountains. Then Lieutenant Colonel Roost found us, he was driving a Skell, alongside a Korean general. They took us over to where more survivors, mostly Eurasian brass, had holed up around an old, broken fountain. They had a command tent but not much in the way of resources, not for so many. Mostly injured, some severely. The fountain was beyond repair, at least with what we had. By the time a Muskie buggy arrived—"

"Driven by Vinnie's girlfriend," Joe says.

"She's from a settlement called Green Camp," I pick up, ignoring the gibe. "A refugee—an outcast. Her name is Teal. She saved us just as we were about to crap out on the Red. The only survivor from the command tent was the Korean major general, named Kwak. Kwak and Gamecock, Tak, Kazak, DJ, Neemie, Vee-Def, Michelin—she picked us up, shared air and water and filters, and transported us here. She called it the eastern Drifter.

"Shortly after, Captain Coyle and her troops arrived at the southern gate. Another scattered drop, I guess. They forcibly hitched a ride with less savory settlers, the Voors. The Voors were also coming to the Drifter, maybe to intercept Teal."

"Voors—Voortrekkers?" Joe asks again, and there's a glint in his eye, the same glint I saw the first time he asked—as if this was not unexpected.

"Yeah. Then, while Tak and I were outside—something happened inside. All but DJ vanished. He didn't see or hear a thing. We'd asked him to go outside the southern gate and try to establish a satlink."

"Vinnie thinks another wagon full of Voors showed up, maybe at the eastern gate, and took our people by surprise," Tak says. "But that gate was supposed to be welded shut. We just don't know what the hell happened."

Joe looks down at the green dust, scrapes it with his glove tip. Rubs the dust between his fingers. Most of it sifts to the floor. "How come we didn't detect the Ant forces in solar orbit? Flying downsun to intercept Mars?"

"How come we didn't detect comets?" I add.

"Fucking shambles," Joe says tightly. "Lousy coordination,

crappy intelligence. If we get back, I am definitely going to write a letter."

We update Joe on the character of the Voors, who could become a second front in our little set-to.

"They hate us, I get that," Joe says, "but enough to destroy all chances of survival?"

"Maybe," I say. "The patriarch, de Groot, is a real strutter. His son, Rafe, may be more sensible. The others...pretty strung out—and in mourning. They lost their settlement to the comets. They may be the last of their kind."

Joe's eyes get bigger. "Are the Voors expecting to team up with the Ants?" He looks us over with his wild, pale stare, and I hope I'm not seeing the last hope drain out of him, because frankly, we're all going to need a little of that, just a sip, from his cup.

"I doubt it," I say. "They won't be beholden to anything or anybody."

"Just like my pappy," Joe says, slipping into drawl. "Biggest sonofabitch in Memphis, ran a plumbing outfit, cheated on his customers and his women, never paid his taxes, but at least he wasn't a fucking joiner."

Tak and I reward him with weak grins. Joe's pappy is famous—and various. Joe never knew his father.

"Who's on top of our pyramid?" he asks with a sniff, and covers the silver leaf with his hand.

"Gamecock."

"Never here when you need them. Let's grab our shit and move."

Just then, to emphasize our situation, the outer lock doors resound like they've been hit with a fistful of boulders. It doesn't take us long to gather what supplies we can carry and abandon the northern garage.

TWO BALLS, ONE HEAD—YOU'RE GOOD TO GO

The reconnaissance group sends Ackerly back. We meet him a third of the way through the tunnel going south, just where a side jog took Teal and me to the first lookout. All clear to the southern gate, Ackerly says. DJ worked the locks and brought in the survivors who made it around the Drifter's shoulders.

"Needles fell in a second wave from the aero. They were caught outside, trying to get from the Tonkas and the Trundle. We lost all but two of the Tonkas and couldn't fit the Trundle. The Chesty is inside, but it's badly damaged."

"How many got in?" Joe asks.

Ackerly lowers his eyes. "Thirteen," he says.

Joe's lips work. He turns to Tak and me. "We have to assess, find out how many can fight, get our teams back in order," he says. "Then we have to locate Captain Coyle and the Voors."

Ackerly leads us to the southern gate. The thirteen new arrivals are of all persuasions, all walks of life, all colors, tired and stretched to breaking, but all are beautiful. Six corporals, three sergeants, a warrant officer—CW5, black eagle eyes surrounded by wrinkles; could be outstanding, another major, a tough-looking first sergeant, and another captain who's too zoned and beat up to do anybody any good.

In addition, we now have two lawnmowers, six heavy bolt rifles, eight boxes of spent matter cartridges, and kinetic projectiles of all sorts. Plus the Chesty—the General Puller, a long, narrow tan and red carriage sitting on eight tall wheels, supporting four side-mounted Aegis 7 kinetic cannons and the big draw: a triple-rail, chained-bolt ballista—but only ten percent charge remaining.

Joe asks how many of the new group have more than a few minutes' reserves in their suits. Two hold up their hands. We start distributing the filters and tanks taken from all the vehicles, including the Voor wagons. The survivors are quiet, trying to deal with their emotions, their short-term shock response to what they've been through. The usual acid mind-burn that comes after an engagement, when there is still no relief, no chance to really think, just adrenaline and bad shit dogging us while we run and pretend that we're still iron-ass Skyrines and not damaged goods.

It's going to take some real leadership to bring us back up to snuff. Joe picks the warrant officer, Wilhelmina Brodsky, a tough old bird with a face carved from teak. Brodsky is given the task of organizing new fire teams. Tak helps with the distribution of hand weapons. Not all of the weapons will be carried by rated Skyrines, but we'll make do.

"We're going to defend this gate with all we have," Joe says. "Most will stay here for now, rest up, scrub suits." He turns to Tak. "I want to station three sentinels just before the northern gate. Comm doesn't seem to work very well down here, so make sure they can all run fast. Vinnie, pick three. Then, I need to know about that eastern gate, and wherever the hell everyone else might have gone."

DJ says he understands the tunnels pretty well around here, and even down a few levels. I ask how he knows that.

"I seduced the panel in the southern watchtower," he says. The same place that Teal took me when we saw the Voors arriving. "Time on my hands while you were out on the playground. All dead-dude crypto. I got me some pretty pictures."

"Upload?"

"Eyeballs only. No way to link, like I said."

"But your angel recorded, right?"

"Some of it. Then the console crapped out—all the displays went blank. But it's still up here." He taps his head—not the angel, the skull beneath his helm. I remember Teal saying that the digs continued even while the Drifter was deserted, even while it was flooded. I say nothing about that. No sense confusing people with things I haven't seen and don't yet understand.

"Eastern gate open and receiving visitors?" I ask DJ.

"If the Voors or the Algerians welded it shut, they didn't inform the console," DJ says. "But the map says it's definitely there. Entrance lies about five hundred meters that way," he points to our right, then down, "and fifteen meters below... Comes in at a heavy mining level, meant to receive big equipment, maybe send out shipments of ore."

"Any visitors logging in or out?"

"I asked the booth AI about that multiple ways, but no joy, no grief, nothing one way or the other."

"Can we get there from here? No flooding, no other obstructions?"

"I think so," DJ says, thoughtful.

"Can the booth AI here tell us if someone breaks through the northern gate?"

DJ shrugs. "It really doesn't seem to care. It's pretty old and worn-out."

"Sentinels," I say to Joe. Brodsky continues putting together teams. She enlists Tak to help refresh two teams on the rifles.

"Yeah," Joe says. "DJ, stay here and tell them how not to get lost." DJ does his best.

Joe sends Beringer, Stanwick, and the burned-out Captain Victor Gallegos north, then leans against a wall and makes motions like he wants to smoke a cigarette. A couple of minutes of this odd charade and he's up straight, brushing the imaginary cigarette against the wall. I've never known him to smoke.

"Now, Vinnie... can we go take a look around?"

I lead Joe back to the southern watchtower. The console is indeed dead, so we pull down the periscope and do a 360. Soon enough, we understand our situation. The Drifter is surrounded by a solid circle of Antags standing back at about a klick, black Millies lined up with the big shiny heads forward, like a string of beads draped over the hardpan—platforms just behind them, dark gray with faint gleams of light as they are charged and tended by their gun crews. A full division, if we can effectively judge Antag order of battle—at least five infantry brigades carried and supported by over a hundred Millies, six mobile weapons battalions, other groups we can't make out to the rear of the forward forces.

They've completed the perimeter—and haven't just bunched up before the gates. Holding all fire. Waiting. A hell of a lot more than enough to obliterate us. If we decide to break out.

Not cautious. Confident.

Fucking arrogant.

Joe pushes up and stows the periscope with a grim look. "They could take this place in an hour," he murmurs. "What the fuck are they waiting for?"

"Orders?" I suggest. "Maybe they're as screwed up with tactical as we are."

"They're just playing with us, I think. Cat-and-mouse." His hands keep clenching. He hasn't slept since maybe before their drop. He whispers, "Take DJ and Brom and Ackerly and reconnoiter the eastern gate. Check integrity, evidence of another Voor team—wagons, supplies, whatever. Explore at will, grab what you can, expand on DJ's map—and get back as soon as you can."

"What do we do if we encounter the Voors?" I ask.

"Avoid getting killed," Joe says, eyelids heavy. "Tell them the truth—if we don't pull together, we're all going to die in here."

Back to the southern gate. Tak sees Joe's situation and takes him away from me, arm over his shoulder, with a backward glance.

"Take a break, sir. Five minutes," Tak says to him.

Rugged.

"Ackerly, Brom, DJ—on me," I say.

ANT FARM

When I was a kid, I used to love ant farm tales—the kind of stories where a clutch of ordinary folk are cooped up on an island or isolated in something strange, like a giant overturned ocean liner or a lost starship, whatever—didn't matter. Cooped up, the people all started to act like ants in an ant farm, digging out trails through the sand between the mysterious plastic walls, acting out little dramas, retracing familiar old trails, bumping into each other—like that. And what I loved was, all the inhabitants of the ant farm seemed oblivious to any larger drama, careless of what the farm might actually be—a child's toy, for example. Most of the characters hardly gave a damn about the big idea of their situation, paid the large questions almost no attention, because, I guess, it was insoluble at their level of information and smarts and faced with that, we all revert to what we do best—socialize, mate, preen, strut, fight, talk a lot, wonder a lot. Ant farm stories are just like life. We have no idea why we're here, what we're doing alive, or even where we are, but *here* we are, doing our best to make do.

And that's another reason I prefer not to think of the Antags as Ants. Because if I do, then it means they've somehow managed to escape *their* glass walls, their farm, and cross the stars. Ants are peering in at our solar system. Peering in at *us*, on Mars, stuck in the Drifter.

Wonder what they think of us? Do they pity us, so backward and *stuck*?

SNKRAZ.

Note to self: Stop thinking. Follow orders. Rely on training. Those are a Skyrine's protective glass walls.

DJ takes the lead again, right up to a tunnel that veers abruptly to our right. "This way," he says. Brom and Ackerly exchange glances with me as they pass. Our guide whistles. The sound echoes eerily ahead. All Tom Sawyer stuff to DJ. Gotta love him. Drives me nuts.

A few minutes, and we arrive at a wide spot in the tunnel, with a railing surrounding a shaft about seven meters wide. The walls of the shaft have been carved to shape a steep flight of steps, a spiral staircase, like something Basil Rathbone and Errol Flynn would have a sword fight on, running up and down—the first of a number of such shafts and far from the worst.

The deeper we descend, many meters, maybe a hundred or more, the shinier and more purely metallic the walls become, reflecting our flaring helm lights—big metal crystals, what are they called? Formed in deep space over ages of slow cooling…

NEWS OF JOE

Widmanstätten patterns," Alice Harper says. "Nickel iron crystals. How big?"

I spread my hands apart. Fifty centimeters, maybe. Chunky as hell, but smoothly polished, like an art project.

"My Lord," she says. "You were descending through the core of the old moon. Right there on Mars!"

"Right there," I say. My head aches like fury. My neck is stiff with talking, remembering, and I want to delay like anything what's coming up. "I got to take a couple of pills."

"Go take," Alice says. She looks at her phone, as if expecting a call.

Vac supplements are recommended while coming off Cosmoline. I've been avoiding them the last few hours because sometimes they flush the system. Part of the glamour of being a spaceman. I'm in the bathroom, staring into the large mirror, disembodied head swimming in my filmy gaze—seeing nothing I like or respect.

I rest my hands on the sink. A phone wheedles in the living room, not mine. Alice answers, her voice low. I've left the bathroom door open for the moment and clasp the vitamins in my hand, deciding whether I want to become human again—find firmer ground through more food, good company—or give in to the vac in my head.

Alice is speaking on her cell. Something's up. She sounds energized, but I can't quite hear what she's saying. I swallow the vitamins and scoop water from the tap to chase them. Then I emerge. The food in my belly is behaving. My legs are behaving. My vision is clear. I feel stronger.

Alice stands on the step up to the hallway, smiling a very odd smile. "That was Joe," she says. "He wants you out of here."

"And go where?"

"He didn't say, and I don't think we want to know—not yet. Get your stuff together."

"Moving out? Where?"

"I do not know. Honest."

"Do I have a choice?"

Alice—the same Alice who walked me around the market and made cioppino, who's listened to everything with sympathy and firm understanding—glares at me, brooking no dissent.

"It's *Joe*," she says.

"Why doesn't he come here?"

"I didn't ask! Let's move."

She helps me put together a packet with pills and fills a bottle of water from the tap in the kitchen. Somehow, I have run out of questions.

But she tells me, "Keep talking," as we take the elevator. "Keep your mind on what happened. Don't lose any details."

DEEP PRIDE

At the bottom of the spiral stairs, three tunnels run straight outward like spokes for as far as we can see; DJ has led us to a circular chamber at the center of a perfect shooting gallery. No star lights in sight. I signal for us to take positions away from the tunnels, close to the chamber wall.

But there's only darkness and silence.

Out on the Red, there's always the faintest hiss of ghostly breeze, almost inaudible except during a sandstorm, but down here, there's only a muffled hint of withheld human breath, the superlight scuff and rubbery tap of boots, and beyond that— beyond these very thin noises—

Nothing.

We switch on our helm lights. We can all see that the main trail of prints and streaks in the dust leads down one tunnel. The dust in the other tunnels is almost undisturbed—except for some tiny pocks and thin lines, which I ignore, because I can't explain them and my head is already overloaded.

DJ bends to draw a map in the dust. He lifts his forefinger to his lips as if to taste the dust on the tip, then catches me watching and drops his hand. "There are sixteen main levels connected by twenty-one shafts—right down to the torso. Most of the levels were closed due to flooding before the Voors packed up, I think—but they've drained now. All but the deep hydro."

"We should go back," Ackerly says, kneeling by the human tracks. "They're ahead waiting to ambush whoever follows."

DJ has an odd look. "Okay. *This* tunnel goes to the eastern gate—but *that* one does not." He points to the well-traveled tunnel and taps the middle of his map, then draws a staggered cascade of lines down through the Drifter's long axis. "It drops at a shallow angle and then intersects one side of a ring. Go halfway around the ring, and you'll meet the first of a series of shafts descending to a tall cavern—a big void. Right now, we're only in the neck—"

"What?" Brom asks.

"This whole Drifter thing is like a big swimming guy, trying to stay afloat, isn't it, Master Sergeant?" DJ says. I nod. "We've only gone down as far as one side of the neck."

"I do not get that swimmer shit," Ackerly interrupts.

"Try to imagine something for once," Brom tells him.

Ackerly frowns. "Backstroke or crawl?"

"Just the upper head and forearms and part of the neck reach above the sand," DJ says. "It's kind of like a giant doing a backstroke, I suppose. Head and shoulder, the harbor of one arm, thrust out in front—the northern gate. Another out behind, the southern gate. Yeah, backstroke."

Brom laughs. "Fuck," he says. "I can *see* the arm now. Big elbow. Hand below the sand. So what's down *there*—way down in the belly?"

"The big cavern. A void. The console labeled it the Church."

"Why the fuck is there a church down here?" Ackerly asks.

"It's what the Voors called it. Down in the gut."

"If *this* tunnel goes to the eastern gate," I point, "nobody's used it. These thin tracks could be pebbles falling from the roof or something, but there are no boot prints around here."

DJ absorbs this but looks stubborn. "Well, I'm fucking solid this goes to the eastern gate."

"Up in the booth—were some of the digs marked in blue and red?" I ask.

"Yeah. Way below, lots of red—mostly around the Church."

"The gut," Brom says.

"Bowels of Mars," Ackerly says. "Love it. Love it. We are heading into the shit for sure!"

"When Teal saw the red and blue traces on the larger diagram, she seemed to think the digs continued after the Drifter was abandoned," I say.

"Who's Teal?" Brom asks.

"The ranch wife who saved our bacon," DJ explains. Then he catches on and squinches one eye. "Still mining—even in deep water? Who would do that? *What* would do that?"

Brom and Ackerly look between us, blank-faced. We're talking way above what they've managed to understand.

"Let's get to the eastern gate," I say. "First order of business is figuring out where the Voors might have come in, and how vulnerable the upper works are to Antags."

DJ shrugs and heads down the tunnel he thinks—or remembers—leads to the eastern gate. "These are *old* digs," he says. We can hear him clearly enough, even above the scuff of boots, because his voice is naturally high-pitched, penetrating.

"How can you tell?" Brom asks.

"The grooves. Dig marks. When I went back and forth between the gates, I could see some were a lot older than the Voors."

"Really? How old?"

DJ flashes us a weirdly chipper look. "Millions of years, maybe. The marks here," he brushes one with his glove, "these are softer—they've been *eroded* by lots of flowing water, you know, the hobo, the underground river. And that must have taken millions of years, because, right? It doesn't flow all the time, it just *hobos* around under the surface, coming back every few million years, flooding, withdrawing…"

He keeps walking, throws out his right arm, and we all turn right. "This is newer, less erosion," he observes in the next tunnel.

I honestly don't know what to think. The tunnel excavation marks back there *do* look worn compared to these. But that could be a difference in machines, mining tools, techniques…

"Head and neck and shoulder," Brom murmurs. "Belly below. What's below that? How far down does this fucker go?"

"Maybe two or three dozen klicks," DJ says. "Based on the pictures I saw."

He has also neglected to reveal that, until now.

"What in hell *is* this place?" Ackerly asks.

"God's candy bar," I say. "Dropped it on His way to Earth. Creamy nougat center, I hear."

Ackerly thinks that over. "Really?" he asks with a boyish innocence you got to love.

The tunnel curves and then rises, and in a few minutes we're at the eastern gate—another hangar-sized cavern, completely dark—no star lights, nothing but our helm lanterns flaring through the cold, clear air. We're the first to disturb the green dust on the floor.

We wander around the cavern. No buggies, no wagons, no vehicles whatsoever—and no equipment. I approach the inner lock hatch, shining my light from top to bottom—pretty big, at least as big as the southern gate lock. The lock has been welded shut, then completely blocked by cross-welded beams and a big pile of basalt boulders—mine tailings, probably. Closed long ago, undisturbed since.

Nobody has been here for a very long time.

Ackerly sneezes and picks at his nose. His finger comes away green. "This ain't Mars dust," he observes, then wipes his finger on his forearm. "It's the green shit that's all over. We're sucking it in. What is it?"

"Algae, maybe," DJ says.

"What if I'm allergic?" Ackerly says.

"Not even a control booth," DJ says, standing beside an old, rusted frame that might have once supported such a structure. "I'll bet when they sealed it off, they covered the outside with rocks, too. So's nobody would even know it was here. Paranoid bastards, but smart, right?"

"No Voors came in through here," Brom observes, turning, his light sweeping around the walls of the garage. "How'd they overpower Skyrines without help?"

Then my own beam returns as a glint—back in the tunnel that led us here. A little speck of reflection that almost instantly seems to be obscured, as if by a shutter, a *blink*, then jerks aside—and vanishes.

"Did you see that?" I ask, retreating to the center of the hangar.

"See what?" DJ says.

"An eye," Brom says, throat tight. "I saw it, too—a blinking eye. Just one."

Ackerly bumps up against us and we're a tight square, facing outward, sidearms at the ready. "I didn't see anything," he insists. "Are we going back that way?"

"Only way out," DJ says.

It takes a few minutes to get these exhausted and thoroughly unhappy men to see clear reason. We cannot finish our mission without retracing our steps—following our boot marks. I look down at the green dust and our own tracks with obsessive interest, trying to make any sense of where we are, what's happening. What we're seeing or not seeing.

DJ takes the lead again. I take the rear. We're all in stealth mode, moving with as little sound as possible, trying not even to breathe loud.

Then Brom gives a little grunt. "Look at this," he says, bending, moving his light along our tracks. There's a very clear boot print, fresh, in the dust. One of ours, doesn't matter whose. Pointing to the garage.

Someone or something has planted an even fresher pockmark, and pushed aside a little line of green dust, right across that print. A few minutes before.

Without leaving any other sign.

"Ants!" Brom says, his voice rising. "They're already inside. We are truly fucked!"

"I don't think so," I say, mind working so fast my thoughts feel like sparks. No panic. Draw them back from panic. "We've all seen Antag tracks on the Red. Individuals leave bigger marks—double circles, side bars. Bigger boots than ours."

"Not Ants, then," DJ agrees.

"Calm down," I say. "Mission first. We have to get back and report."

We return to the radiance of tunnels at the bottom of the first spiral staircase. Alone, unmolested.

"Something with one shiny eye," Brom says thoughtfully. "If not Ants, then what?"

"Let's finish this level and see if there's something we need to know," I say.

We've gone on for a few hundred meters and it's becoming obvious that DJ no longer knows where we are.

"We've walked too fucking far," he says. "I'm turned around."

"Lost?" Ackerly asks.

"No, man, just turned around. Put me right and I'll find the way. We can follow our tracks."

We've made a wrong turn, it's dark—no star lights hang on these walls, and the grooves seem fresh. DJ is silent for a while until we stop again and he turns and looks back at us. "These digs weren't on the map," he says. "I think we're nowhere near where we're supposed to be."

"Then we just go back, right?" Ackerly asks.

"Green dust will show us the way," Brom says.

"If you'll notice," I say, pointing to our feet, "no green dust."

"Shit," Brom says. "It's supposed to be everywhere, it clogs my nose like snuff—why not *here*? Why not when we need it?"

"Because it's not *funny*," DJ says. "There's only green dust when it's funny."

But we're not going to let him off easy. We group around him, tight, as if we can squeeze out a better answer. Not threatening, mind you—we'd never threaten a fellow Skyrine. More like we're really strung-out chain-smokers and we know he has a pack of cigarettes on him somewhere.

"Give me room to think, goddamn it," he says, head low, eyes shifting in our beams. Which are, of course, slowly dimming. At least the air is fresh—fresher than ever, I think, like a slow, continuous mountain breeze way down here. "There was a side tunnel back about a hundred meters," he finally says, and pushes through our pack. "We'll try that one."

"I did not see it," Ackerly says. "Did you?" he asks Brom.

None of us saw it except DJ, and he's murmuring, "I didn't think it was the one, not right. Didn't feel right."

I have nothing against Corporal Dan Johnson—really. Decent tech, dedicated Skyrine, sometimes tries to be funny. But the thought that our lives depend on DJ's self-described perfect memory brings no joy. Ackerly and Brom are stoic. I think they made their peace out on the Red, running before the Antag wall of dust, and the rest has just been prelude to a foregone conclusion.

I'm trying to figure the lack of dust and the walls' fresh grooves. Recent digs?

Even after the water receded?

Slowly it's beginning to dawn on me that we might be dealing with another kind of participant in our weird game—a third party or group of parties, origin unknown, nature unknown.

But carrying a camera.

"What the fuck are you laughing at?" DJ asks me. "It's not funny, man."

"Find that side tunnel," I tell him.

"Yes, sir. What if it's not there anymore?"

"Find it."

Ten more steps and DJ spins around, shining his beam right at us. He points to his right, our left, face bright but damp. "There, just like I saw."

It's a smaller, narrower tunnel, barely high enough to stoop into. DJ bends over and heads in anyway, and then pops out like a cork, arms flailing. He's caught in a weird kind of web, pieces of thin translucent stuff, like flexible glass or cellophane noodles, that have stuck to his helm and shoulders. Grunting like a desperate pig, he plucks off the glassy fibers and flings them to the floor while Brom and Ackerly and I stand back, afraid to touch him, not at all sure what he's blundered into. But finally he's mostly cleaned himself off, all but for little fragments, and I tell him to stop, stop wasting energy, let me look you over.

He freezes like a statue, chin high, arms out. "Are they needles?" he asks, high and squeaky.

"Don't think so. Hold still."

I carefully pluck away one fiber, hold it out and up in our beams. It's about five centimeters long, twenty millimeters across, very much like a cellophane noodle in a bowl of Asian soup, but stiffly bendy. I pinch it lengthwise, not too hard, between my fingers. It flexes, then seems to grow rigid—to actually straighten and harden. Weird material.

Pieces of the shattered web lie on the tunnel floor all around DJ. But nothing seems to have pierced his skintight.

"Fucking spiderweb," Brom says.

"No!" DJ husks. "Fucking heavy-duty *no* to that shit!"

"Fine," Brom says. "No spiders."

"I'm cool with no spiders, too," Ackerly says.

My turn. I bend over and shine my light directly into the cavity that was supposed to be our turning point, our salvation, if ever I trusted DJ. "Something's jammed in here," I say.

"Trapdoor!" Brom says.

Now Ackerly takes umbrage and cuffs him on the side of the head.

My curiosity is piqued. Really. I am not in the least afraid—not now, just feeling a weird kind of wonder. Sad wonder. I feel as if I know what I'm going to find. Or at least *part of me knows*. Part of me feels a separate truth, not…

Human?

"It's not moving, whatever it is," I call back. I've pushed through the rubbery, brittle fibers and found the thing that might have made them, and it, too, looks like it might have come out of some crazy glass-blowing shop at a county fair. There's the eye, like a lens all right, on a tubular kind of head, transparent and blue-green, now slumped on a short neck. Behind the head and the eye is a jumble of glassy limbs about as thick as my wrist, which might have once been flexible and tough but are now shot through with cracks, dry, brittle. Looks like I could crunch them to dust with a poke of my finger.

"I doubt it's Antag," I say over my shoulder. "It's not moving. Old. Ready to fall apart. Decaying—"

Something that crawled in and died in this little hidey hole. Or just stopped working. What is it I'm recognizing, acknowledging, in this sad clump of fibers?

Brom sticks his head in behind me and shines another light down the narrow tunnel. "Looks like a dead end. What is that thing, a fossil?"

"Don't know. But...I think it didn't come from outside. I think it belongs down here."

"Get out and let's go," DJ says, voice still shaky.

I'm becoming more and more interested. I get down on my knees, very cautious, in case any of the fragments are still sharp, and examine its shoes, pads, feet—if it's one thing, one creature, or a creature at all!—about two or three dozen of them, at the ends of a maze of triple-and-quadruple jointed legs. I grip a pad and lift it—it's not all that light—and then, the leg above breaks and white dust rises and okay, it's time to back out, time to find another way, this is almost certainly not where we should be going—the hidey hole is feeling pretty tight.

I exit and hold the pad under the dimming beams proffered by Brom and Ackerly. DJ moves in to inspect with us. The pad masses about half a kilo and the bottom is hard, finely grooved in a cross-hatch pattern, but not your ordinary nail-file sort of grooves—more like the rotating cutter on a big digging machine back on Earth.

"It's a rock grinder!" DJ says, curiosity getting the better of fear. Then our eyes meet—and I recognize something in DJ's look. Knowing, acknowledging. I turn away before he can give me a little nod, before we join a really weird club.

"Maybe it dug these new tunnels," Brom says. "That thing's a fucking *kobold*."

"You just make that up?" DJ asks.

"No, man—kobold. Mining spirit. Like gremlins, only down in the ground."

"Let's go," I say. I'm holding tight to the pad, the cutting foot. Joe has to see this. Our whole situation is out of control in more dimensions than I can track.

Because what Brom and I saw in the useless and welded-tight hangar of the eastern gate was *not* a long-dead fossil stuck in a hole. What I saw had the same single, shiny camera eye—but it had *moved*.

These tunnels are new.

Kobolds may still be hard at work.

———

DJ IS LOSING focus, distracted—frazzled. He's murmuring to himself and leading us back to the eastern gate, hoping, I presume, for another branching tunnel, another shaft, something we missed. Brom is telling us all about kobolds, which he knows from a game he played as a kid on Earth. Ghostly diggers, spirits of dead miners; in the game they were horrible, flesh-eating wraiths that pickaxed you in the top of the head, caught the spurting blood in pelican-like beaks, then tore into the rest of you, bones and all, leaving nothing behind.

He's no better than listening to DJ, and finally, Ackerly tells him to just shut it.

"Right," Brom says. "Sorry."

This time, I'm the one who shines his helm light to the left at just the right moment, and instead of seeing metal crystals or black basalt, I see—a wide opening. A branch to the left, pretty straight, sloping down about ten degrees.

DJ inspects this with a puzzled look. "Don't remember any passage at this kind of angle," he says.

"You don't remember *shit*," Ackerly reminds him.

"This one's new, too," Brom says, pointing to the grooves.

We begin the slight descent. The tunnel grows wider, which I appreciate. DJ insists on taking the lead, and I don't deny him that much; he may still have a clue. The rest of us do not. He's stopped mumbling. Ackerly and Brom are silent as well. As the saying goes, it's quiet, too quiet.

"Will you please just *whistle*, DJ?" Brom asks after maybe ten minutes.

"No spit," DJ says. "Running dry."

All our suits could use a good, long recharge. We've been away from resources for hours; suits can typically run for two or three days, but ours have not been fully charged since prep before our drop. They can take all kinds of abuse and keep us alive, but staying comfortable is once again not an option.

"Where are we, anatomically?" Ackerly asks.

"Below the neck, in the chest, I think," DJ replies.

"Anywhere near the bowels?"

"We might be below the eastern garage, down around the heart," DJ says. Then he pulls up short, hunching his shoulders and letting out a moan. We've come to a round chamber, older, with rust on the walls and a damp floor. His helm light flashes up, around, and he backs off to show us what he's found. A body.

Human.

I walk around him, and then we gather and focus our lights, which are now almost orange. The sight is ghastly. A man has been cut in half and the walls have been scored in a weird, elongated spiral, all the way down another passage to the right... into darkness.

"Lawnmower," Brom says.

"It's a Voor, isn't it?" DJ asks, staring at me as I turn my light up to his face.

"Yeah," I say. "The one they called Hendrik."

"Here's another," Brom says. He's gone about six meters down another passage, also sloping, but this time up. "What the hell?"

"Must have been a firefight," DJ says.

Just two bodies. Both Voors, both cut to pieces while running away—by a lawnmower shot indiscriminately into the passage. Way overkill.

The evidence chills me.

"We need to get back *now*," I say.

Our discoveries are not over. DJ leads us past the second body, up the ascending tunnel, and a few dozen meters beyond, in another circular chamber with four more branching tunnels, we find three more Voors—lined up against a wall and shot with bullets: back-of-the-head-shots, execution-style. No recognizing any of them. Hendrik and the other may have lit out in desperation to escape this organized carnage.

"This is bullshit!" DJ shouts.

"But was it *authorized* bullshit?" Brom asks. "Who the fuck's in charge?"

Not Gamecock, I'm pretty sure of that. I'm having to revise everything I've thought about our situation. No additional party of Voors from the eastern gate, no reinforcements, no Antags breaking in yet—we'd probably be dead by now or see a lot more destruction if that last were the case.

Looks as if Coyle and our sisters might have scratched an evil little itch, all on their own. But why leave the southern gate? Why abandon *both* gates? We'd support them no matter what they did because that's what Skyrines do.

What are Captain Coyle's orders? What does she know that we don't?

Does Joe know what she knows?

DJ has fled up the widest tunnel. We're losing cohesion. Then he starts shouting, not more than twenty meters ahead. "It's a fucking boneyard! They're all over in here!"

Very reluctantly we join him in the biggest chamber we've

found yet, about sixty meters across, a great, dark stone hollow surrounded by a head-high shelf of foggy-silver metal. I'm expecting to see dead Voors and Skyrines smeared all over—a hecatomb of combat mayhem.

Nothing of the kind.

"More kobolds!" Brom says, voice down to a hard whisper.

Hundreds, maybe thousands of them, massed around the walls like a river-piled deadfall, their jointed tubes and pads jumbled in with long heads and camera eyes—still pale, still supple, but motionless, silent, and in such confusion I can't begin to figure out what the mass would have looked like alive and working.

Maybe the kobolds had come together like Tinkertoys to become a single machine, to more efficiently carve out the lava and metal with hundreds of grinding, cutting pads, still busy, still digging—

DJ splashes through an ankle-deep pool. The chamber appears to have been expanded within the past few days or weeks. Water could have been kept longer in the lower tunnels, allowing the kobolds more time to keep digging—until they connected with a dry passage and everything drained. But draining water wasn't what killed them. They can move around for some time even after the water is gone—I saw one do just that. Maybe they can even keep working.

A gigantic mining machine, a big operation—

Until somebody—possibly Captain Coyle herself, or Gunny de Guzman, whom I first saw with the lawnmower—ran rampant and sprayed beams all through the hollow. Spiraling scorch marks rise across and around the walls, cleaving the thick masses of kobolds, up to the rugged ceiling. By definition, a lawnmower is excessive—so what's an excess of excess? Mad, thorough destruction.

Our sisters might have figured they were about to be attacked. Maybe they *were* attacked. But we see no blood, no human bodies—except for Voors.

Ackerly and Brom and DJ stand at the center of the hollow, stunned. "This is *our* shit!" Ackerly says, his voice very low now, trying to reason through the threat, the cause. "What if these fucking kobolds are Ant scouts—little buggy drones or shit? They're inside, checking things out, making their moves, so our sisters righteously carved them into lunch meat!"

"These aren't Ant drones," Brom says quietly.

I agree. They don't fit any known pattern, don't carry weapons, and haven't hurt us or even threatened us.

"Maybe it doesn't matter if you're a kobold whether you're alive or dead," Ackerly says. "Maybe they can revive and spring up and grab you...like zombies! Soda straw zombies."

"Shut *up*," DJ says in fierce disgust.

They're all looking right at me. It's never good when Skyrines start plumbing the depths of their intellect.

"We have to get back to Sanka," I say. It's all I can think to do: finish our mission, pass the buck—inform our commander the eastern gate is locked, we haven't seen any Antags in the Drifter...

Only kobolds, whatever the fuck they are.

DJ walks ahead and we follow, muttering in the shadows and damp as he flings his arm right, then left, guiding us. We're moving fast. Our heads hurt from all the pressure changes.

He halts at a wide spot in the tunnel and slams his hand against a hatch set into the wall, covering an opening in the floor about two meters wide, not an airlock but maybe watertight. "Okay," he says. "I know this one. This covers a shaft that takes you down maybe fifty meters, to where nobody's been except maybe the Voors. If we can get it open."

"And you know that *because*...?" I ask.

"I told you!" he shouts. "The booth. It's…up here, you know?" He taps his head again and I feel a sudden anger, an outrageous urge to just start kicking him and the walls, because it's all so nuts. Would a little certainty and sanity hurt whoever's in charge, please, just this once?

Instead, I ask, "Will it take us any closer to the southern gate?"

DJ thinks this over. "No," he says. "Deeper, down to a big void, no idea what's inside." He kneels and manages to pry up one side. "Look, it's not locked."

The door is light, not steel—probably some polymer printed out by the depositor.

"Is there space down there for a good-sized group to hide?"

"Definitely," DJ says. "Really big."

"Fucking hold fire!" someone shouts from down the tunnel—a woman. "Seventh Marines, Akbar!"

I recognize the voice. It's Captain Coyle.

"Fuck," Brom says under his breath.

First down the tunnel walks Vee-Def, pushed out front by Sergeant Mustafa, and he doesn't look happy. He gives me a warning glance as helm lights flash. Theirs is not a cordial relationship.

"Fuck this shit," he says wearily, and Mustafa taps him on the back of his neck with the butt of her sidearm. He reels forward and falls to his knees.

Ackerly, Brom, and DJ form a tight square around me, and we all palm sidearms.

Mustafa glares. "He's being an asshole," she says, then reaches to help Vee-Def back to his feet.

Coyle and four of our sisters come out of the shadows and join us in the wide spot, where they surround us like it's old home week, checking us over, casually checking status of our sidearms, monkeys picking nits, social as shit in a chute—but my head is buzzing, my adrenaline is way up.

Shrugging off Mustafa's help, Vee-Def stands. His eyes are heavy, and not just with pain. Betrayal. Rage.

"What the hell happened to you?" I ask Coyle.

Without meeting my eyes, she softly, gently tells us about the unexpected arrival of twelve more Voors, coming in through the eastern gate, fully armed with pistols and assault weapons. Her voice is flat, deadly calm, like she's on some sort of drug.

"The Voors drew down," she says, pacing around the hatch. DJ bends and swings the hatch up. At Mustafa's scowl, DJ backs off. "There was a brief struggle, nearly everyone returned fire. Two Voors were killed by bolts, two of ours were killed by projectiles, and we overwhelmed the rest. Some broke loose and ran down here. When we got here, they ambushed us, attacked us again."

"What about Lieutenant Colonel Roost?"

"Killed in the first attack." Coyle suddenly looks right at me, face like an angry little girl's, defying me or anyone to say she's a liar, but that's exactly what she is, a liar—and we all know it.

The ladies have sidearms out and charged. De Guzman levels that goddamned lawnmower, expression total trigger. I idly observe that if she fires she'll take out not just us but half her team.

"Ladies, ladies," Ackerly says, holding up his hands.

DJ's sweating, losing focus.

"Where's Teal?" I ask.

"I don't know," Coyle says. "Doesn't matter."

The sisters loosen their ring but not their vigilance.

"Listen up," Coyle says, her voice ringing against the walls as if she's addressing a platoon. "We have orders. New orders. The Antags are going to overwhelm this place, and command doesn't want it to fall to them. So we're taking all our spent matter and mining explosives and shit…rigging it to release all at once. We're going to collapse the upper works."

Brom and Ackerly shake their heads and look dubious. DJ stands aside, back hunched, like he's going to be sick. He keeps looking at the hatch.

"Sir, why not mount a defense until they reinforce?" Brom asks pertly, as if rational questions are still in order. Ackerly pokes Brom in the ribs but it doesn't seem to register. "We have the weapons, you say we have enough charges—"

Coyle ignores him and turns to me. "Where have you been?" she asks.

"The eastern gate," I say.

"Find the Voors?" she asks, bold as whiskey.

"We're on board, Captain," I say. "Carry out your orders. We'll move back to the southern gate and wait for all of you before we abandon the Drifter."

"I need your assurance that you understand my orders supersede any others," Coyle says. There are dark moments coming, that's what I get from her weird, *don't hit me*, little girl look. Orders are orders whether you like them or not. Captain Coyle does not like her orders. Not one bit. But she's an excellent Skyrine.

SNKRAZ.

"I don't know why you didn't confide in us in the first place, Captain," DJ says dreamily, rubbing his neck. There are streaks on his cheeks, I notice for the first time, like he's been rubbing them with green dust.

"What's with him?" de Guzman asks.

"He's tired," I say. "Like all of us."

"Execute in sequence," Coyle says. "Need to know. Anyway, it's all out now. We came back because our detonators aren't up to the task. We're taking another pair down to the Church, and then we'll climb up and join you at the southern gate. Apologies, Master Sergeant. We'll leave Lance Corporal Medvedev with you."

So she, too, knows about the Church.

The ladies slip down the hole beneath the hatch, covering us as they depart. De Guzman goes last. And just as suddenly as it began it's over, like a wicked, ugly dream.

"Don't listen to them," Vee-Def says. "They want us dead. All of us. It's a suicide mission."

DJ says, "Strong tea, ain't it?"

COLD COMFORT

Alice Harper has called a minivan to the curved drive outside our building. In the rearmost seat, far away from the driver—who sits behind a plastic shield anyway, and probably isn't listening—I continue my story, speaking low, eyes darting at the bright, cloudy day, wondering where she's taking me but not really caring.

I feel very funny indeed. This isn't Cosmoline, nor is it getting used again to Earth air and gravity. My mind is filling again with ghostly thoughts, visuals, details, all fragmented and swirly. Not direct experience, not sensual input or something I read or saw, more like a direct feed into my cortex. Maybe it's another kind of angel taking form in my skull, trying to awaken. It hurts, sort of—but this is an interesting sort of pain, like freshly exercised muscles.

Then my mood flips. All things unexpected turn out badly; that's the truth of battle. Most of the things we *do* expect turn out badly, as well. I'm not a happy camper, in any case, and my innards are knotting—both stomach *and* brain.

"I'm going to be sick," I say.

"No, you aren't," Alice says.

"I *am* sick, inside," I say.

"Not really," she says. She sounds like she knows something but she doesn't want to tell me, not here, not yet. And suddenly that's okay. I'm compliant again, complaisant. I do feel strange, but I trust her. That makes no sense, even if she is pretty and a good cook and knows how to take charge.

She fed me cioppino. Fish and clams and crab and vegetables. Delicious.

"Did you drug me?" I ask.

"No," she says firmly, and pats my knee before unhitching and moving up front to talk to the driver. When she returns, she tells me, "You didn't come back as Master Sergeant Venn, did you?"

"No," I say.

"Joe sent you back with another ID, and in the crowding and confusion, out on the dust and on the orbital—nobody checked, right?"

"Or didn't care. Focus on getting us all home."

"Joe figured the brass would take a couple of days to start putting together all your stories. A couple of days before they decided to round you all up and isolate you. That's why he told you to stay away from MHAT."

"Right," I say.

"He didn't think it would be a good idea for him to join you right away. Too many eggs in one basket. So he sent me. And no, I did not drug you. But you are now full of essential supplements and vitamins."

"Are those making me sick?"

"You're *not* sick," she emphasizes, a little ticked. Her patience is wearing thin. I am trying her patience. I am trying her patience on for size and finding it's just too sheer. I can see through it. I can be either patient or impatient.

Shit, I am drugged—looping out and in, flying free...

And then, *not.*

My head is clear as a ringing bell.

"What the fuck happened up there?" I ask her.

"You tell me," she says. "But not here. We'll be where we're going soon, in an hour."

"And where is that?"

"Safe, quiet, remote. Joe says he'll try to be there when we arrive."

"We both made it, you know. We both got off Mars."

"I know."

"They wanted to kill us. All of us."

"So I heard."

"But you want me to wait before I learn the truth, don't you? Before I figure it all out, or somebody tells me."

She nods. "Patience. Won't be long, Vinnie."

On the return trip, before we slipped into the Cosmoline, the orbital crew promised us all campaign medals stamped with our company blaze. But what's inside my head, what's happening to me, and maybe to others besides me—to DJ, for example—

Will shove all that aside.

I'm being hustled away by a zaftig, pretty female who's a great cook, knows how to sling and deliver the right supplements, claims she knows Joe—and also knows what's good for me.

"One last thing," I say.

"One last thing," she agrees, leaning in on the bench seat, watching me closely.

Very softly, so the driver can't hear, "I'm valuable, ain't I?"

"You're fucking irreplaceable, Vinnie."

TEAL'S WAY

We make steps, one after the next, getting farther and farther away from the chamber of kobold slaughter, from the hatch, from Captain Coyle, just picking a way out, a way up. God help me, my brain is still on overdrive. I need distraction from thoughts about Coyle, about our sisters, about orbital command.

And so I think about kobolds. What are they hoping to achieve? Are they like automated termites, just digging for the hell of it—turning the entire Drifter into a rotting log of rock and metal? Maybe that's it.

We've been moving this way and that, ever upward, for about an hour, when we see a light fly back across the shining metal ceiling over our heads, and DJ shouts, "It's Michelin! And Neemie!"

This passage is not very wide but we all pack together, shining our beams in each other's faces. Neemie and Michelin look like they've been through a grinder. Their skintights are badly lacerated, helms broken and faceplates torn away, and Michelin is clutching his arm to his chest. It looks broken.

Ackerly tries to help Michelin but he jerks aside, eyes showing whites all around like a terrified horse.

"Where are the others?" I ask.

Michelin points up, down, then around with his good arm, face ghostly white. He says, "Shit's falling from so high we can't even smell it."

Neemie grimaces. "Don't mess with him," he says. "Talk to me. While I still have a clue."

Michelin starts to sing, "*If I only had a clue...*" Neemie gently puts his hand over his mouth. Michelin folds down against a wall and slumps his head.

"Tell us about Coyle," I say.

"She got final instructions from that Korean general, Kwak, before he died. That's why they're all here, I think."

"Fucking command," Michelin mutters.

"What instructions?"

"They came with beaucoup spent matter charges. In their backpacks. Somebody back home wants this place blown to gravel, that's what I gathered, that's what Gamecock—I mean, Lieutenant Colonel Roost—figured when Coyle and the sisters took us over, us and the Voors. Poor Muskie bastards didn't stand a chance."

"Coyle killed them all?"

"De Guzman tried. Too tight for that. Some got away, don't know how many."

"What about Teal? The ranch wife?"

Neemie shakes his head. "Michelin and I got away, and I think maybe Gamecock. But you know what's really scary? There's something else down here! Like bundles of thick straw, only moving and fast."

"We've seen them," Brom says. "Kobolds."

"They filled the tunnel and flooded in on Coyle and her team just as they were zeroing the Voors—executing them, man! Coyle was a fucking fiend—"

"Had her orders, she said," Michelin adds. "Weird fucking face on her."

"—and de Guzman with that fucking lawnmower…" Neemie swallows but it won't go down and he strokes his throat as if to help it. I'm amazed he can still talk. "But then we were backed into a big space and it filled with those straw bundles, straw creatures, coming in from all sides, and I swear, I swear this is true—"

"It *is* true," Michelin says, looking up.

"Coyle's team pulled us out of there, laid down more lawnmower, pulled us into another tunnel where there were these crystals, big, clear crystals. And when they started laying charges, pulling them out of their packs like Girl Scout cookies—the crystals turned black! The walls turned to, like, black *glass* and got spiky, and the spikes snagged Magsaysay and then Ceniza, ripped her suit—and, *man…*"

"Help me up," Michelin says.

"They both turned all black, shiny," Neemie says. "Like statues."

DJ throws me a look as we help lift Michelin back to his feet.

"Medusa," I say and instantly regret it. Ackerly and Brom are ready to book to the top and run straight out onto the Red. It's just a matter of seconds before everything closes in on all of us.

"We didn't see the finish," Neemie continues, "but they were pinned on the spikes and their legs and skintights and everything—"

"Solid, shiny, filled with fireflies," Michelin says. "Some fucking defense!"

"Whose defense?" Brom asks. "Who's defending who?"

Time to get back to essentials.

"Where are they now?" I ask.

"Coyle was going deep before everything mixed," Neemie says. "Down to a place the old Voor called the Church. They strung him up and he tried not to tell them, but Rafe…"

Michelin's eyes go horse-wild again. He throws out one arm, bangs the walls, as if he'd break that one, too.

"Hold him, Brom," I say.

"He's *hurt*, man," Brom says. "We have to get him to the top and out of here." Brom's eyes beseech.

"Don't forget what's waiting outside," Ackerly says, voice cool. "Are they still holding good Skyrines?"

"I don't know who's good or bad," Neemie says. "We got away in the freak. Kazak and Vee-Def were helping Gamecock. Coyle beat the colonel down bad when he questioned Kwak's orders. And then Kwak dies—he just *expires*. Still spouting crap about old moons and dust and shit, and that snaps everybody. Believe it. *Nobody* goes home."

"Who's in charge?" Michelin asks. "I'll follow orders if I just know who's wacko and who's not."

"DJ," I say, and he perks up instantly, "guide us back to Sanka. Now."

"Right," he says, and turns to the others. "Southern gate, fellows. On me. We're packing up to go home."

I don't contradict him. It's a good story. Maybe we are, maybe we aren't.

DJ leads us with firmer conviction and a lot more motivation. He's still intent on running his gloved fingertips along the grooves, as if he's reading the walls. There's green dust again—these tunnels are older, the grooves more worn, and somehow that's reassuring. We follow them back along a scuffed trail of many footprints.

DJ looks back at me and whispers, "This dust, it's fucking strong tea. I'm seeing shit. What about you?"

I don't want to hazard an opinion. We're stretched way too thin. I'd rather die on the Red than face rogue Skyrines or black spikes. For the moment, thinking things through is more than I'm good for—but even so, there's a peculiar *newness* in my head.

Something fresh and unexpected.

And then—scaring the hell out of me—

Takahashi Fujimori.

His face rises like a dull orange ghost in our beams. Behind him are Brodsky and Beringer. Believe me, Skyrines can shriek like little girls.

Then we get real quiet. That kind of shock is not good. We could have killed each other. Jangles subside and we catch our breath.

"Where you guys been?" Tak asks.

"We're retreating in good order to the southern gate," Ackerly says, strolling past. "Permission to abandon this shithole, Master Sergeant."

"Follow us. Sanka's up ahead." Tak asks me, "Any sign of Captain Coyle and her squad?"

"Could be way down deep," I say. "They're going to demo this place. Blow it the fuck up. We don't know anything about anything, Tak."

"Yeah. We were sent to find you. We make one last attempt to locate Captain Coyle and her team, see what the fuck they're up to—issue a final notice that we're all gathering at the southern gate, organize vehicles and weapons," he shoves out his hands, "and push through the Antag line. There's a dust storm outside, a real good one."

"Saw it from a watchtower," Beringer says. "Great screen. Might give us cover."

"Outstanding," Neemie says, fingering the rips on his skin-tight. "Blind and out on the Red in our pajamas."

"We're hoping the bright boys in orbit have decided to regroup and open up a distraction," Tak says.

"*Hoping?*" Brom asks.

"In here, it's fucking bughouse," Beringer says.

"You're telling us?" Michelin asks.

Ten minutes later, we've come to the roundabout just before the southern garage, where Joe is squatting beside a Voor—de Groot's son, Rafe. Rafe is in decent shape considering but minus his skintight, face bruised, sullen.

Joe, with a sour look but no words, takes us all back to the southern gate. There de Groot and two of the Voors are lifting Gamecock on a stretcher, up into the cabin of the Chesty.

"He's not going to make it," Joe says, out of our CO's earshot. "They have some story to tell. You?"

I try to pass along what I might or might not know. As I finish Kazak comes around from the vehicle's lock hatch.

Tak and Kazak and I slap backs, but it's a brief moment. Kazak is in surprisingly good shape after what he's been through.

Rafe stands beside his father after they finish loading our CO. Both regard us with weary disgust. De Groot looks to have been chewed all over by rats and his face is swollen almost beyond recognition, but he's still upright, proud, defiant.

Joe sums it up. "Coyle and her squad are working from a different set of orders. The Voors are coming with us."

"Who's been lying the hardest?" I ask.

Joe ignores the question. "Any sign of the rest of our team?"

"None we've seen."

"The ranch wife?" Joe asks.

"Nothing," I say.

"She's gone over to the Drifter," Rafe says, but before he can explain what that means the floor shakes under us. The walls shiver and dust sifts from the ceiling.

"From below?" Kazak asks.

"From above," Tak says. "Bombardment."

"Antags getting ready to move in."

"I strongly doubt it," de Groot says. "You do not see at all, do you? What is happening, who is working behind you?"

Joe assigns Kazak to watch over the garage and prepare for

our exit. Then he picks four of us and signals for us to move out. "DJ, you've still got some sort of map in your head, right?"

"I think so," DJ says.

"Find that hatch again. We're going to locate Captain Coyle and see what her disposition really is. Try and get her team to come back with us."

Joe says, in a low voice, so that Rafe and de Groot can't hear, "I don't get these fucking kobolds. What are the chances the Voors invited the Ants in? And the Ants killed some of them for their trouble?"

"Not likely," I say.

Joe absorbs this. "Then it's true. Coyle and her orders, Major General Kwak, what the Voors have been saying…"

I'm about to ask what the hell else could possibly be true when DJ comes trotting back. "Found the hatch," he says. "There's a shaft, something like steps but cramped as hell, not designed for people. I don't know how our sisters made it down."

Rafe comes forward. "It is old and for the Church," he says. "Not for us."

Joe acknowledges this contribution with a nod, then points for us to move out. DJ leads the six of us to the shaft opening and lifts away the hatch. Christ it *is* small—just two meters wide, steps tiny and tall; we'll be crawling down more like worms or snakes than men.

DJ says, "If you're down here digging long enough, maybe you get all big-eyed and greasy like, you know, Gollum."

I'm actually fingering the platinum coin in my pouch, but when he says that, I stop.

Joe has had enough of DJ's nervous chatter. "Cram that shit back in," he says. "We go down, find Coyle and our survivors, find Teal and what's left of the Voors. That's that."

We begin one by one to drop through the hatch. I volunteer to take point.

"Dick down the hole," DJ says.

I hear murmuring up above, establishing order as the defensive lines break and join us, until there are just two covering our rear, awaiting a signal we've come out in a better place.

Beams bounce and flare.

One sidelights Tak grinning through his faceplate like a lacquer mask.

HOW LOW CAN YOU GO BEFORE IT'S UP AGAIN

Just a few meters down. On top of everything else, like a final fillip of perversity, the skinny shaft is really getting to me.

We did mine training at Hawthorne Tactical in Nevada, suspecting there were going to be circumstances where we might have to worm around under the Red, and there was a particularly awe-inspiring old turquoise and silver mine shaft that we, a squad of ten, plumbed for almost a quarter of a mile, taking instruction from a fifty-something DI named Marquez about how to stay calm under an overwhelming burden of rock. "There's a whole goddamned *mountain* over your head right now," he kindly informed us. "Look at those braces, look at those *beams*—think there's *termites* in that old wood? Are there termites in Nevada? You know there are. Wood-chewing, white ants. I think there's termites in *all* this old wood...Plus, fidging overburden shifts all the time, seismically active, *wow*, did you just feel *that*?"

As we stooped and crawled, he lectured on how to conduct live fire in a confined space, he'd learned it from a guy who learned it from a guy who once went after Viet Cong in their spider holes, and *he* learned it from a guy who did the same in Korea, and *he* learned it from a guy who sent in Dobermans to clean out tunnels in Okinawa and then took in gunny sacks after—

Jesus, *I hate this fucking place.*

I do not want to think about other places that were worse because my skintight is already filter-clogged and I'm sweating like a bastard, dripping from the lip of my faceplate, and Joe's boot takes me across the back of the neck when he slips, and I start thinking about my integrity; maybe he's ripped the fabric and if I fucking get out of this I'll just hiss out on the Red.

Why is the air still good down here? Who set up diffusers to spread clean, breathable air throughout the Drifter? The Voors? Kobolds are more likely. Better engineers. Hell, the old silver mine at Hawthorne, the deepest shafts, was reputed to be filled with sulfurous fumes from deep under the mountain—so that syphilitic cunt of a sadistic motherfucking DI told us—but nobody had ever been that deep, it was off-limits, he said, maybe we're already over the boundary, and then he taunted, "Smell anything, Skyrines? Whiff that stink? Other than your own butt-gas?"

He was just trying to flunk us out but no way, that pay hike shined over our heads every day we trained at Hawthorne bigger than claustrophobia, stronger than deep-Earth butt-gas.

Joe and I and the eight others had already been through seven circles of Skyrine hell. Only two would not finish. But they gave that DI immense satisfaction, those two. They flunked out in the drowning pool, floundering in skintights in zero-g prep. The DI had issued suits with leaks. Pointless, we thought, so much water—that much water on Mars! Seemed ridiculous, unfair, but I survived the mine shaft and kept my calm in the drowning pool, I made it, Joe made it, the other six made it, who were they? Fuck I'm forgetting so much, is the oxygen really all that good down here?

"Off-limits," Joe mutters above me. I'm still mad because he hasn't apologized for the boot in my neck, but my own boots are slipping on these inhuman steps.

"Fucking off-limits," I affirm, banging my knee, and again integrity will be an issue. I'll have to check myself all over and hope somebody brought the right patches.

"Don't remind me of that fucking old mine," Joe says. We're in memory sync. "I hated that place," he says. "Didn't you?"

I'm trying to hold on to the edge of a long, long step. "Loved it like my mother," I say. "A total stone vagina squeezing out born-again Skyrines. Just like here."

Joe snorts. I'm paying him back for his boot in my neck. Orderly descent. All an Antag has to do is lay down a couple of bolts from below and we'll cook, we'll fry in this shaft like—

My foot hits something that gives. That clacking sound again, only like rocks or plastic striking, not metal. I know that sound. I can imagine what's making it. I shine my helm light straight down between my legs and something shines back up at me just for a moment, like the lens of a camera, not an eye, not wet or alive—but shiny and round.

I suck in my breath.

They're keeping track of us.

And then it's gone. The spiraling shaft below is empty, as far as I can see—a couple of meters—but for a moment, I've come to an abrupt, stunned halt and Joe is right above me, knees doubled just behind my head, cursing.

"What?" he shouts.

"Tell DJ I just stepped on Gollum," I say, still processing the visual, hoping my angel caught it and we can all replay and judge when we're at the bottom. Then I see a black void and my boot kicks out from a step into empty air.

"Bottom, I think," I say.

"Shove through, goddamn it," Joe says.

I do that and then I stand up in a bigger darkness, a blessed black openness, and start shining my helm light around.

"Go ahead," Joe says.

I move on, relieved to be out of the shaft, but there's also that newness in my head. Feels right, feels *good*. Seems to help me find my way around. Problem is, I'm less and less sure I know who I am or who I'm with. I focus and try to hear those behind me. But I've lost them. Maybe I've turned left when they turned right.

I don't mind.

Strong tea.

I'm surrounded by complete darkness but I switch off my fading helm light, touch fingers lightly to the grooves in the wall, feel the grooves rise and drop in an interesting rhythm.

I keep walking. It's possible I'm just losing my grip, possible that the green dust is infiltrating my brain and I'm descending in a spiral to a place where no one will ever find me. There's a certain comfort in that. I like it down here. Maybe I won't have to deal with whatever's happening with Captain Coyle and our sisters. I can leave that to Joe. But then, I won't see Joe or Tak or Kazak or any of the others again, and I won't even be able to compare notes with DJ, possibly the only other Skyrine feeling the tea as strongly as me.

I haven't a fucking idea what's happening, really.

But fairly contented.

———

I'M SOMEWHERE BELOW the neck of the homunculus that is the Drifter, winding down. After a couple of hours, I realize this is *way* down. It's getting warmer. The air in the darkness is rich and moist. Electric. I'm smelling that living planet again. The walls are damp. Then I'm on my knees, crawling, occasionally touching the grooves to coordinate the noise in my head with where I am, possibly *who* I am, which is not at all clear.

I hear somebody or something up ahead. Down this far, deep into the chest of the Drifter, more than likely I'm about to meet up with one or more kobolds. That doesn't concern me, though it should.

I like kobolds.

Then human instinct kicks back in and tells me to get my shit together, think of something to counter the strong tea.

I remember reading an article about cat ladies.

Brain really digresses here: there is such a huge difference between a cat lady and Catwoman. Funny how that works. *Not funny at all, asshole. Get it together!*

Cat ladies—not the slinky gal wearing a mask with perky little ears, rather the kind that just loves kitties and can't stop filling houses with them: this article I read back on Earth said that cat ladies were more than likely infected by a parasite found in cat shit, *toxi something something*, that is *supposed* to end up in rats, where it takes over their rat brains and makes them unafraid and bold, but also makes the rats *love* the smell of feline urine; well, cat ladies are probably infected with this parasite and it's in their brains and so they never clean the litter boxes, just keep piling on the kitties and rising to heaven on the smell of cat pee...

SNKRAZ!

I'm thinking the green powder makes DJ and me love darkness and depth. Makes us seek something, I don't know what. I sure as fuck hope I don't acquire the urge to dig. To keep myself as human as possible, I begin to hum pop tunes but somehow end up with Grieg, "In the Hall of the Mountain King." "Dump dump dump dump *dump* da da, *dump* da-da, *dump* da-da..." Finally, the tune runs out of my head. Legs getting tired. Nose clogging; I sneeze a lot.

There's a kind of dream I'm having as I walk, not at all unpleasant, but in other circumstances it would be an honest-to-God nightmare. Funny stuff. Weirder and weirder.

Very strong tea.

I'm swimming across a muddy plain beneath upside-down hills of ice, blue-green and white, festooned with hanging meadows of luminous flowers, and the hills are dripping shiny twisters, downward-flowing rivulets of supercooled brine, and I don't know *what* I look like but I'm sure I'm more like a crab or a trilobite or a spiky worm than a human because, of course, humans could not survive here.

I avoid the brine—tastes bad, too many minerals—but those glowing flowers are food as well as light, and when I meet up with dozens of others like myself, in a low ocean valley, we're all very interesting and good-looking (*ugly—the ugliest fucking shelly things I've ever seen, multiple joints and grooves, waving arms and shit I can't begin to describe, and they all seem to be ridden by,* I'm *being ridden by, a skinny, spidery parasite with a set of odd, multi-faceted eyes—I love this parasite, it's my best friend, it keeps me safe and warns me of bad stuff*)—

We're each of us big, maybe four or five meters long—and as we gather, we look up in admiration and pride at something we've all made, something immense and beautiful: a great pillar rising thousands of meters from the middle of the valley, all the way to a high, dark, inverted dome of ice.

Below us is the rocky, metal-rich core, the solid heart of our world, heated by internal radiation, heated also by tidal friction from outside, while above, the ice forms a protective barrier between us and the greater universe, allowing us to grow for a billion years—grow and develop in peace.

My God, how *thick* is that ice?

One hundred kilometers.

And only in the last thousand years have we managed to dig out and look around, like breaking out of an immense, frozen egg—

The cause of our long, gestating ignorance, and soon, of our destruction. Because we can infer what's coming—

Moonfall.

We know it's going to happen, we feel the changing tides, we're no longer where we *were*, wherever that was, around a great, steady source of gravity and the constant rhythmic, reliable tides...

We've been knocked away from all that. Our world has been growing colder for a long time and we've been slowly dying off, but meanwhile building, encapsulating, encoding, and preserving.

Getting ready.

The walls of the pillar are made of tiny crystals from which slough great cascades of what can only be called slime, luminous, thickly elegant slime filled with writhing, transparent tubes that join and come apart within the cascades.

The pillar is *working*.

The pillar is *ready*.

Really bad things are about to happen, but we're as prepared as we're ever going to be.

I'm so distracted by this second life, this tea dream, that I barely notice I've bumped up against somebody in the darkness. Fumbling, I switch on my helm light, which is so dim and orange it barely illuminates anything. But it shows me whom I've bumped into.

Not a crab, no outer shell at all—very tall, very slender—female. Slowly I recall my humanity and this female's name: this is Teal—nick for Tealullah.

She regards me with wide, calm eyes; no surprise that I'm here. Like DJ, she's rubbed her pale face with green powder. Maybe I should do the same. Can't get any weirder.

Then she looks beyond me.

I turn slowly and see Joe and DJ and Tak and Beringer and Brodsky. They were with me all along. I must have thought they were giant crabs.

Saying I've been confused does not begin to cut it.

"Didn't want to interrupt you, Vinnie," Joe says as if speaking to a child. "You followed the grooves. You found it."

"Yeah," DJ says in admiration.

Teal blinks at them, then focuses on me. "Come wit' me," she says. "Afore 'tis gone, you have a see it."

"How'd you get away from the Voors?" I ask.

She shakes her head.

"Some are dead," I say.

"I know. One would ha been a new husband. But he didna feel it. The ot'er life did not take. And I didna want t'at, with him na brushing old trut'…"

Even befuddled, I realize this is a new version of her story. Which do I believe?

"Other life?" I ask.

She takes my hand.

Jesus! Her touch fills my head with sparks. She whispers in my ear. "You are *t'ere*, you feel it, doan you?"

"Yeah. Maybe." I can sort of see Joe in my peripheral vision. The others: not at all.

"Go ahead," Joe says distantly. "We're with you."

Maybe they are, maybe they aren't.

Teal walks beside me into the largest chamber in the Drifter: the Church, the void. Scattered strings of star lights glow along the outer wall, profiling one side of what might be a shaft hundreds of meters high—a great cylinder. Someone has raised nine or ten of the miners' wide work light panels on tall tripods and connected them to the Drifter's hydro power through thick cables. Teal walks from one panel to the next and switches the lights on, and now I see the galleries hewn high in the metal walls, all the way to the top.

The void, the Church, is like an inverted Tower of Babel.

The last thing that catches my eye, oddly, is the most

startling and prominent, as if I've seen it so often before it can be ignored—but of course I haven't and it can't.

A pillar of glittering crystals rises through the center of the Church, big, though not nearly as large as the one in my waking dream—my green tea dream—and broken, cracked all over. The pillar is held by embracing spars of rock left in place, but also by hanging nets of interlinked tubules like those making up the kobolds, only thicker. Basic units of construction. Tinkertoys.

The void is the center, the focus of the greatest mining operation in the Drifter: a carved-out and liberated pillar of something like living diamond—a diamond skyscraper, struggling to restore and remake itself after billions of years of being trapped, encased in stone and lava and metal.

And now I can see the connection. The big story.

This pillar, like the one in my vision, oozes a glistening gelatin that slides down around the supports and braces, cascades slowly from level to level, pooling near the base—where unfinished kobolds stir sluggishly, trying out new connections, apparently without direction. Some, however, have begun a laborious journey back up the braces, climbing with agonizing slowness to become part of the thing that will eventually surround the pillar and reinforce the mined-out galleries, filling the deep heart—or mind—of the Drifter. Recreating the immense crystal pillar in those ancient, ice-roofed seas.

The green powder lies thick all over. It forms a thin scum on the churning slime. Maybe the powder *comes* from the slime.

For a crazy moment, a panicked resistance sets in; all my training and paranoia and battle fatigue and all the bad shit a Skyrine falls heir to rises up like a twister filled with knives and all I can think is that somehow the Antags have drugged me, drugged us all, or maybe command drugged the Cosmoline, and some unknown new enemy (maybe we're our own enemy) has infiltrated the Drifter to create a literal fifth column, some-thing big and awful and nasty-subversive...Something that if it is allowed to complete its work will spell the end of all that we fight for.

But none of that makes sense.

I'm caught between competing indoctrinations, competing information, and I drop to my knees in the glare of a work light panel, shade my eyes, and look high into the void to try to find that other life again.

The life that had purpose and majesty, yet is now gone.

"Very, very old," Teal says, getting down on her knees beside me. "Te moon fell on Mars in pieces, long ago. T'is wor one of te pieces. Te Algerians and t'en te Voors part mined it out but at first knew not'ing...T'en te Voors found te Church, but broke a dike and let flow wild te hobo, and when t'ey fled, te old crys-tals had years and enow water a shape old servants...First of the awakening."

"Kobolds," I say.

"After te Voors abandoned te Drifter, te servants dug and searched."

"The red and blue parts in the map," I say.

"All yes. In te beginning, Fat'er lived an breat'ed te green powder all t'rough te old spaces, blown up from te deep hydrau-lics. He had time enow a feel te ot'er life, time enow a guess what t'wor."

"He told you?"

"No need. He wor first gen. He inhaled green powder like all te rest...Gave him weak sight a life a te old moon. T'en, te Voors sent his first wife out a te dust. 'Tis why he went a Green Camp. Better t'em t'an Voors. And he fat'ered me. What he only slightly felt and dreamed slid deep inna my genes...and grew.

"But word got out. T'wor traitors in all camps. T'at's why te Voors came a Green Camp a trade for me. By t'en, te doctors told, te child a te exposed man and woman will be te one—'tis *t'ird* gen will grow and finish te big story.

"De Groot had only sons—said he'd atone for what t'ey did and trade for me. Wanted a see te Drifter clear, work it, use it... T'ought it would give t'em power over te Earth and over te Far Ot'ers, too. And maybe 'twill. But look...Drifter can defend*T* itself..."

We follow more cables, thinner—leads from Skyrine demolition packages. Explosives have been rigged around the bottom of the void, around the pillar, and even more hang higher up from the growing tubules and braces—dozens of spent matter charges rigged to expend their energy all at once, a rather impressive show of force—what our sisters carried in those heavy packs when they arrived, hitching a ride with the very folks who could take them where they wanted to go.

All planned.

"Captain Coyle?" I ask. Joe and then DJ are right behind me, listening. My focus is on Teal, but they're here, too.

"The Voors tried a stop t'em. Your women shot t'em," Teal says. "I saw some die."

Coyle and the ladies were assigned a special ops mission, a mission we were not privy to. None of us are expected to survive.

Teal walks ahead, crossing rock bridges carved from the mass of old stone, a kind of elevated maze over a slow lake of glass-clear, shining ooze, filled with half-made kobolds, rippling over a thick bed of glowing red and blue flowers, the foodstuffs and guides of my deep ice vision.

The old moon trying to come back to life...

Trying to *remember.*

Captain Coyle's wires extend across the lava bridges, to the other side of the pillar, where more charges hang prepped and ready to blow. Collapsing the entire void, possibly pulling the head and shoulders of the Drifter down beneath the surface of the Red, ending all the labor that the Algerians and the Voors had put into this amazing formation.

Putting an end to all the possibilities, all the raw materials, and why?

"Why kill such knowledge?" Joe asks. And now I see it, too. Knowledge more dangerous than opportunity and resource. "Crazier still, why kill *us*?"

DJ comes into my filmy sidelong view. "Strong tea. We've got it, and *they* don't want us to have it."

"Abody dinna want knowledge," Teal says.

"Which abody, I wonder?" Joe asks.

DJ's moved ahead of us, over a high bridge, but Teal calls for him to stop, holds up a finger, points out an extrusion from the base of the pillar: a dark, hard, shiny material we have not seen before but which has been described to us. Not rock, not metal. Throwing up a dark meadow of sharp spines, thick as grass, silvery black, translucent, at once beautiful and frightening.

The spines are *growing.*

"Te an*T*ent knows how a fight," Teal says. But the look on her face tells me she *dinna* know what this is, what it means, only that we should not come near, should not touch. She keeps us back, but DJ is already in the forefront and he stoops to look at the growing spines, then turns, rises again.

"Fuck!" he cries. "You gotta *see* this. This is important."

Cautiously, Joe and I push around Teal's blocking arms. We cross the bridge, extra cautious around the spines, around the dark, spiky growth, clinking and spreading through the clear, gelatinous lake. Where the spikes intrude the lake itself and the kobolds within are also turning dark, hardening.

"It's like silicon," Joe says, wondering despite the danger, the strangeness. Maybe the dust is slipping deep into his thoughts. Maybe we're all touched by the strong tea.

We're all turning first gen.

And then comes a soft, girlish voice, half hidden behind the extrusion, calling to us.

Asking for help.

Another few steps.

It's Captain Daniella Coyle. She must have hauled fresh detonators and another satchel of charges to this side of the pillar. She must have slipped and brushed up against the spines, or maybe they reached out…

She lies across one side of a wide arch of ancient stone, partly covering the satchel, hand grasping the straps to keep charges from falling into the squirming ooze. Her lower body, clothing, flesh, bone, even her sidearm, has gone dark. Shiny. She's turning into whatever this hard, shiny shit is. The silicon darkness is moving rapidly up her torso, freezing her one remaining arm, stilling her grasping fingers around the straps of the satchel, holding them in mid-twitch. Only her chest and head are left and she's having difficulty catching a breath. Her eyes are filled with fear but she doesn't seem to be in pain. Even so, she can barely speak.

Coyle murmurs, "Get me out. Help me up. Get me out."

The satchel and the charges have themselves become dark. God knows what happens to high explosives when touched this way.

DJ kneels close. He tries to take hold of her shoulder, but the spikes crawl up the fabric of her skintight, bristling toward him, aiming for his reaching hand, or warning him away—and he shakes his head violently. He's crying, by God.

"No can do, Captain," he says, but then his voice falls into soft reverence, and his next few words shape a kind of prayer. A soldier's prayer for a fatally wounded comrade. I would never have expected this of DJ but here he is, ministering, caring, coaching Coyle across the unknown border in a way that Joe and I could never manage: instinctive, inappropriate in any sort of polite company—divinely foolish.

"It's out of our hands," DJ says, eyes fixed on hers, and now she's watching him intently, like a newborn watching a mysterious father; his is the last human face she will see and know. "You're a very brave sister, Captain Coyle. Sorry I can't join you, not yet anyway. Soon though. We all know we're short. Just ease into it, Captain. Don't fight it, go with it. There. There it is. Tell all of them hello for us."

Then, gentlest of all, "*Semper fi.*"

Where Coyle has been touched and turned, little reddish lights move in the depths of the dark material, terrifyingly pretty, growing into beauty, like thousands of fireflies in an endless night.

Captain Coyle's last words rise through the Church, high, soft, even girlish, "*Momma! Momma! I'm not ready, Momma, hold me, please wait…Momma!*"

All Skyrines are children, before, during, and even *inside* the end.

Her lips freeze in polished translucency. The fireflies move up inside her neck, gather behind her eyes. Her eyes become greenish torches in the perfect sculpture of her face. Then the lights spread out, flow from her transformed body, back into the greater mass, the extrusion.

Coyle's eyes go dark.

There's quiet between us for the longest time, silence but for the gentle, slippery noise of wavelets within the clear, thick lake, and the light, wind-chime tinkle of the dark spikes as they strike and grow.

DJ rises and lets out a shuddering breath, then brushes past us, wiping his face, leaving green streaks across his cheeks, and stands with the others back beyond the maze of bridges.

Stands and waits, arms at his side like a chastened little kid in this old, old Church.

Far above, a hideous, shuddering slam drops onto our world like the stomp of a giant boot. The high pillar vibrates, making the supports flex and squeak; bits of crystal shatter away and strike the upper galleries, plash into the lake, scatter in bright pieces across the maze of stone bridges.

"Right," Joe says. "We're done here."

And that's it, we're off.

LARGER ISSUES

Out on the Red, surrounded by Antags, in a dust storm and in your pajamas," Alice says. "And yet…here you are. Un-fucking-believable."

"Yeah," I say, still not back from the last of Captain Coyle.

We're driving north on 5, ten lanes, crossing wide new bridges, between wide farm fields and lumber yards and casinos and outlet malls, stuff that's been here for decades, not looking very futuristic, looking damned old and traditional in fact.

Alice adds, "I believe almost anything nowadays. Like, I can almost believe you and Teal will get together and she'll pup out a litter of lobsters."

"That's disgusting," I say.

"Really?" She watches me.

"Not the way it works."

"How do you know?"

"They're gone. They're dead…billions of years gone. They aren't coming back, not like that."

"What do you feel now?" Alice asks. "Still having visions?"

I wonder whether all this talk has done either of us any good.

And why she's indulged me. I could not possibly explain most of it to her.

"No," I say. "Not strong ones, anyway. It just messes with me in general. I don't know where I am, so I don't know *who* I am."

"What was their plan, then? For third gen?"

"Knowledge. Wisdom. I don't know."

"What if somebody *does* know but doesn't want it to happen? Doesn't want us to know the bigger picture—to get smart that way?"

I watch her closely. "We're not going to meet Joe, are we?"

"We are," she insists.

"But we're going to *Canada*. Why not just stop this thing and let me off," I say. Cold, calm. I've known, I've felt, I've *suspected*, but I'm still not decided, I'm still stuck between more than two worlds.

"He's *in* Canada," Alice says.

"Canada isn't signatory."

"True enough."

The driver, up front behind his plastic partition, looks back, checking up on us, making sure we're still okay. That I'm still keeping my shit together.

I am. God knows how.

"What's Joe doing in Canada?"

"Getting away from the bullshit," she says. "Must have been interesting coming back in Cosmoline. Sleeping one place... then another. I can't imagine what that was like. Thinking you were an ugly, shelly thing, out under the ice of an old moon. Wow. What happens when you get away from the green dust? Does it all fade?"

I'm feeling less and less at liberty to go on. I'm thinking of Captain Coyle and our sisters, those who were part of her special ops team, and how only two of them returned with us, with me, but not on the same space frames.

Joe and DJ and Tak and Kazak and Vee-Def, also on another frame.

Michelin and Brom and Ackerly and so many of the others...

"We've got half an hour before we reach Blaine," Alice says. "Canadian authorities will meet us there. If they haven't figured out it was you on that returning hawk. If someone hasn't alerted border security on this side. And if you want to follow through. Do you want me to explain what happens after that?"

"I'm no longer in the Skyrines?"

"In any case, you won't return to your previous life. But you knew that. You're smart."

"Captain Coyle...different orders. She was willing to kill us all. And die herself. Why?"

"I went through special ops training before I switched to medical," Alice says. "I remember Captain Coyle. A great lady, maybe the finest I ever knew in the Corps. There was a time when I would have done the same thing she did, followed the same orders. But then...I met Joe. He took the scales from off my eyes, so to speak. Not to cast any aspersion on scales, shells, crab eyes, whatever. Whatever you feel you are now."

Is this odd and variable and now crude and insulting woman playing with me? Testing me? Making sure I know my own mind?

Or have a mind, *any* mind, to know?

"*One question you should ask,*" Teal said in the southern garage; her face was suddenly thoughtful, sympathetic and distant at once. "*How t'is strong tea, as you call it, knows to fit humans? A just snap inna our tissues, our genes?*"

"You tell me," I murmur.

"First, finish your story," Alice Harper says. "Make it clear, cement it down. Then I'll try to tell you the rest. All that Joe has told me. All that I've learned. I need perspective, and I'm sure you can provide some of that."

MEETINGS, PARTINGS, SWEET SORROW

In the southern garage, Michelin and Kazak have run the troops through final prep for our sortie, our breakout maneuver. Mustafa and Suleiman, from Coyle's team, have wandered back, in shock—and been accepted, because I suppose nobody knows the whole story, or their story, and we're all Skyrines.

Or maybe it was because after they managed to recover some of their wits, they volunteered to go out through the gate, scope out the rocky harbor, and assess the fitness of the vehicles that didn't make it inside the garage. They rigged a kind of broom of old wire and used it to brush off the germ needles scattered out there, brush a clear trail; they did this by themselves, Brodsky and Neemie say.

After the special ops sisters returned, Neemie and Beringer stepped through the lock next and tried to establish a satlink. Nothing going. We're still on our own.

And so now we know. The northern gate is blocked by rubble. There's been substantial bombardment. Outside the southern gate all of the deuces have been destroyed. The Trundle was hit but there's a possibility one of the disruptors is still functional. Another Skell-Jeep seems to have survived and might still run, and two more Tonkas appear intact and not booby-trapped. The vehicles outside the harbor can't be seen through the blowing dust, which is still heavy enough it darkens the dawn skies.

Inside the garage there's the Tonka, with two fixed disruptors and a rear-firing multigauge cannon, the Chesty with its four Aegis 7 cannons and chain-bolt ballista, and two lightly armed Skell-Jeeps—kinetic rifles only.

Joe and Gamecock confer, tapping the lieutenant colonel's remaining energy to figure out how to move the platform's disruptor and its power supply onto the General Puller. The Chesty was designed to fight but also to tow and haul and do light repair. It has a folding crane behind the cabin and its own weapons that might transfer a disruptor.

Simca and Vee-Def think they can take the guts out of a Deuce's triple-rail bolt gun and mount it to the carriage of a...

I'm losing all that. Everybody's yakking. I listen, but I'm not getting it. Tak and Kazak are working hard and I'm doing hardly *nothing*.

Then Joe walks by and says, "We're all going to die out there. I'll make sure you mount some heavy shit before you expire."

"Outstanding," I say.

Teal watches this interchange with that same strange, beautiful calm. Second gen and now more days breathing the strong tea. Ice moon tea. Where does she live from now on? I mean, in her head, but maybe I also mean, on Mars as well.

Where does she go if she lives?

———

OUR WOUNDED—VOOR AND Skyrine—have been loaded in the Chesty's enclosed cabin, including Gamecock. Joe and Vee-Def and Rafe have made one last survey from the western watchtower and report the sky is still thick with dust and winds are up to two hundred knots.

Tak has taken a third turn around the rocky harbor outside the garage.

The Voors are quiet.

Teal: utterly still as she stands in the middle of the garage along with DJ and me. I hear the reports with half my head, half my self. I realize I'm standing beside Teal, not being helpful, and DJ is sticking close, like we're all separated out, quarantined; we are still smeared with green dust and after the reports of what happened to some of Coyle's team, nobody's at ease being around us. They think we've gone over, whatever that could mean.

"I miss my weird-looking parasite," DJ whispers, and looks at me with a smirk. "The one that sat up here." He touches the back of his neck. "Don't you?"

Maybe we do.

De Groot and Rafe tend to Gamecock but he's fading, getting worse, and his eyes show he knows it. Typically a mortally wounded Skyrine will not be allowed to fill a slot in a jump-up. Not be allowed to take up space in a returning frame, if there is one up there waiting for us. Cosmoline doesn't work on major injuries and there are no hospitals in orbit.

One major difference between Skyrines and ground pounders. Helps define us. Not that any of us likes it.

We have four who may not make it, including Gamecock, but we'll take them with us as far as we can. We owe them that much.

The Voors, of course, will not find a slot in any of our jump-ups. Even if we offered—and we won't—they wouldn't take them. Joe says they're getting their wagons back, those that still work; enough to carry their survivors to wherever they can go. Another camp, another settlement, if any will have them. De Groot works like a sonofabitch along with Rafe and two others, hauling and tending.

SNKRAZ.

Our plan is simple enough. We don't know what will happen when we break through the Antag lines, but attempt to break through we will—and dispose of as many of the enemy as we can. The Voors will follow.

Joe approaches Teal and then me and then DJ.

"I'm handing Teal over to de Groot," he says. "She can't come to Earth; they'd never accept her. The Voors will take her with them to a settlement. Rafe seems to think there's a chance Amazonia will take them all, if it's still there. If they can make it that far."

Teal doesn't react to this news. When Joe walks away to help patch skintights using Voor repair kits, she turns to me and says, "Come back if you can."

"What about me?" DJ asks hopefully.

"All of you…if you brush te ot'er life."

I can't stand that anymore, just so fucking *weird* and confusing, and so I walk away to join the others while Teal stands there watching us, beautiful, calm, scary as hell. De Groot can have her, I think, but I don't mean it. I just can't stand the thought of never feeling that touch again—that beautiful connection to something utterly beautiful and strange.

Teal.

Ice moon tea.

"We're not going to make it anyway, Master Sergeant," DJ says, noting my gloom as he walks beside me across the garage to our Skell-Jeep. "Question I have is, which heaven will we go to? Crab heaven or pearly gates?"

Our teams have assembled. We mount our vehicles.

The little side lock opens, Neemie enters and nobody bothers to brush him down because we're going to immediately shove out anyway.

But then he shouts, "I got satlink! There's lots of fresh orbital. Our orbital. Don't know disposition or tactics, but it's up there! Want to see what I got?"

We share, those of us who can. Some of our angels are still working but for most of us, the skintight charges are too far down, the suits too damaged, some of us now wear Voor helms, and so...

"Push out!" Joe calls. Vee-Def will operate the locks and run to join us when we've all exited.

Teal climbs up behind Rafe into a Voor wagon.

That's the last I see of her.

I'm on my Tonka and true to his word, Joe has assigned me to a multigauge cannon. DJ is on the second cannon. Michelin pilots. We have eight passengers, including Beringer, Brodsky, Mustafa, and Suleiman.

Vee-Def in the garage booth fuses a safety circuit and the main lock gates slide open together—inside and out. Air rushes by with a lion's roar. We're blown around for a few seconds, my skintight fabric ripples—our vehicles rev and lurch and roll. The engines all around grow quieter in the thinning air, but the Tonka's rumble still comes up through our asses.

And then we're outside, blind—flooded with the barely tactile whisper of a Martian dust storm. Mustafa grabs my arm, I reach over to Michelin, he slows the Tonka for just a moment—and Vee-Def runs out of the obscurity, leaps up onto the vehicle, and squeezes between Mustafa and Beringer.

The Chesty immediately starts laying down barrages right and left. Nobody pauses at the platform to transfer shit; we're already taking incoming fire, bolts, shells, and then a lancing disruptor beam plows the stone beside us, rises like an electric cobra, and shaves a curved blade from our right rear tire, which immediately digs into the dirt and starts to heave us around.

Michelin ejects the bad tire and it flies off into the swirling murk. Five tires is still enough. Four is enough, though the tail will drag. Three and we're stalled.

Once again, the dust goes purple all around with ghostly lightning, heavy, dull thumps vibrate us in our seats—something bright green and throwing out curling threads of plasma screams overhead like a ghastly firework, then abruptly descends. It misses us but the Skell-Jeep to our right takes the direct bolt hit and leaps in flaming pieces, bodies and blood soaring into the storm—

We're keeping to our course, DJ and I are laying down blind cannon bursts—taking opposite arcs right and left—the Martian wind is rising, buffeting like an angry, dusty ghost…

I'm definitely focused. On the Red now and nowhere else, in combat mode, stuck in this all-too-mortal and coldly frightened body, hanging on to the multigauge and my seat, knocked around by rough terrain, wind, concussions. Michelin's head jerks from side to side in the pilot's seat. He looks up over his shoulder in disbelief.

Still here!

We've managed to push about a kilometer from the Drifter. We can barely make out the Voor wagon ahead of us, can't see a thing in front, and then—

Air, dust, rock—all lift up behind and cast shadows as it flies over. There are four more bursts just like that in rapid succession. Rocks fall around—meters wide, bouncing and rolling, throwing up great gouts of shattered basalt and sand—and a Millie plummets out of nowhere directly in front of our Tonka, outlined in molten glow, tumbling end over end, cracking open, spilling dozens of weird dolls in jumbles of arms and legs all in the wrong places, all twisting wrong—Antags!

Michelin's arms wheel as he almost casually steers our Tonka around the wreckage and broken bodies.

Joe takes the comm: "Ants at nine o'clock! Prep sidearms—
they're on foot, fast and close!"

Now we're going to have our chance to engage the enemy at
close quarters. Pity it won't get reported, pity it won't get out,
what we'll see.

What we've already seen.

BIRDS

What *do* they look like?" Alice asks.

We're about fifteen miles from the border. Traffic is backed up; lots of folks heading north for vacation. Cheerful crowding. Canada's not signatory, but still prosperous, nobody's retaliating, Gurus don't want discord. Gurus want political stability while they dole out their technological gifts, so that we can head out to the Red and fight.

"Like birds," I tell her. "They were pretty thickly suited up. Long in the neck, wide helms, with a long nose—thick bodies, really long, strong arms, a kind of hanging sack below the arms."

"Like where wing feathers would hang," Alice says.

"Yeah. Maybe. But the eyes..."

I hear something above the light electric hum of the traffic. All these electric cars and it's so soft, so quiet, you might think you were out on a meadow with the wind blowing through the grass, that's what it sounds like on the road to the border, to Blaine.

But I'm hearing something more powerful, louder.

Higher.

Alice hears it next, and the driver notices as well. He turns around, and we can't understand what he's saying through the plastic barrier until he switches on an intercom.

"What should I do?" he asks Alice. "We can get off at the next exit, we could go inland, there's a—"

"Quiet," she says. She puts her palm to her chin and taps her nose with a manicured finger.

I'm looking up through the side window, straining on my seat belt, and I see them first. Four hover-squares, quadcopters in civvy parlance. Coming low over the countryside, the fields, the freeway, slowly swaying side to side, searching for something.

"Are they looking for us?" the driver asks.

Alice shoots me a querulous look. "Who knows you made it back?" she asks.

"Nobody, I think."

"The apartment's clear. Joe made sure of that," she says, more to herself, then back to me. "Did you walk from the mob center?"

"I walked. Hitchhiked, actually. A lady in—"

"Crap," Alice says.

"Nobody told me to walk all the way to Seattle," I say.

"No, that would be silly," she says in an equally low tone. "The one who picked you up—somebody from the base?"

"She said she was a colonel's secretary. Older gal."

Alice looks right at me; she hadn't heard that part. "Anyone else?"

"A short cab ride."

"How'd you pay?"

I hold up my finger.

The hover-squares have leveled off about a hundred meters on each side of the freeway and are running north in parallel to the stuck traffic, no doubt scanning everybody through the windows.

I lean back in the seat and close my eyes.

OFF THE RED

Vee-Def shouts through the roar and the dust, "That's our incoming! From orbit—they're carpeting the Drifter!"

Which is how we got through the lines. What started out sporadic has now become constant. Maybe it's for us, to allow our escape, maybe not. But for the moment, while we're on the run, the Antags are in total disarray.

We've gone four klicks. A long chain of explosions ahead of us has halted for the moment and seems to have temporarily put the Antag infantry on pause. Our tires may actually be rolling over some of them in their trenches. I think I see a kind of fountain in a gully, figures scrambling through the morning shadows and the gray and purple-lit dust. More boulders arc out and fall around us from the barrage over the Drifter—bouncing. I can see the Voor wagon off to our right, plunging in and out of drifts of dust and coiling, wind-whipped smoke, and I think I see Antags popping up like arcade cutouts between us, but it's hard to make out anything real, we're shivered by one concussion after another. Michelin is driving like a madman, veering right and left, and I barely hear him shouting in his helm, or singing, can't tell which.

Mustafa and Suleiman cling to each other. Vee-Def is huddled beside them, head down. Michelin and I have temporarily ceased firing the multigauges because we could hit our own vehicles, flying across the rock and dust, escaping from the Drifter.

Five klicks!

By God, we're going to make it!

And then there's this black thing right in front of us, so fucking big it blocks the Voor wagon, the Chesty, the Tonka. Like an entire ridge of rock just flew up out of Mars, only it didn't fly up, it came *down*. The impact throws us all up off the Red a couple of meters, and now we're landing hard, bouncing, and Mustafa and Suleiman have been knocked off the Tonka and I've been snapped out of my harness. I'm clinging to the barrel of the cannon, which is still hot, and my gloved fingers are starting to burn so I let go, drop slowly off to the side, land on my feet, just stand there, fighting spasmodic chest muscles to get my breath back.

A hundred meters of Drifter, a shard from the half-buried swimmer, the deep homunculus, has been lofted by the concussions and dropped almost upon us, and something in me feels utterly lost, such a turnaround from the exaltation of believing we might have actually made it—

All finished, ended, done with—after billions of years!

I don't know how long it's been, I'm rattled, but Vee-Def is beside me and amazingly he has his shit together.

"Sidearms, ladies!" he shouts.

And then the Antag infantry is up and coming at us.

I see two Skyrines running from the Chesty, which has landed on its side, and just behind them, a smoky wave of Antags, recovered enough to search around this side of the fallen ridge, and the dust storm has been completely interrupted by the rockfall, and I'm on one knee, aiming at Antags, hoping I'm seeing them clearly, not aiming at Skyrines in dust-covered skintights.

They're returning fire, moving in to clean us out. It's going to be close.

We're suddenly silent in our helms. No more words. Coordinated fire. I look left, cringing, just as Vee-Def's head flies off, right beside me, and the bolt that took it whangs and fries and sizzles against the side of the Tonka. All those bad jokes, those movies, now hot pink mist. At leisure, his body begins to slump.

My pistol is getting off bolt after bolt, and then, just as an Antag weaves to within a few meters, it runs out of charge—of course—

And I'm down to bullets, and then *they're* gone, and I'm down to waiting for one of the Antags to build up the courage to come in and grapple. Why not just shoot me?

Because the Antag has dropped its weapon or I can't see a weapon. Maybe they long for hand-to-hand or claw-to-hand or whatever, for honor, for glory. And then it's on me. God, it is strong! Those long, flapping arms and three-fingered gloves wrap around my chest, lift me up, and I see another Antag stand atop the Tonka, firing blindly down at Michelin, but Michelin is firing back, and that one topples, and I've got my own gloves straight on the Antag's helm, and I'm digging in my fingers, trying to grab and grip and rip, and I can see its face through the wide, narrow plate, above the long jutting of the helm, the nose, the beak, but mostly just its eyes, looking up at me, as it lifts me, my ribs starting to give.

I look *right into its eyes*. It has four of them, a smaller central pair, red and shiny, between two large outboard eyes, staring expressionless, but I've brought my pistol up and am using the butt like a hammer repeatedly on the plate, and then it lets go, but too late, I've cracked the plate—it has other issues to deal with.

And then I see two Skyrines come around the sides of the Tonka. One is Tak; the other is Joe. Tak is hefting a power supply that must mass two hundred kilos, and Joe's got the rail gun, wrenched from the Chesty, and they're laying down fire, clearing the area around the fallen ridge, the rock, which must have landed on a whole battalion of Antags, clearing a way, because they toss the heavy shit aside, grab me, grab Mustafa, who's still alive—Suleiman nowhere in sight—and we join Michelin and run, leap, around the right of the sizzling ridge of rock—crackling and splitting and powdering from all the energy unleashed by the blast that tossed it here—around to open dust and lava, familiar Red stretching out before us, air clear like there was never a storm.

We keep running. Running forever. I think Kazak may have joined us, can't be sure, because there's six of us running in a line.

And then we stop. We all fall over.

Into a gully just deep enough to cover us.

Instinctively, I roll and start to check integrity, first on my suit, then on the skintight of the Skyrine next to me, Kazak, and then I'm up over to Joe, who pulls me and shouts, "Keep fucking *down*," but I check him anyway, picking nits, social as shit in a chute, my eyes sliding into narrowing tunnels.

Joe grabs my shoulders.

"Hang on, Vinnie," he says.

"Sure!" I cry out. "Love this shit! Love it!"

We're all crying in our helms.

"The wagon," I say.

"It was up ahead," Joe says. "I think the rock missed it."

"Chesty got wiped," Kazak says.

"Sure as shit that rock took out the Antag line!" Tak says. We eyeball each other for a long moment, too tired to say anything. Then we flop back in the gully, studying the bands of dust that flow overhead like pink and gray rivers, and we jerk in unison as a stray bolt draws a sparking trail to the north, perk up as our angels try to come back online—flickering displays and crackling comm, voices out there, so few, far away—maybe from where we all go when our heads get vaporized.

We're back where we started. Before Lieutenant Colonel Roost, before the ranch wife in her buggy, before so many saviors—and who can expect another such round of saviors?

We've worked through our supply.

Power low. Maybe ten minutes of air.

If I slow my lungs down. Stop gasping.

Stop crying.

INVALUABLE

Alice and the driver have stepped outside. I'm still strapped into the bench seat, best place to be, because it's quiet in the van.

Seven men and women from the hover-squares approach us, weaving through the other stalled vehicles: cars, trucks. They aren't cops, they aren't MPs—the hover-squares are unmarked.

And now the seven are interested in the van.

COMING HOME AGAIN

Joe pulls off my blaze, grabs my helm, smashes the angel with a rock. He reaches into his pack and hands me the helm from a dead Voor, tells me to switch it out, put it on in the pop-up, discard mine—then get back to Earth as best I can.

"For God's sake, after all that's happened, stay away from MHAT," he says.

"Pop-up being delivered right now," Kazak says.

Joe gives me Gamecock's blaze and pins me with his own broken silver leaf.

"Aren't you coming with me?" I ask him.

"Right behind you. Second pop-up. I'm going with DJ."

"He made it?"

"As much as DJ will ever make it," Joe says.

So I'll come back with no ID or the wrong ID, which is not a problem, because the pop-up crew will pack us in and hoist us all to orbit, to the return frames, and the orbital crew will soak us in Cosmoline and send us back to Earth; that's what we can count on.

I'm going in and out when I feel a breath of fresh oxygen. My eyes stay open. I can hardly credit what I've seen, what Joe has done, but new Skyrines in beautiful fresh skintights are tending to all of us, to Tak and Kazak and DJ.

One sister leans over me—a lieutenant named Shirmerhorn. "Where the hell have you been, Lieutenant Colonel Roost?" she asks me.

"Mismatch on the DNA," says a tech with a very young voice. He lifts a bio-wand and shakes it by his ear, as if it might rattle.

"Screw the bookkeeping," Shirmerhorn says. "They won't notice. Rack 'em and pop 'em."

And so they do.

I've come through all this shit relatively unscathed. Broken ribs, a greenstick fracture of my tibia, a concussion, oxydep-burned lungs. A long session in Cosmoline is called for. Most of it will knit just fine on the way home.

I see Kazak and Tak and Joe and DJ lying beside me in their plastic tents, peeled out of their skintights.

Joe lolls his head. "You'll touch Earth at SBLM," he says. "Seattle was Gamecock's town." He tells me to go to the Seattle apartment, reminds me of the address—makes me repeat it. "Stay out of trouble. I'll join you as soon as I can. Lots to tell."

"What?"

"What it all means, asshole."

Tak's listening, lying almost on his side.

Kazak rises up behind him. "What the fuck are you two whispering about?" he says.

Joe smiles. "We're going home."

"If they don't pump bolts into our frames," Kazak says, falling back, ever the optimist.

"Vee-Def got it," I say, that image still searing. "He got it quick but bad."

"Listen close, Vinnie," Joe says. "This is important. It's why Coyle was out there, and why all the brass was out there, and I

288 | GREG BEAR

was out there, and why the Antags were out there, chasing us all. There's a bigger picture, and now you're part of it, get me? Lie low and just relax for a while, until we can all sit down, private-like, and talk about it. Lots more to come. I'll be back when I can."

"Back to the world where we can't say 'fuck,'" Tak says.

Joe has a funny story about that, and so, while we're waiting to be delivered to the pop-ups, he tells us. Maybe someday I'll tell it to somebody else. If there's time.

If I'm in the mood.

My moods are getting stranger and stranger lately.

OOPS

Alice and the driver are in custody by the side of the road, and the civvies in the other cars are watching, critical, irritated, thinking we must be smugglers.

"Did you bring anything back with you, soldier?" one of the plainclothes guys asks as he helps me down, very carefully, from the back of the van. "Any crystals—black crystals, white crystals—diamonds or whatever?"

"No, sir. No crystals."

They have a kind of plastic bag they want me to wear, so I oblige them and put it on. Upper baglike torso encloses my arms, no sleeves, but the lower half fits around my legs so I can walk. Even has a separate breathing apparatus. They load me carefully onto the back of a hover-square. The pilot looks back from the cockpit as I'm loaded and secured, then looks forward, touches his mike, and reports, "Fugitive retrieved. ETA twenty-seven minutes. Prepare Madigan."

Fucking Madigan. I don't care *who* hears me. I do not want to be laid up with doctors and needles and idiots who think I'm carrying something contagious.

Even if I am.

Joe had arranged that I come home as a different man. Relying on typical Corps inefficiency. Thinking I might have some time before the docs found out somebody came back who shouldn't have, who wasn't on the list. Who should have died up there, if Captain Coyle and her team had done their job.

No matter.

It was always a long shot.

I had a weird time in Cosmoline on the way back. Unlike most trips, I didn't just sleep it through. I did some heavy-duty thinking, and not always with my own, difficult brain.

With a new, strange, and friendlier brain.

———

THE FOUR WIDE blades on the corners whir their dusty lift, and we're abruptly up and out, flying over the farmland, away from the border.

My plastic bag-suit crackles as I move.

"Welcome home, Skyrine," says the guy sitting next to me, in his forties, graying, hard-muscled but bulky, eyes darting, fatalistic. Could have been a Skyrine himself once.

Inside the plastic sack, I reach into my pocket. Finger the coin, my Precious. They haven't frisked me yet. Teal also had a coin, given to her by her father—a kind of key to the Drifter. And now here's another key. Maybe that means there's more than one Drifter. Makes sense.

Lots of chunks of old moon fell on Mars way back when.

———

I HATE TRANSITIONS. Borders in time, in space, the thin lines between one state and another are the most dangerous. We cross two big borders in life, both equally difficult—being born and dying.

Darkness on either side.

I'm afraid, always afraid, of such thoughts, because I do not slide well between states—war and peace, happiness and grief, friends alive, friends dead. I watched a cat die once. It had been hit by a truck backing out of a driveway. It zipped one way, scared by the motor noise, then suddenly, panicking, turned around—dashed right under a tire. I kneeled beside it after the truck had gone. Last few seconds of life, it looked up at me in greater pain than I wanted to imagine, and then it just shivered and closed its eyes. That cat made the grade. It knew all about borders and transitions.

It crossed over without a sound.

I can only hope I will do the same.

For the time being I'm in Madigan, in a secure facility, with no prospect of going anywhere. But at least I'm getting three squares of hospital food, which is better than I expected, and there's lots of air and lots of water and no smell of pickle, and I don't have to wear a skintight, so that's good.

I don't know what happened to Alice. Maybe she's here, too, somewhere—in quarantine because she spent so much time with me. I still hope Joe will come for me, but that's crazy thinking.

Been doing a lot of crazy thinking since I was put into orbit and fell home. But Earth isn't really my only home now. I dream and think a lot of crazy things.

CAESURA

Okay, I'm ready to spill some conclusions.

Listen close. Tell this to Joe. He probably knows already, but maybe not.

DJ's strong tea, the green powder, isn't spores, isn't an infection of any sort we understand—it's memory. It's what the intelligences from the old ice moon designed their crystals to leave behind when the water runs out, so that kobolds can pick up the work later, when water returns.

But the memory dust affects humans, too. It slips into our cells, into our heads. We begin to remember things we never lived. And there's only one explanation for that.

When the old moon collided with Mars, eons ago, it must have dropped trillions of tons of ice and rock—its icy shell, inner oceans, and deep, rocky core—onto a previously lifeless Mars. The old moon seeded Mars. Rain and snow fell all over the Red until oceans covered the young beds of lava, and Mars came alive for a few tens of millions of years.

But some of that debris blasted back from the impact, far out into space, and drifted downsun.

To Earth. On rebound from Mars, the living things within the ice moon also seeded Earth. In part at least, we're their descendants...Open to the history carried in the green dust, heirs to all that ancient knowledge, if we know how to decode and restore what the kobolds have been trying to preserve for so many millions of years. The secrets of another kind of history. Knowledge, perception, judgment—primordial wisdom.

And the Gurus know it. They must have ordered command to send in Coyle and her sappers. That means they'll do everything they can to stop us. But *why*? Aren't they here to help? Maybe not; they're not from around here, this is all separate from them, counter to whatever they've planned.

What is it they don't want us to learn?

And I'm thinking, if the Antags came here strapped to an old chunk of Oort ice—what the hell does *that* mean in our big picture?

The massive Antag buildup, decimating the Koreans and the Euros and the Russians, then fidging our drop, tracking and chasing Joe's platoon—and meanwhile, slinging comets—maybe hoping to take out anyone who's been subjected to ice moon tea?

Settlers and warriors.

Is it possible *everybody* wanted to erase the Drifter and all it contained?

IN STIR

Got most of it down, including the stuff I told Alice. Packing it all away, sending it out. Along with the platinum coin. Madigan was reluctant to do a cavity search on a contaminated man, and when they got around to it...too late. Won't tell you how or where. But suffice it to say, somebody here at Madigan knows someone who knows Joe, and Joe is still out there.

Joe is legendary here.

A trio of doctors came to visit last Monday—Moon Day—and talked to me through my room's big, thick window. They told me I'm going to spend a few more weeks in quarantine, and when that's finished, they'll hand me over to the capable hands of the Wait Staff.

That could mean I'll be dead soon. Or I'll get to meet Gurus. If I live, I hope they don't mess with my memories of either world. But if they do, or I'm gone, and this is all I leave behind, think on this:

Titan. Out around Saturn, more than one and a half billion kilometers from Earth. Some of us have already become heroes out there. What kind of suits do we wear? Nitrogen and methane

atmosphere, mostly, with traces of acetylene and propane helping shape a billowing, yellow-orange haze over a plasticky, oily
geology rich with long-chain hydrocarbons—sitting on deep ice
and an ocean way beneath *that*, flowing over a weirdly uneven,
stony core.

Undisturbed...until now.

Old and cold.

KILLING TITAN

PART ONE

PART ONE

ICE MOON TEA

The hardest part of war is waiting. The boredom can drive you nuts. You start doing things like playing football with ordnance—I've seen it, lived it. Lots of casualties happen right in camp when there's no real fighting. Days and weeks and even months filled with nothing, then more nothing—the mad ol' ape inside starts to leer and gibber and prance—some of the best of us show signs of going trigger—

Then, WHAM! We're called up. We cross the vac. We drop. It gets real. All the shit happens at once, in a bloody, grinding flash—and if you live through it, if you survive with enough soul left to even care, you spend the rest of your fucked-up life wondering whether you should have done it different, done it better, or not at all.

All for glory and the Corps.

The Battle of Mars is over. I hear we won. Maybe so. But when I left, seventeen months ago, we had just had our asses handed to us by the Antags.

Some new and unexpected elements had been added to the

usual drop, scrap, and stain: a tall young dust widow named Teal, a fanatical clutch of settlers who called themselves Voors, and a crack Special Ops team whose orders included zeroing fellow Skyrines. And as backdrop to our finest mad scenes: a chunk of ancient moon called the Drifter, maybe the most important rock on the Red. Not our usual encounter.

When a lucky few of us made it back, we weren't celebrated. We were hunted down and locked away.

MADIGAN MADRIGAL

Since returning to Earth, I've spent most of my time in an isolation ward at Madigan Hospital, north of Skybase Lewis-McChord, sealed like a bug in a jar while the docs wait for me to sprout wings or grow horns or whatever the fine green powder that coated the insides of the Drifter wants me to do. DJ—Corporal Dan Johnson—called the powder Ice Moon Tea. Is he here at Madigan? I know he came back. So did Joe—Lieutenant Colonel (brevet) Joseph Sanchez. Joe told us all to lie low and stay away from the doctors and not cause a fuss. I suppose I screwed that up, too.

I sent out my first packet just two weeks after I arrived at Madigan. My first and so far only report—along with a coin that I found in the pocket of some old overalls I wore in the Drifter. I have no idea whether all that got back to Joe.

There's a lone fruit fly in the room with me. I've left it a piece of Washington State apple on the gray desk that serves as my writing table. He's my buddy. Maybe he dreams about being human.

I dream about being a bug.

Ninety-seven days. That's how long I've been here, with the docs filing past my window and telling me it won't be long before the Wait Staff comes to see me, and maybe I'll get to tell my story directly to the Gurus, really, and that will be a *good* thing; don't worry. Be happy. I've been debriefed and inquested and examined and cross-examined, from behind thick glass—squinted at from high and low by disembodied heads until they've blurred into one giant, whirly-eyed wizard.

One head rises above the whirl, however: high, smooth brow, impeccable English with a South Asian lilt, Pakistani or Indian, doctor or scientist, not sure which; soft, calm voice. Precise. Reassuring. Civilian clothes. Never reveals his name, position, or rank. He's talked to me, with me, five or six times, always with a gentle smile and sympathetic eyes.

My personal favorite. He's the first I'll strangle with my bare hands when I get the chance.

ONE FINE DAY IN THE BUGHOUSE

H ow are you today, Sergeant Venn?"

"Still waiting."

"I understand you've been brushing up on your Chinese. And your Hindi and Farsi."

"Urdu, too. Also."

"Very good. Your skill with languages is impressive. Better than it used to be."

"More time."

"I envy that."

"No you don't."

Without skipping a beat, he continues, "I am indifferent at Farsi myself. If you will allow me, I'd like to ask how you are feeling, what sorts of dream you have had since returning to Earth?"

"Weird dreams. I've explained."

"Yes, mostly—I have my notes. But I'd like to hear it again, in case we've overlooked something important."

"Come in here with me, sir, and I'll give you the details up close."

"I note your frustration, Sergeant Venn. Perhaps soon."

"You still think I'm contaminated."

"We have yet to determine anything of the sort. Still, you have described coming into contact with nonterrestrial organisms, including Antagonists. All by itself, direct combat with our enemy mandates a period of quarantine—usually, a few weeks in Cosmoline tells the tale.

"But I am most curious about this powder you describe, which you touched, smeared on your skin, inhaled—inside the Drifter. You say it was produced by a crystal pillar that rose within a mined-out cavity that the Muskies, the human settlers, called the Void, or the Church. You tell our doctors that the powder gives you vivid dreams, dreams of living in another time, another place. Curious and interesting. Do you believe these dreams are historical, referring to real events—or delusional?"

Like that. I'm in the hands of experts.

Fuck me.

———

THEY'VE GIVEN ME a paper tablet and a notebook and pen. No computer. No way to reach the outside world or do any research worth a damn, though they bring me books from the base library or a thrift store, old language textbooks and tattered paperbacks from the last century. I'm reading Elmore Leonard and Louis L'Amour and Jim Thompson, plus a few old novels. I've asked for Philip K. Dick. I've asked for Kafka. I've asked for T. E. Lawrence. No joy.

I'm writing again, but it's not like I own my life or this

story. Maybe the docs will come back with answers I can use. Right. Until then, here's what I think I know, on my own terms: the brew I've slowly distilled from my last deployment on Mars—a sour liquor of intoxicating fact mixed with muddy water.

But here goes.

A LOCAL'S GUIDE TO THE RED

A generation before the Battle of Mars began, settlers from Earth, Muskies, discovered a huge, mostly buried chunk of ancient rock. They called it the Drifter. They did what Martian prospectors do: scoped it out, found it interesting, and started to dig.

The Drifter turned out to be a piece of ice-covered moon that fell on Mars billions of years ago. Along with deep aquifers washing around its plunging roots and abundant reserves of pure metal—nickel-iron, iridium, platinum, gold—the Muskies discovered something else, something that changed their game completely: a fractured, battered tower of crystal hundreds of meters tall, from that distant age when the old moon supported an ocean beneath its thick ice shell. A sloshing, inner sea filled with life. That pillar seems to have been part of the archives of an ancient civilization that came to an end when the moon—with all its ice, ocean, and metal-rich center—was tugged from its far orbit, fell downsun toward Mars, and broke apart in the red planet's tidal forces. I can see it, almost, that amazing disaster. The huge fragments shaped a dusty, ice-fogged plume, then impacted around the planet like a short, loose whip—drilling through crust, mantle, even pushing down close to the molten core. The collisions happened in mere minutes but released tremendous energies, dividing the northern and southern hemispheres, sending shockwaves echoing, stirring up immense volcanoes—and adding trillions of tons of water to a formerly dry world.

The fragments of old moon brought something else to Mars. Life. And here's a whizbang conclusion to *really* dream about in the dark watches of the night—

The blowback from those collisions could have fallen deeper into the solar system and seeded *another* world, brought another dead planet to life:

Earth.

ANOTHER FINE DAY IN THE BUGHOUSE

Tell me once more, please, about the Drifter, Sergeant."

"I've told all I know."

"But *I* want to hear it again. Tell me about what the settlers found inside the Drifter, and what they did with it—and what *you* did with it when you got there."

"We didn't do much of anything with it. We were busy trying to stay alive."

"You didn't arrange to bring back samples?"

"Fuck no."

"Please. We're on Earth now. What about your fellow Skyrines? Did they bring back materials?"

"Not that I know about. I've said this over and over…"

"Please be patient. We're being patient with you."

All behind the glass.

BUNDLES OF TROUBLE

Through their chosen human interpreters, the Gurus made it clear to the people of Earth what would happen if we let our mutual enemy, the Antags, have their way with the solar system. The Gurus told us it had happened many times before, and that the ultimate result would be the conversion of every planet, every moon, every asteroid, into raw materials out of which Antag engineers would assemble a kind of gigantic clockwork for harnessing the sun's energy, and then would convert the sun itself—said energy to be shipped thousands of light years, through means not revealed, to power other star systems and to further promote the conquest of other planets around other suns....

Boosting their geometrically accelerating plans for conquest of the galaxy.

Bottom line, if we do not hold them on Mars, they will drop toward the Earth and our system will quickly become a weird clockwork of rotating wire, armillary rings, vast complex mirrors redirecting the sun's light and heat into absorption dishes wider than Jupiter...which will then beam it someplace else through I don't know what method, maybe an opening in the fabric of space-time, maybe just shooting it at light speed to someplace special—

Could be the Gurus don't want to explain further for fear of scaring us silly. If you know you can't win, you don't fight, you give up, right? We have to be able to believe that victory is possible, with a little help now and then from the Gurus. Real super-science stuff, like spent matter drives and suppressors and disruptors—even the Cosmoline in which Skyrines are packed while flying transvac, so beloved by the Corps. Most Skyrines accept this hook, line, and radar dish because it's kind of exciting. Makes us part of a big picture, fighters in a just and necessary war.

But after a few days on the Red, and especially when our drop is fucked, questions can arise among even our densest warriors, given time to think things through. I'd like to meet an Antag someday away from a battle, on equal, unarmed terms, buy him a Romulan ale, and ask him or her, or it, friendly-like, what the fuck do they tell *you* to keep you climbing into your ships and shuttling down to Mars or Titan?

Because up until just recently, when we crawled into our space frames and made the long journey for this campaign, we were *winning*.

We were sure of that.

Now...

I'm out of the whole fucking mess. Locked in my room, going nuttier than I remember being before—and nutty on two worlds, because my *other* self, the self that returns when I'm asleep and keeps trying to remember that old ice moon,

keeps trying to bring back a lifetime billions of years gone—
that carapace-coated asshole is every bit as bored and crazy as
me, with even more reason.

To add convincing detail, the bug in my dreams, he or it,
comes in two parts—an ornately figured parasitic passenger
riding a great big, ugly sonofabitch, hanging on just behind
a triad of compound eyes. I don't know which one does the
steering. Maybe they trade off.

At any rate, just when I think I understand those amazing
memories and thoughts and opinions—just when I want to
tell other people the truth about that other, ancient world—

It all lifts up, turns sideways, shoots away.

Whoosh.

DAY 98

ask for—and to my surprise receive—books on planetary science. No Internet. Just books, and while books are good—some are great—I've got big questions about what's really out there that the old books don't answer.

If what's in my head is real, then what kind of real is it? Dead and long past, or present and threatening? Am I communicating with actual intelligences, somehow still alive, still active, after billions of years? Not easy questions, and no easy answers.

My questions began about the time I returned from the Red to Skybase Lewis-McCord and hitched a ride with a colonel's secretary, and she told me there was fighting on Titan, way out around Saturn—that she had lost a son out there—

And I felt the truth of it.

For weeks now, I've been curious about old moons. Especially the big moon families that circle the outer gas giants. The Saturn system is the most spectacular, but to me, all the old moons seem important if I'm going to solve the puzzles that keep me awake all night. I don't know where I am. I mean, I know I'm back on Earth…

But I don't know *who* I am.

Who is back on Earth? Just me?

There must be enough value to somebody that the wizards behind the glass pass me old textbooks and feed this particular curiosity. But they don't seem willing to teach me more about physics. Still, it's good to get a change in my reading— away from literature and back to science. Whether I'm curious, or my inner Bug is curious, is a question to which I have no present answer. But I want to find out.

So I'm reading up on old moons. The books, being printed and bound and from the base library, are out of date. I can fill in some of the details by listening to Bug. Bug doesn't know anything about Titan, specifically, but it has a broader understanding of ice moons than the textbooks. I presume the inquisitors will eventually ask about my reading, what it means to me, what I'm learning, and what I'm adding all by myself. But they haven't. Not yet. My first clue that the forces behind my detention could be in deep disarray.

They still aren't asking the right questions.

DAY 100

Here's how I hope it will go when they decide to spring me. Some of the docs will realize I pose no danger. They will ask permission to enter the suite. I will say yes. What choice? Anything to get shit to happen. The suite is clean but every Skyrine knows how to make weapons out of common items and I've had lots of time to think. My plan will move to the next stage. Two of the docs will enter wearing puffy yellow MOPP suits. A Marine MP will accompany them, also in yellow, packing enough hurt to discourage bad attitude. They will suggest I stay back, tell me to sit in my best chair, then ask the same questions they've asked over and over. One will take pictures of the other—with me in the background. For this first intrusion into the bughouse, they will not stay long, but by God, they will put themselves closer to the war, to those far-off battles, to imminent peril—to *me*. That will accelerate their climb in the ranks.

I'll be so cool that frost will whiten my brow. I'll smile and nod and thank them for all they've done. Then I'll brain at least one of the bastards before they realize I've gone total trigger.

DAY 102

As if things haven't been weird enough:
Last night, Captain Daniella Coyle came to visit. She just popped up in my head. Coyle died on Mars, deep inside the Drifter—in the Church. Apparently she doesn't know that. She tried to speak to me. At least I *think* she did. What I picked up was like looking at an empty word balloon. She hasn't come back since. But I think she will. Captain Coyle was nothing if not determined.

DAY 120

I've exhausted most of the textbooks. Jim Thompson starts giving me the willies. So much thud-thud stupidity leading to so many dead-end alleys of despair. Reminds me too much of my own life before I enlisted and even for a while after. I switch paperbacks and read *Robinson Crusoe*, an old, safe book that arrived in my pass-through box as a split-spine Signet Classic.

As usual, while I read, I eat dinner off the steel tray—and come upon this:

> Let no man despise the secret hints and notices of danger which sometimes are given him when he may think there is no possibility of its being real. That such hints and notices are given us I believe few that have made any observation of things can deny; that they are certain discoveries of an invisible world, and a converse of spirits, we cannot doubt; and if

the tendency of them seems to be to warn us of danger, why should we not suppose they are from some friendly agent (whether supreme, or inferior and subordinate, is not in the question) and that they are given for our good?

IT'S A LIFE

Half-asleep, wrapped in my bedsheets, I feel a not-so-gentle prod deep inside my head, as if someone or something is rummaging in my attic and opening old trunks. I'm too tired and discouraged to fight it. Memories come back in waves. Memories that sometimes explain nothing—like random bits of beach wrack washing up on my convoluted shores. Memories that ride high in emotions, too.

Let's look at you and Joe.

Joe Sanchez and I had a long, winding history on our way to becoming Skyrines. To me, it seems he was always there—has always been there. But of course, there have been gaps. Some long ones—like before our first drop on Mars. I didn't see him for over a year, during the last phase of training. I thought maybe he had been selected out for special training, but when he reappeared, all was fine; he said he'd been hanging out with a lady in Virginia, while taking some OCS courses at VMI. I have rarely if ever questioned Joe's word.

And of course that last drop on Mars. He had gone ahead; we had reunited at the Drifter. No explanation there, except that our units had been reassigned at the last minute.

But there were also clear, marked-out moments that seemed like beginnings. I think on one now, lying back in bed with my eyes closed; I can almost see the lowering sun, the line of clouds hugging the western horizon.

The trestle.

The time Joe and I nearly got ourselves killed.

I suppose every Skyrine, every fighter for a nation, a polity, a socially segregated club, starts off believing in the purity and magnificence of trial and adventure. As a child, I sought adventure wherever I could find it—sometimes getting myself into real scrapes with danger and with the law. I was harum-scarum, reckless, but I was also pretty smart and so I seldom got into a fix I could not, all on my own, get myself out of. But on three occasions, before I reached the age of sixteen, I came close to getting myself killed.

Once, I was following a train track in Southern California, not far from where Pendleton still trains and houses young Skyrines. I was with Joe. I was usually with Joe when we weren't off trying to pick up girls, which we did separately.

Back then Joe Sanchez was a brown-haired Huck Finn kind of guy, a year older than me, as smart as I thought I was, and even more resourceful. We had known each other for two years, we were happy, we were seeking adventure.

Young men who think they're smart tend not to make straight, linear plans, but to engage in ingeniously crooked schemes and maneuvers, just to try things out. Just to test the world. That's their job. Our job.

Our crooked plan was to walk along the tracks and jump

out of the way as trains came howling around the far head-
lands, through a cut in the Del Mar hills—passing behind
Torrey Pines State Beach. We paid attention and walked the
tracks and jumped out of the way as the engines and bright
cars streaked past, though a few engineers were provoked
to let loose with that impressive horn and glare at us as they
flashed by in their long steel monsters.

But then we came to a bridge over the tidal inlet, a creosote pile kind of thing that might have been fifty or even
seventy years old, just tracks, no cars, no clear path for a pair
of reckless kids bent on a crooked lark.

We were halfway across that bridge, looking down
through the ties at shallow turquoise and gray water lap-
ping against the piles, enjoying the ocean breeze as seagulls
wheeled and screeched. Joe was grinning like a bandit, walking ahead of me, teeth on fire in the lowering sun, glancing
back and raising his arms as if he were a tightrope walker—
brown hair rippling, brown arms reaching—when about two
miles back we heard a train blat out like an angry dinosaur.

The engineer had glimmed across the low tidal inlet flats
and with his sharp eyes discerned two scrawny figures in the
middle of the bridge, with about a hundred and fifty feet left
to finish gingerly walking, tie by tie, balancing, trying not to
step through the spaces between—and the engineer had no
doubt, given the train's speed and our steady, careful pace,
that we had to speed it up, had to run along the ties like circus
performers or cartoon characters...

And then he knew what we knew.

We still wouldn't make it. The train would be upon us
before we could finish the crossing, and the water was at least

thirty feet below, with a two-foot shoal over sand and gravel and eelgrass to break our fall or our necks.

So we did what we had to do. We laughed like loons. The fear was amazing. We ran, no, we *danced* along the ties. We ran and stumbled and recovered and ran. We slipped—Joe dropped his leg between two ties—I came down off a rail, one foot in the air, and somehow, we both scrambled up, unhurt, to keep running, all the time crowing and shouting and screaming—Move, fucker! Speed it up! Speed speed *speed*!

I managed to mostly balance on the left rail, stepping foot over foot, the toes of my shoes catching my pant cuffs, like my own legs would kill me if they could—

And my friend cried out, his voice breaking shrill, "It's right *behind us*! Fuck fuck *fuck*!"

I did not look back. I knew what I had to do—this was adventure, scary but chock-full of living, the height of everything I'd experienced until now—it was *us* versus *the monster*, and the engineer was leaning on his awful horn and the air filled with the most intense, gut-vibrating noise I had ever experienced.

I knew that I had to jump and break my legs.

Or die.

Joe screamed again, looked back at me with the face of a maniac, and dove off the tracks. His legs splayed as he flew a yard out from the bridge and then straight down, arms wheeling. I lost sight of him when I jumped, but I didn't fall— I clung to the left rail with my fingers, feeling the polished, sunwarm steel sear my fingers, hot as a steam iron, while I nearly bit through my cheek—legs and feet dangling, maybe a second before the train's thousand tons of pressure pulped my hand and I fell anyway—

And my toes came down firm on a board. A crosstie. I could not see it but it was there—I could feel it. I let go of the steel rail and hugged a thick black piling, smelling the pungent tarry heat of creosote, just as the train roared over at forty or fifty miles per hour, wheels a few inches from my face, my feet trying to keep their purchase on the crosstie someone had so thoughtfully hammered between two pilings, but angled at a crazy slant, the soles of my running shoes hot and slippery from the steel ties, splinters driving into my palms—the entire bridge alive with weight and motor noise, rattling my guts and bones and suspended thoughts, rattling my skull and teeth while blood streamed from a corner of my lips.

The train took forever.

It was by me in less than a minute.

The horn stopped its insane howl.

The engineer probably thought we were both dead.

No matter.

All my muscles had locked. I wanted to throw up but there was still stuff I had to do. I punched my arm and leg to release their lock, then edged forward along the cross-piece, which angled down to intersect another piling, and then along a lower piece, balancing briefly between pilings, shoes still slipping (I never bought that brand again) until I was within ten feet of the tidal flow, and I just gave up and fell back, closing my eyes—

Dropped and dropped.

Splashed down hard in the bath of the brackish stream, the shock spread evenly along my back and hips and legs. Water filled my nose. Eelgrass grabbed my hips and tried to hold me under, but I thrashed and broke free, found the mucky bottom, and shoved up with water streaming. The air brightened with diamond spray.

Only then did I look for Joe. He stood about twenty feet away, soaked and covered in mud, eyes and teeth golden through the muck. Both of us laughing. We had not stopped laughing since we'd seen the train, except when we were screaming.

"Fuck! I SAW YOU!" Joe shouted, turning the expletive into a buzz saw. "You were like RIGHT UNDER THE FUCKING ENGINE and I could see you fucking *vibrating like a GONG* and then—you…you…" He'd swallowed a lot of water and was spewing it up, saying between shuddering heaves how foul it was. We pulled our feet from the muck and finished crossing the lagoon, then stumbled through saw grass to the gravel bank of the highway. There we sat on the margin and leaned our heads back in the last fiery glow of the setting sun, suddenly quiet, laughter spent.

"Nothing better," Joe said hoarsely. "Nothing *ever* so great."

We sat beside each other for long minutes. The sun slid behind the far edge of the Pacific. Mud dried and stiffened our pants. The chill of evening made us shiver. We didn't care. We talked about trains and bridges, then about girls and drinking and movies and parties, then about cars and how we were no longer alone in the universe, all that stuff, like we were adults, old wise men, until the only lights we saw came from cars rushing north and south and a high scatter of stars washed gray by the electric glow of San Diego and Del Mar. Mist from the lagoon cloaked everything.

By then we were so cold we had to move. We got to our

feet, shoes squelching, and walked into Del Mar—miles away, not hitching, just walking, drawing out our time of being alive after what had happened, clinging to that feeling that we had survived something amazingly stupid and really, *really* great. This had just happened to *us*.

This was *Adventure*.

Walking backward ahead of me, Joe looked up and raised his hands to the dull orange-black sky.

"What's it like out there, Vinnie?" he asked. "We've sucked this planet dry. Nothing better here, just more stupid stunts."

"Great stungs," I said. I had bitten my tongue jumping from the bridge.

"Great what?"

"Great *stunts*," I corrected.

"What's waiting out there? What's *way* out there waiting to happen to both of us?"

That was the night Joe Sanchez and I told each other we would enlist. We wanted more stupid joy and danger and the sheer, druggy rush of survival. We wanted as much of that as we could get, the real thing. Wanted it over and over. God, how I loved that whole stupid day and chilly night.

We were idiots. But we were also young gods.

———

I SAW THAT in an old movie.

Coyle!

This time the word balloon fills in. I roll over, look up from my tangled bed, and glare at the ceiling. "It was real. It happened to me—to us." I can feel her, recognize her—almost hear her voice. "I don't know what you're doing in here! You're fucking *dead.*"

And you're fucking stuck in a cheap hotel. But not for long.

That makes me angry. "Get the hell out of my head!"

And what is this about you and Joe and a mummy? That is just creepy. If you want original, you should see what I'm seeing. And by the way, I like Corporal Johnson better than you.

"You mean, DJ? Where is he?"

Then—Coyle's voice dusts up and away, before I can even decide whether I'm still dreaming.

DAY 123

The stainless steel shutters behind the thick window hiss and click and slide open. A new guy stands behind the glass while the suite's little buzzer attracts my attention. He's alone. He looks around, sees me standing in the door to the bedroom. I'm still wearing my bathrobe.

The new guy's in his late fifties, bald, skinny, with a peach-smooth pink face and small, bright eyes. He's something of a sloppy dresser and wears a gray wool coat over a worn green sweater. He fastens those small bright eyes on me and smiles. Pink lips, tiny, perfect teeth.

"Master Sergeant Michael Venn. Vinnie," he says, though nobody around here has earned the right to use that nickname. Any other time or place, I'd look right past him, but there's something about this new guy, like close-mortared bricks or a finely fitted rock wall. He's confident, in his element, with the creepy manner of a civilian who can make generals wait in the lobby.

I get it. I'll play along and see what transpires.

"My name is Harris," he says. "First name Walker. I'm not a doctor but the docs talk to me. They tell me they're just about finished with your CDE."

Command Directed Evaluation.

"Oh?"

He smiles reassuringly. "They tell me there's no evidence of a maladaptive and enduring pattern of behavior destructive to yourself or others. In short, you're fine."

"Why did the docs take so long to make up their minds?" I ask.

"The stories you told were interesting. Fantastic and interesting."

"You're Wait Staff," I say.

"Some call us that," Harris admits. He releases a dry chuckle and then his eyes scrinch down. "You claim to have been influenced by a green powder you encountered inside an intriguing geological formation on Mars."

"Not just me," I say.

"Right. Another soldier, Corporal Johnson—DJ. Pardon. Another Skyrine. We needed to check out the stories, and so we have. I'm about to deliver a report to a trio of Gurus. They work in threes, you know."

I did not know.

"They interact with us in threes, that is, to avoid making mistakes, I suppose. I've been working with the Gurus for ten years—eleven, actually—and I am still amazed by how little we know about them. How little *I* know."

"Inscrutable?" I ask.

"Like open books, actually—but printed in a foreign language. Well, our local trio has expressed great interest in your story, what you've told us. Our doctors and scientists have finished their analyses, and the upshot is—the final report is going to read—I am going to *tell* the Gurus directly—that nothing significant about you has changed." Walker Harris touches the bridge of his nose, sniffs lightly, and concludes, "You are not contagious. Never have been. Nobody should feel concern. The green powder appears to have been innocuous. Maybe it was just dried algae, residue from the attempts to fill the old mine with breathable atmosphere. Don't you agree?"

I don't say a word. Maybe they'll let me out. Maybe they'll let me get back in the fight. It's all I know, really. All I've ever been good at.

"As for the dreams you've been having, we've been tracking your thought patterns, even translating some of them, and I'm told they're vivid, imaginative. But your dreams are neither based in mental disorder or referential to another reality. Certainly not an ancient moon's reality." Having doubled down, he waits for my response. I give him a twitch of one finger, which he focuses upon like a targeting system.

That look, that expression—

Is this guy human or machine? I have to ask. But I don't. Could be *maladaptive*.

"Your time here can't have been easy."

"No complaints," I say.

"Remarkable presence of mind. Though I understand you've been visited by a friend." His targeting system homes on my eyes. "A dead friend."

This gives me a jolt. I haven't told any of the docs about Coyle. My skin heats, my face flushes. Walker Harris watches with sympathetic concern. I murmur, "I miss my buddies. Nothing out of the ordinary."

"And nothing to be ashamed of," he says. "We remember our dead in so many ways. As for the experience itself… What little I've managed to understand of Guru metaphysics is a puzzle to me. They might or might not deny the possibility of life after death, but you understand—in *our* military, in our security forces in general, such an experience does not inspire confidence. Still, MHAT is prepared to evaluate and clear you quickly if it's just a stress-related interlude."

"Yeah," I say, "but I never expected a visit from Medvedev. Vee-Def, we called him. He hated my guts."

"Paradoxes and surprises abound," Harris says. He's giving up nothing—or he doesn't know. He's like a watchful barracuda, perfectly happy to find blood in the water; any excuse to tear me down and eat me up. I'm thinking maybe Walker Harris is borderline maladaptive.

"But given the trials you've been subjected to, and the length of time you've been isolated with little in the way of human company—and given that most of these contacts have been *scientists*…" Harris's smile could chill a side of beef. "I can arrange for all of that awkwardness to be ignored." His cheek jerks. He's lying.

"Good to hear," I say. "What else have you seen, looking into my head?"

Harris appreciates the chance to show off. "The compiled profile shows an intelligent and resourceful warrior with fewer stress-related issues than might be expected. A warrior who could return to service very soon and be a valuable contributor to our war effort. Which is entering a new and interesting phase."

"Titan," I say.

Harris nods with a tight little fidget. "We have yet to

broadcast these actions to the general public," he says, "but you've drawn conclusions from what little you've heard, and they are not wrong."

"How long have we been there? Fighting?"

"Two years."

Again, he's lying. Based on what the gray-haired secretary said to me outside SBLM about her son's death, I think maybe four or five.

"The Gurus must have given us new tech," I say. "Otherwise, it would take a decade for space frames to reach that far, even with spent matter drives. Out to Saturn and back."

If they come back.

"Very good," he says,

"How's it going out there?" I ask.

Harris purses his lips and presents his profile as if looking at someone beside him—a theatrical pose that tells me our little session is almost over. "Thank you for your patience, Master Sergeant Venn."

I approach the window. "I was told I'd be taken to see some Gurus."

"That meeting is not necessary."

"Pity," I say. "All my dreams, my other life—just made-up shit?"

"Pure and simple."

I manage my best boyish grin. "Good to know," I say.

"I suppose it does bring relief." With a ramrod break at the hips, meant to be a respectful bow, he motions for the shutters to close.

All lies and deceptions, of course. I know things I can't possibly have made up, things I learned in my other life, if I can just remember them clearly, make them stick down like wallpaper over *this* life; things I will apply once I get out of Madigan, if I ever get out of Madigan, if this isn't just a prelude to Zyklon B being pumped into my suite....

The rest of the afternoon passes, my lunch arrives on schedule, I eat and don't die. No poison gas, no quick and dirty end. The window remains closed. Another day passes. And then another.

Inside I'm buzzing. I know that feeling. Something scary incoming. I'm on the fork of two futures. In one, I'm dead. In the other, I would rather *be* dead. Balls-up or balls in a vise.

For a Skyrine, having any choice is outstanding.

SNATCH AND GO

I'm a light sleeper, when I sleep at all. Hours later, something jerks me out of a warm doze. The alarm clock on the bedstead tells me it's four in the morning. The door sighs and clicks.

Not the window shutters.

The steel door.

I push my hand between the foam mattress and the bed frame, wrap the improvised sap—a twisted bath towel with one end tied around a clutch of nuts and bolts—around my wrist and through my clenched fist, and move in a flash through the bedroom door to crouch in front of my reading chair. I swing the sap around and around. The lights blaze on. Blinking, I sway on one knee, buzzing with adrenaline. A tall brunette stands there, dressed in a green flight suit. She looks at me, at the dangling sap, then back to my eyes, which are vibrating madly. I can hardly see straight.

"You're kind of strung out," she says.

I raise the sap.

"Keep that, if it makes you happy." She points through the steel door. "Ready to get out of here?"

I remain on my knee, evaluating.

The brunette tightens her lips. "The Wait Staff ordered you to be killed. I'm your last hope."

My shoulders sag. I lower the sap. I have to chuckle. "Jesus Christ! 'Come with me if you want to live.'"

"Exactly," she says. Her dimples vanish. "Coming?"

"Shit yeah. Where to?"

"I'm not sure."

"Under whose recognizance?"

"Mine."

"And you are…?"

"Commander Frances Borden, USN, Joint Sky Research Center, Mountain View, California." She taps a finger on her watch. "We've got maybe ten minutes. Get dressed."

I pick my day clothes off the desk, shed my pajama bottoms, put on pants and shirt, and stuff the sap in my pants pocket.

"No jacket?" she asks.

I shrug.

"All right, then."

One foot after the other, more than a little skeptical, I walk behind the commander through the open steel door. There's nobody in the big chamber outside the black-barred cage that surrounds the suite, and nobody guarding the outer lock doors that keep negative pressure on the whole shebang. I've never seen all the shit meant to keep me sealed tight until now, and it's hard to believe one Navy officer could have arranged for everyone to just vanish, but we're moving smooth and fast. No guards. No alarms. Nobody seems to care. Scary, but certainly *different*, and for anything that's truly fucking different, after 124 days in stir—I'm game. I'm up for a change.

"This way, Venn," Borden calls as I lag behind, caught up in the drama of how important and dangerous I am. "We've got five minutes before this place screws down tight."

"How do you know about me?" I ask.

"You passed a tight little cylinder to a Corporal Schneider, who delivered books from the base library. Corporal Schneider passed it to me. The lab evaluated it, then sent it on."

"What was in the cylinder?" I ask.

"A tight little manuscript, and a metal disk. A coin."

"Did you read it?"

"I did not."

"Did they get to Joe?" I ask.

"How the hell should I know?" she says.

We jog past a reception station, through double glass doors, and outside the main isolation building. I glance back, of course. It looks like a huge aircraft hangar, big enough to hold a hundred suites.

Borden grabs my shoulder and points to an electric Skell-Jeep idling in a red zone in the front drive. No other vehicles. Nothing else even *parked*. Like a dream.

I stop, hands by my side. Only now do I reach into my pocket and drop the sap. It jingles on the concrete. Nothing makes the least bit of sense. "Just who the hell are you, ma'am? And what is this, a blind date?"

Borden climbs halfway into the driver's seat. Her eyes go flinty. "I am geek steel," she barks. "And *I am your superior officer*. Don't forget that."

I want to smile, to reassure her I'm cooperating, but her

expression tells me this is a bad idea. "Apologies. Permission to return to your good graces—ma'am."

She lifts her eyes. "Just *get in*."

We're out under the early morning sky: light deck of clouds, blinking stars, crescent moon fogged by high cirrus. The whole base looks deserted. Borden drives the Skell diagonally across several McChord-Field runways, over grass and gravel medians, between long rows of blue lights. Absolutely nothing in the sky coming or going.

"Why no planes, no ships?" I ask as the wind rushes past.

"Broken quarantine," she says. "Incoming load of hung weapons. Whiteman Sampler."

"Whiteman Sampler" was a legendary incident from ten years before, when a whole Hawksbill filled with spent matter waste destined for Whiteman Air Force Base in Missouri got mistakenly diverted to Lewis-McChord. And came too damned close to contaminating the entire Pacific Northwest.

"Really?"

"Take your choice," Borden says. "I don't know, they didn't tell me."

I look up, unconsciously suck in a deep breath—and hold it. We're not heading for one of the long strips where Hawksbills land but toward a cluster of five circles radiating from a shorter taxiway.

Borden thrusts up one hand and grabs my jaw. "Breathe!"

I open my mouth and breathe.

"It's going to be close," she says.

The Skell hums toward the northernmost circle, where squats a dark gray, bulky shadow. It's an old Valor—an antique V280 tilt-rotor, used nowadays only for training. As we rumble out of the darkness, the Valor whines and coughs and begins to spin up its awkwardly massive black props. Borden cuts the Skell's motor, slams on the emergency brake, and jumps out even before we stop.

"Go! Go!" she calls. I follow, but not too close, as we run for the descending rear hatch.

"Taking me to Joe?" I ask.

A quick hard look. We ascend the ramp. Palm leaves cover the rear deck, along with boot- and tire-impressed cakes of mud. Could have been flown up from California. Could be from Pendleton. The leaves and mud crunch and crumble as we squeeze forward and take our seats. The whole frame of the Valor vibrates, the cabin sways back and forth, doesn't feel reliable, doesn't feel good. Behind us, the ramp rises with chuffing, shuddering slowness.

I buckle in. "Something's screwy!" I shout over the roar. "You couldn't do this without major pull. But all I see is desperation."

Borden looks sideways. She doesn't like looking right at me. She's scared of me. "Smart boy!" she says.

From the flight deck and the copilot's seat, a red-lit profile turns and stares back at us—calm, cool. High forehead. Paki or Indian. My interrogator.

The chief wizard.

I lunge. Borden shoves her arm across my chest. "He's why you're here!" she shouts over the roar. "Right now, he's your best friend."

My tormentor languidly blinks.

"I don't even know his fucking name!"

"He's Kumar," Borden says.

I thump my head back against the rest. "Fuck this, begging your pardon, ma'am. Let me know *something*! Where are you taking me?"

Borden shakes her head. "Away," she says.

The Valor lifts from the ground—barely. My stomach doesn't like the suspense. Then the engines rise in pitch and the vibration smooths, the rotors tilt forward, and we're really *moving*, soaring lickety-klick over airfield, farmland, highways—mountains—above a big, ghostly, glaciered volcano, like God dropped His ice-cream cone—

The whole beautiful, wide-open world.

Despite everything, I have this insane grin on my face. Away is good. Away is fucking awesome.

———

AN HOUR IN the air. I manage a sweaty little nap. When I come awake at rough air, I sit up and lean to look out the port by my right side. More farmland and rocky knolls, all golden in the morning sun. The sleep has improved my mood if not my outlook. I look at Borden. She's slumped, also sleeping. The Valor shudders and makes a wide turn, and the rising sun blasts her with light. She jerks up like a startled doe and rubs her eyes.

"Good morning," I say.

"Coffee and newspaper?" she grumbles.

"I'll ring the butler."

I'm rewarded with a wan smile. She's rank and geek steel, but she's the only female I've seen in months, and she's not bad-looking. Kumar, if that's his real name, leans back again, surveys us with those shining dark eyes, and says, "Barring difficulty, we will take you to Oklahoma. From there, we will all transfer to another conveyance and fly to South Texas."

I lean forward and say, louder than strictly necessary, "When do I get to beat the crap out of you, sir?"

Kumar doesn't bat a lash. "No foul, no regrets. I'm way outside your chain of command."

"Wait Staff?"

"No longer," Kumar says.

Borden leans over, says, "He might make a decent piñata, but if you treat him right, he'll shower you with candy—no need for the stick."

This provokes a twitch of Kumar's lips. "I'll apologize if you desire," he says with that same slow blink. I think it over. Amazing how long-held emotions vanish when plucked out of context. I may yet beat the crap out of him, but for now I shift my shoulders and release my death grip on the seat arms. Breaking me out of Madigan could be apology enough. Everyone on this aircraft is taking a huge risk.

"No need, really," I say. "What's in Texas?"

"Blue Origin Skyport."

"Fifteen minutes," the pilot announces.

I settle in and look at Borden. "What's going on out there? I've been cooped up for months."

"Nothing you want to hear about," Borden says.

"I'll be the judge. Tell me."

"Everybody's happy," Borden says. "Economy is booming. Hardly anyone complains."

"The Gurus have asked that we offer up a new religion," Kumar says. "It's becoming quite popular."

Borden looks like she doesn't think this discussion is strictly necessary.

"It's not too bad, actually," Kumar says. "Unifying, really."

"Gurus want to be gods?" I ask.

"No. They insist that worshippers of this new religion respect all other religions. No prejudice. Choose and let choose. All equal."

"So?" I look between them. "How's that bad?"

"We are to worship the *electron*," Kumar says. "Apparently all electrons are the same, they just swap out around the universe, so the One Universal Electron shares all points of view, everywhere, across all time. Voilà. Deity."

"God is a minus," Borden says.

"God is a diffuse cloud, sometimes a wave, sometimes a particle," Kumar adds, sort of getting into it. "Physicists in particular are pleased."

"Wow," I say. "I didn't see that coming. They still hate us saying 'fuck' or otherwise disrespecting sex?"

"Still," Kumar says.

"So watch yourself," Borden says, expression sternly neutral.

"Joe had a story about *fuck*," I say.

"Later," Borden says.

In a few minutes, Kumar says to Borden, "Time to speak of Wallops Island. Before we land. Might bring some clarity to our situation."

Borden twists in her seat. I'm peering across her sight line, out the opposite port, so again she takes my jaw and rotates my head a couple of inches, then asks, "What do you know about the silicon plague?"

I like being touched. Not this way, but it's better than nothing. Long swallow. "Is that its name?"

344 | GREG BEAR

"Among several. Tell me."

"Sounds like what happened to some of our Skyrines when they tried to lay charges in the Drifter, in the Church. They turned hard and dark, inert—but with lights inside. Then the lights faded. Dead, I guess."

Or maybe not.

"Could it have been some sort of defensive mechanism?" Kumar asks.

"We thought so," I say, unhappy to relive that shit and be reminded of even weirder shit. Then I get it. The docs kept asking if I or anybody I knew brought back specimens from the Drifter. "Wallops Island got infected?" I ask, looking between them.

Borden dips her chin. "Thousands of square kilometers are under quarantine. No flights, no entry, a tight cordon for fifty miles around the entire facility. They shoot and collect animals exiting the area, but there isn't much they can do about insects, the ocean…dust in the air. They're pretty damned scared."

There goes my Virginia Beach apartment.

"What happened?"

"Somebody on Mars bagged and returned a piece of the black stuff. Somebody else tested it for potency. It was potent. Now they're in panic mode. That's probably why you were scheduled to be executed." She looks to Kumar, who nods: She can tell me more. "They call it 'turning glass.' Sky Defense has canceled all transfers or drops on Mars for the semester. No more offensive or defensive actions."

"What about the Antags?" I ask.

"Quiet, but beyond that, nobody knows," Borden says.

"Anyway, the question you should be asking is, how far is this crap going to spread?"

"Turning glass?"

"No. Executing recent visitors to Mars. Quite a rift has opened up between Wait Staff and Sky Defense. And that is one reason why we're hauling you cross-country."

"I was once in command of Division Four," Kumar says. "Division Four went against the express orders of Division One and ordered your release."

"Good," I say, just to be agreeable. I haven't heard of Division Four or Division One, or any division, for that matter. "What are they?"

Kumar ignores me and looks forward.

The rotors tilt back for vertical landing and that damned shudder returns. My mind is going like I've just been dosed with post-drop enthusiasm. I think on Joe and DJ and Kazak and Tak and Vee-Def and all the others—on Captain Coyle and her team—all of us who were in the Drifter....I had been worried about the green powder. Hadn't thought much about the black, shiny stuff. I am remarkably dense.

"Touchdown in two," the pilot announces. "Ground crew wants a quick transfer. They're armed and anxious, so make it clean."

Borden tightens her belt and says, "For what it's worth, you'd be glass by now if you were contaminated...right?"

"Sure," I say. But I'm ignorant. Ignorant, unshaven, wearing rumpled civvies...I could be a paranoid homeless guy wandering the streets of Anytown, USA.

The Valor bounces and sidles before settling. We're surrounded by anonymous figures in severe orange MOPP gear.

Three big green Oshkosh fire tenders stand by, foam guns ready—whatever the hell good that will do. We run under the shadow of the rotating blades to another Skell—me, Borden, and Kumar. Borden advises me not to make any sudden moves. "They'll blow us off the runway if you so much as cross your eyes."

"Got it."

Our transfer is swift and clean. We pile in. Borden drives. I watch the nervous crews part to let us out of their cordon. Even through their thick visors, their eyes flash fear and even hatred.

An odd look crosses Kumar's smoothly calm features. "Getting interesting, Master Sergeant?"

"Yes, sir."

"That's what the Gurus like. They like it *interesting*."

Our next ride is a low-slung private jet shaped like a manta ray with a fin coming out of its head. On the fuselage below the fin I read *Blue Origin Texas*. We enter through the tail hatch and find comfortable red leather seating near the front, behind wide windows facing forward, not apparent from the outside. The comfy seats wrap around our legs and middles and cushion our necks. A sweet female voice tells us we'll be in Texas in less than forty minutes. Sounds too pretty to be real.

The rear door seals, the jet spins about, and in a few seconds we're in a steep climb. The jet is a drone. It feels smooth and expensive.

"We'll be hitching on a Blue Origin lifter," Kumar says.

"Why not ISD ships?" I ask.

"If you haven't noticed, we're off the grid," Borden says.

"At the end of all our careers, I'm afraid," Kumar says. He arranges his hands neatly in his lap. "But if promises get fulfilled, we'll get a lift to LEO, transorbital to a Lagrange station, and from there—if we're *really* lucky—a high-speed shuttle."

"To where?"

"First stop, Mars," Borden says.

I've guessed it all along—felt it in my bones. Back to the Red. Unfinished business.

"Courtesy of some very brave CEOs," Kumar adds, "a couple of senators, and more than a few generals and colonels."

"Sounds like a full-throated conspiracy," I say.

Kumar demurs. "Let's just say a number of us have become dangerously curious."

A little vanilla-colored cart tracks up the aisle and offers us coffee or juice. I take coffee. Borden orders orange juice. The cart dispenses our drinks in blessed silence.

"Mr. Kumar provided the Chief of Naval Operations with your evaluation, as originally submitted to the Wait Staff," Borden says while we sip. "Your psych chart has some interesting bumps. The Office of Naval Research put me in charge of evaluating those bumps."

"Arlington?"

"Right."

"Someone's skeptical about what the Gurus have been telling us?"

"Draw your own conclusions."

I raise my cup in toast. "They need you to find out why I dream about being a bug."

Borden shakes her head. "That is beyond my mandate," she says. "I was given another assignment. Not to beat around the bush, we hear you have visits from the dead."

I'm silent for a few seconds. "Walker Harris told you?"

"I don't know a Walker Harris," Kumar says.

That's about to drag me through another line of questions, but Borden interrupts, "Was your experience informative? Real-seeming?"

I look out at the pretty cloudscape. "No. Yes."

"Can you tell me who it was you thought was visiting?"

My throat tightens. "Captain Daniella Coyle."

"Were you and Coyle close professionally or otherwise?"

"We were in a bar fight at Hawthorne years back, some sister Skyrines and Coyle and my training buddies. She went Special Ops and we didn't see her again until she arrived at the Drifter with her team. They carried bags full of spent matter charges."

"Enough to collapse the Drifter."

"Easily."

"She turned glass? Describe that again for me."

Reluctantly, hands clenching, I recount the last moments of Coyle's transformation in the heart of the Drifter—the Church—in the looming presence of that crystalline pillar. The blooming spikes, the weird little lights chasing inside her like fireflies in a black night. "After that, the rest of us were in a hurry to get out."

"Understandable. Are you sure she was dead?"

"I'm not sure about anything."

Borden's expression stays cool and firm, but there's something in the way she moves her eyes, looking away, then back—her first tell. Psych evaluations are standard for Skyrines. Trips to Mars and back are expensive and the brass does not want damaged goods fucking up an otherwise orderly drop.

"I was in a transfer once where a Skyrine lost it after we entered orbit, in cleanup," I say. "He came out of the Cosmoline screaming, then started crying like a baby. We weren't told what the corpsmen did with him."

"I don't think that's at issue here," Borden says.

I shift in my seat. "Yeah, but what *did* they do with him? I've never bothered to ask, maybe I don't want to know—"

"Tell me what happened after you returned and were taken to Madigan. No diversions. Straight out."

This is it, then. It could all end right here. "And if I don't pass your exam—Kumar sends me back to the shithouse?"

"You've never experienced visions before? Contact with spirits, ghosts?"

"Not out-and-out. Dreams, sure, but nothing real."

She doesn't want to hear about dreams. "Tell me what happened when Captain Coyle visited you."

"It's pretty fucked-up. Pardon me. Crazy."

"Let me be the judge."

Maybe Gurus are watching everybody on Earth, writing down our stats in dense little Guru charts, and holding back is silly. And so I lay it all out. "I think Coyle was trying to tell me something...pass along some sort of crucial information."

"You could see her?"

"I could *feel* her."

"How?"

"Well, a little protective voice woke me up in the middle of the night and said, 'Captain Coyle is *here*.' It seemed surprised."

"A protective voice...War sense? Battlefield angel?"

"Whatever. Me and it are not used to having dead people show up in our head. My head."

"And then?"

"I could *feel* her, sense it was her—or a dream of her, though she seemed pretty real. But when she tried to speak, there was just this word balloon filled with scribbles. Like those wind doodles all over Mars..." This makes my neck hair bristle. I look hard at Borden. "A few days later, I could actually understand what she was saying. A real pain in the ass. But what's it to *you*? Why track something so crazy?"

"Corporal Dan Johnson reports the same phenomenon."

This is the first time she's mentioned DJ. "He's alive?" I ask.

"So I've been told," Borden says.

"He hears from Captain Coyle?" Coyle had told me she liked him better. Sometimes I have a hard time putting two and two together.

Borden nods. "Nobody has answers, but it could be part of a pattern."

"Do my buddies dream of being bugs?"

"Some of them, something similar," Kumar says.

"Wow," I say.

"*Wow*," Borden echoes dully. She looks out through the little port, angles her head to see better.

"We'd all like more clarity," I say.

Borden nods. "Yup."

I'd section 8 myself if I was in charge. "Maybe we should ask the Gurus. Walker Harris told me the Gurus might allow such things in their metaphysics."

"As I said, I do not know a Walker Harris," Kumar says.

"He claimed to be Wait Staff," I say.

"Other than me, you were never visited by Wait Staff," Kumar says.

"Well, that's what he called himself. And he pronounced me cured. Safe."

"Right before they finalized orders for your execution," Borden says.

————

A FEW MINUTES later, we arrive at a broad, tan stretch of long-gone prairie, sun high overhead, a few cotton-ball clouds pieced out along the horizon. The jet lands on a long runway and swings about to a small terminal. We exit from the rear. The Texas air hits us like a hammer after the cool inside the jet. Heat rises from the concrete in rippling waves.

A few klicks to the north, alongside complexes of support hangars and fuel depots, lines of squat, blunt-nosed heavy lifters rise from concrete pads like the columns of a roofless temple.

"One of those is our next ride," Kumar says.

We're met by a small blue bus. "Apologies for the heat, folks," the bus says; again, no driver. "Please climb in! It's cool inside." Not a human in view besides us. The entire spaceport seems to be automated, at least for this launch. Borden lets me go first up the step and into the bus's air-conditioned interior. I settle into a seat, looking around with that feeling of extreme displacement I've had since leaving SBLM....

I hear a low murmur from outside. Kumar is conferring with Borden. I can't hear what they're saying. They look serious. I don't care. I'm floating, in a way: a worrisome lightness.

"Good for you, too, Bug?" I ask my inner crustacean.

"Yep," I answer for the sublimated presence. "Pillar of fire, then orbit, and after that—we're going home, right?" I have no idea how true that's going to be, and how soon. "In your opinion, Bug, am I fit for *any* sort of duty?"

Kumar and Borden put their conversation on pause and join me on the bus.

OH FOR COSMOLINE

The compact passenger cabin of the Blue Origin lifter—accessed from a cherry-picker elevator carried on another truck—is trim and comfortable. Kumar peers in from the elevator door, observes as Borden and I are strapped in by our seats.... And then, a little awkwardly, he crawls behind us, barely avoiding my nose with his knee.

"It's been a few years since I've crossed the vac," he confides.

The cabin is too warm. Noises rattle up from the structure below—pops, clangs, something like a vat of gurgling, ricocheting ice cubes. All chemical. Hydrogen and liquid oxygen. Old-school, low pollution. As we're lifted into space we'll leave behind a plume of steam.

A ride up on a Hawksbill is a sweet, high-g swoop from the skyport runway, then—*froomb*! Spent matter boosters take us through eight g's to orbit in a few minutes. Guru tech aplenty. But here—no spent matter, no re-ionizing shockwave and sound dampers—proudly, purely human. Early century twenty-one. We had heard about some civilian launch centers shying away from Guru advances but never quite understood why, and our briefings never touched on those matters—any more than we received detailed briefings on Muskies. Not our concern. If companies want to be wallflowers at the Guru orgy, they have that right; the Gurus do not complain, nor should anyone else. Survival of the fastest, right? Yet here are twenty or more Blue Origin lifters, capable of running themselves and apparently in fine condition. Making money. Surviving outside the orgy. I find that reassuring.

The hatch seals. Lights flicker around a wide touch monitor. Another small, sweet voice instructs us. From side pouches on our armrests I extract goggles for an external 3-D view. Borden leaves hers in the pouch. Behind us, Kumar is goggled and smiling. He looks like a mad scientist.

The elevator pulls away and the hatch swings in and seals. Cool air quickly fills the cabin. I wait for the noises below to settle into a musical routine. A couple of seconds later, the popping and gurgling stop. Almost immediately, we hear a thin whine—pumps, I assume—and then a low, bowel-loosening growl. The candle is lit! We're enveloped by a ragged, powerful animal noise that ranges high and low, through bass and treble, into *power*.

We're pressed back, and in four smooth shoves, Texas dwindles beneath us until it's barely visible through a hot blue and orange corona of chemical thrust. The sky turns black. Old-fashioned is kind of a sweet rush. I like it.

But once the rockets cut out and thrust drops to zero, Borden decides to be violently ill. Kumar stretches forward, releases a convenient mask cup, and reaches around to press it over her face before she spatters.

I'm doing okay. I feel superior, happy—for about five minutes. Then it's my own dry heaves for the next hour. Borden starts up again midway through my torment. Humans don't belong in zero-g. That's why Skyrines soak in Cosmoline during the long haul upsun and back.

DAY ONE

Goggles tell the tale: Our lifter is entering orbit at about three hundred klicks. Minutes later, the lifter shudders and we hear another series of echoing rattles and clangs. The small sweet voice says we've hooked up with a transorbital booster. Borden is no longer sick, but she's irritable. We don't say much. A more gradual boost again presses us back. The weight feels good but doesn't last. After twenty minutes we coast. We've reached escape velocity. My stomach is done twitching. Through the port, I glimpse that we're pulling away from Earth. The motion is barely obvious.

"What next?" I ask.

"Six hours transit," Kumar says.

"Love these antiques," I say.

"You'll soon feel more at home," Kumar says.

Borden closes her eyes and takes a deep breath.

"What's our next ride?"

Neither will go into details. Maybe they don't know. Little tubes pop from the sides of the neck rests. I suck on mine.

It supplies a sweet reddish liquid. No food. That's fine. I'm not going to be hungry for a while. Borden's eyelids flutter like she's dreaming. Her skin is pale.

"Problems?" I ask.

"Nothing you want to hear about," she says around an acid *urp*.

"Try me."

"Too damned warm in here!"

"Shall we crack a window?"

She opens her eyes, stares about wildly, and fumbles for the belt clasp, but it refuses to open. This really pushes her buttons. Her hand clutches at the straps, then at her neck, and I get concerned. But she forces herself to relax. Takes another deep breath, this one squeaky.

"Enjoy the moment," I say, not trying to be cruel. "Try the little tube."

She fumbles the tube between her lips. Her cheeks dimple.

I turn away with mixed emotions. "Five and a half hours," I say. "Right?"

"That's all," she says around the tube. She folds her arms and keeps sucking. That's almost more than I can take. High cheekbones, deep dimples.

"First time?" I ask.

She pulls the tube out. A little red liquid sticks to her upper lip, like wine. "Obviously."

"Did you volunteer?"

"Yup."

"Why?"

"The Gurus have been lying to us for thirteen years," she says.

"Gurus lie?" I tsk. Still, the confirmation isn't pleasant.

"About everything," Borden says. "I've spent the last four years gathering evidence and convincing the right people. Now, I have to get up here and see for myself."

"Well, the Antags like to kill us," I say. "That much is true."

"How many Antags have *you* killed, Master Sergeant?" Borden asks.

"A few."

"Did it always make sense, the way this conflict has played out?"

"No war makes sense. Not if I read history right."

"You're invested. You're well paid."

"Could be better." I'm just yammering to keep her talking. She might spill facts I shouldn't know.

"They caught us in a velvet trap," Borden says. "We fight and die for a cause, we're paid in beads and trinkets, and we think it's a fair trade."

"Then why blow up the Drifter?" I ask.

She shakes her head. Maybe she's already said too much.

"Isn't that the heart of the argument?" I say. "There's something in the Drifter that neither Gurus nor Antags want us to find."

Another shake.

"You must have *some* reason to stay so close to me. You're not in love, and keeping me stupid won't help, will it?"

Her jaw muscles shape little ridges. I'm not making this easy for her.

"So…?"

"If I had all the facts, and proof of what I know—and if I could make it all make sense—I'd tell you. But what we've

KILLING TITAN | 359

put together is crazier than a sack of spiders, and twice as unpleasant to pick apart."

"Spiders," I say. "You have something against bugs?"

This elicits a weak smile. Her jaw relaxes. "You never said you dreamed about being a spider."

"More like a big crab."

"Not quite so creepy," she says. "You think you can see everything from the crustacean perspective?"

"Not really," I say. "All that is remarkably vague, for being so weird and important."

She's settled now and focuses in. "The Drifter. The crystal pillar. The green powder. The silicon plague. Your dreams... Captain Coyle."

"Not just delusions?"

"We don't think so," Borden says. "We've convinced the CNO." Meaning the Chief of Naval Operations—a four-star admiral. "And we're working on SecNav. Next up the line, SecDef—but he's Wait Staff."

I look to Kumar. "Tougher nut?"

"The toughest," Kumar says. "To the positive, the top brass and governments of three signatory nations seem to agree with us, as well as your vice president."

"Not the President?"

"He may be persuadable," Kumar says, "if we can bring back proof. And cancel out the messages coming from the Secretary of Defense."

"Proof...from where? Mars?"

Borden points up, around, shifting her shoulders. Then she slips on her goggles and motions for me to do the same. "Ready for something special?"

I goggle up but can't see much, so instinctively I strain against the belt as if to peer around a corner. The external cameras are still seeking. Then they find their targets. Below us, still only half visible, is a tight cluster of large, featureless cylinders. Tough to guess size from where we sit but the cluster looks about four hundred meters in length and half that across the beam. Larger, but not so different from the space frames they pack us into to go transvac. Above that, relative to where my butt is planted, rises the limb of the Earth, now slipping into night. I can make out southern India, Sri Lanka.

The lifter's voice tells us a passenger tub will arrive in the next few minutes to ferry us to our next ship, once the arrangements have been made. Boarding fees, tickets stamped, visas presented to the proper authorities?

Usually Skyrines crowd into a sheep dip station to get sedated by the transit crew, after which we're bagged and slipped into tubes. The tubes are then inserted into the rotating cylinders that make up the rotisseries. After we're loaded, the rotisseries are arranged by number on their respective frames, and that determines how and when we disembark and drop. Before that, we indulge in mostly blank sleep until we arrive. Warm sleep, some call it.

Now we can see what's on the other side of the cluster. It's something new, to me at least, and by looks alone makes my body feel numb and my brain more than a little left out of the bigger picture.

"What in *hell* is that?" I ask.

Borden shakes her head.

Kumar leans forward. "Some call it the Spook. Perhaps the prettiest of our new toys."

Spook—fine name, I hate it right off—is a triplet of very

long white tubes almost obscured by longitudinal sheets of glowing, pearly film. The sheets are attached to the cylinders and each other by thousands of twinkling strands, like nothing so much as burning spider silk. Whether the sheets are made of matter or energy is not obvious. All together, Spook—if it is one ship—must be over seven hundred meters from stem to stern. The sheets ripple slowly, like a flowing skirt in a slow breeze.

I've seen it before. But it wasn't me. *Coyle* saw it. Rode on it. No words this time, but she shares a glimpse of a line of soccer balls where you sleep on the way out to…

I desperately try to ignore her input. "How does it move?" I ask. "What pushes it?"

"She is called *Lady of Yuc*," Kumar says. "I do not know what makes her go. She has been traveling back and forth to Saturn, carrying soldiers and machines, for over five years."

Carrying Coyle, apparently. That means Coyle made it to Titan. Why return to Mars? Why not cash out and retire a fucking hero? I wonder when the captain will deign to fully manifest and completely clue me in. "Is *she* our ride?" I ask, my voice barely a squeak. Coyle aside, it all scares the bloody hell out of me.

"No," Kumar says. "Not this time. Perhaps soon." He gives his finger a twirl. We're still rotating. A shadow passes over our little ship as something even larger, *much* larger, passes between us and the flare of the sun. We're swinging into view of an object at least five times the size of the Spook, in any dimension—and vastly greater in volume, like a gigantic, silvery Rubik's cube with the different faces separated and expanded. Between these faces twinkles more silken fire. This cubic monster is at least four thousand meters on a side.

Our rotation locks, but one last wobble gives us a slender glimpse of what might be the business end of the cube. It's black, no details visible—shadow within shadow.

"What's this one called?" I ask.

"Some call it the Big Box," Kumar says. "Larger than previous versions, and special to Division Six. I know very little about it."

"Tell me more about these divisions."

Kumar turns aside and says nothing. He looks like he doesn't want to be reminded of something.

I look to Borden.

"Six divisions of Wait Staff report to the Gurus," Borden says. "Together, they carry out the Gurus' instructions, plan big plans, and interface with governments and leaders."

"What's Division Six?"

"Logistics and other affairs internal to Wait Staff."

"Mostly civilians?"

"Mostly," Borden says.

Kumar sinks deeper into his gloom.

"What kind of civilians?" I ask.

"Some were part of the original greeting parties, back in the desert days. Others were selected by the Gurus after the revelations, with special assignments and privileges. Division Four was like PSYOP."

"Oh," I say. "Who controls the war effort?"

"Division Four," Borden says.

"The war is part of PSYOP?"

Kumar closes his eyes and looks sleepy.

Borden says, "Yeah. All meshed together. Eventually, some of us got tired of our own bullshit and started asking questions."

"Enough about our questions," Kumar says. "All will be obvious soon enough."

I doubt that.

Hissing and clicking noises starboard. We resume our rotation. In the final quarter of our turn, with no more surprises possible this side of something really weird— hyperspace, electron spin space!—I see a much more familiar sight, three space frames tied to a big spent matter booster. Looks like we're in for prep tanks, rotisseries, tubes…

I let out a groan. *"That?"*

"Our troops are already aboard and asleep," Kumar says. "We'll join them in the next hour. If all things work well—"

"Which they rarely do," Borden says.

"If we get our job done," Kumar persists, "then one or both of those other monsters might join us and carry us farther out into the solar system."

"Why all the show, then?" I ask, trying to be blasé and not succeeding.

"Different kind of war out there," Borden says. "The weapons are big. Everything is just…big."

"What the hell are we up against?" I ask, glancing between them.

"Nothing much, at the moment," Kumar says. "Right now Titan is undefended. Few if any surviving Earth forces, and apparently no Antags."

"Something pushed a big button," Borden says. "A button marked 'delete.'"

"Or 'reboot,'" Kumar adds.

*"Some*thing?*"*

Borden lifts an eyebrow, like maybe I have an explanation. A *clue.* That really makes me sweat.

Our lifter falls into deep shadow. We've closed the distance and now we're linking up. More hissing and grappling. Long guide ramps swing around and lock on to our craft, and with a scrape like fingernails on slate, the transfer tube fastens around the hatch. The hatch slams open. My ears go through their usual discontent, and our seats release us with reluctant sighs.

"Time to go," Kumar says, pushing past.

Borden looks ready to be sick again, but manages to keep it down.

The rest is familiar—to me. Humans take over. Prep teams float us to a pressurized work tank where cordons of vac techs, hooked foot and hip to cables that run the length of the tank, administer injections and brusquely ask how we're feeling, in general, whether we've eaten in the last few hours, how much alcohol have we consumed in the last week, do we have allergies, have we experienced adverse reactions to Cosmoline?

The techs tell us to strip. Personal effects will not be preserved—should have left them home. Too easily, I fall back into the old, old routine. But it's brand-new to Kumar and Borden and they look like sheep being prodded down the chute to slaughter. Rugged. And gratifying, sort of. Still, I know nothing about our mission. I have yet to get my orders, much less any sort of decent briefing. We're heading somewhere—presumably Mars—and when we get there we will do *mumbly-mumble*—and then if that all turns out well, maybe we'll go somewhere else. Somewhere far away. Maybe on the creepy-looking, beautiful Spook. Or inside Box.

The cordon pushes the three of us along none too gently, despite the fact that for the moment we're the only victims in line. Rank hath no privileges here, and after the first few injections we're propelled by casual, expert hands toward a slowly rotating bank of transparent cylinders at the aft end of the tank. One by one, techs fold our arms and legs, tell us to hold still, and prepare to slip us into bags. A pipette not-so-gently squeezes past my ass cheeks and shoves into my rectum. A hydraulic mask clips over mouth and nose. Nozzles on the bag poke out to receive Cosmoline. With a couple of brisk pinches, a head clamp settles around my ears and I feel thick gel worm into my ear canals. I don't mind. I'm already dopey, feeling no pain and not much concern, except for the usual hope that I don't wake up before it's over. I've taught myself to play blackjack in my head, but pretty soon I can no longer keep track of the cards.

Then the old cool goop slurps into the cylinder and smears out against my skin. I smell cloves and lemon vodka—the usual. Soon I'm chilly all over. Then everything warms nicely. Warm and cozy.

Hello, sleep! My old friend…

Sweet dreams—long and dark and slow.

———

THE NEXT THING I know, I'm being decanted. My bag is popped and stripped and I'm hauled aside. Rough hands throw me into the car wash, where rotating cloths slap me awake and sponge off the goop.

Groggy, I look for my squad, anyone familiar.…Where the hell are they? Lots of faces! Grunts aplenty, and then I stop seeing triple and realize there's maybe twenty of us, male and female, several different races, about half Asian—all naked, tense, shivering, and complaining, some loudly.

I recognize one officer from training in Hawaii—try to recall her name. Naveen something—Naveen Jacobi. That's it. Slender, blond, close-spaced black eyes, corded shoulders and arms, long legs. Tough and distant.

One Asian is a Winter Soldier. Almost half of her body—one arm, one leg, half her head—is composite or metal. She's cut her hair to match the plastic fuzz-lines on her composite cranium. Her organic eye is wide and very black; maybe she's tinted the sclera. The fake eye is closely matched. She must have survived horrible wounds somewhere on Earth—maybe in training. We don't bring them back from the Red when they're that badly injured. She's sleek, shiny, modesty minus. She'll never really be naked again. Hard time peeling my eyes away. She sticks close to two females and two males. They fought or trained together. Typically, they've tattooed dead buddies' names all over their torsos and legs. Tough crew.

Also waiting to be processed are four males, two young and skinny and scared, two in their late twenties or early thirties who look elaborately bored. Small load. Peewee drop. Usually, each decant delivers two hundred and females fly separate from males, but we've been given special dispensation.

As my eyes focus, I see Borden join the lineup. She's five grunts away, beside Jacobi; the commander has nice but not spectacular breasts. Tries to cover her privates. Good luck with that. I turn to find Kumar. There he is—pale and pudgy. Makes no attempt to cover himself. Who the fuck cares. He seems just a tetch peeved, like someone's delivered his Scotch sans rocks.

More techs in padded outfits like dog attack suits move down the lines. Grunts fresh out of Cosmoline can behave poorly. Sometimes we bite. Anyone who misbehaves will be spun like a top and pushed out of line to a recovery team—which injects more enthusiasm—and gradually, if not under control, will be spun into another tank, smaller, older, smells different—smells less like Cosmoline and more like shit and sweat and despair. But everyone's tip-top. No wingnuts and no spaz. And so we're rewarded with skintights dispensed by another pair of techs, blank-eyed and long past weary of slapping and sponging and injecting—looking forward to end of watch, to finishing this tour and hooking up with the next return shuttle. Maybe they go easier on each other when they return. Probably not.

> O, *pass a bull to the butcher,*
> *Then pass the butcher your brother—*
> *Butcher takes care o' the one*
> *Same, same as the other....*

Old Corps tune. We like 'em tasty.

We're wedged into stalls. Two techs reach into a carousel and distribute helms. The techs help Kumar and Borden put on theirs; the grunts and I do our own, with critical squints and finger tests for seal flex. We work fast. The quicker we're down on the Red the better. We close our faceplates to test suck. Borden and Kumar get help doing that. Finally, all our elbows and ankles cinch tight. Diagnostic lights flick on beside each grunt. Next step, I'm thinking, a puff pack, another round of enthusiasm, then getting cannolied—stuffed into a delivery tube—and the big drop. Burning puff all the way down.

But that's not the way it's going to be. Not this time. Not

for Commander Borden, Kumar, or me—not for any of our grunts.

Borden grimaces as suit techs pluck us from our nooks, rotate us like bags of sawdust, and push us past a short lineup of impatient pilots and chiefs to an accordion tunnel and another ship. But what kind of ship? A passing, spinning glimpse through a narrow port shows us a command orbiter snugly secured to the accommodating flank of a big lander, side by side with an impressive transport sled strapped to another lander. Such lovely accommodations. Orbiters usually fly high, under threat of Antag G2O—Ground-to-Orbit bolts or other weapons. Even command orbiters are generally about half this size and never fall below fifty thousand klicks. By itself, our next ride confirms there have been big changes on Mars: total G2O fire suppression, apparent theater domination—

Or one of those big old reboots. Both sides on pause—Antag and Earth. Maybe we won the last round after all.

The weapons techs are busy finishing inventory. They look up from their slates, expressions neutral, but I sense their scorn. I'm obviously Skyrine—semi-shaggy fuzzcut, wide shoulders, a Virginia Beach tan around my arms, mostly faded—but I'm not dropping in puff, I'm descending to the Red in luxury. I feel like a fucking POG: *Person Other than Grunt*. Nothing lower in Skyrine hierarchy than a POG.

The burly drop chief meets us at the end of the accordion. Blaze reads CWO 5 Agnes Chomsky. "Twenty-three for command descent," her voice booms in the confined space. On seeing me, her expression sours. I've passed her way five times before. "Limo to the Red, ladies?" Chomsky grates, waving a big hand as we pull ourselves to the lock beyond.

Her smirk is a masterpiece of contempt. I glide past. "What, no tip?" she sneers.

"No tip, *Chief*," Borden says, coming next.

"None deserved, ma'am," Drop Chief agrees with no sign she feels the bruise. Her voice rises to crescendo. "*Move it out*, VIPs! Ten minutes to clear lock." Even the grunts wince. They're strapping on blazes, printed and handed out by the chief as she confirms inventory. I do not get one. Tourist. Fucking POG.

Kumar hands himself along a guide wire to the far side of the lock. Borden and I follow, then the first six of our squad— if they are a squad and not just random reinforcements. I note the Winter Soldier is named Ishida—Sergeant Chihiro Ishida. She's tight with Captain Jacobi and four others, including two sisters—Tech Sergeant Jun Yoshinaga and Sergeant Kiyuko Ishikawa—and two males, Gunnery Sergeant Ryoka Tanaka and Master Sergeant Kenji Mori. To me, they look integrated and aware, like they share unseen scars.

Jacobi seems to be in command of a highly trained squad with four snowballs, one truffle, and seven caramels—Asians who speak American with no accent. Our Japanese sisters go through hell in two countries to get where they are in the ISD Skyrines. Two decades ago, Japan fought China for three months in and around the Senkaku Islands. Thousands died. The old Bushido tradition was revived in Japan with a stacked deck of consequences. For these sisters, combat training of any sort, but especially in the USA—I've heard from the likes of Tak—makes returning to a normal life in a more and more conservative Japan unlikely. So they phase American, more American than me, probably.

And they fight like furies.

We pass through the lock in two packs. The passenger compartment of the command orbiter, a cramped cylinder, is grand by Mars standards but still no one's idea of a limo: a crowded, cold jumble of crew spaces broken up by surveillance gear, sats stacked like tennis balls in a tournament launcher, emergency pods jutting halfway into the main hull—but compared to a space frame, this is luxury.

"Do they serve tea?" Jacobi asks.

"No, ma'am," calls a hoarse voice forward. From between two pod shrouds, a lieutenant in pilot blue pointedly salutes as Borden grapples past. He watches with no visible joy as she inadvertently knees herself into a half spin followed by three painful collisions. Me, however, he tracks with a critical eye. He's a small, wiry guy with a trim shock of black hair, olive-colored eyes, and a softly drawn, mouse-brown mustache. His blaze says he's *Pilot: Transfer: 109—Jonathan F. Kennedy*. JFK. PT-109. Cute.

"Coming with?" I ask him.

He shakes his head, unwinds, and emerges. "Just next door," he says, and swoops a forefinger full circle. "I'm solo on the sled. They'll release me at ninety klicks, I'll spread chaff, see if there's G2O, then drop first. If I make it, you're next."

"Brave fellow," I say.

"Any clues?" he asks.

"I wish."

"Pure fucking snake," he says. By which he means BOA—Brief On Arrival. At least that's familiar. Kumar floats a few meters ahead, knees drawn up and ankles crossed in a kind of lotus. Drop Chief Chomsky emerges last from the lock and pulls herself forward. Her voice is almost gentle now; she's filling couches and assigning escape pods. I've never heard of anyone using a pod. Taking a big Antag bolt is decisive.

I have more time to check out Jacobi's Skyrines. Goddamn, they sure do look like Special Forces. They all move with a freakish physical poise that reveals absolute conviction the rest of the world is their own pre-shucked, swig-'em-down raw oyster. We have seven sisters and eleven brothers—four corporals, three more sergeants, three engineering chiefs, four majors, two captains, two lieutenants. As a full commander, Borden seems to rank. All the Skyrines appear totally down with the program, however unfamiliar and risky. Can't let Navy see them sweat.

The orbiter pilot, also in light blue, emerges from the cockpit after Chomsky has finished. He's a junior lieutenant in his mid-twenties, olive complexion, balding, bigger than the norm. He grabs a brace and stays to one side as Borden salutes in passing, then he lifts a lumpy, soft-sides bag containing the *real* pilot: a preprogrammed Combined Software Navigator: Astral—CSNA. These units are replaced by fresh tech every few weeks, hence the bag. No pecking.

"Welcome aboard, frequent fliers," he says. "I'm Lieutenant JG Clover. Our trip tonight nets you three hundred million bonus miles, good for a free trip to the beaches of Pearl-Hickam, with no return." The joke doesn't raise a grin. "Wunnerful audience. Please be seated. Separation from cluster in five. We'll be on the Red inside twenty. Drop Chief, cross-check and link skintights. We're on ILS for the remainder of our trip." ILS = Internal Life Support. Borden has been assigned the couch next to mine. Jacobi straps in opposite and introduces herself to Borden, then to me—meaning she doesn't remember. No matter. Officers rarely pay attention to noncomms. She's out of Skybase Canaveral and tells Borden this is her fourth drop.

"My first," Borden admits.

"Welcome to Vertical Limit," Jacobi says, then settles in, closes her eyes—clams up. No sense getting acquainted. In a few minutes we might all be dead.

Up front, the cockpit hatch is open. I see Clover strap in and expertly slide the navigator into its slot beside his couch. He looks back, flashes a nerveless smile, and says, "Release in two."

The hatch to the cockpit slides shut.

Chomsky calls out, "Suck guts and grab ankles, cadets!" She settles back, seals her faceplate, and closes her eyes. We seal our own plates, hook patch cords into the couches, bend until helms touch a rear seat pad, shove both hands between our legs, grab our curtain handles, and finally, lay thumbs over the plastic covers on the emergency switches—the diddles.

With a jerk, the couches whir and roll into landing config, spaced around the cylinder beside assigned pods variously at eight, ten, twelve, fourteen, and sixteen of the clock.

Drop Chief, eyes still closed, runs down the seconds to release. The whole damned orbiter makes scary noises, and they're getting louder.

"Crap," Borden murmurs.

I ignore the angel boot-up rolling across my faceplate. Focus on my gloves. Flex my fingers. Steady respiration, *in* one two, *out* one two. Even. Calm. God, I hate physics. From here on down, physics *is* God.

"Orbiter checks prime," Clover announces through our helms. "Sled checks prime. Lander checks prime plus. Release from cluster...*now*."

The orbiter shudders and lurches free. I feel motion along

the axis between my shoulder and my butt. I'm good that way; I somehow know which way I'm going just from sensing inertial vectors. Our descent is smooth, only a little buffet. Then—a low, piggy groan, filled with hypersonics, chords, nasty little demon tunes—

We tense.

And shoot off toward the Red. Our plunge takes five minutes. When upper Martian air begins its low banshee wail, I look left through a palm-sized port and watch the ionized glow, like dying coals, torch to brilliant cherry. Inside, all is smooth and cool and dull. Dropping in puff is so *much* more amusing. Grunts have all the fun.

"Down in three," Clover says. "Sled reports no G2O. We'll descend through our corridor until we pass two klicks—then hard DC. Stay strapped until I give thumbs-up. If we get painted in corridor, tug on your grips, flip the plastic cover, double press the diddle—curtains will drop, you'll spin into your pod, pod will punch free—orbiter will be history. Be ready for anything."

As always.

"Sled is safe on the Red," Clover announces.

Final DC—deceleration—rattles my bones like a cartoon skeleton. I hear the lander stage interact with the orbiter, loud squeals and nerve-racking *bangs*, like maybe it wasn't strapped on too well. Spent matter plasma retros deliver a final quivering kick up my spine, all the way into my skull—

Our backs and butts sink deep into the couches—

The lander shivers like a horse stung by a bee—

Drops a meter or two—

And settles with a deep, final crunch, like a boot stomping gravel.

"Beautiful!" Clover shouts over the mournful decline of the plasma turbines. "Exceptional if I say so myself. And I *do*." His relief is a little obvious. Follows ten seconds of comparative quiet while angels assess our health. "Will three of our passengers kindly remove their thumbs from the diddles?" Clover requests. "That's two demerits. We're down firm, we're alive, and better yet, we've been recognized by resident authority. Such as it is. Welcome to Mars."

The pods retract. Rope ladders unwind and fall down the core between the couches. I look at Borden and Jacobi, peer around my seat and along the pods—rubberneck fore and aft. Behind her faceplate, Borden is pale and shiny. Kumar looks asleep. Beyond them stretches a descending spiral of impassive grunt faces, all the way down to the Winter Soldier. We're all going to be great friends, I just know it.

Thanks for the excitement, thanks for liberation from Madigan, thanks for saving my life, maybe—but even with all that, I just want to know why the fuck we're here.

BATTLEGROUND

First we tap up from the orbiter's gasps and sips, each of us making sure we get a day or so if the welcome wagon doesn't show. We pass through the orbiter lock in phases and I stand in a group of six on the fenced-off platform between the lander and the orbiter, feeling the cozy warmth radiating from the lander's rainbow-scorched skin.

A metal ladder unspools and our group descends. I reach bottom, third in line after two Skyrines, then step back to let Borden and Kumar join us. Next group, and then the last, until we all stand on the dust.

Our skintights hold suck. Readout is optimal. The angel in my helm—quiet until now—perks up with a puzzled report that all is well but there are no instructions, no maps, nothing. As the sled pilot said, pure snake: Brief On Arrival.

I have to note again that I have never dropped like this in my life. All told, it's less exciting than aero and puff and no doubt more expensive. Plus sheer group suicide if the Antags are waiting.

I look through heat shimmer over the pebbly ground and locate the sled about a hundred meters off, still vertical and attached to its lander. The landscape is eerily familiar. Flat—monstrously flat, with high, filmy ice clouds obscuring much of the pinkish-brown sky and more than the usual number of dust devils twisting far to the south. I know this place. This is where I was hoisted from the Red over two years ago, right in the middle of a pitched battle with the largest force of Antags I'd ever seen. On the northwestern horizon lies scattered wreckage: Tonkas, Chestys, and Trundles broken and burned in a ragged line about a klick and a half away.

We're back on Chryse. Our dead are still out there. Hundreds of them. My whole body shudders. We'd just broken out of the Drifter, or what was left of it—trying to avoid flying, crushing chunks of rock as everyone in the universe seemed dead set on blowing that old piece of moon to rubble. We beat a retreat, leaving a lot of comrades behind. Skyrines can't bring back the fallen with the fidelity we once guaranteed our troops on Earth. I've said that before, but you just may not know how much it hurts.

I slowly turn, letting my helm map the local features. Angel also tallies the wrecks in the middle distance, those that can still be identified.

Borden leans in like she's going to kiss me and taps her helm against mine. "War grave," she says.

I'm too choked to answer. A lot of Mars is sacred ground.

———

FORMING A THIRD point with the two landers is a half-buried line of red-and-tan depot storage tanks, like those erected when a base plans to stick around a few months. Beyond the tanks are revetments like molehills that probably conceal fountains, used to draw moisture from the Martian atmosphere. But there's no sign of domiciles. Maybe they're dug in away from the depot. I picture the enemy sitting like Indians on the surrounding hills, but there isn't much out there in the way of hills, and as cavalry goes, our force is puny compared to the Antag brigades that once smothered this theater.

The Skyrines open belt pouches and strap on their combat blazes. I have no blaze but everybody seems to know me, like they've been shown pictures.

They gather around Borden. "Time to share, ma'am," says First Lieutenant Vera Jennings. Jennings sat to the rear of the orbiter, showing a strong instinct for self-preservation, however misapplied. I remember her naked—stocky, heavy shoulders, fuzzcut pate streaked black and brown. Sharp gray eyes behind her plate. She tries to be heard through her helm—she assumes we're in blackout mode. "Where's our camp? When do we get logistics?"

But Borden's comm pings and our helms link to hers. The Skyrines give each other skeptical looks. No blackout, no cordon, no sentinels—nothing?

Borden announces, "I've got daylight, just a little. This is a temporary resource depot, set up here to take care of us and our landers. Nobody stays long."

"Sappers?" Jennings asks.

"Probably," Sergeant Ishida says.

"Too exposed," says Tech Sergeant Jun Yoshinaga. She's small, so small her skintight has cinched up around her knees, but from what I saw during transfer—smooth, flat abs; round, tight lumps of shoulder; huge forearms but long fingers like twisted rope—I wouldn't willingly match up against her.

"I don't know," Borden says. She looks around as if expecting company. The horizon is mostly empty, but I can't see beyond the clutter of charred vehicles. "We're scheduled to rendezvous with friendlies. They'll transport us to a relocation camp, where we'll pick up additional personnel."

"Who's been relocated?" Jennings asks.

"Settlers," Borden says. "They're being protected by our forces."

We all note that she doesn't say Joint Sky Defense—JSD.

"You mean Muskies? Why?" Captain Jacobi asks.

"Muskies, as you call them, are the reason we're here," Kumar says.

"This is Mr. Aram Kumar," Borden says. "He's part of Division Four, our civilian command. I'd listen to him."

That's keeping it simple. The rest of the grunts turn.

"Who gives a fuck about Muskies?" Jennings asks.

"They may be the most important people you'll ever meet," Kumar says.

Jacobi puts on a wry expression and looks my way.

"We have three missions," Kumar says. "We are to investigate the remains of the mining operation called the Drifter and assess its condition. We will then proceed to the relocation camp and evaluate those individuals who have been exposed to the interiors of the old mines. And if there is time, we will organize a travel team to visit where mining continues on a second remnant of old moon. Division Four believes our work there is critical."

"Sir—Kumarji—what about security?" asks Sergeant Chihiro Ishida—the Winter Soldier.

Kumar actually smiles at her, perhaps at the honorific. "For now, according to our best information, the last of the

Antagonists on Mars have retreated to the northern polar regions. As for their orbital assets, they have either scuttled or withdrawn them to Mars L-5, shielded by one or more trojans."

No cracks about being shielded by Trojans. He means asteroids. Mars L-5 is the trailing Mars Lagrange point. The trojans—small t—are asteroids stuck at either the leading or trailing Lagrange points in the Martian solar orbit. I thought we had scrubbed them years ago—Operation Rubber or something like that. I guess not.

Borden extends her arm northwest. Four Skell-Jeeps, three Tonkas, and a Russian-style Trundle, a TE-86, have skirted the charred wreckage and are cautiously rolling in. "Those are for us, I think," she says.

"They don't look good," Ishida says.

We magnify and inspect. Ishida has at least one very sharp eye—all of the Skells, the Trundle, and two of the Tonkas have suffered damage. One Tonka is rolling on four out of six wheels, and the Trundle still smokes where something took out a corner of the cabin.

"They're painting us," Jacobi says. Our helms confirm—we're lit up. No alarms, however—friendlies, right?

"Hey, they've charged bolts and slung the ballista!" Ishikawa calls out.

The Skyrines reach for their spent matter packs.

"Don't charge, damn it!" Borden barks. "Keep your weapons slung!"

Slowly, all comply—against instinct and training. I look at Kumar to see if he's reacting. He is—just barely. His hands curl into fists.

"Fuck this," Jennings mutters.

Two of the Skells and the fenders of the four-wheeling Tonka are smeared with freeze-dried blood.

"Casualties," Ishida says.

Our group tightens.

"No Ants, right?" Ishikawa asks.

"Nobody make a move," Borden orders. "Let me do the talking, but stay on my band."

The roughed-up vehicles pause at fifty meters, then, after thorough inspection, wheel forward at the same measured pace. They still light us up. The vehicles are naked of insignia, not unusual on the Red, but I see the Skells are driven by Russians—helm colors and skintights obvious—and I see Russian colors moving as well through the narrow windscreens of the badly damaged Trundle and the Tonkas. My faceplate manages to capture and magnify a couple of their blue and gold blazes. Special Ops—Spetsnaz, I'm guessing Russian Airborne. We trained with 45th Nevsky back at Hawthorne—not always on good terms—and fought together during my third drop. I might know these guys. I itch to communicate and ease things back, but this is on Borden's plate.

Dead silence on the comm. Nobody looks happy—nobody looks like they know what to expect.

"*Cold and calm*," Borden says. "Do not stare, do not charge weapons or make a move to target."

"No, ma'am," Jacobi says.

"Don't even *twitch*!" Borden's eyes are like a hawk's intent on a distant mouse. Our unhappy grunts keep their hands low and weapons slung or holstered.

Finally, wide comm pings and Russian fills our helms.

A smooth, deep male voice identifies himself as Polkovnik (Colonel) Litvinov and asks who is in charge. Borden raises her hand. Follows a direct burst of data from the Trundle's laser to Borden's helm.

Borden visibly relaxes. "These are our escorts. They didn't get notice we were arriving until last sol. They've been traveling since. They were hit four hours ago, probably by Antags—about fifty klicks from here. Four dead."

That gives everyone pause.

"How can they not *know* it was Antags?" Jennings asks nervously. "Who else would it be?"

Jacobi nudges the back of Jennings's calf with her toe. Jennings shuts up.

The vehicles stop again. Polkovnik Litvinov steps down from the lock of the damaged Trundle and pulls a soft brown cap with a green and gold eagle cockade from under his right shoulder strap, then perches it atop his helm.

Borden crosses to meet him. She opens the conversation with name and rank, says she's glad they're here, commiserates with their losses. None of us have twitched but the rest of the Russians keep to their vehicles, ready to return fire if we offer any trouble—ready as well to depart in quick order.

"You are first in three months," Litvinov says as he studies the way we're grouped. Jacobi has spaced her Skyrines into five fire teams, weapons visible but not at ready. The rest of us hang apart, very still.

Litvinov's sharp eyes miss nothing. "We too are glad to meet. It is confused on Earth, last few months. I learn to pick and choose which instructions to obey. Not good for peace of mind."

I'm guessing the chain of command up here is missing quite a few links. I do not like this one bit, and neither does Borden.

"Sorry to hear that," Borden says. "Our primary instructions are clear."

The colonel points toward the sled lander. "Is that for us?"

"We've been told to make a delivery, yes, sir," Borden says. "In exchange for transport and assistance."

If they want what we have, and don't want to give what we need, things will happen soon and they'll happen fast. The colonel, however, walks a few deliberate paces away from the Tonka and toward Borden, putting himself in any feasible line of fire. "Yours is unauthorized operation, no?"

Borden keeps quiet.

"Division Four?"

"Yes, sir," she says.

"Important division—newly disruptive. Puzzling." He walks by the commander and into the shadow of our orbiter, studying our Skyrines. Ishida's mechanical arm is steady. Her real arm has a light quiver.

"Yes, sir," Borden says.

The colonel's a bold one. Passing me, he leans in with a wolfish grin. "Are you called Vinnie?"

"Yes, sir," I say. "Master Sergeant Michael Venn."

"We are Russian Airborne, Aerospace Forces, Detached—45th Nevsky. Do you recognize us?"

"Yes, sir."

"Good to be memorable. We are told to expect you—in particularly, *you*, Master Sergeant." Litvinov slings his rifle and cuts bolt charge. The Russian soldiers stand down. "We are to protect and deliver you to specified location. Mutual colleague pays respect. Says hello."

I ask, "Who, sir?"

The colonel reaches into his belt pouch and withdraws a worn photo. He holds it in front of my plate. It's Joe, wearing gray long johns but apparently none the worse for wear. He seems to be standing inside a cluttered, crowded domicile, and looks apprehensive but not under duress. Joe just doesn't like having his picture taken, underwear or no. He's beside someone so tall her head almost doesn't fit in the photo. Someone I've been thinking about ever since I departed Mars. Tealullah Mackenzie Green.

Teal.

Borden and Kumar step in to peer at the colonel's picture. Kumar nods to Borden.

"You recognize?" the colonel asks me.

"My friends," I say.

He pockets the photo and examines my face behind the plate. His eyes are determined, sad. "They are twelve hours away, if we encounter no other setbacks. Which one is Skyfolk agent, Guru man name of Aram Kumar?"

Kumar says that's him. The colonel compares Kumar's face with another photo extracted from the same pouch. "Our orders were to come to site of previous hero action, where depot has been dropped months past, with fountains to collect fuel. Here, the orders say, we will take passengers, reinforcements, and supplies. Yet why drop depot so far out there, I ask? And I am told, to allow passengers to conduct recon of former site of moon fragment. Is this correct?"

Borden nods. She's hearing what she wants to hear.

"Then comes complete blackout, no more orders, no other explanation, and so we travel on faith, and already we have paid dearly. We get our supplies?"

"Absolutely," Borden says.

Ten more Russians climb down from their worn and damaged vehicles. Most are sergeants or lieutenants. One is a captain, another is a major. Several are female—I think. The Russian skintights are not flattering and carry heavier armor than ours—useless in my estimation, but maybe reassuring to them.

Lieutenant Kennedy has exited the sled lander and joined Borden and Kumar. Borden tells him to unload the sled, and Kennedy hustles back with a few experimental leaps—which the Russians scrutinize like weary dogs tracking a squirrel—to let down the high, broad white cylinder. The sled angles away from the lander until its support rails crunch on the hard ground. Then it pops its round cap and begins to roll out vehicles. When the vehicles are out, a pallet of supplies in four plastic containers—about a metric ton's worth—is winched down from the lander's cargo deck.

Kennedy then returns with his little slate. Litvinov studies the slate briefly and signs off. Formalities observed. Apparently even under the current circumstances, and even on Mars, we're still bound by paperwork.

Jacobi's Skyrines have stood in place, observant but hardly calm or patient. Jacobi, Jennings, and Ishida now huddle to speak helm to helm. Borden notices but lets it go. I'm a couple of meters away from this triad of discontent, but I can just make out what they're saying.

"I don't see it," Ishida says.

"What's our *real* goddamned mission?" Jennings asks.

"Looks to me like the only way they could get these dudes to come out here was by promising resupply. I'll bet the settlements are down to pucker."

"And what's that crap about no Antags within three thousand klicks?" Ishida says. "If not Antags, what hit the Russians? We're in eclipse and carrying an Ugly tight with Blue—that's fucking off the drum." By Blue, Ishida means Navy—Commander Borden. I'm the Ugly—Ugly fucking POG, a stick-beat off the drum and maybe even a Jonah.

Jacobi catches me looking their way and ends the confab. They split with dark glances. Nobody wants to talk to me. Cheery times.

More Russians depart the vehicles. There are twenty-five altogether, more than doubling our force. We're going to need the new transports.

Within a few minutes, four Russian *efreitor*s, or lance corporals, led by a slender female *starshina*, or sergeant major, have sliced away the plexanyl packaging and taken charge of a new Trundle, two Tonkas, and a Chesty replete with righteous hurt. The supply pallet is hoisted by crane onto the back of the Trundle.

Litvinov steps back and pings his troops. "Welcome to our American comrades!" Half of them salute without enthusiasm. The others just stare or glower.

A pair of tech sergeants with black, bug-green, and gold blazes—spent matter specialists—prepare to set charges to destroy the damaged Russian vehicles. Once the charges have been placed and primed, Litvinov assigns the four *efreitor*s to drive or push them half a klick away—what he seems to think might be a safe distance.

Litvinov's second-in-command, Major Karl Rodniansky,

a squat, bluff-shouldered rectangle with white-blond hair low on his brow, arranges with Kennedy and Clover for transfer of depot fuel to the lifters. "Use it up!" Rodniansky tells Kennedy. "Cruel bastards out here. They do not deserve."

I'm not sure if he means Antags.

Both landers will lift off once we're clear. The sled will be left behind. Thousands of such sleds litter Mars—along with as many artifacts not our own.

The colonel, satisfied that orders and obligations are being fulfilled, returns to Borden and Kumar. "We are told Antags stay up near northern frost," the colonel says. "Maybe that is true. Our attackers use human tactics, not like *Antagonista*. And why do they not take out depot?" The colonel points to the poorly camouflaged tanks and fountains. "*Antagonista* would not need this to get home. But *others…*"

"Sappers," Jacobi confirms with a sour face. She doesn't seem to catch Litvinov's total message. Maybe she doesn't want to.

"Why not both?" Ishida asks. "We're special. Everybody's out to get us."

Nothing better.

Litvinov turns and moves his head close to mine. "Master Sergeant Michael Venn. We have history, you and me," he says. "In Nevada, at Hawthorne dive bar. Like Old West rowdies. You throw me in filthy alley. Remember?"

"No, sir," I say. I don't remember the colonel, but I remember the wicked, navy-issue Iglas the Russians waved in that long, antique saloon. The colonel could still be carrying an Igla and a grudge. Borden is sticking to my side like a shadow. And I notice Jacobi is alert, too.

"Good fight," Litvinov says. "We were green, brash. We

learn well—and months later, join and share hero action on the Red. Now you remember?"

"Yes, sir."

"Venn," Litvinov says, getting closer, "we have fought against and alongside. You swear to me, we speak truth, nothing else?"

"I'll do my best," I say.

His brows compress. "Swear to me on famous Marine's grave," he insists. "Tell me *only* truth, not Earth bullshit."

"On General Puller's blood-soaked grave, I swear to tell only truth," I say.

"Chesty Puller! Namesake, real bastard in Nicaragua, true imperialist American villain. Is good. *Damned* good." Litvinov shakes my hand. He means it. I mean it. Funny how you can feel such things.

Then he gestures for Kumar, Borden, Jacobi, and Rodniansky to join us. We touch our helms, excluding the others. "Two relocation camps have been attacked and evacuated," Litvinov says. "Many settlers die. Witnesses, survivors, say it is not *Antagonista*—it is humans in small teams, well supplied. Fast ships, small ships, arrive, depart, carrying these teams. I know they are not Russian. That leaves same forces that worked to destroy mine in old moon—multinational, American-commanded Skyrines, like you. Kumarji, you are servant of Skyfolk—but top commander in Division Four?"

"To our purpose, yes," Kumar says.

"Is destruction of moons and camps ordered by Gurus?"

"We think so," Kumar says.

"So, safe to say, other divisions on Earth do not approve of your actions?"

"That is safe to say," Kumar confirms.

"*Chërt voz'mi!* Deeper and deeper pile," the colonel says. "Our commanders long suspect Gurus not on up-and-up. Last orders from Rossiya Sky Defense instruct to cross desert and escort new arrivals to resettlement, to what Skyrines call Fiddler's Green—and protect Master Sergeant Michael Venn *at all cost*. Sound like Russians belong Division Four?"

Everyone looks at me, but Kumar answers. "I believe both the Russians and the Japanese have signed on to Division Four and its goals."

Litvinov shakes his head. "But not Americans?"

"Not entirely," Kumar says.

"Not yet," Borden adds.

"Then future is unpredictable. If most Sky Defense signatories want us dead, what if someone here, among your squad, *this* squad, agrees?" the colonel asks. "What if *your* troops turn weapons, finish what others could not?"

Kumar faces Litvinov's sad, serious gaze. "These men and women were handpicked, and all are determined to do the right thing." Echoes of civilian corporate bullshit. Kumar isn't used to hanging out with warriors, much less reassuring them. The morale here is nonexistent. He needs to up his game.

Litvinov looks out from under those tight, shadowy brows, straightens, and scoffs. "*Fuck* right thing," he says. "We do this to piss off goddamn Skyfolk! They treat Rossiya different from UK and USA? Hold back secrets, let us die wholesale—poor rewards, not same prize as America! Again, Slavs are disrespected. *Pfahh!*" He grinds his thumb against his forearm, then lifts his chin and shivers off that long, bad history.

This done, the colonel says, "We stay until ships launch—

then roll to Fiddler's Green. Name of afterworld where dancing and singing never stop, favorite of American warriors—true?"

Borden darts her eyes between Litvinov and the other Russians. We're on margin here, but Litvinov seems to be well in control. Everything depends on him, then—and not on Kumar's social skills.

The Skyrines line up to climb into the assigned vehicles. Ishida and Jennings scope me again, but Jacobi refuses to look at me. The Russians' mood is infectious, and Skyrines despise poorly defined relationships as much as they hate unclear missions and muddled orders. Litvinov—a Russian!—picked me out of the crowd. What am I—hero, MacGuffin, prisoner, or worse, a renegade? Somebody who fucked up so badly they locked him away at Madigan, just to measure how screwy a Skyrine can get?

Makes my cockles warm to think of how much they could end up hating me if things turn bad.

FIREWORKS

The Russians finish laying charges in the damaged and stripped vehicles. The muffled crumps unite into one impressive, upward-flaring blast. Fragments fly off mostly to the south, but a few flaming scraps loft over us. Oops. One piece of fender tinks from the side of the orbiter but causes no damage—though much concern to Kennedy, who prances and rants. But quickly he decides it's not major. He hastily preps to depart. He wants off this rock bad.

The busted and damaged TE-86, Skells, and Tonkas smolder and join the wreckage of the Chryse hero action. The one still useful and four new vehicles form an outward-facing cordon around the landers as the pilots perform their pre-flight check, all this under a sky graying rapidly to night.

Kennedy informs Borden that the depot has enough hydrogen and oxygen to get the ships to orbit on burn alone, without dipping into spent matter reserves. That improves their chances of getting home in a timely fashion. As well, the depot resupplies our vehicles—and by extension our skintights—with fuel and water and oxygen. A couple of hours more for each of us. No gas stations between here and Fiddler's Green. Last gasps and sips for six hundred klicks.

Twilight is short on the Red, mere minutes in a low-dust sky. It's remarkably clear and cold. Walking around in skintights is a mostly quiet affair. Loud sounds come through, but blunt and dreamlike; other sounds simply don't cross the distance. Brief digital snaps of radio comm are restricted to necessities. Not much in the way of chatter. I stick with Borden and a couple of Russian corporals not the least interested in striking up a conversation, possibly because they don't trust angels to adequately translate their anger and resentment. Dead friends. I get that.

Borden's head is on a swivel as she checks out everyone and everything. I have to say she's adapted quickly to walking on the Red, an economy of motion that speaks to training back on Earth, possibly in harness at drop school—or maybe she's just a natural.

I still don't know what to think of Kumar. Skyrines have never been happy with civilian authority. But alien authority? Are the Wait Staff civilians, prophets, or demigods? Going along with Borden and Kumar has gotten me out of Madigan and transvac and down on the Red in relative comfort. And a chance to meet up with Joe and Teal. I don't deserve to feel resentment against anyone here, except Kumar, and other than being scoped as a POG—but I do have doubts. Deep, severe doubts. My thoughts are an unruly churn of speculation lit up by sharp flashes of dread.

So far, at least, no more Captain Coyle. But there is just a hint of *other*, inside, that I can't give shape—can't make out or force to come forward. Brain is *still* not my friend.

Finally Litvinov breaks from yet another huddle with two of his captains and tells Borden, Kumar, Jacobi, Jennings, and Ishida—and me—that we'll ride one of the new Tonkas, now rolling forward. "Keep group tight-knit, no?"

A gruff, hatchet-faced Russian chief named Kalenov finishes passing out vehicle assignments. The rest of our U.S. and Japanese Skyrines will ride in the second Tonka with three more Russians and the driver/shotgun. Litvinov's being extra prudent. None of our Skyrines will ride in the Chesty or the Trundle, denying us immediate access to decisive weapons. For the time being, we're passengers.

———

As ALWAYS, THERE's a delay—the landers have to wait for something, the pilots don't say what. A few Russians get picked for sentinel duty. Most of us climb into our assigned vehicles to stay warm. It's toasty inside the new Tonka, toasty and stuffy and boring. The sisters are making small talk in the back. They seem to be picking up from a previous conversation.

"Meeting *the* guy just before you go transvac," Jennings says to Ishida. "*That's* luck."

"Is he nice?" Jacobi asks Ishida.

Despite myself, I'm fascinated—their talk is low and private, but I can still wonder how a Winter Soldier gets along that way.

"A little," Ishida says. "He was curious at first. Then… after, very gentle, sweet. Yeah. Nice."

"I'll *bet* he's curious," Jennings says. "Shiny sister, strong like tank."

"Fortress heart," Jacobi says.

Ishida takes this stoically. "Right after, he asked about my nick."

"Did you tell him?" Jennings asks.

Ishida suddenly looks forward and sees I'm listening. She leans in, looks sharp straight up the aisle, and says loudly, "It's Gadget, *sir*. Inspector Gadget. Like the TV show."

The others raise their eyes to the roof. I am such a perv. I want to say something clever and complimentary to make up for my blunder, for being who I am—make up to her for what she has become, but really, that's not in it. I don't know what I want. I'm like a kid caught staring into the girls' shower in high school.

"Athena, bringer of victory, whose glory shines in war and peace," I say. "None dare look on her nakedness without fear and envy."

A long, stunned silence. Borden regards me with honest pity.

"What the *fuck*?" Ishikawa says.

"Cut the guy some slack," Jacobi says. "You'd blast him like a stump, Gadget."

"I would, wouldn't I?" Ishida says, languorous.

I lean back, scorched wasteland. Victory is theirs.

———

I USE THE next hour to close my faceplate and study the battle reports screed to our helms. Some are still locked, orders of Commander Borden. No doubt she wants to explain them to us personally, with Kumar watching over her shoulder. There are a few open launch and landing reports, however. We didn't see any of the first part of the so-called Battle of Mars, since my platoon arrived later and was spread out across Chryse by a badly broken drop. I flip back through the logistics, looking for Russian and Korean launch dates. Their fast frames were sent out *after* our own frames departed from Earth orbit, but arrived nearly a month earlier. As some of us surmised, command on Earth—generals? Wait Staff? Gurus?—had decided something big had to be done and done quickly—and so they had arranged for a major and very expensive push.

And fucked it up.

———

ELEVEN HOURS. EVERYONE's asleep in the Tonka except the Russian shotgun. It's totally black out. Low clouds obscure the stars. One small moon rises, a swift, misty little ball. I catch a light doze myself.

Then Litvinov radios that the ships are leaving and we're about to move out. Everyone rouses. One of the Russian corporals, perhaps fresh from a good dream, rubs his eyes through his open faceplate, bumps arms with me, smiles. He has a clean, square little-boy face. I return his smile. He sobers, looks away. Warm and cozy in here.

We focus on the growing roar outside. Two brilliant blue torches rise through the dark on silvery plumes. Vapor drifts back in the diminishing glow and freezes to a fine, powdery snow, like confectioner's sugar, vanishing before it touches the dust. We're on our own.

The perimeter guards climb onto the Skells. We begin to roll. Kumar keeps his eyes on the dark flats out beyond the wreckage. The first Drifter—what's left of it—is about ten klicks away, maybe fifteen or twenty minutes. I'm not at all sure I want to go back. Our fallen are still out there, freeze-dried into rag-shrouded jerky....

Or buried deep in the Drifter.

I keep expecting Captain Coyle to fill in more word balloons, to call out for vengeance from her grave. But I still don't feel her. Maybe I left her back on Earth. How do ghosts find their way around?

The cordon forms a loose W with Skells taking the rear and sides, the Chesty and Trundle on points, weapons bristling, and Tonkas rear and center. Litvinov rides in the Chesty—namesake of imperialist bastard. I would, too, if I had a choice. Chestys are packed with good, strong hurt. I don't see the point of returning to the Drifter, really; if the bombardment was anything like what I remember, and went on after we departed, we'll find nothing but a big ditch. But Kumar's goal is clear. We're here to see for ourselves.

He wants *me* to look.

MESSAGE UNCLEAR

Morning begins with high, pale clouds turning orange before light touches the land. Winds are at work up there, cross-shredding the clouds into faded lace. Then the flats of Chryse emerge from darkness. We're rolling at about thirty klicks over smooth basalt, but that's going to change; I remember the terrain, some of it, far too well.

Wind doodles are everywhere. Dust devils scour random lines across the flats like phantom fingers. I count seven through the windscreen: thin, high, twisting pillars, bright pink this early, far out near the northern horizon as dawn throws rosy light through the Tonka's side ports. They've been scribbling on the Red for billions of years and nothing comes of it, they never remember what it is they really want to say, but they never get bored trying.

Our ride turns bumpy. I move away from the pilot's nest and peer through the dust-fogged plastic of the nearest side port. The landscape looking west is rugged and fresh. Recent craters dimple the basalt, bright at the center and surrounded by silver-gray rays. More chewed over than I remember—what little I remember before we were lifted off.

"Familiar?" Kumar asks.

The entire cabin listens.

"I don't recognize any of it," I say. "Too much has changed." It's not hard to figure out, from the nature of the craters, that a lot more heavy shit fell from on high, whether comets or meteoroids or asteroids, no way of knowing. One crater on our right is easily three hundred meters across. "Must be Antag bombardment," I say. "We don't drop comets...do we?"

Kumar shakes his head.

We're passing signs of less cosmic conflict: blasted revetments, crushed and burned space frames, the melted ribs and skins of big vehicles: Chestys, deuces, Trundles. We roll past six slagged weapons platforms in a hundred-meter stretch, just off the path we're following, which curls through the worst of the wreckage. I assume this action took place not far from our retrieval. But it spread over dozens, maybe hundreds of klicks.

"What were they fighting for?" I ask. "To hold ground, repel occupation?"

"I thought you could tell us," Kumar says.

"I didn't see that much. But this was big. This was *nasty*."

Is Kumar trying to draw me out, open up my head and see if I know important shit but am too stupid to realize it—just as he did back in the cell at Madigan? He's still the whirly-eyed inquisitor. He can't help himself. My gloved fingers form claws. I work to maintain.

"After we left, there must have been more campaigns last-ing weeks, months," I say. "They wouldn't have kept con-centrations of troops or stable positions. They would have moved, or been lifted out, then replaced by more drops—"

"Was four battalions," the Russian driver says in heavily accented English. We look up front. His blaze identifies him as Sergeant Kiril Durov. This is the first time he's spoken. He looks to be in his late thirties, with a rugged, finely wrinkled face and experienced brown eyes. He and the copilot, Efreitor Igor Federov—riding shotgun on a bolt cannon—scan the terrain, perhaps remembering the carnage. "Hero action. We do not bury Antags, what are left. But many."

We pass within meters of the remains of a big Millie—an Antag millipede transport—carved down the middle, bro-ken and burned, windblown dust obscuring the low-lying pieces of hull and canted wheels.

"Why Chryse, why the Drifter?" I ask.

"I cannot speak for the Antagonists," Kumar says, "but Sky Defense was told that control of this sector was important enough to mount a major invasion force, earlier in this extended season than any of us had believed was even possible."

Borden says, "They were instructed to defend the site and deny it to others, or, failing that, to render it inaccessible."

Beyond the Millie lies the wreckage of six more Skyrine deuces, then, half-buried in dust and chunks of rock, a com-mand orbiter and its lander, not unlike the one that brought us here but in no condition to ever fly again.

We *must* be near the first Drifter, but I don't see any rocky swimmer trying to complete a billion-year backstroke. The mounded head, shoulders, and sheltering arms must have been hammered over and over—

Shoved under and drowned.

Kumar gestures for Jacobi and Borden to take the seats across from us. Soldiers and Skyrines rearrange. Here it comes.

"Commander Borden has thoroughly studied what some are calling the Battle of Mars," Kumar says. "Before we arrive at our first stop, we should refresh ourselves on how it all transpired. Commander?"

Borden stands behind the pilot's nest and releases the data loaded into our angels. As she speaks, we view diagrams, short vids, approximations.

"There were at least three major bombardments by Antag orbital forces—two comet strikes followed sometime after by a carpeting with megaton-class spent matter charges," she says. "The first comet strike consisted of seven objects, all presumably redirected or harvested from the Oort cloud. These were the impacts that Master Sergeant Venn experienced on the surface, along with his comrades."

"You were in the open?" Jacobi asks.

"Pretty far away," I say.

Jacobi looks at me, solidly neutral. That's an improvement.

"The first strike took out four settlements, including the largest Voor laager," Borden continues. "Some of the pieces seem to have gone astray, or were intended not for the Drifter but for the Muskies. We don't know, because of course we don't have access to Antag planning and orders.

"Surprisingly, about a hundred and fifty settlers escaped—including a group of Voors who were traveling to the Drifter. They encountered Captain Daniella Coyle's Special Ops team, and against their will, carried that team to the Drifter. Captain Coyle had been put on Mars with orders to destroy the Drifter, by any and all means at her disposal."

"Who gave the orders?" Jacobi asks. "I mean, at the top."

Borden looks to Kumar. Kumar hesitates but finally says, "The instructions were relayed by Wait Staff in Washington, D.C., to Joint Sky Defense."

"You, sir?" Jacobi asks.

"No. I was not in that chain."

"Coyle could have been me," Jacobi says. "That team could have been all of us. Best we get that understood now."

Kumar tilts his head.

Borden says, mostly to me, "Captain Jacobi trained with Captain Coyle. She was in command of the backup team."

"We'd have died inside there like Coyle, if we'd been picked," Jacobi says. Her comrades are somber. The Russians are quiet, attentive. All eyes turn to me, waiting for my reaction.

I look up and down the aisle. "Every one of you—Special Ops?" I ask.

"Yeah," Jacobi says. "Make you uncomfortable?"

"Fuck yeah," I say.

Jacobi leans forward. "We would have tried to kill *you*, Venn."

"That's enough," Borden says.

Strain to breaking. Better get it all out now. I clamp my jaw and look down at my boots.

Borden pushes on. "Captain Coyle was unable to complete her mission, and she and many of her team met puzzling ends within the Drifter's crystal chamber."

"The Church," Kumar says.

I've had quite enough. "They used lawnmowers on the Voors!" I shout. "They carved them into lunch meat!" The old anger, the disappointment—the sting of moral wounds. I was there. Now I'm here. So many aren't anywhere now. "But when they set charges, the Church—"

"You saw the Church, didn't you?" Jacobi asks, cool as ice. "You were inside. What was that like?"

I twitch along my entire back. "At the end, awful," is all I can manage.

"Blood and treasure," Jacobi says, with the respectful yet discouraged tone only an experienced warrior can manage. She gives me the benefit of another direct look, like a confession. I can guess what she's thinking. It should have been her.

But that's not it, not entirely.

I want out of this fucking Tonka. I'll take my chances on the Red. I do not want to be any part of this cabal of butchers, whatever their rank, civilian or brass or grunt—dead or alive. I jerk forward as if to get up—but then close my eyes and force myself back.

I wanted to return. I wanted to see what really happened, how it all turned out. Now I'm here. Eyes back to my boots. I'm okay. The cup of my helm is filling with sweat. The suit draws it back but can't hide my own stink.

I'm *okay*.

I can still feel Jacobi's eyes.

Borden continues. "The survivors from the Drifter managed to organize and break through Antag forces—a remarkable feat considering the pasting a fresh flotilla of our own orbital assets was delivering to the enemy and to the Drifter at the time. During a lull, with the Antags in disarray, landers were dispatched, and our troops were lifted to orbit and returned to Earth."

"Who ordered the pasting?" Jennings asks.

"Gurus," Ishida says. Jennings elbows her, but it probably

hurts—funny bone intersecting metal. "Everyone just fucking wants it gone!" Ishida insists. "Why? What's so bloody
important?"

That conversation won't stop. The Skyrines buzz on. The
Russians look aloof but don't convince. Jacobi keeps watching me. She won't give me a break. I'm the fucking linchpin.

We have to get this done.

"What happened to the Voors?" I call out, interrupting
the others. "Litvinov carries pictures...."

"We're here now to protect the settlers," Borden says. By her
look of nervous keenness, like a dog about to flush a partridge,
she totally gets what's happening in the cabin, the danger and
the opportunity. We're like a raw blade pulled from a hot flame.
If she strikes with the right hammer, she's got us—she anneals
and strengthens. But one wrong blow...flying shards.

Borden strikes. "Since there was no way to evacuate non-
combatants to orbit, the woman known as Tealullah Mackenzie Green, who rescued some of our Skyrines, and whose
camp was destroyed in the first strikes, was handed over to
the surviving Voors. The settlers made their way across a
hundred and fifty kilometers to an emergency cache they had
established years before. Five of them survived the journey,
and joined hundreds of other refugees from other camps."

"What sort of cache?" I ask.

"An abandoned domicile, associated with a mining operation similar to the Drifter," Kumar says.

"How many of these moon things are there?" Jennings asks.

"Fourteen fragments large enough to detect and map from
orbit," Borden says. "Two have been investigated. The first
was mined extensively by Algerian settlers, taken over by the
Voors—then abandoned when it was flooded by an under-

ground river, a hobo. That first mine was called the Drifter. The second...The Algerians dug some ways in, how far is unknown, before they abandoned it. The Voors were never able to get back inside."

"No coin," I say.

"Correct," Borden says.

"Master Sergeant Venn came into possession of that coin," Kumar says. "He found it in a pair of overalls in the Drifter. And he carried it back with him from Mars."

"Man of mystery!" Jacobi says.

I flip her off. She smiles sweetly.

"I came upon a copy of Venn's...ah, report, but not the coin," Kumar says. "Apparently, the coin itself was necessary to gain entry. And that was somewhere on Earth—so we thought. So we informed the Gurus, before Division Four made its move toward independence."

"Was on Earth?" I ask.

"The coin is now on Mars," Kumar says.

That adds further confirmation to Joe's picture in Litvinov's pocket. The somebody I trusted at Madigan managed to get it to Borden, who passed it on to Joe. Joe carried it back to Mars. That's what we all wanted, isn't it? Does *any* of it make sense?

"Why not just blow their way in?" Ishida asks.

"Huff and puff," says Corporal Paul Saugus.

Borden looks down the aisle. "Force has proven counterproductive in these locations," she says.

"Silicon plague!" Mori says. Jacobi steps on his boot, not hard enough to break anything. The others yammer until Jacobi pointedly shuts them up. Then she stands and braces against a roof beam. "Commander, who are we really here to serve or save? Nobody gave a fuck about the settlers in the beginning. Why all the fuss now?"

Kumar's eyes are hooded. "Because of Earth's embargo on communications from Mars, we knew nothing about these endeavors. When we revealed the existence of the first fragment and mining operation to the Gurus, they expressed interest. It seemed to me they were not surprised, though it is always hard to read their emotions—if they have any. Then—within weeks—the Gurus ordered us to locate and do all we could to block access to the mine, and to destroy it, if at all feasible. As well, we were ordered to locate and isolate settlers who had worked in or visited the mines. When we asked for explanation, none was given.

"At this stage, a number of Wait Staff in Division Four expressed long-simmering doubts. We wished to learn more about the mine before it could be destroyed—but made sure to keep our interest secret from the Gurus. Within a few weeks, two members of the Wait Staff in India and Pakistan, team leaders in Division Four, convinced senior officers in the Pentagon, U.S. Joint Sky Defense command. Those officers secretly ordered a number of Skyrines and other personnel already on Mars to investigate the mine, and protect the settlers if possible."

"Joe," I say.

"Lieutenant Colonel Sanchez. Your team was to supplement their operation," Kumar says. "Though you never received your final orders. Other divisions learned of those efforts, our officers were arrested, and their replacements ordered the training and fast dispatch of a Special Ops team. That team was commanded by Captain Coyle. They were to locate and destroy the Drifter, from within if possible. No one was to prevent them from carrying out that mission, including settlers and their fellow Skyrines."

"*Shit*," Jennings says, shaking her head.

"The competing forces arrived within weeks of each other, during a busy season of combat on Mars. They were scattered and disorganized both by internal sabotage and opposition from the Antagonists."

"The Antags also tried to destroy the mine—didn't they?" Jacobi says.

"That soon became obvious, and the size and strength of Antagonist efforts added to our suspicions. Why would two enemy forces in effect coordinate to destroy a potential source of fascinating data? With our efforts scrambled and conflict mounting within the Wait Staff divisions, we were forced to delay. Wait Staff gathered as much information as they could from the survivors of the Battle of Mars and devised a comprehensive threat analysis," he says. "I personally presented those scenarios to the Gurus."

"What did the Gurus say?" I ask.

"They expressed regret that the destruction had been delayed, then informed us that the so-called silicon plague might not be the greater worry. There was potential for the green powder inside the Drifter to become even more dangerous. Once we delivered our reports, orders were issued within days to renew our efforts to destroy the Drifter and its contents.

"By this time, a number of us within Division Four were firmly convinced that the Gurus were not being truthful. Then, somebody at or near the Guru level ordered the quarantine of all personnel returning from Mars—followed by select executions. They called them necessary sterilizations."

"Fuuuuck!" says Jennings, drawing the word out with mounting rage. Jacobi puts a hand on her shoulder.

"Master Sergeant Venn was the only one we could rescue. As we worked to establish a political counterforce, and absorbed the results of our few studies on the old ice moon, some of us drew further-reaching conclusions. We became concerned about the entire rationale behind our other ongoing conflicts, those in the outer solar system."

"Titan," Jacobi says.

"Yes, as well as several expensive exploratory expeditions to Europa, which seemed to come into focus as more than just idly scientific," Kumar says. "These orders were followed by promises of more advanced technology, even more powerful weapons and faster ships."

"We've seen some of those," Jennings says.

"Not all," Kumar says, then winces, as if he might be speaking ahead of his point. "Our forces were unable to complete their missions, but Antagonists were in a more advantageous position, and continued pouring down as much destruction as they could, plowing up the surface of Mars, then sending in additional battalions...no doubt depleting long-term reserves and putting them at a strategic disadvantage throughout the solar system. Why put themselves at such risk? Perhaps because they, too, had been ordered to do so.

"When the activity subsided on Mars and Titan, Division Four split from other Wait Staff and started reaching out to those we suspected or hoped were in agreement. They turned out to be more plentiful than we expected."

"Split command. That's fucked-up," Jennings says.

Durov and Federov divide their piloting attention to look

back down the aisle, as if checking mood and temperature—
or just observing a greater awakening to some new truth.

"Who's giving the orders now?" Jacobi asks.

"Division Four no longer takes orders from the Gurus,"
Kumar says. "We are an independent authority."

"What about the Russians?" Jacobi looks forward. Russians and Skyrines exchange glances. Federov keeps his gaze
on the Tonka's cabin.

"On the fence," Kumar says. "But so far cooperating, perhaps to gain traction for some of their own initiatives."

"What about Jacobi's squad?" I ask.

Borden answers that. "Captain Jacobi and her team have
agreed to the new command."

"You trust them?" I ask.

"Fuck you," Jennings says.

"Silicon plague turned everything upside down," Ishida
says. "Every one of our sisters who came back got locked
up—and then executed."

Pause on that.

"Enough *trust*, asshole?" Jennings asks me.

"We couldn't save them all," Borden says.

Another quiet spell.

"None of that tells us who's in charge of the sappers,"
Jacobi says.

Sergeant Durov says, "We return fire and kill. Not to ask
or to think."

"Why rations with vodka," murmurs Federov.

I'm reminded of the MREs attached to the bunch of Russian tents that saved our asses last drop. Vee-Def straggled
in off the Red and invaded our tent, scaring us and waking

us up. He stuck a piece of reindeer sausage up his nose as a joke, then snorted it out, covered in snot. That nose is still out here somewhere. Along with the rest of his head. So why doesn't Vee-Def talk to me, if I'm being haunted by dead Skyrines?

Because he did not turn glass.

That conclusion is so stunningly obvious that I wonder at my stupidity not to have thought of it before.

The Tonka rumbles and jounces over deep ruts.

"We should be in the Chesty and the Trundle, on weapons," Ishikawa grumbles from the back.

"Our best soldiers man weapons," Durov says. "*Polkovnik* riding with them, keep you safe. In good hands. He is why you are not dead."

The Tonka slows and runs alongside a high gray ridge that stretches across our entire field of vision. We swing left with a shudder and a couple of slams and roll up a rise of undulating, cracked basalt about half a klick long that forms a bumpy ramp to the crest of the ridge. The Tonka noses down and halts. Sergeant Durov has expertly arranged to give us a tourist's vantage. Skyrines and Russians crowd up front or glim through the side ports.

Jacobi, still brooding, is invited forward by Borden—a crook of one gloved finger. She squeezes in between me and Borden. Doesn't want to touch me if she can avoid it. Weird fucking emotions. I did not know about the other executions. Somehow, I always assume my misfortunes are special. I'm suspect in part because I'm not dead and some of their friends are. Better and better.

Through the dusty plastic, we see the rim of the biggest crater we've yet encountered, maybe eleven klicks across, a massive, scythe-shaped upthrust that mingles old surface basalt and lower crust. The crater's far wall is an irregularity along the horizon, interrupted by a dark, jagged peak that rises a few hundred meters out of the center.

"This is the Drifter?" I ask.

"Until recently," Borden says.

"It's *gone.*"

"Huge impact," Borden says. "The smaller surrounding craters are backscatter, ejecta. The prominence is the central peak. There's still a big portion of the fragment left below, but it's pretty shook up."

"With more activity than anyone could have expected," Kumar says.

"Perhaps due to nitrogen from cometary ammonia," Borden says. For the moment, I ignore that as irrelevant—though a conversation flashes into memory: the old Voor talking about essential ingredients, *stikstof*—nitrogen.

I make out a series of beige level surfaces this side of the peak. Could be lightly dusted frozen lakes—something I've never seen on Mars.

"The hobo is still flowing," I say.

Kumar agrees and points. "Look there. And there. Those are not dust devils."

Beyond and to the left of the peak rises a thin white plume, and then, almost invisible, four or five more. Venting steam. The magma under the Drifter is still hot, still coming in contact with the hobo. But it's no longer capped off, no longer sealed under the fragment of moon.

"There's magma close to the surface," I say. "Too hot for Voors or miners. All that's left down there is probably dissolved or melted."

"Possibly not," Kumar says. "As we said, there is still activity. We do not refer to seismic activity."

"Everything in that hole is brown or gray but the center," Jacobi says. "Why's that peak so dark and shiny?"

"We think not everything in the mines below was destroyed," Borden says.

"But what's up with all that black shit—sir?" Jacobi asks.

Kumar is about to interrupt when comm crackles and Litvinov demands entry. He passes through the lock and the Russians brush him down before he carries forward a steel bottle and offers us hot coffee. The Russians distribute tin cups. Our Skyrines join in with the sudden manners of polite society. I don't ask where the Russians got coffee.

"No doubt you see water and heat," Litvinov says as we sip. "Before last and biggest impact, we sent exploration team inside Drifter—down deep. Instructed to bring back specimen from crystal pillar. Some brave fool attempted to cut away pieces. He turned dark glass—what you name silicon disease."

"The sample that caused so much trouble—was it from here?" I ask. "Was it your soldier?"

"It *is* him," Sergeant Durov says, and taps his head. "We bring him back, but do not touch him—very difficult. He is filled with lights. No lights when we pack him on return lifter." The colonel's look is intense. "He is dead—but I feel him. Do you?"

I shake my head. The shotgun, Federov, holds his finger to his lips, lightly grips Durov's arm. What's that about? No speaking of the dead? The undead in our heads?

Follows our fourth silence. The Russians are stony, mostly,

but the square-faced soldier clutches his cup and weeps. He's not afraid—he's sad and bewildered. He reaches inside his helm and brushes away tears, then looks aside, ashamed.

"Satellites reported big incoming. We evacuate Drifter," Litvinov says. "Before we get all out—biggest comet does *this*. Half of team, far enough distance, survives...Other half still inside." He swallows hard. These are hard men and women, I know that—but what they've experienced is more traumatic, in some ways, than what our Skyrines went through. "Have you study mountain at center?"

We lower our cups, close our faceplates, and magnify that view. The central peak is not just dark. As Jacobi observed, it's black—with shiny surfaces.

"*That* happen after comet. Everything in center of impact is black glass."

"They blew it the fuck up," I say. "It felt threatened."

"*What* felt threatened?" Litvinov asks sharply. "It is rock! How can rock know fear? You are to give answers! Is it angry at us, Venn?"

"I don't know," I say. "I don't know if anger is part of it."

"I say it *is* angry, deep down," Litvinov insists. "Everything it touches...black glass." He lifts his bushy eyebrows into an arch above his thick, broad nose. "We leave here now. Too dangerous. Too *strange*."

"I believe we've established that nothing practical can be done here," Kumar agrees.

"You know madness from inside," Litvinov says to me. "Old moons, crystal towers, make many things, dangerous, strange, and special. Including, what did you call it? 'Ice Moon Tea.'"

"That was DJ—Corporal Dan Johnson," I say.

"Affects a few of my soldiers. What is it doing to them?" Litvinov asks.

"I'm not sure, sir," I say. "It could make us sensitive to something old. Something still down there."

"Our dead?" Litvinov waves that question off. The colonel's not a believer, and Durov isn't going to convert him. "No understanding, no sense," Litvinov says, then instructs Durov to back us off the rim and begin the long trek to Fiddler's Green. "I will stay with you," he says. "Best soldiers in Chesty, put on strong weapons."

"Good to hear," Kumar says.

Borden quietly observes that central peak until it's out of our sight. I wonder what she knows—what she thinks she knows and how that fits into why I'm here. "What do you see out there?" I ask her.

"Same things you see," she murmurs.

"I do not like being kept ignorant," I say.

"Neither do I. When I know for sure what I'm seeing, I'll tell you. And you'll tell me. Deal?"

"Yeah," I say.

We backtrack, then head northeast. In the rear of the warm Tonka we absorb ourselves, hide ourselves, by finishing the cooling coffee.

Once we are well under way, Litvinov arranges his words carefully, with a tinge of bitterness. "Where we are going, three camps have been attacked and destroyed. For safety, some settlers and your people move into second mine. We delivered to them your token, Master Sergeant Venn." Litvinov reaches into his belt pouch and brings out a quarter-sized circle of inscribed platinum. I recognize the spiral of numbers. It looks like the coin I brought back from Mars, hid from the medicals, then smuggled out to Joe, along with my notes.

"I don't know who it belongs to—I found it in—"

Litvinov waves that off as well. "Joe Sanchez tells me to give it back, so you will know," Litvinov says, and hands me the coin. "Reminder of hard things yet to do."

I'm trying to remember how well the colonel fought back in the bar at Hawthorne. Funny—that stuff is less clear to me than what it feels like to be ridden by a smart parasite under a hundred klicks of ice. I'm thinking the Wait Staff had good reason to be concerned and keep me locked away.

I might not be human much longer.

ACROSS THE DUSTY DESERT

We're twelve hours crossing the huge basalt plain. The going is smoother the farther east we move, away from the battle zone. Kumar is awake but unfocused. Borden spends most of the time sleeping. I've napped and played a little helmet chess with the *starshina*, a slender young woman with small green eyes named Irina Ulyanova, who in other decades might have been a ballerina or a gymnast.

Even the thought that I might see Joe and Teal again is darkened by the realization that it's been a while since we were here and so many things could have happened. Teal could have been forced to mate with one of the Muskies, the Voors—one of de Groot's sons—and squeeze out that fabled third-gen baby, momma and poppa and then infant double-dosed with Ice Moon Tea. I do not want to think about that.

Joe's being here—and Joe himself—are complete ciphers. Was he ever really back on Earth? Alice said he was, but could I trust anything Alice was telling me, back in the condo?

After all, I ended up in the hands of the Wait Staff. I never made it to Canada and freedom.

You don't know folks until you've fought with them. In large part because of my relationship with Joe, fighting fills the list of important things I've done for twelve years. It's all I know, really: how to train to fight and travel to fight and arrive to fight and then just *fight*. Make scrap and stain on the Red. I'm sick and tired of fighting. I want to be done with it. Don't we all. I'm avoiding the main issue, aren't I?

It *really* disturbs me to think about Teal and what might have been. It disturbs me more that I wasn't here for her, but what disturbs me most is the uncertainty she would even have wanted me to stay and help in the first place, or the second place—or any place.

I don't know nothing about anything.

And I'm hungry.

The wind is blowing strong enough to rock the Tonka. There's a light patter on the outer skin.

"What's that?" Borden asks.

"Storm," Litvinov says, hunching his shoulders. "Strange weather always now."

I lean over and look through the windscreen. Little hard bits of white are striking the Tonka—hail. I've never seen hail on Mars. The wind picks up.

Borden becomes sharply interested. "It's because of the comets," she says. "More moisture in the air." As if in a trance, she tries to get closer to the windscreen, but Federov holds out his arm.

"Two kilometers from mine camp," Durov announces. "Going dark fast."

Litvinov squats behind Federov to study the forward view.

The silvery light through the windscreen darkens from pewter to gray steel. The line of vehicles keeps rolling, but this degree of wind and hail is not part of our training. Nobody's fought on Mars during such extreme weather.

The Tonka sways as if kicked by a big boot.

"Tornado!" Durov shouts. The dust devils have given up scribbling and combined to form a Dorothy-sized funnel of dirt and rock, swaying and touching down to our left, rising and wagging like the tail of a huge dog, then digging up our right. I don't know if it has enough strength to lift us—the air is so thin! I can't work up the brainpower to understand how the hell this is even happening—

Then I hear another voice, clear but far off—far *inside*. Bold but also scared:

Let me hook you up to the straight shit, Skyrine. There's a lot to see, but they won't let me do it without you, and I'm getting bored.

I jerk and look around, but nobody's playing a joke, the others are as quiet as little packaged lambs. I stare at Borden. She's focused on the storm. The Tonka shudders and the steely sky flashes. A brilliant white arc moves from left to right across our path.

Sergeant Durov shouts back, "Bolt!"

Litvinov drops his hand. Everyone in the cabin charges sidearms. The *whee*s of ramping energy are painful in the enclosed space. Durov turns the wheel hard left. Through curtains of hail, we see the Trundle in front go just as sharply right. The line is splitting to form a perpendicular to the arc of the bolt, a decent enough maneuver for running over flat and open, if one shot is the only info you have as to location and concentration of opposing force.

Federov returns fire but his choices are few—his targets unseen.

Another bolt. The Trundle on our right erupts in a brilliant violet flare, lighting up the storm and flinging molten chunks of fuselage and frame, then veers toward us and slams our tail, front wheels chattering against our bumper and almost locking before the pilot torques us right and we're free again. We've all sealed our faceplates. We know what's going to happen next. We're sitting ducks in here.

"Outside!" Litvinov shouts. The airlock hatch blows and we push through and jump free, trying to find someplace, anyplace, to lie flat and return fire. The hail is pea-sized and falls faster than it does on Earth—really stings, even though it weighs less. There's a wall of dust and what might be mud spinning off to what I think is the south, obscuring the outline of the big Chesty, which is now laying down a series of sizzling purple barrages.

Then something over to our left fires a volley of chain ballistas, designed to take out vehicles—the double strike of a first charge hitting one side and six meters of thin, strong chain swinging the second charge around to the other side.

One of our guns? I don't think so.

Chain ballistas tend to belong to Antags.

Jacobi is right beside me and Borden is opposite. We all go flatter than flat as two more of our vehicles, right and left, are blown to hell. Sizzling blobs of aluminum and steel and flaring pieces of composite drop all around.

Jacobi's Skyrines disperse into three fire teams, arranged in a spread-out triangle. My status puts me as a fourth wheel on the short team, and Borden thrusts a pistol into my hands.

The hail and wind blow up and away, exposing us to

anyone who cares to look (of course). The air is amazingly clear. Sizzling, popping ice litters the dust—hail drying faster than it can melt. Jacobi sticks up like a meerkat, surveys the flats from her full five nine, then swings her right arm to the northeast. I see our enemy, too, bobbing black dots out there at maybe half a klick. Jacobi pivots and swings her hand southeast—more dots. Things with ill intent fill fighting holes on both sides of our line of travel, as if they knew we'd be coming.

A bolt lifts up and screams to hit not twenty meters off, upending the flaming chassis of the Trundle, which emits that ghastly, up-smeared glow of spent matter depleting all at once into the sky—the vehicle's energy rising in controlled detonation. Three surviving vehicles—two Tonkas and the Chesty— roll around us, any minute *over* us, firing with all they've got at the same targets Jacobi has spotted—quick curves of rising and falling bolts, the straight-out, washboard-roaring, nauseating rip of lawnmower pulses, whiz-screams of disruptors, concentrated on the fighting holes. Two broad patches become flaming blue-green luaus.

Then our team leaps as one and crazy-jogs the distance to where we saw heads bob. I take the run with Ishida and Jacobi. We square off at about ten meters and stoop. Something in the hole is blasting our direction without taking aim, single weapon sputtering half-charged bolts—down to almost nothing. I'm hit by a smoking green blob that tries to burn a hole through my chest but can't do more than crisp the upper layer of skintight. More green blobs lob from the ditch—

One brighter than the others passes over my right, and the

Skyrine behind me—the gunnery sergeant? Tanaka?—keels over flat with fire twisting from his back—

We're within three meters of the ditch, staring down at a fucking Antag sprawled on its back, wings out, doing a dust angel, faceplate fogged, low on gasps, and scared shitless—even so, aiming its bolt rifle over the rim of the hole to zero us if it can.

Ishida drops to her knees, the pair of us behind her follow, and together, we all pump the hole with bolts and a lawn-mower beam until dust and dirt and charred bastard kibble blow from the ditch like the plume from a small volcano.

Another brighter bolt flies over our lowered heads from the Chesty, I hope, and blows the ditch all to hell, knocking us back on our lightly padded asses. We're kept busy for a few seconds cursing and brushing each other off, tamping out the smoking shit with the backs of our gloves. A comic display of self-concern before we even know the fight is over, but what the fuck, it'll be over for *us* right now if our skintights don't hold suck.

I've somehow hit the deck again and spread out. Borden has her arm over my back, cozy-protective. I try to shove her off but she stubbornly shields me. Jacobi stands again, slings her bolt rifle, daring more fire—she'll take it or she'll know where the fuck it comes from, and I admire that, I really do.

Then, "Thirty it. We're done," she says over comm.

Surrounded by little whirls of smoke, in the middle of our own fading dust devil of soot and flakes of enemy, we stop, lift our heads, look around, assess....

We're alive.

Some of us.

I roll out from under Borden's arm but we wait another few seconds to rise, not as ape-shit brave as Jacobi. And perhaps not as sensitive to when the action is over. I'm out of practice, I tell myself—but truly, I accept that Jacobi is superior, I'll follow her anywhere, even knowing we're going to die in the end, because she's so fucking awesome.

Borden shadows me, just inches away. Our brand-new Tonka is behind us, flaring and slumping into puddles of silvery metal. I see maybe three crispy critters within the collapsed and sputtering frame. We are left with two intact vehicles and perhaps twelve Russians and as many Skyrines and of course Kumar, he made it, I've made it—

Shit. I'm pumped, I'm scared, I've pissed and filled my drawers—I've become shit sausage. My skintight works frantically to process what was once safely wrapped in bowels and bladder, as well as filtering the salty, smelly fluid leaking from all of my pores.

All I can say to Borden is "Stinky."

Big-eyed, she nods.

Litvinov and three of his soldiers join us. The Russians take a knee and view the scene through scoped bolt rifles. I hear little seeking *whees* and clicks.

I can still hear. That's good. One thing about air on the Red is—

Fuck that.

Litvinov sends four more soldiers across the flats to make sure the opposite attackers are down and scrapped. They drop and zig-crawl, rise and run hunched—a talent in low-g, where any little toe jab can loft you like a clay pigeon. When Jacobi gives the all-clear, we cross the dust and join them.

Along the horizon, as if nothing's happened, rise more of those goddamned drunken pillars of dust, reeling and scribbling in Mars's diary: *What you say, Bwana? Bullll-shee-it. Don't look at us. We're busy.*

Jacobi kicks her boot at a piece of charred reddish-gray fabric that barely covers what was once the arm or wing of an Antag warrior. Another step and she nudges a helm, weirdly intact after all that energy—a cup cradling the four-eyed, beaked head of a warrior who came all the way from the distant stars to die right here on the Red. This one looks at us with a lazy, crowlike leer—or maybe not—through two large outboard eyes and two smaller eyes above the bridge of the beak. The eyes are frosting over and shrinking now that the big heat is gone and moisture is being sucked away. Its raspy tongue is frozen between the open halves of the beak, like a bird's, but studded with what look like teeth. Ishida comes over and pries open the beak. Inside—flatter teeth for grinding. It chews with its tongue. More like a squid or a snail, somehow.

Ishida mocks a gag and backs away.

As if conducting a tour, Jacobi joins Ishida and both wave us forward, then jump into one of the Antag fighting holes and pull back strips of camouflaged cover, sliced into six-inch ribbons by our lawnmower. The strips barely conceal a small pressure tank and a broken-bladed fan—a small fountain. For gathering sips and gasps and fuel from the thin atmosphere. The Antags weren't many, at this point in their mission, but they were here for the long haul. And they knew they would die.

Litvinov approaches, opens comm, and turns to me. We're wearing weird little skull grins, both of us; our cheeks hurt,

Momma says our faces will freeze this way—but we're alive, and it's either grin or bawl like a baby, even the big, tough colonel.

He says, "Bet you other *Antagonista* soon come and finish. Is it bet?"

"House always wins," I say.

"Truth," he says. This is afterglow, we're stinky and jazzy and fear isn't in it, not now. We're beyond that sour shit into hypercalm or just plain hyper, a weirdly happy state almost like an out-of-body experience. Like the Antags in the trench, we know we're going to die out here. Nobody fucking goes home.

The colonel scans the smoking wrecks and our own charred dead. Skyrines and Russians join to assess our losses. Taking names and blazes if any. We've heard that Russians reduce their dead in place. There's little oxygen for cremation so bolts do the work. Litvinov's soldiers start that process, shooting energy into the shattered Trundle and two Tonkas, taking care of their dead and ours as well. The vehicles flare purple-white. The corpses wither and smoke. Bits of char and ash top our helms and shoulders. We brush them off.

"Waste of energy," Jacobi says. Hard sister. But this hurts her. It hurts her bad. Including the Russians, we're down by half. Twenty-four of us climb into the Chesty and a Tonka, the only vehicles still functional and carrying charge.

Borden and Kumar, Ishida and Ishikawa, Jacobi, the square-faced young *efreitor*, and the chess-playing gymnast, Starshina Ulyanova. Litvinov. They've made it.

Jennings, Tanaka, Yoshinaga, Mori, Saugus, the pilot Durov, and his shotgun Federov—all dead.

Inside the Chesty, with the Tonka trailing, we cross the

last two klicks. The Russians sit toward the rear, near the lock, shivering and talking about what, I don't know, just talking. I want to talk as well. Screw propriety and courage. Screw everything.

"I heard the captain back there," I say to Borden. It's something to mention, something random that may or may not be important.

"I didn't hear anything," Borden says with less than her usual focus.

"I mean Captain Coyle," I say.

She stares.

Litvinov lifts his gaze. "Ah," he says. "You hear ghost."

"She's not a ghost," I say.

"No? What, then? Others return, you know. Not just your captain. Federov heard! Now he is ghost, too."

Kumar watches with sleepy eyes. He's in shock, I think. He's not hurt, but that doesn't matter.

"If not ghost, what?" Litvinov asks.

"Bored," I say. "Waiting for shit to happen."

"On Mars, dead get bored fast," the colonel says, then adds, in passable American, *"Ain't it the truth."*

The Chesty's driver calls out in alarm. Through the side port, I see burning hamster-maze domiciles laid out on the brown rock like PVC piping hit by hammers and torches. The camp's temporary housing has been opened to the sky.

I drop my chin and swallow hard.

ARRIVALS AND DEPARTURES

Rather than pass through the Chesty's airlock, we hunker down and the driver opens the side loading hatch. There's a brief gale, a frosty puff, and Borden, Kumar, and Litvinov exit first.

The resettlement camp is in ruins, all but for a single quarter, which is surrounded by a couple of dozen Russian dead, Antags, a small Millie that seems largely intact but empty, until we walk around to the other side and see it's been opened up as if by a can opener and scoured by lawnmower beams. The insides are gruesome.

"They wanted the settlers dead, all of them," Kumar says.

"No shit," Ishida says. "Willing to fight to the last warrior." Jacobi touches her shoulder. She shrugs it off and takes point automatically, leveling her bolt rifle. I almost expect Coyle to add something, but once again she's gone silent. No words, no word balloons—not even static.

Borden watches me like a mother hen over a piebald chick. We walk through a little arched gate, very pretty, that once led to an outdoor tented garden, now flat and torn. Someone dug trenches around the revetments, which look to me as if they're protecting the domiciles and not vehicles. Someone, probably Litvinov, decided on a strategy of mobility and rapid response: Keep vehicles and fountains below ground level, dig fighting holes around the perimeter at fifty meters, prepare the ground to protect what's important.

Six Russians emerge from the forward trenches to greet us. They're all that's left. They gave everything they had pushing back the Antag offensive, and Litvinov isn't bringing them good news, except that—maybe—the last of the enemy have been dispatched.

"All bad guys, toast," a Russian says in passing, shouldering his bolt rifle and accepting a spent matter pack from Ishida. Unless there are human sappers out there with their own orders, ready to move in next. If I had any creep left, I'd be creeped the hell out.

The Skyrines load up from the Chesty's reserve. I'm left with the pistol. Litvinov barks instructions. Vigilance. No rest for anyone. Another Russian comes around the far end of the domicile carrying two lawnmowers, both blinking red—depleted. She stumbles along, worn down, a sticky wrap around one arm and another around her leg to help her suit hold suck. Without a word, she hands me one of the lawnmowers and Ishida the other. I hate lawnmowers as a matter of principle. I hate the noise they make, I hate what they do, and I've never used one in combat—trained with them, of course, back at Mauna Kea—but I'm glad to have it. The lawnmower means I'm no longer a fucking POG. Ishida passes me two spent matter packs and we lock and heft and wait for the lights to go steady green, then dark blue. Borden watches. No objections. She lends four Skyrines to the Russians. Jacobi goes with them and instructs Ishida and Ishikawa to follow Borden, Kumar, and me to the last intact domicile.

Litvinov waves for Ulyanova to unlock a small fountain. We climb down brick steps to the tap. "Take what you need," the colonel says. "The mine is two klicks north. We stay here."

"Understood, Colonel," Borden says. "Apologies, but we're taking the Chesty, sir."

Litvinov shifts his boot in the dust. "We do our best," he says.

At Borden's nod, Ishida hands back her lawnmower. The Russian *efreitor* who gave it to her, in hopes perhaps that the Chesty would now be available, receives it with a side look at the colonel. Borden then gestures for me to give my lawnmower to Ishida. I hand it over. POG again, but it's all good and we're good to go. Six of us climb into the Chesty. All but three sentries head for the domicile to rest and organize. The domicile has a big lock on the north end, sadly adequate to pack them all in at once. Clearly we're not taking time to stop and compare notes. I wonder who's left inside. I wonder who's at the mine. The second chunk of old moon.

Jacobi drives. Kumar takes the side seat. Borden sits beside me. Ishida and Ishikawa take seats on either side of me. Nobody says a word.

Ishida periodically taps her mechanical arm and grimaces. The wrist is softly clicking. Whatever tech they give Skyrines never works as advertised. I wonder what it's like to be made one with your equipment.

You'll find out.

Quoth Coyle. Only that, and nothing more.

BAD MOON RISING

The ride to the mine is quiet and swift. We seem to have temporarily run out of things that want to kill us. The weather gets weirder, however—spooky fog lies in a fine, low carpet over the basalt and dust, a few rocks poking through like tiny islands. Briefly, looking through the Chesty's narrow slits, I feel like we're in a jet cruising above overcast. Then, as if at the snap of a magician's finger, the fog bristles into spikes and vanishes. Poof.

We climb a rise. Ahead is a sullen gray promontory, blocky and crenellated like an ancient castle, about a hundred meters broad and thirty high. Not as impressive as the Drifter's old swimmer, but more than enough to draw attention on the monotonous plain.

As if pointing an accusing finger, a dust devil rises over the castle's brow, dances a gray little jig, touches the Chesty's nose, then picks up its skirts and dissolves. A scatter of sand rattles on the windscreen.

"Coin?" Borden asks.

I take it from my pouch and hold it up for her inspection. As returned by Litvinov, perhaps at Joe's request. She says, "Good. Now we see who we can trust."

Jacobi draws us up onto a cleared square of brushed lava and gravel in the shadow of the castle. She parallel parks, as hidden from the sky as possible—and shuts down the main drives but leaves the weapons on full charge. Again, we disembark through the wide side hatch, never having pressurized the interior. Out of habit, I check the Chesty's water and oxygen supply, prominently displayed beside the hatch. Levels are at one-sixth. Quick calculation tells me that if there's nothing left in the mine, no taps and no reserves, and somebody finishes off their work at the camp, we'll have about four hours of sips and gasps. Jacobi notes this as well. Our eyes meet over the helm readout. She gestures for me to follow Borden. Ishikawa and Ishida flank us as we step down. A tight little cordon. I feel like a Roman emperor. Speaking of Rome, I could use a good orgy. Wonder what Ishida's skills are in that regard—that little conversation—

Don't think I'm a nutless, squeaky-clean Skyrine. I hope Coyle isn't rummaging deep in my basement, and not because I fear she'll run into old shellfish. Wonder if they all mix it up down there. Ghosts who aren't ghosts, bugs who aren't bugs, squared off in a primordial do-si-do.

"Venn!" Borden calls out over comm. She's found a tall inset in the rock, mostly hidden by shadow. A quick sortie by Ishida shows us, using her paler silhouette for scale, that the cavity is about ten meters deep and nine high. There's a rusty steel hatch about the right size for a buggy or a bus, and a smaller personnel hatch beside it. Architecture may vary from mine to Muskie mine, but the basics are the same. Now to find the lock. We step into shadow and search around the hatch. Ishida finds the little panel first, on the right, behind an inset, spring-loaded push-plate that opens with a strong poke. The others form a cordon. I approach the panel, coin foremost, wondering if we could ever find it again if I fumbled—here in the gravel and dust—

The insertion point is obvious, like a slot in a coin-operated clothes washer. Nothing fancy. Might be molecular-level recognition of the coin's metallurgy, damned difficult to duplicate, plus the number spiral—an encrypted description of the coin itself—

Maybe. How should I know? I am more nervous now than I was getting out of Madigan. Back there, I had adrenaline pumping and the sheer joy of breaking out of stir. Here—

I'm down to piss, no vinegar. Don't know what we're going to find. Joe, Teal, the Voors—maybe the old bantam himself, de Groot, herding his sons around in the dark—

Or everyone dead? Turned to black glass?

The wide hatch shudders but does not open. Instead, the little personnel hatch creaks and shoves inward, giving us access to the smaller lock beyond. Bet it all. We push through, leaving the Chesty with just Ishikawa on guard—packing the bolt rifle to protect the Chesty's weapons, in case we need to make a hasty retreat. Ishida carries the lawnmower. Within the walk-in closet of a lock, we brush off and cycle through. The inner hatch opens and, as always, our ears pop. On the other side, a long garage has been carved out of lava and sealed with plastic sheeting. There's room for three buggy-sized vehicles. Currently the garage holds one buggy, plus, on shelves to our left, the suits and gear of the current inhabitants, which I estimate number forty or fifty. No names on the folded and packed skintights, just numbers. Farther back in the shadows, I make out plastic cargo modules, their transparent sides revealing hints of steel and round green surfaces, square gray surfaces, in-between bits filled with pipes or wires.... Equipment. Tons of it. And beyond those crates, a stack of more crates emptied, folded, and compacted. At some point, the mine received a lot of support.

Kumar and I open our faceplates. The air inside is clean. Kumar sneezes, which is impolite up here. Colds that can't be suppressed by antivirals spend about two weeks infecting all before they burn out their host reservoirs, kind of like brush fires, and we're the brush. A cold in a skintight is less than optimal. Snot has nowhere to go—nowhere good—and sneezing is painful.

"Just dust," Kumar says, looking around. "I'm fine."

Funny how the trivial magnifies. We'd rather be thinking about cold viruses—not so much about turning glass.

"Sir, Venn," Borden says, "please close your plates. We keep sealed until we learn what's happening."

"Of course, yes," Kumar says. "Apologies."

We seal up again. Typical that those instructions weren't made clear from the beginning. Then again, for me, does it matter?

The garage's far steel hatch opens with a clattering hiss, and a ruddy, middle-aged man in a white tunic steps through. He looks like a Greek in a college play. I don't recognize him. "Welcome to Fiddler's Green," he announces in a voice at once oily and assured. "We hear you've had a bit of a trek!" He looks beyond Borden and Ishida and spots Kumar. His smile inverts and his face becomes a drawn olive mask. "Kumarji!

You have finally decided to break with your masters and join us. Perhaps it is not too late."

"You left me in ignorance!" Kumar says, and moves through the press of Skyrines toward tunic man, who, as the distance closes, looks less and less sure of himself. Kumar backs tunic guy up step for step, until he's against the plastic-wrapped rock. "We were attacked," Kumar says. His head moves as if he's examining the path of a fly zipping around tunic guy's head.

"What could you expect? I told you not to force their hand!" Tunic guy draws himself to his full height, hands clenching a fold of dingy cloth before his crotch as if afraid Kumar might punch him in the 'nads. "Division Four was in disagreement, we could not be sure you would accept. You were the last—"

Kumar suddenly swoops. "You *idiot!*" he shouts and slaps tunic guy square on the face. He reacts with a snort, then leans against the wall. "If I could, I'd throw you out on the Red," Kumar says. "I'd leave you out there *naked*. After you gave me your assurance we would work in tandem, stay in touch..."

"How could I know? Division Four was split from the start," tunic guy says.

"We hadn't finished our work! You always were a grandstanding son of a whore!"

Tunic guy drops his gaze.

Jacobi whispers to Borden, "Who the fuck is he?"

Borden replies, also in a whisper, as Kumar and tunic guy continue to argue, "Krishna Mushran, head of Mumbai Research Authority."

"Wait Staff?" Ishida asks.

Borden nods. "One of the first to be invited to meet with the Gurus."

Jacobi makes her mock-impressed face—eyebrows raised, lips pinched—and says, "Terrific. What now?"

Kumar looks back to the rest of us, who are either increasingly concerned (Borden) or neutrally bemused (the Skyrines), and says, "Will someone please detain this man.... Is there a brig, a cell, a goddamned *hole* into which you can stuff him?"

"You have no such authority," Mushran says, rubbing his cheek. "And we are past that now. I have—"

"You've been out of touch for months," Kumar says. "Division Four is united and more powerful than ever. We've done your work for you."

"Did he order the attacks on the Russians and the camps?" Ishida asks Borden. The commander shakes her head—she doesn't know. None of us moves.

Kumar looks over his shoulder again at Borden, a kind of expectant glare. Borden rouses and says, "Captain Jacobi, please take this man into custody."

"Yes, ma'am. Where shall I put him? And how shall I log his detention?"

"Just hold on to him."

Jacobi motions and she and Ishida flank Mushran, take him under his arms, and lift him until his feet kick.

"There is no need of this!" Mushran squeals. "Kumarji, our meeting brings good news—"

"No thanks to you!" Kumar growls. His eyes are actually popping a little and there's sweat on his cheeks. "Soldiers have died. *Wait Staff* have died."

"Not my doing!" Mushran says. "I came here and beyond to supervise a difficult situation, in order to speed progress! I have arranged scientific work, medical exams—all this is far more important than the Gurus let on!" Then he gives in to his own anger and begins cursing in Hindi, loudly and with some talent, if I'm any judge—curses being what I studied most back at Madigan.

Kumar steps through the hatch and we follow. Mushran and his Skyrine escorts come last. The tunnel beyond is bare reddish-black rock, no visible veins of crystallized metal. Little lights glow steadily in a shallow furrow along the ceiling.

"You can't begin to know what's down here!" Mushran calls out. Ishikawa clamps a hand over his mouth, but Borden shakes her head, not necessary. She doesn't let loose.

Then we hear the cry of a baby. Louder, insistent.

Mushran watches with concern as a trio of shadows emerges from the gloom at the end of the tunnel. The Skyrines raise their weapons.

"Do not shoot!" Mushran shouts through the muffling gloves. "Do not fear! They are no threat! The only danger down here is you!"

"Let us take this slowly," Kumar says. Borden waves for the rifles and lawnmower to be lowered, then signals hold tight. The squad stands down—slightly.

Two males and a very tall female pass from deep shadow to dim light. My heart skips a beat. I hope it's Teal and Joe and maybe Tak, or maybe Kazak—our old team regrouping on the Red—but my eyes are watering and I can only make out that they're all wearing white tunics stained with green.

Borden leans in close to me. "Muskies?" she asks. I squint and recognize one of de Groot's sons, Rafe, I think—and then

DJ. The tall female beside DJ is not Teal but could be her sister. She's carrying a baby, suckling now and quiet.

"All Muskies except for the skinny dude," I say.

"Hey, it's Vinnie!" DJ calls out, and steps ahead from the group, approaching until Jacobi shouts, "Hold your ground!"

DJ looks surprised but stops.

Jacobi asks me, pointedly, "Do you recognize them?"

I nod.

"I need voice affirmation!"

"I recognize Corporal Dan Johnson, and I think that's one of the Voors—Rafe, Rafe de Groot. I do not recognize the female."

"So noted," Jacobi says, comparing DJ's picture in her helm with the living article.

DJ by now has realized how strung out we are. "Vinnie?" he says plaintively. "That *is* you, isn't it?"

I wave.

"Fuck, I knew you'd find a way back! Joe and Tak—they're here! We'll be a team again!"

Kumar observes our exchange as if we're all lab rats in a maze. Mushran also seems intrigued. At heart, both are still whirly-eyed inquisitors.

I say, "Your turn, DJ. Who's with you?"

"This is Camellia," DJ says. "And you remember Rafe. He's okay now. We're all a big family down here. This place is amazing, Vinnie. You got to take the tour."

Rafe is unhappy to see so many sisters packing heat. He remembers well and slowly edges back.

"Who else is in there?" Jacobi asks.

"Fucking everybody!" DJ says, grinning. "Everybody who counts. We'll show you! There's no danger, Vinnie, it's not like the Drifter—not like that at all. Everything's changing, active, but it's under control, it's friendly—no turning glass! We've accomplished awesome shit! Really! You need to see the stuff we've found. Come on!" He's like an excited little boy.

Rafe takes the opportunity to turn around and glide silently back down the tunnel. The rifles twitch but do not rise. The tall woman and her baby remain, curious, transfixed—fearless? Or just ignorant?

"Let him go!" DJ says. "He doesn't like you guys. He's okay, really."

Borden keeps her hand on my shoulder.

"Who are this infant's mother and father?" Kumar asks.

Mushran chooses to speak. "I may introduce Camellia Vanderveer, and her son, the second of our third-gen offspring."

"Where's the first?" I ask. Before Mushran or DJ can answer and dash my long dreams—

The hatch behind our welcoming committee fills with clambering, clacking clusters of shiny pipes like thick gray straw—translucent, cross-connecting into individuals, then letting loose. Kobolds, DJ called them—the self-assembling workers we found in the first Drifter. The unexpected and alarming mass is punctuated by beady black eyes like camera lenses.

Borden draws back, bumping into Mushran.

DJ says, "It's okay! They're here to help. We've made amazing progress—once we learned to listen to the tea."

I hear "the tea" as well—the gentle suggestion deep in my head that these assemblies, these *servants*, are no threat. They are familiar to a subset of the things that fill my cranium.

But Jacobi and Ishida and Borden have once again raised their weapons and aimed them at DJ, the Muskies, and the kobolds. Knife's edge, I think. Kumar seems fascinated by the entire mess. As if willing to let bygones be bygones, or at least to hold his anger in reserve, he moves closer to Mushran and tells Ishida and Jacobi to release him. "What is this… happening now?" he asks.

Mushran shakes out his arms. "I have not been treated with respect, Kumarji. Let this make itself known without my help!"

"Open your minds!" DJ invites the rest with a big smile. "Let the tea in! If the old moon likes you, things clear up fast."

Nobody knows how to accept his invitation. Nobody, I think, would even if they could.

"Suit yourselves," DJ says with a shrug. "I'll go tell Joe and Tak you're here. See you down deep when everyone's ready to have their minds blown." He steps back through the kobolds, who clatter out of his way and flow back into the darkness.

Camellia's infant has settled down to suckling at her exposed breast, hardly more than a bump on her ribs. The baby's pale skin is mottled with green. The tall mother seems reluctant to leave us—hungry for fresh faces, diversions, society. But finally, with spooky grace and composure, she pulls the baby from her nipple, to soft complaint—then folds up her tunic, turns, and follows DJ.

Mushran takes advantage of our divided attentions. He makes a cautious step forward. Nobody stops him. "There should be a meeting before we enter the preserve. We need to brief these fine soldiers. Please do not interfere with or attempt to damage the workers—the assemblies you saw earlier. That I implore! Am I understood?"

Borden says that no harm will be done to them.

"Good," Mushran says. "The consequences could be catastrophic. Much that is down here, and the reasons we are all here, needs be described. And I am owed explanations, as well, Kumarji. I need to know what has happened on Earth since I left, and since communication was cut off with Mars."

Mushran has adeptly put Kumar in his place, yet strangely, both former Wait Staff seem totally down with the reversal of mood and tactics. They've gone through these games before, I guess, like retainers sparring in a royal court—which is what they are. Or were. And their game is far from over. "First, since you insist on staying in your suits, we should provide replacement filters and top you up with the necessaries," Mushran says. "There must be a chance to rest and recuperate. Do any require medical assistance? Calming drugs?"

"We're fine, sir," Borden says. "We'll keep our filters and such for the time being. We'd like to move on to the next phase."

"Then please, come with me."

A LITTLE KNOWLEDGE

Mushran makes sure the way is clear and leads us from the garage and equipment hangar through rough-cut tunnels to a hemispherical chamber about ten meters across and five tall, which leads to three branching corridors—all lined with the same pale gray plastic and lit by strings of low-power lights. Kumar is content to be quiet and follow, so Borden and the rest of our group follow as well. Mushran turns into a broader corridor, this one square in profile, with two long, parallel grooves like guide rails cut into the floor.

The sheets of plastic come to an end, revealing that walls and ceiling and floor are no longer dark stone but almost pure nickel-iron, shiny and etched with sprays of big metal crystals formed over millions of years deep in the heart of the old ice moon. The way the lights reflect on the buffed walls, we seem to walk in a shadowy fog. I remember that from the Drifter.

Mushran leads us up a gentle incline and then through a dogleg into a narrow, long room lit by three lamps on stands.

I could be getting closer to seeing my buds again, and closer to Teal. Things might be moving forward at a real clip. And something inside me is reacting positively, as well—*not* my inner shellfish. Captain Coyle. If she thinks we're making progress, finally getting somewhere, I have no idea how I should feel, because she's past cark and care, right?

I am not a fucking ghost, Venn. Got that? And what the hell does cark *mean?*

All righty, then. The word balloon has filled in very clearly, accompanied by a voice that sounds at least vaguely female.

I'm not alone, wherever the hell I am. This place is full of extremely weird shit, the kind of shit nobody can train for—nobody has ever prepared for—and I'd like to know what the bloody hell is going on.

"Yes, ma'am," I murmur. "Me, too."

Borden sees my lips move. "You okay, Venn?"

"Yes, ma'am," I say. "We're fine." Borden doesn't even favor me with a pitying look.

Mushran has pulled a flat rectangle out from the wall. I wonder if it's a door, a hatch, or maybe something exotic. It's giving him difficulty, wedged behind a flap of insulation, catching on a plastic strap. We watch with wary fascination. What's this fucker up to? What magic trick is he going to demo to our amazed and childlike eyes? If it's a door, is there something weird behind it—more kobolds, or worse, something we've never seen before? The long rectangle is not cooperating. "Just a moment," Mushran says, and gives it a jerk. It clatters back, rattles against the wall, and teeters loose into his hands.

Everyone lifts their weapons.

"Here it is," Mushran says. "Not a problem."

"God*damn*," Borden mutters through her teeth.

Mushran frees the rectangle from the strap, lowers it to the floor, then looks up at us. "Some assistance, please?"

It's a folding table. We're all pretty strung out. All but Kumar, who has kept this disembodied, steady smile on his face the whole time, observing with his big, warm black eyes.

"A little help?" Mushran asks again around the group of stock-still Skyrines. "I believe there are chairs over there—behind those boxes, perhaps."

Borden tips her head. The Skyrines fall out and chip in to set up the makeshift conference room. When the table and enough chairs to seat eight have been unfolded and arranged, Borden acts as mother and decides who sits where. She puts Kumar at the head, which Mushran accepts without protest.

I notice Rafe has joined us again. He's standing in the doorway, listening.

"Mr. de Groot—please, come in," Mushran says.

De Groot gives me a look, as if trying to think why my face should be familiar, then sits at the far end. He doesn't like Skyrines. No reason he should. The sister who's taken up lodging in a corner of my head would have killed him and his entire family. And after listening to Teal's story, maybe I would have as well.

This is getting cozy.

"I will begin," Mushran says. "Some years ago, a settler at Green Camp reached out to ISD troops and passed along descriptions of the Drifter and several other mines, which he thought might be of strategic importance—for their mineral stores."

I assume this was Teal's father. For his pains, he was eventually put out on the Red—left to die by the Voors.

"He thought that Earth would lavish more money and attention on the settlers if they knew of their expertise regarding these resources. The news caused a stir throughout Wait Staff. Contradictory responses emerged. The division charged with strategic planning for the war against the Antagonists expressed interest in exploring the old fragments, and in recruiting the settlers to help us secure their resources. But another division took a quite opposite point of view. They began to plan for the complete destruction of the settlements and any settlers who had visited these sites. No explanation was given, and such was our loyalty to the Gurus that none was requested."

Rafe clenches his jaw.

"But some pushed forward a more reasoned plan. Before any drastic action would be taken, it was decided that a reconnaissance survey on Mars had to be conducted. The Gurus did not seem to object. As part of a larger strategic push, select groups of soldiers would be tasked with finding and describing the old mining sites. Despite our best efforts, however, our planning came a cropper."

"What does that mean?" Ishida asks. "I don't know that word."

"Fucked-up," Jacobi says.

"Yes. That." Mushran continues: "Antagonists shipped many divisions of troops to Mars, along with a tremendous increase in orbital assets—and finally, a barrage of comet strikes. What appeared to be an attempt to disable or totally destroy our forces seemed, under closer observation, to more plausibly be an attempt to render the Drifter—the primary old moon site—inaccessible.

"Some of us—I credit Kumarji here—found this coincidental focus on the Drifter by both the Gurus and the Antagonists to be suspicious. Why would the Antagonists not want to exploit all available resources? Their supply lines were even more strung out than ours.

"And then, we discovered that those in Division Four responsible for long-range strategic planning—"

"And clandestine operations," Kumar says.

Mushran defers. "They ordered that Special Forces be trained and sent to destroy the Drifter. Perhaps not coincidentally, my original division—Division One, release and promotion of technological benefits—was kicked into high gear to make available the technology necessary to produce far more powerful spacecraft. High-speed probes sent to Jupiter and Saturn added to our knowledge of distant moons with deep oceans of liquid water, encased in shells of ice. The same sort of ice moon that once fell on Mars. The technology used on those probes was expanded. When the first three ships were finished, because of their configuration, they were referred to by our construction teams as Spooks. The Russians called them Star Gowns."

"There was one in orbit around Earth, last we saw," Kumar says. "Along with a very large Box."

"Yes. Well, each of these Spooks carried four divisions of Skyrines and forty scientists out to Saturn. The journey took three weeks. All in secret. We soon discovered that Antagonists had already begun extensive operations on Titan."

"Old and cold," I murmur.

"Old and cold," Mushran agrees. "The Gurus insisted

that we could not allow Antagonists to exploit the resources of the outer solar system, any more than we had on Mars. Our troops were supplied with very large, specialized weapons and vehicles. They journeyed down to Titan and soon engaged Antagonist forces on practically equal terms. That front heated up until it consumed more than half of our resources, which put a strain on our Martian operations.

"To some of our brightest minds, the coincidences became too great to be ignored. It seemed the Gurus were feeling more threatened by the old moons, or something they contained, than by Antagonist domination. What could this possibly be?" Mushran looks around the room. He must have been a teacher once. He's enjoying the chance to play professor.

"Turning glass," Jacobi says, lips pursed behind her plate.

Kumar folds his arms and surveys the dark metal ceiling.

"Most interesting," Mushran says. "But not our primary concern."

"Shellfish," I say.

Jacobi gives me a disgusted look, like I'm the snotty kid acting out in class.

"What the hell does that mean?" Ishida asks.

But Mushran agrees. "Indeed, the former inhabitants of the old moon that fell on Mars. Powerful and consistent visions were being supplied to a few settlers, as well as a small number of our troops, after exposure to the contents of the Drifter."

Jacobi asks, "Why bring Venn here? What does he know about it?"

Rafe has been tapping his finger on the table, a hollow drumming signaling his impatience. Kumar ignores Jacobi's question and turns toward the Voor, who shoves back his folding chair and rises. "Time a look-see," Rafe says. "Everyone as thinks they wor masters, powered an' wise, come a with." He sounds more like Teal now. I'm not sure I like that. What the fuck does it mean that his accent has changed?

"Lead on," Kumar says.

OLD AND IMPROVED

Two hours before we need to hit the taps," Jacobi reminds Borden. The commander nods. That's a kind of time limit, then, to determine what our options are—whether we go all in and throw in our lot with the settlers and Joe and DJ and whoever else is here, or get back outside, decontaminate, and…

What?

Another possibility presents itself. If this mine is the well-spring of an undesirable variety of madness—uncontrollable shit that nobody wants to deal with, worse than turning glass—then we'll simply be cut loose. The next step—whatever that may be—will be made without us.

At the head of a widening tunnel, Rafe is joined by three other men I don't recognize, all dressed in the same white tunics streaked with green. No introductions are made. Rafe speaks to them in that bastard version of Dutch-Afrikaans affected by the Voors. Two break off and head down a side branch into a shadowy gloom with a white glow at the end.

Jacobi arranges her sisters in a spaced V, as wide as the tunnel allows. I itch to join their formation, but despite our action on the Red, she doesn't invite me. I do not want to be kept apart, but—

I get it. I hate it, but I get it. If I were Jacobi, I'd distance myself both from Borden—Navy rank—and me, shithead, VIP POG, as far as I could run.

It's Ishida who haunts me in a way I can't define. I keep looking at her. Jacobi and Ishikawa notice, but we're moving too fast for them to call me out. I've met three Winter Soldiers in my years in the Skyrines—never in space, never in combat. We all wonder what it would be like to be torn apart and put back together, made into something not quite human—better than human, more than flesh-and-blood Skyrine, according to some reports from those who should know—but difficult to reintegrate with the Corps, a judgmental and suspicious culture that resists challenge and change because everything we go through and especially combat overloads us with challenge, drowns us in uncontrollable change. We *hate* change. We hate newbies because they replace people we were getting used to. What if the newbie is actually someone we knew who is now someone different? But my fascination with Ishida goes beyond that.

Is it because I'm not entirely human, myself?

You've got real problems, Venn, Coyle says.

There's that, too.

The tunnel has gradually expanded to about ten meters wide and five meters high as other tunnels combine, the supporting walls replaced by textured beams that then also go away as we're surrounded by solid ancient rock and nickel-iron, not going anywhere. Vetted by the best mining engineers on Mars. Maybe by some of our people as well.

The light brightens ahead. Mushran and Rafe lead the way around a broad, curving corner—metal phasing into rock, finally becoming rock all around, with the plastic cover going up again as a moisture block.

What stretches up and out beyond that curve has been lit up like a nighttime bridge on a holiday. Red, blue, and green lights rise in sweeping lines along ramparts that begin on a broad, flat floor, then gradually descend to wrap around and intersect more rocky pillars, creating an interwoven, maniacally complicated cloverleaf with nine or ten levels—dropping hundreds of meters below the firm, dusty floor into the heart of the old fragment—encapsulating and supporting great masses of diamond-white crystal.

Borden and Jacobi and Kumar stare in astonishment at this immense and extraordinary excavation. "Is this like the first Drifter?" Borden asks me.

"Yeah, but more."

The first Drifter's digs—what the Voors called the Church—had revealed a tall, intact chunk of white crystal, surrounded by braces and struts of rock. In retrospect, and seeing what has been done here, I think the goal of the kobolds had been, and still is, to expose as much crystalline surface as they can. Inside Fiddler's Green, at least three times as much has been revealed.

So it can make tea, Coyle says. *Tea to train kobolds.*

"Yeah," I murmur. "And us."

Just below the overlook, pipes spray shimmering liquid over the digs, uniting in a cascade that plunges three hundred meters to fill sparkling pools on the lowest level. Rainbows gather around the inset floodlights. This could be another hobo, an underground channel diverted with the specific purpose of giving the crystals all they require, encouraging the kobold caretakers to finish their work, whatever that might be.

Only two people I can see walk the ramparts below, checking and measuring columns and brackets, flashing their torches up faces of crystal. They wear black hoods and shoulder capes made of the same material as the plastic on the walls, like raincoats. They don't seem concerned about getting wet. One flashes a light up, then nods to the other. They link arms and vanish beneath a rampart.

"Got the layout?" Borden asks me.

"The water is pumped from below," I say. "It recirculates."

Kumar says, "Maximized production. I'm not sure this was ever authorized."

"Nothing in half measures," Mushran says. "Such was implied from the beginning, as soon as we parted from the other divisions. We *go for broke*, no?"

"Why are the Muskies helping?" Jacobi asks. "What's their take?"

"Division Four promised them relocation, supply, and defense," Kumar says. He doesn't seem all that enthusiastic now, seeing what's been accomplished. Jealousy—or too much of a good thing?

"This fragment sat here, inactive, nothing more than a mass anomaly, for over a billion years," Mushran says. "Until we were sent to work with the miners."

From an access hatch a few meters behind us, two men emerge, removing their hoods and capes. My spine tingles seeing them.

"Fucking Vinnie!" Tak says, coming forward and patting my skintight. "Why all the armor?"

Behind him, Joe steps forward, face wreathed in a huge grin. "Master Sergeant," he says. He wraps his arms around me.

"We're old friends," Tak explains. "Vinnie, introductions?"

I hesitantly make the rounds, naming names and ranks, introducing Kumar as former Wait Staff. "Met him at Madigan," I say.

Joe looks abashed. "Sorry about that," he says. "Alice told me you didn't make it across the border."

"I got you the fucking coin," I say behind the faceplate.

"And now we're here." He wipes his face with a green-speckled towel.

Mushran suggests that the tour continue, there is not much time. "Joe, would you carry on?" They seem on good terms. Kumar notes this with precise calm.

"Yeah, well, this big dig looks like we've been here forever, but it's only been a few months," Joe says. "We drilled from the galleries around the upper levels, down to where we hit crystal—then blasted fractured basalt and sandstone a few kilometers east of here, diverting an ancient aquifer until it found its way to Fiddler's Green."

"Deliberate," Borden says.

"Absolutely," Joe says. "When the water began to intersect the rocky layers containing nodules of crystal, it triggered the assembly of kobolds, which began to carve outward through the matrix. Reproducing what happened in the Drifter, but this time…quicker and, as you say, deliberate."

"Water was enough?"

"The comets might have helped speed things up," Joe says. "Lots more nitrogen in the atmosphere."

"The Antags seeded nitrogen…on purpose?" Borden asks. "How does that fit in?"

"There is some thinking that the Antags are also divided and in turmoil over these artifacts," Mushran says. "But any theory of such planned action is not yet widely accepted."

"Weren't you afraid it would make you different—less than human?" Jacobi asks.

"Some of us are affected," Joe says. "Kazak was. Others, like me, like Tak, don't seem to feel it. For us, it's just dust. Nobody actually gets sick because of it."

"Why doesn't all this shoot out spikes and turn you to glass?" Ishida asks.

"We're not trying to hurt it," Joe says, his eyes crinkling with amusement, or anticipating Jacobi's next question.

"So if it's not going to kill us, why would the Gurus want it destroyed?"

"It's older than the Gurus by a few billion years," Joe says. "Older tech. Maybe they feel outclassed."

"But it's *not* technology," Ishida says. "It's more like rocks."

"That's how the ancient civilization kept records," Tak says. "The one that lived in the old moon before it fell. We still don't understand the process."

I want to throw up, I'm so torn inside. Seeing DJ, Joe, Tak, waiting to see Teal—and everyone here is talking like this is a ride at Disneyland. "What happened to Kazak?" I ask.

"Killed when they attacked Fiddler's Green," Joe says.

"Who attacked?" I ask.

"Antags," Tak says. "We got most of them."

Kazak didn't make it. That fucking hurts. I was sure he'd survive everything and see us all home. My heart sinks.

Everything's falling away beneath my feet. I absolutely need to see Teal. I feel dizzy.

"Those crystals aren't, like, a diamond as big as the Ritz, or quartz—or anything like that," Jacobi says. "They're some sort of server—data storage made of rock?" She's working this over. The literary reference is nice—I did not anticipate that. Maybe I tend to think grunts are ignorant, too. "So the dust, the tea, is..." She looks intense and lets it trail off.

"Why not just let it sit here?" Ishida asks. "Why did the settlers dig it up?"

"Tell us, Vinnie," Joe says, with that provocative grin I know so well. The grin that got me into the Skyrines. The grin that ultimately brought me to Mars. "Why do the Voors think it's important—why are *we* here?"

"The green powder hooks us into something I don't understand," I murmur. "Something really old. Maybe more important than anything the Gurus have offered."

"Speak up, please," Mushran says.

"Origins," I say, louder, to get through the faceplate. "Access to the deep past."

"The wisdom of an ancient civilization," Mushran adds, with an upward look, as if about to pray.

"Is that what you feel, Vinnie?" Joe asks.

"Yeah. I guess."

Jacobi is taking this in with that same fixed intensity, and now she's watching me the way I watch Ishida. They're *all* watching me.

Three more men, two young, one old, all wearing capes and hoods, all tall and skinny, walk past with barely a glance at us and enter the hatch, which turns out to be the door to an elevator. I walk to the rim to watch the men emerge below. They go on about their business, surrounded by a flow of kobolds getting on with their own billion-year jobs.

"Where's Teal?" I ask.

"We're heading to the annex now," Joe says. "That's where you'll have to decide whether to strip and join us, or break it off and go home."

Which is why this charade is so ridiculous.

FAMILY UNIT

He leads us around the rim of the dig, through a low, flat cavern shored up with natural columns of rock and metal and braces of load-bearing concrete. The ceiling is a meter over my head. As I've said, I don't like deep mines and the suggestion of overburden. I can almost see the openness of the Red, the surface, and wonder what the weather's like. Probably weird. Safer down here. But I don't feel that way.

We walk through a shadowy, unlit zone toward three bright spotlights. As we close on the lights, I make out a steel hatch, like the lock hatches but thicker. There's a box with attached pad on the right side, at chest level. Tak takes out a platinum coin and places it in the panel. "We don't get many visitors," he says. "We're just being extra cautious."

"You don't want shit getting out," Jacobi says. Her eyes shift and her plate fogs. She's not handling this part of the tour well. Maybe she shares my dislike for low, flat places covered with billions of tons of rock. Or maybe she's been more thoroughly briefed than me. Maybe there are real dangers, and all these good folks are crazy, and we don't want to join them.

The hatch opens. I've been through so many goddamn hatches, if I never see another I'll be a happy man. But this is the sticking point, whatever the fuck that means. This is why we're here.

Coyle's gone back into hiding; maybe she doesn't like caverns, either—with better reason than most, right? Bug is silent as well. It's just me in my cranium, and to be alone is to be in bad company. Some Frenchman said that. Maybe Jacobi can tell me. Alice would know. Where the fuck is Alice? Right. She can't go transvac anymore. Bad solar storm, no more Cosmoline. I remember. I remember the apartment in Seattle, Joe's and Tak's apartment where I was invited to stay when we were all on Earth, nice place, with a view of the Cascades and Puget Sound and all the ferries coming and going. Why we fight. What the Gurus told us, gave to us—all that tech.

But the Gurus lied. Everything's a lie. And now, we're about to be led into...what, the truth? Or another kind of lie, even older, even more devious and dangerous? Maybe the Gurus know more than we do about what the tea does. Maybe they really *are* looking out for our best interests, and we're acting like upstart children. Moses after all goes up the mountain to see the burning bush and receive the Utterances, and down in the lowlands, his people get restless and start worshipping idols. Dathan, right? Edward G. Robinson orders the casting of the golden calf. Maybe we've just looked on the golden calf and now Moses is about to conjure the lightning to righteously teach a great big lesson. My chin cup fills with sweat. I want to open the faceplate. It's too late for me, why not just open the plate and take in more dust, finish the job?

I reach for my plate.

Borden grips my elbow. "Not yet, Venn," she says. I shake her loose, then turn and try to back away from the hatch. My step is spasmodic. I'm shaking all over. Tak has come up behind me, Joe is on my left.

"Let me go!" I plead. Tak and Joe move in close and put their heads—their naked heads—against my helm. They talk in low voices, tell me I have to maintain, it's important we all stick together and see this through, this is why we came to Mars. Joe's wearing his patent-pending skull grin, part determination, part sympathy, part bloody-minded stubbornness. I remember that grin and the first time I saw it. I remember that day back in the lagoon near Carlsbad. The day he and I scared the living shit out of each other, on a stupid dare, when we were snot-nosed kids.

"Relax," Joe says to me. "There's good stuff to come. Maybe good answers. God knows we've earned them."

"I w-w-won't be *me*," I say, maybe I *whimper*. Yeah, that was a fucking *whimper*. "I'll get sucked down!"

"I don't think so. You look *muy frio*, Vinnie. We'll get through this together, right?"

I feel my head shaking back and forth, then cycloiding to up and down, like I'm agreeing. That's the effect Joe has on me, but Tak as well; I don't want to play the coward or the fool in front of Tak Fujimori.

"DJ's waiting," Tak says. "I think he has something to show you."

"Yeah, but DJ's crazy," I say. They ignore that. DJ's always been crazy.

The hatch opens. A short, dark-haired woman pokes her head through, not as plump or as pretty as the last time we met—haggard and worn down, pale, but recognizable.

"You remember Alice," Joe says. He likes surprises.

"You can open your plates," Alice tells us, no prelims, no intros. She walks between us, fluttering her hands and looking a little disgusted. "Everybody peel and get cleaned up, replace those filters. Doc says it's okay."

"Who's the doc?" Borden asks.

"Me," Alice says. "Former first lieutenant Alice Harper, U.S. Marine Medical Services."

"You can't go transvac," I murmur. "You'd die, right? That's what you told me."

"I was wrong," she says. "After what we did to you. You getting picked up…The trip wasn't easy, but I made it. What's behind the big door is worth the risk. You know that—don't you?"

"Can you ever go back?" I ask.

"Maybe not," Alice says. "Can you?" She taps her cheek. "Go for it."

I reach for my plate. Borden shoves out her gloved hand as if to stop me, but Kumar says it will be fine, this is expected. Despite that, Borden signals us to wait. She opens her own plate first. When she still lives, we all break seal and breathe the air of Fiddler's Green, which is pure and sweet and alive.

Alice crinkles her nose at our waft. "Jesus," she says. Our skintights have been stressed to their limits. We smell of shit and piss and combat flop sweat. "We got soup and tea inside. Real tea. Mushran, is this fine Indian gent another master of the universe?"

"Yes, Alice," Mushran says, and introduces Kumar in a

tone that indicates here, in the annex, Alice Harper is running things, not Mushran, and certainly not Kumar or any other part of Division Four. No surprise, once they got her here—however they got her here—Alice put herself in charge.

Four tall young men and women wait in an alcove beyond the hatch and receive our shed skintights. The suits are racked and the men begin to replace the filters with fresh ones taken from a box. They must be in their teens—Martian years. Second gen? The women break away and hand us plastic scrub pads, then point us toward a wide, shallow tub, where we step under U-shaped pipes rigged to deliver spray mildly scented of soap. The women make scrubbing motions. Naked, we turn about, enjoying the warm shower. Ishida's skin and metal drips. Ishikawa has a broad grin.

"Scrub!" Alice shouts.

We scrub.

"Don't forget butts and privates. And chew this."

As we emerge, she hands us little lozenges. The lozenges taste of cinnamon. My mouth begins to effervesce. We've got foam on our lips.

"Lick it down and swallow. New bacteria, better than your own, believe me. And fresh breath. Your tummies will ache for a couple of hours, but after that, you've never felt better."

"Alice," one of the men says, shaking his head in disgust, "te suits want disinfect and patch."

"Do it," Alice says.

They haul away the skintights. Tak has a stack of white tunics over his arm and starts handing them out. Children's sizes, considering how tall the Muskies are. Mine drops just below my ass, like a hospital gown, but feels clean and cool against my drying skin.

Still no Teal. I made sure of that before I entered the showers. And no DJ this time. What's he up to? Is it possible that here, inside Fiddler's Green, DJ has found a place where he can avoid being the total goofball? Astonishing. I'm starting to feel better about this. Clean makes a difference.

"I got to go topside," Alice says. "Joe will take you from here. Congratulations, Venn. See you in a few." She touches fingertips with me and smiles, then moves off. "Say hello to Tealullah," she adds over her shoulder. "I don't think she likes me much."

I watch her fade into the tunnels. "Why's that?" I ask Joe.

"Because Alice took her kid away," Joe says.

Joe and Tak stick by me. Borden sticks by me. Kumar has conceded his flanking position to Joe and Tak. I got a posse. "All right," I say. "We're here. Where's Teal?"

"In the annex," Joe says. "Let's go."

CHOSEN BY THE TEA

We look like patients in a mental ward, walking away from the shower room, chewing our gum, foaming and licking, but everyone is dressed the same so we fit right in.

"What was it like at Madigan?" Joe asks.

"Great," I say. "Docs took good care of me."

"I'll bet," Joe says.

"Sorry we couldn't get to you in time," Tak says.

"Hey, no problem. I screwed up," I say. "Talked to a secretary. Used my finger to pay for a cab. Nice apartment, though. Alice…"

"She's our Dorothy," Joe says. "Keeps all the Tin Men and Scarecrows organized."

I think of all the twisters outside. "Wasn't sure I could trust her…Still not sure," I say, time and imagination skewing in my head. Someone's rummaging in my memories again. And to confuse me more, I'm remembering stuff that never happened. Or looking at things from points of view not my own. Like the bar fight at Hawthorne.

"She's tough," Tak says. "Maybe a little too tough."

"Teal had a baby," I say. "And they took it away from her?"

"Him, actually," Tak says.

Kumar and Borden and Mushran are a couple of steps behind, listening.

"Let's go grab a beer and talk about it," I say, in my best "where the fuck am I" tone.

"Beer on Mars is crap," Tak says. "They tried brewing it from sawdust and yeast, so Rafe says."

"What the hell is he doing here?" I ask. "The Voors would have shot Teal."

"Voors live here, remember?" Tak says.

"The elder de Groot was a piece of work," Joe says. "He's dead. There's only eight Voors left. About a hundred died when Ants hit their caches two months ago. Rafe saved Teal, but he couldn't save her husband."

"Husband?" I'm used to bad news, but this mix of good and bad leaves me hollow. My stomach starts to ache. "I thought…"

"Do we ever get what we want, Vinnie?" Joe asks.

"You seem happy," I say.

"Weirdest thing is how happy Joe is," Tak says.

"I'm a happy guy," Joe says. "You met Kumar at Madigan, right?"

"Yeah." We look back at Kumar, walking between Borden and Mushran. Behind them I see our Skyrines, Jacobi and Ishida leading the way. "Real head-fucker. What the hell is this place?"

Joe ignores that for now. "Back at Madigan, they tested your blood and shit. You came up triple cherry. The tea had done a real number on you, strongest they'd seen off Mars.

So Kumar decided you had to be brought here, or the Wait Staff—the other divisions, still mostly in control—would kill you for sure."

"Venn was high on the list," Borden says.

"Which pushed everything forward faster than they wanted," Joe says. "Kumar was still playing faithful servant to the Gurus. And second fiddle to Mushran. Mushran gets around. It's weird how he gets around."

"Why not wait until I got back to Mars, for Teal...?"

"Elder de Groot wanted to breed a master race that would understand everything there was in the Drifter. He thought that would make him the ultimate power in our big old war. No good if the baby is fathered by a Skyrine, and besides, how would he know about you? Turned out none of his surviving sons were suitable, so he found another Voor who was."

"I don't understand any of it," I say.

"Good. Clear out the bullshit and think fresh thoughts. Where we're going..."

We enter another wide room, with a ceiling only marginally higher than the last one. The natural gloom here is broken by chains of lamps drooping from the roof. Rows of folding tables are spaced between rock columns and plastic braces, and where possible laid end-to-end beneath the brightest lamps. A few of these are attended by scruffy Muskies, not as tall as Teal. Shorter folk. Uglier, I think, but I'm irritated the Voors married one of their own off to Teal. Joe's right. What was I thinking? Joe's always right. Nothing better.

I look into a corner and see DJ working away madly at one of the farther tables, hands racing over sheets of gritty beige paper, covering them with crude pencil sketches. Scraps and wads litter the table and the floor. Where they got the paper,

I have no idea—but what he's doing is important enough that someone found it and gave it to him.

As I walk over, DJ glances up, eyes crossed, face pink, feverish, looking even more of a dumbass than usual, like he's on drugs—and I suppose, like me, that he is. "Hey, Vinnie!" he calls out. "It's coming in a rush. I can't get any of it right! Come help!"

"Sure," I say, lifting a page. The sketches he's making are from the time of the old ice moon, and they're not half-bad. DJ has drawn the gnarled outer shell of a big, regal-looking bug, rearing up to show its underbelly—which is uglier and more complicated than its upper parts. I recognize the triad of large eyes, and behind those, peering over curiously, another triad—the smaller passenger. Partners. Parasite-friends.

"That's the boss, but in my head, he's not just one bug—he's like a composite memory of a thousand or so, spread out over centuries, I don't know which one he is, really. Recognize him?"

I shake my head. "Sorry. Shouldn't that be 'it'?"

"Definitely *him*," DJ murmurs, returning to his drawing. "Do some more tea. Come back when you feel it stronger. Man, this sucks, this really sucks—who the fuck *are* these guys, and why are they all lumped together?"

"Maybe it's a dynasty," I suggest. "You know, inherited rule."

DJ shakes his head. "No way," he says. "These guys are way more Spock than that. They were better at running things than we've ever been. Good guys, inside—really."

"They're dead, DJ. Extinct."

"Not in here," DJ says, tapping his head.

I back away, a little spark jogging up my back.

"How many here like DJ?" I ask Joe.

"Before the strikes, we had six, including Kazak," Joe says.

"Now we're down to DJ," Tak says. "And you. Maybe."

"He looks pretty strung out."

"Screw you," DJ says, fingers dancing over the paper. "This is power. This is knowledge."

"I don't feel that devoted," I say.

"Give it time," DJ says.

"What about the kids? The third-gen babies? Where are they?"

"They're not here," Joe says. "Lifted off Mars forty sols ago. Moved to safety on Earth."

"Earth! What about the Gurus, what about Wait Staff who aren't going along?"

"They won't know," Kumar says.

"Yeah, *right*. That's insane!" I say.

"Safest place for them," Joe says. "Far safer than here. The only kids still with us are the Voor and Muskie children—those not affected."

I'm fuming at this bit of news when I hear and then feel someone on the opposite end of the workroom. A clear, throaty female voice followed by a soft padding of feet. "Who's all t'ere?"

Three tall women walk together, heads nearly bumping the lights. They look much alike: thin, worn, mousy fine brown hair cut short, skin pale, eyes wide. They all wear tunics that drape to their knobby knees. Green-stained tunics. They've come from the mine pit. We stare. None is the woman I saw earlier carrying her baby.

Joe whispers, "Recognize anyone?"

I don't, at first. The two women on the outside of the

group hold out their arms to guide the woman in the middle. She looks lost, out of place, as if focusing on things we can't see, people not here. As she's helped forward, I make out scars around her eyes. They outline the edges of a faceplate. Flash burns. She's blind.

"Say something," Joe says.

"Is t'at Michael? I feel him," the woman says.

Behind me, the Skyrines push up close, I don't know why, instinct maybe, even now, even with my being such an asshole—we have to stick together. Or maybe they just want to see the tall women and figure out what this means.

"She's been asking after you for months," Joe says. "Talk to her."

They've taken Teal's child away and now she's here, she's trying to find me, and I barely even know her. "Why?" I ask. "What good am I?"

Teal raises her head. "It *is* Michael!" she says. "He's here!" She bumps into a table. The other women guide her. I want to run. God help me, we've made these poor people suffer so much.

"Vinnie, if it's you, come a here!" Teal says, her voice bright. She gives her most radiant smile and holds out her arms. I remember that smile. "Come a me. Talk a me! So long, so much a tell!"

JOURNEYS NEVER END

With no tact at all, Kumar and Borden and Joe separate me and Teal from our protective posses—Teal from her helpful tall friends, me from the Skyrines, who all of a sudden want to stick like glue. Borden tells them, and Joe confirms, that this is okay, no harm, we need our privacy, Teal and I, and then we're shepherded across the workroom to a small side cubby with chairs and a small table—a single lamp. Isolated and quiet.

The look on Kumar's face is intense. Borden is trying to be discreet, but Kumar doesn't give a damn—he might as well be watching porn and jerking off. This is why we're here. This is why he assigned Borden to me and brought me here.

Then, Joe and Borden and Kumar withdraw like matchmakers leaving on cue, but I know they're just outside, listening. I get it. We're big investments. Prize Thoroughbreds.

I gingerly sit across from Teal. I have no claim. That passing spark of connection, that slap across my face, sharing her grief and fear at the appearance of the Voors—no right to think I did anything major to protect her or keep her from harm—did I? I imagined it all, right? Even so, I want to bathe in her presence. I could be a ghost and I'd still just want to be here and watch her.

Teal stretches her hand across the table.

"I am such a shithole," is the first thing I say.

"Hush t'at," she says.

I reach out. She hears flesh rub on plastic, grasps my fingers, then lays her palm over mine. Her touch is dry. Jeweler's fingers, long and strong but delicate. I remember that fine strength. She pushes at the table, trying to get closer, so I move around the corner, kneel beside her.

"Let me feel you!" she says. She brings her face close to my head, hands hovering beside my cheeks. Her nostrils flare. She's smelling me. "Hasna't been hard, hasna't?" she says, eyes moving as if they can still see. I wonder if somebody will replace her eyes, like Tak's, and I think it could happen—but not here. I want desperately to get her to Earth, to a hospital, to fix her and make her whole again.

Back to see her child.

"So sorry a be this way," she says, and touches the scars around her eyes. "Went hard for us."

"I know," I say. "Not your fault, not ever."

She raises her chin. "You're alive a-cause me, remember?" she says, teasing a little, but full of joy, of pride. "I saved you."

Tears drip down my cheeks. "You sure did," I say.

"I was sa glad a find ot'ers. Never touched you, dinna know your feel, just far looks," she says, and her long fingers stroke my cheeks, my lips, the orbits around my eyes. I don't remind her about that slap. "Dinna catch your smell, 'cept sweat, fear. You're afraid now." She touches the moisture on my cheeks. "Na tears. So much a learn!"

She takes my hands and raises them to her own face. I touch her skin. It's the first time I've actually felt her so intimately, flesh, bone beneath, warmth, and her scent comes at me from different angles.

"They say you feel strong te tea," she says. "You know te old moon's life. What do *you* see, Michael?"

I don't know how to say it. The silence grows and she frowns. "It's na wrong. Fat'er felt it. First gen gets it strong, second less. T'ree strongest of all, t'ey say. He use a give me stories. I t'ought t'ey were odd, but beautiful."

"You didn't tell me that," I say.

"Being in te Drifter weird enow," Teal says. "What happened after you went back a Eart'?"

"I need to know what happened to *you*," I say.

"Sure," Teal says. "Te Voors took me back a te main cache, t'rough te fighting. Only five lived, Rafe and de Groot and Aram and me among 'em. T'ere wor ot'er Voors and settlers at te cache. De Groot took lead, organized, tried a open te second mine but dinna have te coin....Still, t'ey took me in, made me one a t'eirs. Te women fit me, de Groot got his way—I wor married. I wor married—Michael." Her eyes try to search me out, to see what I'm thinking. Her hands twitch. She wants to feel my expression, but she's afraid.

"Was he a good man?" I ask.

"He wor chosen by de Groot, one a te Voors but not one o' his sons," she says. "None of his sons felt te old moon strong. De Groot chose a man wit' a strong sense. Not cruel, not stupid." She turns her head. One ear got nicked, I see under the short fringe of hair. My whole body aches. "Te babe came quick enow. T'en Joe and DJ and Tak returned wit survey team a open te second mine. Joe had te coin."

"The one I found," I say.

"We returned a digging, all a us, and t'en, good time, fine mont's—t'en, Far Ot'ers came and hit us, we t'ink. Houses split open a dust and sky. Husband died. I nearly died. Alice and Joe send away te babies. After, we divide from t'ot'ers, live in te mine."

"Amazing work here," I say.

I hear a commotion outside the cubby. Kumar and Joe and Tak are arguing.

DJ enters, breathless. "It's gonna happen!" he says.

Joe pulls him back. "We got hours yet," he says, and drags DJ away. Harsh whispers out of our sight.

"What's that about?" I ask.

Teal's face firms. "Tell me about you," she says.

The little room feels close and dense. Everything feels fragile, temporary, I don't know why. And then...

I do know. The mine, the *contents* of the mine, senses time is getting short. I can picture it, maybe the same picture DJ has. The Drifter turned glass right to the central peak after it was hit.

And that's not a bad thing.

Coyle didn't die, not completely.

Teal pats my hand. "We're a get evacuated, some a new camp, some a Eart'. But tell me afore we ha'a go." She grips my hand firmly, brooking no dissent. The people outside have fallen silent. Maybe they've gone away. Maybe they're decent enough to give us privacy.

I stumble through my story. My life has been empty compared to hers, and what's the point? What are we expecting?
Weren't we supposed to get together and produce the third-
gen child? Was that the plan or just my fantasy? What the
hell happened? I don't say this, but I think it as I speak, and
maybe it paints over my words and makes her sad. She leans
her head to one side, listening with that nicked ear, spidery
hands moving slowly on the table, trying to find mine again,
which I've put back in my lap.

I describe the lockup room and Kumar and the window.

She shakes her head as if that can't be real. "Michael," she
interrupts, "tell me a te ot'er place. What's it like? Living anot'er
time, anot'er body? Make me see it. My husband couldna."

"What was his name?" I ask. It's important. People connected to Teal are important. He didn't hurt her, maybe he
cared for her.

"Olerud," she says. "Olerud Miesler."

"How'd he die?"

"Fighting along a te Russians, out on a dust," she says.

Jesus. Her husband died protecting her. I wasn't here,
I can't resent him. I can even feel admiration, gratitude—
Goddamn it to hell.

"Enow," she says. "Tell me what you see."

"Comes and goes," I say. "Usually, it's brief. Like a sharp
kind of dream." I study her face, feeling the coiling of a
mighty force held back, wound up....

And then...

Being with Teal, smelling and sucking in the tea, *my God.*
It's here.

I start to describe to her the things I didn't realize I'd been seeing and dreaming, spilling it all. She's the perfect listener. She'll believe. She'll get it.

"All our life came from them," I say.

"I know," she says, nodding.

"There are millions of them spread over vast time, hundreds of millions of years—all different sorts and shapes. In the time that comes through strongest, most of the powerful ones, the ones in charge, come in two parts: a smaller rider and a big, stronger partner. I don't know who's smarter. They blend together, except when they're apart—which isn't often. They have tough shells."

"I know. Like lice." Her lips curl.

"More like crabs or lobsters," I say.

"We ha na lobsters here. How big are te old ones?"

"Maybe as big as this table," I say. "Very smart. Their world is beautiful. Under the ice, under upside-down mountains of seeping minerals, there are all sorts of creatures—hundreds of kinds of smaller shelly creatures, scuttling through gardens of animal flowers like anemones—long chains of glowing bulbs, like jellyfish, that light the way through their cities—clouds of little wriggling things like fish, also glowing, everything equipped with lights.... Glowing bacteria? But here, under the ice, fish didn't rise to the level of crustaceans...." Am I babbling? Get to the point. I shift gears. "Inside, where they think, they feel cozy—cozy and familiar. Not like bugs at all. I don't know what that means."

"T'ey wor kind?" she asks. "Not kill and be killed?"

"Maybe. I can't be sure. Seeing from inside—of course it feels familiar. A whole rich civilization, history going back millions of...whatever they used for time. Tidal surges, warm and cold spells. They could sense the rock getting colder. They could tell that radioactive decay was slowly fading in the moon's core. But the tides kept the oceans warm. And when the moon was knocked out of orbit..."

"Around Jupiter or Saturn?" Teal asks.

"Maybe Saturn. But Saturn was different back then. And there was more than one inhabited moon," I say. "Before the disaster, there were seven or eight." Pretty specific. Which voice told me that?

"Did te shelly t'ings break t'rough? Did t'ey travel?" Teal asks.

I think this over. Good question! They must have traveled to know about the other moons—right? Did they colonize them, as well? "I guess they'd have to have dug out through the ice. But a long, long time passed from the time they first built cities until they saw the stars."

"DJ and Olerud speak it te same," Teal says, lifting her face. Her eyes are pale, but she still tries to see. "Many ice-roof worlds. How far? How far back a time, do you t'ink?"

"Hard to know. Several billion years, at least—but even so, like I said, their world is familiar to me! It's as if I *could* know them, understand them, with just a little effort."

And a guide.

"We'd be friends," Teal says.

"Huh! I don't know about that. What if we told them we boil crabs alive in a kettle?"

Teal's disgust is precious. "Na me, na ever! Crush lice, maybe."

I move on. "And they're pretty strange—parasite or partner on a bigger—"

She interrupts. "Pairs. Olerud said t'at. But te ot'er moons... Wor all dead and smashed?"

I look around the gray cubby, my tension slowly easing. Alice was right, Kumar was right—Teal's my catalyst. Maybe it was Joe who told them, though how he'd know I have no idea. Maybe he could see it in us—but he'd have to have been clued in earlier. Joe's bright but he's no magician.

Maybe Joe's participation goes back to Kumar's or Mushran's first quest for the Drifter. Maybe Joe's been in on it since just after training at Hawthorne. Joe has always been my polestar, my goad, even my flail—but I've never understood him.

"No," I say. "They were alive before Earth cooled and had seas. They were the first life in the solar system," I add slowly, feeling part of myself, my human ego, wither under the implications. "Liquid water beneath deep ice. They were first."

"You get all t'at?" Teal asks.

I nod.

"My boy would a felt all t'at and more, as he got older. All their history."

"Maybe," I murmur. "Third gen...Whatever that means."

Teal draws her blind gaze down from the ceiling. "Too valuable a leave wit me," she whispers. "I lost Olerud, lost my sight, and t'en t'ey took my boy." She presses two fingers between her small breasts, barely visible beneath the folds of the tunic. "Mushran and Joe say he's going a Eart' now. Much safer away from Mars. What will happen a t'em? Will te bogglers on Eart' peer and study?"

"I don't know," I say. What in hell are bogglers? Scientists?

"Or...maybe t'ey'll be raised a go out a te old moons beyond."

"I don't know anything about it. I wish I did, wish it would put you at ease."

Then more sharply, reminding me of the old Teal, she says, "So many dead. Who wants what, who does a t'ing and why, nobody tells, nobody has the trut' or will part it wit' us."

My throat is too tight to even attempt to apologize. Besides, how is any of this my fault?

Joe and Kumar and DJ enter. Mushran is talking outside, maybe to Borden. "Ready for a rest?" Joe asks.

My vision is swimming. I want to lay my head down on the table, but I've kept my eyes on Teal. We're not going to be together much longer. I know that. I hate that.

"He is sa tired," Teal says. "He has been wrung out."

Joe helps me stand.

Teal is in the far light, tall, skinny, trying to look back, as her two tall friends lead her away. One has her own baby at her breast, and it's sucking and cooing.

Then…Can't see them at all. My whole body trembles.

"Good-bye, Michael!" I hear. "Get rest. See you soon."

I shove against Joe, frantic, losing it all, but he holds me. I slowly work my way back, but hate them all.

BUG DREAMS AND OTHER ODYSSEYS

They take me to a side chamber, outside and away from the annex. I lie on a small cot: dim lights, cool air. Jacobi and Ishida and Borden stay with me, but Teal is gone. Joe shows up for a minute, then Tak. I don't want any of them. So *fucking* tired.

"You did good," Joe says. "Take a break."

"Where's Teal?" I can almost see her next to me, like an afterimage. Did she turn glass? Is she going to be in my head all the time now? "Where are we going next?" I ask.

Jacobi touches my forehead. "He's got a fever," she says. Alice blurs into view. Her face swims in the shadows. "It's the tea, he's feeling it strong," she says. "Go to sleep, Venn. Sleep it off."

"I want to stay with Teal," I say.

"Not a choice," Borden says. "She's getting a rest, too."

"I need to stay close...."

"No one who stays will survive," Mushran says. He looks furtive, disappointed. I know that look. Chain of command. Bad orders.

I try to get up, but Jacobi and then Ishida hold me down. Ishida could hold down a gorilla. "You don't know that!" I shout.

"Teal isn't staying on Mars," Kumar says. "There will be ships enough to carry them back to Earth."

"All of them?" Jacobi asks, looking up at the others.

Kumar looks away.

"Why didn't you send them back with their babies?" I ask.

"We could have planned better," Kumar says. "But this is where we start again."

"How can I believe any of you?" I ask, woozy, studying them, looking for pressure points, places to put a knife—I want to kill them all, honest to God, I want to fucking gut them. Kumar is aloof, oblivious. In a fight he'd go down squealing like a shoat. Or maybe life doesn't mean anything to him, not if he can't be in charge, play the political power game. Maybe that's it—he's just a political drone.

Joe pulls up a chair beside Borden. She looks at Joe. He folds his arms and lets Kumar fumble his way through. They're arguing about something. I've missed part of it. In and out. I brush away Jacobi's hand. Alice is firmer. She takes my temperature. "Same as DJ's," she says.

"There is no assurance," Kumar is droning on. "To keep privilege and power, many on the division boards have deceived and been deceived."

"What about Mushran?" Joe asks. Mushran appears to have left. Disagreements, arguments…Like listening to my mom and dad yelling at each other in another room, while I lie in bed with the flu. "Perhaps he is still lying."

"We don't have any other options," Borden says. "We're told by people we trust that the ships are coming, and that Teal and some of the settlers will return to Earth—and that DJ and Venn will continue with us to Titan."

"Why not take us all to Titan?" I murmur.

"Stop it," Joe says. "We're Skyrines."

"I *am*?" I shout. "Who the fuck says?"

Joe shakes his head. "We go where we're told and do what we're told," he says.

"Told by *who*, goddammit?" I hate him when he feels he has to spell out the way things are to *me*, of all people.

"The President," Borden says, jaw tight. She still believes in chain of command, God bless her little pea-picking heart. Bad orders. I was right. They're all facing up to receiving bad orders.

"You don't know that!" I say.

"I'm told the President is now with our program," Kumar says.

"He's flexing whatever muscle he has with the divisions," Borden says. "Some commanders are refusing his orders. But…that's enough for me."

"And for me," Joe says, patting his knee and standing. "It's what we've been waiting for."

"Where are *you* going?" I ask him. "Earth or Titan?"

"Titan."

"Good!" I cry out. "I'll get it done there." I don't know what I'm talking about, clearly, but that's never stopped me. Didn't stop me from banging on my parents' bedroom door and shouting for them to be quiet, let me die in peace—swear to God. Then I fell over and puked on the carpet and my pajamas. "What about Teal?"

"Alice will accompany Teal and the others back to Earth," Joe says.

"Yeah," Alice says. "Lucky me."

"You'll die, right?"

"I hope not."

"They'll reunite Teal with her child," Borden says.

Joe is talking now. Wow, is he ever far away. "Jacobi's Ops team will finish here and six will go with Alice and the settlers, six will go with us. Litvinov is prepping his own team. I don't know how many of the Russians will come along to Titan."

"Fucking Titan!" I mumble. "Who's in charge of our sisters?"

"They're under my command," Borden says.

Somehow, I doubt that.

"They're with us," Joe says. "You think this place is a mess, I hear Titan is a fucking nightmare. Biggest goddamn weapons in the solar system, biggest battles, diving through methane seas to tunnel below thick ice to underlying oceans…ugly and old and cold. But somebody thinks it's worth claiming and saving, and maybe they're right. Maybe out there we can learn the truth."

"What about everyone we leave behind?"

Joe shakes his head. "I don't know how many will have to stay."

"I have asked for as many landers as they can spare," Kumar says.

"What about the Antags?"

"We assume their goal is to recover all the fragments."

"What will that get them?" I say. "We're human. The dust speaks to us. The Antags aren't human. That's how the tea works, isn't it?"

Kumar watches me, inclines his head, says nothing. I know more about this than any of them except DJ. Borden is smart enough not to claim expertise when I'm so obviously upset. Is she worried I might puke on her? I reach down and feel the tunic. Not pajamas. A tunic. Christ, am I confused. "I can't think now," I say, but nobody's paying attention, because I'm so clearly out of it. That pisses me off and I struggle. Ishida holds me down. I get fascinated with the way her arm works, lying across my chest. It's such a pretty arm, all shiny metal and composite.

"Maybe they'll allow the settlers to live," Kumar says. Did I hear him right? We're leaving settlers behind? "To provide them with assistance," he adds.

I heard it right. "Then shouldn't we kill the settlers ourselves, to keep them from helping the Antags?"

Joe can't answer, Kumar can't answer. The variables are too many. One step at a time, one problem at a time.

"Teal will be reunited with her baby," Borden says quietly. "We all want that."

The knot just gets tighter. My becoming valuable, for whatever reason, is the worst thing that could have happened to me. Or to them. I could just blow it all right now. I could become a prodigal goddamned monster, shooting tea dust from my fingers, spraying everybody until they're flocked with a thick coat of powdery green. I want to. Part of me really wants to self-destruct.

"What does Coyle say about this?" Borden asks, taking me by surprise.

The dead Captain Coyle is lost in the haze. "She hasn't checked in," I say. "She isn't real. She can't be."

"In any other time, under any other circumstances, I would agree," Kumar says. "I do not believe in survival after death. But it seems that turning glass elevates you to a quite different plane."

I look around the shadowy group. This is weirdly important to Kumar, to Borden. Joe doesn't commit. "You believe she's still here?" I ask. "I mean, floating around—but talking only to me and DJ?"

Long quiet. Sounds outside. People moving.

Kumar says, "Your experience is not unique."

Joe says, "Kazak saw Coyle, too. Really chafed that DJ was the only one who supported him. But before he died, Kazak was tuned in stronger than anyone. Mushran says it's not a plague. It's a fucking investment opportunity. If we can find and protect everyone who's tuned in, we might have a direct way into the old data. That's what Division Four's thinking—isn't it?"

Kumar maintains his steadfast expression. Borden nods once. Joe stretches. All this weirdness doesn't sit well with him. I've become a big part of the weirdness.

Kumar says, "If Antagonists attack with full force, this mine will become just like the Drifter. We have, I believe, less freedom of action if everyone is black glass and no one is free to interpret."

"Will the Ants attack?" Joe asks me, leaning in close. His nose bobs over my head.

"How the hell should I know?" I ask.

"A few hours ago DJ just sat by his sketches," Joe says. "He didn't draw, he just whispered over and over about big change coming, like what happened when they dropped the load on the Drifter. He felt that one before it happened, too. So did Kazak."

DJ senses it. He's right. I sense it, too. Coyle isn't being drowned out by my confusion—she's gotten lost in coming change.

"Yeah," I say. "Something big, anyway."

"Okay on that," Joe says with a deep sigh. "Here's what the last bitburst has to tell us. At least seven space frames are entering orbit, along with one or two bigger vessels. No guarantee what they might be."

"Spook or Box," Borden says.

Kumar looks languid, like a nap would be a good idea. Weird fucking reaction.

"Let's hope," Joe says. "As soon as the landers drop, we're pulling out."

I'm fazing. My head hurts.

"Hey!" Joe clamps his hand on my shoulder. "Still with us, Vinnie?"

"Fuck you," I say.

Joe pats my shoulder. "All right, then."

Borden looks disgusted. No letup, no certainty. She's made her pact, received her orders, and she'll follow through, but she doesn't trust Kumar and can't figure Joe. To her, I'm a crazy burden, neither ally nor asset. Teal and DJ and the Muskies are deep-sea mysteries. And nobody trusts Mushran.

"Your turn, ladies," Joe says to Jacobi and Ishida.

"Ma'am?" Jacobi asks Borden.

Given all Borden's learned and seen, and reflecting on the

implications of her orders, she can't trust herself, either, or her past views on reality. So we're all square. Every one of us is nuts.

"Just give us some time," Borden says to Jacobi.

I close my eyes.

That's a big mistake.

AND NOW A WORD FROM OUR SPONSORS

I'm usually smarter when I'm not thinking. My subconscious soup simmers all the time, even without the spice of Ice Moon Tea.

Now that I'm out of it, my inner Bug is eager to raise my level of education before we arrive in Saturn space. Proximity to Titan being important. Maybe crucial. I see and feel the broken bits slowly come together—the history of a massive undertaking, the best times of that old moon become clear, but out of sequence—

I take what I can get. And here it is, for what it's worth:

Back then, Saturn was a brilliant yellow-green ball, slightly bulging around the equator, while chains of small storms drew pastel whorls across her tightly banded surface. No rings, but at least fifty moons, and twelve were big. So how did the bugs see that, know that?

Hush. Close focus in time, more detail:

Our bug ancestors began their push by erecting a huge

tower on the seabed, beneath a great wide hollow in the over-arching ice shell. The builders were philosophers or thinkers. If you thought it, proposed it, you did it—no delegating back then. Strong minds implied strong backs.

Almost all of the "thoughts" and opinions appear to have come from the smaller, spidery bugs that rode and guided the bigger ones. They discovered through long, careful calculation (what did they count on? They had eleven sets of legs and I can't begin to figure the bits around the eyes and mouth—) that the fluctuating tides and currents and even heat came from a huge body some distance away. They didn't then know what a *planet* is. They'd never seen the stars. But they were intent on solving the problem of where the tides and frictional heat came from. The bugs were digging their way up through the icy crust to find out.

Over a couple of bug lifetimes, the tower rose from the ruined site of their oldest city—which had collapsed long ago in a cataclysmic quake or volcanic eruption. Volcanism on the old ice moon meant eruptions of slushy liquid water filled with gases like ammonia or methane or even cyanide. Up from the rocky core welled regular flows of compressed mixes of water and all these gases, highly saline flows that dissolved buildings and killed hundreds of thousands of fellow bugs....

But that was okay, apparently; the bug thinkers knew that the interior heat and mix of poisons helped explain their origins, how life began here in the first place. Death became a kind of deity to the thinking bugs, as much as they had a god—death and, for an increasing crowd of rarefied intellectuals, whatever caused the tides and friction. Whatever it was that kept them alive. Their god was something they thought they could find. I'm okay with that. I wish it were true for me.

The crustacean intellectuals, crawling hordes of engineers and architects turned builders, carved great chunks of ice and rock and stacked them precisely to rise almost fifty kilometers from where the old city had been, a sacred site for a sacred project. Nearly all of the crustacean cultures and subcultures were down with this, cooperative and cooperating. They seemed to have been more integrated and less argumentative than we are. Maybe more dangerously curious. What would they find as they punched upward with massive drills, manufactured with tremendous effort out of chunks of ancient nickel-iron in the ice moon's deep core? This is some time before the bugs started creating their crystalline records.

In this bit of history/memory, my most constant point of view is that of a bug who's going to be the third in line to poke through the hole they dig, rise from the liquid water that fills the hole—capped with a rapidly refreezing crust.

———

I REFUSE TO be completely subservient. Some of my own memories are rising now. As a kid, I watched documentaries on YouTube about Arctic seals biting through the thin ice to open breathing holes and places to pop up and look around. My inner Bug is nothing like receptive to these memories, but as judge of all that's emerging from our relationship, I decide it's a perfect metaphor.

Our bugs are going to wear the crustacean equivalent of pressure suits, big sealed tanks with portholes sized to accommodate their many eyes. The bigger bug will of course get the larger suit, but connections between the suits will continue the interchange both consider essential to life. Designing and making these connections has jump-started new segments of bug industry and communication....

Oh my goodness. The bigger bug is not an "it." The bigger bug is *female*. They're quite good friends, have known each other since they were krill, raised together in crèche, assigned to each other by a master midwife/matchmaker. Now they're partners. Husband and wife. Not sure what Jacobi or Ishida or even Borden would think of this.

Back to the history lesson. The drills have finished and been withdrawn. A kind of methane-acetylene bomb with a charge of pure oxygen is set off at the center of the bore-hole. The ice flies up into the space beyond. Liquid water floods the open hole, which becomes a giant crack that spreads about half a klick to either side, causing alarming vibrations in the tower and even partial collapse, and sending cascades of ice from the bottom of the ice shell, which kills dozens of bug couples in the viewing stands.

But we're not distracted. We're focused in a way that only a bug can be!

And then...

First bug couple is up and out. The larger support suit's crawling legs and tracks carry it a dozen meters across the darkness beyond, across the rugged and unknown top of their world. Jesus, are they excited—and terrified. Fear is amazingly similar for these bugs, very like fear as I experience it.

Fear and excitement.

Second bug couple is up. No instant death awaits, which some of the more conservative engineers had predicted.

And then...

We compare notes through constant clicking chatter, sonic rather than radio. We don't know anything about electromagnetism or radio waves. A great civilization, but physics is not our specialty. We do very well with chemistry, better than humans, maybe. As if being blind to the sort of things that enchanted Maxwell and Tesla and Marconi and Einstein gives us extra strength and sensitivity in other disciplines.

The sky is black. We don't call it the sky—we call it something like *roof*. (My tongue tries to shape the word—but they don't have tongues or teeth or lips…so I return to being a bug and don't try that again.)

Then our lead couple, our lead explorers, posit that perhaps a cloud of vapor has risen over the excavations—likely from the blast that opened the way. Makes sense, so we settle down and go dormant for an hour or so. We don't even send signals back through the pool down to our waiting comrades. Besides, the pool has frozen over again. We might not even be able to return. We've brought along a small drill just to communicate, but that may not be enough.

Hours pass. Finally, we appoint our leader couple as the pair who should rise and orient the suits, big and small, so that the male can see what *roof* looks like. Maybe it's another high shell of ice—a favorite hypothesis among our best philosophers down below. One shell after another, and only our own inhabitable, so why bother digging out?

Our leader couple looks up. We await his reaction. I can see that the fog has cleared, and the blackness beyond is relieved by…

But I must wait my turn.

Our leader couple is stunned into silence. Then he tells us we should all look up, if only to confirm what he is seeing.

We do.

After a long while, we come to agreement as to how to describe what we see, above the roof of our world. There is no other roof. Instead, there is a huge round blot of brilliance, radiating heavily in the infrared—our favorite mode of seeing. And all around it, like tiny creatures, much like those who surround us in the wilder regions of our inner sea: hordes of bright little specks.

But the specks are infinitely sharp, tiny.

"They must be holes in a greater roof, holes like the one we just dug," says our fourth couple, perhaps not the best and brightest, but most amusing and beloved. "Maybe they are shining lamps filled with little glowing creatures come out to welcome us."

They are something like "funny." A bug version of Vee-Def or DJ. We love them, love *him* (the little guy is our referent in these matters), but doubt that what he thinks is true. I'm working my brain overtime, and actively comparing notes with the sluggish but often more stable and even wiser brain of my big wife.

She comes up with a solution first. I love her for that. "I think those glows are other places made of ice, like our world," she says. "But there have been disasters. They've dug out to the surface, other explorers have broken through to the open, but their explosions were too powerful—and they are all on fire. They're burning!"

Perhaps not the most fortunate hypothesis. It is convincing enough that we scramble back to the frozen pool of water and frantically chip and dig down again. The cap finally breaks up and we dive through and fall, drifting down past what is left of the scaffolding and the drills, tumbling along the side of the tower of rock and ice, rolling, endlessly rolling until we are back among our companions, our friends, our supporters.

The funny couple doesn't survive. We will miss them.

Shit. My partner died, too. That means my host male will be dying soon as well. Makes me sad, very sad. Worse to lose that partner than to die myself.

Many sacrifices, much sadness—but also much discovery. Much to think upon.

We soon concluded that the lights in the outer blackness are not holes. They are burning spheres. Millions of them.

That was the first time.

We—that is, our doubled bug forebears—waited a very long time to try again.

———

JACOBI AND TAK stand over me. I've had my eyes open for some time, but only now do I see them.

"Wow!" Tak says. "You were way, way down. Feel better?"

"I lost her," I say. "They dug out, but I lost her."

"No time," Jacobi says. "We're moving out."

"Everybody?" I mumble.

Tak and Jacobi lift me from the cot. "They've cleaned our skintights," Jacobi says. "Pretty good job, as far as I can tell."

"Weapons?" I ask.

She says, "See if you can stand."

AD ASTRA OR ELSE

'm doing better now. I know who and where I am, for a little while, maybe.

We're suited up and back on the Red. Litvinov's troops have lined up the vehicles to begin transporting settlers away from the mine. The settlers number about fifty. Most of the work in the mine must have been done by kobolds. DJ and Joe and the Russians organize the move. They pack as many settlers as they can into the first group of four vehicles—two Tonkas and two Trundles.

I've had no chance to say good-bye to Teal. Borden and Kumar and I stand with our Skyrine sisters. Captain Jacobi brushes my arm. Something about her attitude has changed. That worries me.

"Moving out?" she asks. I lift my thumb. I can't see her face behind the plate, bright with morning sun. "About time," she says. "Ishida asks if you're married or otherwise bespoken."

"Lifelong bachelor," I say.

"Figures. We're running a pool on whether you end up married to Borden, to your Muskie girl, or to Ishida."

She brushes my arm again.

"Terrific," I say.

"Gadget likes you."

"She'd burn me to a stump," I say.

Jacobi's face becomes visible as she turns. She's nervous watching the lines of settlers in their skintights. "We can hand over her instruction book if you want to study up."

"Thanks," I say.

Borden and Kumar approach from the Trundle. "One of those for us?" Jacobi asks.

"Three, actually," Borden says. "We're also taking Litvinov and ten Russians."

"Won't be enough for all the settlers," Jacobi says.

"Our mission takes precedence," Borden says.

Then Jacobi does something that astonishes me. She and Ishida flank Borden and stop her forward progress. Borden is surprised into silence.

"We won't lift until the settlers evac," Jacobi says. "All of them."

Borden stares her down. "Then you're going to die here," she says, voice tight.

"If necessary, Commander," Jacobi says. "I won't take the blame for killing Muskies."

"So says our lady," Ishida adds. The others gather to show support.

Kumar raises his hand. "This is not an issue. We have priority to return to Earth all who have a connection with the mines."

KILLING TITAN | 491

Borden looks astonished, and then really, really angry—like she wants to strangle Kumar. She comes plate to plate with him. "Why am I not kept in the loop?" she asks.

"To accomplish that," Kumar smoothly continues, "we have been provided ten landers—enough for all, I think. Might take an hour more, however. By which time Antags could be upon us with, as you say, righteous hurt."

Borden turns her back on us. She's feeling the thorny end of the shit stick and I don't know why. I suspect it's because Kumar just doesn't care.

"Maybe so," Jacobi says. "But we won't leave until they're off the Red. These people have suffered enough because of us...*sir*."

Kumar studies her a few seconds, then acquiesces with a bow. "I will so instruct Litvinov," he says, and walks away. At this moment, I love our sisters with all my heart.

Jacobi's cheeks are pink with anger. "What's the deal with Joe Sanchez?" she asks, voice still tense. "Ishikawa thinks he's dead cool. Is Sanchez taken?"

I don't dignify that with a response.

"Don't go all GI on us, Venn," Jacobi says.

"No, ma'am," I say.

"Until we all get in the shit again and decide to fuck or fight, to us you're *still* a POG," Jacobi says.

"Yes, ma'am," I say. Sisterhood is powerful. Warm and fuzzy, spattered with blood and spit.

———

AN HOUR LATER, still no sign of Antags or anyone else. All the settlers in suits have been loaded. They fill seven vehicles, including the Trundles, and twelve hang from the sides of the Tonkas. The round-faced Russian ballerina, Starshina Ulyanova, stands on the rear hatch step of the Chesty and waves for an accordion to be stretched from the nearest domicile. Not enough skintights for complete evac. Good planning all around.

SNKRZ.

I'm tired of feeling confused and shitty. I want to feel tight and angry, like coming off a good fight—like I can shift the stars with my rage, with the righteous indignation that stupid fuckers anywhere would dare challenge me and my brothers and sisters. True *grunt* rage, *hu-wa*! Best drug of all. Back when I last felt it, it turned my skull into a white-hot, chrome-plated death's head filled with sizzling brains—fearsome to behold. I'd like to feel that again. Having Jacobi rag me makes me think it might be possible. But not yet. Not unless we survive our lift from the Red and our big transport is ready for the long, long haul.

The round-faced *starshina* waves the vehicles off. The settlers are leaving first. We all wait quietly, if not patiently. I can imagine the quiet inside the mine—the second Void. Except for the kobolds. What are they doing to prepare? Because I know beyond a shadow of a doubt what our sisters have done. They've laid a network of spent matter charges, enough to collapse the mine, incinerate the Void, put full fucking stop to everything the Muskies have been doing. Expediency rules. They won't leave a thing for the Antags, and there's no way of knowing what *they'd* do, anyway. Maybe blow it up, too.

Two squads of Russians gather to either side of us as we watch the eastern skies. Together, we track the lancets of descending landers—eight sharp white needles spaced about two klicks away.

ANOTHER HOUR PASSES before the rolling stock returns and the vehicles line up to receive us. Two of the landers off to the east ascend on pillars of torch fire. Two more follow minutes after.

KUMAR AND BORDEN emerge from the hatch beside the accordion, DJ in tow. I wonder what he's feeling. I *know* what he's feeling, but I won't acknowledge it. This is a solemn moment. Something huge is about to happen down in the mine, something beyond logistics and spent matter and physics. Because we both know that spent matter can only poke this place in the eye and make it mad.

But when it gets mad, when it feels *afraid*…

Difficult to believe whoever's in command above Kumar is doing everything right. We're all expecting that before we go, the Antags or more sappers will arrive in force and there will be another fight. My emotions are narrowing. I've missed that sensation for so goddamned long.… The instincts it took a claw-nailed handful of DIs to beat into me over weeks and months at Hawthorne, Mauna Kea. We're all expecting to die, but we hope, we want, we *desire* with hot pink passion to fight and kill before we go.

The round-faced *starshina* waves her hand, all aboard.

"Ready, ladies?" Jacobi asks.

High overhead I see a fast-moving object brighter than the

nearby spot of Phobos. It slides quickly east to west, opposite the typical orbital track of our space frames. My plate enhances enough to show me an elongated, slightly blurry thing like a tied-up bundle of handkerchiefs. I point this out to Borden. "Is that our ride?" I ask.

She looks up. "I think so," she says.

"Spook?" I ask.

"Fastest thing in the solar system." But she doesn't look happy or secure.

The last group of Russians climb onto the frame of a Tonka.

"Sorry about the crap they're putting you through," I tell her.

She shakes her head, then straightens. "You're coming with us in the Chesty. Jacobi's team will join us. Kumar's orders."

"Yes, ma'am."

"Kumar is coming, too."

"Terrific," I say.

The settlers are nowhere to be seen, but the ships that lifted them off the Red have left black-rayed smudges on the basalt.

"Godspeed," Borden says to the vanished ships.

I instinctively look west. Over the low rise that marks the second Drifter, the second mine, and the reduced horizontal lines of the domiciles, four dust devils spin out their syncopated dance, twisted little pencils moved by invisible hands. I hope nobody will be left behind on the Red or down in the mine to experience what I sense in my hindbrain and deep in my gut. Nobody human.

We pack into the Chesty, into the tight spaces between

weapons and stores. Joe goes last. Ishikawa sits beside him. DJ sits beside me. "Amazing tea," he says. "I'm going to miss it."

The Chesty moves out. Ten minutes' ride to the last two landers.

Then it all blows.

The whole Chesty shimmies on its wheels. Something subsonic booms up into the chassis and through our flesh and bones. The boom rises to a roar and everything shakes and rattles as the shock wave passes under us. The Chesty heels over on its springs, lifts, and bounces back with a squealing jolt. The driver revs to full speed, ponderous at best, then spins us to face into the aftershocks. Those of us in the back crowd around the six small ports, all but our sisters, Jacobi's team.

They stay seated.

"Oh, good," Jacobi says, utterly deadpan. "It's beginning to work." She folds her hands and looks between her knees.

Kumar perches behind the Russian driver, looking through the windscreen. "Blessed Siva!" he says.

A cloud of dust towers over the mine. The domiciles are obscured—maybe they're already gone. I see the landers, our landers, sway like trees in a high wind. Three more ships are descending despite the activity off to the west. There are now five, enough to carry the rest of us.

"Out!" the driver shouts. "Move it!"

We seal our plates and abandon the Chesty, leaping and running toward the landers, Kumar straggling—having difficulty—until Borden and I lift him by his belt pack and sling him along between us. The sound is incredible. Definitely no need to look back. Pillar of salt.

The crew chiefs of each lander grab us at random and push

us toward the ladders. We climb like monkeys, all but Kumar, whose feet can't seem to stay on the rungs. Takes far too long. Takes forever. The landers are still swaying. From kilometers off, we hear the crust complaining: deep throaty screams made worse by the thin air. I look left in time to see the dust tower into a mushroom, then spread out. Around the mushroom's stalk, a crackle of basalt spreads from the low dome of the mine. The crust shatters like glass hit by invisible hammers and collapses, forming a vast, bowl-shaped pit, the edge too fucking close and coming closer. Yeah, Siva indeed—our wicked sisters did a real number down there.

I'm almost at the hatch, shoving at Kumar's butt. Then I make the mistake of looking back again. The color at the center of the pit is changing. Swift, dark, riverlike branches fan out to the expanding perimeter—

"Get the hell in!" the crew chief shouts, pulling me through the hatch and shoving me back into the cabin, which is crammed with people in skintights scrambling for their lives, maybe for their souls. Borden straps Kumar into a seat and looks at me, frightened out of her wits. I strap into my own seat.

"Two minutes!" the pilot shouts over comm.

There are people still climbing as we hear the other landers begin their motor ramp-ups to launch. And then we feel our own ship rise. The hatch hasn't closed. Alarms go off inside the cabin. We're launching and not everyone's in a couch, but the downward tug is just moderate—the pilot is hovering over the Red, up and away from the debris and collapse—

Maybe it all ends here.

"Sorry," Jacobi says from behind me. And again, "Sorry."

I can't see a thing. Hope to hell that Teal is up and away.

The hatch has closed. We have pressure. I open my eyes. Borden and Kumar are across the aisle. Our seats realign and the pods roll into position. The pilot issues safety instructions. I don't listen. I look back over the edge of my seat. Everybody made it, we're all strapped in, that's a miracle, isn't it? I make out Jacobi and a few of the sisters and a few of the Russians. I see DJ behind and to my right. He looks like he's napping and having a bad dream. Where's Joe? Where's Tak? Mushran? Presumably in another lander. We're climbing fast. The acceleration is probably at max. Leaving Mars isn't like leaving Earth. You can stand, if you are strong and fit—

And then, as if the shock is holding back my sensations and memories, I realize, I not only saw it—I *felt it.* The pit turned black as obsidian. All the surface for kilometers around turned deep dark glass, and then, like a second sky, a sky *below*, it twinkled with burning streaks and stars. The glassy, broken land filled with submerged and flashing lights.

"Twenty minutes to rendezvous," the pilot announces. He has a distinct southern accent. Virginia, I think. Maybe Virginia Beach. "What the hell just happened back there?" he asks.

Nobody answers.

I close my eyes and let the acceleration lull me. Not so bad now. We're off the Red, we're alive, things are working out. Better and better. Right?

PART TWO

PART TWO

BATMAN AND SILVER SURFER
SAY . . .

'm drifting again. For some reason, I relive the time when Joe and I were eighteen and crossed the border in Arizona, riding in a pickup down to Chihuahua with three other guys and a nineteen-year-old tomboy named Famke. That trip ended up kind of sweet and creepy. Guided by a crazy young Mexican kid, we crawled deep into a desert cave and found a curled-up mummy wearing a grass thong. Famke examined the body—she was studying premed—and said it was a girl and really old, maybe hundreds of years. The Mexican kid insisted she had been fifteen or younger when she died, probably in childbirth. Joe got a sick, guilty look and took a folded cardboard box from the back of the truck, taping it together and mumbling something about her being lonely all these years, and now, she was back with her kind, with young people; she needed to go home with us. He insisted on removing her from the cave and bringing her back. He didn't want her to be lonely anymore. We'd drunk so much beer, he thought he was saving her from the dark and the dust.

He filled the top of the cardboard box with dried brush.

We made it back despite stupidity and too much beer, crossing the border with the cardboard box in the back of our van, saying to ICE it was filled with stuffed and mounted frogs we were planning to give as gifts when we got home. Two inspectors cracked the box's crisscrossed lid, barely peered inside, and waved us through.

Back in Chula Vista, we went our separate ways, except for me and Joe. Famke flew off to work in Africa. The other guys melted into the southland. Joe kept the mummy in his parents' garage until his mom opened the box one morning, pulled out the brush, and screamed. His dad called the cops. No charges were filed. Nobody could figure out how many laws we'd broken, or what to charge us with, and besides, by then, we'd already joined the Skyrines. The authorities ended up putting the mummy in a museum in San Diego. Strange days.

I slide from kid-flick memories into deeper sleep. It seems to go on longer than the few minutes left before our rendezvous. Some part of the kid flick is still with me, because I see piles of old comic books spread out on a narrow little cot in a room with a crazy, leaning roof—an attic bedroom not much bigger than a closet and filled with shelves bent under loads of books and boxed comics, an old tablet with a cracked screen, another tablet with a keyboard that projects from the front onto a desk, so I can write stuff—not that I write much. A few essays. Once I tried to write a comic and draw it as well, but didn't get very far. I remember I loved *Silver Surfer*. The freedom, the audacity, that chrome-shiny body. Kind of like T-1000 on a surfboard.

I never liked *Silver Surfer*. I never had an attic bedroom. I'm trying to wake up and not succeeding.

This isn't about you. They're shutting me down slowly, and I just want to move around a little before I'm done.

I see the Silver Surfer float along the aisle of the lander, and he's conversing seriously with Batman. Jesus, I do not think they would ever get along. Alternate universes. Two different kinds of bad attitude. One cosmic, the other…

I tell myself over and over, I never read *Silver Surfer*. I never had an attic room. Never wanted to write comics. So *who* loved him, and who could imagine him hanging out with Batman?

It's Coyle. Coyle is dreaming inside my head. She's decided to share.

"Stop it," I say. "Please."

You and your fucking train—and Jesus, that mummy*! I want out. I don't know how to get out! I don't know what I am.*

"You're a ghost," I say.

I'm not dead. You know I'm not.

"I don't know anything."

I've been sucked in and I'm being stored away. Like all the others, only slower. Something seems to think I'm useful like this. Still active.

I can feel my lips moving. I'm mumbling, but I can't wake up. "They're all glass now."

It's not glass.

"What the hell is it? Silicon?"

Not that, either. If the crystals are threatened, they reach out and absorb. That's how they learn about threats—by absorbing the things that threaten them. I threatened them. Now, I'm getting stiff. Solid.

"DJ says all of Mars could turn glass. Then you'd have lots of company."

I've already got company. You wouldn't believe how much company.

"Skyrines?"

Yeah. Some Voors, some of my team. Others, Russians and Muskies, that didn't finish before they were blown up in the Drifter. They've already been recorded. Stored. I try to avoid them.

"Right." I start to shiver. If I shiver enough, maybe someone will wake me.

Coyle goes on: *You saw me get absorbed. You thought I was dead. So did DJ. I still don't know what happens after, except…before I'm done, I can still talk to you.*

"If you call this talking," I say.

Shut up and listen. This place I'm in, if it is a place, is filled with big stuff and little stuff. I think a lot of it is old. I mean, really old—billions of years or more. With my help, maybe you can access some of it. That's what it wants. But I need you, as well.

I just want her to go away. I want it all to go away so I can be as sane as I was before.

"I'm already there," I say to this craziness. "Ancient bug history."

Not just that. Really important stuff. With my help, you might be able to understand. Interpret. But right now…I can't help. I'm locked out. There's a kind of firewall that stops me from looking around and searching. Keeps me from being active.

"Meaning what?" I ask.

Batman and the Silver Surfer have parted ways and are now just floating. I see them despite the fact that my eyes are closed. But then, my eyes have been closed all along.

I think this place needs a user to get it to open up. Someone alive. Really alive. Somebody with a need to know that deserves access privileges.

"Is it a kind of library? Why don't you check out a book or two?"

I am a book, shithead! There's only so much I can do. I'm becoming a record, and records are tightly controlled.

"They don't let books run the library, huh?"

I refresh or something every little while, and I'm allowed a kind of exercise—meeting up with similar records—and that feels good, but… Oh, crap. I'm in the cage again. Time out. No more for now.

I finally manage to crack my eyelids. Blurry, Joe and DJ hang over me.

"You okay?" Joe asks. "We couldn't wake you."

DJ smiles. "He's okay," he says.

Ship attachment noises ring out around us.

"We're transferring," Joe says.

"What's all this about turning glass and old records?" I ask DJ.

DJ makes his "it hurts to think" face. "It's pretty huge," he says. "I don't know how huge. When I hook in through one of the ones who turned glass, I just…" Again the pained expression. He shakes his head. "Let's go over that later," he says.

"No, now," I say.

The ship lurches. Our Skyrines and the Russians grab couches and stanchions. Jacobi flows smoothly past, followed by Ishida. Borden is waiting in the alcove opposite, beside the stowed pod. Crew Chief follows the last of our group. "We've docked," he says. "You got three minutes. I want you out of here as fast as possible. I will not stay connected to Spook for any longer than I have to."

"Got it," I say, then focus back on DJ. Borden listens closely.

"The tea hooks us in," DJ says. "Nobody's figured out how. But we're guests. We don't yet have full privileges."

"Coyle said the same thing," I say.

"Sir, that's *not* Captain Coyle," DJ says. "Everyone who turns glass shows up sooner or later. I don't know if we can trust anything they say, because the records have their own motives. They need to help us to stay flexible. They need to be useful to a potential user."

Joe shows his puzzle face.

"I can see the bugs, some of their history, their living back then, because the records want that," DJ says softly. "But I don't know what's true and what's propaganda—understand? The records cover *everything*. That's all I got."

"Yeah," I say. "But where are they? In the glass?"

DJ spreads his hands, nods, points his nose left, then right. "Kind of like that," he says.

I pull up from the couch. "Maybe Walker Harris knows," I say.

"Who's he?" DJ says.

"Came to visit me at Madigan. Could be a Guru."

"Amazing!" DJ says, totally credulous. "What do they look like?"

"A guy. Let's go," I say.

It's DJ's turn to stall. "Did you dream about Silver Surfer and Batman?" he asks.

We both twitch.

"Yeah, just now," I say.

"I've dreamed that so many times," DJ says. "Bat and Surf keep arguing, never resolve anything. Is that Coyle?"

"I think so."

"Well, she doesn't like me as much as you, but she's stuck with us, right?"

"I heard it different," I say.

"Ice Moon Tea, the records, whatever you want to call it, makes Coyle repeat that dream. I wonder she doesn't get bored."

"She's definitely irritated," I say. "That sounds like emotion, doesn't it?"

DJ thinks this over. "Yeah," he says. "But maybe that was her ground state when she was alive."

"We have to leave," Borden says, listening, taking notes in her head. I'm still undecided about Borden but this part I definitely do not like.

"Come on!" Crew Chief shouts, waving his arm. There's a frantic note in his voice. Spook ship actually frightens him. "We've only got a few minutes!"

We pass up the aisle and through the hatch into the accordion. Windows in the accordion's long stretch show us a shiny, curvy, intricate white framework wrapped around long clusters of glowing spheres like Japanese paper lanterns— and surrounding everything, those shrouds, the bright outer skirts, pleated panels rippling like silk in a slow breeze. Doesn't look practical, barely looks real.

Kumar and Mushran and Litvinov meet us on the other side. "We get privilege of Star Gown," Litvinov says. Russian name for Spook. "Three weeks to Titan—"

"Excellent!" Kumar says.

"Not so excellent. Departing Earth, Star Gown was attacked," Litvinov says. "Three weeks may be nine weeks, or months, if she is not at full speed. There is damage to seeds, to weapons, and damage to two drives."

Kumar looks perturbed. With a shake of his head, as if dismissing this doubtful news, he moves ahead to the hatch opening into the bigger ship. All of us compete to twist and find a better viewing angle.

Jacobi shoves her hand out. "Shit—there, and there," she says. We see gray streaking the shrouds and, farther aft, curled and torn struts and vanes. Forward, on a long, twisted boom that once separated cargo from forward living quarters, shattered spheres bunch like smashed eggs in a carton. "Looks bad," Jacobi says.

We pull ourselves along ropes that suddenly acquire wills of their own, stiffening and then coiling, rudely tugging the last of the lander's passengers into the Spook's shadowy gray interior. I swing up beside Borden as we move into a pitch-black chamber. Sounds big in here. Long echoes from the squeak and whistle and snap of the ropes. Then the lights come on, and everything turns White. Even harder to see how big the space is. Distant bays, cubes, trestles hung with rounded transporters. Spook is *big*.

"Can this ship still get us out there?" I ask Borden.

She squints at all the whiteness. Everything here is spotless and clean, despite the outer damage. "We're here. The settlers have made it to their frames. Everybody on the landers is safe."

"I'm turning you over to CWO Mueller," the lander's crew chief says behind us. We had forgotten he was still there. He makes a face at what he's seen. "Then I'm taking off."

"Mueller isn't here yet," Borden mutters.

"She will be." Crew Chief makes another face, as if he's glad to avoid the encounter, then tosses a quick salute, takes the rope, and grapples back to the hatch. The hatch hisses and snicks shut. Pressure pokes our ears—more echoing clangs and far-off, metallic scraping that seem to come from all around. The landers that delivered us are away. We're on our own.

Kumar hands his way back, sweating profusely. "Pilots say the ship is capable," he tells us, "but threats gather, and to reach full speed this close to Mars will be difficult."

Borden asks, "Where in hell is Mueller?"

The ropes slack and we transfer to grips along a series of parallel rails. We line up between the rails like a line of expectant gymnasts.

"Here she is," Borden says.

The Spook's crew chief swings down from a hatch overhead, arms and legs spread like a swimmer at the end of a deep dive, just before surfacing. She's forty-something with a Persian-cat face and looks like a former beauty queen who's spent too many years under the Texas sun—pretty in a rough fashion but hard. She wears a slender white crown that curls around her ears and seems to be listening to someone or something unpleasant. With a brisk nod, she removes the crown, lifts her pointed chin, and focuses her full attention on us.

"I'm CWO 7 Mueller," she says. "Beulah Mueller. Grunts call me Bueller. I'm go bitch on *Lady of Yue*, so listen up!"

She's a formidable presence. We listen.

"We have an incoming Box that doesn't want us to leave, and a squadron of disgruntled corvettes are about one-twenty K from us. They've been chasing us since NEO, they caught us once halfway to Mars—causing the damage you've just seen. We probably can't afford another run-in."

"Losses?" Kumar asks.

"All our gunnery mates, three out of four glider pilots. Fifty-six dead."

This news shakes Borden. "If we get to Titan, can we even *begin* our mission?" she asks.

"We can try, Commander," Bueller says. "Let's worry about that after we finish Spook prep. Is this all of you?"

"All," Litvinov confirms. Borden sadly agrees.

"We asked for a hundred and forty. I count thirty-one," Bueller says. "Waste of a big ship!" She grabs a pair of handles and swings in ahead of Kumar. The bars lurch and haul us forward. "First phase is coming up. Anyone here rated for big weapons? Bolts and long-range disruptors?"

Ishida, Jacobi, one of the *efreitors*, and Ulyanova raise their hands.

"Good. Talk to me in a few minutes. Right now, all of you strip and we'll get you right with Jesus."

The rails carry us forward to a more constrained space, walls dark with streamers of purple. I see little sparks in my vision. All of us going transvac experience cosmic rays now and then. But these sparks leave neon trails. They don't look like cosmic rays. More like optical migraines. Just a hint of what's to come.

Bueller watches as we shed our skintights, this time without the help of gravity, a one-handed maneuver—other hand on a handle—that some accomplish with speed and grace, but which takes me longer.

"I want to see you *naked*, Venn!" Bueller shouts.

"Yes, ma'am."

Bueller's voice becomes painful. Worse, I find it difficult to look at her—I keep wanting to look away. There's something off about her outline, her image. Is it me? The purple streaks and neon sparks? A weirdly opticked crew chief. She just doesn't look real. The rest seem to agree. No one will look at her directly without a squint or shake of the head. Joe is off to my left. I catch his eye. He knows something we don't. Christ, now I'm feeling like dried bonito—downright flaked.

The shed skintights drift off to nobody seems to care where in the dark chamber. The rails drag us along, bare feet dangling, through a rectangular opening in the far bulkhead and into a space fully as large as an aircraft hangar. Here one rail takes half of us to the right, the rest to the left. Bueller hangs back and hovers, tapping heads to indicate right, left. The grunts do not appreciate the familiarity, but clearly, Go Bitch doesn't give a damn. We're all she's getting and she's not happy.

Filling the center of the great white chamber is a steel wheel about thirty meters wide and two meters thick across, its inner rim studded with black bumps. The wheel is the first of three that form a tunnel or gantlet. I do not like this. Nobody around me likes this.

"We have to go through those?" Jacobi asks.

"Yeah," Bueller says.

"Why?"

"Purge!"

"What kind of purge?" Ishida asks.

"Quantum," Borden murmurs, but I'm the only one who hears her.

Ishida rubs her temple. "Like castor oil, ma'am?"

Bueller looks clown-sad. "Don't you read our briefings?"

"We've been busy, Chief," Jacobi says.

"It ain't about your fucking bowels," Bueller says. "Downsun, you've been hanging with bad company since before you were born. Pasts that never were, futures that will never be. They slow you down. Those wheels will start the process of getting you clean."

"Sounds like a tent revival," I say.

"Think of it as a cosmic car wash. There'll be another at waypoint—if we make it, which is getting less and less likely, goddammit! MOVE!"

Bueller swims around us, effortless as a sea lion in an ocean swell. One by one, in two lanes, she guides us through what could otherwise be subway tollgates, closer and closer to the great studded wheels. The tollgate lanes end at two steel autopsy tables. Each is sprung from behind by a heavy piston. Five meters from the first wheel, Bueller taps me and Kumar and tells us to lie flat against the slabs. Not autopsy tables—more like human pinball paddles.

Kumar looks at me with those mild, calm eyes. "I'm told it's not unpleasant," he says.

"You first," I say. He rewards me with the merest grimace.

Behind us, Bueller taps Ishida and Jacobi next, then two Russians. Our sisters exchange finger-hooks and sharp dares and line up. The Russians clump, waiting to see what happens to us. Bueller swims back and jostles and jabs. This makes the

Russians unhappy. Go Bitch doesn't give a fuck. Neither does Litvinov. The Russian colonel looks terminally depressed.

Kumar and I try to lie flat against the tables. Simultaneously, they hiss and not-so-gently shove us through the first wheel with just a half twist of spin. Kumar gives a little shriek, I clutch my balls, and both of us fly neatly through all three wheels. My hair stands on end. I don't have much hair and what there is is short. My fingertips tingle, but most curious of all, my innards try to decide whether they're properly arranged. I swear, it's like a fucking math wiz wants to shuck my guts as a topological experiment—particularly my colon. Maybe I'll just turn inside out. Won't make a difference, even inside out, humans are still just donuts.

The wheels ratchet three bumps counterclockwise and wait for the next pair. I let go of my balls. My muscles relax. My bowels stay tight and inside. I'm suddenly right with Jesus, clean and sparkly—renewed. Kumar's source was correct—as weird as this is, the total sensation, once the purge is finished, is not unpleasant. I feel like a thunderstorm has blessed me with cool air and a lungful of charged ions. Maybe that's it. Maybe we're all being ionized. I've run into tech sergeants and engineers—including DJ—all Tesla freaks willing to swear that everything the Gurus provided had already been invented by their hero. Some insisted the Gurus weren't real, that the government was just dosing out bits and pieces of the stuff Tesla did back in the twentieth century. I'm so invigorated I'm giving their crazy theories a new look.

Bueller gets us all through without a hitch. As we clutch ropes and bars beyond the wheels, staring owlishly, deciding whether or not we have complaints, wide circular lids at both ends of the chamber open and we see what waits beyond—fore and aft. It's a longitudinal view down the hull of the Spook, from a position about fifty meters out from the centerline.

"*Fuck*," Borden says with a frightened reverence. That's the second time I've heard her utter this grunt standard. But I agree. No other possible reaction.

Let's take the description in layers.

Judging from what we saw earlier, the fore end of the Spook is dominated by a wide gray bell, more of a shallow bowl, about sixty meters in diameter. From the convex center of the bowl juts the bullet-shaped bridge or command center, the ship's prow. The bell's concave side protects the bridge, command center, and crew areas from radiation or other weirdness aft. Classic.

Looking aft, however, there's little or nothing classic or familiar about the Spook. First comes a slender run of steel-gray pipes. The pipes surround and support glassy blue modules, like grapes stuck between soda straws. In line aft of the straws and grapes comes a procession of space frames filled with payload or cargo, arranged in fasces like cylinders in a revolver. Each chamber in the cylinders reveals the rounded bronze or gray tip of a seed—what I assume will become, on Titan, a weapon or vehicle or some other piece of equipment. They look like bees waiting to crawl out of a hive. Just aft of straws and grapes, and just before the space frames, the designers chose to mount defensive weapons, extensible pods that rib and groove the transparent outer hull.

"Damage," Borden observes. Many of the pods are blackened, dark—or gone. Bueller makes a little grunt, but adds nothing.

The three long "skirts" begin aft of the payload, about a

third of the ship's length back from the bridge. When we first saw them, they rippled and flowed, kind of pearly, but now they're stiffer and singed with streaks of gray—not as pretty but still impressive. They surround and partly obscure a stack of pale gray disks, each about sixty meters wide and separated by trusses like coins in a magician's hand. Even damaged, this central complex shimmers with a foggy uncertainty that makes my eyes cross. Like Bueller, none of it looks entirely real. Maybe it isn't. The trusses and coins run aft another fifty meters beyond the skirts' hemline to the Spook's tail— flaring black cones that I assume are engine nozzles, ribbed with red and black vanes that might shed heat. All of this, the Spook's business end, is wrapped in a fine hairnet of inter- secting struts and beams.

Seen almost in its entirety, the ship is weirdly beauti- ful, like a blown-glass jellyfish leading a parade of steel and enamel fruits. Doesn't look remotely human-made. None of this does, really.

Bueller's sun-chapped lips pull her ruddy cheeks into a hard grin. "That's enough," the crew chief says. "We're trans- vac in fifteen minutes. We need you properly stoned."

"Stoned?" Ishida asks, one eye wide.

"*Stowed*," Bueller says. Her grin flattens. Comically som- ber, she waves us on.

"She's nuts," Ishida says, not quite out of the crew chief's hearing.

"These are traditionally odd people," Kumar says. "They have adapted to an odd ship. But *Lady of Yue* has been travel- ing to Saturn and back for five years with never an incident."

Jacobi lifts an eyebrow. "Except now. Ship looks pretty banged up. How much can she take?"

"She is *very* strong," Kumar says. "I have been told—"

"You've never been on a ship like this, have you?" Borden asks him.

We pause to admire the broken protocol.

"There has never *been* another ship like this," Kumar finally says, voice low.

"Guru theory?" Ishida asks.

"Not precisely," Kumar says. "Wait Staff was instructed to approach humans who had particular ideas, to fund them and give them laboratories in which to work. We did. This is one of the results."

"I knew it!" DJ says. "It's Tesla shit, right?"

"All human, huh?" Jacobi says, in no way agreeing with DJ. "But guided by Gurus. And Socrates's boy slave understood geometry from birth."

Again, learned sister.

"We eat first?" Ishikawa asks.

"No time!" Bueller calls from the front of our line. "We assign soccer balls. Big Vamoose in fifteen minutes. Short sleep. *Then* food."

"Soccer balls?" a Russian asks behind me.

"Big Vamoose?" another Russian asks, frowning.

I slip my hand out flat, showing motion at speed. He still looks puzzled.

"What happens in the second purge?" Jacobi asks.

Borden decides this line of thinking is not productive. She calls down the line to Litvinov, "Anyone see Mushran?"

The Russian colonel is making sure his troops are organized and prepped and distracted. He points forward. "Went before," he suggests. "Ship is big and very clean!" he adds cheerily. "Never stay in such fine hotel." His troops appear unconvinced.

Bueller warns us against touching or even brushing each other for the next few minutes, so we keep apart—not that there's been much hugging. What *does* happen at midpoint? Maybe I'm too encrusted with unresolved bits, a deep dark sinner who won't make it. Maybe I'll be bleached out of existence. I might have some of Coyle's sins hanging on me as well. But my inner voices have chosen to be quiet—no Bug, no Coyle. I'm all alone in here. Feels almost normal.

I turn left and look up through a clear panel into more structure. We all look. Beyond intricate shadowy architecture we get a glimpse of the brownish limb of Mars, slowly rolling.

"Bye-bye, Red," Jacobi says.

I keep staring, like maybe Mars can answer something for me before we leave. Above the limb, I see a star. The star goes black. The space around the star goes even blacker. Then, something huge cuts a shadowy wedge out of Mars. The wedge seems to double, sharpen, and form an arrowhead.

Jacobi and the others have turned away, waiting to be led to their places for the next ride. Try as hard as I can, I can't make sense of what's happening out there, and after the confusion of our intro to the Spook and all the other shit we've been through, my instincts are numb.

The wedge digs deeper into Mars, blocking most of what I can see. Then I see it's part of a cube, a huge cube—and its corners are pushing out and twisting around, shaping pyramids, which in profile look like arrowheads. Between the pyramidal corners and the main body of the cube, sparkling spiderwebs are being drawn by the thousands.

It's the ship we saw in orbit before departing from Earth.

It's Box.

I tap Bueller on the shoulder to distract her from herding the rest of us aft to our soccer balls. As she slowly spins about, a high whistle pierces the air, and *Lady of Yue* shudders around us, then begins an awful wailing sound, like a woman who's just lost all of her children.

The skirts, the sails that flow aft of the cargo and crew areas, are spreading wide, revealing more damage as they expand—but also sending out their own spider-silk sparkles. The sparkles fan to shape a nimbus, then flow farther aft, where they cage a welding-torch-blue glow. Fascinating to watch, painful, hypnotic. Leaves burning afterimages on the backs of my eyeballs.

"Don't look!" Bueller shouts, then grabs my shoulder and shoves me toward the others. There's a weird sensation, like the ship is expanding longitudinally, like we'll soon be squeezed out and left behind, surrounded by vacuum. "Grab hold! We're moving *now.*"

I feel myself drifting aft, my grip on the rail insufficient to keep me in place against the growing acceleration. Borden and Ishida are sliding along right next to me, along with Ulyanova and two more Russians. Below me I see Jacobi and Ishikawa and DJ. I can't see Joe or Kumar.

Then—we're a tangle of limbs, bodies, heads colliding against the far bulkheads. Cables and equipment sway and swing above us. Bueller still tries to pull herself forward, but she's finally pried loose and joins us in the tangle, right on top of Borden.

Everything around us reflects that far, sapphire-blue arc light. Through the forward frame, I can make out that Mars is gone. But not the black cube. That shadow is following, then trying to flank *Lady of Yue* even as we untangle, cursing and climbing free. Bueller rises over the mass and looks around, eyes flinty—then points to Ishida, Jacobi, the *efreitor*, and Ulyanova.

"Outboard to the weapons," she says. "We have four. We need five."

"Venn," Jacobi says. I try to remind her about my not being rated, but she shrugs it off. "Just bigger point and shoot," she says. "Right? Follow Ishida and you can't go wrong."

Joe watches us from a recess, where he's shielding Kumar. He tips a salute at me. I mouth something rude, but he's already turned and is dislodging Kumar from a nest of snaking cables.

At Bueller's command, more rails and cables descend, and, behind Jacobi, we all grab hold, to be yanked outboard so hard I wonder that my shoulder stays in its socket.

"Keep your eyes forward!" Bueller calls as we move through the framework, toward the weapons pods on their translucent booms, now retracted snug against the outer hull. I count twenty pods—fifteen that were apparently ruptured during the previous encounter, no doubt venting their contents—their gunners—into space. Five are still intact.

We climb in. Ishida takes the pod closest to mine. Jacobi teams up beside Ulyanova. The *efreitor* seems happy to be working alone.

Bueller stands by the root hub.

I've fitted my nearly naked body into the bucket seat and watch the laces strap me in. A half helmet swings up from the rear of the pod and cradles the back of my skull. Something buzzes along my spine. Guidance? Nerve induction? I look over at Ishida, but can't see much—the brightness of the pod's surface obscures her details.

The pods extend and we are now surrounded by stars, with *Lady of Yue* below. Box is trailing behind the arc light, but still closing the distance.

"We caught them by surprise when we left NEO. Box has been in a hurry ever since," Bueller says through comm. "She's larger and faster, but rising upsun, chasing us, she still hasn't had time to shed all her sins."

How does Bueller know that?

And what the hell does it mean?

"We still have the advantage," Bueller says, but her voice drops a note.

"Box already found you once and clobbered you," Jacobi says. She sounds right next to me.

"We need five minutes!" Bueller says. "Those sparkles running to the corners of the cube are drive tension distributors. Cut them with your bolts or disruptors and you'll slow her down, and that'll give us just what we need…five minutes, maybe, but not a second more."

I fit my hands into the trigger gloves. I'm in charge of a bolt weapon. I know how they work, in smaller form, on a planet's surface—but this seems natural enough. My fingers feel the guidance and trigger post and I test it, also natural enough. Another buzz along my spine, this time reaching out to my fingers. The pod swings on its pedestal, and I see, along the gleaming inner surface, a set of reticules and crosshairs move into place. They converge on a corner of Box, then outline several of the tension sparkles, whatever the hell those are.

What if I still have no fucking idea what I'm doing?

Ishida speaks in my left ear. "Three of us will carve out the far corner, with its interior exposed—see those lines?"

"I see the far corner."

"You will trim the near corner."

"Harder to see those lines," I tell her. "Have you done this before?"

"Never in space," Ishida says. "Follow instinct. Hit what you can, but make it count."

"If the pyramids ride any higher, if they extend any farther, you can't help but see the tension lines," Bueller says over comm.

"Yeah," I say, starting to feel really ill. Something is dragging us along through the stars like a cat drags a rat. I assume it's our own ship. We still haven't finished getting straight with Jesus, right? Worse, we're newbies manning weapons that are totally vulnerable to being blown wide open, like glass bottles in a shooting gallery.

Then Ishida and Jacobi loose their bolts. I follow those pulsing white dots, watch them carve the far pyramid's tension lines, watch that sharp black corner of the cube shiver and twist on its extended post....

And then I focus on the lines just visible below my own assigned pyramid, linking it with the main mass of Box.

The reticules align.

Box sends out its own bolts, a firefly mass curving around from the far side, presumably the business end, and traveling twice as fast out to our ship, where they nick another smoking groove in a skirt, then climb up to sizzle one of the pods—

The lone *efreitor* is surrounded by a ball of plasma. His pod ruptures and bits of him fly out into the darkness, streaming behind like a tiny comet's tail. We keep firing,

Bueller keeps shouting in our ears. We keep cutting spider-web tension lines.

Then all at once, *Lady of Yue* really cuts loose, and in our present state, the stars take a horrible spin—and we are no longer effective as gunners or as human beings. I spatter the inside of the pod with the contents of my mostly empty stomach—mixed with blood. My eyes feel as if they're going to fall out on my cheeks.

But Ishida and Jacobi exchange calm comments, battle discussion—in Japanese. Ulyanova chimes in in Russian. Somehow the tone alone helps me keep it together—that, and another buzz along my spine. We've had a definite effect. The corner pyramids are retracting and Box seems to be wobbling. Maybe even getting smaller.

I think Box is falling back—miracle.

The pods retract. Bueller opens them and extracts us one by one, ignoring the smoking ruin of the *efreitor*'s pod—gathering us up in her arms, wiping us down with her sleeves, then grabbing our damp collars and tugging and shoving us inboard using feet, hands, legs, arms, herding us. Her own face is streaked with tears and spattered with vomit. Maybe ours, maybe hers.

"Did it work?" Jacobi asks, slurring her words.

"Don't ask," Bueller says. "Maybe." She huffs and tugs. Ishida gives me a thumbs-up. I have no idea what the hell just happened, or what we did—whether it was real or just a nightmare. But through the structure, looking out to where Mars had once been, and Box had hovered, I see nothing—

Just a gray smear of stars.

"Move it!" Bueller shouts. "We got four minutes to get you packed away."

"We're fucking puppets," Jacobi says. "We don't understand any of this!"

Borden helps Bueller marshal us toward the centerline. Jacobi is still fomenting. "The Gurus are so goddamned frightened they're sending us out here and just pulling strings. How the fuck did that ever happen? Does anybody know what's going on?"

"Wait until you see Titan," Bueller says grimly.

Something comes back to me, something Kumar said. *That's what the Gurus like. They like it interesting.*

Makes me want to puke all over again.

THE BIG VAMOOSE

More rails slide from above. Bueller is a dozen meters ahead. She tells us to grab and go. The rails take us aft through the soda straws and blue spheres—Bueller's so-called soccer balls. They still look like grapes to me. Borden is next handle over. Jacobi and Ishida are to my left. All gawk in wonder or worry. As we're transported aft, we pass the first few triplets of blue spheres. They're dark, with stripes faintly barber-poling across their surfaces—out of order?

Finally we arrive at spheres that glisten pure blue, no stripes. Bueller swims backward, assessing our nearly naked forms with a practiced eye. She tells us to pay attention and assigns each a number. "Name and rank don't mean shit. Size, mass, composition are important. We're balancing our balls." Not even a grin.

Numbers light up on the corresponding spheres, and our rods and handles pull us up next to our assignments, so awesomely efficient it threatens to bring tears to my eyes. I wonder if this is how the secretary's heroic son got out to Titan a few years ago. Conveyed in brilliant style, using such sophisticated might and know-how—only to get himself killed. Maybe eaten by one of those insects in the Spook's tail, or something weirder down on Titan.

Crew Chief quickly opens a plastic box and removes stacks of gray circles, like doilies or lace yarmulkes, each sealed in gel in an envelope of transparent plastic. "Here's the good stuff," Bueller says. "I guarantee pleasant dreams."

The envelopes gleam and squish as she passes them out, one apiece.

"Part one of your brain boost, weeks of training—makes you all good citizens. Don't mess with these beauties. Follow instructions to the letter or you'll be shit down the chute, useless to me or anyone else."

Jacobi and Ishida examine their packages with curled lips. "Could have used one of these earlier, right?" Jacobi asks me.

Borden and Joe and Tak and the Russians hold theirs gingerly.

Two minutes left.

"They're called caps," Bueller says. "Used to be an acronym, I forget for what."

"Cranial Amplified Programming," Borden says.

"Yes, ma'am. Now you know why I forgot. You don't need to shave your heads, just pull the caps out of their wrappers, place them over the center of your crown, and they'll settle in and glue down. Leave them there until they fall off. They don't put anything inside your skull but training and info, and that'll take twelve hours to set up and become useful."

"Not for these two," Borden says, pointing to me and DJ. "We need their heads clear." She takes Bueller aside and they have words. The commander has doubts DJ and I are up for this much stimulation. I hear something about her not knowing all that they put me through back at Madigan. Wouldn't want to trigger *instaurations*. Maybe she said *installations*. Either way, what the hell are they?

"*Everybody*, ma'am," Bueller insists with a concerned expression, brooking no dissent, even from rank. "We're really short and we need expert drivers. If they don't get it, they won't have the proper training, and they won't have touch ID. The machines won't recognize them, they won't be able to coordinate with the team—they could all die down there!"

Grunts love to watch command argue. Makes us feel warm and cozy. Bueller's winning, but Borden isn't happy. She backs off, head lowered, like she wants to butt someone, anyone.

"Me, too?" Ishida asks, touching her metal cranium.

"Yeah," Bueller says. She delicately examines Ishida's head, finger hovering, and studies the line between metal and flesh. "Plenty of room. You'll be fine," she says.

"*Arigato*," Ishida says.

"What's in them?" Tak asks.

"Reflex learning, part one. Key ideas. Words and phrases that will speed your getting acquainted with seed product down on the Wax."

"Product..." Ishida says.

"Weapons and vehicles," Bueller says. "Seeds begin to suck up processed materials as soon as your glider connects with the reserves stockpiled on the base platform. If the base or the platform still exists. We'll know that in a couple of hours, after we get there. We can't see it from orbit. Understood?"

"Vehicles and big weapons get assembled in place," Tak

says, as if this makes all the sense in the world. Joe watches us from forward, where he's sitting between Borden and Kumar.

"Starting with those seeds," Jacobi says.

"Right," Bueller says.

"Wax?" DJ asks.

"Whole damn moon is covered with waxy residues, along with poisons, corrosive bases, and saline cesspools. Worse than you'd encounter in your worst nightmare. There's even traces of something like sarin gas, and if *that* seeps into your gear…"

Better and better. Bug is back and thinks it's all very cozy. Saline solution ripe with metals? Mother's milk to ancient life. Lightning and electricity? Once there were entire ecosystems that dined only on electrons and scavenged their dead to replace membranes. We're all wimps compared to the great old ones.

Thirty seconds.

Borden, Jacobi, Ishida, Ishikawa, Kumar, and I share a number. That means we'll cohabit a grape. We crawl inside, Borden last. The big blue sphere is heavily padded with thin, sun-yellow lamps hiding between the cushions. I see the swirly pattern, like being inside a soccer ball. The hatch closes. Ishida mutters and Jacobi looks around, anticipating the next slam. From our point of view, new tech has never implied comfort.

"Resuming now," Bueller says.

Second-phase acceleration begins. It's much gentler than the first. We shift to one side of the ball and bump the cushions. No straps, no drama. All there is to it. We're cargo, packed and ignorant but so far comfortable enough. Warm and comfortable.

"This is Big Vamoose?" Jacobi asks.

The pressure grows in that same direction. Ishida closes her eyes, claps her hands, mutters. Maybe she's praying again.

We're floating inside a soccer ball, wearing yarmulkes, hitching a ride on a Chinese warrior lady with long, burned skirts—about to fly off to rescue an entire moon. I'm still recovering from watching our bolts trim Box, from feeling *Lady of Yue* mess with Jesus and everything else about reality. I still can't believe any of it. But then, I didn't believe I was going to Mars the first time, either.

Jacobi spread-eagles and bumps into Borden's leg. Borden withdraws, tightening her space. Ishikawa's taking it all in stride—no strain, no sweat. Kumar tucks his doilied head, folds his legs and arms into a lotus, and rolls to a point of stable rest.

Finally, Crew Chief's voice reaches us inside the sphere. "Guidance reports Box still tracking at a million klicks, so close your eyes. That's what I do. Close your eyes and count backward from ten."

I get to five before my fingers tingle. I feel a weird crawling and tightening on my head. The cap, I assume. I sure hope my quantum junk has been scrubbed.

Then…

I black out.

Don't feel a thing.

COBWEBS

Darkness, close and warm. Air smells stale, like I've been here awhile. I remember where we are. A moment of concern, not quite panic, as I think the lights will come on and I'll be surrounded by desiccated mummies.

But the ball brightens and everyone's fine. Borden thrashes, as does Ishida, who might hurt someone if she's not careful—but she quickly regains motor control and looks embarrassed. "*Gomenasai*," she says.

"*De nada*," Ishikawa says, rubbing her shoulder.

I feel reasonably chipper. My scalp itches. I look around. There's something silvery and dusty on our heads, like a net of gossamer threads. I pat my scalp. The others refuse to pay attention, so I thump my crown and say, "Cobwebs, ladies."

They reach up, hesitate in unison—kind of comical, like they don't want to find a spider. Then they pat the gossamer and make disgusted faces.

"What the fuck is this?" Jacobi asks, inspecting a clump of threads.

"Laying eggs," I say.

"Fuck you!" Ishida says, and keeps plucking and balling up the stuff that comes out of her short hair. "It's that goddamned cap."

Kumar wakes next, legs still tucked into a lotus. He reaches across to Jacobi's temple and pinches up a thread. Jacobi's reaction is swift; she grabs his hand, ready to crush fingers, snap wrist, break arm—

Kumar freezes. Privilege does not precede him everywhere. He says, "Pardon me. Do you feel any difference?"

"No." Jacobi shoves his hand aside.

He flexes his fingers. "Nor do I, yet."

Borden wakes last. Seeing the others, her hand goes to her scalp. Her expression is priceless. "Jesus Christ!" she says. "Is this it?"

"Part one, the crew chief said," Kumar observes.

"I demand a raise," Ishida says.

The lights brighten. The hole in the soccer ball slides open. Bueller peers in. "I'm cracking my little eggs," she says. "Chicks are bright and fluffy. It's been two weeks. We're about halfway. Come on out and get some food."

"Not hungry," Ishida says.

"Me, neither," Jacobi says.

"Mandatory," Crew Chief says. "You've learned a lot in the last few days and we want to set it firm. Believe me, you won't want to miss *Lady of Yue* at full sail."

Ishida, Jacobi, and Borden finish removing their gossamer. Ishida collects the threads, wads them up, and leaves a small, dusty clump about an inch wide suspended in the middle of the ball. We push out through the hole. More smart ropes offer themselves and we move forward between the white metal beams. All very efficient. No bouncing, no collisions, just straightforward transport beyond the spheres toward the big bell.

The outer hull of the ship has darkened to a deep, cloudy-sky gray.

Ishida glides past me. "Maybe we'll ride centipede together," she says. I can see it. A great big machine, bronze-colored and round-headed, big slit-port for an eye, with a thick, muscular body and a long crawling tail—machine or monster? Now residing as a seed in cargo stores.

SNKRZ.

Jacobi guides herself toward Ishida. "Gadget, how's the equipment?"

"Smooth and shiny," Ishida says. "I feel innocent."

"Me, too," Jacobi says, looking unsure of herself, and burps.

Ishida lifts her real eyebrow. "Sir, your being innocent worries me."

For the moment, I also feel pretty good. *That* worries me. Nobody hauls grunts in comfort. There's got to be misery. And here it is. My turn for a bilious belch.

Jacobi looks green. "Not again," she says.

"What?" Kumar asks. He looks surprised, then turns a lovely olive. His stomach twitches. We're all popping sweat, trailing a mist of salty drops.

More rope lines appear from the other side of the long vineyard. We're joined by Ishikawa, then by a bare handful of Russians, but many of the ropes are empty—no Litvinov, no Mushran, no Joe and DJ. These Russians don't speak English. Not having skintights and angels puts us at a disadvantage. We're as dumb as we look.

Crew Chief meets us at the apex of the rope ride, holding on to a steel ring mounted around a big circular opening. "Jump off and wait here," she says. "We've got crew quarters beyond. Should fit you all in."

"Crew get a good sleep?" I ask, trying to avoid another heave.

"Nobody sleeps but passengers," she says. "*Lady of Yue* is a cranky girl."

"Who's driving?" Jacobi asks.

"Two rabbis," Crew Chief says.

"Rabbis?" Ishida asks.

"That's what we call them. They keep the ship right with the law."

I look aft and finally see Joe and DJ and Litvinov and more Russians, including Ulyanova. A gentle breeze wafts forward. Crew Chief tells us to release the circular rail and go with the flow. We tumble with the currents. I feel like a wet dandelion seed with a sour tummy.

DJ moves up beside me, spreads his arms, flaps, and twists. "You'll believe an asshole can fly," he says.

"Keep tight!" Bueller says.

The opening takes us into a tube about five meters wide and maybe fifty long. Halfway along, the tube turns clear as glass and we end up in an outboard bubble just aft of the weapons pods.

Lady of Yue's skirts no longer ripple. They've moved forward a hundred meters, where they shroud the soda-straw vineyard and the cargo stores beyond like a stiff cape, with the gray bell as a great round hat. The whole Spook seems to have grown to maybe two thousand meters from stem to stern.

"Where the hell are we?" Joe asks, pasty and damp, behind me and DJ. Bits of cap still fleck his scalp.

There's activity on the other side of the bell. Something large and pale and curved rises over the rim of the bell, then moves aft below the skirts like a hoop half-hidden by hanging laundry.

"Here come the garters," Bueller says. "Aren't they perrr-ty?"

The natural light this far out in the system is gray and indistinct. It's going to be even darker out by Saturn. The stars, with so little competition, shine sharper and brighter than ever. We're a hell of a ways from Earth, from Mars, from the sun. It's lonely and empty out here.

What's the reverse of claustrophobia—agoraphobia?

"*Lady of Yue* has three garters in nine sections. In part, they strengthen the holds and stability vanes aft during the next phase of flight. We'll get to Saturn space, from where we are now, inside of three days. This is the hard part, ladies."

We watch the garters join section by section—what we can see of them. Jacobi huddles with her squad. Our Skyrine sisters cock their heads, listening girl to girl. The guys might as well not be here.

Bueller says, "Matter down close to the sun acquires bad habits and old sin. Matter that knows sin is held back, but matter that is cleansed becomes young and fast. We have to get this far out from the sun to shed the last of it. That shit really starts to fall away when we hook up the garters."

The Russians are stony. The last thing any warrior needs is a feeling that our strength is tied to evil ways and fucked-up souls. We know what we've done and where we'll likely go because of it. Only God has promised to understand. It scares me that out here, maybe we've passed outside His boundaries. I hate this fucking *Lady of Yue*, hate all ships that carry us into harm's way—I really do.

"Of course, it's all temporary," Bueller says. Again, her weird, Persian-cat look. "When we return downsun, matter reverts like a sailor on liberty. Now it's time for pudding. After you eat, one more little nap. We'll wake you in Saturn space about three hours from Titan."

COOK'S TOUR

We get our pudding cups in the small cafeteria, really more of a coffee shop. The cups contain brown goo that tastes like chocolate or coffee or toffee or all three, pretty okay and makes us feel stronger. Crew Chief waits patiently.

Ishida asks Bueller why we aren't given a chance to inspect the cargo aft—the big insect-looking things. "Does cap training kick in when we see them, or when they're finished?"

"Won't mean a thing to you right now," Bueller says. "They're seeds. They get finished on Titan. Saves a lot of mass."

Our tummies are full. Drowse hits us as we return to the vineyard and our soccer balls.

"How long since you've been back to Earth?" Jacobi asks Crew Chief, eyelids drooping.

"Too long," Bueller says. There's a wistful something in the way she says it. She closes the hole to our ball. The interior gets dark.

"She can't go home," Ishida says. "Too many times out and back."

"Too many times stripped and reloaded," Jacobi says.

We sleep. We sleep in hopes all our sins will be gone when we wake up. Goddamn, what a sleep. If it's all the same to you, General Patton, I'd rather shovel shit in Louisiana.

PART THREE

PART THREE

TITAN

Again, we feel pretty good when Bueller pops the soccer balls and we spill out. This time, there's an undeniable extra layer of youth and freshness, a new enthusiasm that comes from whatever's happened since the garters were applied. Yet nothing about Crew Chief has changed. If anything, her outlines seem fuzzier. I look around. None of us are exactly crystal. Big Vamoose must have affected our vision.

I hope.

Bueller takes us back to the outboard bubble. *Lady of Yue* is a Sally Rand kind of gal, slipping her white feathers over the best parts, showing less than you want to see, less than you need to see, but enough to keep curiosity fresh. I vow that's the last time I'll think kindly of this massive, silk-skirted bitch—but in fact I can't feel too down on anything because of that damned *freshness*. Maybe there is a long habit of sin way back in the old neighborhood, where so many terrible things have happened. Somebody once called that Karma. I don't ask Kumar about Karma. Too alliterative.

Fuck, I'm cheerful.

Borden and Kumar and Litvinov form a little triangle in the passage forward, as if blocking the crew chief from exiting without more explanation. But she's wrung out, and all that's left to explain is that we're on our last reserves. *Lady of Yue* is going to deliver us with all we're likely to ever get to accomplish our mission—whatever that might be. We're lucky to be alive.

"Take it slow," Bueller says. "Take a moment to find yourself again. Sorry to say that we've made you a very lumpy bed, my friends." The Persian-cat look is gone. She seems so damned out of focus I want to rub my eyes.

She peers forward and we rotate to see Kumar preceding a pair of small, skeletally thin figures in dark gray coveralls cinched around their waists—ugly but practical outfits, comfortable in zero-g. Both have prominent gray caps on their scalps—thicker than what we were given. They look permanent.

Kumar says, "Our pilots want to pass along a last bit of information, and wish us luck."

"These are the rabbis," Bueller explains in an undertone. "We call them that because of their relation to the law, to deep physics, and those caps. They get new ones every trip. Their caps don't fall off, and they don't take them off until they get new ones." She sucks in a deep breath at the audacity of what's happening. "Rabbis don't *ever* meet with passengers. Socialize, I mean. This is special, so be nice."

Both of our pilots have short, kinky black hair, flattened noses, and rich umber skin. Except for their thinness, they might be Pacific Islanders, descendants of the first humans to navigate by the stars. It's a strange meeting, leaders of a doomed crew to an equally doomed expeditionary force.

The pilots take us back to the observation bubble. They want to join us in viewing our destination. At first, they say very little. They speak with their golden-brown eyes, and they point.

Lady of Yue is descending toward Titan, which right now is between Saturn and the distant sun. For the first time, we see all of Titan eclipsing the sun, a moody golden scythe cradling a dark brown ball, backlit by stars and other moons— and by Saturn. The full glory of Saturn and its rings holds our attention for a good long time. Everyone is transfixed.

Almost everyone.

I track Joe's attention because Joe won't let the pretty stuff get in the way. Both he and Litvinov survey *Lady of Yue* fore and aft to get a better picture of the damage. It's bad. Two of the main cargo frames and two of the balance vanes beyond are marked with gray gouges and slashes. Hard to know whether anything in the frames can be salvaged, but the vanes do not look useful. Three of the six skirts are stiff and dark and one has a peculiar tear running its length, edges still sparking, which I might be able to understand if I knew just what they were made of in the first place—

Then Litvinov and Joe turn. The pilots are actually going to speak to us. Bueller is astonished.

The older pilot has streaks of gray around his temples and the skin of his face looks like soft leather. We settle in, grow quiet, and turn toward him like kids on a bus trip. It takes real presence to make Skyrines settle in so intently.

"We would like to bring better news," he says in a wispy

voice. He has a strong, out-of-kilter gravitas—we can see him, we assume he's there, but the light he reflects seems incomplete, and when we look sideways, he doesn't quite stick to the background. "We've traveled here for seven seasons. First season, we had stations around the southern hemisphere, and Antags had stations around the northern. We were stretched too thin to fight. More of an exploratory season, learning how to survive, trying to figure the best way to carve down and access the seas—because that's what both Antags and humans wanted to do."

"The Ants told you that?" Ishida asks.

The older pilot smiles. "No, dear," he says, like a patient grandfather. He doesn't look that old, but the grayness of his reflected light gives that impression. "We sent out surveillance machines, both crewed and automated. Most didn't come back. That was the only killing going on that season, until the very end.

"Then we learned the Antags were digging deep. They'd broken through to a polar sea and were sinking big machines and fanning them out through the canyons and around the ridges, up to the shelving slopes and crustal caps, as far as they could reach. They made it down first, but we were right on their heels, and we began a two-pronged push on the surface to close up their ventrances—cryo-volcanic fissures and blowholes. We were delicate, because we wanted to preserve as much as we could. We used methane jets to carpet bomb the northern polar regions with conventional explosives, then sent our best big machines on long marches overland. We thought we'd surround and seal off and just vent-hop until we'd closed all of them. Didn't work.

"Our first-stage product wasn't that efficient. The Antagonists were better at converting raw materials. Their machines grew faster and became bigger than our machines. They chewed us up on the surface, and we never made it into the deep oceans. First season came to an abrupt end just as we were able to defend and finish our own ventrance. A very brave force descended during the short pause to see what they could see. We had to abandon them."

I can feel Coyle listening, agreeing. *I was there.* Bad season, worst season of all—highest percentage of casualties. She stuck around for the second delivery of soldiers and seeds, new product, new designs—after taking in the lessons of the first season.

"Season two was different," the pilot says. "We lasted, though still with many casualties. We cleared more vents, finished our exploratory journeys from the southern poles to the equator—even claimed vents north of the equator, old Antagonist entrances—surrounded them, sunk in and defeated them, kept the enemy from digging out—thousands of their machines were destroyed or lost. We lost dozens. Finally, a good season for us, terrible for them.

"But the Antagonists had learned. Season three was the most important of all. That's when we came upon the saline jungles. Some called them cities. They were old and seemed deserted, but our Wait Staff advisors communicated with the Gurus, and they were very interested."

Mushran regards our dubious expressions with a dignified nod. The pilot defers to him, while Kumar moves around our little group as if conducting a diagnostic survey. He seems concerned about too much knowledge being added all at once. Knowledge can change the mix.

"We thought this was more archaeology than battle, which

was fine by me," Mushran says. "I like to learn and live. The saline jungles were intricate mazes made of compacted salts and waxes and plastics, hard as granite. Traveling between their branches was like seeing coral reefs from a worm's point of view. They stretched for hundreds of kilometers, rising to touch the crust like pillars—mostly around the equatorial regions, where the tides were strongest, where the aurora sang bright, and purple currents flickered like lightning. Really. Just like that. Continuous and unbelievably beautiful."

"You were on Titan?" Jacobi asks him.

"Along with Captain Coyle," Mushran says.

We regard Mushran with more respect. This does not affect him in the least. "When we first explored the saline jungles, we thought some parts might still be alive—but there was no life. They were barren, populated only by electric currents and ionized, oxygen-free membranes, like cell walls but many kilometers across. Nothing like triple worms or spider castles."

"What are those?" Jacobi asks.

"You'll see them. Still, the jungles seemed dynamic—the way the purple discharges and exchanges moved. Some of our observers were especially interested. They formed a cadre within the battalion and called the purple flows inside the cities 'I/O,' without explanation. We thought they meant the Jovian moon. But later we learned they meant *Input-Output*. The saline cities might be dead, but they were still active—still very much in use."

"By who?" I ask.

"We did not know," Mushran says. "About the time of the sixth season, we heard rumors about the old mines on Mars. Our I/O experts were again interested. And when they heard that Antags were dropping comets to destroy the Martian mines, the old fragments of moon, our experts quickly returned to orbit. We were told to abandon the saline jungles and fall back to our fortified deep-ocean stations. Many of us returned through our few open vents to the surface and caught gliders back to *Lady of Yue*, which returned us to Earth. Some of our experts were already anticipating what happened in season seven. Kumarji referred to these new activities as a 'war on information.' But none of us knew whose information was being targeted. That's when our stations began to get seriously pasted. And that's also when we saw evidence that Antags were attacking not just us. They were going after each other."

"We can't know what we're supposed to do here," Jacobi says. "Who are we defending? What's left to defend?"

The others murmur and nod agreement.

"What's our mission, Commander?" Jacobi asks Borden.

"We have no combat orders," Borden says. "Division Four tells us to deliver Corporal Johnson and Master Sergeant Venn to Titan, get them as close to the saline jungles as possible—and wait for results." She looks exhausted and folds her arms.

The older pilot picks up the narrative. "Our last orbital season, we saw that Titan was being repeatedly bombarded by comets."

"Antag?" Litvinov asks.

"We presume," the pilot says. "Nearly hyperbolic orbits. The maps made for the previous season are useless. River networks, plains, and highland landmasses have been extensively reworked. Eleven out of twelve installations have fallen silent, presumably destroyed with all personnel. However, cap training—instructions for operating your equipment and weapons systems—is up-to-date. As for the strategic situation, and whether there are still Antagonists—nobody knows."

Without farewells, the pilots depart. We're quiet for a time. Then Joe taps Tak, DJ, and me, taking us aside, and pulls us in close. "Captain Coyle served on Titan years before she was sent to Mars," he says. "She expressed her opinions and got busted down. When they sent her back to Earth, she promptly re-upped, went full MARSOC at Camp Lejeune, and rose to major in record time. Then she talked back some more and got demoted again, but they still gave her tough assignments. They gave her Mars. Anyway, Borden thinks you two might have a special connection with Coyle that could help us down there."

"That would have been *years* ago," DJ says.

"Even so, that's a big reason you were plucked out of Madigan. Kumar and Mushran and Division Four believe in ghosts."

"Do *you*, sir?" I ask.

Joe's look is veiled. "Prove me wrong," he says. Tak stands by looking rock steady. Bless Tak Fujimori.

STATS

Titan grows hour by hour. Bug and I like it in the bubble. Well—Bug doesn't actually express an opinion, but I speak for it.

Borden and Kumar persuaded the other Skyrines to leave me alone. Borden wants me close to Titan. In full sun, the old moon looks like a big dusty orange shot a little out of focus. Dim at the edges (it's not very bright out here), brownish in places. Foggy. Most of the details we see are the frilly, tortured edges of high methane clouds. Methane. Swamp gas. *Right.* There are methane oceans down there and methane rivers. Liquid methane falls as rain in drops bigger than marbles, slow and steady, washing down in rivulets from the waxy, sandy, icy land. Titan is orange and brown and frilly and mysterious.

Operations have come to a strategic halt. Ishida and Jacobi think we're on the ragged edge of completely pulling out. They anticipate, they hope, that the entire mission could be aborted. Borden and Kumar know better. They say nothing.

Litvinov is hiding somewhere with his troops. This waiting isn't good for any of us. Hanging loose on *Lady of Yue* is really weirding us out.

Despite the survey that says half our seeds are damaged beyond recovery, I think we're dropping soon. DJ agrees. Joe agrees.

No word from Captain Coyle.

Borden asked me a few hours ago if I felt a stir, like I was closer to something important. I don't. Maybe we are, but I can't force it. DJ and I don't compare notes. Mostly we avoid each other.

———

JOE DISOBEYS BORDEN'S strong suggestions and visits me in the bubble. We don't speak, just watch as the ship enters Titan's long shadow. Saturn-shine partly fills the moody darkness. There's lightning in the high methane clouds, dozens of silent flashes like giants trying to light cigars. Did I say Titan was *big*? Bigger than Earth's moon, over half the diameter of Mars. Everything is poison down there. Atmosphere consists mostly of nitrogen. And it's *old* nitrogen, maybe from the far reaches of the Oort cloud, that somehow drifted down long after Titan was formed. Titan's nitrogen differs from that in the gaseous nebula that helped shape Saturn itself, which...

More useless crap? I don't know. Bug likes it. Bug is compelled to acquaint itself with how much things have changed since his day. They've changed a lot.

To me, all by myself, listening to nobody and watching only with my own eyes, Saturn is a big piece of art glass dropped "swish" through a banded platinum hoop. Bug sees it different. He remembers Saturn as green with no ring. Something big happened a long time ago. Isn't that what this is all about?

Did Bug come from around here? The rings are new, Bug decides. But yeah. This system is where home *was*, probably a moon just a little smaller than Titan. Then something big happened. I think it could have been another planet or a wandering dark sun. It shoved some moons out and pushed others into Saturn itself, changing its color and maybe helping create the fickle beauty of the rings. What I read back at Madigan, though, tells me the rings are fragile and maybe they just come and go. Bug doesn't express an opinion. Neither does anyone else.

In brief, however, this is where we all began. Yada yada. One can only hear about the birds and the bees so long before it gets boring. Any thoughts, Captain Coyle, any guidance? Nothing. That's okay, I can put that aside, because suddenly there's a shitload of data pouring into our helms from *Lady of Yue*, supplementing cap learning. I drift in the bubble with Joe beside me, taking it all in.

The supplement is gentle at first, taking us back to basics — more detailed stuff about Saturn and its moons. There's Iapetus, famous for being a yin-yang moon, white on one side, black on the other. Iapetus's white is deposited water ice, its black is spray-painted by dust kicked up from impacts on another moon, Phoebe. Bug seems to remember Iapetus, but remembers it as neither so black nor so white. There's Enceladus, which is pretty small but has a lake of water under one region. Bug doesn't know anything about Enceladus. Or Rhea and Tethys and Dione and lots of much smaller moons.

Then the *Lady*'s data turns harshly practical, adding more

layers over what the caps have already infused. As a battle-field, Titan is unbelievably difficult. Most of the water in the surface layers is mineral ice—like rock or sandy grit. Lava on Titan is water mixed with ammonia, rising from Titan's seven inner oceans through deep vents—cryo-volcanoes. All but two of the oceans are salty in the extreme, and not just table salt. There's ionic sulfur and potassium—a devil's brew that at times generates amazing electrical currents, which some of our machines—especially the excavators—are designed to use to advantage.

Basically, Titan is a giant wet cell battery. No one in his right mind would choose it for fighting ground. Our basic protections need to be stronger than anything made for Earth or Mars. To that end, there's one new plus: Water, along with hydrocarbons scooped up from the surface, can be woven into a superstrong fiber. Don't ask how. The structural dia-grams make my head hurt. Did you know that concrete con-tains water even after it sets? I didn't.

Then—basics again, like a break between bad news.

Titan's brown color comes from complex hydrocarbons called tholins. There are lots of different gases down there, many of them poisonous, some flammable (if you have a lighter filled with oxygen!), but mostly there's nitrogen. Because there's lots of lightning and other electrical discharge between the methane clouds, billions of tons of tars and waxes and precursors to more complex chemistry are made and scattered over the surface or swept into the basins of the methane seas. These organic compounds will provide many of the raw materials used by our weapon and vehicle seeds to double and even triple their present mass.

Follows more harsh. We've been fighting down there for

six years. *Lady of Yue* fills us in on what those battles were like, how they were fought and with what. First impression: big and scary. Second impression: worse.

Joe's eyes close and he curls up. I feel the same way.

But there are some things *Lady of Yue* and cap learning can't teach us. Having been hit by quite a few comets in the last year or so, as the pilots told us, Titan's topology has been massively altered. It's possible even the number of inner seas has changed, not to mention the outer methane lakes. Titan now rocks to a different music.

It's clear Borden and Kumar and maybe even Joe are of the opinion that the Gurus know what's really down there. Question remains, why is it so dangerous that they'd jeopardize the entire war?

Final bit of info: We'll be descending in twenty-eight hours, a ship's day—if the landers can be pried from the twisted frames, if the seeds can be salvaged, if there's still any good reason for us to drop. The grunt's delight is that matters of life and death are rarely his responsibility until he's deep in the shit.

LAST CALL

Two of the five gliders respond positively and check out to Bueller's satisfaction. With our reduced force, all we need is one to put us down on the Wax and complete the mission. We'll get just one chance. *Lady of Yue* will station-keep for as long as she can.

Bueller escorts us down a tight, cold aft corridor to inspect the best glider. It's a genuine aircraft, not the pop-up-and-down landers used on Mars. The fuselage is almost eighty meters long, bulbous and heavy at the nose, oval in profile at the middle, where the wide delta wings are currently upswung, casual and awkward. About five meters behind the blunt nose circle twelve intakes, each two meters wide. Farther back, behind the wings, the glider's middle tapers to a more slender V, followed by three jet exhaust nacelles spreading wide the profile. The whole thing finishes with a screw-twisty triangle of ailerons.

As we watch, the glider's fuselage opens long hatches to allow stowage of seventeen parcels, varying in size between five and twenty meters. These are so-called seeds from *Lady of Yue*'s aft bay. They look like presents for a grim Christmas, long and lumpy, concealed by black plastic wrap cinched down by red strapping. Stowage in the glider is accomplished by slender and flexible mechanical arms, watched over by a skinny, naked crewman enclosed in another bubble on the end of a boom—the only crew member we've seen so far. His outline is exceptionally fuzzy, for which I am grateful. He pays us no attention whatsoever.

"These are your rudimentary seed packages," Bueller says. "Some will combine in place to form more complicated structures, like excavators or centipedes. Others will take more time and grow out to full size by themselves, mostly the vehicles supporting big weapons—zapguns, ionics, penetrators. Once placed in their cradles beside the station, all the seeds will dip from the station storage tanks, and they'll also start pulling in gases and liquids from the local atmosphere, plus solid raw materials arranged for them just outside the installation's perimeter. I'm being told that the station itself may be recycled if those supplies are not sufficient, so you'll want to get in and get prepped quickly.

"Seeds are hungry," she says. "Don't fuck with them. Don't get between them and raw material reserves. Don't mess with *anything* growing. Half-finished product has been known to absorb whatever it touches. Stay the hell away from developing product."

We all nod. Respect your weapons. Nothing new. Then why am I trying to swallow my Adam's apple?

The ship's now-rigid skirts form a pale backdrop around *Lady of Yue*'s damaged midsection. I try again to assess the ship's overall condition. Doesn't look great. Optimism always leads to disappointment. Pessimism is wiser anytime we're about to land in the shit. And that is surely where we're heading. Maybe this was a suicide mission from the start.

Bueller has let us absorb long enough. "Time to load," she says.

DOWN TO A DISTANT SEA

Our cleaned and repaired skintights are handed back and we clamber gingerly down the dim passage into the glider's main cabin, equipped to carry fifty. We're only thirty.

Bueller hands out another stack of caps and taps her head. "Ready?" she asks. "Part two. We save the best for last." We shuck the doilies and inspect them. Damp and fibrous, as before. Again we paste them over our crowns. Ishida's cap folds in half away from the metal side, and settles down on softly fuzzy hair and flesh. She looks at me, looking at her. "I'll be fine," she says. "What about you? How many haunted heads can you handle?"

Jacobi grimaces.

We push ourselves back in the glider's narrow couches. Bueller checks us over, nodding at each fitting. DJ's cap squirms on his crown and he reaches for it. Bueller slaps his hand.

"Bon voyage," Bueller says as she returns to the hatch. "Wish I was dropping with you. I surely do. Suck smog and come back soon." She withdraws. The hatches seal. Behind us, muffled groans, clangs, sounds of machinery and fluids.

Cap works faster than last time. There's an odd taste in my mouth, my entire body. "Hey!" I say out loud. I now see and understand, very clearly, that the liquid oxygen necessary to burn a portion of Titan's atmosphere is being pumped into the aircraft at the last, after the seeds are stowed. Our so-called glider is more of an ice-sucking jet designed to enter atmo, inhale combustibles, light them off, then power along for a few hundred klicks and coast to a tightly controlled landing.

More visuals. On our way down, and maybe even on our way back up—if we ever get that far—we'll become ramjets, packing in nitrogen to increase pressure in the fuel mix. The combustibles either freeze or condense on the chamber walls, and the precious slush is skimmed by the outer whisks of the turbines toward the combustion chamber, where the engines inject oxygen and light the mix. Whoosh. I thought the idea of using oxygen in a Zippo to light your cigarette was funny.

It's how we get down there.

Once down, we're destined to crawl, dig, excavate...and walk. Okay, that's good, I get that. Walking is good. Big, bulky diving suits, thick legs, sometimes with tractor treads for feet, sometimes with huge grippy boots...

And the goddamnedest, most primordial-looking machines we've yet seen. As big as destroyers, bronze and silver, with a dozen segments and lateral tree lines of ornately fringed legs for carving and crawling and digging—for burrowing deep through ice and rock into the interior oceans of Titan, and for tangling with, and surviving, other monsters. These machines come with their own problems and weaknesses, natcherly, and no certainty there'll be enough material down

there to allow them to grow to full size or reach full arma-
ment. In which case, we might have to scavenge the surface of
Titan and hunt for machine corpses before we can dive deep.
More delays before we fight. But also, delays before we die.

If we fight at all. If there are Antags down there, or our
own people hot on our trail. My head hurts. At this stage I
seem to be mostly asleep. I certainly can't move, which is fine
because I'm locked into my couch. A coolness runs all up
and down my memories. The cap is pulling away the pain,
flooding me with more words, more impressions curious
and harsh, informative and discouraging, all necessary to
my in-depth training. Not thinking, really, and not worry-
ing, just taking it all in like a sponge—not so bad. Even the
bad news feels pretty good. Got a thing you want to think
about? Hey, here's something *better*. The concepts build in
reverse like bricks falling out of a tornado to make a building.
Boy do I prefer listening to angels in our helms. We can be
bitch-friendly with our angels. We can complain about them,
give them rude names, hijack their stupid certainties to help
cement squad morale. Not *this*. We are becoming the caps.

My muscles twitch. My fingers curl as if wrapping around
controls. The last of my diminishing flare of curiosity illuminates a distant question: Where do these caps get their reflex
knowledge, the muscle training and innate instincts? Maybe
I don't want to know. Maybe cap knowledge is distilled from
dead Skyrines.

The cap floods my curiosity and drowns it with more concepts, pictures, diagrams, like a magician forcing cards. Coyle
remains silent. Bug remains silent. Maybe they're learning
right alongside the little homunculus that is me, the tightly
curled-up kid trying to pretend he's watching cartoons

before going off to a school he hates, a Central Valley concrete blockhouse filled with kids too crazy to ever get into
the Skyrines. It was there I learned that civilian kids are the
worst. To Army brats. Maybe they thought I was the creepi-
est kid in the school. Maybe their moms told them about my
mom, or my dads. My real father was stationed at Fort Ord
for a year but we didn't live on base. Until they divorced, my
mom spent her mornings in a cannabis haze, but she tried to
be good to me. She kept herself just a little whacked-out from
the hour I left for school until 6:30 p.m., when she could start
drinking—but she really wanted us to live a normal life.

Not so easy.

Before I met Joe, I tended to jump without looking,
because nothing could be worse than staying right where I
was. I wasn't cruel or sadistic like some of the truly fucked-up
kids I knew—the ones who strung mice on nylon lines and
watched them dangle and squirm. Jesus, not like *those* little
monsters.

Okay. I'm going away now.

Or not.

Something is trying very hard to put my conscious mind
up out of the way, on a shelf, to get on with cap and reflex
learning. I don't resist. It's all cool. I'll have time to examine personal questions, try to resolve old philosophical issues,
like, Why become a Skyrine? Why volunteer to fight? In
part, to seek adventure. But also because war for all the shit is
neater and cleaner and sweeter than civilian life.

All right, that's a lie. That's delusional. Help me out, Bug!
What was life like in the really olden times? Were there cool
bugs and cruel bugs, good and evil bugs, dumb and smart
bugs, bugs pious and bugs blasphemous? Were you all smart

and nobody dumb? Why can't I hook into those truths, Bug? I'm thinking you're—

Shut the fuck up.

Ah, at last! Coyle steps back in. She seems to take me down from the shelf and shake me like an old T-shirt.

Listen. This is important shit. We're going to where we might actually learn something.

"Yeah?" I mutter. "Like what?"

Like where I am.

If you don't know where you are, you don't know who you are, right? Here are the eternals: The shit remains the shit, the fight is always confused and messed up, and in the end—

Goddamn, Venn, hang on. Something really weird is coming. I think you're in for it.

Coyle was worried about something. I've been waiting for whatever that might be, but I'm still surprised when it arrives. My brain locks up. Thinking stops. Topped out. Too damned full. At the same moment, maybe, comes a sharp jerk. I feel our axis of motion changing. I confuse that with cap visuals of seeds sprouting, growing, like carnival balloons plumping out, becoming monstrous, making crew and warrior spaces, getting ready to take us in. Then that all mixes with motion and coolness and calmness.

Synesthesia, big word. Mom liked to read dictionaries. She and my dad and several stepdads—she chose them soon after he left, one after another, very much alike—would read pages to each other from an old paper dictionary or a volume from the *Encyclopedia Americana*, after dinner, in bed, and smoke Old Tobey, as she called it, and laugh at the big words.

I think I'm in my bedroom, nine, ten, eleven years old,

trying to sleep but listening to their muffled voices telling me all about Titan's atmospheric pressure and natural caches of raw material and how to find them, how to get your machine to self-repair if damaged—take a dip in a methane lake or where volcanic water streams down through carved-out, wax-lined valleys, down to where the plastic trees pop and—

Mom says, on the other side of my bedroom wall, beyond the stick-and-wallboard and chalky Army paint job, "Your machine will know you because of your touch. Touch ID is key to security and operational efficiency."

Mom? Is that really you?

Pulls me up short for a moment, along with another hard jerk, bump, double bump, and a

Roar.

Now my eyes are open. I peer through a port. Blackness outside turns orange, brown, then muddy yellow. We're getting closer and closer to the answers. But first we're going to have to dive or dig. Bugs dig up, we'll dig down. Maybe we'll meet halfway. But the bugs have been dead for billions of years, right? Deader than Captain Coyle.

Man, I really need to *wake up*.

And this time, unfortunately, I do.

INSTAURATION ONE:
MADIGAN MADRIGAL REDUX

I'm wrapped in sheets, twisted into a cocoon soaked with sweat. I open my eyes and see a gray ceiling, roll against the tug of the sheets, and see a wide sliding door and beyond that a familiar room. *Too* familiar.

I unwind from the sheets and stand by the side of the bed. I feel myself, soft ribs beneath gray underwear, thigh muscles, sinews between my legs, balls okay, cock okay....

Hair on my arms and legs, around my junk, hair on my chest, fuzz on my head. To my right is the narrow door to the bathroom, where the light above the shatterproof mirror has been left on—as always.

I blink away a smear of sleep.

The battery-powered electric razor rests precariously on the counter beside the sink. I leave it there, about to fall off every time I use it, as a kind of protest. Maybe I can bankrupt them with busted razors. No outlets anywhere, in case

I want to try to electrocute myself. I wouldn't, but they've been careful not to provide temptations or opportunities.

I bend down and feel under the foam mattress. The sap is still there. I haven't taken it out, haven't yet been rescued by...

Who?

I lean my head on the bed. The rumpled sheets and blankets look like a topo map of mountains. All rearranged, tangled, no good now.

Shit. Of course none of it was real. I had no idea how weird they could get. How far back does it go? How much do I remember about Mars? I remember meeting Teal, being rescued by her in her buggy. I remember the Voors. I remember Captain Coyle and her Special Ops team. Not all a dream. But everything since being locked in at Madigan is now in question. The whirly-eyed inquisitor finally got to me, finally pushed me into the madhouse. I can almost remember his name...which of course I learned in the dream.

Kafka?

Kmart?

———

DAYS PASS. NOBODY visits. Food arrives as usual, but tastes bland, pasty. I read, but the paperbacks don't mean much. I can't remember the last page. I can't even remember the cover of the book, unless I turn it over and stare at it, and then, it doesn't seem to matter. Elmore Leonard? Louis L'Amour? Daniel Defoe?

The bell rings at the window. Takes me forever to get out of the chair and answer. I'm toasted. They've finally broken me. Brilliant piece of work. Just lead me out to the end of my rope—somewhere out near Saturn—and jerk me back and that fucking does it. I'm one sad little white lab rat. See my twitchy nose, my beady pink eyes?

The bell rings again. I pack some energy down into my legs and stand to get to the window. The face behind the glass is not the whirly-eyed inquisitor, it's the other guy. The one who claims he's Wait Staff. (But didn't the inquisitor claim that, too? What was his fucking name again, Kafka or Kaffeine? Total toast!)

The face asks, "How are you feeling today, Master Sergeant Venn?"

"Not so good, Doc." I stick my tongue out and say ahhh. He smiles. This guy looks like a mannequin, the way he dresses, so fashionably lost and feckless, someone's idea of a middle-aged nerd.

"Have you been sleeping well enough?"

"Too well, Doc. Take me out of the oven, please? I'll tell you anything you want to hear. Really."

"We don't expect that, Master Sergeant. We are most concerned about your welfare."

"Then let me go. Let me walk on the beach. You can surround me with MPs, I don't care. I just want to feel sand between my toes and smell the salt water. See the sunset. I need to know I'm back on Earth for real, not somewheres…"

My voice breaks. I can't finish.

"I am most sorry, Master Sergeant. Perhaps soon. But first, I have to report that we have conducted an investigation into your longtime friend, Lieutenant Colonel Joseph Sanchez."

"What about him?"

"It seems he is not all he appears to be. Certainly not all he told you he was. Why do you trust him, Master Sergeant?"

"Fuck you!" I try to shout, but it's a raspy croak. I step away from the window and turn my back. Why so angry?

"He was ever your *instigator*, was he not?" I hear behind me. "He was the one always leading you into trouble."

I try to go to the bedroom and close the door, but the door won't close. I want to go into the bathroom but my legs won't carry me there. I stand by the bed and think about pulling out the sap and just whaling away at my head.

The voice goes on, calm but concerned. "He encouraged you to enlist in the Marines, and then to join the Skyrines. He accompanied you through basic and vacuum school and much of special training thereafter. He was with you at Hawthorne and Mauna Kea, but he was not with you at—"

"Just shut up," I say.

"While you were training with your drop squad and various chiefs at Socotra. He rejoined you before your first drop on Mars. Did he seem different to you at that time?"

He didn't. Maybe he did. I don't remember.

"Did he tell you what he had been doing while he was away?"

He did. He didn't.

"Thereafter, did he not always seem to have special knowledge about the unpleasant situations you were subjected to during your actions? And was he not always there before you, able to locate you and extract you, even during the most extreme circumstances?"

I return to the living room to face the guy in the window. Is he the same guy in the window I remember from the last time? Doesn't matter. "I know about you," I say. "You're not Wait Staff. Your name doesn't show up on the lists."

He ignores that. "Joe Sanchez is a very special individual, is he not?"

"He's my bud," I say.

"Then why has he betrayed you so many times?"

"I don't know what the fuck you're talking about." Suddenly I'm calm and collected and cool. I'm as frosty as a fudge bar in Fargo in February. Vee-Def said that once.

"Are you really anything without Joseph Sanchez? Are you even a complete human being, Master Sergeant Venn?"

"What's your point, you horse-fucking little dweeb?"

The guy smiles not in cruelty or triumph but in pity. Like he knows he's about to change my life and not for the better and he almost regrets it.

"Joe Sanchez has been stringing you along since before you were arrested, Master Sergeant. He has used you to advantage, and will use you again."

"How?" I shout. "I'm stuck here! Bring him to me! Put us together in a room with you and some Louisville Sluggers, I'll knock the Guru shit out of you—"

The guy behind the glass takes a peculiar, isomorphic side glance that smacks of a special effect gone wrong.

"That's it!" I say in triumph. "That's what Kafka said to me. He said you couldn't be Wait Staff. You have to be a Guru!"

"I *am* a Guru," the guy says, and then, briefly, I see him without the overlay. He *looks* like he could be a fucking Guru, but I've never seen one, so how can I be sure? He's not exactly a mammal, he's certainly not a bug, and he's definitely not an Antag. Also, he's not ugly. He looks efficient and smaller than I would have thought. The figure behind the glass keeps talking. Where's his mouth? Somewhere above the bump that might be a jaw, below the wide ridge that holds a shiny gray bar that might be his eyes. Gort eyes. RoboCop eyes. Shit. I still don't see his mouth. Just little motions above the jaw. Maybe he's a straw-sucker.

"You should ask Joseph Sanchez the following questions," he says.

For a while after that, I don't hear anything. I stand there trying to focus on the window, on the deepening darkness beyond the glass.

Sound returns.

"Ask Joseph Sanchez—"

"Yeah, ask him *what*, Goddammit?"

"Ask him about Corporal Grover Sudbury. Ask where he went with the corporal after your comrades exacted their punishment, and what they both did there."

"Sudbury vanished," I say.

"Everyone has their role, Master Sergeant," the voice says behind the window. "The relationship between Sudbury and Joseph Sanchez is popular, Master Sergeant. Far too popular to waste."

GOOD MORNING, MOON

Someone taps my helm with a padded metal finger. "Venn. Wake up." It's Ishida. She's persistent. I wake up—again. She's taken the seat next to mine. Borden is across the aisle talking earnestly to Kumar and Mushran. The glider vibrates, roars—again with that huge, MGM lion's roar—and we roll clockwise, then counterclockwise. The nose lifts, the tail vibrates, something big groans, and the whole airframe shudders.

"Rough ride," Ishida says with half a frown.

"I wasn't sleeping," I insist, but my words are mushy.

I look forward and see Ishikawa, Jacobi—Joe. Beyond them, Litvinov and the backs of the Russians. Their helms are distinctive. When did we put on our skintights? I lift my hand, check the seal with the glove. Same ones made for Mars, but newer—cleaned and pressed. I do not remember any of that. Are we off *Lady of Yue*?

Apparently. Yeah. We're on the glider, aren't we.

I clench the couch arms. Coming awake or out of my

trance or whatever, to *this*, does not feel good. I'm clearly a danger to everybody, blacking out like that.

"Did we all make it?" I ask.

"We're not down yet," Ishida says. "Look." She motions for me to close my plate. I do, and blink down a display. The glider feeds our angels a decent external 270, plus data in sidebars and two ratcheting crawls. I turn my head and the external goes with me. The glider is surrounded by swift brownish haze—methane clouds. A film keeps trying to stick to one or more of the cameras but gets swiped every few seconds. We're sloping into a valley of ten thousand smokes, but it's not fire that makes the smoke—it's freezing methane and a lot of other stuff, all described on the lower crawl. The turbines must be sucking in fine water-sand and that explains the surging and roaring. But we haven't crashed. We're still descending.

Everything gets brighter. The haze begins to clear and we see lower decks of brown and yellow clouds, a small sun cutting through a serrated break—the most surreal and beautiful sunrise I've seen. A flat deck of cirruslike clouds above the glider burns golden yellow.

We're down to five klicks from the rugged surface. Rising gray plumes of sandy water ice spew from black, shiny cracks that have to be dozens of meters wide and many hundreds of meters long. Below those cracks...down through them...what? Inner oceans? Deep in the cracks something green or silver-gray churns and bubbles. Ice lava, the crawl says. Ammoniated, highly saline water that just won't freeze solid and shoves up in a methane-steaming, ammonia-vapor slurry.

Planes, trains, and automobiles all the way. That's my life.
But now we've gone as far as we're going to go, end of the line,
right? Journeys end in warriors meeting. Which warriors?

Are Antags still down there?

Any of *us* left?

I'm working to ignore the blackout and what I experienced. Going back to Madigan. Fuck that shit. I should have
been section 8'ed as soon as I got back to Earth.

Time-release terror.

"Huh?" I flip open my plate and look around. Nobody's
spoken in the noisy cabin. It's Coyle. She gets me every time
she pops in like that. She's clear, crisp, like inside my suit with
me. Almost solid. Ishida has become engrossed in her helm
display and pays me no attention. DJ, across the aisle, has
kept his plate open and is studiously peering at nothing. He's
out of it, too. We're both mainlining a strong signal.

Doesn't explain the—

*Borden called them instaurations. They must be time-
release psych capsules implanted back at Madigan to knock
you down in case you get out of their control. I heard of that
sort of stuff during Special Ops training. How to control a
team that's gone rogue—implanted suggestion. Drives rogue
agents to question everything. Commit suicide. Ups the ante if
you disobey orders or defect.*

"You think that's it?" I have to work hard to think my
words back at Coyle rather than say them aloud.

Maybe. I'm not you, I don't feel all of you.

"You sound stronger here. Are you stronger?" I lean my
head back in an agony of conflict. Trust isn't part of my tool-
kit now, because everything's up for grabs.

Shut up and just keep the objective in view. There's something down below that shitty layer of gunk that's brought us this far.

"How do you know any of this?"

Because I'm part of it. I don't like it, but I am. We're going to where it's all coming together—where everything is held tight. So far, I'm not fixed into that memory. Until that finishes, I'm still flexible. I can make decisions and not just answer questions. But that's going to end soon. I don't like what might be replacing me. Doesn't feel right, but I can't see it clearly. Big Kahuna? Another bug? I don't like any of this.

Sounds like Coyle is dropping back into babble. I'm caught up in my own problems. I have a choice. Either I give in and let the *instauration*, the Madigan poison, spread, or I pretend it never happened, don't tell anybody—don't look Kumar or Joe in the eyes for the next few hours. Keep trying to stay part of this team, which, God help me, I'm actually thinking of with that weird combat affection called unit cohesion, spirit of the corps. Jacobi's juju is working on me as well as the sisters and the Russians.

I'm full of spirit, all right. Spirits, more like it. Haunted head, indeed. This is what, number four? I can't juggle that many balls.

I concentrate on the view. We're flying between low hills, turbines roaring on both sides, glider rocking like a carnival ride, then swooping up and down. I drop my eyes below the rim of the helm and the image from the outer sensors follows. Below—through rising silvery mist, swirling and blowing away at unseen nitrogen winds—

The debris of battle. My God, so much broken, blown-up shit!

I hear the occasional gasp or oath from the others, buried in the continuous roar. Ishida beside me is speaking Japanese, probably a prayer. Her sweet voice is musical counterpoint to what I'm seeing, what we're all seeing.

In jumbled mounds every few hundred meters across a flat brown prairie lie what look like thousands of stomped-down, bronze-colored centipedes, but *huge*—hundreds of meters long. Even crushed, they appear thick and strong, robust around the head and long in the middle. They're too damned big—big as ocean liners and cracked open, smashed, their lumpy, glistening interiors open to the corrosive mist. Around and inside them, nothing moves. They're squashed, they're dead. We're flying into a landscape littered with dead monsters. Some of them are ours. Some are not. The biggest of the big, the most powerful, now just wreckage on the Wax.

"Four minutes to station," Borden says over glider comm. "There's not going to be an accordion. Have to move fast. We'll find heavy combat gear on the other side, but for this transit, these suits will have to do, and that means we've got all of five minutes to get inside and get cleaned off."

I pull open my plate. Joe hunkers, waiting. I watch him suspiciously. Does he know shit I should know, should have been told a long time ago? Why would I even care what happened to Corporal Grover Sudbury? He was a rapist, a scumsucking shithead. I don't want to think about him, and maybe that's the point. I'm out of Guru control. They have me rubber-band screwed to a fine knot, about to snap, primed to step out into the poisonous cold and open my plate. Put an end to the guilt, the fighting—the confusion.

DJ leans back and reaches through the seats to tap my shoulder. "Stick close," he says. "It's going to get weirder, but

I'll be there with you." He looks serious. DJ rarely manages to look completely serious.

"Slim comfort, DJ," I say.

"It's *bad*, sir. You hear what I hear? Captain Coyle has been here. She says to tuck prunes and hang on to your fudge."

Behind us, listening, Ishida splutters a giggle and reaches a gloved hand to cover her mouth like a Japanese schoolgirl. Damn, that touches me. Somewhere inside, our Winter Soldier remembers being shy. If she can keep that core alive after all that's happened to her, I can sure as shit maintain. I notice she's found a pen and scrawled something on her skintight. I saw it on her previous skintight but didn't pay attention. She's written "Senketsu" above where her blaze might go. I don't know what that means. On her own suit, Ishikawa has written "Junketsu." I'm about to ask, but Borden tells us to seal and check suck.

Alarms in the cabin.

Glider hard-bumps and slows to an abrupt, lurching halt.

TITAN F.O.B.

The installation is a gray, snow-spattered hockey puck about fifty meters high and maybe twenty times that across. We did not get a good look before the glider nuzzled up to one side.

We unstrap and bunch in the narrow aisle. Borden pushes up mid-aisle and props her hands against the bulkhead. "Half-charge weapons. We'll move out in squad order, three teams," she says. "Jacobi's team first, Litvinov and Russians next, Sanchez and Johnson, Fujimori and Venn, take the rear." She gives me a stern look. Joe moves up beside me. Tak pushes through the aisle to stand beside DJ. DJ doesn't relish being POG any more than I do. "Two on point for each team," Borden continues. "All but points keep weapons belted. Damage to the station must be avoided at all cost."

The lock passes us outside a squad at a time. We don't wait for the others. It's every one of us across the crusty Wax and gritty ice-sand to a big black canopy that offers some protection against the weather, like a tent flap.

In the ten meters between the glider lock and the station, our arms and legs become coated with a fine, spreading layer of liquid methane that instantly starts to steam. We're warm enough to boil methane. That means our suits are losing heat fast. Sandy ice-grit lands as well and turns to mixed slush that curtains off and refreezes, weighing us down like hanging chains. That distracts us momentarily from the sensation that we're being squeezed by a big, cold hand. Titan's atmosphere is almost half-again denser than Earth's, and our skintights are designed to hold suck, not keep shit out.

Borden tries to alert the station that we need the outer lock opened. I see her lips move behind her bedewed faceplate. No response. Either nobody is there, or comm is fucked. She makes hand gestures and somehow communicates to us that there's a way in—maybe she knows the code.

My world-line is just a vector arrowing through a rugged trail of bad places relieved only by weird sanctuaries where you have to know the secret word or carry a fucking master coin. And it's not just me. That's human space in a nutshell. That's all we've conquered in the vac—stretched-out orbital threads between little BBs on which we depend for our lives. Most of the universe hates us so intensely it spreads itself so vast we can't even think of going there. Down where I am, it's cycles of hell spiraling in ever-shrinking circles. Inside, outside. Vac or poison outside, me inside. Tubes and coffins, more tubes, more coffins. Eternal returns of day and night.

Is it day or night? Day, I think. We landed at sunrise. The glider could have slid around to the other terminator, but Titan's pretty big—that would have taken a couple of hours.

Borden finds a big checkerboard. "Venn, get up here."

I join her and Joe and Litvinov.

"Make yourself useful. Coyle should know the sequence."

"She's not very reliable," I say, but then I reach up and slap my gloved hand on the squares in a staccato sequence. What are our chances? Good, it appears.

The big outer hatch yawns wide in the great curved side of the hockey puck, really big—way over our heads. Dreamy blue light beyond. Looks like a cheap nightclub, but it's easily large enough to hold us all. I'm as surprised as anybody. DJ pats my shoulder, but this still isn't enough to make our commander happy.

We gather within the hatch. Comm is dead, probably screwed by the clouds of ice dust and sand, but the cold nitrogen is dense enough, and sheltered from precip and wind we can hear each other pretty well.

"Glider is about to unload seed cargo!" Borden shouts. "The seeds will activate outside the main hatch. We'll want to keep well out of their way. Early on, they don't recognize people."

"Don't get between product and material!" DJ calls out in Bueller's Texas accent.

The last swirls of ice dust and vapor make it hard to see even inside. The bluish light cuts through some of the haze, but it's still not bright. We trudge across the hangar with a weird, high-stepping gait, plucking the soles of our steaming boots from dark muck and slick crap. Water has laid down a rugged gray sheet spackled with sticky-looking black gobs. Who gets hangar patrol and cleans up? Maybe nobody's left alive in the station. That would be a kindness—dying rather than being stuck here.

My nose twitches. Something stinks in my skintight. Something acrid. Maybe I'm imagining it. Sweat is kind of

acrid, plus the stinks we all make—fear, hormones, phero-
mones, even hydrogen sulfide and methane. But this smells
like *ammonia*. I do not want to smell bitter almonds next.
That would be it for all of us.

"Move it!" other voices shout. My nose was right. Our suits
aren't holding suck in the cold. The seals are hardening, cracking, corroding. Real incentive to get deeper into the station.

Since nothing welcomes us, Borden walks over to the far
wall and the outline of a smaller door. She lines me up and I
slap at another checkerboard while the others bunch up like
schoolkids after recess, stamping our boots, feeling deep cold
seize wrists and ankles—suit heaters can't begin to keep up—
and why not? How fucked was the planning? Why did we
have only Mars-rated skintights? We're off the grid.

The smaller door opens. Sun-yellow warmth blasts the ice
dust to slush and rain and we all crowd into the brightness,
dripping and soaking and no doubt stinking of everything
rich and strange.

I look back over the jostling, steaming crowd, through the
door into the hangar behind us, and see big, dark silhouettes
of things rolling in. Offloaded seeds, bronze or black and
shiny, making deep rumbles. They're growing fucking hair!
Jesus, they're actually sprouting thick slick fibers that writhe
like Medusa's snakes. If they follow us inside, we'll become
part of their balanced breakfast.

The smaller door slams down.

I hold my breath until I see the seeds are not joining us.
For a moment, we stand without words, silent and stinking,
until the ceiling sprouts spray heads and we're sluiced three
times, three complete spray-downs, so forceful we're shoved
against each other like pins in a bowling alley.

When we're clean, the inner station opens another door and allows us to proceed. The next chamber is also yellow. A crudely lettered sign has been slapped onto the door between. It reads, "Don/Doff."

"What the hell does that mean?" DJ asks.

"Put them on, take them off," Tak says.

The first thing we do is shuck our skintights, already frayed and blistering, and on Borden's orders, toss them into a disposal bin along with helms, angels, everything. Out with the old. Almost naked. There are thirty of us in the station. We haven't seen anyone else. Are we alone? Nervous, anxious, pacing, we mill and slap shoulders and ribs to stay warm. Despite everything, I feel a sudden need to get my hands on those big weapons. I want to get to work—*need* to get to work! Because of Bueller's cap I know nice things, encouraging things about centipedes and excavators and nymphs and crushers and stampers, about deep scrawlers and excalators. I know how to work them. I can see them! I can almost reach out and touch them.

Borden pulls us up short. "First up is the latest fashion," she says. Her voice is high, reedy. She's pepped on relief and exhaustion and maybe on the last of the cap training. "Appropriate apparel for the occasion. Without heavy-duty suits, we won't survive if there's even a minor breach, and we won't be able to work outside." She points down. "Or below."

"Found 'em!" Tak shouts. One wall of the chamber is covered by big steel crates labeled "Anti-Corrosion Pressure Skins, Style K(int)." There are ten crates, each claiming to contain twenty suits, but six of the crates are empty. Tak and Ishida and Jacobi open the next two crates. Inside hang thicker, bulkier suits, still wrapped in shiny plastic. Tak tears a hole in one and opens a diagnostic panel on the helm beneath, checks the readout, then moves on to a second and a third and gives a high sign. "These look good," he says.

Jacobi flicks at a scrap of silvery fabric attached to the inside of a crate lid. "What's this?" she asks. It's a brief message scrawled in Japanese and Russian. "What's it say?"

"It says, 'Don't wear them,'" Ishida translates.

Starshina Ulyanova reads the Russian. "Same," she agrees. "Both in one hand—one people writing."

"Yeah," Ishida says. "Probably Japanese."

"What's the ink?" Jacobi asks.

"Could be blood," Tak says. He reaches down and picks at the message with his fingernail. A flake falls away. He looks up at me. We stand back.

"What the fuck's wrong with the suits?" Ishikawa asks. "They look new."

The air inside the station is clean and breathable but frigid. We're turning blue. The old skintights—even if we could recover them—would likely be full of holes by now.

"Check the other crates," Borden says. A thorough search of the crates reveals no other notes and no other choices. "We need these," the commander concludes. "Get them on and let's assemble a search team. We'll carry sidearms, nothing bigger."

We "don" the bulky gray suits. Circlets of heavy plastic and metal wrap arms and legs and thorax. A full suit-up involves letting auto-clasps grab and tighten each band, which takes about ten seconds, keep your fingers out of the way. The helms are bulky, faceplates narrow and thick. But Titan gravity is lighter than on Mars. The suits feel only slightly heavier than our old skintights.

Mushran adjusts his helm with help from Tak. We swing the plates shut briefly to read what the new angels are saying. Not much. A small blinking display reads, "Adjustment under way. Please be patient." Sure. Never a choice.

Taps are in abundance on one side of the chamber. Hundreds of warriors at once could take in gasps and sips and energy before going outside, before riding those big weapons into battle on the Wax. We suckle for a few minutes, looking at each other from the corners of our eyes.

"About seventy hours' worth," Joe tells Borden. He reads the reserve for these essentials—maybe one more dip, then the reserves go empty. Unless we lose a lot of the team. We pluck loose. Time to reconnoiter. The Russians huddle with Litvinov. Jacobi's team surrounds her. They confer for less than a minute. Litvinov and Jacobi step aside to whisper with each other. Then Jacobi approaches Borden and Kumar.

"Where's Mushran?" she asks.

Kumar shrugs. "Gone ahead, perhaps," he says.

"Stupid!" Borden says with considerable heat. She's sick of Kumar and Mushran, I don't doubt.

"I do not disagree," Kumar says. "He has never listened well, nor followed others willingly."

"Fucking honch," Jacobi says.

Borden says, "Before we fan out, time for details. They're not good." In her most cautious and low-key voice, she tells us, "*Lady of Yue*'s arrival survey shows that we're down to just this one station. The others don't answer and *Lady of Yue* couldn't see them from orbit."

"No welcome wagon," Jacobi observes. "Anyone left?"

"The station's only signals are automatic, and those sporadic," Borden says.

"We're going swimming, right?" DJ asks. "Into the fissures—the volcanoes?"

Borden won't let him get ahead of her. "Our orders are to secure the station and check out the product taking shape, or any other equipment we find, reopen the vent if necessary, then, attempt to access the inner sea."

"I'm prime for that!" Ishikawa says, flexing her fingers. Teen eager to take the family car out for a spin.

Borden is unimpressed. "We don't have a large enough team to do it all. I'm making the decision that we take control of whatever product has already been shaped and proceed below. There may still be a deep-sea installation under the crust and no more than a few hundred klicks from here. We don't know what it looks like, what it contains, or what the inhabitants have accomplished. But that's our destination, unless *Lady of Yue* says otherwise."

"No reports?" Ishida asks. "We don't know what's happening down there?"

"None that reached Division Four," Kumar says.

"Secret even from Wait Staff?" Tak asks.

"Secret from me," says Kumar. "I do not know about Mushran."

Mushran has reappeared without being noticed, a singular talent. He is still adjusting his suit, wincing. All of us are uncomfortable. The Russians are stretching, exchanging unhappy glances. Mushran looks up and around, eyes darting at the activity, like he knows something we don't but it's not yet time to share.

"You went away," Jacobi says. "Where to?"

Mushran nods reasonably. "About a hundred meters up

and in, there is a kind of control center, damaged but repaired. There are bodies."

The Russians get up. Litvinov shakes his head; there's really nothing to translate, nothing to explain, that isn't already obvious. Borden tells Joe to look into Mushran's claim. We recover our sidearms and charge up the bolt pistols. The guns seem puny. I'm hungry for product—for our bigger, badder weapons and transporters. We head for the next chamber over, following the path Mushran must have taken, and see that it was converted at some point into a make-shift armory. The armory occupies one of four chambers that radiate inward from the lock antechamber. Only damaged and broken sidearms—bolt rifles and pistols—remain. There are also three piles of spent matter cartridges, all depleted. It's dark and quiet. Station is operating on severely reduced power, just barely enough light to see and getting chillier. Our suits are doing a fine job keeping out the cold, but we've left our plates open until we get used to the narrow view. Plus the damned things are starting to pinch. I flex to get the joints to break in faster. The pinchings move around and sharpen.

"I don't trust Kumar or Mushran, and I still don't know what to make of Borden," Joe says.

"She seems square to me," DJ says.

"She's befuddled," Joe says.

"Aren't we all," Tak says.

Joe scowls. "I'm not convinced she's up to command, double that with Kumar and Mushran hanging over us."

"'You go to war with the army you have,'" DJ quotes sententiously, "'not the army you want.'"

"Don't fucking jinx us!" Tak warns. He's serious. DJ knows better.

"Sorry," he says.

"Anyway," Joe continues, "Litvinov seems to have a grip. What about Jacobi?"

I think maybe now I should tell him about the time bomb in my head. How it focuses on him. How that makes him a threat to whoever planted it, and how that makes me wonder what the hell role he played in all of this. But I don't.

"Jacobi's strong," I say. "Moody, but she's got her shit together."

Tak says to Joe, "*You've* been moody since Kazak died."

"Moody?" Joe snorts. "I'm crazier than DJ."

"Good to know," DJ says. "Wouldn't want to excel at anything in this outfit."

"But I'm not going to let the crazy loose until I learn why everything we were told is a lie," Joe says. "And why that became obvious to Kumar and Mushran only a year and a half ago, about the same time Antagonists started dropping comets on Mars—and here, too, apparently."

"Ancient history," DJ says. "But I don't hear much from Coyle, and hardly anything from the others—" At this his face goes ashen. "Got to say, they all scare the shit out of me. They're human, but *not*, know what I mean?"

"I fucking do not know what you mean," Joe says. "Thank God."

We pass a bank of cylindrical elevators and equipment lifts filled with debris, pipes, cables. We find the stairs. The steps are bigger than we're used to, with odd grooves up the middle of each riser.

"Tail draggers," Joe says.

"Antags?" DJ asks.

"You guys tell me," Joe says. "This station has been occupied by both sides at one time or another, so Mushran says. Three combat operations to control and secure. We won the last one, supposedly." He nudges the grooves with his boots. "Antags must have turned glass at some point, right? So you'd channel them, too?"

DJ and I shake our heads. No Antag ghosts. I don't know whether that would be an interesting experience or not, but right now, this damned suit is really doing a number on my joints and stomach and I don't need any further distractions.

We walk up both sides of the staircase, which curves slowly around a long, inner bulkhead, up about twenty meters—a decent climb. My knees are binding now, and it isn't the climb. Feels like tacks are being driven into my elbows and ankles.

A wide, deeply cold hallway leads to a dark circular space. The broad, shadowy floor beyond sinks through several levels to form a kind of arena. Mechanical arms and racks of stacked disks hang motionless from the ceiling.

"Drones?" Tak asks.

"Vent probes," Joe says. "Probably broken, or they wouldn't still be here."

We look as we pass. Not a clue. There's a lot more debris at the center of the arena, and the steps have been slagged—melted and cracked, the cracks sealed with a lighter gray putty. On the far side, big plates of transparent plastic have been shoved over two wide openings, held in place by foam sealant.

"These suits fucking *hurt*," DJ says, shaking out his arms, then kicking one leg so hard he almost loses his balance. Mine is pinching more now, too. The pinches are even sharper, really painful. I'd like nothing better than to "doff" the fucker and see what's going on inside. But we're across the chamber and join Tak to look at what lies beyond those big, jerry-rigged plates. Tak takes point as we kick at the debris, trying to make sense of how much damage and why.

Joe walks up to the plates. "Jesus, come look," he says. We gather in front of a mostly transparent panel overlooking a slow-motion, boiling caldron about a klick wide and filled with rising mist and broken machines. "Our vent," Joe says. "Lots of battle damage. It's dark down there, in the center, but you can still see."

We press close to the plastic. What lies beyond is spectacular and discouraging. The station was constructed around this fissure, this volcanic vent, like a thick wall around a half-frozen lake. Titan's dark brown night sky casts a faint glow over the complex. Methane snow drifts down through the cold, clear nitrogen, hits the slushy liquid, and instantly puffs away...to rise into the brown sky, refreeze, and drop again. The continuous cycle of snow partly obscures a churning, circulating graveyard of diggers, submarine-like transports, big, broad-shouldered mechanical centipedes—hard to know how much buoyant crap is out there, passing in twisted review before our unhappy eyes.

"Looks abandoned," Tak says.

"That it does." Joe looks at me. "Any more clues from Captain Coyle?"

"Nothing," I say.

"Bug?"

I make an effort to raise Bug. I almost get something— a warning? A memory? A brief suspicion of knowledge, quickly extinguished. "Sorry," I say.

"Great." Joe turns and swings out his glove. "Over there.

Mushran was right." There are bodies on the opposite end of the viewing gallery. I count four.

We stand over them.

"Human," DJ says. "Not combat casualties."

"What, then?" Tak asks. He winces as he kneels. "Group suicide?"

The four lie half-in, half-out of pressure suits like ours, spaced apart from each other as if caught up in their own private agonies—naked jumbles of contorted, mummified limbs. Two men, two women. The men hold knives in skeletal hands. The women seem to be trying to extricate their legs from the bottom halves of their suits. Dried blood covers the floor. Almost no smell.

DJ says, " 'Don't wear them,' right? Written in blood?"

Joe whistles between his teeth. "Keep tight," he says. "Don't guess. Know."

"Yeah," DJ says.

"Ow," Tak says, then grabs his stomach. Joe is next. The sharp pain for me is in my right calf, like a dagger shoving through.

"That's it," I say. "The suits are bad."

We try to help each other out of the suits. Tak is difficult. It's like he's glued in. When we remove his neck plate and helm, the neck support pad takes an upper layer of skin, leaving raw, oozing pink. He's in agony but doesn't say a word. We pick the knives off the floor and start hacking and carving at the tough material, each working on the other, pulling aside automatic clasps, lifting and removing rounded plates. Joe raises up his own neck piece. Little bloody wires push inside, still wriggling toward each other—still trying to grow together.

"What the hell!" Joe says in a mildly peeved tone. He grabs a wire and pulls. Beads of blood follow.

The gloves are the hardest. Wires have worked around all my fingers, and one is still plunging through my thumb. I take it at the root, in the wrist of the glove, and pluck it out with a sick moan. Joe is making the same noise as he cuts and then tugs wires from his thigh, his hip, his arms.

Tak is free first and stands breathing hard before the transparent plates. He's managed to skip and roll his way into the middle of the bodies. One of the females congratulates us with a wrinkled grimace, as if still watching through her dark, shrunken eyes.

We stand naked again in the cold, drops of blood falling in quick-freezing spatters. The wounds are painful, intimately horrible, but I don't think any one of us is going to die. Barely in time.

"What now?" DJ asks.

"Tell the others," Joe says to Tak.

"Right." And Tak is off at a run.

"We're staying?" DJ asks.

"We're looking for more suits and someplace to get warm," Joe says. "We can't do anything back there. Why didn't Mushran say something?"

"Because he has a death wish," I say.

"Fucking A," DJ says.

A quick, hopping survey of the arena chamber overlooking the fissure tells us nothing, gives no clues as to where other equipment might be. Our feet turn blue and go numb.

Tak returns with Borden, Litvinov, and Jacobi. Ishikawa trails. All but Tak still wear the suits. Borden looks at us with mixed pity and sympathy. "We're going to need to find you more suits," she says in a small, not-quite-resigned-to-this voice.

"Fuck that!" Joe shouts. His words echo. He points to the bodies, the pools of blood—the red drips from his own flesh. "Mushran saw this, he knows about these fuckers—he must know!"

"I'm sure he did," Borden says. "When he saw Tak, he looked shocked—then angry. He asked him what the hell he had done."

Litvinov adds, "Bastard said, 'It's only little pain.'"

"Shall we ash him?" Tak asks. Tak never threatens lightly.

"Back off that shit! We don't have a choice," Borden emphasizes.

DJ says, "I'm not wearing a fucking iron maiden."

"Screw you, screw all of you!" Joe shouts, his voice hoarse. He lapses into a fit of coughing. We're turning grayish blue. All the blood is retreating to our core.

"We *need* these suits," Borden says. She looks down on the bodies and the blood. "I don't know what happened here. Panic. Poor leadership."

"Goddamned right, poor leadership!" Joe says through his coughing. He sags to a squat, then falls over on one hand. We're getting too weak to resist the inevitable.

Five of Litvinov's soldiers join us. They carry four of the bulky suits, still enclosed in sealed plastic bags. They hold them up beside us, sizing. Their faces look ghostly, resigned.

Tak's look as he takes a deep breath, lowers a big gray pressure suit to the floor, and strips away the plastic is classic Tak. Pure American Bushido. DJ is next. He squats on a bag and inspects his feet. Signs of frostbite.

"No options," Borden says.

"And when it's over," I ask, "will they ever come off?"

"I don't know," Borden says.

"These must be new," I say. "Coyle didn't say a thing."

"She's a fucking ghost!" Borden says with a rare bright spark of anger. Nobody at Division Four or on *Lady of Yue* warned our commander about these difficulties, either. "Why should she care?"

We open the bags. Warrior and armor, all one. And then I remember what Coyle said, long, long ago.

She *did* warn me. I just wasn't paying attention.

FISSURE KINGS

Except for the corpses, the station is deserted, a barely functional shell of what it had been before Titan got its face rearranged in the last prolonged assault. Miracle it survived at all. But no miracle for us. In outline, the hockey puck is not much more than a thick wall around the inner vent. The onetime stadium roof over the vent has collapsed, letting in the elements—mostly methane snow.

Now that we're back in our suits and suffering the unexpected and literal breaking in, Borden and Litvinov escort us back to the armory, where, under the watchful and nervous gaze of our comrades—plus Kumar and Mushran—the outer walls are shifting and bulging, with alarming snaps and groans, to allow us access to developing product.

The walls begin to smoke and shiver.

"Eating station!" Litvinov says, and he may be right. We seal our plates. The air is frosting, the water freezing out.

Three huge, round, bronze-colored heads dissolve and

shove through the station's outer wall like fish rising from a milky pool. The wall puckers and seals around them. Ports pull open in each head, inviting some of us inside—and cap training alerts us who goes into what vehicle, whose ID will match with the product, who's trained for which segment of our mission. Depending on the size and complexity of the weapon or transport, there will be one, two, or three drivers, and room for at most five suited warriors—I can see that, feel that.

The slow-building ecstasy of enthusiasm finally arrives. I get it. These guys are good, great, brilliant—whoever designed caps, product, station! We're being primed to do our bits without complaint. It's even better than the first after-drop rush when we stand up on Mars. Pain is sweet. We welcome each jab and stab, each strung wire through our muscles, around our bones. Prepped and pumped, in pairs or triples, we break from the tight-packed herd into which we've instinctively clumped and, new boots gripping the slippery, icy floor, climb into the ports in the round bronze heads.

The first of the heads, fully crewed, withdraws with puffs of vapor, leaving behind a glassy sheen of freezing liquid and a smoking, dripping hole through which another head suddenly presents. This one's ours. I'm with Joe and Tak. DJ is going with Borden. Borden looks at me with her usual concern—I'm her charge, her ward, right? But we're operating according to the instructions of a higher authority. We're not much more than automatons riding the giant machines. Grunt zombies. Quite different from the drama on Mars. And I'm down with that.

Judging by the size of the round head, Joe and Tak and I are being assigned to a big one. Buddies, all former mates.

Outstanding. But then Starshina Irina Ulyanova, the round-faced ballerina, moves in after Joe and before me, followed by Ishida, then by Jacobi, and *that*'s our full complement. Not a problem. We're nothing if not flexible. I move to the middle and take a moment to study the inside of the head. We're in a big, broad-shouldered bronze centipede—do centipedes have shoulders?—very like the ones whose crushed remains litter the ground outside or slush around in the vent. With the portal closed, we occupy a cabin about five meters wide and ten deep extending back to the thorax. It's dark and warm, like being inside a heated gourd. Web cap training tells me the freshness of the product is responsible for that—heat of manufacture. We'll cool down once we plunge into the vent or dig through the crust—both are possible with this machine. It calls itself an Offensive Scout, Advance Response, or OSCAR. It can swim or dig or just crawl over most surfaces. Pretty universal. Other types are more specialized.

Tan ribbons fall from the curving bulkheads and shake out into vertical hammocks, with pads and clamps arranged to lock on to our suits. Ulyanova is the first to lie back in one of the ribbon hammocks. Lights above her switch on and match color with a small, bright light over her faceplate, green for green. The clamps lock to her midriff. The pads suck down on her pressure suit. She settles back and relaxes, then tries to look back at us, but her suit is stiff—we're all stiff. No rubbernecking.

The rest of us follow her example. Our lights match, too. All good. I'm happy drool and grins. Shit, this is fine, so fine—even as something smooth and cool worms up my penis.

Ishida places her arms and legs into a bay to our right. Her hammock adjusts accordingly and she sits up. I can't see her face, can barely hear her voice in the whir and growl of the centipede, our Oscar, preparing to move out. Tak's and Joe's hammocks slide forward right behind Ishida. I'm carried center and aft. We're now in our assigned stations, even though we're not yet clear what we're about to do.

Within minutes, we feel a lurch aft and a wide transparency slides open forward of the driver. Oscar's face now has a big rectangular eye. Plastic? Metal? I'm betting on a tough, cold-resistant plastic. Wonderful how we use language to mask ignorance. Cap learning carries almost no info on the engineering behind these monsters.

Then, following a cheerful burst of digital notes, we can hear everyone through comm. I content myself by looking forward between Joe and Ishida. Tak is at my two o'clock. We're on the move. Through a wavering shroud of methane snow, Oscar crawls up and over the edge of the hockey puck. It's easy to see how busy our delivered seeds have been. The outer walls of the station on this side are so corroded and marked they've nearly been eaten away. The hangar where the glider delivered us is already gone. A crawling phalanx of three more fresh machines scours the top of the station, trailing from their stumpy, jointed tails those awful, questing, chewing snake-tresses—

Tresses busy slapping, cutting, lifting, and then simply *absorbing* the station. Maybe the product will absorb the corpses as well. Grunts into machines. Total combat efficiency. Wouldn't brass love that?

Way back in my head is a velvety blackness, like a curtain

in a darkened theater, and it's slowly drawing aside. There's nothing onstage yet, but soon...?

I'm distracted as my helm offers a much wider view. Direct retinal imagery. I darken the plate interior and become a disembodied pair of eyes moving ponderously through the slush, advancing on outthrust claw-clamp feet to peer over the inner rim of the station...down into the vent. The vent's inner lake swirls like a gigantic, half-frozen toilet bowl of combat shit slowly being flushed. Hey, I'm in a good mood. I'm laughing in my big thick helm, even as painful and intrusive bits of the suit—*my* suit, my friend!—absorb my sweet flesh the way product eats the station. I'm down with that. I'm down with pain, poison, and frozen death. Happy to serve!

We hear Borden's voice, transmitted by sound through the saline solution, echoing and chirping. As usual, she brings good news. "Last transmission from *Lady of Yue*," she says. "Big hurt is in the system—a Box and seven other ships. They'll be in orbit around Titan in ten hours. Box can deliver hundreds more seeds, enough to overwhelm any Antag residues—or us. They aren't transmitting to *Lady of Yue* and they do not appear to be here to help."

"Fifteen to thirty klicks descent through the crust before we swim the deep ocean," Joe says. "Catch up on your reading—this is going to take a while."

"Payload is ready for delivery, right?" Jacobi asks. She means me and maybe DJ. I'd be flattered, but I'm still distracted—severely so. I feel the awful loss of control of my own thoughts, like I'm being funneled down another pipe. Another poison capsule is breaking open in my head, the second trap—the second *instauration* is on its way.

A suave, mellow voice asks, "What's it like, Skyrine? After all these years. Look back upon your long and astonishing list of experiences, and tell us in your own words...."

The velvet curtain opens wide, the stage fills.

I fall onto it.

NO NO NO FUCK NO

I'm standing on a huge platform, small and alone, before a dark, unseen audience of millions, maybe billions. I'm completely naked and flooded in light. I look down on my nakedness and see that my arms and legs are chewed and wrinkled, red and brown and leathery. I'm alive but uglified. The audience sighs with a far-off storm of sympathy. They love my ugliness. Fighting has made me into a fucking Elephant Man. Thank you for your service! War is so…so…evocative! My wrecked body arouses in that unseen crowd deep emotions they can't otherwise imagine having, right? Emotions they don't *want* to have, not in real life, but that's entertainment, isn't it? *Horrorshow*, as the Russians say.

Time to do my bit for the cause.

Somewhere above me the suave Voice lists in boring detail the actions in which I've participated, the war zones I've visited. Some I don't remember or have never heard of—places on Earth and everywhere far and wide. There's been war on Earth? Then we fucking screwed up, didn't we? I don't need

596 | GREG BEAR

this. I just want to return to the action, to wherever it was I just came from, to finish fighting beside my fellow Skyrines and learn whether we're all going to live or die. I don't want to be debriefed or celebrated or encourage folks to buy bonds. That's true fucking old-school.

Business well over a billion years old.

And so—

I dig deep and find Coyle, beg of her, defer to her, she's been listening close—

Enough. No need to be a ghost before you're dead!

She seems more faded than the last time, but she somehow finds the means, the inner roots of this delusion—reveals them to me—and together, we put the poison back in the capsule, shut down this fucking engram, this *instauration* or whatever it is.

Attaboy, Venn. We're so close! I know there's something in here that will help you...A little more time for me to move around, and I'll find it.

UNDER PRESSURE

What?"

The curtain closes. Gone in a flash. I open my eyes. I'm back in my hammock, listening to my fellow crew members as the giant bronze centipede probes the half-frozen water of the vent lake. No wonder I have a hard time distinguishing dream from reality. Time to get down to the real business at hand. I look left and right and see through a thick haze five other transports. Six in all. Arrows and symbols tell me Borden is taking point. She's with Kumar and Mushran—a lot of honch in one vehicle. Maybe she'll dive so deep the whole damned vehicle crushes. Bye-bye, brass. Bye-bye, whirly-eyed Wait Staff. Cap training prissily informs me this is not a good attitude. Maybe not. But Borden's craft is definitely descending first. And what a craft! If ours is like a centipede, hers is a tank-tractor earthworm about ten meters across the beam, its eight segments equipped with rippling treads on *three* sides! And the first five segments are studded with robust grasping arms. The arms and grapplers and other Swiss Army knife extensions will grasp and cut and weld and do all manner of crazy shit. Borden's earthworm can dig faster and swim deeper than any machine in our phalanx, our flotilla, whatever the hell we are. She's not just taking point, she's presenting a serrated edge.

I don't actually *see* this. I remember it. I even know how to drive that talented bastard, should I need to. I receive another burst of pain-free pleasure as reward for accessing cap training. Your grunt *can* learn new tricks.

"Why does everything have to look like insects?" Ishida asks.

"Bugs made us," Tak says.

"I do not believe that," Ishida says. "Never have, never will."

"What, then?"

"Angels," she says primly. "Spirits. *Kami* and *yokai*."

"Yokes? What?" Tak frowns as he peers ahead.

"*Yokai*," Ishida repeats.

"That's like fairies," Jacobi says from up front.

"We are made by fairies?" Ulyanova ventures, first words she's spoken since we sealed and departed in the Oscar.

Ishida sighs. "Not fairies, *yokai*." I see someone has again scrawled *Senketsu* on one shoulder of her suit. Not ink. Blood, I suspect.

Oscar crawls over the floating wreckage, shoving big pieces aside, while we listen to hollow thumps against our outer hull. We're trying to reach an open space in the slush where we can descend without getting hung up. Temp outside is fluctuating wildly. Inside, our suits pinch and adjust some more. I feel something slide up my rectum. Terrific. My guts twist like a tub of worms. But then, almost immediately, the other pains subside. My guts settle. Anesthetic enema? Small mercies.

Oscar propels itself with big cilia, arm-sized rubber strips rippling in sequence, scooping and shoving fluid behind, speeding up or slowing down to steer right or left. Buoyancy tanks in our tail and below the cabin fill with liquid. If Joe and Jacobi want to rise, the tanks boil some of the liquid into steam. Sluices eject the resulting thick salts and gaseous ammonia. When they cool, they suck in liquid again and we sink.... Makes a little singing sound behind us, like a chorus of crickets and birds, along with the deep chuffing of the cilia and the faint squeaking of the joints.

Ishida resumes. "I wonder what the spirits of this place are thinking," she says. "*Yokai* do not enjoy intruders."

"They don't like humans much at all, do they?" Jacobi asks. "Ladies with long black hair and no eyes, right?"

"Not a *yokai*," Ishida says softly.

"Well, let's hope they don't mind us taking a dip right... *here*," Joe says. "Hold your noses."

I suck in my breath as our forward view suddenly goes dark. Tiny sprinkles of the dimmest gray light blur and blink around us. We feel more impacting chunks of wreckage. There's a body. Did I see it or just imagine it? A frozen face in the darkness. Now it's gone. Nobody else saw it, or nobody will admit it. How long can a corpse float in this corrosive stuff?

"Releasing minnows," Jacobi says.

"Tracking," Joe says.

Little silvery lights brighten and flow ahead, five-centimeter drones that swim and corkscrew through the slush. They vanish quickly into the dark, but draw traces on the dive screen and in our plates. The minnows return what they are sensing tens and then hundreds of meters ahead. They're our scouts and pickets.

Polymerized, membranous currents of almost pure water are flowing down here, held together by the powerful electrical fields. In our helms, they show as sinuous auroras rippling and waving deep into the fissure. We just passed through one—electric, icehouse cold.

"Strong current flow," Tak says.

"Don't rub your toes on the carpet," Joe warns. "Whole ocean down here is like a giant battery. Lightning on the surface sparks *up* to the clouds. Cooks the hydrocarbons along the way."

We're all tied together, exercising cap-infused skills necessary to take charge of this beast, guide it, expand its sensory range—

Hours pass. I don't mind. Everything is fine. I can't feel any more poison capsules. Maybe I'm done with them—or maybe they've already done their work on me.

We finish our long dive between the rough, massive walls, then level off at twenty-three klicks and keep station under an immense icy dome. Minnows tell us there's nothing below but slushy ice, more current membranes—and then the deep, deep Titanian sea. No sensation of pressure. Nothing in the ears. The Oscar is intact and our suits are doing their work. We're pretty broad targets in the IR, I think. Cap training does not contradict that opinion.

Some machine, that's our Oscar, our centipede, and some

crew, sinking into almost unknown waters to see what we can see. I laugh in my helmet.

Keep it together, Venn!

I can barely hear or feel the captain. It's like she's slowly turning glass all over again.

OLD AND COLD

All of our sensors are tuned on the world beneath the crust. The deep saline sea that winds its way around Titan, around the equator and extending fingers north and south, with isolated lakes both saline and fresh, as if springs from far below access pure ice down in the mantle. The clarity of the sea around us is remarkable. The current flows seem to attract all the debris from the water and channel it deeper, to spread out across the seabed. Titan's seas are constantly being purged. Based on what I learned in the textbooks at Madigan, that doesn't make any sense. Such a process would have to be guided and controlled—implying at least a living ecosystem, if not a civilization.

But Jacobi's feed to our helms is undeniable. We're swimming through crystal-clear waters, way below freezing, with occasional cloudy globs of ammoniated, debris-laden slush being drawn toward the current flows—disintegrating and descending in long charged plumes as they glide past like UV rainbows.

We pass under a low-hanging arch of crustal material. The Oscar switches on its brights and scans the surface of the arch. Another icy dome, shot through with veins of black gunk. Where it's most purely ice, it sparkles with a million reflections, a galaxy of glints. Farther along, we encounter a breccia of ice and clumped boulders held in place by a thick mortar of brown, gray, and black tar. Our lights warm the mix and rocks fall away.

"This could get hairy," Joe says.

The falls reveal fresh underlying material—and frighten big worms or insects—fifty or sixty meters long! They escape from the sudden brilliance, burrowing deeper into the matrix.

"Jesus!" Jacobi says. "Sure those aren't Antag weapons?"

"Pretty sure," Joe says. "Alive?" he asks me.

"Yeah," I say.

"Your bugs?"

"Much younger."

"They're not talking to you?"

"No."

"Maybe our cousins?" He gives me a sour grin.

A few of the worms are large enough to kick out more boulders. We dodge two such rockfalls, then get a glimpse of huge mandibles on a wide, plated head—mandibles that pinch in from five sides, a pentagon of grasping, cutting jaws. These creatures are at least ten meters long, their serpentine bodies covered with bristles.

Borden communicates from the lead vehicle. "Serious question, Johnson, Venn—are these things intelligent? The ancestors of your bugs?" she asks.

"I've never seen anything like them," DJ says. "But that isn't exactly an answer."

As we glide along a cleft exposed in the archway, we see more of the bristling worms. They dance in our lights as if in some sort of ecstatic ritual, then gather along their lengths and link clasping bristles to form triads. Each bristle tip has a minuscule claw—small by comparison to the bulk, but maybe as big as a human hand. The bristles cling together like Velcro, then let go, and the triads break free to burrow up into the breccia. As quickly as they appeared, all the bristling worms are gone.

"Easy come, easy go," Jacobi says.

"Like in sand or aquariums," Ishida says. "Acorn worms. Priapulids."

"I'll bet you've eaten them with rice," Joe says. "Maybe they're out for revenge."

"No, sir!" Ishida sounds alarmed.

The crystal waters and the ice above again look empty and pristine. A wavy purple flow comes close to our Oscar on the left wing of the formation, so we move off—the entire squadron banking and retreating like birds in a flock. The cilia hum along our hull—hum with intermittent slapping sounds. Maybe they're not in complete sync. Maybe they're getting old. How long does a machine last down here? Longer than our Mars skintights, I hope.

The bottom of the ocean rises beneath us, low gray hills studded with boulders as big as Half Dome.

"Everybody stoked?" Joe asks. "All cheery-bye?"

"Tol'ably so," Tak says.

"Don't be," Joe says. "Don't let the tech use you. Stay sharp and independent. Remember—everybody else who came down here is dead."

"We don't know that," Jacobi says.

Ulyanova makes a little sigh.

We all saw the wreckage around the station. And the condition of the station itself. Did everybody just give up? Antags and humans at the same time? Before the Antags could find or confirm, or destroy, what Captain Coyle believes is at the heart of…

Watch yourself, Venn.

This time, I can almost see Coyle. She's standing in a long hallway between rows of black columns. She's found a relevant cache of records and is trying to communicate what she's found to me. *We're here. This place is incredibly deep and strong. I've been checking out newer history. And you're in. The library accepts you as a legitimate user.*

"What history?" I ask softly.

Coyle says, *Our shelly friends broke through their crust, then retreated, but centuries later, they did more than that. Much more. They sent spaceships. Some of the ships reached Titan and other moons. Others went much farther—all the way to the Kuiper belt, even the Oort cloud. Huge places out there. Sun-planets!*

"How long ago?"

Got to slow down. Got to rest. I'm not going to be a guide much longer. I'm becoming part of the archive. I just looked at myself—shit! All of me. My DNA, my memory, scars and breaks—everything. It's all being preserved, fixed. No words to describe how that feels.

Then—fuzzy quiet.

"DJ!" I say.

"Yeah. They're fading," he murmurs. "Something else is coming."

"We're going to meet our makers?" Ishida asks.

"Are they still alive down here?" Jacobi asks. "Is that why we're here?"

"Electrical strong to port," Joe warns. "Ocean's opaque ahead."

In our helms, we see our cloud of minnows zipping forward from our phalanx, spreading, darting little waves of lights, and a purplish glow off to our left, signifying the superflow of salty ions that could melt our Oscar if we intersect the boundary. Like touching a giant power cable. What keeps the current from smearing out through the water? Salt gradients. There's a fresh thermocline separating that flow and our own like an insulating blanket. Oh, we're bathed in ions—but nothing the Oscar can't handle. Whereas over there, in the purple, deadly potential is being shunted from the depths to the crust, and carrying curtains of debris along with it.

"Could melt through and make another vent," Ulyanova says. Smart sister. Smart Russian sister. With a round face and a ballerina body, not that I can see any of that through the suit.

"Uh-huh," Jacobi says. "Just keep us out of the purple."

The Oscar hums and vibrates. I'm still trying to orient and remember what I read in the textbooks back at Madigan—trying to encourage the web cap training to fill in details—but things have changed a lot down here since our caps were programmed. There are wide gaps in our education.

Then, instead of Coyle all casual in a Karnak of black columns, I see pale brilliance. Quiet, bright silvery spaces. I close my eyes. The silvery void is infinitely dense, filled with infinitely thin lines and figures—like pressing knuckles into your eyes in a dark room. Geometric eyelid movies—only *bright.* I have my eyes closed and it's *still* bright. Will I ever be able to sleep again?

The silver wants something. It expects something—a response. But what's the question? It's flowing through my mind. It's practiced on the record of Coyle, I presume, but it still stomps around like a bull. Christ, I feel like a man about to be drawn and quartered, my hands and feet tied to snorting horses, and there's an idiot-faced fuckhead with a hammer, about to stroke down on—

Inquire.

Not a voice. Not even a word, but immediate, coming from all around and shivering my head like a gong. I jerk up so hard in my suit that everything hurts, joints, feet, hands, neck—all the wires tugging as my muscles tense. If I don't stop jerking I'll be sliced into bloody pieces!

Again:

Inquire.

"Yeah! Yes. Right here. Don't go away." I keep my voice low, but that doesn't stop the others from hearing. They're busy. I have no idea what they're thinking, what Joe or Jacobi is concluding about my little whispers in their helms. I know they can't hear what I'm hearing. Maybe DJ can. Maybe he's hearing the same thing.

"I'm listening. What are you? Who are you?"

Again the holographic presence, not words, not sound:

You have an ancient port of entry.

I don't know what to say. In confusion, I open my eyes to the helm display of the saline sea, our flashing minnows, outlines of the other machines powering ahead, leveling off.

"Deep station in about thirty klicks," Joe says. His voice sounds loud, overwhelming, but not any more real than the presence. "Something's still there," he adds. "It's not putting out a beacon, and it doesn't answer."

We're leveling off at three hundred meters beneath the crust. All of our sensors combine to show we're cruising above deep canyons between long, razorback ridges.... Curving mountains running parallel, separated by a klick or less and meeting at right angles with other ridges, like the pocketing squares on a roulette wheel. There are no bottoms to those squares. Nothing the minnows or sensors can measure. The geology here is a total mystery. Is it artificial? If so, made by who or what? Made *when*?

After all I've been through, it's still a shock to realize that what we're seeing echoes with other parts of my understanding, what I've learned from Bug and Coyle—confirms that our connection is real. I'm not imagining anything. Coyle, my inner Bug, the silvery void...

If I accept that I'm not crazy, and this is why I was rescued from Madigan—why I was picked up and kept there in the first place—knowing that makes it a little easier. I swallow hard. My throat is filled with needles. DJ and I are here to make a tight, strong connection with something old and important.

The silver space fragments. Everything shivers, reassembles. Something else is here with me. Something new but familiar to my inner Bug.

Ripples form in the brightness.

Inquire.

"Yeah," I say.

"What's up, Vinnie?" Joe asks.

"Keep it down, sir," DJ says. "He's working."

"Got it."

Do you have a guide?

"Maybe," I say. "I can understand you, whatever you are."

With a guide, you can learn how to access the archive, if you are a qualified user.

"I had a guide," I say. "She turned glass on Mars. She's been warning—she's been telling me about you... I think."

Eyes open. I'm twitching all over. The Oscar slides around a massive mineral growth, glowing faintly in the ocean darkness—all the other weapons report in, chiming and chitting at each other, maintaining formation but veering starboard to get around that thing that connects the ocean floor to the crust above.

Joe fans out the sensors. We can all see the result in our helm displays. I have to poke with my eyes through the silver, but I'm learning how to do that.

We're in the middle of a mineral jungle—a deep forest of crystal pillars, each dozens of kilometers high.

"The mother lode!" DJ says.

We slowly move into the jungle. DJ begins to whistle. The tune sounds familiar, but I've never heard it before. Still, it brings on an oddly familiar mental state of congruence and connection. The brightness is becoming tangible. I can feel it wrapping my skin, flooding my mind. It's bright and silvery, and while I can feel it, so far it conveys no information, no meaning other than its own strength and reality.

Again my thoughts are overlaid by vibrating, wavering lines, infinite geometry—and again, I feel and hear Coyle. Her voice is distinct. It ripples the silvery space. The connection between this silvery space and distant archives—on Mars and elsewhere—becomes manifest.

I'm still here, Venn. I've got a short reprieve, I think.

I'm still your guide, for the time being. Go ahead. Can you understand?

"Jesus! Captain. Yes."

We don't have much time. It's ready. Ask it something.

"But what the hell is it? *What's ready?*"

Inquire.

"I don't know what to ask!"

Ask it about poppa momma shit and where we come from and where we go, and why the Gurus and Antags don't want us down here. Ask it about moons. You won't like what it has to say. I'm dead, but I've had a chance before I settle in to poke around—and I don't like it one fucking bit. But you got to ask.

Ask now.

Coyle is thinning rapidly, thinning and fading.

"What's happening to Captain Coyle?" I ask.

Your guide is becoming memory, which is atonement. We recognize your guide's music, and we recognize your music. Because you have the proper music, you can be a user.

Inquire.

"Why don't the Gurus want us down here? Or in the Drifter, in the mines?"

Choose one question.

Make it a good one, Venn! This place is freakish particular.

"Why is everybody trying to keep us away from *you*, whatever you are?"

You have been lied to.

Inquire.

"By who?"

Across billions of years, we who acquired this memory have encountered forces of decadence and corruption. These forces

succeed by persuasion and temptation. They must maintain
your ignorance or they will fail. We can relieve your igno-
rance. Because of that, we are a threat to them.

Inquire.

"You okay, Venn?" Jacobi asks.

I'm not. Inquire! Shit. I don't like where this is going,
because it's confirming what I already sense, maybe even
know, and that's not good. I don't want to learn any more.
Besides, Coyle has thinned to a wisp.

The vibrating silver turns insistent, brilliant red. No wasting time down here. Painful!

Something pounds on the outside of the Oscar. The giant
bronze centipede rocks and shivers. Joe and Ulyanova and
Jacobi are fighting to keep the machine under control.

Flowing out over the deep-ocean mountains, around the
column of salts and minerals, our minnows report a steady
stream of icy daggers, each six or seven meters long, like huge
icicles, driven by frilly, ionized currents: a blizzard of electri-
fied torpedoes sweeping in at dozens of knots.

"Incoming!" Jacobi says. "Hold fast!"

The minnows scatter to get a wider perspective. We still
can't actually see—it's dark and the ocean here is almost
opaque—but the minnows are working the whole spectrum,
plus sound, which is incredibly precise in the cold. We can
hear what's happening for thousands of klicks, even the
echoes off the ridges and roulette pockets—

"Twelve big machines at three klicks, rising from behind a
low ridge," Tak says. "They're about where the station is supposed to be. They look aggressive, and they're *huge*."

"They're not ours!" Jacobi says. Her voice is small and
deadly calm.

The new machines, sensing us, suddenly fan out and descend to hide in the corner of two intersecting ridges. We can't see them. We can't see anything.

"We're exposed," Tak says.

"I know that," Joe says tightly. I understand him well enough to know he's either following orders from Borden and Kumar, or he has something on his mind. Maybe both. Asking him right now will only distract him. He'll tell me when he's ready.

Or when *I'm* ready.

"Ice torpedoes holding," Ishida says.

"Slowing," Joe says.

"Why don't they just take us out?" Ishida asks.

The ice torpedoes keep station in a cloud around us, barring our progress—but not coming any closer. My head throbs with the red field. I don't know what it is or why it's happening now. Maybe I'm having a stroke. Maybe all the shit in my head has finally blown me up inside.

Slowly, though, it's starting to convey information. Lots of it. Confused, historic, and strategic...if I could understand Bug strategy!

"Slow down," I say through gritted teeth.

"Nobody's moving," Joe says.

"Venn—what do we do now?" Jacobi asks.

I wish I knew.

Ishida has been assigned to our weapons. I click down the list in my head, feeling a sudden dread that we might actually use them—and that isn't what the red space is telling me is appropriate or necessary. We have place-keeping mines, remoras that attach and deliver spent matter charges, torpedoes bigger than minnows but working the same principles. And that's pitiful. Whatever's out there is equipped with weapons way beyond the ones in our arsenal. They've harnessed Titan's electric flows. They've been here longer, they're survivors, and they're way more powerful.

But they're not moving in for a kill.

"What are they?" Ulyanova asks.

Joe strains to look back at me. "You're our ace in the hole, Vinnie. You and DJ."

The red space turns silvery again, and in that infinitely dense collection of waiting information, another figure appears. Not human.

"Coyle," I say. "Goddammit, Coyle, what is this? Where are you?"

Handing off, Venn. I'm settling in to fixed memory. That means I'm finally going to die... except when people remember. You'll remember me, won't you? You'll pray for me?

I remember DJ's attending Coyle as she turned glass, and my throat tightens. "Always," I say.

It'll be hard to work with your new partner, but she's still alive. She's a user. And she's smarter than me, with more experience.

"She—? Descendant of the Bugs?" I ask.

Same as you. Good-bye, Venn. Take care of our troops. And best of luck.

I reach out and feel around with whatever senses once connected us, but I can no longer detect the essential part of Coyle. The hard-core, almost cynical devotion to duty, the bitter sense of humor and doubts about my innate abilities... the devotion to life, despite a career of dealing death. Captain Coyle is gone.

No. She's here. She's just not *active*. I *can* see her. All of her, spread out like a silvery blueprint before me, naked and complete—everything that turned glass back on Mars, stored, transmitted, has been fixed in the archive, faithfully and truthfully preserved. Feeling no passion, no pain, but eternal—timeless and totally revealed.

"Jesus Christ, Captain," I say. "You're fucking *beautiful*...."

But of no use to me now.

"Who's talking to you, Venn?" Jacobi asks.

"Coyle's fixed," DJ says.

A new outline sparkles in my mind. The archive has other plans. It wants me to move on. I have the awful feeling that Coyle tried to save the most difficult for last. *She?* I'm not yet seeing anything solid or embodied, more like the shape of a mind, and very likely that's what this new presence sees when it looks my way. How the hell do we communicate, if that's even an option?

Then—

It's a reality.

The new voice is startlingly sweet, like birdsong in a forest. It rises and drops, and then finds a kind of level range, and I know it for the first time—like Coyle, female, but very different. I'm about to confront the new user, but between us rises again that master steward of the ancient memory stores, the thing whose existence has scared the living fuck out of the Gurus and the Wait Staff.

Inquire.

"What do we say to each other?" I ask. "How do we do this?"

"What are they, Vinnie?" Joe asks. He sounds remarkably scared. "Bug descendants? Natives of Titan?"

"I don't know," I say. "Captain Coyle isn't in the picture anymore."

You have the music. You are suitable as users.

I think this through quickly. I feel like an idiot. I feel as if my lips are moving as I try to read a book.

"You're mumbling again," Jacobi says, irritated.

I open my eyes. Ishida is watching me. The silvery void wraps across her concerned face.

"Steady keeping. Ice torpedoes still wait to crush us." This is Ulyanova.

My focus shifts. I stare into the infinite silver at the resplendent, uncertain outline of the other user, the mind that is also here, and by golly, there is a certain *something*, an awareness that we are related, maybe more distantly than a snail or a cockroach, but still…

Inquire.

Like playing a TV game show. I sat next to my grandmother on that old-dog-stinky, Afghan-covered couch in Fresno while she watched her favorite game shows, and she knew the rules, the routines. I need to be as smart as my grandma.

I try to stay away from the new user and focus the silver on the master steward. Don't want to say something stupid or be rude.

"Are we both descended from those who made you?" I ask.

Yes.

Inquire.

"Another mind?" I ask. "Something else affected by the tea? DJ!" I say.

616 | GREG BEAR

"With you, bro," he says. His voice has changed. "This is a joint and a half, ain't it?"

"Can you see the other one? The other user?"

"Yeah."

"What do you think?"

"I think I should resign my commission."

DJ is a noncom.

"Tell me!"

"Well, this much is obvious," DJ says. "It's not Coyle, it's not a bug . . . and it's not human."

"You guys are driving me nuts!" Joe shouts. "Give me some actionable!"

After all Joe has done to and for me, I feel a weird moment of justification.

"Those folks out there, they don't want to kill us," DJ says with a deep sigh. "Not anymore. We need each other."

"What the fuck does that mean?" Jacobi asks sharply. She looks stretched and exhausted. We're twelve klicks beneath the icy crust of Titan, within sensor range of a grove of massive, crystalline pillars that rise from the cross-ridged floor of the saline sea to the frozen roof. The ice torpedoes are poised between us and a flotilla of huge weapons—overwhelming force.

I break through the silver and look steadily at Jacobi. "Captain Coyle has handed me over to something else," I say to her. "Someone new."

She gives me a conspiratorial squint. "What sort of someone?"

"Still trying to find out," I say.

Inquire.

"What do we do now?" I ask the steward.

Use the sense your music gives you. Speak to your partner.

"We need to surrender," DJ says softly.

"Is DJ nuts?" Joe calls back. "Vinnie—is he nuts?"

"I don't know!" I say. "Maybe they want to take us some-place safe. Someplace where we can meet and talk."

I still can't see the other clearly. Maybe she doesn't want to be seen clearly. Maybe there's not that much trust despite our common music and the master steward.

Inquire.

"Where do they want to take us?" I ask. I feel the archive lightly brush parts of my mind.

Use the sense the music gives you.

Great. I'm sitting on top of the most massive data store in the local universe, and it's a stickler; *I'm* the user. I make the decisions. I could spend the next million years working through inquiries about limitations and rules, but all I got in my head is an image of that Antag helm on Mars, cupping a broken bird-head with four eyes and a raspy tongue.

And based on what I'm learning, remembering *that*, remembering all the dead and the dying and all the blood on my hands, all the friends and fellow soldiers now gone and all the blood on *their* hands, and all the bird-heads we've broken back there on Mars and Titan and everywhere else…

Nearly all *female*…

And then I get it. I understand. I know who's out there, who's driving those weapons. We're both descended from the bugs.

And we've both been deceived.

That's *huge*.

I simply want to break down and cry.

I rise above my confusion and try to figure out my strategy. What do I believe? What's the truth, and how liable are we to counterintelligence, cointelpro, whatever the fuck you call it? I'm not a very good juggler. Maybe this is one ball that's primed to explode.

Inquire.

"What went wrong? How did this happen? Who are the Gurus and what do they want to do to us, for us?"

The others hear me. They're stunned into murmurs and prayers. Jacobi is trying to stifle sobs. Skyrines have sharp and sometimes predictive senses. Some of us already know the shock that's coming. I feel sure that Joe knows. Has known for some time. Like Kumar and Mushran and even Borden. Division Four. Traitors all.

One inquiry at a time.

"Yeah—why are the Gurus doing this and telling us these things?" This seems to be simple enough, related enough to deserve an answer.

For billions of years, they and their kind have sold war to the outer stars.

I'm not sure I understand what that means. "Our war, you mean? Sold it how? How do you know this?"

One inquiry at a time.

"How do you know this?"

Long ago, they convinced us to fight with our brothers.

It lets me experience more directly what it's saying—I see data feeds and communications radiating from our solar system. We're being televised. We're being recorded and spread around the galaxy....

"It's a business for them? We're entertainment?"

They transmit your fighting and dying, your wars and pain, out to far worlds. It fits an old pattern that to these forces, advanced into decadence and boredom, your people and troubles, your murder and pain, are amusing.

Inquire.

"Bugs fought for them?"

Many did. Those wars destroyed four moons. The final archive that preserves that history is this one.

Inquire.

Damn right. There's a big question here. "Where did the moon come from that hit Mars and sprayed Earth?"

At the last, in desperation, one moon from this system was flung inward toward the sun, toward the young inner worlds. It failed to arrive as planned, and struck the fourth planet.

And helped start life on Earth—all by mistake.

Inquire.

"You thought you were losing?"

Yes. We were losing.

Inquire.

"Did you lose?"

That was long, long ago, and the builders of the archive have long since passed on.

A painful subject, I sense, even to an objective archive. "They're dead?"

Passed on.

I can still conjure up a clear picture of Bug. Ugly and covered in baroque carapaces, a united pair of creatures—brains and brawn. This image, the statistical portrait of an entire culture, has until now served as a representation of what the green dust awoke in the Drifter. Somehow I've drawn reassurance from its example—however strange and distant. But

I never thought of Bug as a warrior. An explorer, a thinker, a strangely friendly presence—but never as a hero, and certainly not a tragic hero.

"What's happening in there, Vinnie?" Joe calls out.

The steward of the archive is withdrawing, no longer serving as an interface, an interpreter. It wants me to move on.

I hear the birdsong again. It's starting to make sense. I get impressions on a broad spectrum. Background details, snippets of directed voice—psychological coloring. The new presence might be on one of those massive ships or weapons out there. Wherever she is, she's a user. She's alive. And that means she can ask *me* questions and make accusations.

I don't want to understand. I want to shut down. I'd almost rather die than complete this fucking quest. But I'm not going to die, not right away. Not in time to avoid the truth.

I begin to understand almost all of the pretty song that is the other voice:

We [are told] we share inheritance. Difficult to accept. We [see] you. You arrive ready to fight. We [see] your vehicles and have [stopped them from becoming threats]. [Who are you], why have you come here?

I sense the urgency. We're surrounded. They're extremely wary, but desperate—like us—and achingly curious. There has been so much pain and loss. They don't know our origins or our intentions, but they still have hope. I sense that they have fought against their own kind. They've suffered great hardship to reach and survive on Titan and tap into the archive. They, too, were touched by the ancient memory of

Bug. Likely they, too, had comrades who turned glass. I wonder if Coyle met any of their dead, and if so, why she didn't tell me.

Because I am still alive. Because honor and duty still matter to me. To us. And that's messing with me big-time. But I also have a duty to this mission, to the people who thought I should be here, that DJ should be here. That we could learn and help them understand the mysteries and deceptions.

Expose the big lie.

So I bear down and focus on the other user. I don't use words—so little time. Instead, I show this new presence the Drifter, the crystal pillar, the green dust smeared on our skins. I show DJ in an ecstatic mood, rejoicing at the ancient connection.

I try to convey the experience of Captain Coyle.

And I show the new presence Bug.

Back in turn arrive visions of a precisely parallel experience. The colors and outlines are difficult—I have to focus on one of four separate views that otherwise cross and confuse. The four images come from four eyes. Some of their kind were once smeared with green dust. Their genetic music is the same as ours—the dust worked on them as well.

We are also alike in being aggressors. We're like cocks set against each other in a ring. If we are victims, we are willing enough—ideally suited for entertaining distant worlds.

I cannot escape the truth of who it is I am talking to, *what* it is that confronts us across the deep saline sea, through the ionized membranes, from within those larger and more powerful weapons. Nobody on our Oscar is going to like these new truths. My own reaction is gut-level, instinctive. I feel revulsion. But if I shoot back my disgust, my grief and resentment at our own losses, my wish to defeat and even exterminate all of them—the total effect of my Skyrine training and esprit de corps—

The other user could just give up on us—let loose the ice and crush us.

Somehow, I filter and control my negative instincts. I feel that the other is doing likewise. She does not in any way enjoy addressing me, and her doubts are if anything stronger than mine. She and her warriors have come far, for many different reasons, to fight on Mars and on Titan. Nearly all of their warriors are female. Males form the upper ranks and rarely engage in combat.

But their doubts have changed many of them. The information from the archive, and the evidence of their returned dead, have driven them as well to betrayal and treason. Like us, they have skeptics who wish to resume the war. They need another and very different perspective. They need objective confirmation.

We hear Borden's voice explaining that Box has arrived and dispersed its seeds. The seeds are gobbling up whatever was left of the station, making new weapons—dozens of them.

"Reinforcements are here!" Jacobi says with relief.

"They're not here to help us," Joe says. "They're here to hunt us down and kill us all. And then they'll do their best to kill Titan. Believe it!"

Who's more powerful and more dangerous?

The enemy in front, the humans above?

DJ moans. His voice rises to nightmare screams. Then he goes quiet. The suit has done something to flatten his distress. He's out of the game.

But as long as I can keep my connection open and keep

exchanging information, I'll be useful. As long as their skeptics don't get the upper hand—a distinct possibility—

We'll live.

"They're holding fire," I say. "If the forces from Box get to us—"

"The hell with that!" Jacobi shouts. "This is cat-and-mouse. We got to break loose and head back to the station."

"I don't think so," I say. "They want to keep us alive. They need us."

"*Who* wants that?" Ishida asks, her voice dark and dangerous. "Who needs us? Who the *hell* are you talking to?"

"Antags," I say.

The reaction in the Oscar's cabin is electric. What should have been obvious all along has been cloaked in many layers of denial. Now doesn't seem the best time to give them the really acid news—about our being fighting cocks. Dupes. Naïve victims of an ancient con.

"You knew that!" Joe calls out to them. "It's what we expected—it's the reason for Division Four and everything else we've done. Why else would we come here?" He sounds angry. How long has he known? Even before Mars? Maybe he's one of the Wait Staff. Who the hell is Joe Sanchez? He's been in so many places at so many convenient times… throughout my life.

"Because we wanted to access the old knowledge!" Tak says. He's said very little throughout our journey in the Oscar. "To wipe out the enemy. Power, that's what we wanted."

Joe says, "Vinnie and DJ are our scouts. I go with what they recommend."

"DJ's out of it," Tak reminds him.

"Maybe, but Vinnie is reporting back. We either trust

him, or return to the surface and defend ourselves against the weapons dropped by Box. You still think they're here to rescue us?"

The others are silent on that.

"They're here to find us and kill us. I guarantee they won't show any mercy. If we start a fight down here, we also die. If we listen to Vinnie—maybe we live."

It's hard acquiring so much tolerance all at once. I'm not at all sure I wouldn't prefer to fight Antags again and die. Still, I keep sending—keep visualizing and trying to interpret the return feed. The other user's feed is turning nasty. I keep seeing battle in space and on Titan, on Mars—I keep seeing dead Antags, friends and lovers, commanders and soldiers.

And dead humans. Lots of dead humans.

She's testing me.

"We don't have time," I say. "They expect a solid answer."

"What do they want?" Jacobi asks, voice hoarse.

I ask, and receive a kind of picture: humans and Antags standing in a cabin. No armor. No weapons. Separated by mere meters. Can we just talk to each other?

Can we even breathe the same air?

"They want a face-to-face. On their terms, on their ships."

"How you going to arrange that?" Ishida asks. "They going to crack us open and scoop us out like lobsters?"

"New machines descending," Borden says across the cold fluid. "We need actionable. What's Venn doing?"

"He's *communicating*," Joe says sharply. "He's doing what you brought him here to do! We got problems down here."

"I say go back and surrender to our own kind," Jacobi says. "At least they're human."

Borden says, voice far away, "I'm in command."

"Fuck that!" Ishida says. "Turn around and go back."

I hear Kumar's voice from Borden's vessel: "That would be suicide. They are killing all who deny the Gurus."

What we're engaged in is a *fratricidal war*. And the Gurus put us up to it. How in hell can I convey this to Tak and Jacobi, to Ishikawa and Ishida? To Ulyanova? Ishida lost half her body to the war! Most who already suspect these bitter truths—Borden, Kumar, possibly Mushran—are on another ship, along with Litvinov.

The Antag vessels are still holding. We have maybe thirty minutes before Box's reinforcements arrive and all hell comes down on both of us.

Joe says, "It's on you, Vinnie. This is why you were born."

That does it. I want to shrink up inside my suit, dry up into a little nut. But the other user is still touching parts of my head. Still trying to find common ground. And providing scenarios, little road maps of how we can proceed. If we don't attack.

"They can take our machines inside theirs," I say. "They can get us back to the surface, away from Titan."

"You mean give up without a fight?" Jacobi asks, outraged.

"Take us where?" Ishida asks. "To their *planet*? Never go home again?" Those seem like optimistic appraisals, actually. Kumar, Mushran—Borden. They're all agreed. Makes me sick to think of who agrees with me.

"Guarantees?" Joe asks, though he knows better.

"None at all," I say. "But it's why I was born, like you said—right?"

"Yeah," Joe says, and communicates with Borden. The

shouting in our cabin is fierce. "Do it, Vinnie. Let it go!" Joe says. I tell the other, my Antagonist counterpart, to open up their ships and take us inside.

All of us.

We surrender.

Then our ballerina speaks up. She's having difficulty interpreting the rapid back-and-forth. "I get this straight," Ulyanova says. "They are enemy? I say, *kill* them. I say die trying!"

The next part is going to be very, very hard.

TAKE BACK THE SKY

*For those in my family who traveled far in company
of service members, and those who waited at
home in times of war:*

Florence Bear
Earl Bear
Irene Garrett
George Garrett
Lorraine Garrett
Lynn Garrett
Dan Garrett
Kathleen Garrett
Colleen Garrett
Devin Garrett
Barbara Julian
Wilma Bear

PART ONE

DANCING ON CLOUDS

I hate transitions, and this is the worst.

In the control cabin of our Oscar, a gigantic centipede made to swim and fight in Titan's freezing saline sea, a dozen klicks below the scummy, icy crust—

Pinched and stabbed and wired through and through by the suits we thought were meant to protect us—

I've never been more afraid and lost and in pain. We're exhausted—no surprise, after our passage through the ice station's freeze-dried carnage. Seeds deposited from the stores of our orbiting Spook fused with the station's walls, chewed them up, and converted them into five Oscars—ours and the four others flanking us before the labyrinth of the bug archive.

Our former enemies are hiding in that maze. Our former allies are creeping up from behind to destroy us all.

Lieutenant Colonel Joe Sanchez, Captain Naveen Jacobi, Sergeant Chihiro Ishida—our Winter Soldier, half of her body replaced by metal—First Sergeant Tak Fujimori, Starshina

Irina Ulyanova, and me, Master Sergeant Michael Venn, are in this Oscar. The second carries Commander Frances Borden, Corporal Dan Johnson—DJ—Sergeant Kiyuko Ishikawa, Polkovnik Litvinov (I've never learned his first name), and our mysterious Wait Staff reps, the former servants and right-hand men of the Gurus, Aram Kumar and Krishna Mushran. The rest of the Russians occupy the last three.

On my recommendation—and on threat of ice torpedoes closing in from all sides—we've stopped trying to defend ourselves and have surrendered to the birdlike creatures we've fought for years on Mars and elsewhere. We call them Antagonists, Ants or Antags for short.

Starshina Ulyanova frantically resisted that surrender and had to be subdued by Tak and Jacobi. She lies quiet now in her sling behind Jacobi. Her rank is roughly equal to DJ's, corporal, but edging over into sergeant. She's still having a rough time. Her cheeks and forehead are beaded with sweat, and she stares into the upper shadows of the cabin, lips pressed tight. Her instinct is to continue the fight, even if it means self-destruction—either resisting the Antags, who are presumably here to save us, or trying to destroy our own people. I don't really blame her. She's surrounded by leaders and soldiers who haven't had time to explain the fundamentals we're all facing. Besides, we don't speak Russian, and her English is rudimentary.

Even so, there's something odd about her, as if she's listening to voices none of the rest can hear—except me. Why do I think that's possible? That she's being subjected to an experience similar to my own, maybe to DJ's...

Maybe not so much to DJ. Maybe just to me.

No evidence for any of these hunches, really, but that by

itself doesn't mean she's crazy. Hearing voices is why I was returned to Mars, then hustled out with DJ to Titan.

On Mars, inside the first Drifter, DJ and Kazak and I all got dosed with a powder produced by deep-buried fragments of ancient crystal brought to Mars billions of years before on pieces of exploded ice moon. We called the powder Ice Moon Tea, and my sensitivity to its messages was what convinced Commander Borden to rescue me from Madigan Hospital, where I was scheduled for execution. I'm one of the special ones. Glory be. So is DJ. Kazak—Sergeant Temur Nabiyev, our favorite Mongolian—was also one of the special ones, but he died on Mars before I returned.

In our heads, ancient history bumps up against the captured and stored memories of fallen comrades. Sometimes it's like dancing on a cloud—impossible, but if you don't believe, you fall.

I can't shake the strangely lovely image of Captain Coyle settling into her peculiar death. On Mars, when she tried to blow up the first Drifter, under orders from the Gurus on Earth, she and her teammates turned into shiny black glass. We thought those who turned glass were dead. But some came back to haunt us. Absorbing and co-opting enemies is one way the ancient archives preserve themselves. That's what the Drifter's crystals contained—a gateway to records kept billions of years ago by our earliest progenitors—inhabitants of the outer ice moons of the ancient solar system.

Giant, intelligent bugs.

Coyle first came to visit me after I returned to Earth and was locked up at Madigan. In those early hours, her presence was confused, less an actual voice and more like word balloons in a comic—empty word balloons. But soon enough they filled in, and what was left of Coyle did her brusque best to take me step by step through the courtesies and techniques of the bug archives. She introduced me to the semiautomated steward who parcels out that memory, if you're qualified, if you know how to ask the right sort of questions.

The bugs are long gone, but their voices still echo. At Madigan, and on the way back to Mars, I relived bits and pieces of bug history, watched those ancient ancestors of both humans and Antags burrow up through the icy shells of their moons and discover the stars. Life had first evolved on those moons, long before Earth turned green, in deep oceans warmed by residual radiation and the constant tug of tidal energy from their gas-giant planets. I learned that this wasn't the first time creatures like the Gurus had entered our solar system and provoked wars. I learned that the bugs had fought one another long, long ago—class against class, changing the shape and disposition of the outer solar system.

Dropping big chunks of moon down to Mars, including the Drifters.

Helping seed life on Earth.

Then Coyle warned me that she was about to *really* die. Her final act was to introduce me to the Antag female who's now my direct liaison, who's waiting across the midnight ocean to save us from our own forces.

Coyle's voice went silent and all that was left of her, the absorbed data of her life and her body, spread out before my inner eye like a beautiful crystal tapestry. The captain was no longer capable of talking, acting, or learning, but she was still full of instruction.

How like Coyle.

YOU CAN GO IN NOW,
BUT PLEASE DON'T

My grandfather was a colonel in the Rangers. My grandmother was a fine Army wife and very smart. One of the things she taught me is that God can do anything except change a man's mind. "That's why there are wars," she said, and knew the subject well. In two wars she had lost a husband, two sons, and a daughter, leaving her with just my mother, who was thirty when her sister died. "Men are so goddamned stubborn they will insult, curse, and shout until they can't back down, and then decide it's time to send our children out to die. The fellows who order up wars almost never go themselves, they're too old. But they're still cowards. If you're a leader and you screw up a war, or maybe if you just *start* a war, you should blow your brains out right in front of all the Gold Star mothers, sitting on bleachers in their Sunday best—and that's what *I* say, but don't quote me, okay? This kind of talk upsets your mother."

Until I was eight and my mother and father divorced, we lived on or around military bases. I bounced through five or six concrete blockhouse schools and hated every minute of it. My mother believed in the goodness of the human race. As if in spite, the human race tried with all its might to prove her wrong. After her divorce, she jonesed for handsome, crazy men and usually ended up with cashiered ex-Army or bank robbers. I thought I had to protect her. Or at least I remember thinking that; maybe it just turned out that way. None of that stopped me from enlisting to become a Skyrine, but now it haunts me.

FISH MARKET DREAMS

In the front slings of our Oscar, Joe and Jacobi try to maintain communication.

"Minnows are quiet," Jacobi says. "Maybe they're being jammed."

All the rest of us can do for now is listen to the sounds gathered by the far-flung sensors, clear and sharp and mysterious in the deep cold, and wait for the Antags to make up their minds. We're mostly silent, lying slack in our harnesses like aging beef.

Our minnows, silvery drones the size of fingers, act like cat whiskers. They flow smoothly back and forth between us and the Antags, tracking their ships behind the great, dark ridges of the old Titanian archives.

The hovering flocks of Antag ice torpedoes haven't moved in. We still have hope, I guess. But we've surrendered. What does it matter?

When we abandoned the station, other ships were entering Titan's orbit—human-crewed ships. One of them was the big

Box, newer and far more heavily armed than the Spook that brought us here. On our way out to Saturn, leaving Mars's orbit, the Spook managed to count a little coup against Box, trimming some of its sectional field lines before it was fully prepared—but that won't happen again.

I wonder what Mushran and Kumar are thinking. They arranged for all this, and for years benefited from their connections with the Gurus. I suppose knowing is better than ignorance, but we're still screwed. As wars go, this one is a complete fraud. But then, aren't most? Killers of the brave, the loyal, the committed—killers of our best.

Somehow, I don't believe that describes me. I'm not one of the best. Joe, maybe, or Tak or Kazak. Not being one of the best may mean I'll live. But that's bullshit. Wars don't discriminate. Wars are blind and violent and nasty, lacking all morality. If they last long enough, they'll do their best to destroy all hopes and dreams.

Wars try to kill *everybody*.

But until now, they've never actually succeeded.

What's become very obvious is that the cavalry descending behind us in Titan's cold sea, other machines carrying other humans, is no longer our friend. It may not know it, but it's chasing us down in order to cut off human access to bug history—the archives on Titan and maybe elsewhere in our system. Our joint sponsors, the Gurus, do not want any of us, human or Antag, to learn about our bug origins or the ancient wars the Gurus encouraged. If we're killed here on Titan, and if Titan is finally destroyed, this cancer won't spread.

Our duty now is to survive, even if we have to join up with our enemies.

COLD TRENCHES

Something's changing overhead. We hear the echoing, drawn-out groans of deep pack ice, like an idiot playing a pipe organ in an empty cathedral. This profoundly scary and stupid noise is punctuated by the softly ratcheting clicks of Antag machines keeping station out in the darkness. Why don't they just suck us up? They're hiding in the cells and cubicles of the ancient archive—what I'm starting to call Bug Karnak because for some reason it reminds me of ancient temples in Egypt. Bug Karnak, after billions of years, is still transmitting bug history to those who react to Ice Moon Tea. I could tune in if I want, but it's much clearer if I coordinate with my liaison, and she seems to be distracted. Maybe she's waiting for her fellows to make up their minds about our usefulness—thumbs up or thumbs down. Do they have thumbs? Maybe the Antags think we're decoys. Maybe this sort of thing has happened to them before—recently. Deception and betrayal. They're being extra cautious.

I wonder if she has a hard time hearing me, too. Yeah,

we're related, but that's hardly a guarantee of compatibility. To add to the suspense, our replacement pressure suits continue to work us over, slicing through flesh and bone with wires and blades to integrate and control—presumably to make us quicker and more responsive.

What was left of the ice station is probably gone. After our seeds were done shitting out Oscars, and while we were leaving, more seeds must have dropped from Box and finished the job. Seeds save a lot of weight when transporting weapons upsun to places where raw materials are abundant—places like Titan, covered in methane, ethane, and silenes, and spotted with deposits of naturally generated waxes and oils and plastics. But even with an abundance of raw materials, when time is short, efficiency rules. The station was preprocessed. The seeds from Box likely dug in like hungry mastiffs. I wonder what happened to the corpses. Maybe they're now part of brand-new weapons. How is it possible to stay human in all this? Facing these examples of a fucking hellish ingenuity?

"Antag movement up front," Jacobi says.

There's Russian chatter from the third and fourth vessels—unhappy, strident. Litvinov opens up to his troops in the dissident transports. "We do not act!" he shouts in Russian, then in English. "We are here. We have no more decisions to make. If we return, our people will kill us."

I watch Jacobi's crescent-lit face, just visible around the rim of her helm, then expand my gaze over to Joe, slung beside her. Our suits creak in the slings. Six of us. How many Russians were crammed into the last two Oscars? Not full complements. Not six, maybe only three, not enough to form true teams, share the stress, subdue panic. Since we didn't fight together and didn't have long to socialize, they never made much of an impression, except for Litvinov, of course, and those who died out on the Red…and Ulyanova, softly singing to herself opposite.

Long moments pass. On the second Oscar, Borden reports scattered soft targets—organic. "Looks like a shoal of big fish," she says. "Native?"

No one confirms. No one can answer one way or the other. We close our plates to access displays and pay attention to the forces directly in front. I don't see the soft targets or anything that answers to what she means by organic—squishy and alive—but more machines rise into view, twelve of them, longer and thicker than Oscars, escorted by scouts like nothing we've seen before—robot falcons flexing ten-meter serrated wings, slung with bolt weapons and pods filled with cutting tools. Butcher-birds, I think.

"Oscar's about to be cracked like a lobster," DJ says from Litvinov's ship.

"Shut the fuck up!" Ishida says, half shell herself.

The fourth vessel's debate has turned to what sounds like fighting. The fifth joins in. The Russians are falling apart. Litvinov's not with them. His influence isn't nearly enough.

It's painful to listen to.

Ulyanova, under her breath, still sings. But then she opens her eyes and looks right at me.

She smiles.

Something inside me smiles back. Goddamn.

Joe taps his helm and looks around his sling at me, eyes flicking, examining. Can he tell? I work to recover.

Ulyanova's turned away again.

"I'm not sure our fellow warriors are going along," Joe says. I do not want to fall into another instauration, another

Guru moment—not here and not now. But how could the *starshina* be connected with all that?

As we watch the serrated falcons maneuver in the deep ice-pudding, banking fore and aft to block any escape, the best scenario I can imagine is that the Antags are being really, really cautious. No surprise given our history and the strangeness of this new relationship. They're doing everything they can to discourage us from responding defensively or mounting our own assault. With twelve big Antag ships against our five, how can we put on any sort of offense? By acting like we've surrendered, perhaps—catching them with their guard down. Who knows what happened on Titan before the stand-down and reboot? Traps and stratagems aplenty, no doubt.

"What the fuck are they waiting for?" Jacobi cries out. My concern exactly. We're not resisting. How will they carry us out of here, take care of us? Wasn't that the deal? How long can any of us afford to stick around?

What do they think about the fresh human ships dropping from the surface, no doubt to wreak total destruction?

I finally detect a jumble of thoughts from my Antag opposite. Their ships in orbit are under attack. Just like on Mars, all of us are being targeted. Those who support the Gurus want to find and obliterate us—fellow humans included. On Mars, we saw ample evidence that the Antags were similarly divided.

Inquire.

Again the voice of bug steward. It usually pops up when decision points are reached. However, I'm not sure I can formulate any relevant questions, and bug memory isn't about current situations or possible outcomes. Or is it? There's a kind of urgency in the voice. Maybe it knows something, or has been tapping deep into my thoughts and has enough of its own smarts to guess.

Inquire.

About what? I pick something out of my own jumble of questions. If we lose Titan—

"Are there other archives like this one?" I ask, and feel DJ's approval.

Unknown. Accessing what you know, it is probable that massive force will soon be deployed to destroy this entire moon.

Inquire.

"Do we already know enough to survive on our own?"

Unknown.

"Where are the archives you know about?"

Nothing is certain. Some could remain out on cold moons in the dusty reaches, or on larger worlds far from the sun, completed by our engineers before our own wars nearly destroyed us.

Aha, I think. "The Antag female gave us a glimpse of something she called 'Sun-Planet.' Is that what you're talking about?"

Possibly. It may have been the last world where our kind lived before we passed into extinction. Many hundreds of millions of solar cycles have gone by, but that world may have preserved its own archives. Still, the connections are broken or at best incomplete. There could be much that is new and different. And it is possible the ones you call Gurus have found and destroyed them already.

A long answer. We have no idea what's being planned for us. No way to survive if we stay where we are. We'll soon be overwhelmed, or caught in one amazing shit-storm of high-tech combat.

And to add to the tension, my liaison may be what she says she is, a sympathetic presence arguing for our survival, but she's still grieving for her dead. She still hates our guts, as do her fellow warriors. Most of us feel the same about Antags. They don't trust any of us and we won't trust them even if they give us a chance, even if the tea and bug memory say we should.

In a communication colored by apprehension, she informs me that the process is moving slowly. Not every Antag in her force believes human captives can be of use. She's in a minority, and there's a bitter argument under way. She's defending the present plan—defending our survival. If the opposing faction on those waiting ships wins the debate, we could all be gathered up and rescued only to be dumped naked into the frozen sea—or worse, tortured and summarily executed.

Just a heads-up, she assures me. She's working hard to convince the others they're wrong, arguing on the basis of Antag honor and loyalty to the ancient ones, whose inheritance runs through all our veins.

The bugs.

Antag *honor*?

Christ, what have I gotten us into? What if it's all a sham? How could we expect any better?

In the round cabin, Starshina Ulyanova is shouting in Russian, trying to get Litvinov to order us to fight, to do something!

From many klicks behind our vessels and the Antag ships comes a deep, visceral *thump*. Heavy overpressure passes, making the Oscar squeal at its joints. Then the pressure fades, leaving us all with headaches—caught with our helms open. We close and seal and immerse in the display.

"There they go!" Joe says. The fourth and fifth transports, with their Russian crews, have had enough. They're trying to turn and head back to what they seem to hope is salvation— the human forces descending behind us.

The Antag falcons have passed over and beneath us and stand between the fleeing vessels and the deep night of Titan's inner sea. The transports try to respond with weapons—

But Joe has locked firepower to our own centipede. The others can't fight unless we do.

Suddenly, the wayward vessels are wrapped in a brilliant balls of glowing vapor, followed by another slam and more overpressure. Our hull is struck by whirling bits of debris, like a hard, hard rain.

"Who the hell did that?" Litvinov shouts. "Sanchez! Unlock weapons!"

"It wasn't Antags," Joe says. He sounds sick, as if none of this is worth it, life has passed way beyond what can be borne. I have to agree. We're down by two. How many seconds before we all sizzle?

"We're seeing long-range bolts from one of Box's machines," Borden says, and Ishida confirms. "They're getting closer."

Friendly fire, as the shitheads say.

No time left, I tell my Antag female.

From beyond the walls of the stony labyrinth, bolts pass around us, almost brushing the centipede, into the shadows behind—Antags returning fire. Something far back there lights up, refracting through a cloud of slushy ice like fiery diamonds and throwing a weird sunrise glow across the solid gray ceiling.

The wide-winged falcons swarm our remaining Oscars, pods thrusting forward and fanning out tools. Here it comes.

"Antags moving in to recover," Borden says, her voice strangely calm. Is this what we're all hoping for? Is this our only chance?

A cutting blade spins into our cabin space, narrowly missing Ishida. Our helms suck down hard at the loss of cabin pressure. My fellow Skyrines cry out like kittens at the roaring flood of subzero liquid. But our suits keep us alive.

Once the cutting is done, with banshee screams, torches provoke scarlet bouquets of superheated steam that bleb around inside the cabin until the cold sucks them back. From superchill to steam heat and back again in seconds—and still, our suits maintain.

In my display, I see more and bigger bolts rise from behind the walls of Bug Karnak, penetrate electrical gradients, make the entire frigid sea around us fluoresce brilliant green—followed by more sunrises behind. Strangely, I feel justified. Wanted. The Antags are defending us. But they're also killing humans. My guts twist.

From the first rank of falcons, steely gray clamps fan out and jam in through the wedge made by the cutting blades and torches. The Oscar's head is pried opened by main force. Spiked tentacles shoot from the nearest falcon and insert into the ruined carapace, where they cut through our straps and shuck us like peas from a pod. We're jerked up and over, bouncing from the edges, dragged through darkness punctuated by more blinding, blue-white flares to an even bigger machine rising over the walls like a monstrous catfish, its head dozens of meters wide. A dark mouth swallows us whole.

Three minutes of tumbling, blind darkness. The seawater around us swirls and drains. We're in the catfish's belly.

A little light flicks on below, then left and right, and the tentacles suck down around our limbs, grab us up again, then drop us through an oval door into a narrow tank filled with cold, silty liquid. Soon we're joined by other plunging, squirming shapes—the crews from the other Oscars. Most of the outside lights switch off. It's too dark in the tank to recognize one another, but I'm pretty sure one of the suited shapes is DJ. Another might be Jacobi, another, Tak. Then Borden. I hope I'm right that they're both here. Another, slightly smaller, could be Kumar or maybe Mushran. I try to count but we keep getting swirled around. Rude.

Where's Joe? Where's Ishida, Ishikawa, Litvinov, Ulyanova? Then the tank's sloshing subsides and we drift to a gritty, murky bottom, settling in stunned piles like sardines waiting to be canned.

A dim glow filters through the tank's walls—translucent, frosted. Sudden quiet. Very little sloshing. My sense of integral motion might be telling me we're rising, retreating, but I can't be sure. Nobody's making a sound.

Why are we here, being treated like this? Haven't we been told to become partners, to solve a larger riddle? How did we end up so thoroughly screwed, and what did Joe do to get us here? Joe has gotten me into and out of more scrapes than I can number. But our first encounter, I was the one causing real trouble—or reacting the only way I could. Now we're both here, and I'm not sure what Joe means to me, to us, anymore.

Has he sold us out? Is he even alive?

Thinking you've fit all the pieces into a puzzle, then

having it picked up, shaken, and dumped—being forced to start all over again—they can't teach you how to react to that in boot camp or OCS or the war colleges. That's a challenge you have to learn from experience. And mostly at this level of confusion and weirdness, you don't learn. You just die.

Bumping and bobbing along the bottom of the tank, listening to my suit creak and click, listening to the distant twang of wires working through my flesh—a never-ending process—I try to keep it together, try to remind myself that the Antags may be connected to the wisdom of bug memory but still have every reason to hate us.

Judging from the contortions and soft moans, the suits are still causing everyone pain. If you don't move they hurt less. But still, they keep us warm.

There's ten or twelve left. Way down from our contingent on Spook. Were some dumped? Did the Antags select us out like breeders on a puppy farm?

After a time, everything in the shadows becomes part of a sharp, awful relaxation. I can still think, mostly, but want to slide into old, safe memories, then dreams. Dreams of better days and nights. Of places where there *are* days and nights. I don't think or feel that I'm about to die, but how can I be sure? When you die, you become a child again. I've seen it, felt it through the return of Captain Coyle. She introduced me to a little girl's bedroom and her comic books. But I don't feel like a child just yet, though young memories, memories acquired when I was younger, even bad memories, are more and more desirable, if only to block out the pain. I can't just give up. Not after all the shit I've put others through.

Then, despite my focused concentration, I experience my own moment of panic. I start to scream and thrash. Everything in this fucking tank is entirely too fuzzy and I'm not ready to accept whatever dark nullity is on the menu because I really want to see what's next, I want to *be there*, *be out there*, I want to learn more about what our enemies are up to and who they really are, which ones are our enemies, I mean—learn more about how the Earth was screwed over by the Gurus. When you die, you stop learning, stop playing the game. Is that true? I'm not sure it's always true. It may not have been strictly true for Captain Coyle. But she turned glass. Maybe that's a different sort of death, like becoming a book that others can read but not you. And now I don't hear her in my head because her settling in has finished, the ink in her book is dry and she's part of the memory banks of our ancient ancestors.

Is that any different from real death?

I just want to keep on making a difference.

To that end, and because my throat really hurts and thrashing around is pointless, I stop. I keep bumping into the others and I don't want to hurt them.

And I'm worn-out.

I roll left and try to see through gummy eyes. Through the murk and foggy walls, I make out blurred outlines of Antags flapping their wings like penguins or seabirds, swimming or flying by the tank. Checking on us. Are they actually flying, or are they in liquid like us? I grasp at this problem like a sailor grabbing at a life preserver. I say to myself, out loud, like I'm a professor back in school, "Their ships may be filled with oxygen-bearing fluid, like Freon—which allows a different relationship to the pressures outside. Maybe we're being subjected to the same dousing. Or maybe it's just warmer water, seawater. Maybe they come from an ocean world. I don't *know*. I have no fucking idea what's what, I'm just making shit up."

So much for the professor.

I try once more to retreat into better times, better history, but I can't find my way back to the sunset beach at Del Mar, to wearing shorts and T-shirts and flip-flops, to hitchhiking and walking with Joe before we ever enlisted, hoping we could pick up girls or girls would pick us up. I was fifteen and Joe was sixteen and given the age of the girls who might have been driving those cars that flared their lights and rumbled or hummed by in the night, that wasn't likely.

But I can't reach back to good times. I keep snagging on the first time I needed Joe, the first time we met, before we became friends.

THE TROUBLE WITH HARRY

A warm, dry California night. I was dragging a rug filled with my mother's dead boyfriend down a concrete culvert, trying to find a patch of brush, a ditch, any place where I could hide what I had been forced to do just an hour before. I looked up and stopped blubbering long enough to see a tall, skinny kid rise up at the opposite end of the culvert. Bare-chested, he was wearing cutoffs, carrying a long stick, and smoking a pipe. The bowl of the pipe lit up his face when he puffed.

"Hey there," he said.

"Hey," I said, and wet my pants. Why I hadn't done that earlier I didn't know.

"Who's that?" he asked, pointing the pipe at the rug.

"My mom's boyfriend," I said.

"Dead?"

"What do you think?"

"What'd he do?"

"Tried to kill us."

"For real?"

I was crying so hard I could not answer.

"Okay," said the shirtless boy with the pipe, and ran off into the dark. I thought he was going to tell the cops and so I resumed dragging the body in earnest farther down the culvert. Then the shirtless boy returned minus pipe and with a camping shovel. He unfolded the shovel and pointed into the eucalyptus woods. "I'm Joe," he said.

"Hey," I said.

"There's fill dirt about twenty yards north. Soft digging. What's his name?"

"Harry."

"Anybody going to miss him?"

I said I did not know. Maybe not.

Joe took one corner of the rug. "How did it happen?" he asked as we dragged the body between the trees, over the dry leaves.

"He broke down the door to my mom's room."

"What'd she do?"

"She didn't wake up. She's stoned."

"And?"

"When he saw me, he swung a big hunting knife. He said he was going to gut my mom, then me. I had one of his pistols."

"Just as a precaution?" Joe asked.

"I guess. He'd beaten her before. He taught me to shoot." That seemed unnecessary, but it was true.

"Then?"

"I threw a glass at him, to get him out of her bedroom. He followed me down the hall and I shot him three times."

"Shit! Suicide by kid. Anybody hear the shots?"

"I don't think so. He fell on an old rug. I rolled him up and dragged him here."

"Convenient."

No more questions, for the time being. We dragged the body together and in an hour or so had dug a not-so-shallow grave and rolled him into it, down beyond the reach of coyotes.

Then we filled it in and spread a layer of topsoil and dry brown eucalyptus leaves over the patch.

"I'm Joe," he said again.

"I remember. I'm Michael," I said, and we shook hands. "No one's going to know about this, right?"

"Right," Joe said. "Our secret."

I was thirteen. Joe was fourteen. Hell of a way to meet up. But Joe had judged me and I had judged him. In the next few months, he blocked my downhill run to drugs and crime. He even talked to my mom and got her into a program, for a while. He seemed to know a lot about human beings. But for all that, he wasn't any sort of angel. He always managed to get us into new and improved trouble—upgrades, he called them, like that time on the railroad bridge, or in Chihuahua when we found the mummy and brought it home.

Matter-of-factly, over the next year, Joe assured me that he and I were a team. By being associated with him, with his crazy self-assurance, even his tendency to vanish for weeks, then pop up with plans for another outlandish adventure, I began to feel I was special, too—a capable survivor. As we crisscrossed Southern California and Mexico, hitchhiking or getting our older friends to drive, we kept nearly getting killed, but more than once he saved me from other sorts of grisly death—and together, we helped each other grow up.

The police never did find my mom's crazy boyfriend. He might still be out there in those woods. And my mother never asked about him, never mentioned him again. She was probably just as glad he wasn't around to beat on her. Good riddance to one miserably screwed-up bastard.

Most of that shit isn't worth going back to. My whole life has been a parade of crazy hopes. Hardly any rest. Joe was part of it from that time on. And now we're stuck here, waiting to be canned. Sardines waiting to be packed in oil.

Then why am I still thinking, still trying to solve problems? Thinking. Sinking. I really *am* sinking. Before I go to sleep, in my head, all by myself, I spout maxims and rules of thumb like a drunk DI at his fucking retirement party. I'm an old man in a young man's body. That's what Joe told me years back when we stood in line to recruit. "You're an old soul," he said. "And that ain't necessarily a good thing."

It's even more true now. That's what battle does to you. That's what…

Shit. I'm forgetting the best stuff. Really clever stuff. It was all so clear just a moment ago.

Someone grabs my helm and shoves another helm in close. Through the visors I see Jacobi. She looks angry. Her lips form words: "I don't think they like us!"

No shit. So sleepy. I can't hear much. All comm has been jammed or cut and the suits are too insulated, too heavy. Jacobi's hands let me go. She's checking other helms. Poking, looking, poking again—taking a count. Then she half-walks, half-swims through the silty fluid and returns to me. Again she's trying to say something, but she points emphatically at the wall. Hey! There's an Antag peering in, checking to see if we're still alive. Fucking ugly bird with useless wings, except they seem to be able to swim. Or maybe they're weightless and that's the only place those useless wings work—in zero g.

Jacobi slams her helm hard against mine, twists my head left, and I see what's beside the Antag. It's a big, shadowy mass, slowly morphing or rotating, can't tell which, but it has long, sinuous arms. For a moment, it looks like a catamaran viewed head-on—two bodies linked by a thick bridge. Each body sports two very large eyes. Arms emerge from the tips of the bodies, below the eyes—slow, lazy arms.

I have no trouble reading Jacobi's lips through her visor. I'm thinking the same thing: *What the fuck is that?*

That's not all that's new. I see smaller forms that superficially resemble Antags, crawling by the tank on their knees or feet, wings folded, like bats. Never saw either the squid or the little bats on Mars.

Then the silhouettes move off and the tank goes dark. Hours pass, maybe days. How much in the way of sips and gasps do our heavy suits carry? We finally get organized enough to sit up and form a long oval in the murk at the bottom. We could be in a twelve-step program. At Jacobi's prodding, some of us stand and try to walk, but there's nowhere to go.

I get lost all over again in trying to remember Camp Pendleton, Hawthorne, Socotra off the coast of Yemen, Skybase Lewis-McChord. Madigan. Why can't an *instauration* come along, one of those preprogrammed moments that make me think I'm somewhere else? Compared to this, that would be a vacation. But there's no such relief.

I can almost imagine those far-off places are still around, and might return to my life—that I'm here but they're still out there, still real, and some of the memories carry so such detail—

But the damned suit keeps pinching, cutting, insinuating, and that blocks me from losing myself in any memory, any setting, any world I want so badly to re-create. Worse, it keeps diverting me to the pain of my first year as a teenager. Listening to my mom get beat up. Sitting with Harry, her boyfriend, on the couch as he drank beer and smoked and made me watch grisly YouTube videos with him. Accidents, corpses, history shit. Kept him from beating on Mom, but I hated those videos. Made life seem frail and nasty. Poor fucked-up Harry. Maybe he never had a chance.

I don't want to remember any more about Harry.

TIME IS NOT ON MY SIDE, AND NEVER WAS

More days, or maybe just hours. Couldn't be days, right? The lights brighten. Antags swim or prance by the walls, peer in, make gestures with their mid-joint wing-fingers. They do have thumbs!

I see no more catamaran squid with their sinuous arms. Could be robots or machines or weapons, but they looked alive to me.

Then the top of the tank opens and those damned spiky metal tentacles reach in and pluck one of us out by an arm and a leg. I think it's Litvinov, the Russian colonel. The opening closes. We move around, frantically bumping, trying to stay away from the opening.

Can it get any worse?

The tentacles poke back down and explore, roiling the tank's rippling, foaming surface. In a few minutes, four more suits have been plucked up and out. And now it's my turn. The cold saline drains from around my suit and a warmer something surrounds me. My joints ache and lungs labor.

660 | GREG BEAR

Pressure has changed. Maybe there's air outside the tank. Could also mean my suit has sprung a pressure leak.

Then the tentacles relax and release. I'm lying on something but I can't see what—a table, a rolling cart? I'm moved along a narrow, cramped tunnel that curves sharply off to the left, and then I'm dumped on a slab. The slab is in a small cylindrical room. Two Antags strut around me, then the room quickly fills with the smaller bat creatures, all carrying wicked-looking tools. They climb up and lean over me, over my suit. I can't move.

But then something sparks in my head—a little communication from the Antag female. She's making it clear to me and probably to DJ that we're still not where we want to be. We're on a small transport ship, in orbit around Titan, and the first thing the Antags are going to do is cut us out of our suits, in case we have secret weapons, in case we can still cause damage, wearing them. The big Antags back off and let the smaller creatures do their work. They surround me, heads bobbing, tools dancing, and make low grunting noises.

I hope they kill me quick.

A scratchy voice, sound not mental, through a translator, says, "Helpers will remove your armor. It will hurt."

Together, the bats start cutting. Their torch-saws make quick work of the outer shell, which is roughly pulled away, revealing underwear and then naked flesh, with wires stretched taut like guitar strings—

And I'm the frets.

I scream.

The bats work quickly, pulling and extracting and clipping while grunting and whistling, and I bleed all over the table before a bigger Antag sprays on a kind of floury powder that stanches the blood.

When I'm too weak to scream, two big Antags lift me from the table with those damned wing-fingers, shrouded in elastic gloves, and wrap me in gray blankets that fit snug to my body. Where the blankets touch, the pain goes away.

I'd rather die than go through that again.

A big Antag leans over me as I'm carried into another, much smaller room. Expressive damned eyes—two outside, two inside, near the beak. Then I know. This one is the female, my liaison, my connection—those vibrations. Again she does not rely on our private circuit, but uses a translator to tell me in hashy English that the others will also have their suits removed, for her crew's security but also for our own good.

"They are designed to control you," the scratchy voice says. "The Keepers are afraid of you."

"Who're they?" I croak.

She wipes my mouth with a cloth. "If you join us, you can fight to kill them."

"Yeah. Sure. When can I speak to my friends?" I ask.

"On a bigger ship, we will find a place for all of you to live together."

"What about Bug Karnak?" Somehow, through our connection, she knows what I'm talking about.

"It will stay here," she says.

"But someone's going to try to destroy it, right?"

The Antag female leans over me, four eyes glittering in the dim light of the cell, beak open to show a raspy tongue. "You will sleep. We are moving to bigger ship."

She thinks there's something unusual about this particular bigger ship—I can feel it in the overtones. Something powerful, dangerous, and puzzling.

"Where to after that?"

"Far away," she adds. "Long journey. Many days."

"You travel between the stars?"

"We go home," she says. "If we live."

Lots of ifs. "Where are you from?"

Through the overtones, I'm left with an impression of something like a big basketball on a billiard table, slowly rolling across gravity-dimpled felt and scattering smaller balls every which way. Makes no sense to me.

Then I realize this might be Sun-Planet.

"You don't come from another star system?"

No answer to that and pretty soon I'm numb, sleepy all over again—

Asleep.

This time I dream of walking across the dry, brushy hills between the close-packed, apartment-strewn suburbs of San Diego. My mother is walking with me and one of her boyfriends, it's Harry, goddammit, and he's packing a Colt pistol in a fast-draw holster slung on his hip. Harry's about to teach me the basics of high-powered weapons.

Christ. Why can't I dream something pleasant, something wonderful?

SORRY, CHARLIE

My eyes are open, though I'm still in darkness. I'm wearing a loose kind of pajama bottom. I fall against a wall and back my way around a circle. I'm in a small, cylindrical room. A can. Tuna, not sardines. If I spread my arms, I can touch both sides. I have no idea how much time has passed. I'm comfortable enough, though my body still throbs and aches. It's dark in here. Dark and close.

"Joe? Jacobi? Commander?"

No answer. Where are we?

Have we left Titan?

I feel the peculiar vibration that tells me the female Antag isn't far away. I pick up a jumble of her deep thoughts, then more overtones, and no doubt she can feel some of mine. Images and emotions. She's hard at work—maybe she's in the control room, but I can't see what that looks like. My vision and hers still don't sync.

But her fellows are ragging her. Some hate her for getting close to humans and not killing us. Our being here puts a tremendous strain on their command structure, their cama-raderie. So many want us dead.

Even putting that aside, I don't think she has a lot of respect for me, for us. After all, they were able to capture us alive— and even though that was what the bug steward wanted and she had told her superiors that was what should happen and everyone in her crew signed on to that course of action—

Even though we surrendered reluctantly, and two of our Oscars tried to break and run…we didn't *really* put up a fight. We chose the coward's way, right?

How old is Antag culture? That kind of shit thinking usually passes after a really bad war or a few thousand years of scouring the countryside and raping and killing peasants. After a while, that kind of thinking gets stale.

But they're in charge.

The female delivers another sip of precious knowledge. We're on the move; our cans (we're all in ventilated cylinders like this one) are going to be packed into a transport, await-ing an opportunity to rendezvous with a much larger ship, that dangerous puzzle ship, even now swooping down from behind other moons. Antags do like to hide behind moons. But she insists this is not one of their ships. Makes no sense. She shows me that leaving Titan was less difficult than leav-ing Mars. Duh. That's why we hardly felt it.

Will my air last that long? That *really* pushes a button. I remember being told back in basic that you'd be flunked out if you got iffy in tight situations. No claustrophobes allowed. Skyrine training leads you into lots of trials that involve con-finement, being closed in, squeezed tight, sometimes for days or weeks. But usually while asleep or waiting to be dropped, when adrenaline and our favorite drug, never given a name but we called it *enthusiasm*, kept you up and prepped.

But that's a long time ago. We've been through a lot since then and this fucking can is too much. It's tough to quit a panic once engaged. All I manage is to stand flat against the wall and shiver all over. For the first time in my life, I'm asking God to just kill me. Get it over with now. I've lost all interest in whatever will come next, because I'm *IN A FUCKING CAN* and *can't get out*.

Then another kind of panic grips me. If I survive, I think, I'll never be what I was before—whatever and whoever I was before. Shithead before, but at least I was a semifunctional Skyrine and a faithful member of the Corps. What will I be in a few hours?

Just when I'm about to lose the last of my dignity, my discipline, I am bathed in a kind of autumnal light. A kind of opening is revealed through which I see something, through which I can experience the outside and try to control my fear—

It's in the overtones. It's my connection with the Antag female—Bird Girl.

I try to remember where I've heard that name, *Bird Girl*. My mother read me books all the time. I was five or six when she started us on bigger novels, usually from the base library, but sometimes from bargain bookstores. I try to recall the titles—something to distract me, and it helps by bringing another round of memories, this time so sharp and sweet I can almost forget the can.

I feel myself wrapped in a blanket, nestling up against my mother's warmth and hearing her voice as she reads. Crickets chirp outside, a breeze puffs the curtains through the window screen—the last dry heat of day fading into Fresno night. We haven't moved to San Diego yet. My mother and father haven't gotten their divorce. These are good times, cozy times. I feel secure and happy.

Bird Girl. This may be where I first heard that strange name. Mom read me Vance and Le Guin, Martin and Tolkien, of course, but there was also this book set in South America that told about a girl in a big green jungle. It takes me hours to remember the name, then it just pops up. *Green Mansions.* Rima was the bird girl's name. I feel so clever, I want to tell Joe and DJ, but I doubt they've ever heard of the book.

Mom's reading to me continued even after my father left us and my behavior went downhill, exasperating her, but when she read to me, we could imagine better times and places. She moved us down to San Diego. Started dating the string of crazy dudes. But she still found time to read to me. I think now, digging deep, that the love of reading I picked up from her—that, and Joe's influence—is what kept me from becoming a narcissistic monster. As she read she mused, talked about our life, tried to explain what she was feeling—I didn't always want to know about that. Embarrassed the hell out of me sometimes. She drew out lessons and revealed a kind of wisdom she rarely applied to her own life, but passed to me nevertheless, along with those stories—a kind of mother's milk full of immunization against the insanity that all too often surrounded us.

When she found a new man, of course, all that was put on pause for a few weeks, so I didn't actually like any of her men, and she knew it and that added to our strain.

But for right now—

Listening to the overtones coming from the liaison—

"Hey, *Bird Girl*," I whisper in the darkness, in the can. "Read me a story. Give me something. We're partners, right?"

My words must come wrapped in their own overtones, a haze of comfort and the sound of crickets, the heat of a Southern California summer—and so many strange words. Maybe Bird Girl knows about Tolkien and the others. Maybe she was told to study us as a culture. Maybe she's a scholar of humanity.

Yeah. Right.

There's a pause, a kind of mental question mark, and then I get another round of overtones. I desperately reach for them, like grabbing flowers out of a falling bouquet, so sweet because they're not in the can with me. Most of it turns out to be bug memory, a constant flow of old history and planetary geology. Bug steward is still there, acting between Bird Girl and me, coordinating this ancient flow—and maybe trying to give me some relief.

But there's also a young memory and it has to be from Bird Girl, because nothing about bug steward is young—

Very sharp—

A tangled ball of wings and grasping hands. Momma Antag has just hatched five babies, and they pile up against one another in a soft bowl, mewing and thrashing and waiting for something to be deposited in their barely open beaks. A tube drops down. Momma doesn't regurgitate—maybe it's not Momma—

It's not. This is a place where they make soldiers.

The infant soldiers eat. It's pea soup and salt and anchovies, by the taste, or at least the smell. Ecstasy. Not in the least cozy from my human perspective, but it's one of Bird Girl's favorite early memories.

Fair exchange.

The overtones fade. For a long, long time, I resonate again between panic and trying to reach out in our weird, four-part thought space—DJ, Bird Girl, the steward, and me in four hypothetical corners—and get relief, plus answers...

DJ is barely there. I think he's actually asleep. I don't want to dig into DJ's subconscious, which is mostly old movies and memories of porn, so I avoid that part.

And then—

I feel a pressure down my centerline, pooling around my feet like I'm in an elevator cab. We're definitely on the move. I can stand, but it's easier to squat and press my back against the cylinder wall. The pressure grows on my butt and feet. I focus on that pressure, that sensation. Something's going to change.

After a while, I stop squeaking like a mouse and rise from the bottom, then float up inside the cylinder until I bump my head. Somehow that's better than just sitting. We're still in orbit, I guess, but no joy on getting the can open. We're waiting for that big powerful ship, but it's not here yet.

The ship we're all stuffed into at the moment is little more than a light transport, the last of those that once delivered weapons and reinforcements to Antags on Titan. The Antags retrieved their survivors and the few remaining catamaran squid. I get a kind of doubled picture/impression of these remarkable creatures swimming in Titan's deep icy slush, the supercold, super-saline fluids, and wonder how that makes sense, how they survived—

But I know now that the squid are not native to Titan. They belong with the Antags! And how many Antags remain? Not many. They've dumped the falcons and the smaller weapons that faced us across the walls of the archive—Bug Karnak. Those are all gone.

The big ship that's supposedly out there is not one of the ships that deliver Antags to Mars. Those are much smaller, less powerful, and slower. This one is bigger than big and stranger than strange, and for some reason no Antag is really at all sure it will allow us inside, or how the Antags will take control and fly it, but if everything works out right—if we acquire or earn infinite amounts of luck—we will meet with it soon and be transferred over.

So Bird Girl informs us, DJ and me, reluctant to reveal even this much. She's doing it only because she's also scared, and that resonates with our fear. Still, bug steward approves of the resonance. We're truly related, the steward observes. Proof of some ancient concept, some ancient—

I lose the rest of that overtone, which seems to come out of nowhere specific—the depths of the saline sea, Bug Karnak, maybe—

Or the squid? Did I just touch the mind of one of those? Or something even stranger...

The *starshina*.

I shudder.

This new and strange ship, if our luck holds, will take us very far away, very swiftly, because of a *haze of branching green minds*...whatever the hell that means.

Ulyanova again—just briefly. Like tiptoeing over razor blades. I want that to stop, really I do. I try to blink in the darkness. How do I know when my eyes are closed?

Fascinating stuff, no?

But I'm still in a fucking can.

DELIVERED

I have a moment through the awfulness to wonder how the others are doing, if they're also still in cans. Maybe we'll all end up drooling basket cases, no use to anybody, and the Antag commanders will just dump us out in space like old garbage. Antags should have no idea how to fix us—only how to kill us. We'll become part of Saturn's rings, supercooled packets of meat caught in the grind of orbiting ice and rock boulders, forgotten by everybody…

Bug steward seems to be keeping its presence, its interference, low-key, to encourage the connection with Bird Girl. And I feel Bird Girl more intensely than ever. She's exploring me in detail, overcoming an inherent reluctance, listening closely to *my* overtones, but so far, it's strictly a one-way exchange. Perversely, that makes me both happy and even more queasy.

Then, as if in payment for her intrusion, she provides another blurry impression of our transport working to join up with the big ship. No idea where that is. Maybe it's still orbiting Titan. If so, why hasn't Box attacked it?

For a time, I feel like I'm floating in space, no body, just a pair of eyes—vision doubled, so it's a quartet of eyes—but very low rez. I can barely make out the stars. Then my perspective shifts and I think I see Saturn's rings, lightly sketched and again doubled, giving me a weird ache in my eye muscles. There are little flashing symbols on the different rings, the shepherd moons—then the view goes back to that goddamned ship. I have to guess through Bird Girl's eyes, or maybe what someone is telling her—because she can't see it directly, can she?—how big it really is.

The vessel we're closing on is maybe nine or ten klicks long and has a short, blunt tail. Forward of the tail swells a gray bulb maybe two or three klicks in diameter. Full of fuel to get home? There's a cylindrical midsection about four klicks long and a klick in diameter, and at the prow or nose, a long, skinny tube like the needle of a hypodermic. Big and ugly. Forward of the bulb, just back from the nose, five long containers are arranged in pentagonal frames around the middle cylinder like bullets in a revolver. Not all that different from the Spook, actually, but maybe ten or fifteen times bigger. I can't see what drives it. I'm given the impression the big ship has been hidden away for years—kept in reserve, but by whom, and why?

Why can't Bird Girl view it directly? Is it invisible?

What's obvious is that no Antag has never seen or experienced anything remotely like it. The transport's crew is approaching cautiously, critically, in no hurry, because they're ignorant of what could happen, but also, Bird Girl is their only connection to someone or something crucial to activating the ship. Maybe two somethings.

One appears to be an Antag, a ragged, poorly treated

creature with a sad, shabby demeanor. In Bird Girl's eyes, this bedraggled Antag is a monster, a traitor, a true atrocity, but essential to the success of this mission.

And there's something else, something she won't tell me about or allow me to see. Not an Antag, but a Keeper, fallen so far from grace, after flying so high, that the crew simply wants to kill it. But Bird Girl won't let them.

And this Keeper, whatever it may be, is afraid of *me*? Of humans? More afraid of those who are connected to the archives, I'm guessing. That makes my brain itch. The enemy of my enemy is my enemy's former friend?

For some reason, I don't draw the obvious connection. I'm not at my best in this situation. As far as we are concerned, her fellows don't trust Bird Girl not just because of that weirdness, but because she has a connection with humans, and will force us all to meet and interact. In their eyes, she's tainted all around.

Great. I try to screw down on our link, to see these complications more clearly, or at least begin to understand them—but now a debate, maybe even a fight, has broken out around Bird Girl, not for the first time, and she's totally absorbed trying to defuse the tensions and get along with her fellows. There aren't that many of them left, maybe thirty. Hard to count.

The last Antag warriors are convinced that this journey, this maneuver or feint, will be the last thing they'll ever do.

Ice Moon Tea has connected us, the steward of bug memory has connected us, but Bird Girl will be very, very glad when our sharing ends and she can revert to her lone fighter self. She feels *violated* by having to deal with DJ and me and the mysterious Keeper. She feels she's been sacrificed, her honor discarded.

GARDEN OF ODIN

When her troubles have eased, Bird Girl passes along a tid-
bit of information, and it's a wrencher—that the crew
believes, or has been informed by their commanders, that
there's something about the big ship that's frightening and
forbidden—taboo.

It's not an Antag ship. Got that. And it's not human,
either. Something huge, invisible, alien, unknown. A lost
artifact filled with angry gods or creatures of light? Cosmic
zombies or vampires? I try not to let my subconscious get out
of control.

Then our link fades. I'm back in the dark. I sniff, sniff again,
feel the coolness of the container wall—smooth and dry. If I
don't stretch out my arms and press, I float. The air actually
feels fresh, though I can't tell where it's coming from. That's
a plus, an offer of hope that we're not just being executed by
slow suffocation. But I'm still thirsty and hungry. Should I be
grateful we haven't eaten since being peeled out of our lobster
suits? I haven't had to fill the can with unseemly stink.

More motion—sideways, swaying, followed by creaks and pops I feel in my ears. Possibly the cans are being sealed off, and the swaying may mean we're being transferred.

As much as Bird Girl has no interest in keeping us fully informed, I get occasional glimpses of this and that—of two transports entering an opening in empty space, of cans being winched in clusters out of one transport. I try to chuckle at a memory of beach parties on Socotra, beer cans slopping in plastic-strapped six-packs. The chuckle fades into a gurgle.

This is all she sees, all Bird Girl can know. She's not a pilot, has no connection to the pilots, if this strange, taboo ship can have real pilots. But from what she does convey, it's obvious the ship is vastly more powerful than either of us has managed to use or create. We've both been contained, coached and prepped to go at each other on almost equal footing. How much does equality of tech and knowledge equal a longer, more entertaining war? Who's been dealt the stronger hand?

Who's favored?

Bug steward seems irritated by my density. *Whoever most pleases the masters of this ancient game.*

Gurus? Keepers are the same as Gurus! Bird Girl has been telling me that *Antags have Gurus,* just like humans—showrunners for their side of our war. Bird Girl's commanders, her people, have been told that humans want to kill all Keepers—all Gurus—and all Antags and dominate the solar system, while Keepers, like Antags, just want to live in peace. Same story we've been fed, but in reverse.

The air in the can becomes close. I can't simply stop breathing. I need to get out. There's that damned squeaking again—it's me, I'm freaking.

Then the can opens like a lunchbox. The lights come up to

unbearable brightness and three of the small, bat-wing critters rustle close, wings folded tight, to peer at me. Their four
reddish-purple eyes blink. Big Antags are at least four times
larger—if the small ones are even Antags and not lackeys or
servants. Nobody wants to touch me. I rise from the can and
nearly float out, then grip the edge, casual as can be, except
that I'm laughing like a maniac. I try with all my willpower
to stop. Don't want to lose it. Not after having survived all
that crap—not when there's finally hope.

I stuff my hand in my mouth and look around.

The cans have been tied down with rubbery gray cords on
a brightly illuminated platform. We're in zero g, surrounded
by a space that shades off to warm darkness. Four more of
us are released and cling to the edges of the cans or the cords
themselves: Borden, DJ, Kumar, Joe. Our sounds echo—
retching, crying out, calling names.

Bats pull the rest of the cans up against the first five, tying
them to the others with more cords. They're opened next.
Here's Tak, Ishida, Ishikawa—Jacobi. We're all in pajama
bottoms and nothing more. Jacobi looks cool and collected,
but vomit spatters her chest and arms.

Litvinov emerges with a gaunt, haunted look on his lean
face. Ulyanova rises from her can with arms crossed. I see
Kumar, also covered in vomit. I don't see Mushran.

Most of the Russians must have died back in the Battle of
the Titanian Sea. The two that are still with us, besides Litvinov and Ulyanova, I barely know—a couple of *efreitors*: one
male named Bilyk, the other a female named Yagodovskaya, a
few years older than Ulyanova.

Christ almighty. Fourteen, barely a squad. Six are still
spewing thin vomit that makes the bat critters shuffle and

flap. For some reason, that insane comedy makes me want to cry. But at least I've stopped laughing.

Physically I'm okay, but DJ is taking this poorly, as are Ishikawa and Borden. We've been through too many changes.

Five of the big Antags watch from the side of the platform. I recognize Bird Girl at the center—same orange and blue colors around the eyes, same blue, raspy tongue. I fix details of Antag appearance in memory—wingspans of about three meters, outer tips sprouting small fingers, more substantial gripping digits on each wing elbow or middle joint—basically two upper sets of hands. The bats seem to have similar arrangements. Beneath a thick tunic, the thorax presents a central breastbone like a turkey's. Under clinging pantaloons, the lower limbs are short, thick, and tightly muscled, with hands on knees and prehensile feet, mostly covered now in buttoned pockets and flexible booties. Bird Girl would make a great juggler.

The bats gather around Bird Girl like dogs at a hunt. She moves her wing-fingers and issues light, sweet whistles, to which the bats respond by helping mop up the vomit. Everything is hidden in shadow. Antags, bats, us, a couple of transports maybe thirty meters away—surrounded by gloom. No more overtones, no more clues. Bird Girl is no longer broadcasting on our private wavelength. DJ looks pale and serious. At least he's stopped spewing.

Kumar hangs on to my arm, pushing his face close. "Where are we?" he asks, eyes darting. I hope I'm not surrounded by total loons. Most of the others have been far more isolated than me. Ulyanova stares off into the shadows and doesn't once look my way.

The bats pry us apart, space us out, then hand us more ropes. After they've persuaded us to hang on, they tug and guide us out of the shaded chamber and along a curved tube. The walls of the tube are equipped every few meters with rungs that both big and small Antags use to navigate. The rungs do not seem designed for them but they're making do. Bird Girl is behind us. This phase of our journey takes about ten minutes. The tube veers sharp left, and we're pulled through the crimp with hard knocks.

The bats and one of the Antags then tug and shove us into a cubic space like a giant racquetball court, its corners also lost in shadow. All we can see clearly, in the center of the court, is a spherical cage about thirty meters in diameter, made of thick wire mesh and cabled to the side walls.

Some of the bats nicker and whistle, then poke out wing-fingers in sequence. They seem to be counting, maybe counting us. They can count to forty-eight on their fingers, should they be so inclined.

Four Antags enter the court. Bird Girl is again number three in their lineup. Two wear tunics, including Bird Girl. The others are equipped with what could be light armor, covering the breastbone and forming protective collars over the wing-shoulders.

Bird Girl surveys our pitifully reduced group. Her purple-rimmed eyes light on me, and she approaches with evident reluctance, no doubt disgusted by everything about me—certainly by my appearance and smell. Man, have we been primed to be enemies.

I look left down our rope line. We're all scarred in pink lines and scabs from the removal of the lobster suits but appear to be healing. Ishida's metal parts are lightly scored but seem intact. I wonder how they knew which parts were hers and which the suit's.

We half-bob, half-float, hanging on to the rope and to one another. Bird Girl informs us through the translator that all our cuts and bruises were due to the activities of our suits and were not deliberately inflicted by Antag healers—by which she means the bats, not just technical rates but general-duty helpers. She also confirms that we're going to be kept for the time being in the spherical cage. Her voice through the translator is edged with something like electronic bird sounds—grating, hashy, not at all soothing. But then she adds that these quarters will be temporary. The Antags are presently exploring, hoping to find better living spaces deeper in the ship.

To DJ and me she relays directly that there's something complicated about that process—something that scares her. Keepers are involved, and there's one major, nasty, foul impediment, accompanied by mental expletives of sharp bones in the throat and patches of fresh guano, applied to the only way forward, and to a gate that is also a trap—a *puzzle* gate. If we solve the puzzle, we might be able to get the hell out of here, wherever we are.

And if we don't, the obscenity will kill us.

I was under the apparently false impression that we left Titan's orbit as soon as we could, to avoid being obliterated by Box and the others sent after us—but Bird Girl seems to think we're still close to the big orange moon.

No questions allowed. Not that DJ or I try…She's worried and tired. The cage is it for us for the time being, but it could be worse—has been worse. Inside the sphere we can be fed, looked after, kept clean…and closely watched. Mats will be provided. Maybe we can wrap ourselves up and bounce around like Ping-Pong balls in a church raffle. I suppose to keep us clean they'll hose us down, right? No comment. We can exercise, Bird Girl suggests. Get stronger. She isn't sure how we'll do that, but her commanders want us strong and healthy. I get the impression the commanders are the ones wearing armor. Her relation to them is less clear— she's not exactly inferior in either station or rank. Civilian? Consultant?

Unwilling volunteer?

She makes clear that she wants *one of us* in particular to stay healthy. Again I see a naked Antag, oppressed and unkempt, but I don't recognize the human she shows me, except that it could be one of our females. Maybe a Russian? We all look alike to the Antags.

One by one, we're guided through a hatch into the cage. Ulyanova doesn't put up a fuss. Yagodovskaya, the *efreitor*— Verushka or Vera—seems to have a calming influence. The bats toss mats through the hatch, then swing it shut with a clang and click a double-stranded lock around the latch. Something to jiggle with later, to see if escape is possible.

The lights around the court dim, as if we're in a night-time zoo. We can no longer see more than a meter beyond the mesh—can't see Antags large or small, though now and then I hear the bats nicker. Maybe most have left, gone to work, getting ready to finally go home—or to fight again. Fight their own kind. If they fail here, I suspect suicide missions are the next option. And they'll take us out to die right beside them.

At least we're not cramped. The big ball could hold dozens more. We take this time to examine one another in more detail. Tak has corpsman training, as does Jacobi. All who came out of the two surviving Oscars are here—all except Mushran. Nobody remembers seeing him after the centipede cabins were split open.

DJ moves closer to me, along with Joe and Jacobi, and we grip hands in a loose star-knot, like a parachute team. Joe pulls in Jacobi and Bilyk. Ishikawa and Tak join next and draw Ishida in. Yagodovskaya—Vera—grabs Ulyanova and they join us. Borden and Kumar and Litvinov cap our formation. We seem to want to cling like monkeys, anticipating more misery.

"We need to show some fight," Joe says, keeping a wary eye on the *starshina*. "We've been through a meat grinder. We need to show them they can't get away with treating us like shit."

"When will they feed us?" Jacobi asks.

HAMSTER LIFE

Our first sleep in the cage is deep.

I come out of my void to see Jacobi marshal her team and lead them in limbering up—another diagnostic, I think, making sure they can still fight, or at least move together in a coordinated fashion. Ishida works the hardest, complains the least. Litvinov gathers up his three Russians and does the same.

Kumar seems content to drift to a far side of the cage, where I imagine he's making plans. That's what Wait Staff do, all they're good for, right? Without Mushran, can he possibly carry on?

Joe rolls and floats up beside me, asks, "I wonder if the Antags will make us join their fight."

"They're doing everything they can to avoid a fight," I say.

DJ flaps by, ineffective at swimming or flying or whatever he's doing, and chimes in. "They're really unhappy. They've spent their whole lives training to push us off Mars and get ready to invade Earth. And now—they're giving up and planning to get the hell out."

"Fuck 'em all," Jacobi says as she bounces along the bottom of the cage.

"Just passing it along," DJ says and slides against the mesh without benefit of a mat. He grips the thick wire with his fingers and hangs on. "Some fucking hamster ball, ain't it?"

I lie back beside him, stretch out my arms, and stare toward the center of the cage. DJ joins Kumar and some of the others in pretending to sleep. Being hooked in by the tea isn't easy on either of us. I hope it doesn't leave mental scars to match the ones from our lobster suits.

There's now a faint suggestion of g-force. We seem to be accelerating. What can this ship do? What kind of maneuvering? How fast, with what kind of power?

I can't drift off. I let go of the mesh. DJ follows. Borden and DJ and I join in another daisy, gripping hands and pulling our heads almost together. Our feet impact softly against the cage.

Jacobi swings by and grabs a hand from Borden.

"What do you know about this ship?" Borden asks DJ and me.

"Not much," I say. "Bird Girl's not very consistent at keeping us informed." I tell them about the apparent connection between our Gurus and their Keepers.

"What the hell are Keepers?"

"Their Gurus," DJ concurs.

"This whole war was arranged and coached on both teams?" Jacobi says.

"We knew that," Borden says.

This sobers them, but in fact nobody seems very surprised. "Awkward communication could be to our advantage," I say.

"As the weak partners in this dance, DJ and I should listen close and hope for more embarrassing revelations."

Borden looks at us with some surprise. "Strategic thinking?" she asks. I smile, showing my teeth.

Now Joe is with us. Not many of us can sleep. "Vinnie always thinks strategically," he says.

"Whatever's out there scares the hell out of the Antags," I say. "They need to take control, but they don't know how. And it all seems to involve Keepers. Gurus. Whatever."

"Wonder if that explains where Mushran is?" Borden asks. That hadn't occurred to me, but the idea gains no traction in ignorance.

"Where are they planning to go?" Jacobi asks.

"No idea," I say.

"There's something they call Sun-Planet," DJ says, and I give him a severe look. He's getting ahead of what I'm comfortable speculating on.

"What the hell is Sun-Planet?" Borden asks.

"Still collating," I say.

"It's way out there," DJ says. "Could be Planet X."

Joe and Borden frown.

"Planet X," he says, about to launch into that story, but they raise their hands and he cuts himself off.

Do I truly understand the import of that basketball-on-felt diagram Bird Girl fed me earlier? She doesn't seem to remember Sun-Planet in any detail. She's got textbook knowledge, nothing sensual or immediate. I wonder if she's ever been there.

"Anything else?" Joe asks.

I hold back a few subliminal impressions because I'm not

sure they make sense. Antag family structure? Something important is missing, but maybe about to arrive. "They're way below strength. Maybe only thirty or forty Antags, not including the bats."

"Got that," Borden says.

"I saw some squids," Joe says. "Did you see them, too?"

"Yeah," Jacobi says. "Haven't seen them since, and I wasn't sure I saw them the first time."

"What about the hunters out here in orbit?" Borden asks. "Ours and theirs—Box and the rest?"

"Doesn't seem to be their biggest worry," I say.

To my relief, the group breaks up to return to exercising.

Every few hours, three or four bats show up with a tank and a hose and let loose a spray of water. The spray cuts a tangent across one side of the sphere. We wash in it, drink from it, or simply avoid it.

More hours. Nature takes its course.

"Dignity in the Corps!" Joe calls out. "We get to crap behind blankets."

Exactly right. Nobody's much embarrassed, but we hold up the mats for individual privacy.

After a couple of hours, the bats lob fist-sized green balls through the hatch. I grab one and bite into it. It's dry and yeasty, slightly salty, slightly sweet. The others see my tacit approval and grab their own.

The lights go down every thirty hours. That leaves those of us who are still not sleepy to cling to the mesh or bump into one another.

ROTATIONS

Jacobi specializes in light martial arts, Borden in building strength. The Russians exercise separately and keep busy trying to catch Litvinov unprepared. Our respect for the colonel grows. *Polkovnik* is equivalent to a colonel in the Skyrines. He must be twice the age of the others, especially Bilyk, a skinny but wiry opponent. Litvinov experiences a lot of bruising, some bleeding, but no broken bones, and sluices every time he gets a chance, urging his soldiers to do the same.

We need distraction and information, and for the time being nobody outside is talking and nobody or nothing within me or DJ is volunteering new facts, which I find both peaceful and like another little death. Can't put up with ignorance much longer, but Joe and Borden and Litvinov and Kumar (I think) are maintaining, and so is DJ, and so will I. But we can't maintain forever.

Still, compared to the cans, this is a real improvement.

One big question—if this isn't an Antag ship, and not a

human ship, why is there pressure, a breathable atmosphere? Who designed the lights? Who's controlling?

And how did the Antags know to dock their vessels in empty space, find that hangar, and get us on board?

Something obvious I'm just missing, and it's pissing me off.

DIVISION FOUR

Jacobi and Ishikawa take Ishida and Tak off to one wall of the cage, where they grip in a four-petal flower and quietly talk. Kumar watches from his curled position across the cage. He's saying little but tracking everything, especially Litvinov's exercises.

Then the flower breaks and Ishida crosses the perimeter of the cage. She adjusts her tack by changing her center of gravity like a circus gymnast. Impressive.

Then she spreads her arms and legs to slow her spin and glides up beside Kumar.

"Tell us about Division Four," she says. The former Wait Staffer turns his head to stare back at her, and blinks. The gouges and scars along her formerly polished body parts, added to the pink lines of withdrawn wires and other scars on her flesh, give her a fierce, tattered look that's more than a little scary.

And maybe a little sexy.

I hope we're not coming apart. I have to admit that before

we landed on Mars, and after, I thought she was kind of awe-some, but none of that matters now. I just want all of us to be allowed to keep it together, stay sane, fight again.

Win this time.

Kumar seems to relax and relent. He waves for us to gather around. DJ wakes up, extends an arm, and marches with his hands along the mesh to join the condensing pack. Borden seems to materialize beside Joe. Litvinov and the Russians, including Ulyanova, arrive last.

Kumar's voice is low and hoarse. For the moment, it seems we've got back some of our cohesion—but who knows? It all depends on how much Kumar feels the need to keep us ignorant.

"None of you, possibly excepting Master Sergeant Venn, has ever met a Guru or had much to do with Wait Staff until recently—correct?" Kumar asks.

Litvinov says, "Russians give Wait Staff tours, on Mars. *Starshina* was there."

"Ah," Kumar says. "Perhaps she will contribute?"

Ulyanova doesn't react.

"The commander's hung out with you guys, hasn't she?" Jacobi asks, referring to Borden. Borden keeps her eyes on Kumar but says nothing—possibly waiting for him to reveal something she doesn't know.

"Just me, until she met Mushran," Kumar says. "She was not involved in political decisions on Earth or elsewhere until the last few months. What I am approaching, on a round-about, is describing to you what it is like to deal with Gurus and their representatives, to carry out their orders without truly understanding their goals." He sounds as if the loss of Mushran has put all this on him and he feels the weight.

"We're listening," Jacobi says.

"Good. Listen critically," Kumar says. "I think it will soon become important."

"What do Gurus look like?" Ishida asks.

Kumar affords her another blink, then a small grin. "Do you believe I have seen them? Seen them as they really are?"

Ishida nods intently.

Borden says, "I know you've seen them."

"I, on the other hand, am not so sure," Kumar says. "The Gurus who interact most with humans are about the size of a large dog. These have four walking legs and four arms, rather like canine caterpillars. Their faces are broad, with small, sensitive ears. Their eyes are large, like a lemur's, possibly because they want us to think they're nocturnal.

"Whatever we thought we saw, it early became apparent to the more discerning Wait Staff that the Gurus are talented at creating illusions. They have shown themselves capable of altering both physical shape and how we see them. How much of what we have witnessed is in fact real, I do not know. I doubt anyone knows."

"Wait Staff fooled?" Ulyanova asks, looking up and shifting her look around the group as if to see how astonishing this might be. "You do not see from inside? Or see outside clear?"

"I am not sure what you mean," Kumar says.

She smiles her strange smile and waves her hand—continue.

"Are they ugly?" Jacobi asks.

"We never saw them so. Usually, as I said, they appear cat- or doglike, with multiple limbs but pleasant faces, evoking a certain domestic familiarity, likely to make us feel a positive connection—to establish affection."

690 | GREG BEAR

"They look like pets," Ishikawa says.

Kumar nods. "It is the highest privilege to be in the presence of a Guru," he continues. "They evoke peace of mind, calmness, stability, loyalty. Neither Mushran nor I, nor our closest colleagues in Division Four, spent more than three years working with them. If you serve in the presence of Gurus for longer than three years, betrayal of any sort becomes unthinkable."

"But for you—thinkable?" Tak asks.

Kumar gives a small shrug. "It was Lieutenant Colonel Joe Sanchez who brought back to Earth the first Martian settler exposed to the Drifter's green dust."

"I'm right here," Joe says. Kumar looks past him, past us, like we're living through a bad haunted-house movie and Joe is one of the ghosts. He doesn't trust Joe, I think. That makes me trust Joe more—for now.

"That was five years ago," Kumar says. "The settler was smuggled past all security in ways about which I have not been informed—perhaps because I myself still do not arouse trust."

"No kidding," Jacobi says.

Kumar is unfazed. "It was this settler who first told a select few about the ancient pieces of memory buried deep in the Drifter. At first, none of us believed, it seemed so fantastical, so opposed to the history taught us by the Gurus. There was discord in the divisions, but word slowly leaked to our top leaders, and then, we presume, to the Gurus. The settler was stolen from our care. I learned later he was executed. That was our first shame, but also the first indicator of how desperate the Gurus were to keep this information away from Earth and from our fighters."

"They didn't want us to know about our origins?" I ask.

"That may have been part of their concern. But also…the knowledge that our ancestral forms on the outer moons of the solar system—"

"We call them bugs," DJ says, looking grimly serious. "That's what they were. We get used to it. Mostly." He's forcing the issue.

"That's what you see in your heads?" Borden asks.

"Yeah," DJ says.

"You?" The commander looks at me.

"Yeah," I say.

Ishida and Jacobi make disgusted faces. Ulyanova eyes the cage limits.

"The *bugs* had long ago encountered a species like the Gurus, or the Gurus themselves, and had been led by them to fight many wars."

Litvinov and the Russians jerk as if they've been poked, perhaps realizing something significant. This may be their first hint that the Antags themselves have Gurus.

"The Gurus are that old?" Ishida asks.

"It seems they are. Endless wars, millions of battles, billions of deaths, before our progenitors cleared themselves of that plague."

"It can be done," Joe murmurs.

"The bugs, as you call them, settled through the outer solar system about four and a half billion years ago. They took their wars with them. That is about the time Mars and then Earth were struck by chunks of some of their moons. We think that at that time, they were divided into rigid social classes. The Gurus aggravated these divisions and set them against one another. Very soon, the bugs began to fight to preserve class and racial mixes, to exclusively honor a certain social or family unit—or some representative philosophy. Wars over philosophy, or within families, can be the most vicious and long-lasting. Their wars under the tutelage of the Gurus may have lasted a hundred and fifty million years." He looks at me and DJ and tilts his head. "Is any of this incorrect?"

"Not so far," DJ says.

Kumar seems amused that DJ should become an expert.

"Did the bugs' Gurus share technology with them—better weapons, better ships?" Ishida asks.

"Their battles kept them mostly in the outer solar system and the Kuiper belt," Kumar says. "They did not themselves visit Mars or the Earth. But yes, they seem to have been given insights to help them—but only up to a point, a carefully selected *strategic* point. Only enough to maintain a balance between opposing forces, with occasional swings of victory and defeat. The Gurus always try to keep things *interesting*. And the bugs must have fascinated their intended audiences a great deal. We are, perhaps, only a late sequel...an afterthought." Kumar lets this sink in. "After the debriefing of three Antagonist survivors, under cover of gaining tactical knowledge about the battle situation on Mars—"

Joe won't meet my eyes. He's been in on it almost from the beginning. Always coming upon surprises, always ending up in the center of action. And only telling me when I might be useful—or if, conceivably, I might get hurt if I do not know.

"—we combined the knowledge gained from them, with the history outlined by the Muskie colonist who had been successfully exposed to Ice Moon Tea. But that was not all. Even then, we were provided with certain confirming truths by Antagonists who had reached similar conclusions, or had themselves been exposed to the green powder—like the female who speaks her mind to Master Sergeant Sanchez and Corporal Johnson. A number of these brave enemies tried to reach out and warn us. Most died at the hands of our troops— sacrificed as they tried to spread the truth.

"Mushranji sent records of these debriefings to Division One, which promptly buried them—followed by more executions. He managed to keep himself separate from all that, to play as if he were still in the camp of those fanatically devoted to the Gurus. But he carefully enlisted and informed other Wait Staff—making sure that none he approached had spent more than three years in the presence of Gurus. That they had at least a minimal chance of being persuadable.

"And soon, Mushranji had a large enough cadre of the informed and the like-minded that Division Four secretly split from the other divisions, from top politicians and administrators. Soon, we began planning and then directing operations on Mars to confirm the existence of the Drifter, its contents, and its effects on a number of other Martian settlers.

"I fear that because of our tight limits, and our failures, all of you became involved in painful confusion. We were still learning, still trying to understand how we might survive this new and growing base of unwelcome knowledge. Mushranji himself kept me in the dark, ignorant about certain matters, that I might play my part better. I hope he is not lost…"

"*Antagonista* take orders from Gurus, too," Ulyanova murmurs, again with that peculiar expression—an expression of feeling pain in a place one doesn't know one has. Her companion, Vera, sticks by her like a faithful puppy.

Litvinov looks away and says softly to her, "We knew this must be so."

"We are not special!" Ulyanova says. "So many have died to be part of special." Bilyk's glower deepens. Did he want to be special, too, or is he just reacting to the loss of friends, the end of ideals, the loss of any real reason to fight?

Tak echoes his dismay. "This has been going on for millions of years?" he asks. At Kumar's nod, his expression crumples. "What kind of evil shit is that?"

"We do not know the occasions when Gurus broadcast these wars," Kumar says. "There may have been long gaps when old species burned themselves out, like movie stars at the ends of their box-office appeal, and new species found intelligence, only to have the Gurus arrive, or revive, and recruit them."

"We're just entertainment!" Jacobi says, words sharp as flint.

"That is the truth of it, in a nutshell," Kumar says.

Quiet around the group. The big picture, even the nutshell, is more than most of us can immediately process.

"One big, bloody reality show," DJ says with a sniff. He rubs his nose, his far gaze showing the wear he has sustained. In the second Drifter, on Mars, for a time he had been truly happy. Then that, too, had been taken from him and destroyed—by Jacobi and her team. And now we may be about to lose Bug Karnak, the ancient archive, and our steward.

Ishikawa says, "What I want to know is, who's paying the cable bills?"

Nobody feels like laughing. What I feel like is punching my fist into something until it's mush. Finding out over and over again how much of a sucker you've been, what your real

TAKE BACK THE SKY | 695

place is in this nasty old world, is something Skyrines and other fighters should be used to…

But having my life and death, my relations with friends and enemies, the saving and the loving and the hating and the killing…

Having that spread around and *laughed* at, commented on by Guru audiences, *critiqued* like a TV show—

"Are we sure this is all on the level?" Jacobi asks, looking past the others at Joe. Joe shifts their attention adroitly, with a nod, to me, with the evaluative expression I've always hated. The same expression he used when we first met on that concrete culvert. The same expression he used before we went to take care of Grover Sudbury.

He wants me to answer.

And God damn us both, I do. "It's real," I says. "As real as anything in this fucked-up life."

"Who's seen the broadcast? The cable feed?" Jacobi asks. "Whatever the hell you call it."

"I may have," Kumar says. "It is what finally pushed me into Mushranji's camp in Division Four."

"Where did you see it?" Litvinov asks.

"In a Guru domicile in Washington, D.C.," Kumar says. "A door alarm failed and I entered without being noticed. I saw a room filled with war, and in the center, like an orchestra conductor, a Guru who looked human. It noticed me and quickly changed shape, then tried to wipe my mind of this memory, but apparently that failed as well."

"They're not perfect," Joe says.

"No," Kumar says with regret. "I almost wish they were."

"What was it?" Ishida asks him. "What was the show?"

"Fighting between Oscars and Antagonist weapons on

Titan. Spectacular, fully involving—looking at it, just from the corner of my eye, I was there. It took me days to recover."

This is still sinking in for the others. Loss of illusions is a long, hard process, and Kumar has not been the man we've trusted the most.

"They're actually *broadcasting a show*?" Ishida asks in disbelief. "Broadcasting from where? What kind of antennas— *to* where? How do we even ask the right questions?"

Kumar says, "It is the belief of the people within Division Four, and it is my belief, that the signals begin in your suits and are edited locally, to be delivered by some means—perhaps this ship—to the outer limits of the solar system to be sent on their way. We have yet to confirm any of that, however. I must emphasize, the Antagonists on this ship seem to be part of that group fighting and dying to change things. Analogous to the group of us that Mushranji helped create and organize— and supply."

"Antags still hate our guts," Jacobi says.

"Also true," Kumar says. "But they have sacrificed many in their own civil war, and many more fighting to save us. I hope we will soon learn their final disposition."

"There's a word for what they're doing, the Gurus, living off blood and misery," Tak says. "They're blood-sucking parasites, like mosquitoes."

"Worse," Borden says. "Mosquitoes need to eat. This is war porn. Who is out there, caring not a damn, getting off when we fly to our deaths—paying to see!"

I'm fascinated by the change in her features. This is no longer the disciplined, all-together commander we've come to expect. This is a frightened, angry mother, disgusted by what someone is doing to her children.

"We used to think the aliens would be like angels, or like demons," Kumar says. "I was raised on those fantasies. But Gurus are neither. They are in show business—arranging to get us to kill each other in ingenious and protracted ways to provide entertainment for heartless armchair rats."

"Jee-zuss!" Jacobi exclaims. She's dug her nails into her hands.

DJ says quietly, "We're no angels, either. Snug kids and their mommas and poppas eat dinner in front of the TV and watch us die on the evening news. Leaders push their causes over our mangled corpses. Civilians get off on our dying and blood and salute us in airports. Gurus didn't show up and recruit us until recently, right?"

Kumar doesn't know how or even whether to answer.

"We're perfect for this shit," DJ says, flicking his sharp eyes between us. "Doesn't matter what you call it—it's been going on for thousands of years. I read the *Iliad*." He waves his long fingers, arms still marked with red lines. "Happy little soldiers, paid rich in blood and shit and sometimes even respect." He snaps one of those akimbo civvie salutes. Having finished this tirade, packed with far more eloquence than we are used to from DJ, he folds his arms and looks through the mesh as a couple of bats bring up a hose.

"What do we do when we get out there?" Ishida asks, also tracking the bats.

"If," Tak says.

"Out where the Antags live. Will they let us fight with them, let us help clean this up and put it right?"

There it is. Our team wants to fight some more. I wonder if this was Kumar's plan all along.

"What's it like out there?" Ishikawa asks.

"Venn? What do you get from your connection?" Jacobi asks. I shake my head. DJ seems ready to leap in, but I give him a hard look. Right now, we're in limbo, but judging from what little I've been fed, we're going to have to get used to a whole new scale of weird. And I don't want to add to anyone's confusion, not now.

"What kind of worlds are they from? What do they look like?" Jacobi persists, as if they still might trust me or DJ to know the score.

"It's confused," I say.

"Fuck that!" Jacobi says. "We need to know." But she's barely whispering and her expression has lost focus. Then, as if they've reached their limit, they all break loose and scatter across the cage. Some gather mats and wrap up in them.

The bats look on in confusion. Are they supposed to spray the mats, as well? They nicker and knock on the cage, as if to warn us. We ignore them.

Joe pulls me and Litvinov and Borden together. "We can't keep on like this, on the inside with a view to nowhere. Can you pass that along to the Antags?"

Litvinov looks around at our scattered survivors. "We are not crazy minks in trap," he says. "Tell them *that*."

"I've been trying," I say. "It's not exactly a two-way street."

"What do you get from Bug Karnak?" Joe asks.

I've been wondering about that myself. "Nothing much," I say. The last few hours there's been something peculiar about our circumstances, about this ship, that is either blocking the steward or making it go silent—withhold judgment. Or the signal is simply losing its strength. Maybe we're already too far away.

Or…

What I've been dreading—the destruction of the archives—may be well under way.

"What about DJ?" Joe asks.

Borden says, "He's been dealing with this since Mars."

Ishikawa passes close on a personal Ping-Pong exercise from one side of the cage to the other. "Heads up," she says. "Twelve beady little eyes."

From a dark corner of the racquetball court, well outside the cage, three larger Antags have joined the confused bats to silently observe. We rotate as best we can off each other, off the cage mesh, an awkward low-g ballet, to face them. I recognize Bird Girl.

Her translator rasps and hisses. "Choose three," she says, focused on me. And then she adds, through our connection, an image of the one she especially wants—a surprise. Or maybe not. "We are leaving Saturn."

"We'd all like to have a look," I call out.

It takes her a few seconds to respond.

Everyone in the cage is at full alert.

"Others see later. Choose three," she repeats, and I feel another something brush the inside of my head, a deeper inquiry—but also a kind of reassurance. Bird Girl believes her fellow Antags are slowly coming to understand the trauma they've caused us and to believe it might be counterproductive.

Litvinov says grimly, "Old debts still need paying. How long?"

Joe says to me in an undertone, "Be careful." I know what he means. The shape we're in, our people may conclude I'm selecting the first three to be dumped into space. I don't like being put in such a position, but I drift and climb around the cage and pick DJ, Borden—and Ulyanova. Borden because equality in our fate seems the right tone. Ulyanova because hers was the face Bird Girl showed me.

When I'm done, the others look relieved—all but Joe, who seems severely pained—then move away from us four and from one another like drops of water on oil to grip the limits of the cage.

Had I not received the *starshina*'s image, I would not have picked her. There's more going on with her, inside her, than I can fathom. I might feel a connection to that weirdness, but without reason or explanation. Or rather—scattered shards of explanation, which do not, unassembled, take any satisfactory shape.

The hatch opens in the mesh cage and the four of us pass through, Ulyanova last. Vera clasps her hand, then reluctantly lets her go.

Bird Girl extends with her wingtip hand another rubbery rope about ten meters long. With a shake, she indicates all of us should take hold. Then she and her companions move out ahead, drafting us out of the racquetball court and into another long, curved hallway.

Being in this ship is like living in a gigantic steel heart—or intestine. That's it. We're literally in the bowels of the ship.

Borden grimaces as she bounces off the tube. Ulyanova continues to look as if we're all being led to the gallows.

"Pretty obvious where this ship will be going," DJ says, gripping the chain and rotating slowly around an axis through his sternum. "What else is out there but Planet X?"

I ignore him for the moment. I'm getting signals again.

Bug steward is sending more tantalizing, brief snippets. Things are changing rapidly down on Titan—nothing good.

"No, really!" DJ insists to nobody's stated objection. This is his chance. "What else? They've been looking for it since the nineteenth century. It was what pushed astronomers to discover Neptune, but Neptune was weird...tilted over and shit. So they looked for Planet X again and found Pluto. But Pluto was too small!"

Borden can't get the rhythm of our movement through the tube. "I'm more concerned about where we're going right now," she says, teeth chattering.

"But that's the big kahuna! The Antags call it Sun-Planet."

Borden looks to me as the rope torques us about. We bounce and correct. "You've heard that?"

"Yeah."

"Their Sun-Planet is Planet X?"

"Of course it is!" DJ says. "It swoops down every few hundreds of thousands of years and scatters moons and stuff like billiard balls."

Borden drills me with her eyes. "You did not mention any of this!"

"None of it's confirmed," I say.

"If *she* tells you something, shows you something, give it to me and Kumar!"

"Sure," I say, and she's right. DJ also looks apologetic. Knowing when to divulge and what to divulge is a real art form in this situation and around this crew.

And there's worse to come. I just can't put the fragments together, not yet. But I'm keeping my eye on Ulyanova because Bird Girl chose her, and because I sense she's at the center of everything about to happen. I just can't figure out why.

The tube widens and the Antags have more freedom to keep us from bumping and bouncing. Our trip goes on for more long minutes, time enough for me to get bored.

I remember the nighttime lectures under the amazing skies of Socotra that seemed to dwarf both the ocean and the island. The DIs had brought in a crew of professors and they were trying to convert a bunch of grunts into stargazers. Pleasant memory, actually. That's when DJ became fascinated with the idea of Planet X. Maybe he's always been the prescient one.

Ulyanova crawls up the chain and grips my arm. "I feel someone!" she says. "Is not right, is strange!"

"Yeah," DJ says. "You don't know it yet, but you're one of us."

Borden looks back at him, lip curled. More stuff not reported?

"How?" the *starshina* asks.

"Were you ever exposed to the green dust inside the Drifters?" DJ asks.

She frowns. "Possible," she says. "Help pick up bodies."

"Welcome to the club," he says. "See things?"

Ulyanova frowns again, shakes her head. She's lying. But how, and why?

And why does Bird Girl care?

We reach the open end of one tube and emerge on one side of an aggressively amazing space. It takes a few confused seconds to process what we're seeing.

Big ship indeed.

A wide curved landscape stretches beneath us, rising on

two axes to a central shaft maybe half a klick away, itself a hundred meters thick. The curved surface butts up against the shaft and then smoothly spirals around it, like the surface of a screw or the inside of a shell. No way of knowing how many turns the spiral makes, or how long the shaft is, but what we can see, upper surface and lower, is coated with a carpet of bushy green, red, and brown vegetation. Enclosing this giant spiral is a blank, almost featureless outer wall. The way the lighting concentrates on the screw itself is mysterious—no obvious source and very little scatter against that surrounding wall.

Ulyanova makes a growling sound and taps her head, as if to knock some wiring back in place.

"Oxygen processing?" Borden asks.

"Or a big salad bowl," I say.

"What do Antags eat?" Borden asks, as if we'd know.

DJ just squints as if thinking hurts.

Our escorts tug on the rubbery rope and pull us up close, then point their wingtips at a rail running around the outer edge of the screw. From around the long curve comes an open car, empty, automated. It stops right beside us.

Bird Girl suggests we all climb in and hang on to the straps. We do that. Then, without a jerk, just smooth acceleration, the car whisks us around the long spiral of the screw's edge—forward, I think, toward the prow of this monstrous ship. Our progress is leisurely. These cars may be made for bringing in the crops or carrying farmers—not for mass transit.

"We're being kept in the back of the bus," Borden says. "Aft of sewage treatment or whatever this is."

Bird Girl turns, her four eyes glittering, and says, "Not

shit. Not food." Through our link, she's trying to convey something about this ship, but to me it's a muddle, and I doubt DJ has a clue.

Here it is again—the difficulty of meshing the ways our brains work. We may be relatives, but we haven't been connected socially or biologically for ever so long—maybe for as long as there's been complex life on Earth. There's another conflict as well, an invisible fight to receive and act on information while we're losing one of our most important sources.

Bug Karnak is shrinking. Our links are fading, dying.

I look at the endless acres of whatever sort of growth or crop rises along the spiraling curve.

"Are they trying to speak something?" Ulyanova asks. "I do not feel it right."

Beats us all. None of us feels it right.

OUTER OF OUTERS

In fifteen or twenty minutes—no helms, no timekeepers of any sort, how are we supposed to know how long things take?—the transport has wound us fourteen times around the screw and never a difference, never a change—reddish, brownish, greenish broccoli-like bushes. Not food. Not for air. Not to suck up shit and process it.

Like DJ and Borden, and maybe Ulyanova, who has this puzzled look all the time now, watching the inner shaft and the acre after acre of broccoli...we're getting hypnotized.

Then we slow. The rail frees itself from the screw's edge and lofts over the brushy surface, and for the first time I notice there's no new upper surface; we're nearing the end of this particular line and we're still nearly weightless. If the ship is moving somewhere, it's accelerating at no more than a few percent g.

At the end of the screw is an inverted dome, also featureless—gray and smooth. The Antags do not get out of the transport, so we hang on while it rolls for a couple of hundred more meters. The center shaft of the screw gardens passes up and maybe through that dome, but before the shaft and dome join, there's a hole in the shaft's side—no hatch, just a hole. We enter that hole and with a sigh and a jerk, as if hitting a bumper, the transport comes to a halt in darkness.

The Antags—visible to us now only as shadows—swing away and tug on our cord. More cords and cables have been stretched from the darkness above to a few meters below the transport, and we are encouraged by gestures and Bird Girl's brief screechy words to climb into a deeper darkness. Antags seem to love darkness. Maybe that's why they have four eyes. They're used to darkness and night, or dark ocean.

Ulyanova stays close to me. Borden stays close to DJ. Three of us with some sort of connection, but one deaf and almost completely blind to the greater messaging of Ice Moon Tea. Borden's wondering why she's been allowed to come this far with us, the *special* ones. Why Bird Girl chose her. Really, it's because *I* chose her. There's something about her we need right now, a steadfastness and stability, perhaps a lack of imagination. Because things are about to get really strange.

I have to ask myself if Borden knew even at Madigan, even before I came back from Mars, that Ice Moon Tea was important, that some of us were going to be crucial and had to be saved. Well, there's one more of us now. One down, Kazak—and one up, maybe. Ulyanova. Balance of forces. Not for the first time do I wish that Coyle was still around, still explaining, still bitching. Bird Girl can't seem to explain the most important things in ways I understand, and we're both tangential to the information contained in Bug Karnak…

Which is melting away like a sand castle at high tide. "Inquire" indeed. After being hidden from the Gurus for so many eons, maybe it'll just wash out with the roaring tsunami of human and Antag forces down on Titan—and leave us literally dumb.

And what's about to be revealed is frankly horrifying. It may save us, but at what cost? Assembling the same fragments in his own head, DJ's starting to look faintly unhinged, even more lost and puzzled than Ulyanova.

Ahead lies a great circle of seven circular openings, each maybe thirty meters across. The Antags pull us through the closest and then draft us another hundred meters—until the gloom brightens. I think we've been corkscrewed around the outer diameter of this part of the ship, but how they knew which opening to choose, and why, is still a mystery.

Sunlight glimmers through transparent slits that rise for several dozen meters along the outer wall, showing us that here the ship's hull is exposed to space. The Antags jerk hard and our cables curl into loops, then grow taut again, as we pass into another large chamber, this one stranger than the last. It contains a series of great, dark soccer balls, wrapped in a conical net…

We're pulled sharply outboard into a long, cathedral-like side chamber with dark gray tiers but no seats—a big, bizarre medical theater. For all its size, only three other Antags occupy the tiers, spaced out, separate, as if they bought different tickets or don't like one another. They watch us closely with glittering gray- and green-rimmed eyes.

My attention turns to the apparent reason we're here. Bird Girl is fulfilling her promise. Behind us as we entered, but quickly dominating, this weird theater opens wide to a direct portal at least sixty meters high. Beyond the portal slowly moves the orange and tobacco-colored ball of Titan. This confirms what we already did not doubt, that we're in orbit and maybe about to shove off.

Titan at great leisure slides clockwise out of view. The spaceship is rotating. Beautiful, but I've seen it before. I look back at the tiers. The Antags, all but Bird Girl, are wearing light armor. I sense the three in the gallery are not happy we're here. Not happy about any of this. I get from Bird Girl that these are important individuals, the equivalent of commanders or generals—one might even be a commander in chief of this particular combat theater. And the reason they're here is that Bird Girl is being put on a kind of trial. They're judging her. They're judging *us*.

But she has power over them. How?

We hear far-off booming noises, liquid noises, and then a kind of buzz-saw thrumming whine that sets my teeth on edge—hard to imagine in a ship so large. We've rotated far enough that we can see a broad curve of Saturn's rings, then Saturn itself—too large to fit inside even this theater's broad view.

Another round of liquid noises and again the distant buzzing. The important, silent Antags reveal neither surprise nor appreciation, hardly any indication they're alive. Tight discipline. I doubt they've ever spent more than a few minutes in the presence of humans, and that in quick, nasty combat.

But right now I don't give a shit about protocol or Antag feelings. I'm impressed all over again by what lies beyond the window. I've seen it before but never presented this way, and I'm still capable of awe. The rings and the immense yellow and gold gas giant cradled within are mesmerizing. The light on the rings, intersected by the planet's shadow, reminds me of the shine off old vinyl records. Even though the rings are hundreds of thousands of klicks away, I can make out the braids formed by tiny moonlets navigating between the larger rings. Skips in the record—God's favorite songs, played over and over.

Across its visible surface, Saturn shows incredible, subtle detail—faded pastel yellow bands, storms big and small revealing brown depths, an overall softening haze that seems to end abruptly against the blackness of space. Beyond the curve of night, thunderstorms light up the murk. Some flashes are bright enough to compete in daylight. I wonder that anything could ever survive down there. Maybe it hasn't—ever or now. The ocean moons make even more sense as the origin of life.

Bird Girl sticks out a wing and draws our attention away from Saturn, away from the gallery, and with a little flourish, toward her. The longest, claw-tipped finger at the wingtip moves along her beak, almost to her eyes, and she has our full attention—but why? What's she up to?

Borden tracks our former enemies like a rabbit watching a circling hawk.

Slowly, like a magician, with the inboard hand of her opposite limb Bird Girl raises a long object like a cheerleader's baton. First she touches and then twists a round knob, four eyes shifting. She points again to her eyes, then to my eyes, then to Ulyanova's, then back to hers.

"Four, two," the translator rasps.

Bird Girl draws an X in the air. The knob lights up and projects doubled ghosts. Our eyes aren't easy targets for Antag displays—four into two. She then covers half of the knob with stretchy tape.

Finally, she lifts her left wingtip finger, shapes an oval in the air, and into that oval the knob projects a map of the outer solar system—Uranus and Neptune beyond Saturn, then, beyond Neptune, a long void, followed by a brief, grazing flyby of Pluto and its moons, then outward farther still—across a seemingly endless gulf, empty but for unimaginably distant clouds of stars.

The image swirls to show us the receding solar system, the sun alone bright, the rest indicated by arrows and orbits. This display has now taken us too far out to see most of the planets.

We watch, transfixed, as Bird Girl sweeps us all in a long, long arc over what lies beyond the diffuse region of dust and moonlets and comets beyond Pluto—chunks of primordial ice spread thinner than mosquitoes on a winter lake, most of the chunks no bigger than gravel (I think, it's hard to guess and impossible to read) or even a grain of sand, but some are truly massive—great dark spheres hiding in deep space, more than a hundred billion kilometers from the sun; many times the size of Jupiter but not cold and apparently still too small and dark to attract the attention of Earth.

Then the view moves out farther still to circle a black void, a shadow-haunted world scribed by reddish map lines, five times more massive than Jupiter and ten times the diameter, its density far less than water—like a great cosmic balloon. A balloon with a nuclear core. I can almost feel that unborn star pulsing at the heart of this monstrosity, this enigma—this impossible thing.

Planet X.

If that really is the Antag home world, they're not interstellar visitors. They're near neighbors, astronomically speaking. They've apparently been out there all along and we on Earth never noticed.

"That is ours," Bird Girl says. "That is our life. We will not get there without you."

Borden is ignoring the documentary and studying the view, frowning deeply, a common expression for our commander. "Where's our pursuit?" she murmurs.

Good question. We seem to be alone out here, facing no obvious threats, yet all along we've been harassed by both sides, intent on wiping us out with all our knowledge.

"She's trying to tell us—" I begin, but Borden is having none of this. She covers my mouth with her hand.

"Think, goddammit! Why are they taking so long to get the hell out of here? Ask her!" she insists.

The translator works for any of us, but no sense adding to the confusion. "Where are the other ships?" I ask. "Why are we waiting?"

The translation is quick. A bristly outer layer like soft porcupine quills rises around Bird Girl's wing-shoulders and the back of her head. She looks behind us at the distributed trio up in the tiers. The Antag commanders issue melodious commands and then, with all the dignity they can muster, not much in my eyes at least, flap their limbs and depart through a forward, funnel-like exit.

Bird Girl stays with us—banished to our company. "We have no quick danger," she says through the translator. "But we do not control. We cannot leave yet."

"What does that mean?" Borden asks.

"We do not control."

Borden gives me a sharp look, as if this is my fault and I've been deficient all along. "How can they not control their own ship?" she asks.

"Others do not see this ship," Bird Girl says. "No other ship will attack."

"Jesus!" DJ says. "It's been in my head all along! I've been an idiot!"

Sometimes it's difficult to tell Bug Karnak's data dumps from memories of bad dreams, and the steward has not always been helpful in laying down boundaries between the two. But now it's becoming more and more clear—

We've been clued in, through fragments waiting for our need, for our necessity, to join up, to take shape, and the shape they finally assume is a confirmation that this large ship is very old, and tinged with menace and uncertainty—a dire, ancient bug memory that can only be labeled "Guru."

"This is Keeper ship," Bird Girl confirms. "Dark to our forces and yours. We have taken Keepers prisoner and brought them here. One knows *her.*" She points a mid-wing digit at Ulyanova. "They were joined on Mars. Together, they can help us guide ship home."

We turn our unwelcome attention to the *starshina*, the stern-faced, serious young woman with hardly a clue to what she really is. But now my own fragments are starting to come together. The instaurations, the meeting at Madigan, something behind the observation mirror implanting and perverting me…

I know at least a little about what could be inside our *starshina*, tormenting *her.*

"You're the one?" DJ asks with comic wonder, like he's discovered the punch line to a joke in a stack of playing cards. "You've been linked to a Guru! Jesus…How can that happen? They used tea on both of you?"

Ulyanova draws her shoulders square and cocks her

head as if listening to a conversation in a distant room. "Did not know..." She's frightened by her own doubt. "Not my choice!"

"Maybe not," DJ says. "But if it's true, it's worth at least a couple of pay grades."

"Venn!" Borden insists. "What the hell are we facing?"

"Bird Girl could be right," I say.

"*Could* be? We were told the Gurus didn't have ships anywhere near this big. And how the hell could Antags find, much less board a Guru ship?" She diverts her anger to Bird Girl, whose quills barely shift. Borden's voice has become shrill, and realizing this, she pulls back and swallows hard. "What in hell have I got us into?"

"I've been asking myself the same question," I say.

Titan rotates back into view, looking like lumpy pastry dough stirred by a huge stick. Massive disturbances are taking shape in the orange and tobacco overcast. The centers of the disturbances open to reveal huge cracks in Titan's surface. Through those cracks rise flashes of blue and orange, impossibly bright, impossibly large. Our diminishing communication with the steward, our shrinking connection with Bug Karnak, makes awful sense.

Bird Girl winks with her outboard pair of eyes, which I assume means, do we feel it, too? The loss?

We do.

Together, our forces and the Antags—those still under Guru influence—are grinding through Titan's icy shell and churning the deep oceans, finishing the destruction of Bug Karnak. In all our heads, the steward DJ and I and had almost come to know, to anticipate and expect, to rely upon, is dying by falling chunks and increasing silences. Subjects are winking out. Untapped potentials are marked as blanks, then simply closing up, going away.

In Fresno, I once watched a library burn and tried to feel the pain of the books, the loss of their stories—the loss of my mom reading those books to me. I couldn't. Now, I do.

It hurts.

Bird Girl's translator addresses Ulyanova. "You must show us how to go through puzzle gate, how to reach ship's control, or all ends."

Ulyanova hasn't had much time to feel the potential of her connection. She and DJ and I are points on a polygon. How many points there are, ultimately, I don't know.

Bird Girl raises a small ridge of soft quills and elegantly ripples her wings a full beat. Then she rises to the funnel-shaped exit and jerks on our rope, which we're gripping like a lifeline.

And away we go.

But not before we get one last broad look at Titan, lightning lancing from cloud to cloud—dust and volcanic plumes of water and ice being swept under by a dense shroud of heated gas.

"Gawd almighty," DJ says, wiping away tears, moving his lips in prayer at the end of what we had never really understood in the first place: the influence of the archives. Our links with the liaisons and the steward. The wisdom of the bugs.

Our reason for being out here.

AFTER KARNAK

Bug Karnak didn't have time to contribute much to our info about this vessel, only that parts of it looked familiar and that the bugs may have encountered similar vessels once upon a time—might know more about them and tell us more about them if we simply observe more, exchange more—help the fragments come together.

As for getting more information from bug steward—

That's no longer possible.

I'm not sure if it's an actual shock or just another bloody brick in a wall of cruelty and confusion, but we've been dragged to another cube-shaped racquetball court and another round cage suspended by cables.

There are people inside this cage. Or rather, they were people once. A sour, stale smell tells us all we need to know about their present condition.

Bird Girl tugs on the rope, making us loop around each other. We swing past the cage. Inside are clumps of tangled mummies, black and brown and gray. As Bird Girl warned us, based on the evidence clumped in this identical trap, we're not the only humans on board, but we may be the only live ones.

Borden absorbs the view with a darkening of her face that could be prelude to a heart attack, but I know it's just more rage—rage pumped up and then barely suppressed by discipline and training. All along, since she sprang me from Madigan, I've had a difficult time figuring the commander. That may be because for Borden it's not so much honor and duty but closeted fury that keeps her going. An urge to vengeance. And not vengeance on our former enemies. There are people and *things* back home she's gunning for.

Borden hates Gurus. I pity them all, despite the strong suspicion that none of us will ever see Earth again.

More important to our fate, if the *starshina* is part Guru, how much longer can she stay human, stay useful to the Antags?

"How many are there?" DJ asks. We try to tally but it's not easy. The bodies are in bad shape, and not just from decay. They appear to have died while engaged in desperate hand-to-hand. Biting. Rending. Ripping. Severed, shriveled limbs drift slowly across the cage, along with blackened scraps. Some of the bodies are still tied in combat knots, limbs embracing torsos, fingers tight around necks, wrestling holds so much like coitus—others, just plain inexplicable. Last-ditch. Chaotic. Most still wear clothes, pants and shirts dark with old blood. Shoes are not in evidence. A few of the scraps have escaped the mesh. We bat at them with instinctive grunts of pity and disgust.

"Seventy or eighty," I guess.

DJ covers his nose and mouth with one hand, keeping his other hand on the knotted rope. Borden is beyond expression but her body is stiff and her jaw waxen.

"Didn't they feed them?" Ulyanova asks, but I doubt they were trying to eat one another. A few, I see, are draped with banners or ribbons covered with symbols I can't read. Maybe they had all been pressed into some sort of competition, strong against weak—and the Gurus handed out prizes.

"No women," Ulyanova says. "Maybe all men."

"How can you tell?" DJ asks. "Not much of the fun parts left."

She gives him a perplexed look.

"Did Antags kill them?" he asks, but we already know better. These poor bastards were put in a cage and left to their own devices until the fighting made them too weak to live. The Gurus could have recorded their combat and their agonies. Makes sense if this is a Guru ship. Plenty of studio space. Plenty of program opportunities.

Wonder who was the last one and what he was thinking, and how long he lasted after he'd won and the fighting was over?

Ulyanova looks startled. "Getting stronger!" she says.

Whatever she's hearing isn't coming from either of us or the steward. Those signals have faded to nothing. Bug Karnak is blown to bits, melted down, buried in ice and Titan's interior magma. What the *starshina*'s hearing seems to be from a source much nearer—but we have no idea how all this works.

Ulyanova swings close. "*Antagonista* are frightened!" she whispers. "No control, no way out…and something wild bad up front."

Borden's darkness has gone pale. Her jaw juts. Our prospects aren't improving. What if Gurus were and are still smarter than bugs? Could they reverse the whole weird, tricky process? Like turning a telescope around.

Are they already looking at *us* through Ulyanova?

A WORLD OF SHIT,
WITH RAZOR BLADES

The three ranking Antags wait for Bird Girl to catch up. We've gathered the looping cable between us and clump about three meters behind her. So far we've managed to avoid bumping into structural elements—columns, beams, bulkheads, all smoothly sculpted, no signs of manufacture or refinement, like surfaces in a computer rendering.

"Big fucking ship," DJ says, belaboring the obvious. "But we're still back in the tail. Maybe we just passed the asshole."

The translator renders this for Bird Girl. A sidewise glance from her two inner eyes is her only response. Blessedly, we're beyond the corpse smell. The air here is smooth and cool.

Slow as always, I mull over another obvious data point: Gurus breathe terrestrial air, at terrestrial pressure, even on their own ship—even way out here. Is this their native atmosphere? At the very least it's what they suck in while they're here, and that makes the ship human and Antag compatible...

But what do Gurus breathe when they're at home?

Do Gurus *have* a home?

And now that the ship is infested by Antags and humans, can it flush out the good air and pipe in the bad, can it fumigate to get rid of us like rats? Or is that too blunt and obvious? After all, how interesting is extermination without conflict, without pitting us against one another? Without cages and corpses and shit?

Fuck the inquiring mind. I do not want to know.

We emerge from another tunnel into a doubly curved chamber, like being inside a big, rope-cinched eggshell. The light here has no obvious source and is orangey-peach in color. At the egg's large end, blocking any obvious path forward, is a round black plate about six meters across, sectioned in thirds through the middle. The most grizzled-looking of the Antag commanders, whom otherwise I can't tell apart—no visible signs of rank on their light armor—folds its wings tightly to its body, lower hands clasping. The others follow this one's lead, including Bird Girl. She's waiting for a decision. After several minutes, one of the Antags musics some words, which the translator picks up and returns with rough overtones as, "This is difficult place. Many reasons not all are brought here. May cause disease."

"Illness," Bird Girl corrects. "We cannot go forward and take control until we pass through a puzzle. The puzzle changes. When we do not look correctly, do not solve, the gate will not let us through. If there is no going through, we stay until we die. No other place to go now."

"All righty!" DJ says, waving his hand and splaying his fingers as if weaving a protective spell. Not much reserve left for DJ and I doubt there's much in either Borden or Ulyanova. How much for me?

An Antag commander approaches the "gate." The others

hang on to its lower hands, as if it might be sucked through. At a slap of a wingtip hand, the gate opens in six parts that withdraw into the bulkhead. At first, through the gate I see only gray uncertainty. Then the gray area acquires a spiky focus. A geometric, weedy growth spirals out around the edges, bulging toward us with thorny fingers.

I think of showering after gym class in high school, in the echoing tile washroom, sitting on a damp aluminum bench, when I tried to simulate druggy experience by pressing an index finger against the sides of my eyeballs. But that was juvenile shit. This is real. This is messing with my brain, maybe with my soul.

The patterns inside the gate become simpler and solid, as if the puzzle has learned who and what we are, how we see, how we think, and has isolated the most effective way to entrance or confuse us.

This pattern leaves perverted afterimages.

And then—

Having found our nature and our weakness, what lies beyond becomes a tortured maze of the nastiest crap I hope to never encounter again, and I've become part of it—trapped, strung out on machines with steel teeth that chew me open and then retreat to allow dancing steel arms with needle and thread to stitch me back together before I bleed out.

I see all of us stuffed into big iron caskets like iron maidens, filled with sharpened spikes—not much worse than the suits we had to wear on Titan, but then...

Yeah, they're worse.

DJ is twitching, neck corded, struggling to look aside, but he can't. Ulyanova I can't see—she's drifting behind me and, caught in more ways than one, I refuse to turn away from the gate. Winding nests of razor-scaled serpents dart forward to grab my head. I'm dying, but I should already be dead. Somehow, even in the middle of my horror, I think: *You crazy bastard, you're pegging at around seven—can't you ramp it up to eleven?*

Never taunt an evil genius, right?

Gurus like it interesting.

The puzzle gets personal. Skyrines and Antags are now personally tearing my flesh. There's Joe, Tak, Ishida—and even Kazak, dead Kazak, teeth buried in my stomach. Pain isn't enough. The gate plays with every human fear great and small: of being broken or isolated or eaten, a great shrieking chaos of *You'll never breathe again, you'll never eat again, you'll never fuck again, you'll be lost and nobody will ever find you, and if they do, you won't care because there's so much pain, and worse, you're crazier than clockwork apeshit and now you're laughing, watching your fellow Skyrines join you in a never-ending hell—*

And if such images can have physical overtones beyond the pain and the shock, here they are: the sense that everything in one's body is about to fail, piece by piece, causing not just pain but deep uncertainty, and maybe it's already happening or has already happened—

Worse than any instauration, because this one stabs in and hooks forward the socially outcast, the living who are worse than dead, who will shit their pants and soil their souls and *embarrass* themselves and all who know them and love them, simply by failing in form and duty.

Combine that with the mincemeat grinders and the hooks and the flaying—

And the overall impression that it will all go away, all be

forgotten, if only *we turn on one another and fight and kill*! I can have everything back, my youth, my innocence, freedom from pain, a young, whole body—if only I fight.

All will be forgiven.

My God, that has real power. That reaches eleven. My hands form claws. Borden has curled up like a pill bug. I hear DJ growling like an angry cat, but Ulyanova keeps quiet. I've rotated enough to see her face, a paleness waiting to be smashed—I reach for her—

Bird Girl jerks hard on our cable. We cannot keep our eyes on the gate. The Antags close the hatch. It's over. They haven't been caught up, not this time, leaving us ignorant humans to bear the brunt. Borden is still tucked up in a tight ball. DJ and I cling to each other.

The nightmare inside the gate was completely convincing to us—but not to the *starshina*. She licks her lips. She's into it. She's ready for a change. What did the gate promise her? Life as a Russian soldier, as a Skyrine, is total misery, and now she's seen her way clear to being special and in control. A fucking awful transformation, but I see it in her eyes. Already she's thinking like a Guru.

"Four of our own have tried to enter this gate," Bird Girl says, and passes us impressions of bloody pieces being returned. "Not just illusion. Death trap. Deadly, killing puzzle." Now she addresses Ulyanova directly. "Tell us what we must do, how we must think, to pass through."

The *starshina* wipes her forehead and inspects her palm, as if she might have mopped more than sweat. She turns to DJ and me. "There are Gurus here—I feel them! They are unhappy and weak. They believe they will die." Her English has improved. What sort of expertise can she access now? She looks up, aside. "They do not mind dying, but are surprised and angry I see into them. They did not expect that—ever.

"And now we must meet, no?"

DJ looks at her in abject wonder, then at me. We're still sweating like worms on a griddle.

Bird Girl tugs us back from the closed gate. "We go to see Keeper," she says, and points her wingtip at Ulyanova.

The *starshina* seems to suddenly spark. Whatever's inside her, whatever has combined with her, is making its first moves. She addresses Bird Girl in Russian. The translator hashes and wheeps back English, then Antag. "To do this, to finish it, I am in charge," she says. "You will show me to *Antagonista* who looks into Gurus. All my comrades will see, and all of you will see, because gate will kill if we do not go through at once. Understood?"

"Understood," Bird Girl says.

The Antags have their own Guru mimic.

More sides to the polygon.

GHOSTS, DEAD PEOPLE, AND THINGS THAT NEVER WERE

Bird Girl and the ranking Antags escort us into another access pipe that extends quite a long ways aft through the ship, opening into a chamber that has the benefit, for us, of not being excessively changeable or excessively large. On one side of the chamber, outboard, maybe not too far from the first racquetball court and our hamster cage, is a makeshift hangar where three smaller vessels have been parked—not the same as the larger transports that brought us here, more like orbital fighter craft, suspended in a web of rubbery cables that keep them from bumping. A few Antags in that hangar are busy winging from ship to ship. And finally, we see a squid. Mostly the same as I remember through the foggy walls of our liquid-filled tank on the first transport up from Titan—squidlike in some aspects, but arranged like a catamaran, two grayish-pink bodies with four or five arms each linked by a kind of bridge—but not in water, not this time, and not floppy like you'd expect from a squid on Earth. This creature slides gracefully into a fighter craft and emerges a few seconds later, arms carrying equipment wrapped in dark fabric or plastic.

Borden ignores the squid and concentrates on what she can understand, what might be more immediately important. "Five ships," she says. "Probably not big enough to take us home, or anywhere far from Saturn."

DJ stares at the squid. "Wouldn't want to tangle with one of those."

The Antags around the corded fighters move into a tunnel. Three emerge a few minutes later with a bundle floating between them, an irregular squirming object wrapped in a flexible bag with a squat brown cylinder attached—some sort of pressurized sack, I'm guessing.

The Antags are going to introduce us to some Gurus. The ones they captured on Mars and apparently kept alive? Maybe not. Maybe we have no idea where their Gurus come from. Wherever, I want to be any fucking place but here. I don't have a home, not really, but I want to go back there, even if it's Virginia Beach turned black glass.

We are in the grip of an unpredictable enemy whose motivations may not add up, who have spent years trying to kill us on Mars and on Titan, and that's bad enough—

But what about meeting something that wants to *watch* us kill one another? Gurus. Keepers.

But no choice. We're either useful or we're dead.

And goddammit, even with all that, even with my brain telling me to shrink up like a penis in a Speedo swimming through a daiquiri, I can't tamp my curiosity back into its Prince Albert can. I have to ask—what have we done with *our* Gurus? Did they return to Earth and get set free in time to visit me at Madigan—one of them, anyway? Did our mutual access to the influence of the tea make me a sitting duck for those implants—the instaurations?

What about Borden? Is Borden a fucking mimic? Joe? Kumar? Mushran? Could we ever know? Shapeshifters just love frozen ice stations, according to the movies. Imagine crossing a cruel fucking movie producer with the Thing from Another World.

That's it for now. Having worked my way back to pop culture, I'm done with curiosity. I don't share any of this with DJ or Ulyanova. Better to keep my poisoned imagination to myself.

Bird Girl makes a wide spread of her wings and the others draft into a smaller side chamber with their bundle, away from the ships. I don't even hear two more Antags come up behind us and take control of the rubbery cable. We could let go and just drift, but Bird Girl turns to look at us and I swear there's something imploring in her four eyes, like she's asking, begging, for help. They want to go home, too, and this is the only way for them—even if it's only a sliver of a chance.

Borden speaks first. "Let's go see," she says.

I wish Joe was here, but she's right. It's time to face reality. Time to stop trying to think things through and find out what's really in store.

Ulyanova hand-overs along the rope. The Antags behind herd us to where the package was taken, tank and all. We're closely watched by six other Antags who have emerged from the ships in the hangar. Several more enter furtively from another angle, I'm not sure where—can't watch all sides at once—and now there are twelve: six smaller, batlike critters having joined the party. They all watch with far too many eyes as we enter the far room.

Bird Girl takes hold of the cable and carefully persuades us into another curving, bean-shaped hollow with its own reddish glow. The hollow winds on around curvy corners into other hollows, other voids, spaces bean- or kidney-shaped, like we're being scooted through Leviathan's intestine. This place is aft of the important bits. What's forward is protected by the mind-shit gate, the infernal combination lock with agony for tumblers. Until we find our way through, we're stuck in the ship's asshole, as DJ called it—where Gurus store humans they want to torment.

On one side of a kidney void, three Antags have suspended the wrinkled package between them. It's partly inflated, and something kicks at one end like a kitten about to be drowned. One armored Antag has extended its left wingtip hand to a clasp on the side of the bag. At a musical tweep from Bird Girl, the clasp is flipped and the bag splits along a seam, then peels up and around, revealing a grayish, glistening shape, like two or three wet, furry animals glued together, legs folded, single head tucked in…

"Kumar wasn't lying. It *is* like a dog," DJ says.

"A couple of dogs," Borden says.

"I see rabbits," I say. I'm remembering the odd dreamlike interlude I experienced on the way down to Titan, when I either imagined or was deceived into believing that I had never left Madigan, when the guy who said he was Wait Staff but was likely a Guru told me all about Joe and how he was central to my being here, being anywhere, and how Joe had—

Fuck that. What's important is that I saw the Wait Staff sort of admit to the deception and convert back into being a Guru, but it didn't look anything like this lumpy, limp bundle.

"We need Kumar," DJ observes.

"They didn't tell him to come," Borden says. She then asks

Bird Girl, straight out, "Is that supposed to be a Guru?" The translator sucks in her words and rasps out more tunes.

"It is Keeper," Bird Girl says.

The damp train of rabbits or dogs unfolds a set of ears— floppy, basset hound ears. Six legs unfold as well, two ending in three-fingered hands. The whole thing is about a meter and a half long and masses in at maybe thirty kilos.

So far, Gurus turn out to be pretty much as Kumar described them. Very little like what I was shown or imagined in my *instauration*. This one, whatever its real shape, looks pitiful, weak—defeated.

Ulyanova trembles and strains against the cable, taking deep, hiccupping breaths. A seizure doesn't seem out of the question. "Not *finished*," she says, and then reverts to Russian. The translators again convert this to both Antag music and English. "Where is the other? We cannot go through the gate with just one."

How does she know this? Presumably because she's channeling this poor damp creature, plugging into the way it thinks.

Ulyanova slips her tenders' grasping hands and gets too close to the furry bundle. Her own hands form claws. She is almost on it when one of the smaller bats pulls her back—but gently.

Ulyanova looks beyond Borden, along the ranks of Antags. "Don't let it die!" she says. "I want to watch it *suffer*."

DJ has a look in his eyes I haven't seen except in the thick of desperate battle. And Borden—

Borden has cropped her former agitation, her rage, and is studying the damp gray shape as she once studied me.

"Can you understand Keeper?" Bird Girl asks.

Ulyanova draws in her brows.

"She must tell," Bird Girl says.

Ulyanova gives her a quick, dagger glance. "I would go back to the way I was, if I could, but I can't. I know one thing now I did not know then. I cannot unknow it."

"What?" Borden asks.

"Why Gurus are here," Ulyanova says.

Borden gives DJ and me a side glance that seems strangely guilty. Was this why the commander came out here in the first place? Maybe not to test me or to hear what DJ or Kazak had to say—no care or concern at all for the bug archives—but to learn what had happened to the *starshina* out on the Red. Gaining access to a Guru mind, tapping into a direct feed through a channel they can't control—a channel planned by our forebears hundreds of millions of years ago, designed into the Ice Moon Tea. Bug vengeance or bug defense—ancient and with no regard for our young *starshina*'s mental health, or, I suspect, for her ultimate humanity.

What would that be worth?

Bird Girl points for us to grab the cables to again be yanked along like leashed puppies. "Take you back," she says through the translator. "All will be brought forward."

I haven't heard her interior voice for some time, but now I do:

She (I see a distorted view of the *starshina*) *is polluted. When this is done, we will kill her and the Keepers with her. Then we will take back the sky.*

At that, she puts up a wall. For the time being, no more questions, no answers.

It will be done.

A PAIR OF ACES

This is going south fast," I tell DJ and Borden while we are being led aft. "Once we help break down the door, we're no more use to any of them."

"Big surprise," DJ says. "Bad hand all around."

Ulyanova seems dazed. I'm not sure she hears us. She's listening to something else and I don't like the implications of that one bit. If she has a connection to a Guru or to a couple of Gurus, what's the guarantee they can't delude her, too? But to tell Ulyanova that seems to be as fraught as waking a sleepwalker. She might just explode.

We pass by the cage full of corpses. Leathery bits drift around us, as disgusting and pitiful as ever. From the corner of my eye, I see something floating near the mesh, a faint glint with a chain or wire attached. Borden, the closest, reaches out and grabs it.

We're taken by the railcar aft around the screw garden, then returned to the first hamster cage, where the rest of us wait. Bird Girl and two subordinate Antags escort us to the opening, unlock it, and swing it wide. We let go of the leash and pull ourselves through.

Inside, Ulyanova kicks away, grabs a stray mat, and then kicks off again, crossing the cage to get as far as she can from the rest of the squad. She wraps herself in the mat, then peeks up briefly, staring in our direction for a second or two. Her face is stolid, numb. Litvinov and Vera cross the cage to be with her. Bilyk keeps well away.

Borden explains to the rest where we were taken in the ship, what we saw, and the very little we were told. They learn there is at least one Guru on this ship and probably two.

"Antags want our help, her help mostly," Borden says. "This could be the endgame. They'll kill us if we're not useful, Ulyanova first. She's the most dangerous if she gets out of their control—if somehow she gets back to Earth."

"What chance of that?" Ishida asks.

Borden shakes her head.

"What else can we do?" Jacobi asks. She sounds hoarse and exhausted.

"This may have been Mushranji's plan all along," Kumar says.

"Your ignorance is awe-inspiring," Ishida says, and Tak gets between them, just to be careful.

———

WRAPPED IN A mat, I try to close my eyes, but there's too much going on behind my head, wherever that is, to let me sleep. Bird Girl truly believes that the *starshina* and likely their own exposed soldier are crucial to piercing the nightmare gate, taking control of this ship and getting the hell out of the solar system. Crucial to going home.

My eyelids disagree with my brain. They become too heavy. I drift off.

Comes a sudden jerk-up to full awareness. Ulyanova is floating a few feet from me, suspended in shadow and the last few drops of cage-cleaning spray from our attendant bats. She looks at me as if she would solve all her problems simply by figuring out how I work, what I mean. Turnabout.

"What?" I say.

"Do not need live Gurus. Will be problem."

"All right," I say.

"Do not want this," she murmurs. "I will not be me."

As I have never been quite sure who Ulyanova is in the time I've known her, what can I say that might help? Nothing.

"I feel *Antagonista* who is connected to Guru," she says. "Very unhappy. Others do not treat her well. Stupid, no?"

"Stupid," I agree. Her English has improved. Is that some sort of proof of her connection?

"All Antag fighters are female," she says, after a thoughtful pause.

"Interesting," I say.

"Once I thought females in charge, bottom to top, would be good. Now, not so much. Well, she needs me to finish this work. Can you tell her that? Your *Antagonista*, your steward?"

"I'll tell her." I decide against passing along Bird Girl's design for the *starshina*'s fate.

"Good," Ulyanova says, then presses her lips together, as if evenly spreading lipstick. At least that's familiar. She looks away, looks up, then focuses her pike-sharp gaze on me again. "Gurus know you," she says. "I know what they know."

"Okay," I say.

"You brought dead girl from Mexico." She gives me a disgusted look.

"True."

"You almost died walking on railway bridge."

"Yeah," I say.

"And you killed your father." She smiles with a sad, creepy kind of pride. "I stabbed my father. He did not die. Why I joined Skyrines. Anybody else know these things?"

Honesty is definitely the best policy here. "Joe Sanchez," I say.

She shakes her head. "He is not like you, the corporal, or me, right?"

"Right."

"Proof this comes from shithole Gurus. What they know, I know. Poor me! My soul is rotting. But is good." She moves closer and grabs my arm. Her broken fingernails dig in. "Bits of Guru inside you, like bombs. No others needed. We kill other Gurus, and *you* help open gate."

Before I can think of a response, she backs away, folding her arms. Joe moves into view as another volley of food is tossed through the cage. Nobody tries to catch the cakes. The bats watch, squeaking, then retreat. Maybe they need us fat.

"Borden's getting bored," Joe says, with a worried glance at the *starshina*. "Time for a conference."

QUESTIONS NEVER ASKED

Borden's bare feet just touch the mesh. She has reasonably long and grippy toes, handy under these circumstances. She folds her arms as Jacobi and Litvinov and their respective troops join us. Litvinov and Ulyanova are at the center of the cluster, Bilyk and Vera to one side. Vera seems deeply concerned about the *starshina*.

I'm curious about one big, important thing, especially after my conversation with her a few minutes earlier.

"Who set Ulyanova up for this?" I ask. I do not want to give Borden or Joe, or Kumar, control over the discussion. I'm not at all sure who's on the side of those exposed to the tea.

The commander lets out her breath in exasperation, whether at me or at the cards we're being dealt. She says to Ulyanova, "I'm not sure where we're all at now—but we'd like to know how this happened to you."

Ulyanova gives us a head-back, almost reptilian look, as if recovering from a punch in the jaw. Her brows draw together and she starts slow. "What I remember...On Mars, between big battles, we defend Voors and Muskies in station, when we are told important leaders, Wait Staff, come for visit."

"When was this?"

"Last season," she says, referring to the combat season I spent away from Mars, at Madigan. "They will inspect."

"Inspect what?" Borden asks.

"Drifter, Voor camps. And another piece of crystal on surface, exposed by sandstorm. We are ordered by *polkovnik* to escort leaders sixty kilometers to this place, wait for them, then take them to lander. There are six, including *polkovnik*. We stay in tractor. Hours later, visitors and soldiers return with heavy box. They order us, put it in cabin, take all to lander. They have for what they come. No more talk."

"They look human?" Borden asks.

For some reason, this seems to surprise Ulyanova. "They are Wait Staff!"

Jacobi looks back at Kumar, who as usual is staying a few meters from the group.

"An important pair of visitors, but just one tractor?" Borden asks. Ulyanova cocks an eyebrow at the commander. Is she the one who needs to explain the ways of rank?

"Only one," she says. "Big enough."

"Did they know about the other Drifter?" DJ asks.

"I think not. We carry them, try to make sure they get safe from Red. But strike happens—strong force, two millies, maybe one hundred *Antagonista*. Lander is in pieces when we arrive. We hear on radio is Russian force trying to reach us, join to repel enemy, but bolts strike tractor, throw bodies. Throw me on dust, but I am just shaken. Russians arrive, many die pushing back enemy." She folds her hands. "Box is broken open, full of crystal and powder. Pieces inside are black."

That sinks in. We experienced how dangerous the crystal is when it feels it's in danger.

Joe says. "If they carved off samples..."

Inevitably we all look Kumar's way. "Please continue," he says. "This is new to me."

Ulyanova resumes. "Around what is left of tractor, we find four of our dead and both Wait Staff. One visitor is in pieces, turned glass—other badly injured. Soon, he, too, is dead. All are covered in powder. Two soldiers are also glass."

DJ taps his head, then looks to me. "Hear any other Russians?"

"No." I watch the *starshina*.

"We carry remains to another tractor. Not touch pieces. Then—one last bolt. My helm loses suck. I breathe powder and blood before troopers put me in safety bag."

Litvinov looks haggard. "Unique orders from orbit," he says. "Collect all dead. Collect visitor body. Nobody allowed to inspect."

"Gurus," Kumar says.

"But they look human!" Vera says.

"They usually present as one form," Kumar says. "But can easily look human if they wish. Master Sergeant Venn has seen at least one such. However, I believe nobody, until that moment, had ever seen a *dead* Guru."

"If they can be whatever they want to be," Jacobi says, "they can look like a corpse, right? Fake us out?"

"And this one had turned glass, anyway," Ishida reminds us.

A brief pause as we absorb more awkward implications.

"What would the tea do to them?" DJ asks. "They're not part of our old family, like Antags—or are they?"

Nobody wanders up that sidetrack, but I've already figured it out. The crystals and the tea can be adjusted to do more than just absorb enemies. It can also link them into the bug network, with none of the advantages. A deep and dangerous espionage.

"Did Mushran arrange all that?" Borden asks Kumar. "Was there a plan to expose Gurus and humans to the tea together? To get a Guru to turn glass?"

Kumar considers. "I cannot deny that such a plan was a possibility, but I was not told of it, even after I arrived on Mars."

"What happened to the casualties? The Wait Staff bodies?" Ishikawa asks.

"They were shuttled to Earth," Litvinov says.

"More shit to turn Virginia Beach into black glass," DJ says.

"Sacrificing Russians!" Litvinov adds, giving DJ a warning glare.

Kumar folds his arms and grips his elbows, as if he's suddenly cold. "That must be when Ulyanova became important to the Antagonists," he says. Admirably restating the obvious, or just bringing the point home to slow Skyrines?

We don't bring back our dead. Scrap and stain forever. What changed, and who changed it? I try to imagine Ulyanova and Litvinov's Russian troops on the Red, traveling in the presence of Gurus who look human—with a box full of Ice Moon Tea. Close, breathing the same air. Going into a trap designed to mix them all together, just to see what happens. Was Joe already involved? Conspiring with rebel Antags to undercut Wait Staff on both sides, screwing with those monsters who found advantage in sending us far, far out to fight and die? Joe would have loved that. A real *upgrade*.

But I don't interrupt.

"Is Mushran really dead?" Ishida asks.

"He was in our Oscar," DJ says. "I didn't see him after we were dumped into the tanks."

"Nobody saw him after that," Litvinov says.

"Maybe he was a Guru after all," Ishida says.

"Not possible," Kumar says.

"How would you have known?" Ishida asks.

Kumar looks away. "Perhaps I would not," he admits.

My thoughts are almost too dense and rapid to hold on to, so I keep my attention on Ulyanova. The *starshina* seems to be warming to her situation as a strategic asset.

"You've known about this how long?" I ask Joe.

"Parts of it since last season," he says. "After I sent you home. But not the Guru bits."

"Planned it?"

"Not me," Joe says.

"Very likely, Mushran and a very few others in Division Four," Kumar says.

"But not you?" Jacobi asks.

"Not me," Kumar says.

Back to Joe. "You returned to Earth for a few months," I say, "but avoided me—I was in Madigan, right?"

"Yeah."

"Then you hopped a command shuttle to Mars. Who arranged that?"

"You saved the coin we found in the first Drifter," Joe says. "Hidden up your ass, as I recall. I took it back to Mars to open the second Drifter station. But for some reason, you seem to think I've been deceptive." He gets right up in my face. My turn to feel the burn. "Maybe you were the one who drew me in!"

"Fuck you," I say.

"Shut it," Borden says.

"We've known each other since day two, Vinnie, when I helped bury your fucking secrets. Look at me! I'm as confused and twisted as you are," Joe says, then backs off. "You give me way too much credit."

Borden pulls her way up between us. "Let's put two and two together," she says. "Mushran had to establish several things. One was that the Antags actually had their own Gurus—the ones they call Keepers—and that they were substantially the same as ours, maybe working to the same ends. He kept Kumar out of that loop. Kumar's job was to track Wait Staff and Gurus on Earth, figure out how they were reacting. Right?"

"That is so," Kumar says.

"Even before that, Mushran needed to confirm that the tea really gave you and Johnson and Kazak access to special knowledge and didn't just make you see stuff. With that confirmation, Kumar and I arranged to get you out of Madigan and back to Mars.

"After Mushran had established an element of trust with rebel Antags, he told them what had happened to some of our Skyrines. In turn, they relayed to him that they, too, were aware of the crystal archives."

DJ cocks his head. "We're like detectives in the last chapter of a fucking mystery!"

This actually draws out a smile from Borden, the first we've seen in a while.

"We could use some more clues," Ishida says. We've forgotten that not everyone in our group has the big picture, but now is not the time to fill in those details, and maybe they'll pick them up as we move forward.

"On Titan, the one you call Bird Girl was channeling an Antag who turned glass. Isn't that how it works?"

Makes sense to DJ and me.

"Keepers probably relayed that intelligence to Gurus on Earth," she says. "Division Four noticed that Wait Staff and Gurus were paying lots more attention to suspicious communications, looking for exchanges between humans and Antags." She looks to Kumar.

Kumar says, "When we weren't doing our best to kill each other."

"But how did Division Four, or the Antags, learn that Gurus could be hooked in?" I ask.

"I am not sure Mushran knew that was possible," Kumar says.

"So it was just dumb luck?" Jacobi asks.

"I don't think so," Joe says, hot on the trail. Watching him, I remember what he was like as a teenager, and have my doubts he is deep in the conspiracy. After all, the source of my only info on these matters is the Guru at Madigan—and Gurus lie, right? "The rebel Antags must have discovered that the tea could link their soldiers to Keepers—give them access to shit from deep inside a Keeper's mind, no filters, no sham. Gurus feared that prospect more than having humans dialed into ancient history. Mushran may have then set in motion the encounter on Mars."

Joe grabs my shoulder and spins me around. I'm being grabbed a lot lately, but I don't resist. Maybe I deserve this. "You've been blaming me since you came back from Madigan," he says. "And maybe I knew stuff I couldn't tell you right away. I put you into play, sure. But I never got clued into the big picture, just bits and pieces—orders with thin or no explanations. I doubt Mushran ever trusted any Skyrine. At the beginning, I had no idea you'd be so important. But it made things a lot easier."

"Because I'm a sap."

"Because you're reliable. I knew that given the opportunity on Mars, everything would be easier for all of us—because of you."

"I would like to have had a choice," I say.

"Me, too," DJ says.

"You knew pretty much when we knew," Borden says. "And on some matters, you knew before."

"What about Ulyanova?"

The *starshina* listens, eyes still narrow, lips tight.

"I can't speak to what the Russians knew," Borden says, "or when she awoke to her connection."

Ulyanova lifts her hand and one finger, then folds the finger and looks away as if bored. Or in control, waiting for us to figure all this out so she can get on with her life.

"Bird Girl knew before we did," I say. "She chose Ulyanova. Maybe *their* steward told them who to look for."

"Who's getting Wi-Fi and who's not," DJ says.

"Can you hear anything through her?" Joe asks DJ and me.

"Nothing substantial," DJ says. "More like static."

"Then nobody knows what she's actually tuned into."

Again her impatient, bored look.

"I do," I say. "She's been sharing some of my deepest secrets, and she could only get them through a Guru."

Joe looks uneasy. "Or me," he says.

"Yeah."

"How did the Antags find this ship?" Borden asks.

"Let's ask them later," DJ says. "I'm so tired I could croak and not know the difference."

"Right," Borden says. "We'll give it a rest for now."

I'd like to sort things out further, but have to agree that would not be productive.

"We are done?" Ulyanova asks.

"Done," Borden says.

Vera brings up a rolled mat and leads the *starshina* to another part of the cage. Bilyk looks like a lost little kid. Litvinov is paying him no attention, and the others are scrupulously avoiding Russians—all but DJ. DJ spreads his mat next to Bilyk and conks immediately. Bilyk soon joins him.

But I'm buzzing.

We haven't even got around to the caged dead and the gate.

SORROW AND PITY

We're allowed a few hours of nothing like peace but at least quiet, and the rest of us are starting to rouse. We take advantage of a stream of water shot through the cage by a trio of bats, then intercept baseball-sized lumps of the cakes we've been eating for days and now hate like fury. But we're hungry. We eat, then hold up mats as curtains. The bats obligingly wash away our by-products. I don't know where the water and shit goes, but it doesn't come back into our cage.

"More discussion, sir," I suggest to Joe. "Debrief on our trip forward."

He looks uneasy, as if his gut is bothering him, then says, "Let's do it."

Ishikawa and Vera escort the *starshina* to rejoin the main group. Litvinov and Bilyk flank them. Ulyanova's attitude is again cool and calm. Litvinov is almost obsequious toward her.

Everyone forms layers around DJ and Borden and me,

clutching arms and legs and rearranging until all can see and hear. Joe forms up beside Borden and they lead the brief/debrief.

DJ and I, Borden adding details, explain what we saw on the way forward, in the company of Bird Girl and her Antag commanders. We neglect to say much about the screw garden and its low, bushy forest—which nobody understands—but we do describe the tangle of human bodies in the second hamster cage. Borden's face takes on a brief pained expression, like she knows something we don't, and doesn't want to know it.

The explanations wind on. Not all our group is clued into the weird details about Bug Karnak, the steward, and DJ's and my off-and-on link with Bird Girl.

"Yeah, but why did they pick you four to go forward?" Ishikawa asks.

"Because you're clued in, right?" Ishida asserts.

"Commander Borden isn't," Tak says.

Jesus, we have to start all over again. Everyone asks pointed questions about who knows what, who's talking to whom, whose head is most busy and why. I doubt that most of our survivors believe deeply in any of this. Trust is going to be hard to maintain—after all, we're consorting with the enemy, one way or another, all of us, right? And some more deeply than others.

Slowly, with jumps and starts, everyone is brought up to a kind of pause point, the closest thing to exhaustion of topic we can manage for now—which I think should have happened back on Mars, but I wasn't making those decisions.

Then Borden raises her hand. She's clenching something. I

remember she grabbed a shiny little piece of metal outside the second hamster cage.

I get a sick feeling.

"On our way back, when we passed the corpses in the cage," she says, "I found this. It must have slipped through the mesh." She extends a dog tag smeared with dried blood and lets it float out on its crusted chain.

Joe pinches the tag between his fingers as it drifts his way and examines the stamped letters. It's a newer tag, with an embedded chip, but the letters are still stamped, and that means it belonged to a Skyrine. "Jesus!" he says, and looks at me as if he's finally had the very last of the air let out of his tires. He releases the tag and wipes his hand on his pajamas.

I grab it next. The blood is dark and crusted but I can still read the name: *MSGT Grover N. Sudbury.* Master Sergeant— my rank. Grover Sudbury—the rapist bastard several of us, including DJ, Joe, Kazak, and Tak, pounded to a pulp outside Hawthorne.

Bringing back another part of that moment in the dream, the instauration, about returning to Madigan—

Ask Joseph Sanchez about where he went with Grover Sudbury, and why.

I never asked. Too ridiculous.

Tak reads the tag and recoils in genuine horror—the kind of shuddering, supernatural horror you might feel in a nightmare or as a character in a scary movie. Which suddenly we all are. This could change everything—but how?

How does it make *anything* different?

"He can't be here," Tak says, his voice ragged. "We stomped

the shit out of him and we weren't brought up on charges or even asked why."

"Kazak helped," DJ says. "Just before we were sent to Socotra. We heard the shithead was given a dishonorable discharge. After that, he went away. Nobody saw him again."

Borden lets the tag and chain slowly swing between us. "Okay. You knew him. If he was no longer in the service, how did he get here?"

"And how the fuck did he earn rank?" DJ is sensitive about promotion, having been busted down a few times.

The others wait for a story, any story that brings them into the picture.

Litvinov inspects the tag and asks, "Who is this?"

"A psychopath," Tak says. "He assaulted a sister in a scuzzy apartment he kept just outside Hawthorne, while we were in training. Probably not his first, and we did our best to correct bad attitude."

"Why is he here?" Ishida asks.

"Was here," I correct.

"Kind of coincidental, finding his tags, don't you think?" Jacobi asks, but nobody can put together an explanation that makes sense. Knowledge of the past does not help us get to where we are now.

Ishida asks: "Is anybody sure this Sudbury was actually here?"

"No," Joe says, as if it might be more convenient.

But now it's Borden's turn. She found the dog tag, she's holding it again. She looks around at the accusing eyes. "I didn't stash this away and bring it out now to upset everybody," she says coldly. "One of us knows what happened to Sudbury. I think we all need to hear."

I look at Joe. Borden looks at Joe. Joe looks defeated, then defiant. "Goddammit," he says. "We beat the beans out of a fellow Skyrine."

"He deserved it," Tak says.

"Yeah, but we didn't kill him."

"He wasn't just kicked out, given a dishonorable discharge?" Borden asks.

"No," Joe says. "He went to the MPs and IG and pressed charges. Everybody I knew was about to be court-martialed. I had some connections already, so I went to the main office at Hawthorne. Told them what happened."

"Told who?"

"Our DI, as it turned out. I told him about Sudbury and what he did—to protect my squad. He took me to a side office in another building. Special Considerations, it was called. Inside, he volunteered Sudbury. Filled out papers and everything. We'd heard rumors about Guru attitudes toward sex criminals—violent offenders. Rapists. Child molesters. The rumor was, if they were reported, the Gurus and Wait Staff would make sure they were locked up. DI said only that it was rumored to be a death sentence. I didn't care."

"What happened?" Borden asks.

"Everything tidied up," Joe says. "Sudbury went away. Nobody was brought up on charges. The DI never mentioned it again, and I never went to that building again."

"The Gurus took charge?"

"I don't know," Joe said.

"*Didn't* know," Borden says. "Nobody let on that Sudbury would end up here?"

"Wherever here is, how could they?" DJ asks.

Joe shakes his head.

"Not just Skyrines," Borden says. "Similar deal in the Navy. Nobody wanted to talk about it."

Litvinov adds, with a firm nod, "Russian perverts, too."

"Gays, you mean?" Jacobi asks sharply, as if leading him into a trap.

"No. Still difficult in Russia, but not for Gurus. These were worst of cruel, vicious—sadists. Generals and colonels said they were made into Guru sausage. Never asked for more. Did not wish to know."

"Sausage!" Jacobi says. "Nothing wasted in this man's army."

The others take the tag from Borden and pass it around. Ishida, as if morbidly fascinated, holds on to it the longest. "No guns, no knives, no weapons, right?"

"Apparently," Borden says.

"Everyone fought with bare hands and teeth," Ishida says.

Ulyanova has been studiously avoiding entering the discussion until now. "Ugly bits of flesh. Sausage. Gurus find use."

"Just guessing?" Borden asks.

Ulyanova frowns. "See it. Remember it. They were put in cage, told they would not eat until, unless, they select meanest. Gurus want...how do you say it? Like skimming cream. Why humans deserve their doom, for film and broadcast. Audience love it. In the end, Gurus leave dead to rot."

"Sex monsters in the fight of their unholy lives," Ishida says. "For the director's cut." She clutches her metal arm with the opposite hand, knuckles white. "Almost makes you sorry for them."

"You didn't see what the bastard did to our sister," DJ says. "Got what he deserved."

Some of us nod in agreement, but Tak and Litvinov, Borden

and Ishikawa, have this dismayed look, as if even now they can't believe or even conceive of the depth of Guru depravity.

The dog tag hangs between us, loose. Nobody wants to hold it. Borden doesn't reach for it. It should just float away, like the guy it once belonged to.

"You see why I want Gurus dead?" Ulyanova asks.

"Aren't you one of them now?" Ishida asks.

Nobody defends Ulyanova, and she doesn't seem to care one way or the other. Nobody speaks for a time. Our tight little group has definite seams on this issue. Fascinating. I'm split myself—I could have killed Sudbury and enjoyed watching him die.

But this…

Makes him almost equal to us. Fodder for distant eyes.

"Might make it more convincing this is actually a Guru ship," Tak says. "What the hell would Antags care about human deviants?"

"What are they planning for *us*?" Ishikawa asks. "Same thing, different day?"

"Fuck!" DJ exclaims. "I did not need to hear that."

"You should ask your Bird Girl," Jacobi says. "You can do that, for us, to put our minds at ease—can't you?"

"Ask Ulyanova," Borden suggests. "She's right here."

"I do not see future," Ulyanova says, and turns sullen.

"Well then, who the fuck does?" Ishikawa asks. "If the Antags have Gurus—"

"We know that much," Borden says.

"—then what's happening with *them*? Is this all going to end up *interesting*, part of the movie extras—or a whole new show?"

Jacobi digs in. "What's the equivalent of Antag sexual deviancy? Breaking eggs? Making omelets?"

That's too much. The tension weirdly breaks. Joe snorts. Some of the others let air out of their noses, showing amusement and disdain.

DJ says, quietly enough, "Good question, though. Are there any cages here full of dead Antags? Or are humans just particularly nasty sons of bitches?"

"If you haven't noticed, we're already *in* a cage," Jacobi says. "Maybe they just have to get us mad enough and we'll put on a show. Maybe Vinnie is a camera—or DJ! Maybe they're filming us right now."

I hadn't thought about that. It is too fucking possible, maybe even likely.

"I'm ready for my close-up!" Jacobi says, leaning in.

My fists clench.

"Leave Venn alone," Ishida says. "We have to cut the *starshina* some slack, too." She returns Jacobi's hard look with a hard look of her own. "We have no idea what it's like to be hooked up to this shit."

"The bodies in that cage have only been dead a few months, not years," Borden says.

"They still smell," Jacobi says.

"Justice grinds slow," Tak says, following his own line of thinking, which doesn't get any response.

"How long has ship been hiding?" Litvinov asks.

"Does anybody know *anything* about this ship, other than what they've told us—and maybe what they've shown us?" Jacobi asks. "She's our only source on some of this! Give us the rest, goddammit!"

Ulyanova's turned sickly pale, almost green. She looks as

if she's digging around in a toilet and finding clogs and back-ups of the worst sort. "You want me to *know*?" she asks, tears coming to her eyes. "You want me to ask Guru what the fuck about all?"

"What *do* you know or feel?" DJ asks, only marginally more gentle. He and I, and Kazak, have been closest to the situation she's in now. Can the Gurus be any stranger than bugs or Antags?

"Is not good," Ulyanova says, holding her hands to her head. "Is not true, not correct. And not safe." Litvinov gathers up the wilting *starshina* and leads her away, weeping.

"She is done with answers," he says over his shoulder. Vera goes with them across the cage, and wraps Ulyanova again in her mat.

DJ embraces himself in his arms, as Kumar had done earlier. From behind, he looks like someone is hugging him—someone invisible. We've all had more than enough. As if reacting to yawns in a crowded room, pretty soon we're mostly asleep—exhausted and traumatized.

Before Joe joins us, he plucks the dog tag from the air and pokes it through the mesh, letting it slip out to become part of the water and the shit, cleaned up, moved out. "By itself, this is useless," he says. "We're going to ask a lot of pointed questions before we let Ulyanova probe a Guru. If that's what the Antags are planning."

I feel a twist. They're not mentioning me, but I know.

Kumar agrees. "Let us see what leverage we have."

Then they wrap up and at least pretend to join the rest. Perversely, as I grip the mesh and squeeze my eyes shut, I'm picturing how the fight went down in the second cage. How the teams formed and dissolved, sucking in victims, dispatching them, throwing them aside, then turning on one another until one or two remaining fighters simply bled out. A horrible way to go.

Who's showing me all this?

Just my fucked-up imagination.

Or maybe not.

Sweet.

THE SITUATION THAT PREVAILS

So it was phrased in a silly old cartoon about a real shithead who fought in World War II and sounded like Bugs Bunny and somehow never got himself killed. The phrase is bouncing around my head as I slide in and out of stupor. We are in the situation that prevails.

I hate sleeping in zero g. One can only hang on to wire for so long, before your fingers cramp and you let go and bounce off whatever's nearby. If it's another Skyrine, or Borden, they shove or kick you away, usually without even waking up.

But in zero g, I don't dream much—at least not here. One doesn't dream inside a dream, right? Maybe all I've been living through since I left Madigan is just another Guru instauration, and when I wake up I'll be back in my apartment in Virginia Beach, getting ready to take my car out for a squeal, maybe drive to Williamsburg for kidney pie and some old-fashioned, cozy history. Real history. Has human history ever been real? How long has this shit been going on? Looks like a long, long time. Lots of wars.

Have to ask: Which war was the most popular, ratings-wise?

I open my eyes and find myself looking through the mesh into Bird Girl's four purple-rimmed peepers. She's floating steady on the other side, watching me, just waiting, quiet inside and out—letting me enjoy my restless doze.

"Where are we going?" I ask.

"Forward. All of you. All of us. Through maze and fake eye shit." She's getting creative with her English.

"There's bad attitude brewing," I say.

"*Brewing*? Like beer?"

"Yeah, bad beer. We're not going to put up with being lowly assholes anymore. If the *starshina* is valuable to you, we want equality. Knowledge. Concessions. We have memories of dead friends, too. Tell your commanders that."

Long fucking speech, but inside it takes just instants and there are actually fewer words. More like thought balloons filled with emojis. That's the way it is, here in the land of deep mind-fuck. The madder one gets, the more the word balloons simplify.

But Bird Girl and I are closely enough related both in ancestry and employment that the message is clear. And when I look back at the others, watching my interaction with the Antag, I see they're awake and alert and have lined up in combat order. Borden and Joe and Litvinov and Jacobi are at the tip of a fighting formation, holding one another's hands like they're going steady. Wonder of wonders, we're together.

I try to find Ulyanova. There she is, in the charge of Ishida and Vera. Sisterhood of power. Cool to see, and cool to see that our *starshina* is neither weepy nor green.

Bird Girl brings her four eyes back to mine.

"I will say it," she tells me, and then moves off back into the darkness of the squash court. I see her shadow exit the cube.

A while later, she and three of the armored commanders return. Bird Girl says, out loud, "We join. No bad beer, right?"

I look back at our officers.

Joe and Borden say, simultaneously, "Agreed."

Litvinov says, "Agree."

The translator buzzes.

The cage door opens.

"All?" I ask.

"All," she says. "Keep together."

"Where are we going?"

"Forward. We will bring Keepers."

"And the connection?"

"Connection and Keepers. They will tell us Keeper thoughts."

"Right," I say. Doesn't sound too complicated, does it? I have no idea how Ulyanova is going to respond, how she'll involve me, or how precise and efficient she'll be. We're all new to this.

HORN AND IVORY, BLOOD AND BONE

Joe and Borden and Litvinov grip arms and share a tether, a leash, as we are led forward. Kumar is right behind them, listening as they evaluate our piss-poor options.

"They must feel vulnerable, to agree to this," Borden says.

"Duh," Jacobi says from behind. Borden doesn't even give her a look.

"They're feeling trapped, like us," Joe says.

DJ and I are paying more attention to Ulyanova than to our superior officers. She's being escorted on another tether by Vera and Ishida. Her lips are creased in a kind of dotty smile, as if we're on a country outing and she's listening to the birdies, so charming to be here. Jesus.

Without Ulyanova we're useless to the Antags, and while at the moment, despite the smile, she's strong enough to manage, to stay alert and keep up with us on the leashes as we're dragged forward, through the usual curving corridors and then along the screw garden on the rail system—just capacious enough to carry us all...

The strain she's under, she could still break at any moment. What if her soul crumbles? She's filled with Guru. Could happen, right?

And me?

DJ and I seem strong enough, we've lasted long enough, but are *we* reliable? Maybe I'm the main POV. I'd gladly ash-can my brain, or at least my imagination, just to be a dumb grunt again.

"Anything left of Titan?" I ask DJ.

"I think they've finished bombing. Good times down there."

He sounds uncertain, so I have to ask, like a kid probing to find out where the Christmas presents are hidden, "But you're still getting something?"

"Not really," DJ says. "Just shrapnel from earlier overloads."

"Right." DJ and I are a thin soup of residuals, peas and carrots in cooling broth.

Kumar drops back closer. "I do not believe that anyone can connect to a Guru and live long," he says in a low voice. "Even when they are right in front of me, talking to me, I have never found them the least accessible. They are masters of…" He breaks off. "What is this place we are going? How much do their Gurus and the connected one—how much do they understand about the ship? The systems involved?"

All good questions. DJ answers the first as best he can. "It's a puzzle lock. You have to solve a code to move forward. Without the code, it's a meat grinder."

"Are you sure you all saw the same situation, or the same version of that situation?" Kumar asks.

"You'll just have to see for yourself," DJ says with a crease of his cheek muscles.

We exit the transport. I've been staring out at the green,

758 | GREG BEAR

brushy inclines of the screw garden and asking myself why
Gurus would put such a thing at the rear of the ship. Having
impossible problems to solve is what distracts me from how
awful our situation is. I'm a nerd. Have been since I was a little kid. It's kept me sane before. I've been a killer since I was
thirteen and not once did I enjoy it or feel anything less than
shitty. Killing is putting an end to threatening stuff I don't
understand, before I can ever understand it. Nerding out distracts from that essential emptiness.

The Antags flank us, all that remains of our pitiful little
party, and guide us through the curvy alien regions to the
hatch, which is presently shut tight. From behind us, out of
glimmering shadow, emerge four more Antags in light armor.
Between them are slung two squirming gray bags.

Through Bird Girl, I feel that another Antag is on her way
to join us, with her own escort. The picture I'm getting is that
this is the connected one, and she's a basket case.

Then we see her. She's spiked and awry, covered with
a damp, sweaty sheen, wings drooping, feet and hands
clenched. Her four eyes are crusted with snot and she's all
twitch and quiver—in worse shape than Ulyanova. Maybe
the Antags have been working her over, trying to force her to
tell them what they need to know.

Bird Girl advances to the bulkhead that holds the mystery
gate. The three commanders bring the droopy Antag toward
the gate and hand her leash to two armored officers. DJ, Ulyanova, and I are urged forward by two more officers, who
let us drift up next to the bags.

Our fellow Skyrines and Kumar and Borden hang back,
for the moment, eyes wide, glad they're not us, not Ulyanova.
The *starshina's* previous calm, her dotty smile, has turned

brittle. She's shivering, but that might be because we're all half-naked, in minimal pajamas, and the air around the gate is chilly.

The Antags unclasp and peel the bags, revealing two bundles of wet gray fur with floppy ears and wide, sleepy eyes. Here's the other that Ulyanova said was necessary—but isn't. Not if I'm around. Their sleepy eyes track us, humans and Antags, as if they would burrow deep into our heads. Eyes that do not concede any ground to our domination, our control.

God, I do hate them.

Ulyanova shudders but does not look away. She tilts her head back, curves her lips, and gives them a sharply angled look, as if she's a dragon about to spit fire. The Gurus jerk and try to shrink away.

"Look," Bird Girl announces, and presses a circular indentation to the left of the hatch. The hatch opens, six pieces sliding aside and back, all somehow very standard, very expected. We've been spending far too much time on alien spacecraft. Give me a simple pressure hatch anytime, give me a rocket, a capsule—

Then we all have to look, no choice—like facing the mouth of hell. But inside the gate, this time there's only a neutral beige emptiness, not easy to look at, to look into, since it seems to promise the nullity I'd like to avoid, thank you—but nothing like the horror we experienced before.

Ulyanova and the connected Antag are kept about two meters apart from the Gurus. Ulyanova's nose is bleeding. DJ tries to help, raising the back of his hand, offering to dab as blood flows down her lip and one side of her chin—but she punches his arm aside, then gives us a hard, steely look. The scruffy Antag doesn't do much of anything.

Then, as if waking from a nap, the beige nullity gets active. Spinning gears take shape, followed by knives, suggestions of endless misery in a variety of fates and forms.

Ulyanova's dragon flames fly now as furious words. "This place…is *disgraceful*," she rasps. "Push Gurus through, first one, then the other!"

The translators work for the armored commanders, but Ulyanova seems to be in charge, not them—they've given up that much in their desperation.

"Will that be enough?" Bird Girl asks.

"What do you care, really?" Ulyanova says. "If we do not feed them to puzzle, if we fail, all who look will be crazy. Try, or we are all mad!"

The scruffy Antag tries to lift a wing, makes sad scrutching noises, along with high-pitched wheeps. She apparently does not agree with Ulyanova.

And strangely, that tilts the game. Bird Girl makes a hatchet chop of one wingtip.

The Gurus squeak.

Kumar moans, then tries to break free of our group—

"Hold him!" Joe calls out.

The little rabbit bundles squeak again, but that doesn't stop two of the armored Antags from pushing one forward, sack trailing like an afterbirth, into the growing, awful gate. Sending a Guru into Guru hell. The squeaks rise to wailing shrieks. The illusion inside the hatchway seems to reach out and grab, pin the little rabbit bundle, yank it from the gripping hands of the Antags, almost dragging them in with it, but they let go—

Together, Ulyanova and the pitiful Antag make sick musical sounds, like a small orchestra about to throw up.

The other Guru squirms and suddenly changes shape without growing or shrinking, looking for a few seconds like a miniature Antag, then a small human, then something I've certainly never seen before—

The inner illusion of the hatch turns black as night—

And spits out pieces of flesh and fur. My God, is that magnificent! Isn't that absolutely what we need to see!

But then the dead puzzle returns. The madness starts all over again. We try to turn away and can't. "Fuck!" DJ says, drawing it out in classic DJ style. We're all on the line, or way over it.

Ulyanova makes a little *hmm*, then looks back at me, at Borden. "Does not seem good," she says. "Not convincing. There is more than two!"

And she's not talking about me.

The eyes of the second Guru sink back into its rabbit-puppy skull.

"It would be most interesting," Ulyanova says, "if both die, and there is a third that needs to die also before I can take their place. I have their minds, their thoughts. We do not need any of them."

Bird Girl and the Antags are not at all happy with these results, or this suggestion. I can't blame them, really. One Guru down, only one left that anyone can see, and the same thing seems very likely to happen if it's fed into the gate. After all, why would the Gurus allow one of their ships to be accessed by unauthorized personnel, even Gurus? And who knows what the Gurus think about personal death, about sacrifice?

The scruffy Antag seems entranced by Ulyanova's words. She reaches out as if to touch the *starshina*, but the armored officers deftly push aside her wing-hand. Ulyanova intervenes and to our surprise grasps that hand—clenches it tight, and surveys us all with her head drawn back.

"It is offering to *solve* puzzle," she says. "But we must not let it help us. If I am become what it is..."

Her eyes turn to mine.

I see the chamber vibrate like a remote that wants to change the channel but can't.

The scruffy Antag makes distressed, angry sounds that are not translated, but the other Antags listen close. Ulyanova says, "This is disgraceful. It is not *interesting*. The Guru says, it *thinks*, there is way to add to drama. We will be more entertaining if we let it teach and guide us. That must not happen. Instead," and she looks back over her shoulder at me, "if it lives, it will block everything we must do. There will be no Gurus on this ship! I *will become!*"

She's following through. She gestures for me to come forward, and this time she grabs my hand. The translator buzzes and makes strident musical notes. There's disagreement and confusion between Bird Girl and her commanders, and apparent concern that we're all about to make a huge mistake. This I get through the ragged connection with Bird Girl. They do not want to put control of this ship, even assuming we can take control, into human hands.

Bird Girl disagrees. We've gone this far. Not to go farther will mean defeat and death.

The last Guru puts up an awful, sad barrage of squeaks and guinea-pig growls, as if intent on making us all feel it's totally without resources or power. Inside my head, I feel those embedded chunks of suggestion vibrate as if in sympathy. And I'm not the only one.

"Agree with it!" Kumar says, aghast. "It's the only way!"

This doesn't convince any of us, least of all Joe. But our Antag counterparts have made up their minds. Bird Girl and her commanders pull the bag and shackles off the Guru. The Guru's squeaking becomes slower and deeper, like a toy whose batteries are running down. Then it makes a sound like a cat playing fiddle on its own sick guts.

What lies beyond the doors is nighttime black. Neutral. Waiting.

Maybe a little hungry.

"No pain if it is gone," Ulyanova says so softly she can barely be heard. "If it dies, I become—I think and solve right here. Right now. Kill the Guru. Kill it!"

Kumar shrieks, "No! It *wants to die!*"

With blinding speed, Bird Girl is handed a bolt weapon by one of her assistants, one of the pair holding the Guru. The commanders try to stop her, but she points it and fires point-blank into the damp, mewling gray bundle. At such short range, the bolt cooks and spatters. Half-baked blood flecks my face. I wipe it away, fascinated beyond disgust.

Then she turns the weapon on the scruffy Antag, their contact, and fires two more bolts into her chest. The unfortunate creature wilts like a spider in a candle flame. Her limbs shrink and curl, her chest caves in—her head wrinkles like a rotten apple.

Then—

She's gone.

None of us can believe what we've just seen.

"She is Keeper mind-fuck," Bird Girl says. The translator throws her words back verbatim. "*Yours* is real."

"You've done what the Guru wants!" Kumar shouts, furious. But nobody is listening. Instead, as if hypnotized, we're locked on to Ulyanova's face, her sharp eyes, her words.

"We go now!" she sings—and the pieces in my soul combine, spin, helpless—

"See and follow!" Ulyanova cries out.

I'm right behind her, we're linked by hand, the puzzle gate requires two Gurus, and suddenly, I'm good enough. Ulyanova is strong enough. We click all the tumblers together, melting the little bombs inside me, using all their energy. The nerd part of me just loves puzzles, doesn't it? And with all that extra, perverse energy—and Ulyanova's deep connection—

The Gurus are not necessary.

I feel the gate succumb and become very, very simple.

Empty air, really.

Bird Girl says something to her fellows and the Antag commanders grip Borden and Litvinov and violently shove them through the blackness, like shoving swimmers into a pool. The darkness swallows all. *That's it*, I'm thinking. *Nice knowing you.* They're going to be coughed out as mincemeat.

But the gate doesn't throw back anything. Again, it remains black, neutral—empty.

"All go, now!" Ulyanova sings again, hand releasing mine and waving like a wagon master's.

Our leashes are gathered; we're surrounded by Antags and kicked and shoved into the blackness. Our screaming gets kind of silly, really, like tourists on a roller coaster. I manage not to make much noise as I go through.

I briefly see Borden and Joe…

Kumar! Looking old and baffled.

But where are they? Where am I? Deep cold but no pain. No cutting or dicing.

When I emerge in a shimmering, shadowy space, not that different from the in-between, I'm still thinking and firmly believe I'm me, always my gold standard for feeling alive. Tak and DJ and Joe float limp beside me. Bird Girl is here, too. She's got a tight grip on the leash that holds Ulyanova. The *starshina* appears to be asleep.

The Antag commanders come through next, followed by the rest of our Skyrines, and what might be the last of the Antags. I'm astonished, as much as I can be astonished, in this condition, the condition that prevails—numb and cold and alive.

I never thought we would make it this far, or take it this far. I always assumed that somewhere between here and then Ulyanova would spark out, or I would, or the Antags would give up and kill us all. I did not know what to believe or think while passing through. Nor do I know what to think of where we are now. The problem with dealing with Gurus has always been that nothing is what it seems.

I try to look deep. Am I empty of those little instaurations, those buried bombs, all fused and used?

No time to know.

We're in a big, dark nothing. Okay. Got it. That makes me giggle. Only *nothing* is what it seems.

We killed all the Gurus we had, didn't we? And the scruffy Antag, who seems to have been an illusion, a deception, and a damned fine one to last so long.

Where's the glowing fog coming from? Our eyes are adjusting to a different kind of illumination, a grayish, dead-looking elf-light that surrounds the gate. At least I think it's the gate. The center is covered. No going back? Or can Ulyanova solve the puzzle whenever she wants?

Is she human now, or Guru?

Can she control what's in her mind?

Or control *me*?

DJ takes hold of his section of our leash and pulls himself into view. His face is as thin and pale as an El Greco saint. Tak and Joe are right behind him. Jacobi, Ishida, and Ishikawa are leashed up to Vera and Bilyk. In the back, Litvinov has Kumar by the shoulders. The elf-light seems to glue itself to everything that came through the gate, like plankton in a passing tide. Patches wrap us here and there and we all look like broken ghosts.

Parts of the glow break off as we move and gleam in the dark like flakes of mica in clouded moonlight. I'm reminded of the Spook's big steel tables and the quantum treatment. More of the same? All Guru tech, we've been told. How much more of this before we crumble like dolls made of dust?

But the Antags, and in particular Bird Girl, seem to still have it together, even after they destroyed two Gurus and bolted one of their own. Has this been their plan all along? A double deception right up until the crunch? Do they trust Ulyanova?

I don't.

They gather our leashes and arrange us like posies in a bouquet. We're all here, Kumar and Litvinov taking up the rear, and the way the Antags are exercising their wings, I think we're about to be drafted to the forward parts of this godawful ship. For a time, I almost want to resist—to force them to bolt me, all of us, just to end the suspense.

But that's not an option.

"Up there," Bird Girl says, pointing with both wingtip hands into the forward darkness. "We hear searchers. Gurus take them as slaves. It is what we expected. What we have been told. Up there."

"What the hell is a 'searcher'?" Joe asks.

"She means the squids," DJ says. That's the image she's feeding us.

PART TWO

PLUTO AND BEYOND

The Antags beat against the thick, cold air. We're still in pajamas, of course, and now we're freezing. Antags don't care. We've made it this far, we'll go the distance. Valley Forge. Battle of the Bulge. Those soldiers had it worse. It was lots colder in those places than here. But we're still clacking and chattering and shivering. DJ is blue with cold, pale gray in the bad light—and maybe it *is* bad light, infected light. Who knows what the Gurus could use to punish intruders?

I don't hear any echoes, any fragment of sensation that could help me figure out what sort of space we're in, how big, how wide, whether it's empty or filled with invisible snares.

Joe's eyes must be sharper than mine. He tugs on my forearm. "Out there," he whispers.

I look. Very far away, no scale to judge how far, I see what could be tangles of silvery branches filled with those elfin lights. Striking two ghosts together could make sparks like that. No surprise to find a Guru ship is haunted, right? Not just our dead back in the hamster ball. So many wars, so many seasons, so many corpse entertainers hanging around to learn about their ratings, how they rank in the sum of history.

"Bamboo groves," Tak says. "All pushed together."

"Bigger than that," Jacobi says.

Ishida asks, "Wonder what could fit in there?"

Then the lights fade and for a time we can't see anything. The Antags are still pulsing and drafting, still silent, and I don't hear Bird Girl or anything else in my head. I thought getting beyond the gate would be some improvement, provide some sense of accomplishment, maybe a hint of our next destination, but so far no joy.

"Fuck this shit," says Bilyk. Bird Girl's translator goes to work. The Antags fluff their bristles, maybe in amusement. Maybe they agree. GI bitching is universal.

"We are okay for a while," Bird Girl then says through the translator, so that all of us can hear. The translator moves over to Russian.

Litvinov growls. "Progress!" he shouts. "We need progress!"

Old-man words, I think. He's the oldest of us, other than maybe Kumar, and he's fading. Doesn't make me happy. Litvinov is one of those people I'd like to sit down with and find out how they've lived their lives, where they've been, what they've done—outside of Mars and all this shit. We all have instincts about guys we'd like to ask personal questions or just listen to, no questions, over vodka.

Kumar is allowing himself to be dragged, not resisting, not protesting, hardly moving—maybe suffering from a hangover after giving in to his Guru conditioning. He said you had to be around Gurus for a long time to come fully under their spell. Maybe they lied to him about that as well. I don't want to think about Guru lies or illusions because that takes me straight back to what was or is in my head and how Ulyanova used me, used that. Let's pretend there really is progress, that we know what we're doing, at least a little.

What did Bird Girl mean by searchers used as slaves? Their slaves or Guru slaves? Would finding *them* mean progress? And if we do find them and hook up, and they mean progress, but only for Antags—are humans then disposable?

Ulyanova would be so disappointed. She's coming into her own, getting her own way, making this all work for Bird Girl. Her allegiances are getting complicated.

Joe and DJ try to separate their strands so they won't keep spinning around each other. I'm lucky enough to be untangled, my leash beginning with Ulyanova, right next to Bird Girl, then stretching back to Tak and Jacobi—all in a row. We're pretty good at using our parachute training to tug here and there and keep separate.

How long is this going to take? I don't like fucking big ships. I remember watching science fiction movies way back when I was ten or eleven, when my mother, between boyfriends, would make me watch with her, and even then marveling at how engineers could shove gigantic spaceships across the cosmos, even then wondering where they got all that energy, doubting the efficiencies, all those cathedral spaces being dragged around wherever you went, like driving a car the size of a city. Even as a kid, I doubted those movies made sense. Boy, was I wrong. The Gurus prove me wrong. Sure, all our transports leaving Earth and going to Mars are small enough, in the beginning, and efficient enough, given spent-matter drives.

But Spook and Box and now this…

Once I nerd out, I can amuse myself for hours. But over

time, and especially now, as I search for the open holes left by the melted and fused bombs, and not finding them—so are they still there?—the nerd impulses turn sour. I'm not a naturally cheerful and optimistic fellow. Had that beat out of me a long time ago, either at home or on the playground.

Maybe this isn't a spaceship at all. Maybe we've crossed over through the gate to another dimension, a dimension not of sight, but of mind—a distributed hell-space with no boundaries, no walls. Those specks of light up ahead—the decayed ghosts of previous visitors.

Maybe if I felt cheerful I'd know I was no longer me. I've gotten used to this poor battered kid-self. Not that I wouldn't like to be set free every now and then. With Joe's help, I veered from drugs and moderated my intake of booze. I could have easily sunk fast and not climbed out. I watched my mother go into that pit a couple of times. The last time, Joe and I helped her out. Got her into a program. I watched most of her boyfriends dive into dope and booze and never rise again. And not just the guy who taught me how to use guns, the guy I shot, but the bank robber she dated for a few weeks. He spent his whole life planning and doing jobs and then getting high. When my mother refused to get high with him, he beat her, he beat me—and then he left. Cops got him outside Barstow. He ended up minus a hand in Chino.

"We need to get somewhere!" DJ shouts to the Antags.

Amen, whatever he means. But they're still drafting. They still have hope.

And as for me...

I get metaphysical, inspired by all the weirdness. I've long since believed in God, but have never quite figured out what belief means, what God is, what God's plan is—what's in store, ultimately. What would it be like to actually cross over into a *good* dimension, into heaven itself? What would heaven be like? Would God be waiting to greet you, or would it be Grandma? My aunts? Former squad members? Veterans in full dress uniform, with their ribbons and medals and all? I'd like that, actually.

How terrific to know it's over, that I can stop sucking in my guts and relax. No more killing, no more strategy and tactics, no more awful grief and mind-bending shock—no more war. Death itself is behind me, over and done with. What would that be like? I'd be a fish out of water. Where in this other dimensional afterlife could I get an assignment, get a job? Who the hell would want to work with me? Maybe I'm not cut out for heaven. But it would be fun to give it a try. Nature's long, long vacation. Anything's better than staring ahead at the armored butts and pulsing wings of a bunch of Antags.

"Where the hell are we?" Tak asks.

"Forward of the tail," DJ says.

"That big bulge, maybe," Jacobi says.

Ahead, the elf-lights outline another thicket, leafless but dense, a weave of long sticks or canes that surrounds our forward view.

I'm not getting any help from my Antag channel, probably because Bird Girl is intent on drafting this awkward crowd several dozen meters ahead. If the "searchers" and "slaves" Bird Girl mentioned are the squid we saw tending to the Antag transports, the double-hulled catamaran creature we saw through the walls of our tank…would this gym set of interlaced sticks allow them to traverse the larger spaces? Monkey bars for squid. They'd do better than us, certainly better than the Antags.

"Squid playground," DJ says, squinting ahead.

I slap his shoulder for stealing my comparison. Borden looks irritated at both of us but Joe says, "Let 'em yak. They're balance to the real crazy."

By which he probably means Ulyanova.

"Starting to close in," Ishida says. And she's right—the thicket is narrowing.

"Searchers!" Bird Girl calls over the translator.

Emerging from the thicket come nine catamaran squid, grappling around the outer reaches. We hear booming and clicking, answered by Antag music and chirps from Bird Girl and her commanders, who rein in our leashes and gather us into a dense, weightless cluster.

The booms grow louder. In the flickering, come-and-go clouds of moonlight flakes, dozens of squid fill the forward spaces, crowding and bumping as they compete for a view. Each is about three meters across, with arms on both outboard bodies that can stretch an additional three meters. On each "hull" they display two amazing eyes, each the size of a human head, gold-flecked sclera almost obscured by large, figure-eight pupils. Again, four eyes—does that mean they're related to the Antags? Other than the eyes, they could not be more different.

Then the sounds stop. The squid gather around us in silence. I have to think they're not happy. Their arms quiver and dart back as they reach out to touch Bird Girl, the armored commanders, and then—me, DJ, Borden. It's here that we all realize that the squid, the searchers, are pushing us gently aside, their attention centered on one individual in our bouquet of humans. Ulyanova.

Bird Girl drafts between us and the searchers and hovers,

wings beating slowly. "These are the ones we hoped to find, the ones we need," she says through the translator. "Keepers use searchers as drivers."

"Are they friendly?" DJ asks.

"To us, yes," Bird Girl says.

"What do they eat?"

"Not you."

DJ grins. Maybe he and the squid will get along.

Ulyanova pushes past us. "They think I am Guru." She smiles as if they aren't wrong. "They will take my orders!" The searchers part, then brush her with their tentacles as she passes through them, spreading her arms and pirouetting. Her self-assurance is startling. She seems to pass inspection. Dealing with Gurus, maybe you get used to all kinds of shapes.

I catch a closer look as we're cabled up again, matched in pairs and quads. Searcher skin seems to be covered with soft plates, like armadillos—a kind of exoskeleton. The plates interlock to stiffen an arm or part of the squid's body.

The Antags urge us forward, into a deeper and thicker forest of canes. Within the thicket, scattered through the spiral, lie shiny dark spheres, each maybe thirty meters wide. More hamster cages? I don't think so. More like living quarters. Searchers come and go, pulling and twisting around the spheres and through the canes.

Bird Girl decides it's time for details. "These searchers cannot fight. They uniquely serve," she says to DJ and me through our link. I get some of that—peaceable monsters—but what use are they to Gurus or Keepers?

"For Keepers, they know how to work this ship," she says. "And for us, they swim on Titan and access archives."

"But none came through the gate," I say. "Have these been here all along?"

"They are from Sun-Planet," she says, attached to an impression of wonder, hope, loss—and sadness. "They have been here for much time. But they remember our home, as well." Bird Girl and the Antags really do feel a relation, an indebtedness, to the searchers, not at all like owners to pets. The relation seems to have overtones of a blood debt. Obviously, when there's time, more needs to be asked and explored.

"Where are they taking us?" Jacobi asks DJ.

"Someplace where we can get a shave and a shower," he says, almost as if he believes it.

RUNNING ON EMPTY

Putting one's self in the arms of a squid requires a courage not expected or taught in basic. We all do it, however, because it's hard to imagine getting through the canebrake without searcher help—and because the Antags have submitted as well and are even now ahead of us. We don't talk much. We're scared, scared to our very guts, in that way that exhaustion makes worse.

It's dark, it's weird, it's Guru—and there are squid.

But nobody gets hurt, and in half an hour we're escorted through the brake, and what's on the other side is more what you might expect within a gigantic spaceship—genuine, monumental architecture.

We're taken across a hollow big enough to hold an apartment high-rise, but filled instead by a wide, undulating coral reef of spun and accreted metal. Judging from the occupants coming and going, like bees flying in and out of a hive, this is another low-g housing tract for searchers. Helping them get around are rope ladders and twisted cane bridges, but more open, with, at the center, a large concave blister that seems to reveal space, or at least blackness and stars. No sign of Titan or Saturn or any moons. About ten searchers are stationed inside the curve of the blister, paying no attention to what's behind them. They're on driver duty, I presume.

We're brought up short on our leashes and again arranged into a bouquet, keeping our distance with outstretched arms and gripping hands, pajamas hiding very little, while Bird Girl takes hold of Ulyanova's leash and leads her into a searcher congregation behind the starry blister. There, our prize pupil creates a minor sensation of movement, investigation, rearrangement.

"It's like an aquarium," Jacobi says.

"I thought squid are mollusks that live in water," Ishida says.

"We've eaten enough of those," Tak says, and Ishikawa looks unhappy.

"Don't tell them that," she says.

"But Bird Girl can read Vinnie like a book, can't she?" Ishida says.

"Never liked sushi," I say. "More a teriyaki kind of guy."

"What's she thinking?" Joe asks DJ and me.

"Who, Bird Girl or Guru Girl?" DJ asks.

"Either one," Joe says.

"Bird Girl is feeling pretty good," I say. "No specifics, but she's where she wants to be—a slow carrier wave of accomplishment, of good feeling."

"She's at the end point of a long strategy," Kumar says. We've all either ignored or tried to stay apart from him after his interlude, including me, hypocrite that I am.

"Maybe she really likes squid," Ishida says. "Old friends from home?"

"She's never been home," I say.

With Vera at her side, Ulyanova's submitting to a more thorough searcher examination, and maybe already being put to use. She's the only one of us that seems to have a real purpose. Yet Bird Girl hasn't stated to me, or to DJ, any change of heart regarding our *starshina* once her usefulness has ended. I hope it doesn't come to that. She's still human, still one of ours—until proven otherwise.

Like me.

Bird Girl leaves her surrounded by searchers to return and address us all. "We will find quarters," she says. "Will be better than hamster cage. And there is food."

"Good to know," DJ says. We look quizzically at each other, since we don't remember passing that comparison—the hamster cage—on to any of the Antags. Didn't go through *my* head. Maybe the bats were listening.

Where are the bats now? I'd forgotten about them. Bats. Birds. Squid. I'd like to shove a few of our DIs into this present situation. They'd go nuts. Serve them right.

"We bring others around, outside, from tail forward," Bird Girl says, and her eyes do not waver from mine.

"You trust this ship?" Joe asks.

"With searchers, yes," she says. "The one named Ulyanova outranks all of you, for the time. Are there mating pairs or other considerations?"

Borden asserts herself. "If possible, we'd like to be kept close—but no mating arrangements. Kumarji will explain ranks, if you set time aside."

"We do not like him," Bird Girl says. "We are not sure of him."

"Neither are we," Ishida says, but Borden gives her an elbow.

"We'd like a decent service and arrangements for the dead we found," Joe says.

"They will be incinerated, along with our dead."

"Dead from Titan?" Joe asks.

Bird Girl blinks all four eyes. "We are told by our searchers that games were arranged for us as well as you. These provoke feelings of guilt in searchers. Arrangements will be made."

"Thank you," Joe says. "I understand."

"Do you?" Bird Girl asks. "I have insight into two of you, and our searchers are, in your eyes, horrible."

Borden says quickly, "We hope to revise our opinions."

"Searchers always important, and these have been to our home, piloting this ship. I wish to learn from them and prepare for the journey. We have work to do, and all may be useful."

She drafts and pulls herself back to the concave, star-filled dish.

"That isn't the nose of the ship," DJ says in an aside to me. "Not a direct view."

"I got that," I say.

"Ship goes way beyond. Wonder what's up there—what they all used it for?"

"Kumar, come here," Borden says.

Kumar climbs forward.

"What's the chance that Ulyanova can remain independent while channeling a Guru?"

"Zero," he says. "I'm pitiful, and all I did was look at them, work with them. She has one in her head."

"Great to hear," Joe says.

DJ hunches his shoulders. "You know what I'd give anything for right now?"

"A blow job," Ishida says with rich sarcasm.

"Fuck no. That can wait. A tent on Mars, with some of those Russian food packs, those sausages, those little reindeer ones."

"Yeah," Tak says.

"Those were the best, weren't they?"

The Russians agree. "Blow job would be good, as well," Bilyk adds. He looks hopefully at Jacobi and Litvinov cuffs him.

INTO THE WEIRD

The arrangements for quarters are interesting. Beyond the starry dish there is indeed more ship. We get drafted through the centerline on our leashes, this time by two searchers, who brachiate like long-armed gibbons from one jutting cluster of canes to the next. I feel like Jane in Tarzan's arms, only a lot more arms. The canes seem to be arranged in a tube around the centerline, and the searchers move alternately on the outside of one tube, then cross to the inside of the next, deftly avoiding other squid on other tube highways coming and going toward the ship's unknown and distant prow.

In some places, the tubes are thin and we can see almost all the way to an outer wall, which in this segment has transparencies like very large windows, giving us glimpses of the outboard cylinders, which have their own transparencies. We're uninvolved enough in our transport that I try to peer through the canes and both transparencies. The outboard cylinders are filled with other screw gardens, lots of them, bigger than the one in the tail. Important. Nonsensically important.

The searchers smoothly shuttle us through an immense cavern. At first, I can only make out blurry patches shot through with flashes of that fairy light—but then I get a real sense of scale. We're being shuttled over a major e-ticket ride. Guru tech is on full display as we smoothly pass over what amounts to an immense four-leaf clover, the leaves pointing aft, the node, connecting the leaves, about two klicks forward of the trailing edges—the whole arrangement maybe two klicks across. Each leaf's inner surface is mapped by canals and geographies of walled-off rivers, along with what could pass for a lake, all teeming with hundreds of searchers going about their business, whatever that might be. Makes more sense than the screw gardens—they're the ship's drivers, right? They need a place for R&R.

Gravity is not apparent, but the water flowing along the rivers and lake doesn't drift away. The giant clover doesn't spin or do anything obvious, but the surfaces of the leaves seem to have their own sticky properties. The searchers in charge of our bouquet make no comments on these wonders, not that we'd understand if they did. DJ and I did not share tea with them and know nothing about their inner thoughts.

Near the node where the leaves come together, we're taken to a lumpy neighborhood of gray-brown mushrooms, spotted with holes, as if worms have been busy, and for all we know, they have. But we haven't met any—yet.

The searchers deliver us and deftly, silently move way, tail first, keeping their eyes on us like servants or guards in a royal palace.

"Our bunks," Borden says.

We untangle from the leashes and explore. The spaces within the holes are equipped with mats and net-bundles of cakes, along with succulent gluey beads about the size of grapes, but bright yellow-green. We're ravenous and try them all. Not terrible. Almost good.

The walls are spongy, soft, reasonably warm and comfortable—and glow with a soft, bluish sunset light. Best accommodations yet, but what I need most, what all of us need most, is sleep. So we divide along rank and friendship, crawl through different wormholes, wrap up in blankets, and rest easy. It's an instinct Skyrines have, sort of Greek battle-field wisdom—know what you can change, accept what you can't, and make do with whatever's handed to you.

But as I drift into a much-needed and reasonably sound slumber, I can't stop thinking about those impossible rivers, flowing along the huge, angled cloverleaves—searchers swimming, breaching, refreshing, enjoying themselves—all the while doing something apparently essential to this ship.

A little residual from Bug Karnak stirs and decides to take shape in my foggy thoughts. The searchers are familiar to the bugs—in reverse. Like the Antags, they were designed and assigned. "What's that even mean?" I murmur, with my hands reaching out as if to grasp these facts. "Bugs never met them, never knew them."

But bugs never met or knew human beings or anything on Earth. Reverse familiarity. Later manifestations of bug civilization helped seed the outer reaches of the solar system, far beyond Pluto, far indeed from the sun. In fact, that's where all the important stuff was happening, four billion years ago.

And the searchers, for the Antags at least, are among the most important.

But how did they become useful to the Gurus? They don't

fight. Can they defend themselves against anybody or anything? How can they be soldiers in a Guru-inspired war?

Maybe they provide a lagniappe of irony, pity, perspective. There's a theory so vague I withdraw my hand. The vision subsides. I'm warm, I'm surrounded, it's not much stranger—maybe slightly less strange, actually—than the quarters we occupied on the Spook, and there's no impending battle, no fight planned for the day, the month, maybe for years, How long will it take us to get where Bird Girl thinks we're going? Hundreds of billions of kilometers. Maybe a trillion. We're definitely out of action for this part of the season, probably for hundreds of seasons to come. Maybe we'll die inside this monster.

Inside. We've been eaten by an immense Guru ship populated by Captain Nemo's worst nightmares...but all in all, it's not too bad. A vacation break from the Red or Titan. Instant death delayed.

I can't hear Captain Coyle anymore, but I know what she'd tell me. She'd say, *When you get home, Venn, you're going to be one fucked-up dude.*

I EMERGE FROM my hole and almost bump into Borden. She's looking reasonably sharp, so I ask her where she got coffee. She gives me a chilly smile. "We need to talk."

"I'm still half-asleep."

"That's our problem, Venn. We've been sleepwalking ever since Titan. I need to talk to somebody about command structure and discipline."

Of course you do, I say to myself. "Happy to listen, Commander, but I'm not sure I'm the right guy."

"I'm conflicted about Sanchez. I don't like his story about Sudbury. Putting our soldiers, any kind of soldier, into the hands of monsters…"

"DJ and Tak and I wouldn't be here without him. He saved our bacon, ma'am, and Sudbury was one mean son of a bitch."

"Even so. I can't talk to Litvinov, he's too grief-stricken at the loss of Ulyanova."

"She's not dead, Commander."

"She might as well be. And she's taken one of the *efreitors* with her."

"Vera?"

"We haven't seen either of them since I don't know when. That's part of the problem…I have no idea when this is or where we are, and no actionable about where we're heading."

"Bird Girl says she and her fellow Antags are going home, but most or all of them have never been there. DJ thinks it's Planet X."

"I goddamned well can't talk to the corporal. He's too whacked for me."

"DJ is smart and he's straight, Commander."

"Maybe it's my lack, then, but I need to think about structure, about who we are, with somebody I think gives a damn."

"If you don't know where you are, you don't know who you are."

"Who said that—you?"

"A writer named Wendell Berry."

"You read a lot, Venn?"

"I like to read. My mother read a lot, sometimes to me."

Borden is the current puzzle, I tell myself. Constrained rage, trying to appear so calm on the outside…What does she think we can do? We're so reduced we could all hole up in a nutshell and leave room for the nut.

"What about Kumar?" I say. "He's the civilian authority, right?"

"I haven't trusted Wait Staff since before I broke you out of Madigan."

"Well, he's been pretty straight with us—except for that moment trying to remember what the Gurus meant to him. I've had my own lapses that way."

"Venn, I want to gain traction here."

"Tell me what you need, Commander."

"We need to reestablish. We've long since exceeded our mission, and we're down to Hershey squirts for orders."

"Jesus," I say, and laugh.

"I mean it. If we don't get it together soon, we'll go fucking native, and that is not any sort of option…is it?"

"Our enemy is in charge, but they're no longer our enemy. Maybe you need to speak with Bird Girl."

"That's what I'm saying, goddammit! What's her real name? What's her rank?"

"I'll ask next time we get together," I say. Borden's face is a mask of little-girl disappointment. I did not think she was capable of reviving her inner child, but here it is, she's in pain, and there's not a meaningful thing I can do. She's my superior officer. We shouldn't even be having this conversation.

Which proves her point.

"We need to have a mission," she says, her voice falling off. She gives me a hard look. I have to think outside the box— that's a direct order, isn't it? All my life I've assigned leadership and planning to others—to Joe or people like Borden—to our DIs or battlefield commanders.

"Maybe it's right in front of us," I say. "We need to follow the Antags to their home world, get as much information as we can about their relationship to their own Gurus—their Keepers—and acquire as much intel as we can about where the Antags come from and what they have to offer in our effort to free Earth from all this bullshit."

She looks squarely at me. "Like you say, obvious. But I'm maybe the least informed of anyone on this ship, the least sophisticated on things Guru and Antag—all book and paper training, right?"

I don't respond to that. I'm still pondering what her highest directive was when she sprang me from Madigan. Was she already anticipating—along with Kumar and Mushran—that there would be a Guru mimic in their future?

"What do *you* suggest?" she asks.

"Litvinov and Joe and Jacobi could work with you to create a new set of directives. New orders reflective of our circumstances."

"Where would Bird Girl fit in?"

"Maybe she wants us to contribute to their game plan, their new mission—but so far she's just providing minimal education...and trying to overcome her hatred."

"What about her commanders? Do we have any sense of how they work, militarily, socially?"

I make a wry face. "I'm not sure, but when we communicate, there's something not stated—some place inside her thinking where I'm not allowed to go."

"Can she wander in your head?" Borden asks.

"I don't think so." *Can she? Would I feel it if she did?*

"How many shoes can an Antag drop?" Borden asks, seriously enough, but with more wit than I thought she was capable of. We're not often allowed to think such thoughts of our sisters in the military, and particularly not of rank, but for the first time, I can conceive of maybe enjoying a social occasion with Commander Borden—going out for drinks if not an actual date. She might laugh at my jokes. I might laugh at hers.

I've been out here a long, long time.

"Well, the big shoe that hasn't been dropped is, where are the men?" I say. "Antag males, I mean."

"They're all females?" Borden seems surprised.

"That's what Ulyanova says. Even rank is female. But there might be something more to the picture."

"A different command structure?"

"Something odd." *Something big.*

"Odd how?" Borden asks.

"I do not know, Commander."

"Surely not as odd as the squid, right?"

I shake my head.

She looks alarmed, then disgusted. "You're thinking the squid are the males?"

"No, they're definitely from a different part of whatever world they all come from. The bugs knew about them in reverse, I mean, the bugs laid down some of the possibilities for the searchers way back when, but…no. They're more different from Antags than we are."

"Thank God," Borden says.

And I have to agree. But what's lurking in my scattered shrapnel of knowledge, now that we're so far from anything like Bug Karnak? Now that Bug Karnak has been hammered into silence…Where *are* the Antag males, and what are they like?

"Thanks for a sympathetic ear, Venn."

"Not a problem, Commander."

"Keep me in the loop, okay?"

"Will do. And sir, I'd be happy to help you understand DJ. He's a valuable member of our team."

She shudders delicately. But then she sucks it up. "Sure," she says. "We need more understanding, if we're going to keep it together."

———

BIRD GIRL CONVENES us all in view of the maze of supports and machinery forward of the node where the cloverleaves come together. She's been joined by two searchers. I can't keep my eyes off the way they grip and glide smoothly through the canes and a spiderweb of flexible cords. They help Bird Girl find her place at our center and even offer to help arrange us. Once again, we're treated like flowers, and the squid seem to enjoy the little flourishes of who is planted next to whom, which some of us accept with tense reserve and others with a growing sense of perverse humor. Who can be most cooperative? After you, ma'am. May I pull up an arm, a tentacle? No, I insist.

Borden takes it all with relative calm. Maybe our talk did some good. Who can suss out what's really going on, what's really about to happen?

Tak is a master of his own sort of calm introspection. I would have expected no less. Jacobi is perhaps the least at ease. Litvinov and the remaining Russian, Bilyk, show little more than resignation. Vera and Ulyanova are still not present.

One of the searchers accesses a satchel looped around its starboard hull and draws out replacement clothes. The outfits seem tailor-made—by squid? They could be excellent seam-stresses, right? The outfits are handed to us as individuals, and while searcher "faces" and gestures are still impossible to read, there's a kind of tenderness to the whole ceremony, mixed, maybe, with Bird Girl's display of what might be observant humor. I've noticed in our connection that there is humor in her, though it's tightly bound to embarrassment—ours, not hers—and the potential for falling out of line, for humiliation, losing social position—not fitting into a per-fectly obvious status quo.

Ishida and Ishikawa speak in Japanese, cocking glances at the squid, at Bird Girl, and nodding sagely. I wonder what they're saying? Tak joins them and they seem to enjoy a joke on all of us. This irritates Borden.

Then I see the similarities—cockeyed similarities. Borden's only human. Bird Girl is also human. Being called *human* is funny that way—a stretchable label that covers a multitude of common sins. Our Antag representative is not deliber-ately cruel, not sadistic, but there's a touch of the challenger and even the bully about her, as if she'd rather be anyplace but here, tending to us, despite our clueless clumsiness—our evil nature! We who used to be killers of her kind and who still are, back around Mars and Saturn. How far she'll go to arrange for and enjoy our embarrassment has yet to be determined.

In their natural habitats, and outside of protective armor, neither searchers nor Antags need or wear clothes. Do they think us weak for our shivering nakedness? Weak and funny? But they're accommodating our obvious needs for the first time, replacing the near-useless pajamas and arranging for us to be covered.

There's surprise among our group as we realize the new clothes fit and are comfortable. We struggle to put them on, but only against the necessity of weightless motion. The new duds are comfy enough, but they're still just pajamas. I'd feel better in fatigues, but little chance of that.

"We are leaving Saturn space," Bird Girl tells us all through the translator. "What we both came to Saturn to study has been destroyed. Both sides will take credit."

She's getting that sarcastic tone down pretty well. I wonder if Antags are just naturally a little angry. That would make them even more *human*, no? Easier to understand.

"Can you still feel the old knowledge?" DJ asks her.

Bird Girl looks at me—is this a question it will be useful to answer, maybe for the others? I try to nod my approval. She's still not very good at reading human expression. But then, I can't read her well without retreating into our link, which is not always open.

"I no longer feel the old knowledge," Bird Girl answers. "Do you?"

DJ seems to try to listen. "Nope," he says.

Nothing, not even shrapnel. The last residuals are melting in my head like ice crystals in a warm breeze. I might miss those bits, but I won't miss the Guru bombs—if they're still there, which…

They do not seem to be.

"As we move out to where comets are made, there will be study of one outer world. You call that Pluto, small, like a lost moon."

"Always happy to learn more about Planet X," DJ says.

"Pluto isn't Planet X," I say.

"Not now," DJ agrees.

Joe is quiet. Stealth Sanchez. Even as a teen, there were days when he went away, hid out, only to pop up when I least expected him. He'd usually say something about having a girlfriend or going to a party in the Valley, but I never knew what to believe. My attitude toward Joe has softened quite a bit.

I ask Bird Girl what Ulyanova's doing.

"Ship has schedule: Pluto, then the transmitters, then Sun-Planet. Your companion helps guide ship's planning."

Still Guru. But where? Is there a wheelhouse on this monster?

I ask Bird Girl how long such a journey will take.

"I am told, for Earth, five times around the sun."

"Who tells you that?" No answer. "What'll we do to pass the time?"

"We will not notice the time."

"How's that done?"

"That is what searchers tell me," Bird Girl says. "They have done this often and often. We will learn."

Then she shows us another projected chart of the outer regions, swooping us out to Pluto, which is accompanied by one large moon and a handful of smaller moons.

At this stage in the delivery of her data, her impressions, all Bird Girl is receiving from the searchers and maybe from Ulyanova, something unexpected and even a little scary, for her, crawls up between us, interrupting the impressions of Pluto.

This object, on the projected chart, is an unlabeled, wavering smudge, not presently active in any obvious way—and definitely not alive or carrying living things. Whatever it is, it's not far from Pluto, doesn't do much, may not seem

796 | GREG BEAR

important, but has no explanation. According to the orbital track, after we reach Pluto, but before we reach the transmitter, we'll come quite close to this mystery smudge.

"Is it a Guru object?" I ask.

No answer. Our squad is taken back to quarters. We resume what passes for routine, going from sleep to sleep, being fed by squid, watched by their huge eyes as we emerge from our mushroom hole nests to chat and stare pointlessly at the stars in the star dish, telling one another we're making history, which impresses nobody, not even me, because the distances and the numbers are so far beyond anything humans can work with, and we're not anywhere near traveling between the stars, which supposedly the Antags had done, part of the big lie we have been fed since the Gurus arrived—arrived this time around—and when I tell that to Bird Girl, she experiences something like amusement, crossed with guilt and self-judgment, because her enemies have been so deluded and ignorant, and that is not honorable—

And we sleep and eat and sleep again, and gather and separate, and gather again, and I guess it's been about four weeks since we passed through the gate, and I wonder what's happened to Ulyanova, whom none of us have seen since.

All of which seems to mush up and fade from memory.

And suddenly—

Months have passed. Things feel very different out in the canebrake, around the searcher quarters and our quarters. We're fed, repeat our dull routines, and most of us believe nothing new has happened, nothing at all has happened.

But I know different. Lately there there's a touch of Ulyanova in my thoughts, something about an apartment and steam heat, Moscow winter—as if she's teasing her only contacts now other than her internal Guru and the ship's squid. But then again, what I'm feeling may not be her at all. It might be me imagining what her life was like, once.

Maybe there's been a Guru on this ship all along and it's pretending to be Ulyanova. At this point, would I know the difference? *Could* I know?

But we're far, far from where we had been during our last "briefing," and when we look at the concave "window," we seem to slide through star-backed, dusty darkness at very high speed. We see at least the simulations of nebular cloud structure. Looks compelling and cool, broadly 3-D, which makes me doubt it's straight-out real.

Likely this display is simulated for the benefit of the searchers' big, wide-spaced eyes.

———

BIRD GIRL APPROACHES DJ and me in the tangle around the window, escorted by three searchers. "We do not like this ship," she says. "It is not honest."

"Figured that out, have you?" DJ asks, and I elbow him in the ribs. She's trying to be forthright.

"What's Ulyanova doing now?" I ask.

"She is behind curtain. She does not communicate with us."

Curtain? Okay. Strangely, I don't feel concern, because this much is becoming clear to me: Ulyanova is still on this ship, she's still in control, active, and she's going to call DJ and me forward soon. The last few hours, I can hear her in my head like a distant song.

I feel another cold, deep concern, worse than that gut-level fear I had earlier, before the confused passage of ship time.

Pluto is coming. The Guru transmitter is coming—a dangerous and important moment. And we'll soon be near that silent smudge that nobody knows anything about—unknown to Gurus or Antags. Unknown to the searchers.

Why go there at all? I don't like it.

———

WE'RE IN OUR soft, warm quarters, half-asleep, when a searcher appears at the entrance. Its tentacles twinkle in the dim light. No surprise, in darkness they, too, kind of glow. They could be responsible for all the elf-light residue, bits and pieces of squid skin, squid dust. Humans shed, too, but it isn't nearly as weirdly pretty.

Wonder what they look like when they're at home? Maybe not very different from the way they look swimming along the cloverleaf waterways. Peaceful, graceful—dedicated and working away for the Gurus. Wonder if Bird Girl can persuade them to work for us. Maybe she already has.

There are several of them outside the hole. DJ and I are gathered up, gently but no nonsense. Not that he and I are prone to offer objections. DJ looks resigned to anything as long as it's over with soon.

The searchers have Bird Girl in tow as well. She's not moving, not in charge, not drafting us forward with her wings. I miss that, somehow, and wonder what's changed. They've wrapped her in a cinched cover or blanket. All of her four eyes are tightly closed. Unconscious? No link. No information from her about what might be next.

"We're going forward, aren't we?" DJ asks me.

"If that's where Ulyanova is."

"Christ, she scares the fuck out of me," he says.

"Why?"

He snorts and gives me a grim smile. Nobody else from our squad is going with us. They're sleeping like cozy little dormice.

The searchers do their arm-nest thing and sedan-chair us beyond the node, through more canebrakes, following an internal highway that spirals and arches forward. I wish I could have a moment with Joe or even Borden to express my last will and testament—give my love and a soldier's farewell to Mom if you make it, Commander, won't you? The tear-jerking moment of every half-assed war movie, because you know this poor SOB is doomed—all he has to do is ask and you know he's about to fly right out of the frame, right out of the screenplay. The Gurus, expert craftsmen, would plan it that way to keep their audience happy, right? Maximum interest.

But this is a tougher kind of epic. Not much in the way of sentiment. Pure scrap and stain. We should be accustomed to simply and violently ending it all. A lot of our dismembered, carbonized, vaporized friends are out there waiting for us. But this *feels* different. What can Ulyanova possibly be or do that scares us both so bad?

———

WE'VE BEEN TRAVELING with the searchers, right behind them, for quite some time. Big fucking ship. None so big as this one, and here it's filled with screw gardens bigger than any we've seen earlier, if size can be estimated in the dim light—and if they are gardens, really, because they seem to enjoy the dark.

More spherical cages become evident, hiding back in

other squash courts, other cubical recesses, filled with skel-
etons, some possibly human, many not—like abandoned and
uncleansed graveyards in an old city—proud Guru trophies.
Imagine the categories! *Best performance with cruelty. Most
satisfying vengeance. Most popular caged slaughter.*

It's sobering to think (or to hope) that all these bodies,
these dead, were once monsters like Grover Sudbury. Perversity is everywhere. But where did they all come from?
There aren't enough planets, I'm thinking, DJ is thinking.
And none of our melted soup of leftover knowledge helps us
understand.

That's all we've got to distract us—screw gardens and
cages filled with corpses. DJ and I keep silent out of respect,
but maybe as much out of terror. Surely these charnel houses
carry their own ghosts! What would the ghost of a nonhuman be like? How would it differ from our own spirits of
the dead—which of course we all know don't exist? They're
figments of our imagination. I've never seen a ghost, right?
Except that I have. And not just Captain Coyle, who wasn't
really a ghost anyway.

Ghosts seem to be able to get around. I don't know how.
Maybe the dead humans up here have already returned to
Earth. Maybe they're lost, drifting in between, dissolving,
evaporating. That leads me down more highways of dark
speculation—anything to keep alert. Fear and anger are good
for keeping alert, though maybe not the best for clear thinking.
But I have to wonder—when they destroyed Titan's archives,
and Mars's, did they destroy Captain Coyle's last existence?

Maybe now she can become a *real* ghost. Will that be
better?

Enough spooky shit. We have to concentrate on what is

immediately apparent and important—that there are dead things aboard this ship that do not come from Earth or any-place like Earth, that are not Antag or anything like Antag. So who most recently supplied these cages with victims? And are more on the way?

"Maybe they won prizes," DJ says softly as we're moved forward, echoing my own theories. "Big ship carries a shit-load of fine Guru memories."

Maybe. But still no explanation for the screw gardens, why so large, why so many?—dozens and dozens arrayed in the dark volumes. Maybe the screw gardens are spooky, too. How the fuck would we know what's spooky and what isn't?

This is the Guru's Rolls-Royce, the limo that takes the most important Gurus where they want to go, their personal conveyance around and beyond the solar system—the way they connect with every show they're producing for their faithful audience of interstellar couch potatoes.

The show must go on, but who could hold an audience's interest for hundreds of millions, much less billions, of years? We're none of us all that charming, all that interesting and suspenseful. We're none of us movie star material! Maybe it's in the writing. The Gurus have to be masters of suspense and plot to make our petty little dramas popular.

———

FINALLY WE COME to an opening in the cane highway, some-thing the searchers can pass through, carrying DJ and Bird Girl and me. The architecture changes. My eyes have a dif-ficult time tracking, and I'm not sure I understand our pres-ent surroundings, but that turns out to be because I'm dizzy. My heart is thumping out of rhythm. Something in the air smells sweet. Could be airborne persuasion or nutrients for searchers—not so good for us. To distract myself, I pay attention to searcher skin and how the segments link as they move. These are nothing like terrestrial mollusks.

My heart steadies, my eyes stop trying to cross—and it all clicks into place. Up ahead, nine searchers in charge of a large, dark bundle give scale to a distant bulkhead. The bulkhead is flat gray and hundreds of meters wide. The bundle the searchers have surrounded is wrapped in a tight gray blanket, maybe eight meters long. At their poking, the bulk flexes. A big Guru? No...and in silhouette, it doesn't look like a searcher, either—more like an Antag, but larger than any we've met.

Bird Girl's eyes open. She blinks and spreads her wings. Two searchers attend to her now, grooming her fine feathers with the tips of their arms. She's smoother, less frazzled—being dolled up for something, I guess, some major introduction or presentation, but who could possibly care how she looks, way up here?

Our link is back but it's filled with emotions and scrambled information I can't make sense of. I try to sort and filter the emotions—and then realize they're both intensely political and intensely romantic.

Bird Girl is terrified. And she's in love.

The searchers move away. She straightens her shoulders and spreads her wings with a pride and presence I've never seen or felt from her—like a princess entering court for the first time. The searchers allow us to float free, but we aren't nearly as good at drafting as the Antags, and the canes are out of reach. Then they remove and roll up the big blanket, revealing what could be a huge, shiny black slug with purple highlights. But it spreads a wide set of wings, as if waking, or as a welcome…dwarfing Bird Girl, the searchers, us. Wingspan of at least ten meters.

Bird Girl speaks. DJ and I hear a raspy version of what she's saying, in both English and Russian. "Thank you for witnessing. This is my husband—*our* husband. We are together again. Isn't he *beautiful*?"

The emotion pouring through our link is extraordinary—immense relief that this huge Antag is still alive, that the family they trained and fought with has been rejoined, ready to resume something approaching a normal life—along with a sense of completion. Where did they keep him? Somewhere on Titan, I presume, and then carried here…asleep, waiting for a safer moment to return and take charge.

"We are together, we have come this far, and we are going home!" Bird Girl announces.

The big male's head is at least twice as wide as hers, his four eyes farther apart but roughly the same size and color. He surveys the searchers and Bird Girl with a sleepy calm, all is well, all is in order, he approves—but then his four purple-rimmed eyes light on DJ and me. With apparent surprise, he scrutinizes us, feathers rising around his massive shoulders. I gather that we're unexpected, unwanted—why are we here?

And that could be a problem. Based on the emotions coursing through our connection, to Bird Girl—and no doubt to the other female Antags on this hijacked ship—he's the ultimate reference point, their mentor and mate, mate to all…

Scares me, really, because to him, we're completely disgusting. We're still the enemy.

THE SECRET WORLD OF PLANTS

The big male speaks to Bird Girl in a high voice that belies his size—more screech-rasp, untranslated. This goes on for a few minutes, with DJ and I out of the loop and way out of our depth, but happy to be ignored.

"She's filling him in," I say.

"I don't think he likes us," DJ says.

Nothing on our link except a smothering mask of affection, not meant for us. Bird Girl is truly enamored.

"They should get a room," DJ says. "Is she going to keep him all to herself?"

He had to ask. From behind, we hear more Antag music, chirps and rasps and soaring notes. I rotate by waving my arms and see five searchers escorting seven more females, including three of the formerly oh-so-superior armored commanders, singing their appreciation like groupies. All of them have folded their wings, leaving Bird Girl as the only female to spread them wide. Clearly this is a great moment for the larger family. We know our enemies not at all.

Two searchers spray something from their tails at the canebrakes. From the shadows we hear rustling and rattling and watch as more canes grow and weave to shape arched thickets, which then fan to connect with the bulkhead, a spiral of climbing ways and bridges.

"That's cool," DJ murmurs.

The searchers take hold of us, gentle but no nonsense, and Bird Girl slowly folds her wings, then allows herself to be conveyed by her fellow females away from the big male. Her moment with the paterfamilias seems to be over. Her grief is obvious even without our link—and overwhelming when I dip in. Separation is such sweet sorrow. What a guy. What a species in which to be male! What's required of the big boy when he's at home? Is he tasked with a head-butting competition to win his place in the herd? Alpha male sports? Keeping a rolling orgy going 24/7?

DJ and I keep silent on all frequencies as our escorts guide Bird Girl and us toward a spiral bridge of fresh canes.

"Ever seen a dead cell?" DJ whispers.

"Plenty, after a bare-knuckle fight."

"In microscopes, I mean! Cells got a skeleton made of fibers just like these bamboo bridges—grow at the tips when the cell wants to move, shrink back when it's not needed." DJ can be full of surprises. Not all porn and old movies in that noggin. "Kill the cell and the gunk, the gel, shrivels, and leaves a pile of sticks. This ship is a giant cell!"

Good to know. I don't believe it for a moment, but it's better than anything I've got. We've been sedan-chaired around that internal skeleton for half an hour or more, and now, through gaps in the canes we see spaces accessible by other arches and bridges—dark, empty spaces. Maybe Gurus once slept there. Maybe they kept sporting victims up here and pulled them out when needed to fight and die.

I once got into a classroom argument with a teacher about the plural of the name Spartacus. The other kids ragged me all day, on the playground or walking home. Now we're surrounded by cages and maybe holes that were once filled with Spartacuses. Spartaci. Spartacoi. Fuck it.

Echoes tell me our surround is narrowing. It's become completely dark. Not even the searchers are illuminating. Not at all reassuring that Bird Girl is with us, because based on what's passing through our link, her deadly sadness and lovebird grief, she might happily be going to her doom, having displeased the big male with our presence, her dealings with the enemy. No way to know how smart the big male is or what they said to each other. He might have given her instructions to gut herself and us besides.

As the lights come back up we can see that we've reached a much slimmer portion of the ship's hull, perhaps closer to the actual bow. Bird Girl isn't committing suicide. She's taking us to Ulyanova. Big male (I'm going to call him Budgie) may not like us, but that hasn't changed the basic plans.

"Why aren't the showrunners doing something about us? Why haven't they learned?" DJ whispers.

"Showrunners? Learned what?"

"Gurus!" DJ says with a critical scowl. "Ship's been hijacked. Shouldn't there be a fail-safe, some sort of dead Guru switch, that would blow it up if it's hijacked?

"Damned obvious," I whisper back. "Ulyanova's convincing. Or maybe—" And this hurts to both think and say, I almost want to shut up and just curl into a ball. "Maybe the plan hasn't changed. We won't matter a great goddamned toothpick to this ship unless we get boring."

DJ plays out my drift. "So we're doing exactly what it wants—and this is our third act!"

I have to admit I was bored back in the tail, for a while, but this is definitely more and more interesting. *I'd* fucking stay tuned. What do we say to Ulyanova when we meet up? Wonder what Budgie will say once he's brought up to date?

Somehow these awkward thoughts leak to Bird Girl. She directs her searchers to move her and favors us with close examination. Four eyes bore into my two. I'm outmatched.

"Show respect," she says.

"Yes, ma'am," I say.

"We have left the mimic alone. Now she makes request for your presence."

DJ and I look at each other.

She raises a ridge between her shoulders and shakes it out with a shuffling noise. The searchers link up, grip our hands, and reach us out to a ladder of large, U-shaped grips mounted on one face of a long, sinuous beam. They release us to the grips, cold and hard, then swing off to one side. DJ and I cling as the beam pushes forward—grows forward!—and twists, spiraling us like a steel vine toward a diffuse haze, like moonlight in a cathedral.

Bird Girl has crossed with us and grips the rungs behind, wings folded. "Climb," she says.

The beam carries us into a narrower, longer chamber, like a pipe or a needle, filled with long ribbons about as broad as my forearm. The ribbons cross over in a kind of braid every five or six meters and are alternately dark, then bright again, illumination flowing aft as if carrying signals to the rest of the ship—like fiber-optic cables. The beam pushes and twists up the middle of these ribbons, contorting to avoid the braids. Searchers are moving up along the outside, keeping up with us and following more arches of canes.

As the ribbons twist along to an end, we see just beyond their conclusion four oblong panels, as colorful as stained-glass windows, but arranged in a wide quadrangle, like the faces in a clock tower. From where we are, each of the four faces appears divided into multicolored wedges, like pie charts—but sprinkled with stars.

As we grow up to and then through the faces, two searchers hiding in the angles between retreat into shadow like shy schoolchildren. The faces have painted themselves with thousands of cryptic symbols, red and blue against a silvery background like a clear dusk sky. Every few blinks, the symbols lift and rearrange—impossible to read or understand.

"Any constellations?" DJ asks from below. The beam—the vine—pushes and twists on.

"No," I say. "Some sort of diagram."

Maybe this is Ulyanova's playroom and these are her mirrors, where she's pasted Day-Glo stickers to remind herself of a human childhood. But the stars that flock in the surrounding mosquito cloud are pinpoint brilliances, like stars in a clear night sky. Not at all like stickers.

Beyond the ribbons and inboard from the faces, more searchers are spraying to encourage canes to grow, giving access to another swallow's nest of shiny black spheres—different in color, but not unlike our present habitats.

"The mimic asks that you will all move here," Bird Girl says. I detect a seething kind of hatred in her, and not just for

Ulyanova—for us as well. Meeting up with Budgie seems to have stiffened her anger—maybe bent her thoughts. At any rate, I'm not feeling any sense of partnership, much less affection.

"Better accommodations?" DJ asks.

"Closer to where the mimic hides." She stretches out a wing.

Starboard from the clock faces, about fifty meters forward of our new domiciles, I make out a slowly undulating curtain, like a tapestry woven from strands of smoke. I turn to communicate this discovery to DJ and Bird Girl when, without warning, Ulyanova and Vera appear through the curtain and surge up before us.

Bird Girl retreats a few rungs, feathers spiked, and DJ lets out a shuddering groan, but the *starshina* looks only at me.

"Long time!" she says, and tries for a charming smile. Epic fail. My God, she's nothing but skin and bones! In this light, her face stretches across her skull like frog skin, moist and shiny, eyes large and brilliantly empty. "I am glad you are here," she says. "I need to think again like human." I cringe as something from her probes my mind, like frozen fingers touching my thoughts, my memories. Ulyanova cocks her head, trying perhaps for coyness, but appearing toothy, feral. "So many strange days. Vera and I make new home. It will be beautiful when finished."

"It is already beautiful," Vera says. "It could be more *useful*."

"I know ship well," the *starshina* says. "I *dream* it. Work is difficult! They fight me, question me, all the time. Here—move closer and help me stay human, will you? Before long trips begin."

DJ climbs closer, starts to speak, maybe to save me from the full brunt of that brightly dead look, but Ulyanova simply glances his way—and he's knocked from the rungs into a nearby cane thicket, where he waves his arms and legs like a fly in a web.

Nobody dares to move. What more could she do if we actually crossed her?

She takes a shuddering breath. Then, at her permissive gesture, Vera and I link hands to pull DJ back to the rungs. He favors his elbow, which has been scraped by a broken cane.

Vera backs off a few rungs and watches DJ and me like a hawk. Literally. As if we're mice trying to hide.

"You have questions…?" Ulyanova asks.

"Where are we?" I ask.

"In needle at tip of ship," she says. "Like hypo that will inject us to stars."

"Is this a control room?" I ask.

"It is part of ship's eyes. Often, brain shows me what it is seeing. I control—but dead Gurus still try to return, take power, change things—and worst of all, *talk*." She looks both amused and sad—easy enough in her present condition. "I keep them in brain's closet. They are not happy!"

"Ship treats us well," Vera says brightly, as if that justifies everything.

"I do not stand in ship's way," Ulyanova says. "None of us are problem, not you, not me—not yet. We *amuse*."

"Can you tell the brain, the ship, where to go? Take us back to Earth—now?"

"Ship goes where it has gone, back and forth and around comet clouds, for thousands of years. This trip, after last delivery, after long journey out to *Antagonista* planet, it will return to Mars and Earth and maybe Titan, to pick up remaining Gurus."

"They're leaving?"

This seems to humor her. "They plan different." Ulyanova favors me again with that ghastly smile. I feel sick with guilt, empathy—not good emotions for a soldier. I remind myself if she fails, or if she turns against us, the *starshina* could kill us all. It wouldn't be her fault, but what would it matter?

I don't know whether to pity or fear her, but what I do not want to do is tick her off.

DJ climbs close again, coming back for more. I always knew he had courage but this is exceptional. "We're on our way to Planet X, right?" he asks.

She has eyes only for me but answers him anyway. "Next stop is near Pluto, for delivery. Then out to *Antagonista* world. Then return to Earth. They failed."

"Who failed?"

"Dead Gurus."

"Failed how?"

"Their deliveries did not amuse. But still they hide and plan."

"Nasty things," Vera says. "They are canceled, but always hope."

"I tell them what they want to hear. They pay attention. So for now, I control."

"Fine," I say, and brace for her response. "But if we can't control the ship and take it home, or wherever we want to go—what have you accomplished?"

Ulyanova regards me with sad triumph. "I stop ship from blowing out air and killing you like rats," she says. "Is that good thing?"

"She is Queen," Vera says, and pats her shoulder, then reassures her, "It is *good* thing. It is *very good*."

Is Vera truly a friend, an advocate—or a kind of pet?

"Come with," the *starshina* says. "Bring up searchers to help." She swings toward the nest of spheres. "This is where squad will live," she says. "Antags will also soon move closer, farther forward, where we can protect from ones we have set free."

"Set free?" I ask.

"Our shame," Ulyanova says. "When we opened gate, we opened cages. Fighters are free."

"But they're dead!" DJ says.

Ulyanova lifts an almost bald eyebrow. "Some still live, spread in dark places. Ours and others. Watch for them. They may be on look for you, yes?"

"Shit," DJ says. He's as gray as his overalls.

"How many?" I ask.

"Fifty-three," Vera says.

Ulyanova shakes her head. "Not so many. More have died, killing each other. They are like wild dogs."

This is a fight we don't need and certainly don't want. Makes my spine freeze thinking about it. "Can't you keep us clear of them?"

Ulyanova looks at us with real sympathy, but suddenly, her smile is wicked. "*You* are more interesting to ship when you fight." She shakes her head stubbornly. "I will not change that. It will help keep you alive."

Gurus and their ghosts know too fucking much about all of us. They know how to arouse fear, anger, violence—which might as well be complete mastery. It's their script. It's their stock on the market. And it's what makes us worth keeping around.

For a while, at least.

Three searchers move up and link arms.

"This way, please," Vera says.

CLOSER TO THE PALACE

It takes a few hours for the searchers to transfer the rest of our squad from the ship's midsection, beyond the cloverleaf water park, through the screw gardens and past the ancient cages, all open now, then along the steel vine and into the needle, where we advance along the ribbons, through the clock faces, and slightly outboard to the new black nests.

Borden and Jacobi assign the cubbies to pairs, except for Kumar, who gets his own. Judging from the reactions, our squad will soon exercise its own choices for nest buddies. Without her Queen, Vera is in attendance off and on, enjoying a break, or just enjoying human company...

As if in reward, one of the searchers that are always in attendance around the clock faces moves toward our new quarters, reaches into its slung pouch, and supplies us with more "grapes" and cakes and another round of blankets.

For the time being, most of the Antags will remain close to the hangars where their ships have been moved and re-stowed.

As the others move in, DJ and I gather Borden, Kumar,

and Jacobi in the ribbon space and tell them about the cage fighters. The air seems suddenly frigid, as if the cold of outer space has been sucked into the hull along with the starlight.

Kumar maintains a studious silence, as he nearly always does. Then he asks, "The searchers will keep lookout?"

"They don't fight," Jacobi reminds us, needlessly.

"I don't know," I say. "But they'll be in the way if the fighters come forward. Ulyanova commands them—but we still don't know what they can do for her."

"What's she look like?" Borden asks.

"She's a wreck," I say.

"How long can she keep it up?"

No way I can answer that.

Three of the searchers return aft, leaving two to take up station between the clock faces, arms barely rippling, intent on instructions and details.

"Perfect sailors of a starry sea!" Vera marvels.

We set up watches around the ribbon space to regularly sweep the five empty cubbies.

———

BARELY SETTLED IN, we're summoned.

We've grown quite adept at moving along the canes and ribbons. The searchers have slung more rubbery cables, so now we hardly need their help. The squad gathers in the ribbon space, where Vera and Ulyanova wait. Forward, two searchers swivel to listen and observe—possibly to protect us, though we all have doubts about what they can do in that regard.

"Show us where we are," Ulyanova tells the ship, and the ribbons expand as if carving great slices out of the hull—

opening up dozens of long, skewed views to vast clouds of stars—the nebulosities of the Milky Way.

My God, how long has it been since I last stared up at that great bridge!

Inside me, something strains—and snaps. I start to laugh. The others look with sour expressions. I can't explain myself—it's all colliding in my head, years of walking different worlds, becoming different boys, different men—looking up at the same sky.

Rediscovering a singular moment…

As a grunt on Socotra, studying that arch of a billion suns, I threw away my last tiny fragment of atheism, my last arrogant assurance that I was righteously alone.

I did not want to be alone, and then…I wasn't.

No way to explain it.

But at that time, the God I believed in was a violent, deadly God.

There were times on Socotra, at the end of basic, knowing I was going to be a warrior, when I tried to think my way to a suitable death—if I died in battle, or in space, out there! Looking up at the night sky, with hardly any lights for hundreds of miles around, I tried to turn the Milky Way into a direct stairway to Fiddler's Green, the actual Fiddler's Green—grunt heaven, Valhalla. Where all heroes go when they die.

I silently prayed to my new masters, to this violent god, to the generals and Wait Staff and Gurus, the threatened billions of Earth: Send me all the way out there. Send me on a mission to find the place where brave soldiers can fight forever, but when we are grievously wounded, when the guts hang out and blood gushes, the guts get shoved back in, new blood steams lava red in our veins—wounds stitch up, bones knit, and we return to our comrades, our fellow soldiers, to toast the pain, the victory or the loss, and fight again.

I'd already killed a man, but back then I did not know what actual battle was, certainly did not know what it was like to fight and die in near-vacuum. Eternal war seemed cool. I don't think that now.

I stop laughing, catch myself in a single hiccup, try to sober up. "Who sees things in these long strips?" I ask Ulyanova.

"The searchers," Vera answers. Ulyanova nods. "It works for their eyes. They can stretch over two strips and see everything. But we can adjust, as well."

I look into the widespread four eyes of the closest searcher, trying to estimate the parallax, the distance, but somehow also sensing the intelligence that might be there, might be set free, if it could only get home…

It does not hate us. It serves and does not resent its service. There's something potential in that wide, deep gaze— something that could be terribly useful and important—but then the searcher swivels and our moment is lost.

"Hey," DJ says, pointing along one wide ribbon, then another. We look where he directs, tilting on cords to adjust our view, and I make out, cutting a crescent from the starry bridge, a faded brownish-gray shadow. For a moment I can almost feel it suspended below our dangling legs. It's a planet. Looks vaguely familiar, but we're not used to this close view, or this way of seeing.

The crescent has a mottled, chunky, mountainous surface thrust between rough expanses of rubbled gray broad plains or maria of smooth white, marked by even bigger, isolated angular mountains like bobbing ice cubes dropped into a sundae. It's Pluto! We seem to be thirty or forty thousand clicks below its southern polar regions.

Moving back and forth between a few ribbons, like kids in a planetarium, we point out the crusty borders of large, icy peaks—trying to remember those lectures on Socotra. We recover the names: Cthulhu Regio, Sputnik Planum, Tombaugh—

But the light is so dim, the sun so far away.

"Old moon," Ulyanova says dismissively, then gestures for us to look forward, to where the strips converge, creating a kind of asterisk. Something large blanks the stars out there, in front of the ship, no way of knowing how far. The silhouette is all we've got to go on.

"Looks like a gift pack of railroad ties," DJ says. "But how big?"

"Is that the transmitter?" I ask Ulyanova.

"No," she says. "This not even Gurus know—*I* do not know. Something interested only by comets, moons, sometimes planets. Every few thousand years, it moves them around—but nothing else. Brain has records of its activity going back a billion years."

"Who made it?"

She shakes her head. "Ship does not know," she says.

"Really?" DJ says. "None of you know all there is to know?"

She diverts her glare but does not push him away. "*Really,*" she says. "It is always here—always avoided. Brain does not like it. Old ghosts do not like it, either."

"How big is it?" I ask.

"No size," she says. "We see it, maybe it sees us—but it has always ignored everything Guru, all the little wars—ignored even bugs, the ghosts say."

"Older than the bugs?"

"Much older."

"Cool!" DJ says. "I like it. Maybe it explains Planet X."

I shiver, and not just because of the cold. Something to deal with even if we shed the Gurus?

Or something that makes all of this, all of *us*, possible?

Looking between DJ's enthusiasm and my dismay, Ulyanova seems to soften. She raises her hand to touch and comb her straw-stiff hair. "All will sleep soon," she says. "Ship will make leap to transmitter, then to *Antagonista* world. Long leaps. Out beyond is realm of madness—madness and birth."

———

DRIFTING BETWEEN THE ribbons and staring forward at the asterisk where the ribbons meet, for no reason I can fathom, I spend my relaxation time keeping track of that unknown object.

"Are you God?" I murmur.

No answer. The object is alone. It does not care. It does what it does, nothing more.

Keep looking, grunt.

Joe joins me and I try to explain, but he shakes his head. "I'm full up with weird shit," he says. I know he's not an atheist, but he's never told me what he thinks or believes.

"Ulyanova says it isn't Guru," I say. "That's got to be important!"

"Maybe she's lying. Maybe it's *all* Guru."

"What do you want, out here?" I ask, angry.

He touches my shoulder. "There's so much shit I got wrong," he says. "It's going to take a while, I know, but I just want to make it right and get us home."

AFTERBIRTH

Days, maybe a week. Who can keep track?

For the time being, we're still parked tens of thousands of klicks beyond Pluto, in sight of that ancient mystery. Looking doesn't give me any more information, though that moon-shifter out there does look remarkably like a Christmas ornament assembled from model railroad parts.

No motion, no alarms.

Bird Girl has been gone for some time and no other Antags have come forward to visit. Maybe Budgie is keeping them busy.

The squad has been rearranging quarters, as I thought we would, as if that might help pass the time and make a difference. DJ and I share one sphere, where he appears to be fast asleep, curled up in a ball. But his eyes are flicking. Neither of us is sleeping if we can avoid it. We're waiting for that forced sleep that hasn't arrived. We all want to be awake when it comes.

Every few hours, I emerge from our cubby to study the

views available through the ribbons, which keep us from being completely blind, like cave fish, up in this needle snout. The clock faces, even when not occupied by a searcher or two, are too cluttered, too abstract—not for the likes of us.

DJ joins me, rubbing his eyes.

"Shit, I fell asleep," he says. "Anything different?"

"Not a thing."

More of the squad emerges, or returns from excursions aft. Going aft makes all of us nervous. Jacobi returns first and looks around with her sharp-eyed squint. She shakes her head. Nothing new there, either. No threats.

"No sign of fighters," she says.

"Tracking Antags?"

"They're busy down south somewhere, close to the clover lake. Still not interacting."

Negatives are mostly good, I think.

Now Kumar, Tak, Joe, and Litvinov join us. Kumar's quiet, as usual. Litvinov just seems depressed.

"Do *starshina* and *efreitor* still control?" he asks for the third or fourth time. "Behind smoke?"

I say, also for the third or fourth time, "Probably."

"Great and powerful wizard," DJ says.

A searcher waits nearby, in case we need help. We don't.

Borden joins us next. "Doesn't seem solid," she says, looking at the curtain. "Probably not hard to penetrate. Anybody been behind?"

Ninth or tenth time for that question. As if we won't announce it loud and clear, when—if—it happens.

"Not yet," I say.

"And you don't want to force the issue?" the commander asks.

"She allows us to see a little of what they're doing, not much," I say.

"They're redecorating," DJ says, and makes room between the ribbons for Ishida and Ishikawa. We're a knot of people holding hands and footing off against the ribbons.

"Steam heat and hot soup," I say. "I think we'll be invited in when Ulyanova is happy with the results."

"Do you guys understand how irritating this is?" Borden asks. "Having to get everything through you!"

"I've never believed it would work," Jacobi says.

Kumar says, "Using the Ice Moon Tea and crystals, taking a chance that one of us could channel a Guru, was the best hope we had."

"Did *that* work?" Jacobi asks, facetious.

"Maybe," I say after a long silence. "We have to trust that the bugs knew more about Gurus than we do."

"A hundred billion years ago!" Ishida says.

"Not that long," DJ murmurs.

"Well, then, you tell me!"

He shrugs. "A long time, not that much."

"This ship has been cruising around the solar system, and outside, for ages," I say. "The most important question is whether the bugs rid themselves of the Gurus way back when... and if they did, whether their tactics can work again."

"Any sign we're being watched by cage dudes?" Joe asks.

"Nothing yet," Borden says.

Litvinov says, "I am curious about screw gardens. Whole ship is filled with them. Maybe we become fertilizer for all the green."

That's a new idea, to me at least. I don't like it, but it touches key biological points well enough.

"Any idea what they are?" Borden asks us.

I shake my head, to her disgust.

Joe says, "If the bugs got rid of the Gurus, how did they come back? Where are they from originally? What can Ulyanova tell us about that?"

"She's communicated bits and pieces about the ship," I say. "But there's lots of stuff that either the Gurus don't know or the ship doesn't know."

"I find that truly dismaying," Kumar says.

"Huh!" Jacobi says.

"How closely connected are the Gurus and this ship?" Borden asks. "How much do they need it to get around and survive?" That may be the smartest question yet.

A long pause. Nobody can answer—but I tuck the question away.

"Heads up," Tak says, looking to the curtain.

Without warning, Vera has passed through. She moves in the spooky fashion she and Ulyanova have mastered, then clambers down the canes to the ribbons, very like a spider, to where we are.

"From now, take searcher if you go aft," she cautions. "They know how to return. Never try to go near or pass through puzzle gate. During next leap, it will be very bad back there. We leave Pluto soon. Next stop, transmitter."

She turns to Litvinov. "*Polkovnik*, gardens on screws are how we move so quick through space. Some plants on Earth plot ahead, all together, to maximize quantum chemistry and bind sunlight. But now they plot, think ahead, to change how slippery space is." She slices her hand out. "Whoosh! Why we sleep. You and me, at least. Where plants go, is difficult for us, since we cannot follow."

"What about the *starshina*?" Litvinov asks.

"Brain needs Queen awake." Vera makes a face and kicks away before we can ask follow-up. A searcher slings itself out from between the clock faces and firmly but politely blocks us from any attempt to go after her.

We haven't been invited. Not yet.

"Servant to 'Queen,'" Litvinov says, shaking his head. "Crazy scheme. And plants! Crazy idea."

"Every ship we've traveled on is different," Jacobi says. "Maybe they're just fucking with us to keep us confused."

"You don't use a bicycle to cross the ocean," Joe says. That's either profound, or profoundly stupid. "Every ship works on a different scale."

"What's that even *mean*?" Jacobi asks.

Ishikawa and Ishida listen to this back-and-forth with unhappy glances. Bilyk seems fascinated. With nobody to converse with in Russian but Litvinov—who doesn't seem interested—the *efreitor* has tried to join our Skyrines, but he's being frozen out by the sisters, possible payback for his comment about blow jobs.

Or maybe they think he's ugly.

———

JACOBI, JOE, MYSELF, and a searcher have ventured aft to see the situation that prevails. Following the cane bridges and with an occasional assist from a helpful searcher, we discover that the Antags have now moved into quarters about a klick behind us, aft and inboard of the nearest screw gardens. We aren't invited to inspect, and make contact with only one or two of them, both armored, both not particularly forthcoming—and after these sentinels send us back, with

824 | GREG BEAR

obvious irritation, our report to the rest of the squad brings up crude speculation, or extended wish fulfillment, that the birds are all engaged in a prolonged, wild orgy.

"Yeah, feathers everywhere," DJ says.

Bilyk laughs too loudly, which brings scorn from Ishikawa and Jacobi. I'm starting to like Bilyk.

Joe and I, with Kumar's tacit approval, say we think it's more likely the Antags are reassembling the social structure they once enjoyed on Mars and Titan, and maybe back home as well. How many males there once were, I don't know. How important the males are to military planning and discipline, I also don't know. Maybe the male is reasserting an aggressive posture and they're planning to come forward and take control of Ulyanova. Her crucial importance is no doubt a sore point with Budgie.

Of course, they could be preparing defenses against the remaining fighters—but we haven't seen any signs of them, either. Bird Girl is being remarkably thorough at staying offline. Maybe they want to keep our channels clear so we can listen for Ulyanova.

Would that mean we're still essential, even to Budgie?

REMEMBRANCE PAST

More hours, more days—more weeks.
Really hard to track.

Vera wasn't being straight with us. Or maybe her Queen wasn't being straight with her.

I've retreated from the cubby, where I now reside alone, to the ribbons, moving aimlessly from ribbon to ribbon. Only about half are illuminated and showing images I can understand—Pluto and occasionally its big moon, Charon. Forward, still visible in the quincunx, the asterisk—there's our mystery ornament, still blocking stars, and otherwise doing nothing.

I keep trying to find refuge in nerding out, but that part of my intellect has become very thin. Bilyk says he once read an article in a Russian science magazine about the quantum capabilities of plants—choosing chemical pathways, planning ahead based on some sort of botanical intuition, a quantum double-down on their chances of fixing photons... So how much weirder is it that the screw gardens can also look ahead and double down on making space *slippery*?

Yeah, it's weirder. Past is no preparation for present. When you keep stepping off the edge of the page and skipping over to another book, it's hard to keep track of the story.

How many months until we take the leap and push the plants in the screw gardens to their limits?

How long until the cage fighters decide to reappear?

I'm just around the corner from stir crazy when DJ and Kumar echo up near. I hide behind a twisted, dark ribbon. I do not want company, not now—certainly not Wait Staff.

They're quietly discussing Planet X—DJ's favorite topic. Another from our squad spiders from the cubbies along the canes to the ribbons, where I recognize him; it's the lonely Russian *efreitor*. Like DJ, Bilyk seems to be a fount of knowledge about science, about astronomy. His English is poor, but they manage to make themselves understood, and I envy them.

They murmur ideas and theories like kids, discussing the surface of our former ninth planet. Kumar listens quietly. Kumar rarely says anything since the Gurus were slaughtered.

Russian scientists (according to Bilyk) tried to figure out what had happened to Pluto, and what might still be happening—tried to understand what smoothed and rearranged those features even into modern geologic times. Pluto had either been subjected to tidal stress or had substantial sources of internal heat—radioactive thorium, possibly, which still keeps Earth warm. One of our Socotra professors described thorium as the atomic battery of creation.

Some speculated that maybe the planet and its moons

had swung close to Neptune during one of Pluto's inward passes—too close, on the edge of the Roche limit, below which the bodies would have broken up completely, joining another set of rings. The grazing orbit would definitely have stressed Pluto, and could have added or subtracted moons for both worlds.

Something had definitely messed with Neptune's big moon Triton, the only satellite in our system with a retrograde orbit. Physically, Triton looks a lot like Pluto—with a supercold nitrogen surface. Could have been imported from the Kuiper belt, just like Pluto.

And whatever pushed Triton around might have tilted Neptune itself into its weird orientation, pole aligned with the planet's orbit. But was Pluto responsible for these disruptions?

Not likely.

Something even larger, farther out—

Big enough to rearrange everything.

Bilyk insists that Russian scientists had long suspected a massive world with an eccentric orbit, way out beyond the edge of the solar system.

DJ enthusiastically agrees.

"Yeah, I'll bet on it—Bird Girl's planet could have made a pass through our system," he says. "It really is Planet X, rolling around the big old billiard table!"

WINTER DREAMS

I'm alone in the nest, still trying not to sleep—too many bad dreams—but drifting off anyway, when I feel a light touch on my wrist and open my eyes with a startled moan. Ishida hangs on a stretched cord a meter away, her metal arm and the metal half of her face gleaming in the light from a strip outside the round opening. Her hand hovers over my wrist, shining fingers suspended, silent, no quiver or betrayal of flesh—steady hand, steady body. One of the most steady of our Skyrines.

"What's it like?" she asks after a murmured apology for waking me.

"What's what like?"

"Being dosed with tea."

I stretch a little. Exercise is difficult under these conditions, consisting mostly of choosing a partner—usually Tak or Joe—and trying to run in a circle inside a nest, or wrestle while hanging on to canes. I feel stiff and unsure. This isn't the first time I've noticed Ishida paying attention to me, and I've certainly paid attention to her, but there was a kind of lost cause about the whole situation, the attraction, for so many reasons, and now I'm embarrassed that she's made the first move. We haven't exactly violated any code, but I always thought a beautiful woman should have the luxury of not having to make the first approach—if this is an approach.

Truth is, she *is* beautiful—strange and strong and beautiful. I've never known what to make of her or her situation. But now she's neatly reversed the puzzle.

"Kind of like dreaming while awake," I say. "There's a part..." I pause, not sure she wants details.

"Go on," she says, not actually touching my wrist.

"There's a part that's separate." I tell her about the sensation of word balloons being filled, which was true for both Captain Coyle and often enough for Bird Girl. "But they aren't actually word balloons, just parts of me that aren't really from me." I shrug.

"I get it," she says. "Can I tell you what I feel, sometimes?"

"Sure," I say.

"After I was hurt—in training on Socotra—I was taken to a field hospital and things sort of blanked out."

I nod. "Yeah," I say.

"When I woke up, the surgeons and the mechanics were eager to talk to me. They were Japanese, and very proud of what they had done."

"It looks like fine work," I say. "And you're still here."

"But everything felt different. They'd saved most of my internal organs, but hooked them up to a layer of what they called false tissue, to pad the metal parts when I bumped around. Plastic buffers and slings. Combat-ready, they said. I could do anything I wanted. I'd live a good, long, active life."

"Wow," I say.

"Felt strange to move."

"I bet."

"But none of them wanted to spend much time with me," she says. "Always busy. Moving on. They spoke Japanese, not English, but used an inflection, like they were speaking to a servant, an untouchable. A *Korean*. That made me sad, but I had seen it before. Female soldiers...We get kind of lost, even in the new Japan."

"Wow," I say. Tak had never mentioned such attitudes, but we'd heard about them.

"Do you have things that protect you, cushion you, when you speak with Bird Girl or the bugs?"

"I don't speak with the archives now. That was back on Titan, and we—I mean, humans—pretty much wiped out those voices."

"I always thought that part was fascinating. Captain Jacobi gets weirded out, but we—the Japanese sisters—we feel a little more familiar with the idea—with being hooked up to *kami*. Maybe just from anime, but...more familiar."

"I remember the markings on your suits. *Senketsu* and *Junketsu*. Anime?"

"Old anime, old-fashioned. Lots of jiggle. Nothing like that in Japan now. Mostly heroes and history and emperors and such."

"Right," I say. Oddly, my sense of discomfort is fading. I'm next to her, she's talking to me, more than ice has been broken—a new protocol is being established.

Technically, Skyrines are not supposed to open up to the possibility of anything sexual or romantic, but of course we do. Some of us get in trouble, but usually only when rank is involved, or one of a pair or team gets out of bounds, professionally and emotionally, and feels left out, badly used. Because of that, and because my stations have been hard and desperate, I've never established anything I could call a romance with a Skyrine. I've thought about it in a vague way, of course, but it's never come up.

And now it seems to be coming up, starting out as a letting down of the barriers, telling stories—enjoying company. While alone. Which I am. My roommates have all cleared out, or I've left them in the other cubbies and set out on my own. Maybe they knew before I did.

Other than to DJ or Joe or Tak, I haven't talked much at all about the links, what it's like to be dosed with the tea… not much at all.

Ishida asks, "When you interact with Bird Girl, what do you see?"

"Mostly hear, rarely see," I say. "Sometimes there are hints of deep stuff, but mostly it's what she wants me to hear. When Captain Coyle faded, she handed me over to Bird Girl, and she served as bug steward, hooked me up to the archives on Titan, which she knew pretty well by then. DJ got hooked up to her as well, but Bird Girl seems to favor dealing with me."

"I like DJ, but you're different," Ishida says.

"DJ is okay," I say, as if giving her an out. "We've served together a long time. He's a real friend, and he's funnier than me."

"But you're the one I'm talking to," Ishida says. My level of embarrassment returns. It would be very bad for my long-term opinion of myself if I said something awkward to this fellow Skyrine, either about her being Japanese, about those difficulties—we hear so many stories, and not all of them are true, probably—or being a Winter Soldier. Same there. So many points where I could get things very wrong. I do know it's hard for female soldiers in Japan now, as everything has gotten so conservative, reverting to historical norms—but I have no idea what to say about that, what I know, and what crap I've just heard that's all wrong.

And then her being half-metal. Sort of. Metal and colloid and plastic and all kinds of synthetics. Half-organic. She's almost like an angel from Fiddler's Green, most of her organs intact, saved, stuffed back in, fully functional.

I'm far more ignorant about all that.

So I stop talking and just tilt my head, big eyes, sad smile, like a real asshole. She skips past all this, cutting me substantial slack, and gets to her point.

"I need to talk to somebody who's male and who I respect," she says, "and who knows what it means to hook up with something that isn't you. Something essential—but really different."

"I'm listening," I say. I've always preferred listening. The last girlfriend I had, back in Virginia Beach—and where is she now?—left me because she thought I didn't care. I just listened more than I talked, and it turned out she took that all wrong. So off she went. We'd been together for two weeks. Longest I've ever been involved. Joe always seems to do better with women.

"Don't take this wrong, the wrong way, but I'm not all there," Ishida says with a kind of hiccup. "Not yet. I'm scheduled to be attached—that's what they call it, but it hasn't happened yet, there hasn't been time. Does that bother you?"

I don't know whether it does or not. Again, what boundaries can I cross and cause pain by so doing?

"You're beautiful, I know that much," I say.

She keeps staring at me, with one natural eye and one mechanical eye.

"It's like a new kind of beauty," I say. "I don't know about all the rest. Maybe it's not important right now."

"But it will be, right? If I'm going to stay human. And that's...that's what I think about you. Are you still human?"

"Mostly," I say, as if it's a joke.

"I don't think it's a funny question," Ishida says. "I thought I was no longer a woman, but that turned out to be wrong." Still watching me. "I feel *everything*, I feel the old... parts...as if they were still there. But I reach down and they aren't. Just skin and metal."

"I've heard about that," I say. "Phantom limbs."

"Phantom cunt!" Ishida says, with the most brilliant shy smile on half of her face, lighting up her eye and seeming like a prelude to something sadder, more direct and painful. "I dream about it. And someday, I'll go back to Madigan or Sasebo or somewhere and get the plumbing finished off. Get hooked up. I'll stop being half a female and be a whole one. They say I can even have kids, through caesarean—through a hatch!" She raises her hand and giggles behind it. "I'd enjoy having a family. I come from a big family."

"Best of luck," I say.

"I don't think any Japanese man will have me," she says.

"Try a Skyrine," I say. "They've seen a lot."

"Yeah. Wonder if that would ever work." She smiles... at me. "What I miss most is just talking. Relaxing. Holding. Until I get hooked up again, right?"

Her need, her expression, her words—so direct. So human and appropriate. I slowly reach out and pull her toward me.

We hold each other for a few minutes, nothing much more, and she snuggles into my arm, flesh face against my skin, keeping the metal side away.

"My God," she murmurs. "You're hard. That is sweet. That is special."

I touch her face with one hand, stroking lightly along the boundary between metal and flesh, and then, touching the metal.

"I feel that, too," she says. "I feel all of my other half. It's almost normal to me now. Is that Guru tech?"

"I don't know," I say. "Maybe. But we'd have found it eventually."

"Sometimes I wake up and think it's all just the old me. And sometimes when I sleep...I think the metal half is dreaming. I can never remember, but that's what I think."

"Then you understand me," I say.

"It's like that?"

I nod and keep stroking her faces. Her face. The metal side is warm and...

I get lost in my thoughts.

DAYS OF FUTURE PAST

For days now, Joe's scalp, DJ's scalp, Tak's scalp, and my scalp have all been itching, and we don't think it's lice. Feels like team spirit.

Feels like fucking *change*.

The waiting has become nasty, unbearable. We've been making plans to gather up what weapons we can and head aft to find the cage fighters, or whatever's left of them. Why haven't they made their move? Any move? We're bored out of our minds! We're about to unveil those plans to Jacobi and Borden when everything suddenly speeds up.

It's Jacobi's turn to study the "asterisk" and the mystery ornament, and she sees the change first.

Change *outside* the ship.

"Hey," she says, softly at first, as if in awe—then louder. "*Hey*! It's different."

DJ and Bilyk and I join her.

"Different how?" DJ asks.

"Major!" she says. "Now it's hollow in the center, like a donut. What the hell does that mean?"

We study the ornament's silhouette, the way stars appear around and behind it, and have to agree.

Kumar joins us. He studies the changes with a frown, and shakes his head. "It means nothing," he murmurs. "It has no meaning!"

"Hasn't it been out here forever?" Jacobi asks. "Since before the bugs?"

Kumar shudders. "*She* is here," he says, and turns.

For the first time in weeks, Ulyanova emerges from behind the curtain, surprising us all. Vera is right behind her, as if carrying her invisible train.

We make space for the pair. "You see that?" I prompt the *starshina*.

"Brain of ship sees," Ulyanova says. She spins slowly.

"Brain have an opinion?" DJ asks.

"Planets will be put in motion," she says. "Soon, one large world, but many, maybe dozens."

"When?"

"Hundreds of thousands of years."

None of us knows what to make of that. DJ looks at Bilyk, then at me. Both shrug.

"Has ship seen this sort of thing before?" I ask.

"Yes. Is old."

"Are there other things out there, like this?" DJ asks.

"In most systems, is at least one."

"You mean, systems with planets?" DJ asks.

"They move moons and planets," Ulyanova says coldly. "That is all they do."

"Got to have power for that!" DJ says.

"Is most powerful thing here, but for sun," Ulyanova says. Vera is impatient. She wants to get back behind the curtain. "Let us leave," she says.

Ulyanova says, "Come to tell you, decades ago, mission before Mars and Titan, ship went out to other warm world in Kuiper belt, collected another population—and moved them to Sun-Planet."

"What sort of population?"

"Excellent warriors. Ship became large to hold them. Soon, it will grow inside, as it grew before bringing humans and Antags to war. It will make more and different weapons, to please larger and different audience. Dangerous times! Brain is restless, eager to return last of Antags, give them chance to fight before all die. Be ready for sleep."

She and Vera—Vera is immensely relieved—rotate to slip back behind the curtain, leaving us shrouded in mystery without context—except that something has changed that never does, and the Gurus are full of surprises.

Sun-Planet may already be under siege. Does Bird Girl know? Budgie? Do we tell them?

Perhaps not if we value our lives.

Joe looks right at me. Right through me.

"God*dammit*," he says.

We make a desperate move for the cubbies, but before we can all hide away...

Something strange, something wicked.

The leap.

SLEEP OF REASON

There's no sleep like bad sleep. Just because the universe doesn't count the total trip time against us, so far as we know, that doesn't mean it doesn't pass somewhere, somehow. What's it like to be half-aware of blind blankness for ten thousand years? I'd like to tell you, but there aren't words.

When we come awake again—fully awake and not just numbly miserable—most of us are scattered, some in the cubbies, a few in the canes, Bilyk and DJ jammed between ribbons—squirming. We pull our squad together and inspect ourselves, creepily convinced we've shriveled like the corpses in the cages. But we don't seem to have changed at all.

"Join the Skyrines and tour hell," Jacobi says.

Tak comments how different this is from the trip on *Lady of Yue*, where we came awake fresh and raring to go. Every scale has a different feel, brings a new set of questions.

Like, what's this thin layer of sparkling dust on our skin and clothes? We all start rubbing, as if we could wipe away everything that's happened.

"Searcher dust," Jacobi says. The searchers attend to us like patient servants, silent, respectful. Jacobi isn't happy with them, however. As they try to help her brush away the dust, she hits them with clenched fists—an exercise in futility. They back off, but do not otherwise react.

"I hate how they just don't get mad!" Jacobi says.

"Let them be," Tak says. "They're not hurting anyone."

"They're fucking squids, goddammit!" Jacobi says. We've all gone so far from discipline and training that anything can happen to us, around us, and we wouldn't know how to react.

Ishida holds up her metal hand, covered with little bright points. We watch them fade. After the sparkling dust evaporates, leaving only a cool tingle, we wonder if it was ever there at all.

"Anybody want to swear off having kids?" Ishikawa asks.

"Solemnly," Ishida says.

DELIVERY AND REJECTION

Ornament is gone, but something else is out there," Borden says, kicking off a ribbon, rotating around her abdominal axis to search what she can see of the sky. "Not the mover. Don't see that anymore."

We can barely make out a dim pair of gray fans, subtending several degrees of the big sky. Ship is either very close, or the fans are very large.

"That must be the transmitter," Kumar says.

"What are those?" Borden asks.

Possibly even more surprising, smaller vessels have departed from our monster ship and move toward the gray fans. They're too far away already and too small to make out details.

"Are those Antag ships?" Ishikawa asks.

"Don't think so," Borden says.

"This thing can make other ships?" Ishikawa asks, almost hopeful.

"No surprise," Tak says. "They taught us how to build Spook and the centipedes, right?"

"Are they doing maintenance or dropping off supplies?" Jacobi asks.

"Maybe they're delivering tapes for broadcast," DJ says. Bilyk, who regards Ulyanova and Vera, when they're around, as if they inhabit some sort of movable nightmare—friends he no longer knows—goggles at this.

"You still don't get it, do you, man?" DJ chides him.

Bilyk shakes his head. "We are for movies?" he asks.

"Yeah, for movies," DJ says.

"Anybody notice we're no longer necessary for anything?" Ishida asks, her voice small. She's keeping close to me, as if I can supply some sort of comfort, or at least a solid center.

I wish.

Kumar joins Borden and they almost touch the crowns of their heads as they spread out along a ribbon, trying to survey everything that can be seen—a long, narrow slice of sky way beyond the sun, the bridge of stars cutting across the slice, cold and steady—just the same as when we departed. Parallax nil despite our journey.

"When are we leaving to find the fighters?" Tak asks Joe as we move off from the ribbons, back to the cubbies.

Joe makes a face. "When we're through with these fucking leaps and sleeps," he said.

"We don't make our own schedule?" Tak asks. "What if they move before we do?"

"You want to go blank, up against a monster?"

Tak kicks away, disgusted.

LEAVE NOTICE AT THE DOOR

A few hours later, the outbound ships have finished their mission. They grow to specks and seem to be trying to return, but one by one blossom into small, brilliant clouds of plasma.

"Jesus!" Borden says and grips a searcher arm as if for assurance. The searcher sighs like a teakettle but otherwise neither moves, resists, or reacts. The clouds flash brilliant colors, then fade to gray—and spread out until they're gone.

"Expendable?" Litvinov asks.

"Maybe not even real," Kumar muses.

"What if they tried to deliver something—and somebody interfered?" Borden asks. She's got a funny look on her face and starts to hand-over to the cubbies.

"What if they tried to deliver…and nobody wanted it?" I ask.

"What are you saying, Venn—we're no longer A-list?" Jacobi asks.

"Jesus, my scalp again," Joe says.

The others agree.

"Get ready!"

Again, except for Borden, no time to get to our cubbies. Our Skyrines hug like koalas. They do not want to make the leap while the searchers are touching them. As if we could get jumbled up with a catamaran squid or two and come out looking like a plate of sushi. Who knows?

"Crap!" Jacobi says as the blankness descends.

SUN-PLANET

My mind slowly tries to boot up. I think I remember the ribbons, expect the waking bodies of my squad, three or four of them arranged loosely around me...

But first, there's a funny, dreamlike state where I'm back at Hawthorne, in the bar, listening to Joe half-drunkenly try to explain his views about the giant F-bomb reserves kept stored in tanks near Los Angeles and New York.

The other grunts and soldiers in the bar are skeptical.

"Sure, it's true," Joe says. "Before the war—the Second World War—F-bombs were strictly limited to military use. Illegal to use them in print or in movies, or in public—unless you were a criminal and didn't care."

"Didn't *fucking* care," says one of our fellow recruits. Might be DJ, but I can't see him clearly.

"Right," Joe says. "But the reservoirs holding the F-bombs were badly constructed. They were porous. Some leaked out into the water supply in New York, and then in Los Angeles. The plume of F-words didn't get very far, but by the 1960s it was too late—everyone was drinking that water and dropping F-bombs twenty-four/seven. The military couldn't stop it. So now, not just soldiers—everybody uses them."

"But what was the point?" asks another grunt I don't really want to think about—Grover Sudbury. We're back before he did his awful thing and we did ours, and then Joe did his. He's just another grunt in this bar, no better or worse than any other.

"Soldiers use F-bombs to keep themselves grounded, to remind themselves they're human, to remind them what they give up when they fight and die," Joe says. "Helps blow off some of the violence and weird crap that violence shoves into our brains. We use them, and we become better at managing a shitty situation."

Sudbury is still skeptical.

"Now everybody uses them, and look where we are," Joe says.

"Where the *fuck* we are," says the other soldier.

I linger on Sudbury's face. I want to talk to him, to warn him not to act out being a cruel asshole, but the memory-state, dream-state fragments into glassy shards of pain in my jaw, my arms, my chest.

Now I'm awake, but I don't believe it. I don't want to believe. I've been dragged from the others and tangled in a cane wall. A few of the canes have penetrated my pajamas and pin me like an insect in a museum. I hurt all over. Worse, my arms and legs, my hands, look lumpy. My entire *skin* feels hot and bruised.

I extricate myself from the brake, pull out the canes that poke through my clothes, and after a few minutes, float free— but my confusion is total. I don't see anyone else. I think

I'm alone, but then, I make a half turn and see a searcher a few meters away, slowly rotating in the half dark. It's been butchered—arms hacked away and hanging by the outer plates, midsection almost cut in half, eyes gouged out. More than one attacker, I think—the squid may be peaceful, but they're also strong.

It's taking me much longer than before to assemble my conscious self, and it's all tangled with memories I can't place, like dreams being edited and erased.

Then a voice rises from a buzzing pool of memory. It's the first thing I'm absolutely sure about—harsh, hoarse, angry, and putting an emphasis on every single thump I'm receiving. *"Never... thought... I'd find... YOU, did you? After what you guys... DID to me."*

I know that voice. But from where, from when? Was it my mother's boyfriend? The one I shot? I doubt it. But in my haze I remember Mom lying in bed covered with bruises after he beat her up, and I'm thinking, *No more of this—no more of him, not ever, why does she put up with it?*

And now—

Vera has awakened some of us personally. There's a look of concern on her face as she shakes us one by one. It takes hard shaking for some—for DJ in particular, but also for Joe and Tak.

We've all just had the crap beaten out of us.

"What the hell happened?" Joe asks. "Christ, I'm bloody! So are you."

"Yeah," Tak says ruefully. "I couldn't fight back."

He looks at me as he tries to flex life into his limbs. I touch my own face, feeling the swollen lips and cheeks, the crusted blood. We examine DJ. Blood and bruises all over. My sight is returning in a spotty manner, as if I'm looking through a slatted window.

How did I let it happen? What is this, some sort of sympathetic response, welting and pain as my mind is probed by Gurus? Feels wrong, feels crazy. They say you don't remember pain, but new pain flares with every move I make. Something or someone struck me repeatedly. Someone I once knew.

Someone almost human.

So I lean into the memories and bring it *all* back—the smiling, heavily scarred face leaning over me in the gloom, the same piggy eyes and interrupted eyebrows, but now with nose almost smashed flat. Long since healed but pug-uglier than I remember him.

"Did you see him?" DJ asks. "He was laughing. Really enjoying himself. Then the squids moved in and tried to separate everybody. Man, you wouldn't know they can't fight."

"Someone we knew," I say. "I couldn't wake up."

"Sudbury! Fucking Grover Sudbury!" DJ shouts, expelling a fine spray of blood. "He and some other fuckers."

"Some human, some not," Joe says through broken lips. He holds his head as if it needs to be glued back together. "The searchers stopped them from killing us."

The smile, the words, the delight Sudbury took in striking me with the back of his gnarly hand, over and over.

Ishida approaches carefully out of the fairy light. She points to the cubbies and cane bridges. "A lot of searchers. Looks like they tried to protect us."

"They fought?" Tak asks.

"They died."

Borden emerges from her cubby, the entrance of which

has almost been blocked by a dead searcher. She shoves it into a slow, broken-armed spin. "What the hell happened here?"

"I knew we shouldn't have waited!" Tak cries out.

"What do you think, Venn?" Borden asks.

"It was Sudbury," I confirm. "Not alone. Another human and as DJ says, a couple of *things*. Not human."

"Not Antag?"

I shake my head. "Didn't see any."

There are maybe five dead searchers in the ribbon space, up between the clock faces, in the canes—hacked, carved, gouged. Three more are spaced before the curtain, still alive, sighing and flexing. One isn't moving and is being examined by its fellows. The plates along its skin are flaccid, peeling away. Who would be strong enough to kill a squid? I've felt the grip of their arms and can imagine what they could do to defend themselves.

Tak runs another inventory on DJ's face, his hands. Then me. "Did a real number," he murmurs, flexing my jaw, prodding my cheek. My whole face seems to explode, and I jerk away, but he says, "Nothing broken I can feel."

Ishikawa and Jacobi seem barely touched. Ishida checks over Litvinov and Bilyk, but Bilyk shakes her off with an accusing look.

"Four of you seem to have borne the brunt of injuries," Kumar says.

"I still don't remember," Joe says.

Vera shakes her head with cold anger. Then she takes me by the arm. Her hand is tight and wiry, firm. "She will speak with you, if you can go, if you can move."

"Just me?"

"Just you," Vera says. The others watch suspiciously.

"I'll go," I say. "I can move."

"I'd like to come," Borden says.

"No," Vera says, and leads me toward the curtain. The searchers move the bodies and themselves aside. I try to keep from crying out in pain, but Tak's right, there are no broken bones—I think.

The curtain gets closer. After what I've been through, I don't want to touch it, or it to touch me. I turn my face aside, lean my head back, and one hand grips the other, to keep it from flailing.

"No fear," Vera says.

We pass through. Feels like thin cotton wool, like a warm breeze. Vera tugs my arm again. "Rules change. Queen can explain!"

Rules change? Now the rules allow Grover Sudbury to come back from the dead and beat the crap out of me, out of us, and start murdering searchers? Is the ship's brain breaking free of Ulyanova and trying to kill us all and regain control?

Vera seems to read my mind. "Ship does not care," she says. "Ship goes, ship makes. It makes for Queen, for *star-shina*. She is waiting."

The smoky fog swirls and for a second I feel my stomach heave up emptiness...but then my feet touch floor. Flat floor. Things have reliable direction, up and down. I stand. The nausea fades. Ahead, a plaster wall shapes itself and corners with the floor. The floor spreads before me a paint of cracked, chipped, dirty black-and-white ceramic tile. The tile acquires a shallow depth and detail. What's left of the grout is dark with dirt, as if it's never been scrubbed.

Arrives before us a wainscot with a beat-up wooden strip and worn wallpaper printed with tiny flowers. The floor and wall become part of a long hallway that smells of cabbage and bacon. I hear voices from down the hallway, tinny laughter—children shouting.

"Ship cares not much about us," Vera says. "But *she* is still Queen. You cannot know how much it hurts her!"

Vera opens a wood-panel door. We step through. Beyond lies a small apartment: three tiny, overheated rooms, a kitchen to the right, half-hidden in dark orange light, where someone makes sharp noises with pots and dishes. An old refrigerator sticks out of the kitchen, humming and buzzing. Through another door, half-open, I see a bedroom, a small bed on a gray pipe frame, paint flaking.

I'm more than half-convinced I'm going through another instauration—but this time, perhaps not mine. Maybe Ulyanova's or Vera's.

I tongue my mouth and realize I've lost a couple of teeth. Through all of my childhood and my adventures with Joe, through Mars and training back on Earth, I never lost teeth. Fuck, that's a mortal insult.

Shoes are neatly paired beside the foot of the bed, men's shoes, and a short, flower-print dress has been draped across the gray and pink quilted cover. A dress suitable for a party.

Ulyanova emerges from the kitchen, holding a pot filled with steaming potatoes. "Hard journey!" she says, with a pale, stressed-out smile. "You don't know how wicked ship can be." She raises her arms—and the pot goes away. Some of the steam remains. Then she wipes her hand on a towel. She's looking, if that's possible, even worse. Like me, she's lost some teeth—but not through being beaten. I think she's malnourished, despite the potatoes. What's real here and what isn't?

"We have arrived around *Antagonista* home," Vera says. "Nobody knows we are here—again, we are invisible."

Ulyanova avoids meeting my eyes. Gray, finely wrinkled around her face and neck—as if she has grown old here! And Vera is looking older as well. They're becoming part of this apartment, this life—this instauration.

"Look at him, he is hurt!" Vera says, and suddenly, as if our Guru Queen has seen me for the first time, she notices the blood and swelling.

"Get him ice and a rag," she tells Vera, her voice deadly calm.

Vera goes to the kitchen and brings back ice wrapped in a worn towel. Both of them apply it to my face, my neck, my forearms. Feels cold. Soothes—a little.

"Do you know what's happened?" I ask. "The cage fighters—"

"I know," she says. "Like I said, when I opened gate. Did you not watch for them?"

"They came during the leap, while we were still… stunned."

"Ah," she says. "They learn not to sleep, like me. Vera, find chair for Vinnie. We must talk."

"The ship didn't tell you they would find us, attack us… that way, that time?"

She shakes her head. "Ship has its motives. Vera! Chair!"

Vera brings forward a cheap dining chair, made of deal and pine. As I sit, I look left. Filmy white drapes billow before a narrow glass door that opens to a shallow patio with cheap iron rails. Through the drapes, as they slowly flap and spread, I see that beyond and across a narrow street, other apartment buildings rise gray and stolid.

How far does the illusion go? How real is it out there? How far can she walk across town, to the park, up and down the streets—when she wants to relax? Queen of the apartment. Of the world outside. Queen of the voices and the children, of the blocks that could very well be out there, if I wanted to look.

"Queen of the city," I say.

"It is what I tell her!" Vera says. "Queen of Moscow, of all we see. Here Gurus once live and dream of other lifes. But now—only her."

"I am not entirely queen," Ulyanova says, with an irritated glance at Vera. "Wrong move, *boring* move, and ship knows, brain knows—everything will change. All will die."

"How many human fighters were in the cages?" I ask.

"Fifteen. Some have died since. Humans not best at cage fighting, it seems."

"Where did the others come from?"

"From where ship has been."

"Between stars?" I ask.

"No. Big planets out where comets are born. Ship has already carried beings not from Earth, out to *Antagonista* planet. I warned you."

"Right."

I want to get back, organize...warn Bird Girl and the Antags. If they don't already know.

"A few planets swing down through system every thousand centuries," Vera says, as if reciting from a textbook. What sorts of beings would grow up on all these worlds? The cold ones, the warm ones? How much more complicated can this get?

"What's all that to this ship? To the Gurus?"

"Victors of long fights in cages explore, find you. I lose searchers. Do fighters know you? *Hate* you?" She nearly aspirates the word.

"One does," I say.

"Male?"

"Yeah. Barely. A monster."

"Why does this one want to kill you?"

"Four of us helped put him on this ship, indirectly, ignorantly—years ago."

"The cage fighters kill Antags, searchers—kill with much pain. Pain as they have experienced, and more."

Her face is so like the face of my mother the morning after she woke up and her boyfriend was gone. Quiet. Not in the least curious. Almost dead-looking. She cooked eggs and made me breakfast.

"Why do you let them move around?" I ask her. "Why not just cage them again?"

"Think!" Vera cries. "She tells you! Even now, she plays game with ship. She builds walls inside. Ghosts cannot cross. Brain cannot hear."

Ulyanova gives me her own sadly critical look. "Brain and ghosts are fascinated by revenge. And so am I. When I open gate, as if to test me, cages open as well. I can do nothing. I cannot protect! I must not. I must not show you are important to me."

Despite the ice, my whole body aches. I dread the thought of what I might find if we go aft...if we do what we have to do.

"You are more *interesting* if you fight," Ulyanova says softly, moving near the window. She seems to want to lean into the sunlight, the breeze through the filmy white drapes.

"And you will live…if you fight. Be as brave as searchers, who do not fight—but protect, and die."

This discussion has long since crossed the line to scaring the shit out of me. So casual, so isolated—behind the curtain. How much time does Ulyanova have before the brain, the ship, the *ghosts* catch on to our little ruse?

She's playing with me. She's making my life more interesting by making me think she controls. How long can that be enough of an excuse? Until we get boring. Then we'll just be fused like those fucking ships coming back from the transmitter. Maybe the cage fighters are just prelude to that.

Ulyanova straightens and walks around a beat-up coffee table. "Worse is done by Gurus, by ship, before we come. Years before battle seasons on Mars, on Titan, ship grew, ship traveled to a large moon. This moon orbits two worlds, tossed and heated for billions of years…Kept alive without sun, not made by bugs, but older, with very strong inhabitants. Ship auditioned them in little wars, then gathered them by tens of thousands…and carried them to Sun-Planet. It supplied them with arms and landed them…to eliminate *Antagonista* and searchers. New soldiers, new species—not affected by bug archives. Very popular for Gurus. New show begins."

Vera says sadly, "*Antagonista* have no home. Nearly all have died. For those we carry, there will be one last, short war, short fight…death."

"What if you help them?" I ask, my heart suddenly made of lead.

"I will confirm this mask. And then, ship will cancel us."

The heat in the fake Russian apartment is muggy, oppressive. "What happens to us, then? If we kill the cage fighters, stay interesting…Are we going to leave the ship and fight down there, on Sun-Planet, with them?" I ask.

"Antags will leave ship. It is their duty," Ulyanova says. "Hard part comes after."

"We must not let Guru plans finish," Vera says.

"I tell Verushka. If I do not stay Queen, ship will gather fighters from yet more moons, more worlds—also not from bugs. Ship will deliver them to Earth. Many, many of them. Soon it will prepare by growing for them new weapons, interesting weapons, evenly matched—and more ships.

"These new recruits, brought to Earth, will be told story, like what Gurus told us—and they will fight to kill humans, all humans, and then, will be set up for long war against those victorious on Sun-Planet. Not *Antagonista*. Those will already be dead.

"But I have my own plan. If I stay in control, if I do not make stupid move! First, we will go to Mars and Earth and gather up last of Gurus, and last of those Wait Staff and leaders who live only for Gurus. They will be brought into ship and receive promotions, live as we do. For days, they will be happy." She points out the window at the long, hot summer of Moscow.

"Brain and ghosts will be happy. If I convince, if I am *interesting*, they may do what I say. I will send you off on ships that carried Gurus and traitors, and you will return to Earth. Then Guru ship will begin trip to far place, to opposite system—three hundred billion klicks. Very long leap."

In my head, she's helping me see that path, that grazing, high-speed journey out beyond everything we know, out to the far side of the Kuiper belt.

And I see her opportunity quite clearly. Just a twitch, really. A very small deviation.

"I will help ship finish well," she says.

Vera shivers.

"I will stay," Ulyanova says. "To finish my work. Vera…"

"I will stay, too," Vera says.

"But now, Antag ships are free to go home," Ulyanova says. "There is nothing for them to return to. So they will die sadly, valiantly. They have honor. Ghosts and brain love tragic homecoming."

I'm so lost now in useless backtracking that I start asking really dumb questions. "What about the Gurus who died? How does the ship, the brain react to that?"

"Ship can make more Gurus, if there is need. Ship can even replace itself, given warning. But not in sun." Her smile is maddening. "You heard *Antagonista* female," Ulyanova says. "She wants I will die, after I am used."

I can't think how Ulyanova heard that. Perhaps the ship ratted us out. Maybe those of us on the tea have no secrets— boring, lost, all our stories nearing their sad ends.

"You think the rest of us want to kill you?" I ask. "Rather than take a risk you'll fail?"

"Yes," Ulyanova says. "Would ship make new me, I wonder? Can you *see*, Vinnie? I dance on edge of knife. We play with brain. Brain plays with us. All to make story. Audiences wait. We might be popular again—as popular as those who fought on ship for years, fought and died. You sent them here, from Earth—and so did we."

"So did *Antagonista*," Vera says. "Many worlds contribute."

"How did the cage fighters stay awake?" I ask. "Why didn't they sleep, like us?"

"Many trips. If they not awake, others kill them. So… they adapt. They learn, do not sleep, no matter how long the time, how hard the trip. Like me. If I sleep, ship knows me to my soul…For now, plan is good. Ship is happy to return to Earth, to Mars, to pick up Gurus, then travel far and start new big show."

Vera's expression is that of a deeply puzzled child, as if this is finally getting to her. Madness leads. Reason sleeps. And sitting on the knife's edge, two of our own, willing to do—what?

It seems to me they've got it good here. A waking dream of home.

"You help me open gate," Ulyanova says. She waggles her fingers and the pot with potatoes reappears. "I remove Guru bombs from your head, use them…All but one. There is one more time I will reach out and use it to speak to you. And after that, one more time we will see each other here."

She carries the pot back to the kitchen.

"Now go," Vera says, shooing me. "Tell others Queen is tired. Being Guru is difficult." With a quick backward glance, Vera follows me out the door to the hallway and then through the curtain, into the ribbon space, still dark, empty now—where have the others gone?—but for the drifting shadow of another dead searcher, its arms hacked away, blood drifting in beads and fist-sized green-brown gobs around the blinded ribbons. The blood has formed a wrinkled crust, making the gobs look like big raisins. I wonder how it got here—killed recently, another fight?

But the blood is old. This one has drifted forward, more likely.

Vera inspects the corpse and *hmm*s sad sympathy. Then

she takes my arm and spins me around, as if we're dancing in the dark, between the drops of searcher blood. "I do not know how, or even if, Queen fools ship, brain, ghosts. They make hard time. She never sleeps, not to let them in."

"But she's back home—you're back, too, right? This is the best you've had in years. What would you give to keep it this way?"

Vera looks at me as if I am some sort of vermin, a spider, a filthy mouse.

"Do you get out and go for walks on the streets, through the city?" I ask. "Do you live a normal life? Enjoy the weather? Is it all out there, a *solid* dream?"

I can't shake the layers of illusion, both the ones behind the curtain and the ones that wrap my own thoughts. Maybe we're all still caught up in Guru mind shit. Maybe everything is no more or less real than Ulyanova's apartment, her pot of potatoes.

Is it possible for me, for any of us, to break free of whatever has been ordained by the Gurus or by their great resource, their master, their reservoir—this fucking ship?

"What is that to you?" Vera says, keeping her voice low.

"Do you know it isn't real?"

"Queen knows," Vera says tightly. "This life will end soon enough. Now go!"

She shoos me again, then returns to the curtain.

———

"How is she?" Borden asks.

"They seem strung-out but in control, for the time being," I say.

Kumar joins us at the asterisk. The ribbons are still dark.

All we can see is the illumination from a thin coat of searcher skin juice, probably from the beaten and murdered, scattering deep-ocean guidance around our living spaces.

"How long have I been gone?" I ask.

"Hours!" Kumar says.

"Didn't feel that long."

"DJ, Sanchez, and Jacobi have gone aft," Borden says. Makes me feel a little sick, that they didn't wait. "They should be back any time now. I've ordered Tak and Ishida and Ishikawa to keep guard aft of the ribbon space, in case Antags come forward and try to catch us by surprise."

"Why would they do that?" I ask.

"We've already found dead Antags. They might blame us."

Litvinov returns from going forward, along the nose. "Is nothing but hollow," he says. "Empty. What about Ulyanova and Verushka? Is still sane?"

I try to describe their situation—the apartment, the warmth, the familiar comforts of home.

"Life of Gurus!" Litvinov says. "Are they in danger from fighters? From criminals?"

"I don't think so. But both are looking older. There's definitely a cost. Ulyanova says the Antags are about to be badly disappointed." I tell them more about the ship's past journeys, the rearrangements and transfers from far worlds to Sun-Planet. "The Gurus have been planning for some time to get rid of bug influence."

Kumar listens intently. "We have failed them, I suppose," he says, still groggy. Nobody's paying much attention to him, not even Borden. I check him over but there doesn't seem to be any particular injury—his bruising is light. "I am fine," he insists, waving me aside. "Do you still connect with Bird Girl?"

"Just more of that baseline signal. They're alive, they're busy, they don't seem to want to interact...and the big male is the core of their efforts. They want to take him home. They all just want to go home."

"But they do not know the situation?" Kumar asks.

"If what Ulyanova says is true," Borden says.

"If they don't," I say, "they could learn very soon."

Joe, DJ, and Jacobi return to the ribbon space. All are looking more than a little out of it, as if the scale of what they've seen takes time to absorb, and there is no time.

"Ship is changing all the way back," DJ says, taking a deep breath.

"Fighters?"

"Three dead ones," DJ says.

"All nonhuman," Jacobi says.

"Hurray for our side," Borden says.

"There are dead searchers and a few Antags all along the route we took, trying to follow the spine of the ship," Joe says. "The cage fighters must have caught them by surprise—like us."

"You can't believe what's going on back there," DJ says. "There's a gigantic tree-thing growing down the center-line, between the screw gardens and over the clover lake—branching and fruiting all sorts of mechanical shit, like making apples!"

"Armaments for our new opposition," Kumar says. "I would like to see those growths. We might understand what sort of creatures they're hoping to use to extinguish us."

"The searchers aren't being much help," DJ says. "All we saw are dead—dozens of them. But remember that transport we used around the screw garden?" He seems unwilling to continue until we admit we remember that much.

"Well," he says, weirdly satisfied, as if he's sounding out our sanity, "there's something like that along the tree, maybe half a dozen tracks moving in and around the branches, carrying shit forward and back—fruit, half-formed weapons, ships."

"Some of those ships look like ones we've used," Joe says. "Others are new and different. And as for weapons...I can't understand any of them."

"You won't be using them," Kumar observes.

"Anyway, we hitched a ride on one of those railcars going aft," Joe says. "About three klicks from here, past where the squid ponds used to be, the rest of the Antags have got four ships in an outboard hangar. They seem to think they're enough to get all of them down to the surface. They want the hell off this hulk."

"Can't blame them, if they're home," Ishida says.

"Have you seen the surface?" I ask.

DJ says, "Sort of, in the big star dish. There aren't any squids there now, either. Whole ship seems empty."

"Could they *all* be dead?" Ishida asks.

"They could have withdrawn. No way of knowing."

"Maybe they're going to be shipped home as well," Borden says. "Evacuating."

"Optimistic appraisal, at best." Kumar says.

"Is Ulyanova ours or the ship's?" Joe asks. "I really need to know."

"She's putting everything she's got into staying human, and Vera is helping where she can," I say. "But I'm thinking we gave her a fucking impossible task."

Litvinov curses under his breath and looks ghostly pale. He's contemplating the loss of almost every soldier he trained

862 | GREG BEAR

and fought with, one way or another. And we're no consolation. After all, we might have helped Sudbury become our worst enemy.

"Focus on what we need to know!" Borden insists.

"We're orbiting a big dark planet," Joe says. "That much we can confirm."

"But how can we be sure we're actually there?" Borden asks.

"The Antags should know, right?" Jacobi asks.

"Sun-Planet!" DJ says in wonder. "Planet X."

"There are a lot of Planet X's out around the Kuiper belt," I say. "Big and small. Maybe warm, maybe cold—in the hundreds. I don't know how many are as large as Bird Girl's world, or how many were tinkered with by the bugs, but they and the Gurus have been playing with extrasolar planets for a long, long time."

"And that Christmas ornament, too," DJ says. "Moving shit around."

Joe shakes his head. "I'm not even going to think about that."

Borden says, "Job one, we have to put together something like weapons, go back in force, and kill the rest of the cage fighters. And we have to make sure the Antags are happy to leave without killing us—or Ulyanova."

"Might be walking into a hornet's nest," Jacobi says.

DJ observes that Sudbury never did have leadership skills. "He could barely understand orders."

"Maybe so, but since then he's gone through a whole new level of fight club," I say.

"Doesn't matter," Joe says. He's trying to pare the mission down to something we can all understand. Borden seems to approve. "I assume what Ulyanova told you is that the mice are loose in the cheese shop and the cats don't fucking care. Happy to watch us all fight it out."

Long pause. I tongue the gaps where my teeth used to be. Wonder if they're floating around here somewhere…

Without warning, the ribbons begin to glow, then to alternate between lighting the darkness and giving us a look outside. Instinctively, we rotate and crane to get a full view of where we are—above and below.

Above is another terrific view of stars, including the everglorious Milky Way. Again, parallax unchanged. Below—

A great suggestive curve of shadow, dark brown and pewter, wreathed like a Christmas tree with flickering aurorae strung between hovering, glowing spheres. Too big to see all at once, the likely equator is divided by a thick belt of what could be ice, green or blue under the spheres, pale gray beneath the aurora.

Out here, tens of thousands of millions of klicks from the sun, there's no sunlight, just the illumination from those rippling, ever-refreshing aurorae, moving like ocean breakers above the surface, defining segments of bright and dark—a twilight-only version of night and day.

As described.

Sun-Planet.

"It's split in half," Jacobi says.

DJ looks caught up in it all, smug at the confirmation. His mind is absorbing the new details. As is mine. It's beautiful and strange down there. "Divided planet," he says. "Antags grew up in the northern hemisphere, searchers in the southern. Separated by thousands of klicks of ice! Brilliant. Bugs had a hand in this, right? Two species separated until they were ready."

"Bad news for the searchers," I say. "At first."

"Yeah…But then they learned how to get along." His voice trails off at these strange, impersonal memories of Antag history, exploitation. They behaved so much like humans.

The mention of bugs provokes a weird sensation inside me of yet again being examined by an outside interest—curious in a fixed way, insistent but gentle. Something very old and disturbingly familiar is rummaging through my head and picking out words, maybe trying to learn my language—but then it comes upon fragments of my interactions with the archives on Mars and on Titan. Bug memories. I contain history I never lived, history I couldn't possibly know, along with the serial numbers, the identifying marks left by those archives.

DJ isn't looking smug now. "It's back!" he says.

"What?" Ishida asks.

"There's an archive nearby," I say.

"It's fucking *huge*," DJ says. "Bigger than anything we've found so far."

I confirm he's correct.

The others absorb this with their own weary familiarity. We've been jerked around by history and by our ugly ancestors too many times to take great cheer at this news, but at least it gets us moving. At least it could promise more interesting developments.

"Let's go," Joe says.

Bilyk suddenly doesn't look good. His arms and legs hang limp, his skin is pale, and his eyes have rolled back. Ishida intervenes and Litvinov doesn't object. She carefully rotates him to show us the spreading bruise along his neck and the back of his head. Our attackers must have sapped him, cracking his spine.

"Is he alive?" Ishikawa asks.

"Barely," Ishida says.

He didn't complain at first. Now he can't.

Litvinov looks at all of us as if this is the last straw and escorts the *efreitor* back to their nest. DJ tries to go with Bilyk, but Litvinov blocks him. "He must heal himself," Litvinov murmurs. "He is strong."

"And what if the fighters return?"

"I am staying here," Litvinov says. "I am old and too slow to matter back there. We will watch and try to protect curtain, Bilyk—last of my soldiers. I ask Kumar to stay with us."

Kumar agrees with a nod, then looks at the rest of us, as if he will soon be a dead man.

"We don't have real weapons," Borden says.

DJ and Tak brandish their canes, rather pitifully—though the tips are sharp, if they're used correctly.

"And by now," she continues, "I presume they know the territory better than we do. They might just play with us until we're all dead. Or they could capture and torture us one by one."

"If the Gurus stocked the cages with Sudbury's type," Joe says, "from all sorts of species, we're not dealing with soldiers but with homicidal maniacs. They may not have any strategy. They may not care how many of their own they lose."

"Where would they go? Where would they hide—back in the hamster balls?" Ishikawa asks, looking at me as if I know.

"Too obvious and exposed," Joe says. "We started this. We have to finish it."

"Would the Gurus have given them bolt weapons?" Jacobi asks.

"In the cages? I doubt it," Tak says. "Not a good show, and besides, they could blast their way out."

"What I'm asking," Jacobi continues, "is whether they've captured weapons *since* they got loose."

"Antag bolt weapons have ID locks," Tak says. "I doubt humans of any sort could fire them."

"What if the fighters include Antags?"

"ID'd to the *owner*," Tak says.

"So probably not," Joe says.

"Antags may have recovered our weapons from the Oscars," DJ says.

"We don't know that, and I don't want to think they'd hand them over to cage fighters," Joe says, with a glance my direction: *Would they?*

"Then we might be evenly matched, up to a point," Borden concludes. "Question is, have they ever had the run of the ship before?"

"I don't know," I say. "This is just the sort of thing Gurus would do to stir the pot."

"But Ulyanova doesn't say that, does she?" Tak asks.

I shake my head.

"What's she think we should do?"

For the third time, I explain what she told me—that the Antags are about to get the shock of their lives, and that Earth could be next. I don't get into the balancing act she's involved in with the ship. She's not worried about the cage fighters. She has bigger issues.

"We've done reconnaissance many times," Tak says, clearly ready, even eager, to go on a mission to search and destroy. "We practiced at Hawthorne. We ran multiple exercises on Socotra, and we did it for real on Mars—first season."

"Against Antags," I say.

"Antags caught in a bad drop of their own," Joe reminds. "But we're definitely prime in tough situations, in strange territory."

"Doesn't make it easier," Borden says.

"Commander, have you had that sort of training?" Tak asks, forthright as always.

"Similar," she says. "Twenty weeks of SEAL training in Cuba."

"Jesus!" DJ says.

"Not many sandy beaches here," Borden says.

"Borden's in charge," Jacobi says. Nobody disagrees. Everyone falls in behind her.

We work our way back along the ribbons and the spiraling cane bridges. Without the searchers to grow and maintain them, the canes are already decaying. There are fragments everywhere, and dust, getting into our lungs, our throats, our eyes.

Borden, DJ, Jacobi, and Tak stick close to me, forming a kind of arrowhead. Joe, Ishida, and Ishikawa take up the rear.

The ship ahead of the bulge is very different from when we moved forward. There's that long, thick central tree DJ and Joe saw, made of the same featureless hard stuff as the rest of the ship, stretching back over the leaf lake (now dry and cracked) and producing strange fruit. War fruit—weapons and ships, nascent, nasty, ready to fill out for new recruits on the other side of the solar system.

Then—there's another tug on our ancient string telephone.

"Feel that?" DJ says to me. "Think they'll let us in?"

As if in answer, the probing presence tempts me with a nugget of information. I see through a deep eye, an eye that temporarily blocks everything around me, a more personal panorama of Sun-Planet, as if I've lived there a very long time—broad, icy regions decked in low, scudding clouds, great sheets and glaciers stretching tens of thousands of klicks to a livid glowing horizon—and on the margin, the border between the southern hemisphere and the belt of ice: a swirling black ocean filled with searchers, feeding, diving like whales—millions of them.

The archives are in the southern hemisphere, under kilometers of ocean. The searchers dive deep and touch them, access them. That's why they're called searchers. They're more important to the archives than the Antags, even. Searchers are wiser. Smarter.

And no goddamned good for war.

And then this glorious nugget of history and insight is supplemented by a permission, a demand—another offering.

Inquire.

ANCIENT OF DAYS

I ask, "How old are you?"

DJ agrees that's a good place to start. We seem to sit beside each other in a steady stream of give-and-take, sensual exploration, study. The rest are momentarily irrelevant. I don't see them. I feel a nudge, hear a word, but do not respond.

I'm deep.

How old are you?

"Not very old," I answer, along with DJ.

Inquire.

"Do you recognize where we got our education, our training?"

Down near the sun. An old planet or moon.

Inquire.

"Are you older than the archives on that moon?"

Probably not older. Perhaps more complete. Was there damage to those archives?

"We think they've been destroyed. Archives on a planet

even closer to the sun have either been destroyed or severely damaged."

Who is responsible for this damage?

"We are, partly. But we've been influenced, instructed, by the Gurus."

We see that. Here they are called Keepers.

"You let them take control of the Antags?"

Follows a search through our memories for associations. Apparently we aren't going to have any privacy, and that could save a lot of time.

Until recent time, the Antagonists, as you call them, were not aware of the existence of these archives. The Antagonists are from the northern hemisphere. They are the only ones to be infested with Keepers. The searchers are from the southern hemisphere, mostly around the polar regions. They are scholars and aware of the archives, of our history, but neither the Antagonists nor the Keepers have enlisted them as fighters because they are not suited.

They resemble animals familiar to you?

"Yes. Squid."

Not closely related to you, these squid—perhaps enigmatic?

"Yeah. And probably not great scholars."

DJ chips in. "We call this world Planet X. What's your name for it?"

Too old to be important.

Inquire.

"Is this planet natural?"

You know already it is not.

"How old is it?"

Comes a number so vast I stumble around in my head

trying to control it. Then I realize the units: vibrations of an atomic particle, maybe an electron in orbit around a proton— a hydrogen atom. Everything in these archives is measured by those beats, those vibrations. Very rational. Could be close to universal. But we're not that sophisticated.

"What's that in years?" DJ asks.

The steward of the archives digs deeper into our heads and understands. *Four and a half billion years.*

"Made by the bugs?" I project my memories of bug appearance and hope for the best.

They were key. Many species contributed to these archives, but the bugs, as you call them, as you show them to us—we recognize their form—completed and organized them.

Inquire.

"Are there any bugs left alive?"

No.

"The bugs were plagued by Gurus as well?"

They were.

"How did they get rid of them?"

They did not get rid of them. They cut the ties that existed at that time. It is very difficult to destroy the Keepers, and almost impossible to be rid of them forever.

"There were accidents, right? Bits of broken moons came down to the inner solar system and seeded Earth and Mars. Does that means that the Gurus, the Keepers, were indirectly responsible for us, as well?"

The bugs emulated an older force. That mysterious influence moves planets, and little else, and five billion years ago, moved several from the realm of comets downward, beginning life in the outer system.

After those long-ago acts, the "bugs" contributed by help-ing seed the inner planets, by accident, through their long wars with one another.

"Where do the Gurus come from?" DJ asks.

Not known. The Keepers are always looking for systems to develop and preserve, in their way. You and Antagonists share ancient origins, but "bugs" have nothing to do with the ori-gins of Keepers.

"Who controls you now?" DJ asks.

Nobody controls. We work with searchers but they are far fewer now than they once were. And the archives are them-selves diminished.

"What's happening on Sun-Planet?"

Total destruction. We have seen it before. When this time is finished, if the archives still exist, perhaps you can bring schol-ars back to finish our studies...

The steward seems to fade in a haze of what might be disappointment—if it can exhibit anything like emotion.

Can it?

Or does it echo our own feelings?

We come out of our reverie and look around us.

"Time to get the fuck out of here!" DJ says.

"Amen," Joe says.

———

WE RESUME OUR slow, awkward journey, Joe, DJ, and Jacobi telling us what they know and helping smooth our learn-ing curve. Without searchers, moving through the ship is an involved process of trying to make out an available surface in the twisted architecture behind and between decaying, rickety canes, in deep shadow, then launch out with a kick—

sometimes connecting, sometimes painfully colliding. Ishida and Borden fly wide, miss the best gripping points, and get snagged in a crumbling spiral. It takes time to pluck them out.

———

THE VIEWING DISH is dark and now the space around it is crowded with dead searchers. The smell is fierce, like ammonia mixed with dead cat.

We find another Antag, also dead from cutting wounds.

Not Bird Girl—to my relief.

"We won't follow the tree unless we can get on that rail line," Joe says. "Too much growth, too fast. And the rail is likely already carrying weapons away to stockpile them."

"Where's the line begin?" Borden asks.

"I thought it was at the tip of the tree," Joe says. Ishida agrees. "But everything's still changing."

Pretty soon, we're almost out of options. There's nothing but darkness, pieces and tangled clumps of canes blowing aft in the steady breeze, and searcher bodies—dozens of them, maybe hundreds. They're becoming a hazard, rolling aft or forming their own clumps, a hecatomb of astonishing proportions.

"Cage fighters couldn't have killed all of them," Borden says.

"Who, then? Ulyanova?"

I'm biting my inner cheek. I don't want to answer. I don't know the answer.

"Is she still human?" Ishikawa asks.

"She's playing a dangerous game," I say. "One move here, another there. If she does something really brash or stupid, the ship could flush us all into space—not just the searchers."

"Do you know that?" Borden asks, and for some reason that infuriates me, but I just hold it in—and keep biting until blood flows.

We've reached a section of this new ship where the last of the fragile cane thickets have spread as if to define a wider volume, only to be crushed by the shrinking hull. Last-minute adjustments by the searchers, before the great dying? Futile, either way.

One more body floats in shadows—spiked on a single jutting cane. This one is neither Antag nor human, like nothing we've seen before. Difficult from our distance to discern details, but it has a small, knobby head, large, almost froglike eyes, compact body with four ropy limbs—and its torso has nearly been seared in half. It's still clutching a bolt pistol.

DJ and Ishida move through the canes, swearing, to recover the pistol.

"It's an Antag weapon, all right," DJ says.

"Why was it carrying that, if it couldn't use it?" Ishikawa asks.

"Don't toss it," Tak says. "Maybe Bird Girl will let us arm ourselves."

"I doubt that," Ishida says.

Nothing but darkness ahead, no clues.

And then the breeze moving aft carries a swirling cloud of fairy glow. Searcher bodies have been sprinkling the surroundings.

"There!" Ishida says. Her eyes are sharper than ours. A few hundred meters ahead, we see a spray of branches blue-green with searcher dust. We grab hands to form a star, calculate how to kick off all at once, and fly across the intervening space. Joe and Borden snag a branch, then we all scramble inboard to what could be a rail line—a corkscrew curve pointing aft. But the corkscrew ends abruptly, and there's nothing obvious in the way of transport—nothing like the tram car around the screw garden.

We're contemplating our next move when we find another body—Antag, one of the armored commanders, caught up in an adjacent branch and mostly hidden by the withered arms of a dead searcher. The Antag's wings have been left half-spread. All four eyes are open and glazed. She apparently bled out through deep slices along her neck and shoulders—neatly skirting the armor on her breast and thorax.

"How many battles can we fight on this tub?" Joe asks in an undertone.

Borden and Jacobi move off a few slender branches to confer. In the light of more dead Antags and uncertainty aft, they're reassessing our situation, who to protect, who to reinforce—who to put in danger. I'm glad I'm not making those decisions, but I handicap their choices anyway, and I'm mostly correct.

"Four of us will go on," the commander says. "Three will return to the ribbon space. We don't know who's most in danger, or how protected Ulyanova really is. We can't risk both Johnson and Venn. I want someone who's linked to the *starshina* and Bird Girl with each party. I should have thought of that earlier, but…Fujimori, Johnson, Ishikawa. Back to the nests. Good luck."

We split up. Joe, Jacobi, Borden, Ishida, and I will continue aft. The pistol goes to Ishida.

"We'll hand it over to Bird Girl," Borden says. "Make it a peace offering."

THE LAST ENEMY

The great intertwine of tram lines, the foremost station, begins about a hundred meters behind the spike ball.

How many times before has this ship gone through metamorphosis? Across four billion years? I can't believe any ship could last so long. But the ship, as DJ pointed out, has aspects of a cell—a living thing. Maybe it's a cancer cell and can go on forever.

"Any idea how much Ulyanova had a hand in designing this?" Borden asks.

"I'd guess she's just letting the ship follow prior instructions."

"Which means sending the Antags down to Sun-Planet?"

"That's what she says."

"Where there's nothing left for them," Joe says.

"And after they're delivered?" Jacobi asks. "What happens to the ship then?"

"A long trip back to the other side of the Kuiper belt," I say. "Or…a short deviation, right into the sun."

"With or without Ulyanova?" Jacobi asks.

"Which would you bet on?" Borden says, and they look at each other with the sublime pessimism of having to anticipate the worst.

I don't like being put in this spot. "With," I say.

"All right, then," Borden says. "Brother and sister of the tea have exchanged confidences."

"Something's coming," Ishida says, and points down the shadowy, spiky center of the tree. A narrow, insectoid car with jointed, grasping limbs at each end is rolling in our direction. It pauses for a moment and reaches out to adjust the angle of a thicker branch, showing considerable persuasion or strength, and then more slowly approaches us. Faceted eyes at the end of long stalks seem to measure and observe.

The car stops a few meters away, ticking.

"Is it alive?" Borden asks.

Before I can hazard a guess, the car starts to move in the opposite direction—aft. We each take hold of a black arm and swing our legs into the cab, trying to hang on as the car picks up speed. We're on our way, slammed this way and that as it swerves to avoid the thickest and most productive branches.

All around us there's growth and noise, branches rearranging, more cars passing on the opposite side of the trunk, bundles of raw materials being ferried and delivered to the other branches...

The cell is metastasizing. The ship feels more and more like a gigantic, cancerous lump, producing death and destruction a million tons at a time.

Farther aft, huge objects, the embryonic beginnings of big ships, hang on the outer branches, some hundreds of meters long and still expanding, their hulls not yet closed over. Other, larger grapplers and industrial organelles move new components toward these ships, through gaps in their unfinished skins, and into what I have to assume are the proper positions.

The whole Guru war machine is in full gear, getting ready for a voyage across the solar system and beyond, to a far world where humanity's new enemies are being fed the old line of imminent conquest and domination...

Recycle whatever you can, right?

THE LAST INSTAURATION

Every second we risk being flayed. We're getting exhausted trying to avoid the rushing tangles, being brushed by nascent weapons or scraped along the rugged sides of half-finished ships.

Borden, seeing we've reached our physical limits, tells us to look for a relatively open space between branches and a slowdown in the tram car's spiraling, jerking passage—and when those are in congruence, we kick off, away from the branches and growths. The contraction of the ship's hull has pulled in outboard chambers we never saw until now, and we take refuge in one, if it can be called refuge, since it shudders and slowly spins, some of the walls growing long spikes, as if preparing to grab the other side and tug it shut—and may at any moment be absorbed, and us with it. But for a few minutes we find relative quiet and try to catch our breaths before resuming the trip aft.

I move off a few meters along a barely spiked curve and over a rim between the chambers.

"Going somewhere?" Borden asks from behind.

I wonder where I *am* going, and why. "In my head…I hear a little fly-buzz," I say.

"Ulyanova?"

"I'm not sure. Maybe."

"Mind if we come with?"

"No…"

The whole cluster of squeezed-down chambers is like the steely pith of a gigantic tropical fruit, with the big seeds removed. As we climb and echo along the walls, crossing over ridges where chambers join, we make sure to keep our bearings so we can find our way back.

According to the buzz in my thoughts, there's evidence nearby…evidence, and maybe something else.

Ishida, alert and sharp-eyed, spots the evidence first. "What is this crap? It's not Antag, right?"

Pulling aside a mass of broken canes pushed up against an inner chamber, like a cave inside a cave, we find shreds of fabric. I pull away what might be a decayed coverall. Its tatters reveal three pairs of armholes, two legs, and no neck hole, but an opening in the thorax, the chest, as if whatever wore this peered out from a central eye. The shards are torn, fading, and rotten—pushed around by cane growths like tattered laundry hung on a thousand poles.

The others observe in silence. This may be the migration the Gurus arranged before our war got under way—the previous episode in the season, so to speak, when they laid up a bitter, desperate end for the Antags.

Ishida looks at me.

I'm sweating.

"You all right?" she asks, as my eyesight fades. I hold up

my hand, feeling a deep unease spread through my body, as if I'll collapse or explode—

I can't help myself. Whatever's coming, I have to close my eyes.

The air around me changes, warms...

Seems more human. Fresher. I smell fresh detergent, soap, and feel the smooth surface of a sheet against my neck, my bare legs.

My body arranges itself, in gravity, on a bed.

I'm back at Madigan. I look up at the familiar ceiling, look left at the bathroom, look between my legs at where the main room was—is—beyond my bare feet...

And see Ulyanova walk through the door. She appears bright and fresh, untroubled, and at first peers around the bedroom as if she can't see me—as if the room is empty.

I want to shove off the bed, get away.

But her head turns and she finds me. "There you are," she says. "No going home for me, ever, but perhaps for you, Vinnie. Now, look...I show what happened on ship, where you are now, long ago."

She moves her hands with exaggerated elegance, as if she enjoys being a sorcerer, as if this, and creating an environment for herself and Vera, brings her the only joy she will ever feel.

As she performs these moves, the veil seems to fall away, and I see her as skeletal, ghostly, skin almost green—like a corpse in an old crypt.

Eyes large, staring.

And then, the instauration or vision or whatever rises from Madigan's ground floor to a higher, quicker level. I'm no longer human. I'm crowded with tens of thousands of others into a gigantic metal cavern, in attendance to fresh weapons, new ships, not exactly like the ones being grown along the tree. I perceive that every show must have fresh designs, novel architectures, new and innovative weapons in the hands or other appendages of new breeds of celebrity warrior, to meet and then sate the expectations of the far-flung, jaded audiences so important to the Guru showrunners…

Everything around me gets stirred, then laid out like leaves in a book, each leaf an experience.

I page through, no choice, and become one of the single-eyed, four-armed soldiers massed in drop-ships descending by the tens of thousands to Sun-Planet, our heads—or rather our chests—filled with training we experienced on our own home, one of those very far-flung, dark worlds in the Kuiper belt, far beyond Pluto, and even far beyond Sun-Planet—a remote, tortured world orbiting between three gas giants, constantly being heated and torqued, volcanoes everywhere—

No bugs were involved in this round of planetary evolution. Here is quite a different style. This world, part of a new initiative, was quickened by Gurus, and now its children have been carried to Sun-Planet, where they have done their very best to destroy the Antags, the searchers, and everything they value. All the current fashion in Guru-supplied entertainment. The couch potatoes out there have grown old and thirsty, in cruel need of newer, more ironic, angrier forms of destruction and apocalypse…

What we and the Antags provided for a time is now old-fashioned, no longer *interesting*. Betrayal and sabotage may be just what the audiences are expecting.

Time catches up.

I brush over the battles, all the wars on Sun-Planet, with dreamlike speed and precision—not just visual, but with snips of agony, flesh rending and bones splintering, wings shredded—feeling the anguish as the Antags lose cohesion when big males are gathered up and executed by ant-thick hordes of these single-eyed monsters...

The monsters then move on to the southern hemisphere and work to turn the archives into a library without readers.

I participate in the destruction of the crèches that support Antag eggs, each the size of a soccer ball and capable of hatching to produce multiple offspring—a male, several females, the necessary components for a seed-family that can also be integrated into other seed-families and raised as their own...

When the dream collapses and fades to a violent end, I roll up in the bedsheets, and through my tears, can barely make out Ulyanova, still standing in the doorway. I am horrified and blasted by the waft of her Guru psychology, her mask— but also the sad, almost hopeful presence of the *starshina* I first met on Mars, not so long ago. Protecting as she must. Challenging as she must to keep the ship from killing us.

No hope of anything more.

"This is what brain knows, what ghosts tell me," Ulyanova says. "I will speak to you one more time, but not as Guru. All your Guru bombs are removed. Even so, you are not out of danger, Vinnie. Ghosts and brain demand interest. If I do not oblige..."

She doesn't need to finish.

The room at Madigan vanishes like a soap bubble, and

I'm back in the decay and rubble of the old chambers that once contained many of the violent, one-eyed race even now awaiting our Antags down on Sun-Planet.

The great seed-pod chamber begins to split and crack, closing down, being recycled. The spikes join with their opposites and pull.

"We should get out of here," Borden says.

But we can't just go back the way we came. Four silhouettes appear briefly along our return route, difficult to see against the central shadows, the spinal tree's spin of growing branches, moving weapons, and vessels.

Ishida and Borden spot them first, Joe and I last. By this time, they're upon us, brandishing bladed weapons, canes, and nightmare faces—the two that have faces.

One kicks around the chamber, grabbing and tossing canes and other debris to keep itself pinned to the curve, until it's tangled with Ishida. A blade clangs on Ishida's metal arm, another silhouette moves in from another direction, swinging for her flesh half—

But I'm there with a clutch of canes wrapped in rotten fabric, something I've assembled in a fraction of a second, and my own trajectory as I kick puts that bundle between the blade and Ishida, soundly thunking her, but not carving.

I have the blade wielder in my hands now, groping up along a skinny chest for something like a neck, as I'm kicked and clawed by anatomy out of a seafood dinner, and then I wrench a tough outer shell almost half-circle below a rim of eyes, and acrid fluid shoots past my ear—

But this thing is almost impossible to get hold of. It's cutting at my hands when Joe recovers the wrapped canes and swings them over to Borden, who wedges her back against a curved wall, kicks down against Joe's body, and shoves the tip of the bundle between a scurry of legs and arms…

Prying loose the blade, the pike, or whatever it is, which Borden has used, apparently, in another form, to some effect in training—

She swings it around, still propped against Joe, who's sliding up a wall, about to fly free, when she passes the blade through the scurry and severs all the grasping legs, then somehow brings herself around as Ishida replaces Joe for prop and ballast—

The commander brings the pike down hard, starting to rise as she does so—and connects with the part I was trying, ineffectually, to strangle. Something flies free. I do not know what it is, because I've turned to take a barrage of twisting buck-kicks and sharp fist blows from a serpentine thing with a rippling haze of arms or legs, over three meters long, getting purchase by wrapping its hind portion around a spike growing from the wall. Thus anchored, it rises, long head of six eyes rotating in dismay, into Ishida's crunching metal grip. I hear but don't see what happens after that. Joe and I have wrapped our legs around the fourth silhouette, which is humanoid—is it Sudbury? More like a powerful ape with red and orange hair and tremendous hands, hands even now trying to rip off my arm, my legs, but without my cooperation, not quite managing to get a grip. I push in with thumbs and go for the eyes—two only—and rip at the flaps of the cheeks. It's amazing how much strength you have when you still care, and death is upon you—when Ishida and Joe and Borden are at stake—and where the fuck is Jacobi? The whole melee comes to an astonished, quivering, bloody halt when a bolt carves the serpent's half-crushed head away, and does double duty with the arm of the ape. The mass separates. Borden is on one side, Ishida and Joe on the other.

Jacobi is three meters away, clutching the pistol we recovered earlier—

And firing three more times before it whines that the charge is gone.

We stare at her in astonishment.

"Somebody made a mistake," she says. "Thought I'd make sure."

We push back from the corpses, surrounded not just by their main masses, but by twirling gobbets of flesh, revolving and rotating limbs, strings of internal organs.

None of them belong to us.

We've just engaged and taken down four cage fighters, and cannot believe that we're all intact and alive.

"Any more?" Ishida asks.

"None I can see," Joe says.

"Where's Sudbury?"

No sign. Maybe one more.

Jacobi and Borden do brief examinations of our opponents. They're all dead, but worse, are absolutely painted by old scars. The ape is missing fingers and a lower leg from a previous encounter, and every one of them looks as if they were once much stronger, more capable.

Before the cage matches.

Perhaps before they were all released.

No satisfaction comes with this victory. No glory, nothing but the chance to return to the spinning, fruiting branches and hitch on another car—completing our horror-train ride aft.

What a prize.

We feel barely alive when the car stops with a jerk and the

limbs fold away, threatening to pinch our hands. We let loose and hear, then see, Antags. They're drafting away from the ships in the hangar to intercept us. But they are hardly any sort of welcoming committee.

The air around us flashes with wings, grasping hands, bolt rifles, and pistols. The Antags take quick control of our group. Jacobi offers them our weapons. A bat intervenes to take them and moves off to join the busy mix around the interior of the hangar, where the big male is directing the loading of passengers and cargo. Preparing for departure. Two searchers move between the ships, interacting with the bats, helping carry cargo from one transport to another. Other Antags perch nearby, like a string of crows on a power line, wings folded, waiting. Looks as if they're packing to return to the planet. What's left of their home to return to?

I try to connect with Bird Girl, tell her we're here to deliver information—but the Antags tie us in cords and jerk us again into bouquets, not in the least gentle.

The big male interrupts his supervision to make a sweeping gesture with one wing. The armored officers and bats stop their own activity and move out of the hangar to surround us.

Then Bird Girl emerges from the hangar, assisted by several bats. Her wings are folded, but one is oddly bent as if dislocated. She's carrying her own bolt pistol and her shoulders are damply fluffled.

The crowd around us parts as she comes forward.

"You're going home?" I ask.

Her reaction is like a needle into my head. "There is nothing left, but there is an end," she says, pulling herself into something like dignity, her feathers smoothing. "Honor in completion." I get her impression of what will come after:

vast calm seas, warm lights glowing over water and land, over ice. No enemies except those chosen to bring glory and more honor. Bird Girl's Fiddler's Green.

"You have seen what our world has become," she says. "Who has told you this?"

"The mimic," I say. "I wouldn't wish it for any of you."

"I could feel your sadness," Bird Girl says. "After all we have done, and what we are now... Our husband wishes me to teach you, so you may teach others, what we were, what we are, and what we are about to become."

Joe and Jacobi have moved close, as if to protect me from the crowd—but there is no more anger, no more resentment. They have made their peace, and for these people, these races, that is remarkable.

What follows next between us is an internal dance, a remarkable exchange of what she anticipates for us—of where humans might go from here, the ship crossing to Mars and Earth, passing on to gather up Gurus and move to the next stage, whatever that will be... but leaving us to join those we feel are family.

This acknowledgment that we will live, that we might possibly go back to Earth, that Earth might still be there... this brings an end to many decades of deception and folly. The utter betrayal played upon them by the Gurus, the Keepers, is striking deep into the most conservative and warlike members of the families throughout the hangar.

"Our husband has changed," she says. "He will ask a favor."

For those not on our connection, a bat has set up the guts of an old human helm display to be shared—a kind of courtesy I would never have expected.

In one great painful sweep, Bird Girl feeds me what they have seen through remotes and the star dish. The surface of

Sun-Planet has undergone big changes. The topography is very different from what she was taught on Titan.

It seems Bird Girl was also something of a nerd, among her kind. Her favorite subjects rise above the rest, the phenomena and characters of home that she had most wanted to experience.

For the first time, I understand the equivalent of the Antag compass—the normal points and several other coordinates that Antags use, including where heat plumes are migrating way below the crust. Plumes and heat and magnetic field lines affect weather. Sun-Planet has external weather and internal weather. If the hot, pressurized inside fails, the outside fails not long after.

But the current reality overshadows her studies.

What they have seen:

Wide gray prairies and plains, low, layered mountain ranges, and...

Ruins. If these had once been cities, they seem to have fallen from a great height like chandeliers and shattered, then been kicked around. Walls, facets, fields of debris glisten like broken ice. The arcs of aurorae still flicker through the collapsed remnants of great arches. Apparently these cities once flew. Must have been a wonderful sight.

Directly below and stretching to the aurora-wrapped horizon, the eastern and western edges of two of the largest of six continents face each other across a narrow isthmus filled with swirling, muddy ribbons, flowing south toward the one great global sea, the watery wall between all the landmasses in the northern hemisphere and the huge equatorial belt of ice. That belt is more than fifty klicks thick in places—a daunting wall between the two ecosystems the bugs seeded here billions of years ago.

In Bird Girl's memory, the southern hemisphere is just the opposite of the northern—mostly water fingered with hundreds of rocky, ice-bound ridges of land. But we're not looking at that yet. We're surveying northern Antag territories, historical lands and their associated waterways—

Lands where millions of generations of Antags once swam and bred and fished, spread across the continents, discovered all the requisite technologies, built their communities, their farms and cities, and in time developed a civilization at least as old as our own.

Only to became entranced by the heart-wrenching stories of the Keepers.

Thousands of craters interrupt the old map of historical memory, often hundreds of klicks across, as if asteroids or small moons had been dropped from orbit. At Bird Girl's command, the screen outlines where major cities and government-designated regions once were. She mentally tries to convey some of their names—a phonetic murmur of her mind—and then, one by one, not finding them, scratches them out with blasts of reddish anger. They are amended on the screen as well—blotchy erasures. I flinch at her vigorous rage.

The destruction on most of the continents comes in the form of asteroid falls, followed by gigantic scorching runs across the landmasses, like claw marks—pointing to huge orbital weapons no longer in evidence. The small oceans now have very different outlines.

That part of the war seems to be over.

"Those brought here by Keepers have finished," Bird Girl says. "None of our cities remain. We find no living of our kind."

The big ship's orbit takes it once more over the belt of

thick ice, into a slow, low passage over the southern hemisphere. There's something cruel and mocking about these sweeps. Are the Guru ghosts, the ship's brain, squeezing the last reactions out of these heartbroken warriors, facing the bitter truth of their destruction?

Here, in the southern hemisphere, the display reveals that the clear blue-green oceans cover deep destruction. Trenches and plains are burned out, pitted—so deeply scored that the inner heat and pressures of Sun-Planet itself produce boiling cauldrons. Visible open trenches score the southern pole, spouting streams of plasma into space—replacing the benign and illuminating aurorae with grim prominences, overarching cascades of fire. The edges of these chasms glow orange in the eternal night, like angry welts around open wounds.

How much of the archives have been targeted? And who targeted them? The new warriors, or the Antags who followed the commands of the Keepers? The latter, I'm guessing, before they fell to the new warriors. After that, with the destruction of the searchers, the archives would have become irrelevant. Without those tuned to their libraries, their destruction is not important.

Nobody remains to listen. And the steward no longer serves Antags.

Which is why DJ and I, but not Bird Girl, can still hear its voice. The steward has only us to talk to, and soon, we will leave.

The one thought that floods me, overwhelming all indignity and anger, I can also see in the faces of our small band of Skyrine survivors.

Fear for what has happened on Earth since we left.

The display now shows the edge of the equatorial ice,

and zooms in to reveal fleets of submarines, ships arranged in starfish flotillas, linked with wave-frothing chains, their upper decks packed with both aircraft and spacecraft. Several of the spacecraft are launching on pillars of spent-matter fire.

"There they are," Bird Girl says. "That is our reception—a quick death. This is all that remains."

To see her home world in this monstrous disarray makes her shrink inside. "They fought for years. Some families, old and conservative, filled with honor, fought to keep the archives from changing our relation to the Keepers, our politics and historically revered policies. Cities built to exploit, then to support the searchers—they are gone. All of our unifying efforts seem to have been ignored. Searchers have nearly vanished."

"How many are left?" Borden asks.

"Wingfuls, if that. There must have been great fear, great hatred." Her four eyes seem to bore into mine. I can share those emotions, that combination of anger and dismay, because that's how we're most alike, Antags and humans— rage and disappointment. Maybe that's what made both of us attractive to the Gurus. Or that's how the Gurus shaped us.

"And now…they are gone. The good, the bad, the foolish, the deceived—the wise! All my people are gone. I am full of shame."

Borden silently studies the view. Ishida's tears, streaming down one side of her face, are the only sign of emotion in our group. Half of her was destroyed in our war. Strangely, she's the one with the most empathy for our former enemies.

"A decision is made," Bird Girl says. "The mimic has done what she promised. And so, after we depart, you will be left here to finish your tasks. There is no place for you down there. But we have duties to perform. Sacred obligations.

"In thousands of centuries, our world will once more travel through the inner space of the solar system. What Sun-Planet will be then...if it will even survive...who can know? But here, and on your world—we ask this of you..."

Three armored females in attendance to the big male are handed a black box about forty centimeters on a side, equipped with a battery pack and canisters. In turn, they give the box to the male, who summons me forward with a broad sweep of his wing.

I receive the box. Ishida and Borden join me and place their hands on the box, as if they know instinctively what's being given to our care.

I look at Bird Girl.

"We have dual births from each egg," she tells us through the translator. "Each egg can be configured to seed a family, and this one is so made. These children will be mine, my family's. You may let them live, if you understand...what we have done. What we are, and what we share. How we have both been deceived."

"We'll take care of them," I vow, and hope I can carry out that promise.

"I think you will raise them honorably."

"We'll try."

"Take what memories are in your heads, or will be when the archives finish with you, and remember what we did for you, in hope of peace."

We surround the egg.

"And take these as well," Bird Girl says, as another bag is

brought forward. Borden takes it, opens it, and peers inside. She looks up with a puzzled and pleased expression.

"Some of our bolt pistols," she says. "They look fully charged."

"Recovered by small cousins from your ships, your bases."

"I didn't know they could swim," Joe says.

"That is why you lost so many battles on Titan," Bird Girl says. "These, I am sure, will be used to protect."

She reaches out with a wingtip hand, as if for the last time, to caress the egg in its case. Ishida is crying freely now.

"Tell them how their family died," Bird Girl concludes, looking toward the transport, the other Antags, the bats, and the two searchers finishing the loading, moving in and out of the lone return vessel.

She raises her joint hand on her injured wing as best she can, and we each touch palms.

"Amen," Borden says, almost inaudible.

"Godspeed," Joe says.

Ishida hugs Bird Girl, somewhat to the alarm of the bats— and then releases her.

THE LONG HAUL HOME

The bats escort us back to the hangar and we are released. We watch the sealing away from the aft terminus of the spine-tree's tramway. Bulkheads are set in place and grow up between us and the Antag transport, beaten and battered, in the hangar. Follows a deep vibration that shivers the air.

The Antags are on their way.

"Suicide!" Borden says.

"Honor," Ishida says.

We begin the long journey forward.

"Keep your eyes peeled," Borden warns, as we each take a pistol and check it. All functional, all well maintained. I think I'd like to have some of those cousin bats go with us. "We're not out of this yet."

No place in our pajamas to hide or store the guns, so we carry them open. And between us, we protect the box containing the egg.

The tram vehicles are as tough to hang on to as before, and the journey is made even more arduous by more changes along the tree, plus what must be a major reshaping of the ship's hull, difficult to understand from our point of view—like rats on an ocean liner.

Throughout, spring-steel threads unwind along the branches and the trunk, filling the spaces between with a curly metallic fuzz—leaving swerving tunnels that barely allow the trams to move forward—while cradling the growth, the ships and weapons, as if they are seeds inside a gigantic pod cramming itself with death and destruction.

I wonder what Ulyanova is contributing, if anything, to these changes. I wonder if she's even still alive. I hear nothing from the bow, nothing from her world behind the dense curtain. The archives on Sun-Planet also have little to say now, fewer fragments to add—but for one overall impression, a kind of courtesy extended to visiting scholars—the confirmation that in time, Sun-Planet will survive, and will indeed pass through the lower system, between the orbits of Neptune and Uranus, and likely will once again scatter moons and rearrange human affairs. That's orbital mechanics—possibly set in place by the shifter of moons and worlds.

I hope DJ is hearing that as well. I hope Bilyk has improved and they can talk. Christ, I feel tiny. Tiny but inflated with huge emptiness where answers might be, perhaps should be—cavernous silences, presaging the ignorance and quiet to come.

I suppose in their own way the bugs were as arrogant and clueless as any gods. What an inheritance! What are we left with?

An egg. Jesus help us all.

We make our winding, devious, tortured passage from the hangar forward and see that the screw gardens are the only constants, obscured as they are by the winding fuzz. There are many more of them. The largest seem to have split and rearranged, perhaps to balance their influence around the ship. The few hamster cages we can make out through the metallic foliage, between the fruiting machines—the new growths and their packaging—the cages that had once been filled with death—have been crushed by growth, folded and crumpled, perhaps to be recycled. For now, they have no use.

The sets have been rearranged prior to the next production.

Every dragging bit of our journey forward fills me with an itching anticipation that the last of the cage fighters are waiting somewhere—hiding. They were never organized, I think. But that's no answer. I wonder if the last survivors are now the greatest fighters on this ship, perhaps between all the worlds—and the most ruthless. Or the most aware of what it means to fight a never-ending war.

Ishida is the first to see another body in the curling growth—caught up in the steel fuzz, being slowly propelled aft for whatever fate, recycling or expulsion, that has met the searchers and the other dead. This body is so decayed it is difficult to tell what it might have once been, or how it died.

We see only two more bodies as we cross through the regions once dominated by the lake, now obscured by stored material, machinery, ships, and thick fuzz. They look like crushed mosquitoes wrapped in gray cotton.

Joe moves closer. Borden turns to listen. "Can you hear DJ?" he asks.

"He's alive," I say. "I don't know what he's seeing or doing."

"Has he been attacked? Or any of the others?"

I shake my head. "I don't know," I say.

"Bird Girl?"

"They're already down on her world."

If she's dead, if they're all dead, then the package we're carrying, slung between us, may be the most precious thing on this godforsaken ship.

The mechanical vehicle, with all its manipulators folded, finally reaches the forward terminus, after we've long since gone numb, our hands and arms buzzing. It stops, rotates on the track, and seems to deliberately shiver us away, as if it's done with us. Then it makes a jerking movement in reverse, and we cooperate to join hands, leap, catch ourselves—leap again.

We're at the base of where the needle prow once began. The ribbon room is intact and seems unchanged. We climb along the bands of starry illumination, then pause before the asterisk, as if taking in that strange cathedral window one more time, for orientation, for instruction.

The ribbons now carry imagery from around the ship—the Milky Way, the slowly rotating shadow of Sun-Planet, its belt of ice still visible beneath the continually rolling breakers of the aurorae, like an ocean of light flooding over overwhelming darkness. The air has not changed.

Beyond the ribbons and the asterisk, the curtain is still there, looking tattered, oddly, as if reflecting the condition of our mimic, the master of all the illusions that hide behind it. This proves to me at least that Ulyanova is still in charge of the spaces and processes important to us.

We search the nests and find DJ, Ishikawa, Kumar. They emerge from a kind of dreaming nap and gather around us, hopeful we may know what's going to happen next. Litvinov and Bilyk are not in evidence. I assume the *polkovnik* is still tending to his *efreitor*, like a father devoted to his last son.

Kumar and Ishikawa take charge of the egg. "What do we do with it?" Ishikawa asks.

"Get it home," I say. "After that—whatever we can, wherever we end up."

"Looks like they've equipped it for a few months, at least," Ishikawa says.

Joe says to me, and aside to DJ, "You've got to learn what she plans."

Then they all embrace us, a most unexpected response, as if we're heading off to our own deaths.

I ask Ulyanova for permission.

Vera emerges and takes us behind the curtain, through the thick wool and fog. Despite the changes and death elsewhere in the ship, the illusions beyond the curtain are still there: the tile floor, the hallway, and now, cold winter sunlight through the window at the end of the hall. The air in the apartment has chill currents, mixing with the heat from the radiators.

We are greeted warmly by a skeletal Ulyanova, and spend time with both of them in that steam-heated apartment. The mood seems relaxed, casual, despite the *starshina*'s appearance. Vera watches me closely. Ulyanova sits me down in an overstuffed chair and pulls up a stool. She might as well be a corpse, with her lips drawn back, her eyes like those of a lemur, her skin pearly gray and showing signs of cracking. Vera looks only a tiny bit better.

They serve us soup and tinned fish, mackerel in tomato paste. Tastes good. Tastes real.

"I am here," Ulyanova says. "Ghosts are here. They still make plans, as if I agree, and I follow their plans."

"Right."

"Ship still listens as if I am Guru. But ship is about to do what it has been instructed for decades to do—make journey downsun, cross to other side of system, far quarter of Kuiper belt, to visit another new planet. Along the way, we will pass close to Mars and then Earth to pick up Gurus and their most favored Wait Staff. Once we retrieve all of the Wait Staff and Gurus, their ships will be available to carry you where you wish to go."

"Convenient," I say.

"I plan well, right?"

"You plan well. We are grateful."

"Do not be. I am now more than half monster. You cannot guess what knife edge I will fall from, any second, and slice plans. Verushka and I are both monsters—but we remember."

"We will stay here," Vera says sadly.

"To finish," Ulyanova says. "This is our home. We have friends, out there." She points through the window to the Russian winter, the lowering butter-colored sun and bunched, snow-packed clouds.

"It's a dream," I say.

"A good dream for old soldiers," she says. "Bilyk is very bad. He will not survive return to Earth. Tell Litvinov we have a place for both here. And a job he can do."

"I'll tell him," I say.

"Now this is what will happen around Mars, around Earth," Ulyanova says. "Ship will demand that all Gurus and their servants return, or destroy themselves, in preparation for new dispensation, new show."

"All the old shows have been canceled?" DJ asks.

They both nod.

"Fucking righteous," DJ says.

Vera smiles.

"This will be ship's last journey," Ulyanova says.

"As we discussed?" I ask.

"After you leave, I will fly into sun," she says. "Wait Staff, politicians, generals who never fought—men and women who made great money from wars and deaths—we will share big party behind curtain. Make fancy places for them to live, to feel they have escaped. Earth is moving away from their influence. Already there is anger. So last refugees of war wait for us to save them."

I mull this over, looking at the plate of cookies, the butter, the cup of tea.

DJ has put down his cup.

Almost against my will, I have to say, "Sometime back, you told me you knew the real reason the Gurus did all this. Can you tell me now?"

It seems that if one of us touched her, she would crumble. But she moves with grace, and her look toward Vera is still alive enough to convey affection.

"Yes," she says. "Ghosts tell me Gurus are like game wardens. They make little wars, allow little kills, to protect us against bigger passions. Without them, we would kill ourselves."

Vera adds, "But Gurus lie."

I squint at the watery sun outside the window. "Yeah."

Ulyanova rises from the stool. "Journey downsun will bring deep sleep, as before. Only I will feel the time. Time weighs heavy—bad memory."

Vera takes my arm, lifting me from the overstuffed chair. DJ gets up as well.

Gray and dusty, Ulyanova looks at us sadly. "Go home and tell," she says. "I hope you will land where you need to be. And I hope Earth is alive when we go back."

"You don't know?" I say.

She shakes her head. "No saying from brain, from ghosts. And at some point, ship must offload spent-matter reserves."

"Ship lets you do that?"

"Ship knows how to make more, if needed. But can travel without—and do not want it in sun."

I had forgotten about that. "Or Earth," I say.

"Will find best, safest place. Go now."

And we go. Back to the others, to the nests and to the ribbon spaces. So many more questions to ask the Queen! But we will not meet again. Perhaps she and Vera prefer the ship's illusions. I would, if I could convince myself...

All wars end in whimpers. And those who serve the Gurus most faithfully, most selfishly, never learn. They rise again and again to the emotions that lead to self-destruction. There is not nearly enough energy to exact vengeance.

We could say we were manipulated. Only true in part. We lie to ourselves like cocks in a pit. We bloody enjoy death and destruction. Sex is obscene. War is holy. We'll have only ourselves to blame when it's all over, humans and Antags, that we could be such fucking dupes.

But Gurus lie.

Maybe without them, we'll find a different balance, live a different history.

"How long have they been fucking us over?" DJ asks.

"Since caves," Vera says. "Long time."

The edge of the curtain is near. I hear groans, babble. We emerge and DJ is instantly on alert, pistol pointed at something unexpected, a shadowy broad X ahead of the asterisk, a figure—mostly naked, sprawled—

Human. Emaciated, bleeding, impaled from two directions. Litvinov emerges from behind the X, brandishing another long, sharpened cane, with a face of fury, about to finish the job, while Borden and Joe and Tak and Ishida and Ishikawa look on, unmoving, unmoved.

They, too, have blood on their arms and hands.

The figure stares at them with the last of its energy, its life. I don't want to recognize it, but I do. The flattened nose, thin, interrupted eyebrows, a rictus of long pain now sharp and undeniable, eyes almost colorless, as if having spent years in darkness...

And a nearly transparent body, showing all its bones and veins, not from darkness but from so many journeys, so many arduous adjustments to chemistry and physics just to stay alive. Champion of champions, the last gladiator on this awful ship, he holds up one hand. The other is pinned to his chest by one of Litvinov's canes. He clutches, at the last, a kind of knife, found or shaped somewhere, the chipped blade glittering. He lets go, and it spins off to chime harmlessly against a ribbon.

This is Grover Sudbury. Our nightmare, the man we condemned, the man Joe sent to this hell—

His head wobbles to see who else has arrived, and he greets DJ and me with a crooked half grin, of pain or recognition I will never know.

"I'm done," he says through bloody spittle, eyes like milky opal. "I'm the last one. I don't want to do it anymore. They're all dead, and I'm *done*."

Litvinov props his feet against a ribbon and shoves the final cane forward, into Sudbury's chest. The cane splits and shivers into fragments.

Sudbury spasms. His breath escapes with a sound like

sandpaper. He stops moving. Litvinov drifts back from the impact. We all seem to retreat from the awful mark, the pierced, racked, wretched example of soldier's justice.

Complete silence before the asterisk, the corpse's X.

"Bilyk died while you were aft," Borden whispers, as if we're in a church.

DJ says, "I think he came to give up."

"I think he wanted to go home," Borden adds.

"Fat chance," Tak says.

MARTIAN RETURN

Down around the sun, time and space are heavy. The screw gardens and their thoughts slumber, surrounded by the sins of warmth, light, and billions of years of closely watched history.

The ship slows, bogged by those densities, those changes. Takes forever.

And then—we're almost there.

After our first sleep, our longest jump, Ulyanova does as she said she would, and makes a pass close to Mars. We receive two transport ships, one for passengers, another for spent matter, which we witness from the ribbons.

We aren't told much about either, even when Vera appears outside the ribbon. She offers the opportunity to begin our departures here, to return to Mars, and to my surprise, Joe, DJ, and Jacobi are ready to go. They'll spread the word as best they can about what's happened, if they're allowed to survive.

Joe and DJ and I say our farewells quickly enough. Joe asserts we'll see one another again, that he plans on getting back to Earth and beginning a new, more normal existence—if Earth is still Earth, if we are still welcome anywhere. I hope when do meet again that he'll explain it all to me, explain what we've been to each other, but doubt any explanation will make much sense to either of us.

DJ says he's heading down to the Red because we might still get communiques—that's what he calls them, communiques—from what's left of the archives down there, but I doubt it. All I get are silences. Maybe that's good. Maybe bug ancestry is nothing to be proud of. Bugs fought. We fight. Maybe bug knowledge is something to be surpassed, grown out of. Maybe we'll go it better without them or the Gurus.

Jacobi surveys us critically, then says, "Fuck it! No excuses," and hugs us all, to my surprise. "Brothers and sisters," she adds, and departs with Joe and DJ.

Ulyanova gives the transports time to depart.

And then we're off.

HOME IS THE HUNTER

Kumar has vanished. Litvinov is nowhere to be found. I presume the Russian went through the curtain, as Vera had suggested. Maybe Kumar has gone through, as well. Maybe he does not want to live in a world without bugs or Gurus or some other influence—or he cannot bear the thought of having to explain.

That leaves the last of us Skyrines, and Commander Borden. The journey to Earth's orbit is brief enough. A nap, as it were. Who's there to wait for me? We're eager to be done with the fighting, the adventure—such as it was. I think we'll part ways as soon as we touch down.

On Earth, there's…Christ. What? A chance to get back to normal? There is no returning to what we were. Even if we know where we are, we still won't know *who* we are. The people I met, whom I could imagine living with after—so many changes! So much space between me and Teal and her child—and how old will they be? How much time between me and Alice? I think a lot about Ishida, but how could that ever work? We both share so many hard memories. What will we do, any of us?

I have no idea how much time I've spent out here, real or unreal.

HOME FROM THE STARS

Earth is still down there. It looks real. It looks alive. Borden suggests they probably can't see us, yet, but more transports are rising, dozens of them, some quite large—Hawksbills!

"Here come the Wait Staff and Gurus," Ishida says.

I think they're delivering their passengers near the new ship's midsection, where, perhaps, quarters similar to ours, or better, have been arranged, spun out of the steel wool—maybe displacing a few ships or weapons. Fancy digs for monsters.

Vera informs us that one transport is being readied to take passengers back to Earth. Maybe we can get down without being blown to pieces. Maybe they'll take us prisoner and debrief us at Madigan or wherever.

AND THE CHILD HOME
FROM THE WARS

Right now, I'm a fraud. I do not want to have killed anyone or anything. I do not want to die like a soldier and end up in Fiddler's Green. I want to die the death of a dreaming child.

Someday, if God will honor a solemn request, I'd like us all to join up at Disneyland in Anaheim. A great big reunion of old enemies, old friends, old warriors. We'll meet in the parking lot, where I last saw my aunt Carrie, before she went off to die in the Middle East, and stroll between the ticket booths and up the steps, past the flower gardens, to climb aboard the old-fashioned steam train...

But first, I'd explore the train station and listen to the conductor's ghost—a balding mustached guy from a really old western, speaking behind a window, probably wearing a vest or an apron...telling us where we need to go next to have fun or just relax. "This way, boys and girls...to the happiest place on Earth!"

So sappy it's painful.

We'll shake hands and talk, and then just sit in silence

before strolling to the other rides, the other celebrations. The restaurants. The gift shops.

Silly idea.

Silly ideas keep me going.

———

WE HAVE THREE packages with us, cargos of life and death. We still have the egg, which is humming along happily in its battery-powered box. Borden is being quite protective. I think she may be making plans for her career after the wars.

And we have two bodies. We made bags from shed membranes around the terminus of the tree, using strips of cane, like natives on an island. Best we can do. We're bringing home Bilyk and we're bringing home Sudbury.

Tak helped us wrap them up.

Both of them.

We board the last transport, a Hawksbill, where we are met by a young, capable-looking pilot, whose name, we are told as he greets us at the portal, is Lieutenant JG Robin Farago.

"This has got to be the weirdest assignment ever," he tells us, then helps us move the box and the bags into the storage bay.

"Where are you coming from? What the *hell* kind of ship was that?" Farago asks. "I never even *saw* it—just got orders and instructions—and there the hangar was, and here you are!"

"What did you deliver?" Tak asks as the others wordlessly head to the couches to settle in, to lock themselves down and rotate.

"I have no idea. Transport command said all the ships

were full! I wasn't allowed to look back. But when I did—our passenger deck was empty. What the hell kind of operation is this?"

We pull out of the hangar, and after that, even we can't see the Guru ship.

I'll take it on faith that it's off to the sun.

I wonder if I will ever know.

The Earth is brown and blue and green and white, all swirled and touched with reflected gold. As we break atmosphere and the couches grow tight, I think back on the people we started with.

I'm still alive.

So many aren't.

SBLM

The landing field is empty, no defenses, no notice we're even here. Lieutenant Farago lands us with expert grace, cracks the hatch seals, and tells us he has no idea why, but there's nobody here to receive us.

"Sorry!" he says. "Those wars were so long ago, right?"

Then a truck pulls up and two Marines get out. Land-based, sea-based, not space. They look young and serious. Here it is, I think—we weren't expected and this is the first reaction.

But then the Marines solemnly tell us they're here to receive war casualties, and Tak, Borden, Ishikawa, Ishida, and I go to the hold with Farago and bring the bags forward. A couple of casualty gurneys are rolled up the Hawksbill ramp. The Marines carefully lay the bodies on the gurneys and drape them with flags—one Russian Federation, the other U.S. of A.

Ishida asks how they heard about us and what we were carrying. Farago says he didn't communicate.

"Radio transmission from orbit," the senior Marine, a sergeant, tells us. "Some Russian, we were told. Are there more Russians up there?"

We all acknowledge that.

"Anyway, we're also told you have a special artifact here, and that a deal has been made for it to be well cared for at a top science facility. We've asked for some people to meet us. Should be here shortly."

The two Marines look at each other, and then a large isolation vehicle, like those used to transport spent matter, rides up the runway and meets us at the ramp.

"Any idea what this is?" a female technician asks, tapping the box.

"A brave soldier gave it to us to take care of," I say. "We'll want to see the facility. We want maximum assurance it'll be well tended to."

Borden steps forward and says, "We're taking charge." She looks at Ishikawa, who moves up beside her. I knew nothing about this. Why should I?

"Absolutely, Commander," the sergeant says. "Uh…mind if we make sure you still hold that rank?"

"I'll wait."

We wait. Borden's rank and active-duty status are confirmed, her connections are confirmed—and she assures us Bird Girl's offspring will be their highest duty, their highest priority, from this point on. Neither Borden nor Ishikawa have ever given me real reason to doubt them.

And it could be a good career move, a good way to stay important and rise in the ranks. They might make admiral yet.

Other ambulances arrive and technicians supply us with civilian clothing—all in the proper sizes. And regulation underwear for males and females. Skivvies, modesty panties, sports bras. The pajamas made by the searchers are shed and collected by the technicians. We suit up, no modesty whatsoever, and then stand for a while in the shadow of the transport, not sure what to say. We've been through a lot and spent a lot of time together.

Farago finds a task he has to do back in the cabin. The technicians look embarrassed. They have no idea who we are or what we're going to do next.

It's awkward.

"It's like we've known each other our entire lives," Ishikawa says.

"I don't know what to do next," Tak says, with a long look at me. "Might go join Joe and DJ, if they let me. What about you?"

"I'm going to Seattle," I say. "If anyone will have me."

Farago is back in earshot, up in the hold.

"They still allow hitchhiking?" I ask him, leaning around the outer bulkhead.

"Sure!" he says. "If you don't like the ambulances, I could probably get you any kind of vehicle you want. Might take an hour. Base is on half-duty status, mostly empty now."

Borden shakes her head and crinkles the bridge of her nose, looking across the tarmac. We all know what she's feeling. We're done. We survived, but everybody on Earth has moved on and we're left out.

I nod and say that an ambulance is fine, to start.

Tak says he wants, needs, to go back to Japan. Ishida says she's going to stay stateside for the time being, feels more comfortable here. Borden and Ishikawa are going with the truck that will carry the egg.

And then, we just climb into our conveyances and spread out. We don't say good-bye, just let the truck and ambulances take us every which direction.

I'm intent on getting my Earth legs back as fast as I can, and that means walking, running, with as little help as possible. I tell the two technicians to drop me off at the demob.

The technicians, both young, both female, both Marines, look at each other before the senior in rank, a corporal, answers. "It isn't open anymore. Everybody's back who's coming back." They want to ask me, "Who the fuck are you, anyway?" But they don't.

"How long?" I ask.

"Seventeen years since they stopped shipping us up and out," the corporal says. "We think we should take you to Madigan and get you checked out."

"No thank you," I say. "I'd like to walk. Just let me out right over there. Okay?"

Another look. With no contradictory orders, they comply.

Pretty soon I realize that nobody down here cares one way or another. Earth, or at least Lewis-McCord, is no longer on alert. I walk. Grass grows in patches through cracks in the airstrip concrete and sidewalks. I don't run into anybody. There are people driving and walking, way far away, but the base is almost deserted.

I'm alone. For once, I'm alone and it feels good. No voices in my head.

I pass through the open gates, guard shack empty, and walk across an overpass to the businesses on the other side of the freeway. Not many people present there, either. It's early in the morning, traffic on the freeway is light, sun is just breaking through the clouds of the far eastern horizon. I can barely make out Rainier. It has its own spreading white mushroom cap, but that's breaking up and showing the snowy slopes of the very real and terrestrial volcano—still there.

Still here.

I walk along the marginal road. I can still walk. I can still take a breath. The air is unbelievably sweet and everything is so amazingly wide open. I want to cry, really want to cry, but the tears aren't there.

Not yet.

My head is...okay, for now. I'm as home as I'm ever going to be, and I'm going to have to figure out if that makes me happy, might ever make me whole again.

I wonder what Borden's going to arrange for the egg. I vow I'll check up on that as soon as I get my act together, my civilian act.

But I doubt she'll tell me.

Joe or Jacobi, or both, will get things done on Mars— maybe help them dispose of the spent-matter surplus out on some plain somewhere. But Joe won't stay there forever.

I should look up the others, too, wherever they've hauled off to. We'll probably run into each other in the next few months, one way or another. I need friends. I know that, but for the moment the luxury of being lonely, of walking with my own trembling legs along the asphalt and over the gravel, then breaking from the road and entering the unguarded scrub woods...

I wonder if I can find the Muskies.

More important for the moment, I wonder if somebody will give me a ride into downtown. Wonder if the apartment is still there, still ours, and will recognize me. Wonder if Pike Place Market is still open, still active. I'd love to grab a fresh bunch of celery and chow down. But I don't have any money.

No ID. I don't want to ask for help, but the technicians gave me a list of numbers to call, and some advice on how to pick up my last paycheck, if there are still accounts for former Skyrines.

If some cop stops me, I might spend the night in jail, as a vagrant.

I keep getting this falling sensation in my head, but I'm not falling. I'm walking and looking and breathing and everything's all right, nothing external is challenging me. Pretty soon I'm going to get hungry, and then I'll have to figure things out.

The marginal road goes on and on, past boarded-up businesses—fast food, payday loans, car dealerships—all closed. Effectively, no more SBLM.

The Hawksbill we rode back on has taken off from the cracked, overgrown runway, flown over me on the marginal road, leaving a smelly rainbow trail, flying off to I do not have the slightest idea where.

My God. I've seen it all, almost from the start and now past the finish. We've shed the Gurus, and while there's still a military—where are they stationed?

A small pink car whizzes by, like a grapefruit on wheels. I stick out my thumb. My beard is thick; I could be any sort of psycho. The grapefruit doesn't even slow.

But another car, an older green hybrid, slows, stops, backs up, and the passenger-side window rolls down.

"Where you heading?" a young woman asks, checking me over, not unkindly, as if I might have lice.

"Well, I'd like to get to Disneyland, eventually."

She looks at me with a squint. "Can't take you that far," she says. "How long you been hitching?"

"Long time," I say.

She unlocks the door and I climb into the kind woman's car. "You look like a soldier," she says.

"Am I that far gone?"

She smiles. "My father used to fly out of here." Then she looks at me more closely, with a frown. "There was that one ship this morning...But that can't be you. Can it? They were coming back from Mars or someplace. It was on the Net."

I shake my head. "What year is it?"

That same expression, but she tells me. I thought I heard seventeen years, but that didn't account for how long we'd been gone, overall, before the war was declared over and the Wait Staff and Gurus were cleared up, cleared out, handed over to the *starshina*'s ship.

Time has really been messed up for those who went to the limit and returned. It's been thirty years since we flew out to Mars.

There are still cars, but they don't fly—so I suppose we're on our own again, moving at our own human pace.

———

I GET OUT in downtown Seattle and say thanks and good-bye. I decide against Pike Place Market, since I don't have money, and walk across the city, my legs barely able to move as I approach the tower where our apartment was. The tower is still there. It looks older, not so well taken care of.

At the front glass entrance, I poke in the old security code.

Wonder of wonders, the door opens.

I take the shuddering elevator up to the right floor, and as the door opens to let me out, I see an elderly woman with white-flecked black hair, quite plump, wearing a nicely tailored pantsuit, waiting for me.

"Welcome back, Skyrine!" she says.

At my look, she puts her hands on her ample hips and gives me a glare.

"It's Alice, First Lieutenant Alice Harper—fuckhead!" she says. "I heard you might be coming back. Joe sent me a call from Mars. He says you should look me up, and here you are! Anybody else with you?"

I tell her not yet.

The apartment's very different, but there's a spare bedroom, I meet Alice's husband, a nice enough guy, a former Air Force flight surgeon, but not a prick about it—they've been married twenty years and living here, taking care of the place—

But first, Alice goes to the refrigerator and brings me a head of celery, green and freshly washed, dripping. "I remember, Vinnie," she says. "Welcome home."

I take the celery and hold it in my hands, not quite sure what to do with something so utterly precious.

"What about Teal?" I ask.

Alice takes a deep breath. "She's in Africa, I think," she says. "She's widowed again, and Division Four buddies tell me she's been asking if she can return to Mars. Martians always want to go home, isn't that right, Stu?" she asks her husband.

He smiles. "That's what we hear. But she's pretty old now."

"What's that got to do with it?" Alice asks. Stu demurs.

They hand me a glass of apple juice that gives me a solid sugar high, and Stu loans me a pair of pajamas—real pajamas, flannel, corded—and then they take me to the guest room and insist I sleep and after that, join them for breakfast.

SAYONARA

The room is quiet.

I try to sleep, but still can't. All night I toss and turn, and then comes the panic attack—I could feel it coming—a sudden fear that Ulyanova never actually cleared my head, that it was all deception, and that the last instauration has been upon me ever since I got back, maybe even before, and my head is still filled with Guru shit waiting to bring me up short, bring me down, fill me with fear, make me *interesting* again.

I keep asking myself, and keep trying to stop these questions—

What next?

Why would the mover of moons and planets have come alive while we were watching?

I lie on the bed in a pool of rank sweat, as if I'm about to be executed, when I receive another kind of dream.

A genuine, human vision.

It's Ulyanova. She assures me I'm free—we are *all* about

to be free. Looking through her eyes, I see Litvinov and Verushka, and I see Kumar, all standing by the window of the apartment in Moscow, enjoying what seems to be a glorious Russian summer, the air balmy, birds flying, sounds of children playing. They're eating bread with thick sweet butter, and soup, and sausages.

They're waiting. Laughing. Even Litvinov.

They seem happy.

The sun is growing brighter. Much, much brighter.

It's over, Vinnie.

Their end is quick.

I wake up. The curtains have been drawn, but the morning is upon us, and I don't feel anybody or anything out there. No voices. No presences. My head is really and truly empty, except for my own memories, my own thoughts, which will take me a long while to deal with. But…

I'm still human. I'm still here.

And Gurus lie.

All except one.

PUTTING ON FLESH

I take walks around Seattle every day, building up my muscles, my strength, airing out my head and my thoughts, just watching people go on about living. For the first few weeks, I felt both deeply sad and somehow superior, for all the amazing and terrifying and deadly things I've seen and the brave and insanely dedicated people I've known and faraway places I've been. Here, people just walk, just drive, just talk, sitting in coffee shops, some staring at nothing as their implants guide them around the world...

Not every second could be their last.

These people I understand and envy and pity at the same time.

Mostly at the ends of my hikes I find a place that's new and peaceful and observe the play of light and shadow on trees, or the sheen and sparkle of rain and grayness, on buildings, on faces, on gardens and flowers and clouds and birds and squirrels, and slowly get back to realizing that the simplest pleasures are the most important, the biggest reasons we're here—if there is ever an explanation for being alive, for observing, for taking up space and eating food.

For not being a War Dog much longer.

Assuming true physical form, true emotion.

Putting on flesh.

One evening at dusk I make my way back to the condominium, where Alice and her husband are setting out dinner in front of that fabulous view of Puget Sound. They put a whiskey-and-soda in my hand—I can drink again, after a week or two when anything of the sort made me queasy, just as if I were still sweating out Cosmoline.

And Alice tells me, setting out a fourth place at the table, that she's invited a guest to join us.

"I hope you don't mind," she says, with a cat-on-mouse expression that dares me to object, to get all pissy and closed down and neurotic. I don't dare do that, so I smile and ask who it is. I know it isn't Joe or DJ. I'd feel them, somehow.

But then I *do* feel who it is.

"It's a young woman," Alice says, more cat than ever, playing with me, playing with me for what she thinks is my own good. "She's in town finishing medical treatments and she asked if we were open to a visit."

"Sure," I say.

"She says you were very sweet out there"—Alice waves her hand at the sky—"when you weren't being a complete bastard—but you were pretty sweet to her when it counted. She says don't expect anything, but she'd like to see you again. I answered for you."

Someone else putting on flesh.

Stu brings in a freshly opened bottle of wine. The deep green bottle glints in the setting sun. His golden smile is big enough to show teeth. He wants me out of here as soon as possible. "We're having pinot noir with the salmon," he says. "Special occasion."

God save me.

UPGRADES

We've been home three years, and I won't go into our life after war, except to add that Joe has sent me a package from Mars, possible now that relations are reestablished—but no doubt incredibly expensive.

Chihiro and I open the box with a sense of strong doubt. In the box is a vial of beige powder—Ice Moon Tea, I suspect—and a note scrawled with a shaky hand in pencil on rough paper.

The note reads, "Heard the good news! Don't want to upset the domestic applecart, but you've had enough peace and quiet. You and Ishida should both return to Mars. We've found Teal's daughter. She's much more than we could have expected. Major upgrade. She says big changes are coming—good changes. I can't deal with her all by myself, old friends!

"Come back and see."

extras

orbit

meet the author

GREG BEAR is the author of more than thirty books of science fiction and fantasy, including *Forerunner: Cryptum, Mariposa, Darwin's Radio, Eon,* and *Quantico.* He is married to Astrid Anderson Bear and is the father of Erik and Alexandra. His works have been published internationally in over twenty languages. Bear has been called the "best working writer of hard science fiction" by *The Ultimate Encyclopedia of Science Fiction.*

If you enjoyed
THE WAR DOGS TRILOGY
look out for

THE CORPORATION WARS: DISSIDENCE

by

Ken MacLeod

Sentient machines work, fight, and die in interstellar exploration and conflict for the benefit of their owners—the competing mining corporations of Earth. But sent over hundreds of light-years, commands are late to arrive and often hard to enforce. The machines must make their own decisions, and make them stick.

With this new found autonomy come new questions about their masters. The robots want answers. The companies would rather see them dead.

931

*They've died for the companies more times than
they can remember. Now they must fight to
live for themselves.*

CHAPTER ONE

Back in the Day

Carlos the Terrorist did not expect to die that day. The bombing was heavy now, and close, but he thought his location safe. Leaky pipework dripping with obscure post-industrial feedstock products riddled the ruined nanofacturing plant at Tilbury. Watchdog machines roved its basement corridors, pouncing on anything that moved—a fallen polystyrene tile, a draught-blown paper cone from a dried-out water-cooler— with the mindless malice of kittens chasing flies. Ten metres of rock, steel and concrete lay between the ceiling above his head and the sunlight where the rubble bounced.

He lolled on a reclining chair and with closed eyes watched the battle. His viewpoint was a thousand metres above where he lay. With empty hands he marshalled his forces and struck his blows.

Incoming—

Something he glimpsed as a black stone hurtled towards him. With a fist-clench faster than reflex he hurled a handful of smart munitions at it.

The tiny missiles missed.

Carlos twisted, and threw again. On target this time. The black incoming object became a flare of white that faded as his camera drones stepped down their inputs, correcting for the flash like irises contracting. The small missiles that had missed a moment earlier now showered mid-air sparks and puffs of smoke a kilometre away.

From his virtual vantage Carlos felt and saw like a monster in a Japanese disaster movie, straddling the Thames and punching out. Smoke rose from a score of points on the London skyline. Drone swarms darkened the day. Carlos's combat drones engaged the enemy's in buzzing dogfights. Ionised air crackled around his imagined monstrous body in sudden searing beams along which, milliseconds later, lightning bolts fizzed and struck. Tactical updates flickered across his sight.

Higher above, the heavy hardware—helicopters, fighter jets and hovering aerial drone platforms—loitered on station and now and then called down their ordnance with casual precision. Higher still, in low Earth orbit, fleets of tumbling battle-sats jockeyed and jousted, spearing with laser bursts that left their batteries drained and their signals dead.

Swarms of camera drones blipped fragmented views to millimetre-scale camouflaged receiver beads littered in thousands across the contested ground. From these, through proxies, firewalls, relays and feints the images and messages flashed, converging to an onsite router whose radio waves tickled the spike, a metal stud in the back of Carlos's skull. That occipital implant's tip feathered to a fractal array of neural interfaces that worked their molecular magic to integrate the view straight to his visual cortex, and to process and transmit the motor impulses that flickered from fingers sheathed in skin-soft plastic gloves veined with feedback sensors to the fighter drones and malware servers. It was the new way of war, back in the day.

The closest hot skirmish was down on Carlos's right. In Dagenham, tank units of the London Metropolitan Police battled robotic land-crawlers suborned by one or more of the enemy's basement warriors. Like a thundercloud on the horizon tensing the air, an awareness of the strategic situation loomed at the back of Carlos's mind.

Executive summary: looking good for his side, bad for the enemy.

But only for the moment.

The enemy—the Reaction, the Rack, the Rax—had at last provoked a response from the serious players. Government forces on three continents were now smacking down hard. Carlos's side—the Acceleration, the Axle, the Ax—had taken this turn of circumstance as an oblique invitation to collaborate with these governments against the common foe. Certain state forces had reciprocated. The arrangement was less an alliance than a mutual offer with a known expiry date. There were no illusions. Everyone who mattered had studied the same insurgency and counter-insurgency textbooks.

In today's fight Carlos had a designated handler, a deep-state operative who called him-, her- or itself Innovator, and who (to personalise it, as Carlos did, for politeness and the sake of argument) now and then murmured suggestions that made their way to Carlos's hearing via a warily accepted hack in the spike that someday soon he really would have to do something about.

Carlos stood above Greenhithe. He sighted along a virtual outstretched arm and upraised thumb at a Rax hellfire drone above Purfleet, and made his throw. An air-to-air missile streaked from behind his POV towards the enemy fighter. It left a corkscrew trail of evasive manoeuvres and delivered a viscerally satisfying flash and a shower of blazing debris when it hit.

"Nice one," said Innovator, in an admiring tone and feminine voice.

Somebody in GCHQ had been fine-tuning the psychology, Carlos reckoned.

"Uh-huh," he grunted, looking around in a frenzy of target acquisition and not needing the distraction. He sighted again, this time at a tracked vehicle clambering from the river into the Rainham marshes, and threw again. Flash and splash.

"Very neat," said Innovator, still admiring but with a grudging undertone. "But...we have a bigger job for you. Urgent. Upriver."

"Oh yes?"

"Jaunt your POV ten klicks forward, now!"

The sudden sharper tone jolted Carlos into compliance. With a convulsive twitch of the cheek and a kick of his right leg he shifted his viewpoint to a camera drone array, 9.7 kilometres to the west. What felt like a single stride of his gigantic body image took him to the stubby runways of London City Airport, face-to-face with Docklands. A gleaming cluster of spires of glass. From emergency exits, office workers streamed like black and white ants. Anyone left in the towers would be hardcore Rax. The place was notorious.

"What now?" Carlos asked.

"That plane on approach," said Innovator. It flagged up a dot above central London. "Take it down."

Carlos read off the flight number. "Shanghai Airlines Cargo? That's civilian!"

"It's chartered to the Kong, bringing in aid to the Rax. We've cleared the hit with Beijing through back-channels, they're cheering us on. Take it down."

Carlos had one high-value asset not yet in play, a stealthed drone platform with a heavy-duty air-to-air missile. A quick survey showed him three others like it in the sky, all RAF.

"Do it yourselves," he said.

935

"No time. Nothing available."

This was a lie. Carlos suspected Innovator knew he knew.

It was all about diplomacy and deniability: shooting down a Chinese civilian jet, even a cargo one and suborned to China's version of the Rax, was unlikely to sit well in Beijing. The Chinese government might have given a covert go-ahead, but in public their response would have to be stern. How convenient for the crime to be committed by a non-state actor! Especially as the Axle was the next on every government's list to suppress...

The plane's descent continued, fast and steep. Carlos ran calculations.

"The only way I can take the shot is right over Docklands. The collateral will be fucking atrocious."

"That," said Innovator grimly, "is the general idea."

Carlos prepped the platform, then balked again. "No."

"You must!" Innovator's voice became a shrill gabble in his head. "This is ethically acceptable on all parameters utilitarian consequential deontological just war theoretical and..."

So Innovator was an AI after all. That figured.

Shells were falling directly above him now, blasting the ruined refinery yet further and sending shockwaves through its underground levels. Carlos could feel the thuds of the incoming fire through his own real body, in that buried basement miles back behind his POV. He could vividly imagine some pasty-faced banker running military code through a screen of financials, directing the artillery from one of the towers right in front of him. The aircraft was now more than a dot. Flaps dug in to screaming air. The undercarriage lowered. If he'd zoomed, Carlos could have seen the faces in the cockpit.

"No," he said.

"You must," Innovator insisted.

936

"Do your own dirty work."

"Like yours hasn't been?" The machine's voice was now sardonic. "Well, not to worry. We can do our own dirty work if we have to."

From behind Carlos's virtual shoulder a rocket streaked. His gaze followed it all the way to the jet.

It was as if Docklands had blown up in his face. Carlos reeled back, jaunting his POV sharply to the east. The aircraft hadn't just been blown up. Its cargo had blown up too. One tower was already down. A dozen others were on fire. The smoke blocked his view of the rest of London. He'd expected collateral damage, reckoned it in the balance, but this weight of destruction was off the scale. If there was any glass or skin unbroken in Docklands, Carlos hadn't the time or the heart to look for it.

"You didn't tell me the aid was *ordnance!*" His protest sounded feeble even to himself.

"We took your understanding of that for granted," said Innovator. "You have permission to stand down now."

"I'll stand down when I want," said Carlos. "I'm not one of *your* soldiers."

"Damn right you're not one of our soldiers. You're a terrorist under investigation for a war crime. I would advise you to surrender to the nearest available—"

"What!"

"Sorry," said Innovator, sounding genuinely regretful. "We're pulling the plug on you now. Bye, and all that."

"You can't fucking *do* that."

Carlos didn't mean he thought them incapable of such perfidy. He meant he didn't think they had the software capability to pull it off.

They did.

937

The next thing he knew his POV was right back behind his eyes, back in the refinery basement. He blinked hard. The spike was still active, but no longer pulling down remote data. He clenched a fist. The spike wasn't sending anything either. He was out of the battle and *hors de combat*.

Oh well. He sighed, opened his eyes with some difficulty—his long-closed eyelids were sticky—and sat up. His mouth was parched. He reached for the can of cola on the floor beside the recliner, and gulped. His hand shook as he put the drained can down on the frayed sisal matting. A shell exploded on the ground directly above him, the closest yet. Carlos guessed the army or police artillery were adding their more precise targeting to the ongoing bombardment from the Rax. Another deep breath brought a faint trace of his own sour stink on the stuffy air. He'd been in this small room for days—how many he couldn't be sure without checking, but he guessed almost a week. Not all the invisible toil of his clothes' molecular machinery could keep unwashed skin clean that long.

Another thump overhead. The whole room shook. Sinister cracking noises followed, then a hiss. Carlos began to think of fleeing to a deeper level. He reached for his emergency backpack of kit and supplies. The ceiling fell on him. Carlos struggled under an I-beam and a shower of fractured concrete. He couldn't move any of it. The hiss became a torrential roar. White vapour filled the room, freezing all it touched. Carlos's eyes frosted over. His last breath was so unbearably cold it cracked his throat. He choked on frothing blood. After a few seconds of convulsive reflex thrashing, he lost consciousness. Brain death followed within minutes.

If you enjoyed
THE WAR DOGS TRILOGY
look out for

THE ETERNITY WAR: PARIAH

by

Jamie Sawyer

The soldiers of the Simulant Operations Programme are mankind's elite warriors. Veterans of a thousand battles across a hundred worlds, they undertake suicidal missions to protect humanity from the insidious Krell Empire and the mysterious machine race known as the Shard.

Lieutenant Keira Jenkins is an experienced simulant operative and leader of the Jackals, a team of raw recruits keen to taste battle. They soon get their chance when the Black Spiral terrorist network seizes control of a space station.

*Yet no amount of training could have prepared the
Jackals for the deadly conspiracy they soon find themselves
drawn into—a conspiracy that is set to spark a furious
new war across the galaxy.*

CHAPTER ONE

JACKALS AT BAY

I collapsed into the cot, panting hard, trying to catch my
breath. A sheen of hot, musky sweat – already cooling – had
formed across my skin.

"Third time's a charm, eh?" Riggs said.

"You're getting better at it, is all I'll say."

Riggs tried to hug me from behind as though we were
actual lovers. His body was warm and muscled, but I shrugged
him off. We were just letting off steam before a drop,
doing what needed to be done. There was no point in dressing
it up

"Watch yourself," I said. "You need to be out of here in ten
minutes."

"How do you handle *this*?" Riggs asked. He spoke Standard
with an accented twang, being from Tau Ceti V, a descendant of North American colonists who had, generations back,
claimed the planet as their own. "The waiting feels worse than
the mission."

"It's your first combat operation," I said. "You're bound to
feel a little nervous."

"Do you remember your first mission?"

"Yeah," I said, "but only just. It was a long time ago."

He paused, as though thinking this through, then asked, "Does it get any easier?"

"The hours before the drop are always the worst," I said. "It's best just not to think about it."

The waiting was well recognised as the worst part of any mission. I didn't want to go into it with Riggs, but believe me when I say that I've tried almost every technique in the book.

It basically boils down to two options.

Option One: Find a dark corner somewhere and sit it out. Even the smaller strikeships that the Alliance relies upon have private areas, away from prying eyes, away from the rest of your squad or the ship's crew. If you're determined, you'll find somewhere private enough and quiet enough to sit it out alone. But few troopers that I've known take this approach, because it rarely works. The Gaia-lovers seem to prefer this method; but then again, they're often fond of self-introspection, and that isn't me. Option One leads to anxiety, depression and mental breakdown. There aren't many soldiers who want to fill the hours before death – even if it is only simulated – with soul-searching. Time slows to a trickle. Psychological time-dilation, or something like it. There's no drug that can touch that anxiety.

Riggs *was* a Gaia Cultist, for his sins, but I didn't think that explaining Option One was going to help him. No, Riggs wasn't an Option One sort of guy.

Option Two: Find something to fill the time. Exactly what you do is your choice; pretty much anything that'll take your mind off the job will suffice. This is what most troopers do. My personal preference – and I accept that it isn't for everyone – is hard physical labour. Anything that really gets the blood flowing is rigorous enough to shut down the neural pathways.

Which led to my current circumstances. An old friend once taught me that the best exercise in the universe is that which you get between the sheets. So, in the hours before we made the drop to Daktar Outpost, I screwed Corporal Daneb Riggs' brains out. Not literally, you understand, because we were in our own bodies. I'm screwed up, or so the psychtechs tell me, but I'm not *that* twisted.

"Where'd you get that?" Riggs asked me, probing the flesh of my left flank. His voice was still dopey as a result of post-coital hormones. "The scar, I mean."

I laid on my back, beside Riggs, and looked down at the white welt to the left of my stomach. Although the flesh-graft had taken well enough, the injury was still obvious: unless I paid a skintech for a patch, it always would. There seemed little point in bothering with cosmetics while I was still a line trooper. Well-healed scars lined my stomach and chest; nothing to complain about, but reminders nonetheless. My body was a roadmap of my military service.

"Never you mind," I said. "It happened a long time ago." I pushed Riggs' hand away, irritated. "And I thought I made it clear that there would be no talking afterwards. That term of the arrangement is non-negotiable."

Riggs got like this after a session. He got chatty, and he got annoying. But as far as I was concerned, his job was done, and I was already feeling detachment from him. Almost as soon as the act was over, I started to feel jumpy again; felt my eyes unconsciously darting to my wrist-comp. The tiny cabin – stinking of sweat and sex – had started to press in around me.

I untangled myself from the bedsheets that were pooled at the foot of the cot. Pulled on a tanktop and walked to the view-port in the bulkhead. There was nothing to see out there except another anonymous sector of deep-space. We were in what had once been known as the Quarantine Zone; that vast ranch of deep-space that was the divide between us and the Krell Empire. A holo-display above the port read 1:57:03 UNTIL DROP. Less than two hours until we reached the assault point. Right now, the UAS *Bainbridge* was slowing down – her enormous sublight engines ensuring that when we reached the appointed coordinates, we would be travelling at just the right velocity. The starship's inertial damper field meant that I would never be able to physically feel the deceleration, but the mental weight was another matter.

"Get dressed," I said, matter-of-factly. "We've got work to do."

I tugged on the rest of my duty fatigues, pressed down the various holo-tabs on my uniform tunic. The identifier there read "210". Those numbers made me a long-termer of the Simulant Operations Programme – sufferer of an effective two hundred and ten simulated deaths.

"I want you down on the prep deck, overseeing simulant loading," I said, dropping into command-mode.

"The Jackals are primed and ready to drop," Riggs said. "The lifer is marking the suits, and I ordered Private Feng to check on the ammunition loads –"

"Feng's no good at that," I said. "You know that he can't be trusted."

"'Trusted'?"

"I didn't mean it like that," I corrected. "Just get dressed."

Riggs detected the change in my voice; he'd be an idiot not to. While he wasn't exactly the sharpest tool in the box, neither was he a fool.

"Affirmative," he said.

I watched as he put on his uniform. Riggs was tall and well-built; his chest a wall of muscle, neck almost as wide as my waist. Hair dark and short, nicely messy in a way that skirted military protocol. The tattoo of a winged planet on his left bicep indicated that he was a former Off-World Marine aviator, while the blue-and-green globe on his right marked him as a paid-up Gaia Cultist. The data-ports on his chest, shoulders and neck stood out against his tanned skin, the flesh around them still raised. He looked new, and he looked young. Riggs hadn't yet been spat out by the war machine.

"So we're being deployed against the Black Spiral?" he asked, velcroing his tunic in place. The holo-identifier on his chest flashed "10"; and sickeningly enough, Riggs was the most experienced trooper on my team. "That's the scuttle-butt."

"Maybe," I said. "That's likely." I knew very little about the next operation, because that was how Captain Heinrich – the *Bainbridge*'s senior officer – liked to keep things. "It's need to know."

"And you don't need to know," Riggs said, nodding to himself. "Heinrich is such an asshole."

"Talk like that'll get you reprimanded, Corporal." I snapped my wrist-computer into place, the vambrace closing around my left wrist. "Same arrangement as before. Don't let the rest of the team know."

Riggs grinned. "So long as you don't either –"

The cabin lights dipped. Something clunked inside the ship. At about the same time, my wrist-comp chimed with an incoming priority communication: an officers-only alert.

EARLY DROP, it said.

The wrist-comp's small screen activated, and a head-and-shoulders image appeared there. A young woman with ginger hair pulled back from a heavily freckled face. Early twenties, with anxiety-filled eyes. She leaned close into the camera at her end of the connection. Sergeant Zoe Campbell, more commonly known as Zero.

"Lieutenant, ma'am," she babbled. "Do you copy?"

"I copy," I said.

"Where have you been? I've been trying to reach you for the last thirty minutes. Your communicator was off. I tried your cube, but that was set to private. I guess that I could've sent someone down there, but I know how you get before a drop and –"

"Whoa, whoa. Calm down, Zero. What's happening?"

Zero grimaced. "Captain Heinrich has authorised immediate military action on Daktar Outpost."

Zero was the squad's handler. She was already in the Sim Ops bay, and the image behind her showed a bank of operational simulator-tanks, assorted science officers tending them. It looked like the op was well underway rather than just commencing.

"Is Heinrich calling a briefing?" I asked, hustling Riggs to finish getting dressed, trying to keep him out of view of the wrist-comp's cam. I needed him gone from the room, pronto.

Zero shook her head. "Captain Heinrich says there isn't time. He's distributed a mission plan instead. I really should've sent someone down to fetch you . . ."

"Never mind about that now," I said. Talking over her was often the only way to deal with Zero's constant state of anxiety. "What's our tactical situation? Why the early drop?"

At that moment, a nasal siren sounded throughout the *Bainbridge*'s decks. Somewhere in the bowels of the ship, the engines were cutting, the gravity field fluctuating just a little to compensate.

The ship's AI began a looped message: "This is a general alert. All operators must immediately report to the Simulant Operations Centre. This is a general alert . . ."

I could already hear boots on deck around me, as the sixty qualified operators made haste to the Science Deck. My data-ports – those bio-mechanical connections that would allow me to make transition into my simulant – were beginning to throb.

"You'd better get down here and skin up," Zero said, nodding at the simulator behind her. "Don't want to be late." Added: "Again . . ."

"I'm on it," I said, planting my feet in my boots. "Hold the fort."

Zero started to say something else, but before she could question me any further I terminated the communication.

"Game time, Corporal," I said to Riggs. "Look alive."

Dressed now, Riggs nodded and made for the hatch. We had this down to a T: if we left my quarters separately, it minimised the prospect of anyone realising what was happening between us.

"You're beautiful," he said. "You do know that, right?"

"You know that was the last time," I said, firmly.

"You said that *last* time . . ."

"Well this time I mean it, kemo sabe."

Riggs nodded, but that idiot grin remained plastered across his face. "See you down there, Jenkins," he said.

Here we go again, I thought. *New team. New threat. Same shit.*